# THE REGIMENT: A TRILOGY

**Baen Books by John Dalmas**

*The Second Coming*

*The Lizard War*
*The Helverti Invasion*

*The Puppet Master*

*Soldiers*

*The Regiment*
*The Regiment's War*
*The Three-Cornered War*
*The Regiment: A Trilogy* (omnibus)

*The Lion of Farside*
*The Bavarian Gate*
*The Lion Returns*

# THE REGIMENT: A TRILOGY

## JOHN DALMAS

THE REGIMENT: A TRILOGY

A Baen Books Megabook

Baen Publishing Enterprises
P.O. Box 1403
Riverdale, NY 10471
www.baen.com

ISBN: 0-7434-8823-7

Cover art by Gary Ruddell

First omnibus printing, May 2004

Library of Congress Cataloging-in-Publication Data

Dalmas, John.
 The regiment : a trilogy / John Dalmas.
    p. cm.
 "A Baen Books Megabook"--T.p. verso.
 ISBN 0-7434-8823-7 (hc)
 1. Life on other planets--Fiction. 2. Mercenary troops--Fiction. 3. Science fiction, American. 4. War stories, American. 5. Soldiers--Fiction. I. Title.

   PS3554.A4373R44 2004
   813'.54--dc22

                                                          2004004241


Distributed by Simon & Schuster
1230 Avenue of the Americas
New York, NY 10020


Production by Windhaven Press, Auburn, NH
Printed in the United States of America

10   9   8   7   6   5   4   3   2   1

# Contents

# THE REGIMENT: A TRILOGY

# The Regiment

# Prologue

... So the woman Ka-Shok, who would become mother of the T'sel, sat in the shade of a fish-hook bush, looking out through the heat shimmers across the gravel pan where the only midday movement was a drill bird flying from thorn jug to thorn jug, to listen and peep, peck and swallow. And Ka-Shok wondered what the truth was of our origins. For to her, the old stories of gods and demons seemed unreal in the world of heat and drought, of hard labor beneath the stars, of bore-worms in the root crops.

It occurred to her then that one should be able to look at a place and see what had been there in its past, seeing things the way they had been instead of the way they were at present. If one knew how. It also seemed to her that she did know how, if she could only do it right.

Now to do something, one must first start. And she decided to start by closing her eyes to what was there at that time; perhaps then she could see the long before. So she closed them, but before long went to sleep and saw only dreams until a scorpion stung her.

That was but her first attempt, for its failure, and the failures that followed, did not discourage her. Before the season of rains came two more times, she had begun to see the past; and not only the past of where she was, but the pasts of other places. And of living people—things that had happened to them before that lifetime, which she had not expected. And she spoke of these things to her husband, who thereupon beat her and called her crazy, and to her daughters and son who, in fear, began to keep her grandchildren away from her.

But she continued looking, seeing more and more, further and further back, only saying no more about it. And it was as if this activity, though pursued in silence, was like a signal fire in the night, attracting seekers. For a certain few people, both old and young, some of them strangers, sought her out, confiding in her their dreams and wonderings, seeking her advice. Until at length, she and some of those few went away, west into the Jubat Hills, where they lived on the sparse catch of snares and fish traps and the roots of certain plants, and together they sought back in time, with her as their guide.

3

Mostly they kept apart from any others. But this one and that would return to their homes from time to time. And when anyone asked them what they had been doing, they answered simply that they had been praying in the hills with an old woman. For what they had seen seemed at the time too strange to tell others, who might beat them for it or drive them away.

Nonetheless, bit by bit, others, not knowing why they did so, decided to go and pray with Ka-Shok, who by then had begun to be wizened and gray-headed. And they became too many to be fed from snares and fish traps. So one who owned land and water rights took Ka-Shok and the others home with him, to the dismay of his son there, and they dug many cells into a hill, that each could have his or her own. And this man declared rules of conduct, and rules of duties, that so far as possible they might continue to seek without the distractions of misconduct, for they did not yet know T'sel.

And not only did they see more and more of what had been in the past, but they began to glimpse behind the Here, and behind the There. And before Ka-Shok departed the ancient husk her body had become, more and more seekers had come to her, until the community moved again, occupying an entire valley and building irrigation works greater than had been seen before on Tyss.

For they had seen marvels in their past, not only of vessels going among the stars, but of the place they had come from. And from the seeing, learned much.

And of even greater import, they had begun to perceive the T'sel.[1]

# PART ONE
## Introduction To Enigma

# 1

Feature Editor Gard Fendel's index finger, stout and hairy, touched *refile,* and the personnel summary for Varlik 681 Lormagen disappeared from the screen. Not that Fendel didn't know the young man personally and professionally, but it had seemed wise to examine the background data.

Lormagen had been in athletics as a boy and youth, and ran and used a health club as assignments permitted. At age thirty he looked physically rather fit. More important, and Fendel hadn't known this, he'd served a three-year enlistment in the military a decade earlier. No combat, but he'd know his way around. The question left was how much stomach young Lormagen had for discomfort and possible danger.

Fendel's finger moved to his intercom. "Derin," he said, "send Lormagen in."

"Yes, sir."

The voice quality of the intercom system was excellent. The slightly metallic timbre had been designed in deliberately, for warships and privateers. It enabled a crewman or officer, intent on something else, to know without looking that the speaker was not someone in the same compartment, and should be acknowledged at once if possible. It also made the words sharper and clearer, helping to ensure they'd be understood.

That had been very long ago, very long forgotten. Now an intercom was just an intercom, made the way intercoms had always been made. They worked very well.

Varlik 681 Lormagen came in, the door sliding smoothly shut behind him. Gard Fendel motioned him to a chair.

"Sit, please."

"Thank you, sir."

Leaning his forearms on the desk, Fendel waited until the younger man was seated.

"You did a very professional, may I say very *Standard,* job in covering the Carlad kidnapping."

Varlik darkened just slightly at the compliment. In the context of journalism, to have one's work called Standard was highly complimentary, if somewhat inappropriate. "Thank you, sir. You honor me."

"I'm considering giving you a new assignment that's even bigger. One that can make your byline one of the majors among our subscribers."

Varlik's alertness level rose. He nodded.

"You're aware of the insurrection on Kettle, of course," Fendel went on, "and that it's continuing. Beast of a place for a civilized man to fight a war, but there it is. Well, it seems now that T'swa mercenaries are being sent there to break its back. That tells me it's worth having someone there to cover it.

"*Two* regiments of T'swa, actually, which really catches my interest. I'll certainly want least one feature on them."

T'swa mercenaries. Varlik had seen a T'swi once, up close: a heavyset elderly man with skin incredibly dark, the color of a blued gun barrel; straight, close-cropped hair gone white; nose bold, hawklike; wide, thin-lipped mouth; unnaturally large eyes shaded by bushy, jutting brows. Despite his white business suit he'd looked so different, so striking, that the image, long unlooked at, was easily recalled.

When Varlik had commented on the man's appearance, someone had told him he was the T'swa ambassador to the Confederation. Tyss was the only gook world allowed diplomatic representation. The ambassador had a staff of two or three, housed in a cubbyhole somewhere in one of the peripheral government complexes. It was doubtful that they did anything. The T'swa had been granted the privilege centuries earlier by one of the Consars, probably Consar XVII, "the Generous," acting as suzerain and administrator general for the Confederation.

"The Department of Armed Forces," Fendel was saying, "admits that this is only the second time in well over a century they've contracted for a T'swa regiment. The last time was in the Drezhtkom Uprising, some eighty years ago."

His eyes stayed on the younger man's face, watching for any sign of reluctance or even tentativeness. He didn't want to send a reporter who'd spend his time there in an air-conditioned, safe-area headquarters.

Lormagen's eyes were steady as he nodded.

"If you're interested," Fendel continued, still testing, "and if I decide to send you, I'll want you to leave day after tomorrow on a military supply ship. It's a twenty-six-day trip, and I'll want you there while the fighting's still going strong. Those T'swa are likely to finish off the local gooks pretty quickly when they arrive."

"Yes, sir. Day after tomorrow, no difficulty. I'd like very much to have the assignment."

Fendel sat back then, decision made. "Fine. It's yours. Call Captain

Benglet at the Army's Media Liaison Office and find out the departure details. The supply ship leaves sometime in the afternoon. And while I'm not expecting full-length video features, of course, take plenty of cubes. This assignment has strong visual potential."

He dismissed the young man then and watched him leave. There'd been no trace of unwillingness. They'd said they wanted someone with energy and imagination; Lormagen definitely had the energy.

*Imagination!* Fendel returned to his screen. *An odd thing to want in a newsman, or in anyone for that matter.* But there were those whose position put them beyond argument, or nearly enough for any practical purpose.

# 2

Excerpt from "The Story of the Confederation," by Brother Banh Dys-T'saben. IN, *The Young Person's Library of Knowing About.*

You have already heard, my friend, of the Confederation of Worlds. But as yet you do not know very much about it. The Confederation of Worlds is an organization of 27 planets on which human beings live. The primaries of some of the 27 can be seen from here on Tyss. Ask your master or your lector to go outside with you some night soon and point out to you those which are visible.

Those 27 are not all of the worlds on which people are known to live in our region of the galaxy. They are simply most of those which have spaceships, and with spaceships, the Confederation worlds can usually control the others and cause them to do certain things that they want them to do. Our own world of Tyss is not one of the 27, of course, and we do not have spaceships. We have the T'sel, and that which grows out of it. That is why the Confederation does not have power over us, although it is all right for them to think they do.

The story of the Confederation of Worlds is quite interesting, and only on Tyss is it known. The first part of it is also the story of how we came to live on Tyss. Very long ago, many thousands of our years ago, people came to this region of space from another region very far away. They came across space in eight very large ships, at a speed much swifter than light, and the distance was so great that it took years to cross it. If you decide to follow The Way of Wisdom and Knowledge, or possibly if you do not, you will be able to visit that time and see that long journey for yourself.

They left their homes to escape a great war. The people who began that war, and who commanded it, were willing to kill to force their own wishes on others. They were willing to kill great numbers of people for that, although few of those killed had chosen for themselves the Way of War.

It was not like any war ever fought in this region, for they used weapons so powerful that they could kill all of the people on a planet in one attack. And that is what they did—they killed all of the people on certain planets, as a warning and threat to others.

On one planet, the government on one great populous island nation bought eight ships, old but large, for they believed that their world would be chosen for destruction. And besides that, they were a people who despised and rejected war, because of the kind of war, called "megawar,"[2] which they had in that region.

Hurriedly they prepared the ships for a very long voyage. Each ship would take several thousand people, and also things they would need when they settled to live on some far world, including seeds and certain animals. For there would be no towns or manufactories* waiting, or even people, but only the native planet in its wild state. Then each sept on the island selected one in 200 of its people to go, and when all had boarded, the great ships left, never to return.

They traveled together on a set course, not stopping anywhere at all until they were far outside the region they knew about. They wanted to be very far away from the war before they chose a new home. After that they continued on the same general course, but deviated* to one side and another to inspect star systems along the way for a planet on which they could live.

In this way they discovered the garthid peoples, who look quite different from humans. The garthids live on planets mostly too hot, and with gravity mostly too strong, for humans. Indeed, our own world of Tyss would seem cold to the garthids, although most humans find Tyss much too hot. But nonetheless, the garthids did not want humans to settle in their sector. So the people of the ships got from them the boundary coordinates* of the garthid sector and went on, not visiting any more worlds until they were well away. Our ancestors did not want anything to do with wars, because the wars they knew had been so indiscriminate* and unethical.

At last the little fleet of ships came to systems far enough away that again they paused here and there to explore for a world they could live on. Soon they found one. It was our own Tyss.

But meanwhile, certain things had happened on the ships. By that time they had been gone from their home planet for more than four of our years. And what did they do, enclosed in a crowded ship for more than four years? The crews were busy, of course, operating the ships and taking care of them. The other people had certain things to do too, such as taking care of children and cleaning. But still, much of the time they had nothing needful to do, and they were quite crowded. So they sat about and talked a great deal. And having nothing like the T'sel, soon they were bickering.* Before long, some of them came to dislike others quite strongly.

Factions arose. A faction is a set of people who feel very strongly in favor of some one thing or set of things, or against some one thing or set of things. It is a group of people who disagree with others, and it exists only in reaction to its polar* opposites. Factions are a major cause of destructive war, which is to say, the kind of war that does not respect the different Ways.

So before they had been very long on their journey, the rulers of the fleet recognized that they carried with them the seeds* of the very kind of war they had fled from! For given time, the factions would surely start to fight among themselves! Therefore the rulers began to counsel together about what they might do to avoid war. But they did not have the T'sel: They could not see how such wars could be avoided.

But they did know that the destructiveness of indiscriminate war is proportional* to the destructiveness of the weapons used. Also, the human mind is prone to explore the operating rules of the physical universe. You already know something about that. When done in a particular systematic* way, following certain rules and limitations, this exploration was known then by the names "science"* and "research."* Certain operating rules of the physical universe, or approximations* of them, which science discovered and described, could be used to do things with, or to make things with. And the doing and making were known as "technology."* The weapons of their huge destructive war had been crafted by technology, by using the knowledge from science.

The rulers recognized all that.

Now, on the ships, not all of the people together had the knowledge to make those hugely destructive weapons. For theirs had not been a world which emphasized science. And indeed, not even their ships' computers,* in which they stored their knowledge, had any great part of the knowledge needed to make those weapons. But the rulers believed that the human mind, free to do research, would in time redevelop that knowledge and once again make those weapons. And this worried them greatly.

Yet they did not want to give up the machines which enabled them to live the way they had been used to. And to continue to make those machines and keep them operating required technology. So they believed they could not do without the technology.

Thus they decided to abolish* research if they could. Without research, without science, they could not redevelop the knowledge with which to reinvent those great weapons. Reactive wars they still might have, but they would not be nearly as destructive as the war they had fled. They would still be able to kill large numbers of non-warriors—those who had not chosen the Way of War—but they would hardly be able to destroy whole populations.

To abolish science was the only thing they could think of to do about it, and they did not at first see how they could accomplish that. All they could do at once was to erase certain knowledge within their computers. So they erased all knowledge which they thought might be dangerous.

But they believed that that would not be enough, for it seemed to them that in time, the knowledge would be rediscovered.

Now, they knew that some of the people with them, called "mentechs," had worked in primitive technologies of the mind, which they regarded entirely as an electrochemical* system. So they sent to the mentechs and asked them if they could suggest anything.

And they could. They thought it might be possible to treat everyone who was on the ships, and their children forever, so that they would never follow the way of science. They could still follow freely the way of technology, but research—the activity of science, the exploration of the rules of the universe—would become impossible. Hopefully, even the possibility of science—the thought that there could be such a thing—would no longer occur to them.

The rulers decided to try it.

But, you may be thinking to yourself, that is going about it in a strange and illogical way. Why not simply decide not to make such weapons? Why not simply respect the different Ways? But they did not have the T'sel. So they did the best they could think of.

Soon the mentechs had developed a sequence* of actions, a treatment. This treatment caused the person to not look for understanding beyond that which people already had. It would not even occur to them that there was any further understanding to be had, and they would dislike and fear and reject any idea of it.

And secret tests showed that it was successful. People treated and then tested thought exactly the way the mentechs had predicted.

Here is how the treatment worked. The person was given a certain special substance which, to put it briefly, made him very susceptible to obeying commands. Whatever the command might be. The commands given him were, in summation,* that the understanding of nature was already as complete as possible; nothing further was knowable. And these commands were enforced by brief shocks of great pain. It did not take long to do this, and numerous people could be treated each day on each ship.

Now, people of different septs had been put to live in different compartments, so far as possible. And when the mental treatment had been tested and proven, the rulers approached the sept leaders. They told them only that they had a mental treatment which would make it impossible to develop great weapons. They did not tell them how it was done, or what the commands were. And they asked them to prepare their people to accept treatment.

And because they feared and hated the great war so much, many agreed to accept the treatment. Some accepted because their leaders told them to; other septs voted, and accepted because a majority agreed. But five septs refused the treatment. They voted, and most of their members said they should not accept. They said that while they abhorred* the great weapons, they did not trust anything which tampered with the mind and would make them less able in any way.

The rulers then discussed whether they should force the treatment on those five septs. But they could not bring themselves to do that, because they had at least some respect for different Ways. On the other hand, they could not make up their minds, at first, on what else to do. So for the time being, the five septs were kept locked up, totally apart from everyone else, and the rest of the people were treated—even the rulers. Even the mentechs. And by so doing they denied themselves the satisfactions of playing or working at science. In fact, there appears to have been some loss of the willingness to question authority on anything.

What that meant was that they became less willing to decide each for himself, and thus tended more than before to follow orders and usual ways in directing their lives.

Soon after that, something happened that helped the rulers make up their minds about the five septs. They were by then far outside the garthid sector, and they found a planet where people could live. It was not a planet where any of them would want to live, for it was too hot there for the people of that time, and the gravity* was stronger than they were used to. But people might survive there. And because the conditions seemed so severe, it was considered that anyone living there would never be able to make great weapons. So they put three of the five septs there, with certain animals and the seeds of certain plants, which they thought might also be able to live there.

That planet was Tyss, our home, and those three septs were our ancestors. And here we have lived for a very long time. Now we think the heat natural, and no more than proper, and the gravity seems just right.

Then the ships went on.

In far later times we learned what happened to the rest of the people.

After Tyss, they found other planets on which people could live. Rather soon they found another that was too hot except in a northern region, and they put there the other two septs that had refused the treatment. And after looking at several more planets, they found one which they liked very much. They called it Iryala, and made it their home.

In time they became very numerous on Iryala, and sent ships out to select other planets where some of them could go to live. Some people on Iryala wanted to follow ways that were not welcome there, and some wanted to adventure, and some, wanting to acquire wealth* and power,* thought it would be easier to do so elsewhere. After thousands of years, they peopled many worlds in this region of space. But Iryala held to itself alone the right to have manufactories to make spaceships, so Iryala was predominant.

Now, when the people of the ships landed on Iryala, they still had the machines used to prevent people from doing basic research, and they could easily make more of them. So it was arranged that each child would also be treated when it was old enough to survive the treatment.

For thousands of years they have done this, and have never regained the concepts* of science or research. The most they could do was to recombine information they already knew into new configurations* and test them, which, of course, was very useful in colonizing Iryala and doing the many things needful to establish a self-sustaining* technology there.

But after several centuries, even making new configurations became disapproved of. So they created the concept of Standard Technology. This assumed that the existing technology was complete and perfect. Any changes in it, they believed, would degrade it from that perfection.

Meanwhile, because of the treatment, they could not know what the treatment was intended to suppress. Except of course at the deepest, least available subconscious level, the commands were no longer understood by the technicians who chanted them. The treatment, which they had named "the Sacrament," was thought of as simply a formula* which would protect the people from great wars.

And after 20,000 years, knowledge of their origins faded to legends among those people because of certain things that happened. . . .

# 3

Mauen 685 Hothmar Lormagen had been home from the shop nearly half an hour. Small, cute, she looked as pretty as the girls in the ads for the beauty aids she sold. Varlik was usually home before her, but there was no sign of him, and no message.

She considered taking out her paints. She was working on a very famous and popular theme—the Coronation of Pertunis. Occasionally Varlik worked quite late, and when he did, might have no chance to call. She might have a long or a short wait, and didn't like to just get started at painting, then have to stop for supper. Intelligent and rational, she understood the demands of his job, and was ambitious for him, but it did have certain drawbacks.

The sun's rays, softened by lateness, came horizontally through open glass doors, tinging the room with gold. Mauen went out onto the west balcony. Spring was in full flush, the trees of the parklike grounds light green with new leaves. Partly screened by the half-woods, she could see the next apartment building, Media Apartments Four, a hundred yards distant. To her left, surrounded by its broad open ring of apartment buildings, stood the heart of Media Village, the towers of the Planetary Media Center. In that direction, her eyes turned four stories down to the sidewalk, on the chance that she would see Varlik just returning, but all she saw was a groundskeeper riding her sibilant lawn mower.

A flutebird sang nearby to the west, a song somehow nostalgic, though Mauen couldn't have said why. Then she heard the door open, and turning, saw her husband enter the apartment. She went in to meet his embrace and kiss. When they were through nuzzling, she stepped back.

"They gave you your new assignment," she said.

"Yes. How did you guess? Ah. Because I'm late."

She nodded. "What would you like me to key up for your supper?"

"I'll eat whatever you eat; I need some extra togetherness this evening." He moved toward the balcony, then looked back as she stepped to the services panel. "Just be sure there's brandy with it," he added.

Outside he leaned on the railing, inhaling deeply through his nose. For him, the smells of spring and autumn had special character, and of the two he liked spring best. He wondered what Kettle would smell like. Not like spring here in Landfall; not like anywhere on Iryala, he supposed.

Kettle, a world generally ignored. The public curriculum treated it—treated all the gook worlds—very slightly: a listing in a table, and perhaps a paragraph or two. Kettle was the Confederation's sole source of technite, and had been these past several centuries. And Kettle was hot, a jungle planet. That was almost all he knew about it, that and the fact of some crazy workers' revolt there. Neither the paper nor the video had much more than mentioned the insurrection, as if it were unimportant.

Mauen came out to stand beside him, her arm around his waist, her head against his shoulder. After a little she looked up at him. "I ordered a chicken casserole, with beng nuts and gondel pods. It will be a few minutes. Tell me about . . . Oh! I almost forgot! I have news, too!"

"News? What news?"

"Hmm. Maybe I ought to wait till later to tell you. You probably won't be interested anyway."

He turned and grabbed her, grinning. "You're teasing! And you know what I do to teases!"

"Um-hm. That's why I tease you." Mauen stepped back from him, smiling, eyes on his. "Tomorrow morning I go to the clinic. We've gotten approval from the genetics board—for three! They finally decided that because our C22.1734 match is so favorable, they can accept the possibility of the C.6.0023 recessives matching. They'll dissolve the Fallopian implants tomorrow morning."

Her happy expectancy faltered at his expression. "Is anything the matter?" she asked.

"How long after the removal before you're receptive?"

"I'm not sure. I'm pretty sure I can have intercourse practically right away, but I don't know when I'll be receptive. I can ask them, though. Varlik, what is it?"

"Come inside and let's sit down. I need to tell you about my new assignment. I'm going to be away from home for a while."

They went inside and sat—he on a fat, lightweight chair, she on the end of the matching couch—leaning toward each other, her knee almost touching his. With the partial setting of the sun, evening had taken the room, the remaining sunlight dusky rose and failing by the moment.

She said nothing, waiting.

"I've been given a great opportunity," Varlik began. His words sounded strange to him—forced, recited. And that seemed unreasonable, because they were patently true. "It's a chance to do a series that can establish me as a really prominent feature writer. Fendel knew that when he gave it to me; he likes my work. But it's going to be a bigger story than he realizes."

As he said it, he believed it. He hadn't thought of it that way before, but now it seemed true beyond doubt.

"Where?" she said.

"On Kettle."

"Kettle?" From her expression, he realized she hadn't heard of the trouble there; she'd probably forgotten the planet since school.

"A gook world, the planet Orlantha. Kettle is its nickname because it's so hot. There's an insurrection there, and I'm going to cover it."

"Is it going to be dangerous?"

"Not really. There's some danger in almost anything. Getting out of bed in the morning. What makes it interesting is that the government is sending in two regiments of T'swa mercenaries—the 'super soldiers' of adventure fiction. That's where the real story is. Usually they get hired into regional wars between governments on this and that trade world, and no one even hears about it until it's over with. Then these hearsay stories come seeping out, ninety-five percent fiction, mostly in the men's magazines. Remember the holo drama, *Memories of a Traitor*? The mercenaries in that were supposed to be T'swa. What I'm going to do is give people an eyewitness report—interviews with real T'swa and video clips—all on the jungle world of Kettle."

It made sense. It was the approach to take, and he could do it nicely. He pulled his attention into the present again. Mauen wasn't staring, just looking quietly at him in the dusk, her face a pale oval with dark eyes.

"How long?" she asked.

"I don't really know. It'll take twenty-six days to get there, and presumably twenty-six back. And I could be there for as long as a dek,[3] I suppose, although Fendel is a little worried that the fighting will be over before I get there." Varlik paused. "Say three deks—four at the outside."

"When do you leave?"

He didn't answer for several seconds. "The day after tomorrow, at 13.20.[4] But I can take tomorrow afternoon off. I took care of most of the preparations today; there's really not that much more. And I can do my background study on the ship!"

He had planned to spend the next afternoon at his desk, calling up material from the archives bank and the Royal Library, but that was selfish thoughtlessness.

"You can get off work tomorrow, can't you?" he asked.

Her response was to get out of the chair and move to the couch beside him.

# 4

"Reasons" as stated and believed are seldom true, and their seniority is illusory. Rather, intentions *and events*, in their order, precede the reasons perceived and give them birth. The most common order is intention, event, reason, but it may also be sometimes event, intention, reason. Be aware also that the operative intention may not be apparent, even to its originator, on this side of reality. On this side he may not be aware of his actual intention, which, of course, originates on the other side.

You may ask how an event can precede the reason. And this brings into question the nature of reasons. More instructive is the question of how the event can precede the intention, which brings into question the nature of time, and once more of reality. But the latter question could only be posed from a this-side viewpoint, which is, of course, very restricted.

> —Master Fo, speaking to Barden Ostrak in the peanut field behind the Dys Hualuun Monastery (unedited from the original cube).

It would be Varlik Lormagen's first time off planet. Space travel was expensive, and why should an Iryalan leave the queen of worlds if he didn't need to?

He sat in the small observation lounge with the vessel's two other civilian passengers, watching a phlegmatic ground crew clear hoses and conveyors, then move aside on hover carts, away from the impending AG distortion that occurred when a large ship activated. The ship moved, almost imperceptibly, the ground crew pausing to watch. One tall heavy man, arms folded high on chest, left a brief image on Varlik's mind as the ship raised. Liftoff was gradual but acceleration constant. The ground fell away, the spaceport shrinking. The city spread its pattern, a grid of indistinct transitways with "villages"—function centers ringed by apartments—at intersects.

Smoothly, with increasing speed, surface features drew together, lost resolution, until the continent spread white and green and tan to a perceptibly curving horizon. Lake Kolmess was a cold-blue, two-hundred-mile pennant far to the south—poleward here, for Landfall was in the southern hemisphere. Then the cobalt ocean, marked with white, appeared over a horizon whose curvature grew as he watched.

He continued watching until their trajectory had left the planet out of sight of his large bulging window, then looked around him. The other two in the viewing compartment were a man and woman—a news team from Iryala Video. He knew who they were, had seen them occasionally but had never met them. There was no hurry to now; he had twenty-six days. He got up and left, not even nodding to them.

There were two men in the officer's lounge, an off-duty mate and a warrant officer. Varlik struck up a conversation. The ship was army, the mate a genial captain in rank who was happy to give him a brief tour. His name was Mikal 676 Brusin. And yes, it was perfectly all right to use any of the ship's library consoles. There would probably always be at least one available. Varlik got the feeling that Brusin was pleased to have him there, that he liked to have new people to talk with.

When they parted, Varlik went back to the library. The consoles were

Standard, of course. The entire ship was the Standard military cargo design. He'd now be able to find his way around any H-class military cargo ship. These things never crossed his mind, though; he took them for granted.

Sitting down, he called up the file on Kettle by its official name, Orlantha. He'd given even less time than intended, the previous day and a half, to background study for the assignment. Mainly he'd reviewed the archives for the little that Central News had said about the war. Even less had been said about it on video, which was understandable. There were always wars of one sort or another on the trade worlds— presumably, it was even worse on the gook worlds—and only devotees paid much attention. But Kettle wasn't your ordinary gook world, sitting out there with no one caring much one way or another. Kettle was where technite was found, the source of the technetium used in steel manufacture throughout the Confederation. The amount used in making a pour of steel was tiny, but it was used in every batch of every alloy; that was Standard.

Kettle had been assigned as a fief to the Confederation planet Rombil, and Rombil had been mining technite there for 279 years—since the Year of Pertunis 432—apparently without earlier trouble with the natives. Now the Rombili had more trouble there than they could handle, and Iryala was bailing them out, obviously because of the importance of technite.

Varlik called up Kettle's planetological parameters and read over them. Most were meaningless or unimportant to him, but some stuck. Surface, 86 percent water. Surface gravity, 0.93—that sounded nice. Rotation period, 0.826 Iryalan Standard—pretty short days. Axial tilt only 2.01 degrees— no seasons, apparently. Briefly, a map appeared beside the text. The inhabited continent, which was the one with the mines, extended from the high middle latitudes in the north to the low middle latitudes in the south.

And hot! Representative daily high and low temperatures on land were, at the equator, 120°F and 105°F respectively; at 25° north latitude, 125°F and 105°F; and at 52° north latitude, 110°F and 90°F. And those temperatures were ordinary! Varlik could imagine what a hot spell would be like. In addition, with so much ocean, the humidity would generally be high; the place was virtually unlivable.

He scanned the summary on bioclimatic zones. The equatorial zone was defined by unbroken jungle, and extended north and south from the equator roughly fifteen degrees of latitude. "Jungle in the extreme," the summary called it, especially in the zone between 10° north and south. Rain was frequent and heavy all year.

As on most free-water planets, planetary circulation made even Kettle's subtropical latitudes relatively dry. The semiarid zones extended roughly between latitudes 20 and 30 in both northern and southern hemispheres. Some semiarid land was desert grassland and some was scrub woodland, grading into forest toward both equator and middle latitudes. Its higher mountains and plateaus were forested.

The middle latitudes lay above about forty degrees latitude, and much of it was jungle or other forest. Some, in the rainshadows of mountains, was savannah or prairie.

According to the summary, the only cool climates on the whole planet occurred on mountains and plateaus above about 12,000 feet. These areas were described as generally extremely wet and misty, an "incredible tangle of smallish trees, standing up at every conceivable angle or lying down, overgrown with vines and lianas and slippery with mosses and saprophytes."

That didn't sound very good either, he thought, then read on. "The exceptions are certain high mountains and plateaus in the arid zone, where the climate tends to be quite pleasant and the landscape ruggedly attractive."

He knew automatically where the Romblit planetary headquarters had to be. And probably the army's.

He skimmed down over material on the geology, flora, and fauna until he came to a summary of Orlantha's history. Very little was known of Orlantha until Y.P. 422, when a survey team found technite there. It wasn't even known from which Confederation world Kettle had been colonized, or at what remote date. The people had sunk into stone-age primitivism, and severe environmental selection, perhaps combined with genetic drift, had produced a very distinct species of *Homo*.

Varlik thought he knew what had happened. Most gook worlds had been settled by one Confederation world or another using them for human dumping grounds—cost-free prisons—long ago. Even several trade worlds had gotten started that way, though in cases where they'd been colonized before the Amberian Erasure, there was only folklore or learned supposition to tell of it. Ordinarily the exiles had been sufficiently equipped to maintain some technology, but Kettle's breeding stock seemed to have been cast away with very little.

Convict dumping had been outlawed when most of the habitable planets in the sector had been settled.

The rest of the historical material on Kettle dealt briefly and summarily with the subjugation of tribes and with mining, and he only skimmed it. He decided to give it a more thorough read tomorrow. Right now he wanted to look into the T'swa mercenaries, and their homeland, Tyss. It was beginning to seem to Varlik more and more that the T'swa were the element to stress in his articles. It was they who would capture reader interest.

# 5

Excerpt from "The Confederation of Worlds," IN, *The Encyclopedia*. Lodge of Kootosh-Lan.

**Pertunis.** With the collapse of the brief Thomsid Empire, the Generals' Junta surveyed the merchant houses of Iryala and subsequently appointed Pertunis of Ordunak as King of Iryala and Emperor of the Worlds. Pertunis's first official act was to dissolve the empire formally. While this was no more than official recognition of the existing situation, it made of Pertunis a sectorwide hero. Indeed, the Confederation numbers the years of its calendar from Pertunis's coronation.

Within 34 years, Pertunis had reestablished the Confederation in much the same form as before the Charter of Halsterbors a millennium earlier. He based it, however, on a network of new trade agreements, the desire of certain rulers to safeguard or regain certain fiefs and other advantages, and, of course, on Iryala's shipbuilding monopoly and military fleet. He did this without any apparent desire for self-aggrandizement. And it served essentially to strengthen the unity, homogeneity, and central guidance— the "Standardness," if you will, of civilized humanity.

The 26 other member worlds were not without differences and ambitions of their own. And their ruling classes could see themselves becoming vassals of the Iryalan throne through the commercial network. But each world had a strong taste for off-planet goods. And each had evolved an economy and developed a standard of living that depended on exports and imports. One by one, Pertunis made them certain guarantees in exchange for their joining the commercial network or for certain modest fees in currency and services. They were also to acknowledge the Iryalan crown as the Administrator General of the network.

Each step into the net seemed the best alternative at the time, the decision to take it the most logical and favorable. And as one after another joined, the remainder began to see that, if they excluded themselves, they would end up in the "trade-world" category, along with the 14 old "junior autonomies," with minimal commercial rights and mostly unable to acquire ships or land like those they had on Confederation member worlds. As trade worlds, they would be outside the Confederation but dependent on it, in positions of considerable economic disadvantage. Only Splenn and Carjath chose ideology over logic, and in their newly reduced positions as trade worlds, neither was long able to maintain a centralized planetary government, nor generally to develop a peaceful and stable alternative. Which of course suited the

Confederation, whose merchants then played the various states against their rivals.

At this writing, life on Splenn and Carjath remains quite stimulating and interesting after nearly 500 Standard years. Their mostly aged, though well-captained ships, keep reasonably busy. Some provide a service important in the farflung Confederation: smuggling.

All the 26 other ex-senior autonomies finally joined Iryala in the network, which in the Year of Pertunis 37 was reproclaimed the Confederation of Worlds.

With the firm establishment of the new confederation, Pertunis was able to give more attention to a project he had worked on at intervals since he'd taken the throne: the development of a logical system of rules, guides, and procedures for the operation of organizations—any organizations—but with special reference to the Iryalan and Confederation bureaucracies. He worked on this, as opportunity allowed, into his final illness. It had begun as a means of rationalizing and lightening the labor of ruling as king and administrator general. In the later stages of the project he elaborated it in extreme detail, in a considerably successful effort to more fully circumvent the bureaucratic stupidities he observed around him. Despite certain weaknesses, it is a true masterwork, of major value to those who are polarized to any major degree. Even to those who are not polarized, it can be well worth contemplating.

After Pertunis's death, this work was declared by the new king, Wilman IX, to constitute "Standard Management." It has markedly reduced operational variation within the Confederation and occupies a place in Confederation life second only to the Standard Technology of "prehistoric" origin.

But while adding efficiency both to government and business, Standard Management further calcified the already rigid Confederation culture.

# 6

Like every army messhall, the officers' mess was a study in stainless steel. Varlik paused as he entered, looking around. Its round tables, more numerous than necessary for the ship's officers, were segregated into a section for senior officers and a larger one for junior officers. Just now they were sparingly occupied.

The mate he'd talked with, Captain Mikal Brusin, looked up and beckoned, and Varlik walked over.

"Might as well eat here with me, Varl. And meet another guest on board, Colonel Carlis Voker." Brusin indicated an officer next to him who wore dress greens instead of the blue tanksuit of most of the working crew. "Colonel Voker's been on Kettle. Went back to Iryala to expedite getting some of the equipment they need, and now he's going back with it."

The mate turned to Voker. "Varlik's the man I mentioned, with Central News, going out to Kettle to report on the war. Served a hitch in the army a few years back; you don't find many media people that have done that, I'll bet five on it."

Without standing, Colonel Carlis Voker looked Varlik over as if inspecting a not very bright recruit. After a few seconds Voker stood and put out his hand. Varlik met it and they shook.

"Served a hitch, eh? Well, at least we won't have to wipe your nose for you and explain the difference between a rocket launcher and a flare pistol. You might even be able to hike all day in a cool-suit without collapsing on your face. Possibly. If you decide to go into the bush."

*Arrogant bastard,* Varlik thought, sitting down with the two officers. Still, it had been a favorable evaluation, even put in rather derisive terms. A messman came over and took Varlik's order while Brusin and Voker continued their conversation, a discussion of stations they both knew. They finished their meal before Varlik was well started, and Voker got up.

"Colonel Voker?" said Varlik.

The officer paused, looking at him, his expression for some reason verging on a scowl. "Yes?"

"May I meet you after supper and ask you some questions? I know very little about the war on Kettle, or about its antecedents."

"Antecedents? You won't learn much about those from me. Or from anyone I know of. But the war I can tell you about. Meet me in the officer's dayroom in"—he looked at his watch—"fifty minutes."

Voker turned on his heel and walked away. Varlik watched him leave, then looked at his own watch.

Mike Brusin grinned at him. "He likes you."

"You could have fooled me."

"He's exasperated from dealing with civilian bureaucrats and army data shufflers for the past ten days—people who use Standard Management to slow things down instead of make them go smoothly. No, he likes you, about as much as he's apt to like any male civilian. He comes from one of those army families you run into—army for generations back.

"The colonel feels that most journalists are too ignorant to report on a military operation. They don't know what they're looking at, so they sort of dub in their own misconceptions. And he's got a low tolerance of anything he considers stupidity."

Brusin paused, grinning. "I confess, I set you up for this. I told Voker about you going to cover the war, and then I watched for you, to call you over. He's basically a combat man, though he's on General Lamons's staff now; I figured he could be valuable to you.

"But after he finished telling me what he thought of journalists in war areas, I decided not to mention *them*." Brusin indicated the video team seated with the junior officers. "They're too ignorant to know the difference between the two sides of the room, and the differences in service that go with them."

Brusin swigged down the last of his joma, wiped his mouth with the cloth napkin at his place, then stood up. "I figured he'd talk to you, though. Anyway, I've got to hit the rack now, Varl. I go on duty again at midnight. See you around."

Carlis Voker sat in the dayroom reading, and looked up. "You're right on time," he said. "What do you know about Kettle?"

"Not much. Too humid-hot for a real human, and a lot of it too overgrown for decent surface mobility. Even the gooks didn't live south of the middle latitudes."

Voker nodded, a jerky nod. "'*Didn't*' is the word. They do now. There's got to be thousands of them in the equatorial jungle and the subequatorial scrub. Lots of thousands."

He looked at Varlik, who sat waiting. Voker went on. "When technetium was discovered there, the initial intention was to mine and refine the ore ourselves. It would give Iryala added leverage, because no one could make steel without getting their technetium from us.

"But about then there was a big upset among member worlds over Iryalan domination. And the worked-out technite mines were on a planet in the Rombil sector; Rombil had been responsible for technite mining throughout recorded history. So Consar XV assigned Kettle to Rombil in fief, with the condition that a royal embassy and a royal military garrison would be kept at a place of the royal choosing and at Romblit expense.

"The Rombili run the place, though—mines, refineries, the whole works. Or they did. There were two technite operations, both in semiarid scrub country—one in the northern hemisphere, a place called Beregesh, and one in the southern.

"For more than two hundred and fifty years, occasional slaves and their women escaped from the compounds. Never any big breakouts, just three or four gooks at a time; no problem. They could easily be replaced and they weren't a danger. The country around the mines was unlivable—scrub woodland with almost no water. That was the key: water was scarce. And when a heat wave moves through, it can be 140° for three or four days at a time. The best thing fugitives could hope to do was work their way up-latitude and try to last twelve or fourteen hundred miles to where the climate eases up. Which of course they could never do. A hundred miles north of Beregesh the hills turned into desert grassland—no shade and no water—while in the southern hemisphere, the continent doesn't extend far enough.

"So went the theory."

Voker's lean face had been intense as he'd talked; now he paused for a moment, his eyes like drill bits, as if to evaluate what his listener was making of it all.

"Of course, a few gooks might find their way onto the plateau south of Beregesh, where it's cooler, and the Rombili considered that a potential problem. So every now and then they'd send floaters over the plateau for any signs of cook smoke or huts or garden patches. Whenever they'd see anything, they'd put down a couple of platoons to clean them out. Then they'd bring in any gook bodies and hang them on the fence of the slave compound as object lessons—just let them hang there and rot.

"But now it looks as if most of them headed for the equatorial jungles, the last thing anyone expected. On the face of it, it made no sense. And the ones that survived must have raised families there. Big families. Gradually they ended up with a whole equatorial population developing under cover of the jungle.

"Then, last year, a force of them attacked the Beregesh Compound, wiped out the garrison, took their weapons, and released the slaves. Not that they didn't already have weapons. They did: rifles, hoses, lobbers, shoulder-fired rockets . . . And no one knows where they got them. Now they've got more."

Voker sat quietly for a long moment, scowling at his thoughts. Varlik didn't speak; he sensed there was more to come.

"They had more than weapons," Voker went on. "They'd learned tactics and coordination somewhere, because about five minutes after the attack started at Beregesh, another force attacked the planetary headquarters on Wexafel Mountain, thirty miles southwest.

"The Rombili had a regular resort at Wexafel Mountain, well guarded but not fortified: a tall wire fence and sentries walking around inside it. Our own token 'garrison' was stationed there at the Royal Embassy—two platoons—and the Rombili had two ornamental marine companies. By Kettle standards it's up in the cool, at 10,800 feet. It's still fairly hot by Iryalan or Romblit standards, but decent—a compromise between heat and an atmospheric pressure acceptable to lard-ass executive types. Sea level pressure on Kettle is a little higher than on Iryala, but only about 85 percent of what they're used to on Rombil.

"Anyway, the gooks wiped them out, too—planetary director and all. I suppose the staff there was running around in circles yammering about what they'd just gotten on the radio from Beregesh and didn't even look out the frigging windows until the shooting started. Probably never even warned their sentries that there might be trouble. And you can guess what sentry discipline would have been like after 280 years without an alarm, unless they had a real ass-kicker C.O., which obviously they didn't."

He shook his head, gaze indrawn beneath a scowl.

"The stupidity didn't end there, though. Three days later another gook force attacked the guard detail at the southern hemisphere site, Kelikut. And the Rombili bungled there, too. They'd begun to build log and dirt fortifications and to patrol a perimeter around the site, but they hadn't sent in reinforcements. They said afterwards they hadn't thought they were needed. They hadn't even set out mine fields! They could enfilade the fields surrounding the compounds with automatic weapons fire, but only from the compound's watch towers, which were nothing more than little air-conditioned tin boxes on legs. They stood up there just inviting someone to hit them with rocket fire.

"Anyway, the patrols were pulled in when it got dark, if you can believe that. So about midnight the gooks hit the guard compound, a couple of hundred yards from the slave compound, and they hit the guard posts at the slave compound at the same time. Total surprise. The Rombili did get one of their patrol floaters up, but it didn't do any good. Another wipeout."

Voker's brooding eyes rested on Varlik's.

"The floater hung around a while, and they claim it attacked the guerrillas effectively. I don't know what they mean by effectively; they lost the place and all personnel, and all the slaves took off. And it was dark, with no one around to make a body count. The floater was lucky to make it up north on the charge it carried."

"Up north?" Varlik said.

"Yeah. The Rombili have a big agricultural operation at Aromanis, 52° north latitude—several thousand acres of grassland country converted to irrigated farmland—and a lumbering operation a couple hundred miles northwest of there in the foothills, all using cheap native labor. This being in native territory, with free natives running around loose, the Rombili had a lot stronger military force there. Why they hadn't flown some of them south to the Kelikut site when they lost Beregesh, I'll never know. Maybe they were too used to getting their instructions from the big brass at Wexafel Mountain, and no one at Aromanis was willing to make a decision like that."

Voker leaned back in his chair now, resting his elbows on the table behind him. "Anyway, that's how it started, more than a year ago."

*More than a year!* That stunned Varlik, and Voker read his expression.

"That's right; more than a year. The landing control ship picked up the distress call during the Beregesh attack, of course, and again at the Wexafel Mountain attack, and sent a message pod to Rombil. Finally, after they lost Kelikut, they sent a request for reinforcements."

He looked at Varlik again, mouth a thin line, eyes smoldering. "And that's how it started. Except it really started a lot earlier. *Because someone had to gather the gooks together and organize them, which couldn't have been easy. And smuggle weapons to them, in quantity, and train them.* We have no idea who, and even less why, but it's got to have something to do with technite."

His demeanor changed then. He turned to his cup, found it empty, and stood up with a lopsided, humorless grin. "You've got twenty-five more days to Kettle," he said. He took his cup over to the stainless steel joma urn to refill it, talking without looking back. "That little mystery ought to give you something to chew on along the way. Solve it and you'll *really* have a story."

Voker wasn't interested in talking anymore that evening, so after a short cup of joma, Varlik went to his tiny cabin and lay down to think. What Voker had told him was shocking. Why hadn't any of it been mentioned in the media so far? It was easy to understand why so little attention would be given to an ordinary gook war, but this one wasn't ordinary at all. Kettle was the technite world, the only one known, and the gooks held the mines.

What the government had released to the media had mentioned none of what Voker had told him. The reader or viewer had been left to assume that it had just sort of grown out of native dissatisfactions, or minor incidents between the natives and the Rombili, the way you might expect an insurrection to start—especially when the natives were supposed to be stone-age primitives.

And Voker said it had been going on for more than a year! Something smelled rotten all right.

Varlik got up abruptly. It was pointless to think about it with no more data than he had. He left his cabin for the library again, to see what he could find to fill the holes.

Voker didn't stay in the officers' dayroom when Varlik left, opting instead to read in his cabin. But Varlik Lormagen stayed in the back of the colonel's mind. It seemed peculiar to give the time he had to the young newsman. But Voker wasn't a man to question his own actions, his own intuition. He'd go with it and see what, if anything, developed.

# 7

Finding technite deposits is facilitated by two observations. First, all past known technite planets, and now Orlantha, were found in the five-parsec Rombil Sector. And second, all known technite sites, including now the Orlanthan sites, are within some area of impact terrain very rich in radioactive elements. The apparency is that, a rather long time ago, each technite area was struck by a large, more or less coherent radioactive mass from space. What the origin of such masses might be is not known.

—From: *Summary Report of the Orlanthan Survey*,
Royal Library, Landfall. Iryala, Y.P. 423.

In the library, Varlik looked at what little the library had on the planet, this time scanning more closely the brief technical summary from the planetological survey. It still didn't do him much good. Then he called up *technetium*. A silvery-gray radioactive metal, said the summary, known only from a rare ore called *technite*. Atomic number 43, half lives up to $2.4 \times 10^6$ Standard years . . .

From the beginning of history, technite had been mined first on a planet called Technite 3, then Technite 4, Technite 5, and finally on Kettle, the first known technite planet to be human-habitable, if just barely. Like Kettle, Technite 3, 4, and 5 were all in the five-parsec Rombil Sector. Other planets in the same sector, with evidence of ancient mining, are assumed to have been Technite 1 and 2. Records of their exploitation do not exist, as the putative Technite 1 and 2 workings predate the organized historical record that began with the First Empire.[5]

Technite is sufficiently radioactive that miners as well as refinery crews had to wear heavy and cumbersome "hot-suits" and breathe bottled oxygen, as protection against radioactive dust. Exhaust fans ran constantly in the mines and refineries to minimize suspended dust in the air. The refined technite was shipped off-planet for extraction of its technetium, as the extraction process required considerable support technology.

It occurred to him to call back the information on Tyss, the homeworld of the T'swa mercenaries, but data on Tyss proved even skimpier than data on Orlantha, because there'd been only a cursory planetological survey. The T'swa sounded like naturals for fighting on Orlantha, because if Orlantha was nicknamed "Kettle," Tyss was often referred to as "Oven." Temperatures ran even hotter on Oven than on Kettle, though the atmosphere was generally much drier; Tyss was a world characterized by deserts, as Kettle was by oceans and jungles. And if Kettle was unique among gook worlds for its technite, Tyss was unique for its exports of fighting men. It wasn't even usually referred to as a gook world like all the other "resource worlds—worlds without significant statutory rights."

The entry listed a minimum of physical parameters and no history at all. He could see nothing relevant that he'd missed earlier. At the end it was cross-referenced to *T'swa Mercenaries* and to *Philosophies: Exotic*. He'd already read the entry on T'swa mercenaries, which in two paragraphs only mentioned their exceptional skill in individual and small-unit combat and barely named some of their more significant military actions. It made him wish he'd had a day or two more on Iryala, where he'd had access to the most complete library bank in the Confederation.

He decided to call up the cross-referenced entry on *philosophy,* and found it obscure and uninformative. The unifying element in human life on Tyss, it said, was a philosophy, *T'sel,* the literal meaning of which was "life on Tyss." It claimed to allow for and codify "every human bent," whatever that meant, and classified the various "Ways" of T'swa life, with a chart showing the categories:

## THE MATRIX OF T'SEL

|         | FUN                                | WISDOM/ KNOWLEDGE                       | GAMES                               | JOBS                                 | WAR                                |
|---------|------------------------------------|-----------------------------------------|-------------------------------------|--------------------------------------|------------------------------------|
| PLAY    | Play just for fun                  | Study as play; learning unimportant     | Games as play; winning unimportant  | Job as play; reward unimportant      | War as play; victory unimportant   |
| STUDY   | Study for fun; learning secondary  | Study for wisdom &/or knowledge          | Study for advantage                 | Study to enhance job accomplishment  | Study for power                    |
| COMPETE | Compete for the fun of winning     | Compete to be wisest or most learned     | Compete to win                      | Job as a challenge                   | War as a contest                   |
| WORK    | Work at playing                    | Work at learning                         | Work for advantage                  | Work for survival                    | Soldiering                         |
| FIGHT   | Fight to control pleasure          | Fight to control knowledge               | Fight to subdue                     | Fight for monopoly                   | Fight to kill or destroy           |

It didn't mean much to Varlik. He read on:

Very briefly, at any time in a person's life, one is said to have a clear mindset for one or another attitude—the rows of the chart—and after childhood these tend to be more or less permanent, with changes toward the lower levels more likely than upward changes. Further, a person is said to be born with a proclivity for certain fields of activity—one will tend to put one's self or find one's self in situations that fall within the columns of the chart. And someone whose mindset is for Work will perform differently on a job from someone whose mindset is for Fight.

As for the terms, *Play* is a nonpolar activity—one without winning or losing positions from the standpoint of the player. The only function of Play is the pleasure of the player.

To *Compete* is to engage in a polar activity—one that has a winning position, a losing position, and partisan spectator positions. The intention is to win, with no intention to destroy or subdue. The primary rules governing Compete, which are universal laws, are generally inaccessible to the competitor. The secondary rules, however, which define and control the specific games, are known or readily knowable and are generally enforced.

*Work* is similarly polar, with success, failure, and partisan spectator positions. The primary rules are generally unknowable to the worker. Secondary rules are generally in place and knowable but in practice are more or less circumvented, ignored, or altered.

*Fight* has winning, losing, and partisan spectator positions, and differs from Compete in that the intention is to subdue and/or destroy, and in having secondary rules which are bypassed at the opportunity and convenience of the participants.

*Study* is also polar, with succeed, fail, and watch positions. (I have some difficulty understanding this level, which Master Gao says is because it is the level I am at, and said that from it I might well attain a great deal of knowledge but not much wisdom. I'm afraid that for me it will have to suffice.)

Levels below *Play* involve increasing amounts of seriousness. There is no seriousness in Play.

Master Gao also pointed out that the chart is a two-dimensional simplification with the sole purpose. . . .

Varlik shook his head impatiently and simply skimmed to the end of the article. He'd had the idea that he would arrive on Kettle armed with a mass of data, well digested, to serve as a framework for understanding, with pigeonholes to fit his observations into. Well, he'd have to do the best he could with what he had. Absently he called for a printout, then cleared the memory. He'd have to try Voker again the next day and see what he could learn about T'swa equipment, tactics, and strategy.

Meanwhile, it was too early to go to bed. He keyed the author index, then called *Hasniker, Gorth* to the screen. Hasniker was a popular adventure novelist who reputedly researched his story situations diligently. Varlik slowly scrolled the annotated titles and, sure enough, there was one that dealt with T'swa mercenaries: *A Crown Prince on Ice.* Maybe, he thought sardonically, Hasniker had found something he hadn't.

✧     ✧     ✧

The next morning, the female half of the video team came into the messhall while Varlik was eating breakfast. Mike Brusin's attention left his plate to pass Varlik's right ear, and Varlik rotated his head enough to see. She was walking over to them, a husky young woman looking like an ex-athlete who'd gained some weight.

"Mind if I sit here?" she asked.

"Be my guest," Brusin replied.

Varlik rose while Brusin was speaking. "I'm Varlik Lormagen, with Central News."

"Konni Wenter, Iryala Video," she answered, and sat down.

The messman arrived to take her order, then left.

"Where's your partner?" Brusin asked.

"Sleeping in, I suppose."

"I thought he might be." Brusin grinned. "He sure knows how to pour it down. Holds it well, but that much is bound to have after-effects."

She avoided the invitation to talk about her partner. "Who do we see to get video cubeage of the war equipment you're carrying to Kettle?"

"You talk to Major Athermon, the ship's executive officer. That's him over there, with the thinning blond hair. And he'll want you to clear it with Colonel Voker, sitting across from him, in green. Colonel Voker is in charge of the ordnance."

"What do you do?" Konni asked.

"I'm the watch officer in charge of the third watch, and I'm also the supercargo." Brusin paused to grin. "And the self-appointed, agreed-upon shepherd of guests. Which one of you is in charge—you or Mr. Bakkis?"

"Bertol's the boss, but he usually puts me in charge, except on a shoot, as long as everything's going all right. He's the creative genius and cameraman. I'm the expediter; I arrange things and do interviews."

*Bertol Bakkis,* thought Varlik. That was the name. The man had won prizes for his coverage of—what was it? The Omsedris flood and—the big fire in the Kolmess Forest.

Varlik finished his chops and fries, then glanced toward Voker. He'd hoped to sit by the colonel again this morning, but the man had been sitting with others, with no available seat adjacent or across from him. Varlik held up his cup and received a nod from the messman, who headed for the joma urn. He'd wait and catch Voker before he left, or follow him, if necessary.

His attention went back to the conversation between Brusin and Konni Wenter. Apparently Brusin was proving uninformative, because Konni turned unexpectedly to Varlik. "What have you been able to learn about Kettle and this war?" she asked.

"Not much," Varlik answered. He'd keep what he knew to himself, although he felt uncomfortable about it. It was his professional edge. "How about you?"

She made a rude sound, not loudly. "I planned to spend a day or two in the royal library, but it only took me about an hour. There was a lot of planetological data, including the mineralogical survey and some old stuff on tribal customs. That's all."

He decided not to ask if she'd found anything on the T'swa merce-naries. Perhaps she didn't know they were involved. Then it struck him that he hadn't brought up the T'swa with Voker, either, and Voker hadn't mentioned them on his own.

Two of the men at Voker's table got up and left, leaving only the ship's executive officer still sitting with him. Meanwhile, Konni Wenter was just starting to eat. Varlik got up, excusing himself, and walked toward the E.O.'s table, joma cup in hand. Voker and the E.O., Major Athermon, had finished eating and were talking, not the most propitious situation to interrupt. Athermon looked up with a slight frown as Varlik arrived. Varlik bobbed a small head bow.

"Excuse me, Major Athermon, Colonel Voker. Major, my name is Varlik Lormagen, with Central News. I just want to ask Colonel Voker if I can meet with him sometime this morning." His eyes moved to the colonel. Surprisingly, Voker smiled.

"Sure, Lormagen. Major Athermon just said he needed to check the bridge." He turned to Athermon. "Lormagen served an enlistment in the army a while back. Made sergeant. Central News is sending him out to report on the Kettle war."

Athermon looked at Varlik and nodded, a nod that was curt without being rude. "Well," said Athermon, "it would be unreal to tell you to enjoy your assignment. Let me wish you long life." He turned to Voker. "Have a good day, colonel. It was nice talking with you."

"Thank you, major. Same to you." Voker and Varlik watched the executive officer out the door before talking further, then Voker spoke mockingly. "Did you have any inspirations after we talked?"

"No, sir. I made further use of a library console, and found essentially nothing. Nothing of value on Kettle, and almost as little on Tyss."

The colonel's eyebrows raised fractionally and he looked around them. "Tell you what," Voker said, "why don't we talk in my cabin? It has the advantage of privacy."

Voker got up without waiting for a reply, and Varlik followed him out of the messroom, down a wide corridor and up a companionway, say-ing nothing, then down another corridor, narrower but nicely carpeted. Ranking officer country, Varlik thought to himself.

Voker's cabin, though small, was twice the size of the cubbyhole Varlik occupied. It even had its own computer terminal. Voker motioned him to a chair, opened a knee-high refrigerator, and took out a bottle.

"Whiskey do?" he asked, and held up a bottle of smooth Crodelan. "One of the little bargains available on out-worlds." He put ice in two glasses, poured a liberal shot in each, then handed one to Varlik and sat down. "I like this stuff too well, so I ration myself to two a day. Might as well have the first one now." He took a small, critical sip. "You mentioned Tyss. I take it you've heard the rumor about T'swa mercenaries. Where?"

A rumor! It could be false then. If it wasn't true, he needed to rethink some things. "From my boss," Varlik answered. "But he considered it fact. It's probably the reason he sent me to Kettle."

"Interesting. Do you know where he heard it?"

"No, but I could make an educated guess. Central News has close connections within His Majesty's administrative staff. We're often chosen to, uh, release selected 'rumors' or 'leaks' to test public reaction. Not that this was anything like that, but it could easily have come from the same kind of source."

Voker looked thoughtful. "I heard it suggested some four deks back, but General Lamons turned it down."

"Why is that?"

"First, he doesn't believe in elite units. They offend his sense of Standardness. Plus the T'swa are as non-Standard as you can get." The colonel's eyes met and held Varlik's as he said it. "Actually, neither Standard Management nor the army's supplemental policies say that elite units aren't all right. Or that non-Standard contractor forces aren't."

Voker slowed as if for effect. "Besides which, there are places for Standardness and there are places for innovation—creative imagination. Every damned thing man has or does was an innovation at some time or other, and imagination before that."

Varlik didn't flinch, but inwardly he squirmed at the concept. Voker saw it, and his slight smile came out awry. "Besides that, Lamons considers that to use mercenaries in a situation like this would be an affront to the Iryalan Army."

"The T'swa would seem to be almost perfect for Kettle, though," Varlik said.

"Exactly. They're adapted to the climate, they're specialists in wildland fighting, and they're more expendable than our own people. T'swa casualties are more acceptable to the public as well as the government. This was pointed out to Lamons, but he refused the logic."

Voker swirled the dark liquor in his glass, eyeing it thoughtfully. "I wouldn't be surprised if what you heard about bringing in T'swa is true, though. Not a bit. The suggestion seemed to have high-ranking interest back home. Someone may have bypassed Lamons and gotten the idea to the Royal Council."

"What, specifically, could the T'swa do that the army can't?" Varlik asked. "Besides stand the heat."

"Huh! What can the Royal Ballet do that the army can't? And a lot of things that the army can do, the T'swa can do quicker and more efficiently." He grimaced wryly at Varlik. "I regret to say."

"Have you ever worked with T'swa?" Varlik asked hopefully.

"No, but I've read a couple of contract monitor debriefs from trade worlds, and the War College study on the T'swa, such as it is. How much do *you* know about them?"

"Not much," Varlik admitted ruefully. "Only that they're supposed to be almost—super-soldiers. Most of what I've read is adventure fiction, I'm afraid. I haven't been able to find anything else."

Voker grunted. "And you checked the ship's library? I'd have expected better of it; any base library would have the War College study on them. Not that many read it; like I said, the T'swa aren't—Standard."

Again Varlik's stomach twisted: The colonel had said the word "Standard" in a tone bordering on condescension.

"You used the term 'super-soldiers,'" Voker went on. "As individuals, that's not an exaggeration. They start their training as little kids. The T'swa philosophy has it that a person is born imprinted with a preference for a particular kind of life, and they claim they can tell what it is when the kid is only five or six years old.

"I know that doesn't make any sense genetically, but it's the basis they operate on, so that's the age they start training them—five or six. From then on that's pretty much all they do—train as warriors and study T'swa philosophy.

"They have *discipline,* of the kind that works best: self-discipline. And maximum individual skills. And their small-unit performance is supposedly the best. Their drawback, such as it is, is that they won't operate as an integral part of large units—armies, corps, divisions. That's undoubtedly part of why Lamons doesn't want 'em: he doesn't know what to do with 'em. Their contracts specify that they operate on their own, subject only to agreed-upon objectives. And they don't hesitate to refuse assignments if they don't fit the contract terms.

"The thing to do with T'swa is, first you know the contract thoroughly, then pick something you need done that no one else can do and that fits the contract terms, which are broad enough. Then you tell them to do it. Nothing hard about that. House-to-house combat, for example: they're great for cleaning out a town. Or fighting in wild country. But to use them, it helps to have a couple teaspoons of imagination."

"What would you tell the T'swa to do?" Varlik asked.

"Easy. I'd tell them to find and hit the guerrillas' main headquarters, capture as many top-ranking officers as they can, and bring them in. Take explosives and blow out a clearing big enough to come in with floaters, then lift out with their prisoners."

"That doesn't sound easy to me."

"I didn't mean it would be easy to do. The *decision* would be easy for me."

"Do you think they could pull off something like that?"

"I wouldn't be surprised. I wouldn't bet a dek's pay on it, but I'd go a week's. Or maybe I would go a dek's pay. Anyway, it'd be worth the try. The T'swa don't mind casualties; they just like to fight. And if they got some really high-ranking prisoners, we could probably find out who's behind the uprising—who provided the weapons, the training. Maybe even why. If we knew that, maybe we could end this war by hitting the source, whatever that is.

"One thing I do know for sure: I don't want to spend the rest of my career trying to root gooks out of the bush at a hundred and thirty degrees of heat."

"How does General Lamons intend to handle the situation?"

"Land heavy forces at Beregesh, take over the surrounding area, fortify the perimeter to keep out the gooks, then rebuild the refinery and reopen the mines."

"Is that practical?"

"If we're willing to commit, say, six divisions there. Lamons is assuming that the gooks have ten or fifteen thousand troops, and I wouldn't argue about that. There are two main problems: One, protecting the engineering and other units while they build an infiltration-proof defensive perimeter that's got to be—oh, maybe twenty miles long. And two, the steambath Beregesh environment. In the mining districts, the troops have to wear cool-suits to function, and they're uncomfortable and damned clumsy. The climate's bad enough up north at Aromanis, but that's a resort compared to Beregesh. At Aromanis we don't need cool-suits."

Voker stopped and regarded Varlik as if something was dawning on him. "Lormagen," he said, "do you have it in mind to feature the T'swa in your articles? Is that what you plan to do?"

"That's what I was thinking about."

"You don't know what you're letting yourself in for. They may be the most interesting thing to write about, or to read about, but frankly, you'll never keep up with them. I'm not sure any Iryalan would be able to, even if they'd have him."

Voker leaned forward, forearms on knees. "Tell you what. You forget about the T'swa and I'll feed you all the leads you can follow up on."

"I really appreciate the opportunity," Varlik answered slowly, "and I hate to turn it down. But what I really want to do is go with the T'swa and let people see them in action—in reality, not in fiction. At least I want to try. There'll be more public interest in them."

To his surprise, Voker grinned. "Got you," said the colonel. "And you'd make a bigger name for yourself. In your shoes I'd feel the same way." He stood, took a case from an open-front cupboard, put it on his bunk, and opened it. There were a number of cubes in it, and he took one out.

"Here," he said, holding it out. "Conversational Tyspi, self-taught. Maybe it didn't occur to you, but the T'swa have their own language; several gook worlds do, more or less. All T'swa mercenaries supposedly speak decent Standard, but among themselves they'll probably talk their own lingo. You'll want to understand as much of it as you can." Varlik took the cube as Voker continued. "Although anyone who thinks as differently as they must . . . But if you can even sort of talk their language, they'll probably like you for it."

He didn't sit down again, but stood as if waiting for Varlik to get up. "And if you're going to tag along with them, you'll have to be in great physical condition. You've got twenty-five days!" He stepped to the door and held it open. Varlik arose, uncertain. "You don't think a man in a cool-suit can keep up with the T'swa, do you?" Voker asked. "You'll have to be in incredible condition and able to take the heat unprotected."

It hadn't occurred to Varlik, and his face showed it.

"Although it just might be possible," Voker said. "If you've got the guts for it. You don't look too bad physically. A prospector team was stranded on Furnace One for three weeks after their suits gave out, and three of them survived. Out of eight. And Furnace One is a lot hotter than Kettle. Like a sauna. Of course, they didn't have to exert themselves."

Voker's grin was wide now. "Come along, bucky boy. We'll get you fixed up with a firefighter's outfit and start you on a good tough stamina routine in the officers' gym. Sweat all the softness out of you and get you ready for the heat. Those firemen's suits can simulate Kettle's climate; with their cooling systems disconnected, they'll keep body heat in as well as they keep external heat out."

# 8

In Tyspi, besides the masculine and feminine personal pronouns *he* and *she, him* and *her,* and the impersonal pronoun *it,* there are neuter personal pronouns, which prove to be quite convenient where male or female identity is not relevant. And outside the military, the neuter personal pronoun is used more than the masculine and feminine pronouns, which in itself tells us something about the T'swa.

—Lecture by Barden Ostrak to the Philosophical Society.

During the 25 remaining days to Kettle, Varlik, enclosed in a fireman's suit, worked out every morning in a cycle of varied and almost nonstop strenuous exercises, mostly steady-paced but occasionally sprinted. Sweat ran down his body and squidged in his socks. He'd complained to Voker, his self-appointed and unwanted overseer, that it was better for the body to have alternate days off. But Voker had scorned the notion, said they weren't trying to build bigger muscles, just toughness, and bullied and browbeat a grim Varlik through it, skirting collapse.

In fact, every day during the first week, Varlik had truthfully expected to collapse from heat prostration. And there'd have been some satisfaction to it; it would have made Voker wrong.

The colonel worked out too, mostly on gymnastics and hand-to-hand combat drills. He exercised strenuously enough, but without a fireman's suit and with numerous breaks to supervise Varlik. When Varlik pointed out the difference, Voker, leaner and harder than any colonel Varlik had ever imagined, pointed out that *he* wasn't going off to follow the T'swa.

Varlik's first two workouts had been an hour each, and left him utterly exhausted. By the fifteenth day, the workouts went on for three hours with a pair of five minute breaks, the soreness forgotten, and Varlik was pleased with his sinewy new physique.

After lunch and a short nap, he studied Tyspi till supper. His progress with the language cube was less satisfying than the physical training, partly because there was no one on board to test him. The colonel had never gotten around to learning it. Varlik could follow the conversation exercises on the recordings well enough, but that wasn't the kind of barracks talk he expected to hear. He couldn't imagine mercenaries speaking with the precise and deliberate diction of the lesson recordings.

After supper he studied Tyspi again, to crowd in as much competence as possible. Relaxation consisted of a drink and idle conversation with Mike Brusin before bedtime, sometimes with Voker sitting in. Occasionally Konni Wenter joined them, twice with a torpid, almost unspeaking Bertol Bakkis, his eyes opaque with seeming disinterest. When they appeared, Varlik kept his mouth shut, excusing himself as soon as he gracefully could.

Following his very first workout, Varlik had asked Colonel Voker if he would record for him a summary of the war to date, to go with his description of its start. Voker had answered that he might if he found time for it. Varlik hadn't pressed the matter. The colonel had already been more than generous with his help and confidences.

Occasionally Varlik had misgivings about attaching himself to the T'swa, and not just because of the Hasniker novel and other fiction depicting the T'swa as ruthless and cruel. Voker had said they began their military life at age five or six! What would men be like who'd spent their childhood in barracks, preparing for life as mercenary killers?

They weren't even *Homo sapiens;* they were *Homo tyssiensis.*

At last Varlik finished his final workout. Tomorrow before lunch they would arrive on Kettle. As he sat freshly showered, putting on his shoes, Voker turned to him. "Lormagen," he said, "I've got something for you in my quarters. I wrote it last night. It's handier than having it on a cube: You won't need a player when you want to refer to it."

Varlik followed him to his cabin, where the colonel gave him an envelope, not thick at all. When he got to his own cabin, he opened it to find a summary of the war indexed by year and dek.

Yr 710.1—Rebels capture mines, as already described.

710.3—Romblit reinforcements arrive Kettle—one division with support units. Brigade assault landing at Beregesh, mine and refinery area retaken and "secured" with no resistance or enemy presence. Found refinery demolished, ditto other structures and mine shafts. Then Kelikut retaken with no resistance; similar destruction found. Troops begin to construct temporary camp and defenses.

710.4—Construction crews arrive from Rombil, begin reconstruction of mines, refineries, etc. Guerrillas infiltrate both areas at night, in force, massacre Romblit construction crews, destroy equipment, pin down garrison remnants. Reserve regiments flown in, land under heavy small-arms fire. Eventually, troops and remaining civilian personnel evacuated under fire, as they cannot reconstruct and maintain air-cooled mines, refineries, camps, in combat situation. Enemy well trained, very effective. Enemy casualties believed substantial due to floater gunnery.

710.6—Rombil lands two additional divisions up north at Aromanis base, along with 1,000+ construction workers and heavy equipment, to establish major military base of operations. Also prefabricated cool-huts, etc., for transfer south to Beregesh. On Rombil, government calls up reserves, begins training. Iryalan government sends military "observer" team to Kettle, headed by General Lamons.

710.8—Full Romblit division lands at Beregesh with strong floater support, under heavy fire from log-and-earth bunkers, including lobbers and blast hoses not evidenced before. Casualties heavy, particularly due to destruction of unarmored troop landers in flight by M-3L rockets, also not used before. Area taken and secured.

710.8.10—Beregesh area fortified under frequent harassment. Casualties moderate, chiefly to patrols.

711.1—Construction crews begin 'round-the-clock work to rebuild refinery and reopen mines. Progress rapid. Considerable pressure from gov't. for technetium.

711.3—Refinery rebuilt to 0.4 of old capacity. First cars of ore from new shafts, using imported contract workers. Enemy floaters, previously unknown, make surprise attack. They bomb and demolish refinery, mine head, worker dormitories, barracks. Mine field breached by aerial bombing, enemy assault troops overrun part of area before withdrawing. Romblit troop casualties moderate; worker casualties heavy because of destruction of refinery and mine head. *This firmly demonstrates enemy policy of withholding unexpected resources for surprise use later.* How far resources will permit continued escalations is not known, but I suspect not much further.

711.5—Surveillance platforms (first direct Iryalan participation) parked on strategic Heaviside coordinates. General Lamons returns to Aromanis with Iryalan Royal Guards regiment and with orders from His Majesty. First Romblit reserve division arrives. More Romblit air attack squadrons begin to arrive.

711.6—Iryalan 12th Division arrives. General Lamons relieves Romblit General Grossel as planetary commander. Iryalan Army assumes direction of the military situation on Kettle, without however relieving Rombil of responsibility as fief holder. I get sent to Iryala to expedite shipping of needed ordnance.

711.9.14—We will arrive at Kettle, you and I. You're tougher than I thought, and you'll need it all. Good luck!

It wasn't all Varlik could have wished, but it was more than he'd thought he'd get. It was something to work from; he could fill it in later, on Kettle.

The last sentences had affected him emotionally, although he didn't examine the fact. Praise and respect were not freely given by an officer like Voker; to receive them could create a magnetic attachment, a sense of loyalty. The colonel knew the value of loyalty in a military organization, and that officers who enjoyed the greatest loyalty were hard taskmasters who demanded much. They drove their men hard, made them perform beyond their self-image, then gave the survivors their respect, at least, and privileges as possible. Their men, in turn, tried to live up to expectations.

Voker had just handled Varlik that way. And with that, Varlik Lormagen was fully committed to going with the T'swa. He didn't analyze it, but to do less would have seemed a retreat from a commitment that Voker respected or even admired.

# 9

On the approach to Kettle, there were again only three people in the small observation lounge—the same three. As he took a seat, Varlik nodded and murmured a quiet hello, actually to Konni. He was surprised that Bakkis was there. The evening before, the man had gotten visibly drunk for the first time on the trip, and it had taken a lot to do it. Drunk, Bakkis had had even less to say than usual.

From space, close on, Kettle was beautiful, showing a lot of blue and cloud white. Inside the atmosphere, the view was still magnificent. At first there was the impression of vast dark forest feathering into greenish tan grassland. Gradually the artificial rectangles of the agricultural district and nearby military base became prominent until, with the intervening prairie, they dominated the view.

On landing, they were called to the airlock—the three of them plus Colonel Voker and two ship's officers. When the door dilated, Varlik realized why they weren't using the ordinary personnel exit: The air temperature outside was somewhat hotter than normal for 52° north latitude on Kettle—115°F at midmorning, nearly twenty degrees hotter than any air temperature he'd experienced before. While in the intense sun . . .

Still, he was encouraged. As they walked to the waiting personnel carrier, forty yards away, he did not find the heat oppressive, merely impressive. The air-conditioned vehicle lifted a foot or so on its AG pressors and sped off down the travelway as if there were some hurry. There didn't seem to be; the young private at the wheel just liked to drive fast. Varlik was glad his stomach didn't feel like Bakkis's must.

The Aromanis Agricultural District was almost three centuries old, and at the edge of his sight he could make out tall planted trees, undoubtedly irrigated, that seemed to line other travelways. The military base was on native prairie without a tree of any description, its grass flattened, beaten, and worn. The drilling troops they passed marched in a cloud of dust that rose tawny gray around them.

Long rows of tents extended from the road, mere roofs above raised floors of boards, their sides rolled open to the usual prairie breeze. At short intervals stood low, premolded buildings topped by air-coolers—the company orderly rooms, mess halls, dispensaries, and other accessory facilities of the units they passed. Quickly enough they approached a broadly rambling complex of connected modules with, in front, the twin-stars flag of Rombil beside and slightly below the Royal Starfield of the Confederation. There were numerous cooling units on the roofs, and a vehicle park spread before it. Their driver parked some seventy yards from the entrance.

"Soldier," Voker said quietly, "why aren't you parking near the entrance?" The question was like the purr of a jungle cat.

"Colonel, sir," the driver said, "that area is unofficially reserved for assigned vehicles, sir. And this is a pool vehicle."

"Fine. What is my rank again?"

Belatedly the driver sensed he was in trouble. "You are a colonel, *sir.*"

"Again?"

"You are a colonel, *sir!*"

"Fine." The purr again. "What is your name and serial number, private?"

The young man answered like someone holding his breath. "Private Jaster Gorlip, 36 928 450, *sir.*"

The response snapped like a whip. "I didn't ask for your rank, private. I can see your rank. I asked for your name and serial number." Then abruptly the soft purr. "Without any unasked-for additions now, what are they?"

"Jaster Gorlip, *sir;* 36 928 450, *sir.*" The driver was answering now like a recruit to his drill sergeant.

Again the purr. "And what is your unit, private?"

"First Army Headquarters Battalion, *sir.*"

Varlik found himself sweating despite the air-conditioned coolness.

"All right, Private Jaster Gorlip, 36 928 450. Let us out thirty feet from the entrance."

Carefully the private drove to a position thirty feet from the entrance, stopped, jumped out, and opened the doors for his passengers, holding Voker's open for him. When they were out, and before the driver closed the door, Voker said, "Thank you, private. Hmm. I seem to have forgotten your name." He turned on his heel then and led the three journalists to the entrance. "Reservist," he murmured to Varlik, and chuckled. "He assumed we were new here, and thought he'd play a little game with us; make us walk in the heat. Regular army would have known better."

He caught Varlik's eye and smiled amusedly. "You wouldn't have done that when you were in, would you?"

"No way. Not with a colonel, not with a sergeant. Maybe with a green junior lieutenant, but I doubt it."

Voker laughed, then held open the door of the headquarters building for them. Inside was not exactly cool, but relatively so by local standards: perhaps ninety, Varlik thought. There was the sound of coolers, communicators, voices. "The place has grown since I left," Voker muttered. "Let's see if they've left the Information Office where it was two deks ago." They had, and after knocking, Voker introduced them to a lieutenant, who looked surprised and pleased to have them.

Lieutenant Brek Trevelos was probably, Varlik decided, the source of the non-news that had been released to the public at home. But the policy would not have been his own; lieutenants didn't set policy, nor did colonels, for that matter. Cheerful and bright looking, Trevelos made sure they'd entered the planetary adjustment factor into their watches, correcting them to Kettle's day length. Then briefly he summarized the army's buildup and preparation here, not mentioning, however, any of the history that Colonel Voker had confided. After that, instead of using his desk comm, he opened the door into an adjacent, somewhat larger office, crowded with several desks.

"Sergeant Wagar!" Trevelos called, and a man came over. "These are newspeople visiting us from the capital." The lieutenant gave their names. "I want you to call the vehicle pool and have them send over an air-conditioned car and driver. When it gets here, I want you to take our guests over to QM and get them fitted with whatever field clothes they need; three sets each. After that, you'll give them a tour of the base. Show them everything. I expect you won't be done by lunch, so at noon, you'll take them to the officers' mess and pick them up there afterward to complete the tour." He turned brightly to the three. "How does that sound?"

Without waiting for their answer, the sergeant went out to make his call. "And now," Trevelos went on, closing the door, "perhaps you have some questions you'd like me to answer while we're waiting for your vehicle."

"Yes," Konni said. "Where will we be quartered?"

"Forgive me, Miss Wenter, I should have mentioned that. We have special air-conditioned quarters for journalists—six sleeping rooms and a large common room. They've never been used. I'll call and have three rooms made up and the coolers turned on so they'll be comfortable. Sergeant Wagar will take you there at the end of your tour, or sooner if you'd like. I suggest you wait an hour, though, for the rooms to be prepared.

"Now, if you'll excuse me for just a moment . . ." He murmured a call code into his communicator and waited for a brief moment. Then faintly they heard the tinny voice at the other end—a voice with no face, for there was no screen. "This is Lieutenant Trevelos, Information Officer," Trevelos said. "Three journalists just arrived from the capital. Their baggage needs to be picked up and delivered at media accommodations. Do you know where that is?"

The tinny voice said something back, about twenty words worth. Trevelos thanked him and hung up, then turned to the three. "A Captain Brusin on the IWS *Quaranth* has already had them sent. Now, is there anything else?"

"I presume we'll be able to stop along the way and ask questions," Varlik said. "Or shoot some video cubeage."

"If you'd like. But this tour is mainly for orientation. You'll be assigned a vehicle to yourselves tomorrow—more than one, if you'd like—and be able to go about more or less as you wish."

It occurred to Varlik to ask about the T'swa then, but he didn't. He still hoped to send home a feature on them before Bakkis and Wenter could, and it seemed possible that they hadn't heard about them.

Then Trevelos issued them media passes, which they signed. The passes would admit them to the officers' mess, commissary, and lounges, among other things. And sooner than they would have thought, their driver arrived.

When they'd had their tour and Bakkis and Wenter had gotten out at the media quarters, Varlik asked the driver to drop him off at headquarters. They left the video team, Konni looking questioningly after him. At headquarters, Varlik went straight to the Information Office and knocked. Trevelos answered him in.

"What can I do for you?"

"I wondered," Varlik said, "where I can find the T'swa mercenaries."

On Trevelos's face, a look of surprise was followed by one that might have been concern. "The T'swa mercenaries?"

"Right. My editor was told by a spokesman on His Majesty's staff that T'swa mercenaries were being contracted with for Kettle. Two regiments." Varlik was not given to lying, and he heard himself say this with some surprise. But it seemed to come out believably enough. "My instructions are to get interviews with them. Where will I find them?"

Trevelos looked clearly worried now, which immediately struck Varlik as odd. Captain Benglet, back on Iryala, had accepted his interest casually enough, and Voker . . .

"Um. Well." Trevelos wasn't sure how to respond. "We don't have any T'swa on Kettle."

"When are they getting here?"

The lieutenant lagged for three or four seconds, then gave in. "They're supposed to land about midnight tonight, in two transports. But not here. They'll land at their bivouac area over east about thirty miles; a landing site has been marked out there for the ships."

"I see. I'll want a vehicle and driver then, at about 19.10 hours local.[6] I'd like to see them come in."

Trevelos nodded. "Of course," he said, and waited for Varlik to leave.

"I'd like you to make the arrangements now," Varlik said, "so I'll be here if there are any questions, or if there's anything I need to know."

Again Trevelos nodded, and murmured a code into his communicator. Again a tinny voice responded. Trevelos spoke.

"This is Lieutenant Trevelos, Information Officer. I want a field vehicle at media accommodations at 19.10 hours tonight. It will pick up a Mr. Varlik Lormagen, a newsman, and transport him to the mercenary bivouac site. The driver will have to know how to get there, and where media accommodations is."

The tinny voice spoke briefly.

"Good. That'll be fine. At 19.10." He hung up and looked at Varlik. "It's all arranged. You took me by surprise. We hadn't realized that anyone off command lines had been informed about this."

"And I hadn't realized you didn't know," Varlik replied. "I guess we surprised each other. Thank you very much for your help."

He started back to media accommodations on foot. Mercenary *bivouac* area. *Odd,* he thought, *how the command here seems to feel about the T'swa.* They hadn't wanted them in the first place, and getting them regardless, were putting them thirty miles away, apparently with no accommodations. Were the reasons Voker had given him all the reasons there were?

Probably, he decided. The military command mind didn't need good reasons. It could be arbitrary, it could be very spiteful, and it was in a position to exercise and enforce both, especially on a planet twenty-six days from home.

It was 120° in the nonexistent shade, a breath-stifling heat that had the sweat oozing again before he'd walked a fifth of the four hundred yards there. After supper he'd shower and lie down, he decided, sleep if he could. It promised to be a busy night, and there was the matter of adjusting to the short days here, and the short hours.

# PART TWO
## *The T'swa*

# 10

A rapping drew Varlik out of sleep, and he sat up abruptly. "Come in," he called. He got off the cot, wearing fatigues but barefoot. His alarm clock looked reproachfully at him. Apparently he'd forgotten to set it— a hell of a way to start. A corporal, husky and square-faced, stood in the short hallway looking in, and gestured at the rectangle of notepaper Varlik had taped to the door.

"Mr. Lormagen?"

"That's right. Come in. What's your name, corporal?"

"Duggan, sir."

"Sit down, Corporal Duggan." Varlik motioned to one of the two folding chairs. "What do your messmates call you?"

"Pat, sir. Short for Patros."

"Pat it is, then. Mine's Varlik."

Varlik pulled on his boots and pressed them snugly closed, snapped his recorder on his belt, slung his video camera under his left arm, slipped the band of his visor-like viewer over his head, then left with the corporal. The night felt strange to him, unreal, like one of the occasional dreams he had of being back in the army in some impossible situation or other. Outside, the air reminded him of a hot pool—all right for sitting in. The vehicle was an uncooled hovercar with the top and windows retracted. The corporal held the door for him.

Aside from their headlamps, almost the only lights in camp were at the few locations where work went on at night—motor pools, the hospital, and, of course, Army Headquarters. The perimeter, about a mile outside the encampment itself, was a barbed wire fence, tall and silent; outside that, accordion wire; and beneath the ground, string mines, no doubt. String mines, at least. A concrete and earth blockhouse stood by the steel-bar gate, which a guard opened for them while others no doubt watched from the blockhouse. Presumably there were other blockhouses at intervals around the camp.

Then they were out, accelerating across the prairie, the treated travelway giving way to the prairie's loose dry soil. A trail of dust rose with their passage. Here the way was only barely marked, as if a reaction dozer had scraped a minimal scalp across the grassland, careful to displace as little soil as possible—almost as if it had backed, dragging its blade behind. At intervals stood marker rods, slender, chest high, catching the head-light beams on reflective surfaces.

The air was still hot, the temperature surely well over a hundred, Varlik decided, and he wondered if the nights here were long enough to allow much cooling. The air that swirled about them seemed hotter, in a way, than it had in stillness outside the hut. But it wasn't really oppressive, not with the sun's fierce rays departed. A person *could* adapt to Kettle, he thought, at least at 52° north latitude.

"What do you think of the camp's defensive perimeter, Pat?" he asked. "Is it adequate? Or is it even necessary?"

Duggan answered without taking his eyes off the cone of their head-lights. "You'd need to ask the general about that, sir, or one of his staff. But one thing you ought to be warned about—don't go trompin' around outside the fence. You're likely to lose a leg, all the way to your windpipe. And that's if someone don't shoot you first. The gooks on this part of the planet have been pacified for three hundred years, damn near, and from what I've heard, they've never been known to join together in anything. But it looks to me like the brass isn't taking anything for granted."

He drove in silence for a minute or so before saying anything more. "And we may not see them, but there's security patrols flying around over the country in light scouts, with scanners and ultra-aud. There's probably one of 'em readin' us right now. We give off a radio signal they recognize. No signal means 'investigate possible hostile.'

"And besides that, there's heavily armed recon floaters that go back and forth over the whole damn region, watching for anything like a mobilization or large movement of gooks. Just in case."

They had left the near-flat vicinity of camp for broadly rolling coun-try, and the camp's few lights had disappeared behind the first gentle hill. What he was seeing now, Varlik realized, was the raw, native planet, marked only by this meager track and the cone of their headlights. Here, low rounded ridges ran almost north and south, and on their east-facing slopes, prairie gave way to savannah, its widely scattered, globular trees lurking darker in the night. Varlik wondered if large animals roved here, and whether any were inclined to attack people. Probably none could catch a hovercar if they tried.

The sky was innocent of city glow, stars myriad against and around the Milky Way's white swath. The present human sector was farther in toward the hub than mankind's earlier home, and the star display a bit richer, although Varlik knew nothing of that. He only knew it was beau-tiful. Scanning it for a recognizable constellation, he found none, and wasn't sure whether that reflected his sketchy knowledge of constellations or his displacement in space, or possibly the fact that he was in the middle northern latitudes here while Landfall was in the southern hemisphere at home.

His misgivings about the T'swa returned again, to mind and gut. He was on his way to meet them, to arrange to live with them, share a squad tent with some of them. A picture flashed in his mind, not for the first time, of large, black, hardbitten men who held life cheap. They were gambling, a fight broke out, knives flashed . . .

Maybe he'd end up with Colonel Voker after all.

And the T'swa would arrive in the middle of night. Captain Trevelos had said they would bivouac, which implied an unimproved area. When they got off the ship, would they have to dig latrines in the darkness and set up kitchens before they retired, besides erecting tents? Welcome to Kettle! They'd be in a great mood!

Or maybe they preferred it that way. Outside the Confederation worlds, and maybe some of the trade worlds, attitudes deviated a bit from Standard. And the T'swa were gooks—barbarians in uniforms, more or less. You couldn't know what they'd consider satisfactory.

After a while the mild hills gave way to an area almost as level as the military camp they'd left, and the hovercar slowed. "It's right about in here, sir," said Duggan. It was the first either of them had spoken for quite a few miles. "Hard to locate exactly in the dark. What we did was, we brought a reaction dozer out, and it sort of scalped a perimeter line around a big square so the ships can find it on the scanners at night. Or they can hang around up there till it gets light, or just set down blind by gravitic coordinates, I suppose; but if they tried that, they might miss the place, depending on how good their coordinates are set."

The corporal's speech was Iryalan instead of Romblit, his diction marking him back-country rural; a lot of soldiers were.

"Would it make any difference where they put down?" Varlik asked. "Couldn't they as well camp in one place as another, way out here?"

"Not very well. We drilled some water wells for 'em; they're going to need 'em when the sun gets up. They're really gonna need those water wells. I've heard their world is as hot as this one, but if they're human, they're gonna want lots of water."

He stopped, and they settled mentally to wait. "Pat," Varlik asked shortly, "what do you think of the Rombili?"

Duggan didn't answer at once, sitting back with one arm leaning on the top of the door. "The Rombili? They seem all right to me. They kind of screwed up the war, but it's easy to see how that would be; nobody had any idea that all those sweatbirds were running around loose down there, or that they had weapons or anything. I've talked to quite a few Rombili, and they're not much different from us."

"Sweatbirds. Is that what you call the gooks here?"

"Right. They got a funny build—long legs, big chest, and kind of skinny. All they need is a long neck and beak for catching fish, and they do have quite a nose. Longish necks, too."

"What do you think about T'swa mercenaries coming out here?"

"Seems good to me." He turned his face to Varlik, a brief reflection of starlight in one eye. "Let the T'swa fight the gooks. I hear they love wars; why not give 'em this one? I'd like to see two divisions of 'em, not just two regiments. Specially if they're as good as you hear."

Varlik watched the man remove something, a small package, from a pocket of his fatigue shirt, take something from it with his fingers, and put the something into his mouth. The spicy smell of nictos reached Varlik's nose. For a moment the corporal chewed, compacting the plug, then spat onto the prairie.

"Is that how most of the men feel about the T'swa? They wish there were two divisions?"

"Or a whole army." His eyes returned to Varlik. "We're not afraid of the gooks. Don't get me wrong. But they've got big jungles down south, hotter than a cookpot. I mean, it's bad up here, but it's supposed to be a lot worse at Beregesh. So there's this bunch of crazy sweatbirds down there, and it's gonna be bloody work doin' anything about 'em. If it wasn't for the technite, I'd say let 'em have the place. And we probably would, too."

He spat again and said nothing for half a minute. Then, "That's kind of what we're trying to do anyway, I guess. What General Lamons has in mind, accordin' to rumor. Just take back the country around the mines, fortify hell out of it, and let the gooks have the rest of the planet. Except for Aromanis.

"And stop usin' slaves. That's where the Rombili screwed up. If they'd have just started mining with mechanicals and contract workers, the gooks wouldn't have even known the Rombili were on the planet."

The corporal paused then, as if uncertain, and peered at Varlik in the starlight. "If I tell you somethin' private between the two of us, will you keep it that way?"

Lormagen extended his right hand. "I guarantee it." They gripped on the promise.

"My best buddy's a computerman, and he called up the staff briefing file on Kettle, to read it. The gooks never even lived where the mines are until the Rombili took slaves down there. And the first batch they took there, a lot of 'em died, because they made 'em work without cool suits. And the women they took down there, some of 'em died when they got pregnant. So the gooks that could take it lived, and the toughest got away to the jungles and had families there. And that's the strain we gotta fight."

He spat again, shrugging. "Not even a gook likes bein' a slave."

Varlik nodded, and the conversation died of contagious introversion and the night. They watched the sky and waited, and after a few minutes they didn't really watch any more, only sat with their faces aimed upward a little.

Then Varlik began to feel something, and his alertness sharpened. He became aware that his driver too had taken life. Carefully they scanned the sky, and realized that within the blackness was a different black, an area poorly defined that showed no stars, moving from what he thought was the east. As they strained to see into it, it grew, encroaching upon the Milky Way, slowly crossing it. Varlik didn't think to lower the visor-like camera monitor. With it down he could have peered beneath it to see normally or cast his glance upward a little to watch through the eye of his camera, which adjusted constantly to target illumination.

Abruptly the night was broken from above by a powerful beam of light that slid across the ground, passing near them, then made an angle nearby.

"Consar's royal balls!" Duggan swore. "I parked in their landing square! Must have missed the dozer scalp somehow; maybe there was a gap in it at the travelway." He laughed as he swung the car around and moved away. "All this empty prairie out here and I parked where they're supposed to put down." They hurried up a mild slope, Varlik with camera busy, then stopped again three hundred yards distant while the powerful light continued to trace a rectangle on the ground. Abruptly it went out, and gradually the vague blackness became a ship settling groundward, no lights showing.

Brief minutes later it rested on the prairie, its powerful lights flooding the area on one side. A second ship took shape above, and five minutes later it rested some hundred yards from the first. More lights brightened the area between the ships, while others flooded thinly a larger area beyond them. Squares opened in the hulls. Hundreds of uniformed men began to file from some of the smaller openings, moving on the double. Some trotted into the thinly lit area, while most formed ranks near the hulls.

Cargo movers floated out with boxes and duffle bags stacked beneath them, setting down their burdens along a line midway between the ships. Then they floated back through the gangways and out of sight for more. A long low pile of material took shape quickly. At one end of it, men were calling and gesturing, and from the ranked troops, squads quick-timed over to pick up gear and trot away with it.

Suddenly, from the darkness to one side of Varlik and Duggan, a voice spoke, seeming not more than a dozen yards away. "Hoy!" it said, quietly but firmly, a neutral, nonthreatening, but attention-taking sound. Varlik's and Duggan's eyes snapped in that direction but saw nothing. Nothing but night.

"Who are you, and what are you doing here?" the voice asked. Its Standard was accented but easily understood.

Varlik's eyes checked the power light on the small recorder at his belt, then he answered in Tyspi. "I've come to speak with the T'swa. My name is Varlik Lormagen. I am from Iryala, and I am . . ." He had no word for journalist. "My job is to tell the people of the Confederation what T'swa warriors are like."

A ring of chuckles sounded softly all around them, and Varlik felt his hackles rise. Even on his bare forearms the hair stood up like tiny antennae. But there was no malice in the laughter. None whatever. Obviously he and Duggan had been spotted on scans from the ships, and a patrol had been sent to check them out.

"You are speaking with a T'swa warrior now," the voice said. "Our commanders are occupied. We will wait here."

This had been said in Tyspi also, and Varlik was surprised to find that the diction was as clear, the speech as easily understood, as the lesson recordings had been. He spoke now in Standard. "Is it all right to talk with you while we wait? If so, I would prefer to speak Standard just now. My driver doesn't know Tyspi, and it would be more courteous if we spoke so he can understand."

There were no more chucklings around them. "Standard will be satisfactory," the voice said in kind, and now, by starlight, Varlik could make out the T'swi as the man walked toward them, a little taller than himself, looking bulky and powerful. Holding the video camera in one hand, Varlik lowered the monitor with the other. In it he could see what the camera saw: dark face, large eyes, hawk nose, wide lipless mouth, and a helmet that seemed quite standard. About ten feet away the T'swi stopped. His sidearms were a holstered pistol and a short sword. He held a rifle ready in his hands.

The sword surprised Varlik. He'd assumed that the swords the T'swa carried in adventure stories had been the writers' creation. Swords were a primitive weapon, seen on gook worlds and perhaps on parts of some more primitive trade worlds. And while the T'swa *were* gooks, they were not supposed to be primitive in the military sense. Even Colonel Voker considered them superb troops.

Now that they were here, in front of him, Varlik had to grope for questions. "How many of you are there?" he asked.

"We are two regiments."

"About thirty-eight hundred men, then?"

"My regiment is the Red Scorpion Regiment. We recently finished a sporadically rather vicious war on Emor Gadny's World, and our numbers are reduced to 934 officers and men."

"In a regiment? You came straight here without refitting or replacing your casualties?"

"No. We refitted on Tyss, and spent two months enjoying our world and our people, healing our wounds and replacing such weapons as were worn out or lost. We do not replace casualties."

Didn't replace casualties! Varlik wondered if somehow he had misunderstood the T'swi. "How many were in your regiment when you went to—what world was that?"

"Emor Gadny's World. An interesting place—beautiful but difficult. We went there four years ago with about twelve hundred. Before that we were on Gwalsey, a dull war, and before that, Splenn. We went to Splenn a virgin regiment, with a full complement of 1,720 officers and men. That was more than fourteen years ago, Standard."

"But . . ." Varlik could not comprehend. They didn't replace their casualties! "How can you call yourself a regiment, then? How many did you say you have now?"

"Nine hundred and thirty-four effectives." The T'swi chuckled. "Abundantly effective effectives. And we will be the Red Scorpion Regiment until there are none of us left."

Varlik pursed his lips and whistled silently. This was something the fictionists hadn't mentioned, probably didn't know about. He imagined for a moment three scarred and gray-haired veterans charging an enemy— or slipping up on them in the dark, more likely.

"How long do you think it will be before you'll be in action? Do you have any idea?"

"It depends on the urgency of the situation. Normally, after landfall we spend two weeks in reconditioning, per contract. The opportunities for exercise are somewhat limited on a troopship, and our manner of combat requires physical excellence."

*This guy,* thought Varlik, *talks like someone out of staff college, not like anyone who'd be sent out to lead a patrol.* "What rank are you?" he asked.

"I am Sergeant Kusu. This is my squad."

"What's your education?"

"We have been educated as warriors of Tyss, by the Lodge of Kootosh-Lan."

Varlik glanced down at the recorder and camera. The tiny red glints reassured him; he wouldn't want to lose any of this. "The Lodge of Kootosh-Lan. I know very little about the T'swa. Does the name Kootosh-Lan have some special significance?"

"Kootosh-Lan founded the lodge, in the year 8,107 of our calendar. That was more than 14,000 of your Standard years ago."

Varlik tried carefully to see the black face more exactly, to read character and mood. *If that is history instead of folklore, their recorded history is a lot older than ours.* He decided to approach the matter indirectly—see if the story had mythic elements. "Was Kootosh-Lan a great warrior?"

A couple of chuckles were audible behind him. "Kootosh-Lan was no warrior at all. She was a teacher, the most renowned master in the history of Tyss. It was she who traced out and codified the Way of the Warrior, then established the first warrior lodge, that those who chose the Way of the Warrior could be properly prepared."

*This Kusu,* Varlik told himself, *is a great interview. Answers everything directly with full pertinent details.*

The sergeant's gaze had moved to the ships; Varlik's attention and camera followed. No longer did the cargo movers float in and out of the freight doors. Troops still picked up gear and carried it away. In the diffusely lit area on the far side was a lot of activity now; they were setting up camp there.

"One ship will leave soon," said Kusu.

"How soon?"

"A few minutes."

*Incredibly quick. They probably drill disembarking,* Varlik decided. "Will the other ship stay?"

"Briefly. While camp is being set up."

"Did the troops unload their own materials, or was that done by crewmen?"

"The ship's crew operates the cargo movers. The ship is T'swa, a troop carrier leased from your own world, and its crew is trained and experienced at unloading military material. They are to their jobs what we are to warring—expert. The Way of Jobs is not less an art than the Way of war. Are you familiar at all with the Ways?"

Varlik recalled vaguely the chart in the *Exotic Philosophies* entry. "Very slightly. I recall seeing a chart showing Ways of, uh, Work, and Fighting, and . . . Study was one. There were others." He wished he could read the T'swi's reactions. Then a movement caught his attention; one of the ships was lifting, and he thumbed the camera's trigger again. In little more than a minute it was lost to darkness. The other ship showed no sign of leaving; its floodlights still illuminated the bivouac area.

Sergeant Kusu interrupted Varlik's watching. "Follow me; I will take you to our colonel now."

Somehow it sounded more an order than suggestion. Kusu had probably been told to bring in whoever was waiting out here. "Okay?" Duggan asked. Varlik nodded. As the corporal activated the AG unit, the burly T'swi turned and trotted off down the slight slope toward the landing site. The others waited behind and to the sides until the vehicle began to follow Kusu, then moved along in its wake.

They drove right through the mustering area. Considerable material remained on the unloading site, unattended now. Two cargo movers were parked there, waiting to transfer more of it, perhaps to the kitchens when they were ready. In about two minutes, Duggan drew the car up to the regimental headquarters site, where already a considerable tent had been erected. A miniature ditch was still being dug around it, to catch and carry off the water from its roof in case of rain. There was a great deal of crisp and purposeful activity roundabout. Squad tents were being raised. These men knew what they were doing, and did it rapidly, with a modest amount of quiet, cheerful talk in Tyspi.

At the regimental headquarters Kusu reported, then introduced Varlik to Colonel Koda. Except for the patrol's black, the T'swa uniforms were a curiously, irregularly blotched green, Koda's included. In the monitor, the colonel looked no older than the sergeant and carried much the same belt gear. Only the shoulder insignia were different. They were standard—cloth wings versus the sergeant's sewn-on patch with the initial $T$.[7] Colonel Koda examined the Iryalan for a brief moment, then spoke in Standard with a slight accent that was mostly a matter of precise diction.

"Varlik Lormagen." He said it as if tasting the name; his eyes were alert, direct but unthreatening. "And you want to tell your people about T'swa warriors. Very well, you can report to—Lieutenant Zimsu of the First Platoon, Company A, in the morning. He will expect you. You can accompany the platoon in its daily routine and observe T'swa warriors to your fill." Then he spoke briefly to his aide in Tyspi before turning again to Varlik.

"Thank you, colonel," Varlik said. To his surprise, the T'swa colonel flashed a quick grin.

"You are welcome," the colonel replied, then dismissed him unmistakably, simply by removing his attention totally.

Unaccompanied now, ignored, Varlik and Duggan climbed into their vehicle and drove away, picking a careful route through the encampment. Hovercars do not ride an air cushion; they operate on the same gravitic principle as floaters. But as hover vehicles are functionally limited to near contact with massive bodies, the turbulence of rapid passage can raise dust. Duggan's caution among the tents avoided this. Even so, he cleared the area quickly enough, and swung around in an arc that would find the marker rods.

Once more on the track, they started back for the Confederation military base, not speaking till they topped the first low hill. Then Duggan swung the vehicle around and stopped for a last look. At almost the moment they stopped, the floodlamps of the ship flicked off, leaving the plain in darkness. There were not even the white sparks of handlamps.

"What do you think of them, Pat?" Varlik asked.

"The T'swa? First-rate soldiers. They set that place up quicker than I ever would have thought. And that patrol! Whoosh! They could have shot us before we ever knew they were around; could have slit our throats, as far as that's concerned." Duggan shook his head in wonder. "They're good, all right. Better'n good."

He paused. "You coming to see 'em again tomorrow?"

"Right."

"Going to stay with 'em while you're here?"

Varlik's misgivings were gone, leaving only a light unease in its stead. The T'swa had seemed both civilized and intriguing, unlike anything his imagination had conjured up.

"You can bet on it," he said.

Duggan nodded as if approving, then swung the car around and started back toward the base. They hardly said anything all the way there.

# 11

Varlik arrived at officers' mess thick-headed and sluggish from the combination of the short Orlanthan diurnal cycle, the army's daybreak reveille, and having gone to bed so late the night before. Before hitting the sack, he'd copied and edited his cube, intercutting his narration, covering not only the T'swa but the Aromanis camp and the heat, with a brief statistical description of Kettle he'd excerpted in the ship's library. It was his first feature on Kettle and the T'swa.

Now, as he stepped into the relative coolness of the mess hall, the pungent smell of fresh-brewed joma met him, along with the different pungency of fried bacon. He'd have liked to take the empty seat at Colonel Voker's table, but the brisk and businesslike pace of eating there warned him away and, at any rate, the media people had their own table assigned here. It might be a breach of etiquette to sit elsewhere uninvited. So instead he crossed to where Konni Wenter and the typically withdrawn-looking Bertol Bakkis sat eating.

A messman in crisp white apron had seen Varlik enter and, tracking him with his eyes, slanted quickly over, stainless steel thermal pitcher in hand, to pour his joma and take his order. Varlik gave it, then unfolded the waiting white cloth napkin onto his lap as the messman left.

"I saw you leave last night," Konni said.

Varlik looked up, noticing Bakkis's opaque gaze on him.

"You did? I'm surprised," Varlik said. "It was close to 19.20 when we left."

"Nineteen-fifteen; I looked. I couldn't get to sleep, so I'd been out walking around to get tired. I saw a car pull up, and five minutes later you left in it."

"Right."

She said nothing then, as if waiting, and he ignored her, testing the scalding joma with a cautious upper lip, deciding that cream was in order, for cooling. If she wanted information, she'd have to be specific.

"Where did you go?" she asked finally as he put down the cream and reached for the sugar.

"Off base." Varlik's eyes moved to Bakkis for a moment; the heavyset cameraman had shifted his attention back to his plate, half cleaned of its eggs and bacon.

"I'd hoped," Konni said, "that we might cooperate here, to some degree at least. It's not as if we're rivals."

She'd hit close to home, and it annoyed Varlik. He finished sweetening his joma before turning his eyes to hers. "I'm afraid I tend to be a loner," he said stiffly.

The messman was approaching with Varlik's breakfast on a large plate, and Varlik gave his attention first to receiving the food, then to opening and buttering a hot roll.

"I suppose you've heard about the T'swa regiments."

The voice as well as the words startled Varlik, and butter knife poised, he turned abruptly to Bakkis. The man had never spoken to him before. "We plan to find out where they keep them," the cameraman went on, "and go out there today. You're welcome to ride with us if you want."

"That's where I was last night," Varlik found himself answering. "I was there when they landed, about thirty miles from here."

"Two regiments, were there?" Bakkis asked.

"Right. Just the way I'd heard back in Landfall."

Bakkis nodded, face still inscrutable. "Do you plan to go back there today?"

"Yes. Matter of fact, I do."

"Be all right to go together, or do you want to go alone?"

Varlik was amazed. He'd thought of Bertol Bakkis as a lump of barely aware flesh, its intelligence pickled in ethanol, operating in some obscure, automatic way along a subconscious thread of journalistic intention. Now the man was talking as casually and intelligently as anyone might, and for the moment it was Konni who sat quietly.

Bakkis had been the icebreaker. While they finished their breakfasts, the three of them talked about the T'swa, about Varlik's brief talk with Colonel Koda, and the invitation to attach himself to Koda's regiment.

"I suppose you got some cubeage of the landing," Bakkis said.

"Some. If you'd like to copy the field cube with your equipment," Varlik found himself saying, "you're welcome to."

"Thanks. I will. And when we get back to our quarters, I'll have Konni interview you on camera. That will make the field shots more meaningful to viewers, and it'll set people up for the feature articles you send."

It made so much sense to Varlik that his earlier guardedness seemed incomprehensible and petty.

After Bakkis had copied parts of his T'swa cube—the landing and the bivouac—and shot Konni's skilled interview, they went to the communications center. On the way, Varlik apologized, not very articulately, for his boorishness, and Konni, for whatever reason, had stiffened at the apology. Bertol's reaction, somewhat amorphous, seemed to say that he hadn't felt aggrieved, but thanks anyway.

The temperature had soared, and sweat had soaked through Varlik's twill shirt; workouts aboard the *Quaranth* had developed his sweat gland function well beyond the ordinary. After filling out brief forms and labels, they left their packaged cubes with the sergeant there for dispatch to Iryala in the day's message pod. Even by message pod, the sergeant told them, it would take 9.83 standard days for reports to reach Iryala— 11.90 Orlanthan days.

From the communications center, it was no more than an eighty-foot walk down a corridor to the information office. At their knock, Trevelos called out to enter, and they did, Varlik holding the door for the other two. Trevelos's almost boyish pleasure of the day before was gone. The expression that met them now was stiff and guarded.

"How can I help you?" he asked.

It was Varlik who answered, "We'd like a vehicle."

Trevelos's expression became stiffer, yet vaguely unhappy. "I'm afraid I can't do that."

Varlik was dumbfounded. "Why? Yesterday you said we could have one or more if we wanted."

Trevelos's discomfort was tangible. "I'm afraid I overspoke myself. If you want to go somewhere, perhaps I can arrange a chauffeured vehicle."

"Okay. We'd like to be taken to the T'swa camp."

Trevelos didn't answer for several seconds. "I'm afraid that's impossible. The T'swa camp is off-limits."

"Off-limits? Why?"

"The T'swa's privacy is to be strictly respected."

"But lieutenant, I was there last night and had a direct invitation from Colonel Koda of the Red Scorpion Regiment to stay with them, to describe them and their training for the Iryalan public. He told me he'd expect me today."

Trevelos actually blushed. "I'm afraid I can't help you with that, Mr. Lormagen. Perhaps something else."

Hormones—something—surged through Varlik's body, with a feeling first of heat, then of internal numbness, incredulity, as he stared at the information officer. Then Bakkis spoke, his tone casual.

"What, specifically, did the general order, lieutenant?"

Varlik's eyes turned to Bakkis's sweaty, somewhat florid face, then to Trevelos again. Bakkis had put his finger on the problem, Varlik was sure: Lamons. But the only result was that Trevelos looked less uncomfortable, as if with a shifting of blame from himself to the general.

"I do not feel I should discuss my orders."

"Of course." Bakkis had taken over, and Varlik was willing, for now, that he should. "We can understand that," Bakkis went on. "In that case, we'd like to see the agricultural operation."

Trevelos brightened. "Certainly. When would you like your car?"

Bakkis looked at Varlik, "Varl?" he said.

"Uh—why not now?" At the moment he didn't care—he had no real interest in the Aromanis farms—but it was an answer.

Trevelos looked almost happily at Bakkis. "I can have a car and driver here in fifteen minutes. And I'll call the farm headquarters so you can have lunch there. Their executive dining room has a marvelous reputation among the general's staff; almost everything they serve is fresh, and the cooks are excellent."

Bakkis asked that they be picked up at their quarters in fifty minutes—half a local hour. After the lieutenant had made arrangements with the motor pool, the three journalists said goodbye and left. When the office door had closed behind them, Bakkis muttered an obscenity, but without heat, and started toward the communications center. "I'm going to dispatch my office and ask them to get this restriction lifted if they can. They were especially interested in the T'swa. Meanwhile, let's keep Trevelos happy and relaxed."

*So Iryala Video had also been especially interested in the T'swa.* "Messages will take ten days Standard each way," Varlik pointed out, "plus whatever time it takes at the other end to get an order issued—if it gets issued."

They had stopped outside the comm center door. "The next time we see Trevelos," Bakkis said quietly, "I'll tell him we've dispatched our offices for a reversal, and that we appreciate what he's done for us. He'll assume we're content to wait, that we're trusting our offices to take care of things for us. That's the way he'd do it. Maybe that will relax him about our wanting to get to the T'swa. Then, in three or four days, we'll try to get a car without a driver, to hop around and interview some Romblit troops. He's already feeling propitiative, and if he'll go for that, screw the restriction; we'll go see the T'swa."

Varlik wondered if that would work, and if Bakkis actually believed it might. One thing was certain: He'd drastically misjudged this man back on the *Quaranth.*

The trip to the farm had been more interesting than Varlik had anticipated. The travelways were lined with tall native trees. The headquarters buildings were comfortable, rambling, air-conditioned, and beautifully landscaped, with everything marvelously clean and well-tended. The cuisine was better than anything he'd experienced before. The Romblit personnel there seemed competent and friendly. Security personnel were numerous, well-armed, and relaxed—were paramilitary employees of Technite, Ltd., the firm that had long operated the Orlanthan fief for the Romblit government. The army apparently restricted itself to patrolling the surroundings, leaving the on-farm scene at something like prewar normal.

Remarkably little powered machinery was used in the agricultural operations; hand labor was compellingly cheap, apparently, and probably more precise for many tasks. Even the removal of weeds in large rowcrop fields was done by a line of tall thin workers, the hoes in their hands rising and falling in unison.

The field workers and domestics had given Varlik his first look at sweatbirds. They were a brownish people, slender except for barrel chests, their coarse brown hair straight and almost crested, their flaring eyebrows like tufts of golden-brown feathers that presumably served to divert sweat. And even those who served in the dining room showed little sign of subcutaneous fat. They reminded Varlik of kerkas, the tall wading birds of Iryala; their noses really were relatively long and pointed, and their necks too long as human necks go. Their physical structure seemed designed to maximize the body's surface/mass ratio for dispersing body heat. They were quite different from the husky T'swa, whose phenotype had evolved under considerably heavier gravity.

Varlik had wondered what the local sweatbirds thought of the war; perhaps, he'd told himself, they didn't even know about it, although all the nearby military activity must have told them something was happening somewhere.

After the farm, Bertol and Konni had been ready for a shower, to be followed by editing their field cubes in air-conditioned comfort. Varlik, though, had decided to take care of one final job, and jogged through dusty 120° heat to headquarters. After the aesthetics of the farm, the drab and dusty military base seemed utterly graceless. He knocked at the information officer's door and identified himself, and Lieutenant Trevelos's voice bade him enter.

"How can I help you?" the lieutenant asked when Varlik had entered.

"I'd like to see the Orlanthan briefing. It will give me a much better sense of the overall situation here."

Immediately the lieutenant looked worried, then apologetic. "Mr. Lormagen, I really dislike telling you this . . ."

"But you can't let me see it."

"That's right. You're neither a staff officer nor a command officer."

Varlik nodded slowly. "Well . . . thank you, anyway."

He turned and left, jogging back to his quarters for the postponed shower. While showering, he rehearsed several scenes with General Lamons, none of which, he knew, would ever occur. A couple of them were probably physically impossible. Then he too sat down to play his field cube of the day and record his article. When he'd finished, he had to admit it was good, something that readers would appreciate. But it wasn't what he was here for.

After supper he found out where Colonel Voker was quartered—a one-room hut of poured concrete in officers' country. Varlik stood hesitantly, unsure he should be there, then knocked. The colonel opened the door and scowled out at him.

"What do you want?"

"I seem to be running into brick walls at the information office. I hoped you could advise me. Again."

Voker's surliness softened slightly, and he gestured Varlik in. His quarters, though military, managed, through the prerogatives and resources of a senior officer, to reflect his personality. The windows were curtained. A small and clearly expensive tapestry softened one wall; a burnished wood bookcase with expensively bound books stood against another. The air conditioner held down the interior temperature to a luxurious 85°. Next to a lightly upholstered chair, a book lay open, face down on a small stand, and a red light glowed in an expensive cube player beside it.

"Specifically?" Voker asked.

Varlik told him of the prohibition against being taken to the T'swa camp, and of Trevelos's refusal to let him see the briefing on Orlantha.

"And this Colonel Koda invited you to stay with them?"

Varlik nodded. "Right."

"Huh." Voker gazed reflectively at him, lips slightly pursed, then abruptly grinned—a grin of pleasure tinged with something else. Malice. "So you still want to live with the T'swa. Well, fine. Be at the headquarters entrance at 05.50 hours tomorrow morning. And carry everything you absolutely need on your person, in case you luck out and make it to the T'swa camp—recorder, camera, toothbrush. The minimum. Don't be obvious—no suitcase. From there it's up to you—your wits and your guts. And your luck.

"And as far as the briefing cube is concerned, you got the essential picture from me aboard the *Quaranth*."

He stepped back to the door and put his hand on the handle. "And I don't mind telling you, I'll be interested in seeing what happens in the morning."

At 16.00 hours, Lieutenant Trevelos, reading a novel on the computer screen in his office, was interrupted by a knock. Irritatedly he cleared the screen before saying, "come in." It was Colonel Voker who opened the door, and Trevelos got quickly to his feet.

"At ease, lieutenant. I just came by to ask a question or two."

Trevelos receded into his chair. "Of course, sir." He looked around. "Would the colonel care to sit?"

Voker waved it off. "The reporter, Varlik Lormagen, and I got to know one another on the *Quaranth*. I ran into him on my way over here, and asked how he's doing. He told me he's been refused access to the Orlantha briefing. Can you give me the background on that refusal?"

"Yes, sir. Last night Mr. Lormagen went out to the T'swa area, and somehow the general heard about it this morning. It made General Lamons very unhappy, and he made it extremely clear to me that under no conditions was I to allow the media to go there again. He was particularly unhappy about Lormagen, and told me—these are his exact words—'You are not to allow this young fart any special privileges.'" Trevelos shrugged, spreading his hands.

Voker nodded thoughtfully. "I get the picture. Thank you, lieutenant. And have a good evening."

In the corridor, Voker allowed himself a chuckle. The situation was exactly as he'd suspected. In fact, he'd have given odds on it, but it was nice to know with certainty. Tomorrow he'd see just how good, and how lucky, young Lormagen was.

# 12

At the Aromanis Base of the Orlanthan Counterinsurgency Army, the working day began at 05.00. Varlik, Konni, and Bertol Bakkis were outside the headquarters building entrance a quarter-hour later, at 05.25, twenty-five minutes before the time Voker had told him. All three were in field uniform, each with a musette bag slung on one shoulder, video camera on the other. The sun was up, but by only a hand's breadth, and it was still "cool"—about ninety-five degrees.

Konni Wenter was thinking how hot it would be in another hour—worse, another two hours—and whether Lormagen had been truthful when he'd told them he didn't know what was supposed to happen, only that something was. And what his real reason might have been in suggesting they be here with him.

Varlik was glad they'd come. He had the definite idea that he was on somebody's shit list, and that he'd be much more subject to counteraction if he were there alone, perhaps being told he couldn't loiter outside the entrance. This way it wasn't Varlik Lormagen standing here, but a group of journalists.

Bakkis's mind was on idle, thinking nothing, an ability he'd always had when there was nothing requiring his conscious attention. He'd been fifteen years old before he'd realized that everyone didn't do that. Only an occasional thought drifted unbidden through his mind. Just now he was aware of moderate soreness in his thighs and abdomen; the evening before he'd gone to the officers' gym, a set of connected modules with assorted equipment, and begun the distasteful task of becoming physically less unfit.

At 05.45, a sergeant came out, followed by a captain, and told them politely to move aside a few yards, which they did. Moments later they could see a hovercar approaching, open to the heat. They watched it come up the surfaced travelway, through the vehicle park, and pull up before the entrance. The occupants were T'swa, their skin blue-black.

As the vehicle slowed, entering the vehicle park, more men issued from the headquarters entrance. Varlik glanced at them, relieved to find that none wore the novaburst of a general. The time, Varlik realized, was definitely at hand; what he didn't know was what to do about it. Almost unaware of what he was doing, he moved closer, out of the background, visor down, belt recorder on, camera in his hands, its red light blinking. Bakkis advanced beside him.

Varlik's eyes were on the T'swa as they dismounted from the light field vehicle. One of them was Colonel Koda, and one of the others also wore the stylized wings of a full colonel. All wore garrison caps tilted to the right, and by daylight their bristly, close-cropped black hair, like their skin, had a distinct bluish tinge. It was when Koda's feet were on the ground that Varlik stepped forward. A subcolonel in charge of the reception group glanced at Varlik angrily, his mouth opening to speak, but Colonel Koda, stopping to look at the reporter, spoke first.

"Lormagen! My visitor at the landing! I had expected you yesterday. Are you no longer interested in my invitation?"

"Very interested, sir. I was refused transportation to your camp; otherwise, I'd have been there."

The white subcolonel's brows had knotted, his mouth a rictus of consternation.

"Ah!" said Koda. "Are you a soldier? Or under military command?"

"No, sir. I'm a journalist. But I depend on the army for accommodations and assistance."

"Then it was only a matter of transportation?"

"That's right, sir."

"Are you available for additional employment, if it does not interfere with your existing assignment?"

This, Varlik realized, was the moment of decision. "Absolutely, colonel."

They stood there for just a moment while the subcolonel fidgeted inwardly.

"Well, then," Koda said casually, "perhaps you will consent to be my civilian aide—my press aide. I have never had a press aide before, but I imagine that your new duties will not interfere with those of your present employment. Perhaps they will even expedite and mutually strengthen each other."

Varlik felt a grin seep up from somewhere to spread over his face.

"I'd like that very much, sir."

"Good. You are now officially in the employ of the Red Scorpion Regiment, of the Lodge of Kootosh-Lan, of the United Lodges of Tyss, as the regimental press aide. You will accompany me until I instruct you otherwise." Koda turned to the other T'swa colonel and nodded. The other in turn spoke to the Iryalan subcolonel.

"Colonel, we are ready to be presented to your general."

The subcolonel was outranked. Stiff, expressionless now, he turned to the headquarters entrance and led the T'swa party—the two colonels, two majors who were their executive officers, and two captains who were their aides, plus Varlik Lormagen—in to meet General Lamons. A standard army headquarters had a briefing room, and it was there that the general awaited them with several other officers, including Colonel Voker and Lieutenant Trevelos. Lamons stared the T'swa coldly into the room, not noticing the uniformed Varlik behind them.

"Colonels," said the general, "I am General Lamons, commanding." He gestured to the officers on either side of him. "This is my executive officer, Brigadier Demler, and this is Major General Grossel, commanding Romblit forces on Orlantha. The other gentlemen are our immediate staff. Welcome."

He was reciting; there was no welcome at all in his words. Chairs stood around a long table, but they were neatly, uniformly shoved beneath it; General Lamons had no intention of inviting them to sit, let alone offering them the quasi-ceremonial courtesy of joma. As he'd spoken, the general's eyes had noticed Varlik, clearly no T'swi, and with his last words of welcome, he looked at the subcolonel who stood beside the T'swa.

"Colonel Fonvill, who is that white man with them?"

"He's their press aide, general."

"Press aide?!"

Trevelos elaborated in a tentative voice. "He's Varlik Lormagen, sir. The journalist from Iryala."

Lamon's face darkened, and he barked out a command as he speared Lormagen with his eyes. "Provost marshal, get that man out of here! Confine him!"

The provost marshal hadn't had time to move when the second T'swa colonel spoke, his voice a flat snap, his black eyes glittering not with rage but with intention.

*"General, no one will touch that man!"*

The general's head jerked as if slapped, his mouth slightly open, face darkening even more, his eyes narrowed. Then, in a calm voice, the T'swi continued. "I am Colonel Biltong, commanding officer of the Night Adder Regiment. More pertinent to the discussion of the moment, I am also the contract officer of the Lodge of Kootosh-Lan for this expedition. You received a copy of our contract, but perhaps you have not fully familiarized yourself with it. We are a military force of a foreign nation, contracted to Confederation service here. Journalist Lormagen is the civilian employee of one of our regiments. Our personnel are not subject to arrest on your order, except for proper, documented, and verified criminal cause, as expressly provided by contract. Any breach of that contract on your part is grounds for our departure."

Lamons's jaw tightened. "Colonel," he bit out, "I would be delighted to contribute to your departure. The sooner, the better. I did not ask for you, I do not want you here, and I will not brook insubordination."

"General, I appreciate your feelings," Biltong said mildly, "but let me point out that if we leave through a breach of contract on your part, the very large advance payment made to our government by your own, and your government's considerable expense in our transportation, are not reimbursable. Per contract. If you were held accountable for that sum, five million dronas on the advance alone, you would be a ruined man, financially and professionally."

The black eyes looked around the room, taking in the faces, shocked or deliberately expressionless, evaluating each in that one glance. The general was not an easy man to serve under; thus, amidst the embarrassment, there was a certain amount of concealed pleasure among his staff.

"Beyond that," Biltong continued, "insubordination is not an issue here. Neither I nor my troops are your subordinates; mine is a contracted independent force. It would be well to read the contract, general; I can recite it verbatim. Now, I believe we have business to discuss."

No one said anything for perhaps ten interminable seconds. Varlik was aware that his military-length hair, already more or less erect, had become almost rigidly so, as if the follicles had spasmed. When at last the general spoke, his voice was rough with emotion.

"Here!" he said, and thrust papers at Biltong. "Your orders."

Biltong took them casually, seemingly without any sense of upset at the hostility he'd met, or of pleasure at his victory thus far. He scanned the two sheets, then looked up at Lamons again. "According to these," he said, "we are ordered to fly to Beregesh in two days, take the area from insurgent forces, and hold it. General, are you familiar with our contract at all?"

"I obtained and read a copy of your standard contract as soon as I heard you might be coming."

"But apparently not thoroughly. And have you studied the specific contract for the employment of our two regiments on this particular planet?"

Lamons seemed to go mentally inert, as if afraid to know what lay behind the question. Biltong turned to his executive officer, who carried a time-worn attache case.

"The contract, please." The man gave it to him.

"General, I understand your confusion. First, your experience has given you no reason to anticipate such a non-Standard situation, nor such non-Standard persons as ourselves. And secondly"—he paused, and held out the contract to Lamons—"in some respects, this is not the usual T'swa contract. Incidentally, I'm not giving you this copy; you've been sent one of your own, I'm sure, which you can study during the two weeks our regiments will spend reconditioning here. But just now I'd like you to look at the signature of the contracting party. It is not, as you will see, your Department of Armed Forces."

For a moment the general only stared at the proffered sheaf of pages, then took them, turned quickly to the signatures page, and paled visibly.

"That's right, general," Biltong continued, quietly now. "Our contract is with the Crown, in the person of His Majesty, Marcus XXVII, King of Iryala and Administrator General of the Confederation of Worlds. That is his signature."

Every white man in the room stood stunned, even Varlik.

"For the benefit of the moment, I will point out that even the usual T'swa contract authorizes us two full weeks to recondition ourselves.

Further, Section 3 of Clause IV.B deals with proper use of T'swa units, and Section 4 states that the T'swa commanders can refuse any assignment that does not meet contract specifications. Incidentally, that section is not often invoked; we are, after all, in the business. But to use special assault troops in routine holding actions is, in the language of the contract, 'a misuse of the contracted force.' It subjects our regiments to debilitating casualties in an action which could as well be carried out by Standard units, wasting our potential as a special force."

Biltong continued more briskly now. "Next, about facilities. To the best of my knowledge, T'swa contracts invariably, and this one definitely, specify that contract forces will have made available to them full and equitable support by the contracting entity *and its agents*—meaning you in this instance, general. And by established legal precedents, that means we are to be provided facilities and other resources equal in kind and quantity to those of the military forces of the contracting entity in comparable circumstances.

"That, of course, has been drastically omitted in this case. However, assuming the situation is corrected without delay, I am willing to register no complaint with His Majesty about the primitive bivouac conditions we've been provided, or their remoteness from base facilities such as hospital, supply depot, and communications center.

"Regarding the communications center, we will of course require unrestricted and uncensored use of message pods, to make regular and irregular reports to our contract control office, which is our embassy on Iryala, and to our lodge on Tyss. Both will be expecting them. Not that censorship would be practical in any event, since our reports are made in Tyspi."

Lamons's bristly stiffness was entirely gone; he stood a defeated man. Now Biltong proceeded to inject the seeds of a working relationship. "It is not unusual, General Lamons, for there to be an initial misunderstanding when a T'swa regiment collaborates with Confederation forces. Confederation general officers are usually unprepared, initially, to assimilate the real meanings of T'swa contract terms, or to understand the uses of T'swa units. We are—too non-Standard for that. And I suppose that, as their adjustments offend the military sense of propriety, none of this is reported in print or taught in your Academy.

"Usually the commanding general of the contracting entity, considering his many and varied responsibilities, will avoid the distraction of working directly with us by assigning an officer of suitable rank to liaise with the T'swa force. And if the liaison officer is one with an interest in the use of small assault units, this will result in more effective planning and coordination.

"We realize that you face a difficult military situation here, and we wish to be of maximum value to you. And not only does the Iryalan Crown have an urgent interest in renewing and securing technite production; it is personally very concerned over the severe military environment on Orlantha. It believes that we, with our unusual experience in wildland conditions and our tolerance of high temperatures, will prove to be an important factor in avoiding a protracted struggle, which the Confederation cannot tolerate. His Majesty expects our ambassador at Landfall to provide him with weekly summaries and, of course, both you and I want the military situation to progress as smoothly and swiftly as possible."

Unexpectedly the T'swi thrust out a hand to the general, who received it with his own, unprepared. They shook hands then, the volition being the colonel's.

"My aide, Captain Dotu, will be here tomorrow to meet with your liaison officer," Biltong continued. "We will want them to begin at once to plan our combat utilization. I will send with Captain Dotu a communications sergeant, who will be in charge of our communications at your communications center. The contract calls for providing him a special office there.

"And general, I regret any trauma this meeting may have caused, and I am sure we will soon find ourselves working together very effectively." Biltong bowed slightly. "To His Majesty's pleasure and our joint success, which are one and the same."

Both Biltong and Koda came to sudden attention then and saluted sharply. The general, after momentary surprise, returned the salute, and the T'swa, including Varlik Lormagen, exited, leaving the general still in shock.

They walked briskly, never pausing, out of the building. Their driver was parked only a few yards away. They climbed in as he started the engine. A moment later they pivoted and left, cruising leisurely out of the vehicle park and down the main travel way. The gate guards, seeing their shoulder insignia, saluted, opened the gate, and let them pass.

Varlik stared back over his shoulder at the retreating base, with an unexpected sinking feeling. He was leaving behind him civilization as he knew it—air-conditioning, comfortable beds, showers, people whose ways he understood . . . and a very hostile general who'd never let him function there now except as the press aide of Colonel Koda.

He looked at the calm, cool colonel beside him.

"Colonel Koda?"

"Yes, Lormagen?"

"What are my duties as your press aide?"

"It is time for the T'swa to make use of something the Iryalan and most other armies have used for a long time—a publicist."

"But I don't know enough about Tyss to prepare publicity for your people. And besides . . ."

"Not for our people, Lormagen. We need you to publicize us on Iryala, to your own people. I suggest you use your usual resources for dissemination—the offices of Central News and any others available to you. Those were journalists outside headquarters with you, were they not? I presume they'll be happy to receive information from you, certainly until we can arrange for them to visit us."

Varlik was aware that the other colonel, Biltong, was looking on, listening.

"We can discuss it further later," Koda was saying, "but I believe I said it when I first proposed this to you: It seems to me that you can go about your journalistic duties for your regular employer quite largely as you'd intended in the first place. That may well be all the publicity we need.

"At least to begin with, you will live with the First Platoon, Company A, First Battalion, accompany them in their training, learn about them. It would be well also to train with them yourself, so far as you are able. Then you can truly tell the people of Iryala what the T'swa are like, and what kind of warriors we are. And when we go south to fight, you can come with us, unless it seems too dangerous, and tell your people what the T'swa are like in battle."

Koda looked away then, sitting calm and quiet, surveying the Orlanthan grassland, as if Varlik had been dismissed, and the rest of the way to the T'swa camp they said almost nothing to each other.

# 13

You ask how the newly entitled T'swa warrior, a youth barely full-grown who has lived from childhood in a warrior lodge, never been off his home world, never seen a city or a ship or a foreigner, seems so considerably educated in what you term "the liberal arts." The answer is that on Tyss, all learn the T'sel, which is translated as "the Ways of Life on Tyss." However, it might as accurately be translated simply "the Ways of Life," for it applies as well anywhere; it is universal. But only on Tyss is it recognized and practiced— thus the term *T'sel*. And it is useful to rational living, which is to say wisdom, for anyone—the follower of any Way—whether on our world or yours. It is not simply a subject for scholars. It is also a subject for warriors, for example— including the young men you have observed and spoken with.

As to how every T'swa warrior can speak your language fluently, be conversant with your history and culture as well as his own, and know more than a little of your technology—it is largely a matter of learning them, which is less difficult than you might suppose for one who knows the T'sel. When your children undertake to learn, they are beset by many hindrances, encounter many obstacles—those from without and, more importantly, those from within. But when our children are still small, they are early helped to . . . let us say, dissolve the inner obstacles and hindrances, at which point those hindrances outside them, already at a practical minimum, become of much less effect and more easily deflected. With that, learning becomes swift and smooth.

And the use of knowledge far easier, which use is part of wisdom.

The Confederation, I must tell you, is fortunate that the T'swa do not lust for power, for we are the swiftest of learners, and the greatest at the exercise of knowledge. But we have looked far, and have seen that such a lust degrades the field for all—for the one who lusts as well as for all others. And indeed, when one knows T'sel, there is no lust. Nor can the T'sel be known while there is lust.

It is not the having of power which ruins; that belief is an error, though an understandable error. There is nothing wrong with having power. *Rather it is the lust itself that ruins, the scale of ruin increasing exponentially with the success of the lust.*

> —Lodge Master Gun-Dasaru to Harden Ostrak,
> following the graduation of the So Binko Regiment of the
> Lodge of Kootosh-Lan (unedited from the recorded comments).

The day promised to be even hotter than the two before, and a line of towering thunderheads were visible along the southwest horizon when the T'swa officers, with Varlik, arrived at the bivouac. On the flat ground behind the encampment, Varlik could see hundreds of men in groups, doing what appeared to be choreographed tumbling in a thin haze of dust. Even at a distance it was a remarkable sight.

And they definitely were not the entire T'swa force; perhaps the rest were on a field march, he told himself.

The hovercar stopped outside the headquarters of the Red Scorpion Regiment, a largish tent that nonetheless seemed to Varlik too small for its function. Its sides were rolled up for maximum ventilation. There he, Colonel Koda, and the colonel's executive officer and aide got out, and the vehicle left to deliver Colonel Biltong and his own E.O. and aide. Inside the tent were only three men besides themselves. Koda, in Tyspi, told the sergeant major to have Varlik put on the rolls as civilian aide in charge of publicity, on the usual warrior's allowances, and to assign him to Lieutenant Zimsu's platoon for purposes of quarters, supply, and mess. When he'd finished, he turned to Varlik, speaking again in Standard.

"Sergeant Kusu told me you spoke Tyspi with him. Did you understand what I just told the sergeant major?"

"Yes, sir," Varlik answered, and repeated it quite closely in Tyspi, without too much stumbling or hesitation. "I expect to do much better with experience," he added.

"Excellent." The colonel's eyes reexamined the Iryalan. "You are very unusual among your people."

Despite himself, Varlik was pleased and embarrassed at the comment. After a pause, Koda continued. "Lormagen, I feel very—optimistic over what we did this morning, you and I. Colonel Biltong and I have intended, since we received this assignment, that the people of Iryala should get a much improved understanding of the T'swa through our regiments, and I have no doubt that you will prove most helpful in this."

Again the colonel withdrew his attention, this time to his desk and in-basket. Varlik looked around, found a folding camp chair, and sat down. With nothing to do for the moment, he felt the heat as a heavy fluid settling around him. The sergeant major, a one-eyed man scarred from hairline to jaw, had used his field communicator, and in two or three minutes another enlisted man entered the tent. Speaking Standard, the sergeant major introduced the soldier as Bao-Raku, with no mention of rank, and told Varlik to follow the man. Then the sergeant major too withdrew his attention, definitely the T'swa form of dismissal, and Varlik left behind a quick-footed, if limping, Bao-Raku.

It took less than a minute to walk to the headquarters tent of Company A, First Battalion. It was not at all like any company orderly room or field headquarters that Varlik had seen in the Iryalan army; it had three small folding tables and a small file cabinet, no computer, and five visible folding chairs. No one at all was there except he and Bao-Raku. The T'swi pulled out a file drawer, removed a chart, sat down, and looked up at Varlik who, after waiting a moment for an invitation, sat down himself, unbidden.

Bao-Raku also spoke in scarcely accented Standard. "I am to assign you to a squad in the First Platoon. Do you have a preference?"

"Not really, unless . . . Except for Colonel Koda, I'm acquainted with only one other man in this regiment, a Sergeant Kusu. I don't suppose he's in this company, though."

"Sergeant Kusu is the leader of the Second Squad, First Platoon. Is that the squad you prefer?"

"Yes."

Coincidence? Or had Koda sent him to this platoon because Kusu was here? That didn't make any sense, but it occurred to him nonetheless.

The company clerk, Varlik supposed the man was, got up. "Have you any clothes besides those you are wearing? Supply will have difficulty providing you with uniforms that fit, until we've had a chance to procure some from the Iryalan Quartermaster."

"I have some on base. I can get them when I go there next."

The man nodded. "Good. And you have eaten today?"

"Yes, I have."

"Then I will take you to your squad."

Without saying anything further, the T'swi went out the door and, despite his limp, broke into a lope, Varlik hurrying behind him through the encampment over trampled bunchgrass clumps. By the time they'd run the quarter mile to the drill ground, sweat was running from Varlik's every pore.

The T'swa troops were in separate groups of ten, squads apparently, each with its own drill square defined and separated from its neighbors by harness belts, with knives and canteens attached, which had been removed for the drill. Each squad trained independently; in a sense, each individual or pair seemed to work independently, for there was no apparent leader. Yet their movements were integrated, whether by long practice or some nonevident communication, Varlik couldn't tell.

"That is the Second Squad of the First Platoon," Bao-Raku said pointing. "They will take a break soon, and you can talk to Kusu then."

Varlik nodded, and the clerk turned and loped away in the direction of the company area. Varlik returned his attention to the drilling troops, recording with his camera.

In part the drill resembled tumbling, in part some strange and acrobatic ritual dance, but withal, it was clearly training for some art of combat. Some of the movements were broad and flowing, others abrupt and accompanied by audible, forceful expulsions of breath. There were gliding movements, striking movements with hands and feet, some independently by an individual trooper, some with two interacting. Or a man might grasp another and throw him to the ground with a quick sweeping movement or a short choppy one, perhaps to be followed without pause by another, somehow all synchronized with the movements of every other. Men rolled smoothly, swiftly, leaped high, bodies amazingly flexible despite their physical bulk. Varlik watched entranced, even as he recorded the scene.

Then, without command, the entire drill stopped, and each T'swi went to his belt and drank from one of his two canteens, synchronization suddenly replaced by individuality. After drinking, men sat on the ground or stood around, most talking or laughing quietly together, while others lay quietly, perhaps with a forearm shielding their eyes from the sun.

Varlik walked over to Kusu, who looked up and rose at his approach. The T'swa face was gray and grinning, greased with muddy sweat.

"So you came," Kusu said in Tyspi, and reached out a hand. "I am glad to see you."

Varlik took it and was startled. He'd expected its hard, beefy strength; what surprised him was its hardness of palm and the inner surface of the fingers, as if they'd been armored with tempered leather. He didn't have callus like that even on his feet! It seemed impossible that it resulted from training—it almost had to be inherent, he thought, inborn—and for a moment his surprise impeded answering.

"Yes," he answered, also in Tyspi. "With the help of your colonels. I'll tell you about it when we have time. I came to report to you; I've been assigned to live with your squad. How long is your break?"

"We still have two or three minutes. But we have only one more drill cycle, of about ten minutes. Then we break for lunch. Wait and watch if you wish."

Varlik retreated outside the square and waited in the intensifying heat. Someone whistled shrilly, a quick piercing pattern, its instrument human lips, and those who'd lain down or sat got up at once, all moving into a pattern of positions. When the drill began again, Varlik once more recorded with his camera until they were done. When it was over and the T'swa formed ranks, Varlik, on his own volition, fell in with them at the end of Kusu's squad, feeling awkward and out of place but doing it nonetheless, then semi-sprinted with them to the encampment's edge, where they halted and were dismissed.

He was enormously pleased that he'd done it, grinning through his sweat as they walked among the tents to that of Kusu's squad, rubbernecking now as he walked. T'swa grinned back at him as they went, the grins friendly, and a few thumbs were raised in his direction, a salute of friendship common enough at home among friends, but surprising him here.

The tent was floored with dirt, and had five cots along each side, with a duffel bag at the foot of each and a barracks bag beneath. From the roof pole hung an insect repeller. On each of the cots sat a field pack attached to a harness, the harness also holding assorted pouches and pockets. A rifle lay beside it.

An eleventh cot stood in the middle of the tent, like the others complete with pad, pad cover, and thin pillow. "That must be yours," Kusu said pointing. There was even a towel, wash cloth, belt with canteens and knife, a potlike helmet with liner, and a small block of what he surmised was a cleaning agent.

Bao-Raku must have brought the things, Varlik told himself. And he'd been half afraid—more than half—that these would be cruel and vicious men! Instead, this. And no one had sneered or needled or even been condescending.

Meanwhile, one of the T'swa had taken a plastic jerry can of water and poured some into each of a row of the potlike helmets outside. There was no rack for the helmets; there'd been nothing to build one with. They'd simply been set into shallow holes dug for them. Borrowing a trenching tool from the nearest T'swi, Varlik quickly gouged out a place and put his own helmet into it, then poured in water and, on his knees, joined in the pre-meal washup—face, hands, wrists.

The T'swa had stripped to their waists, and he was deeply impressed by the massive yet sinewy torsos and arms he saw, muscles sliding and bunching as they washed. Varlik was muscular by Iryalan standards, sinewy now as well, and as tall as most of the T'swa, but almost any of them would outweigh him by more than twenty pounds, all of it muscle.

He wondered what they'd do at day's end in lieu of a shower. In novels, gooks were usually filthy, but clearly not the T'swa, not where there was any choice.

When they'd washed, he followed the casual train of still shirtless black men to the A Company mess tent. Apparently they ate without shirts if they wished! Such a thing was unthinkable in any Standard army. Varlik felt ill at ease now in his shirt, and moved quickly through the mess line. The food seemed of low quality, though doubtlessly nourishing. It consisted of a single, to him unidentifiable, mixture from a pot. Each man scooped his own serving into a broad bowl. In place of joma was some unfamiliar drink, tepid and sweet. Each squad had its own table with a bench on either side—long enough, with a little crowding, for an extra man. Following the example of the T'swa, Varlik poured a sauce onto his food, fortunately with caution, for the sauce was hot, currylike.

There was not much conversation at the meal, and what he heard seemed small talk, although some of it he couldn't follow. Most of the words he knew, but the referents weren't always familiar; he lacked the contexts necessary to give parts of it meaning. An uneasy feeling touched him, not for the last time, a certain sense of unreality that he could not dispel. These T'swa were so *non-Standard!*

Men began to leave, and he left too, his food unfinished, like them scraping his bowl into a garbage can before stacking it. Then he returned to his tent. He too was sweaty, and somewhat dusty. To avoid getting dirt on his bed he lay down on the ground outside, in the shade of the tent. It wasn't as if he was tired. He wasn't, despite the heat, and the humidity which seemed to be increasing. But the others were resting and there wasn't much else for him to do.

Minutes later Kusu arrived, strolled over to him and squatted down on heavy haunches as Varlik sat up. "We are going on a field march this afternoon," Kusu said, in Tyspi again. "But not a very hard one; we're too soon off shipboard. You are welcome to come if you'd like."

"Of course I'll come," Varlik replied. "It's the sort of thing I expected to do. In fact, I trained for it on shipboard, doing heavy workouts in a firefighter's suit, every day coming out from Iryala. If the march is too much for me, I'll find out soon enough by trying."

Kusu nodded. "You have almost an hour then to rest before we fall in. I suggest you sleep; I intend to. And if you are coming with us, you'll need to bring your canteens."

Varlik got up, filled his canteens from a jerry can, then lay back down again, draping the harness belt over his body. He closed his eyes and put his field cap over them, not anticipating sleep, but intending at least to rest. Sleep came nonetheless, to be broken by another shrill pattern of human whistling that brought him awkwardly to his feet, sluggishly aware of hustling bodies. He fastened the belt around his waist, then trotted after them, the dopiness dissipating with exertion, to where the T'swa were forming ranks on the mustering ground.

In ranks, he became aware that the others carried rifles and wore field packs, with magazines and other pouches clipped to their harnesses in front and assorted smaller pouches secured to their belts. Then, without verbal command, another quick whistle pattern started the column in motion at a brisk swinging stride, a column of fours broken into platoons.

He looked around him more alertly now as they moved away from the bivouac area. Rolling hills lay ahead, and in moments they were running through belly-deep prairie grass, where somehow the air seemed hotter, as if the mass of plant stems had trapped or perhaps exuded heat. At about sixty degrees from their line of march and a half-mile distant, he saw a vehicle coming along the track from the Aromanis base. Even from there he recognized it as a staff car, not open like the T'swa field vehicle but enclosed and undoubtedly cooled. Apparently the general wasn't waiting till tomorrow, but had sent someone to meet again with the T'swa. Probably to determine what was needed and wanted in the way of proper facilities for the regiments.

For a brief few seconds he played with the fancy that they had come here to claim him back, and began to imagine the T'swa refusing to give him up. Then a single whistle shrilled, breaking his fantasy, and the column began to jog through the tall grass. In half a hundred yards the ground began to slope upward. The column alternately ran and walked, roughly in quarter-mile installments, the sun beating down on them, the ground heat stirring into sullen life with their passage. At the end of a local hour, another whistle stopped them. After drinking, and licking the salt that a T'swa trooper had offered him, he lay down like the others on the lumpy ground for a break. There was no shade, and the heat was suffocating near the ground. Varlik began to realize what kind of campaign environment this planet was—even here, more than halfway to the pole.

Silently he thanked Colonel Voker for ramrodding him through the twenty-six days of fire-suit workouts on the *Quaranth*.

Then, in about ten minutes, whistling got them up again. They formed ranks, there was another whistling command, and once more the column moved out, walking the first quarter mile, then running again, then walking, and the air he sucked into his lungs seemed stifling hot. After a bit, his legs began to go wooden on him, and he began to worry, wondering if he'd make it. The last thing he wanted to do was fall out, perhaps collapse, so he gathered himself, willing energy to his muscles, strength to his knees. He realized that his eyes had been directed at the ground and the boots of the man in front of him, and raised his face to look ahead.

The long row of thunderheads, though still distant, was nearer now, billows towering to form a single anvil top, an opaque veil of rain slanting from its blue-gray base as it marched on legs of lightning, too far away for thunder to be heard. It seemed to Varlik that if he could hang on till it reached them, he'd be all right.

His eyes soon turned back to the ground without his realizing it, but he persisted, running slack-mouthed, sucking the hot air, his right hand at frequent intervals wiping sweat to keep it from his eyes as much as possible. Then there was whistling again, another break, and somehow he was still with them. Again he drank, the water hot as soup, gratefully licked offered salt, and flopped on the ground, closing his eyes, his face turned away from the sun.

Behind the lids was red, with idly floating spots like tiny oil globules. Then a voice called his name—Sergeant Kusu's voice—and Varlik first sat up, then with an effort stood. A hovercar was coming up from behind—seemingly a T'swa vehicle—and they watched its approach until it drew up a dozen yards to the side.

"Get in," Kusu said gesturing, and despite himself, Varlik started to object. "No, get in," Kusu repeated firmly. "You'll do no one a service collapsed in the base hospital, or maybe dead. It's been standing by, waiting for a call, and I've been watching you. You've done extremely well, but it's time for you to ride."

Varlik found his legs taking him to the vehicle, and he got in, feeling not so weak after all. The sides were open, but the vehicle's top was up to keep the sun off. The steady-eyed driver handed him a vacuum flask— surely a luxury among the T'swa!—with some cool liquid that seemed to be fruit juice.

"Steady there," the driver said, "don't make yourself sick," and Varlik paused in his drinking. Then, after a pause and one more swig, he handed it back, and the T'swi capped it and put it in a bag without taking any himself. In another minute there was whistling again, the ranks reformed, and the battalion moved out, jogging through the grass, the hovercar keeping pace to one side.

Varlik started to take off his shirt to let the hot air flow over his body, the better to cool himself, then became aware of the forgotten camera he'd carried inside it, and raised it to record a few minutes of the march, enough to include one of the run segments, while murmuring comment for its sound pickup. When he felt he'd recorded enough of that, he tucked the camera away again, wondering if any of the T'swa felt resentment at his riding. Somehow, he didn't think so.

He was surprised at how far they went in the hour before the next break, over the rolling hills, curving around to head eastward again in the direction of the bivouac. He licked salt again, drank more of his hot water, then more from the vacuum flask, and all in all felt much recovered. After they stopped, he got out and walked over to Kusu. They shared salt, and he drank again.

"I feel a lot better now," said Varlik. "I'd like to finish this on foot with the rest of you."

Kusu looked him over, smiling a little, and nodded. "Fine," he said, "if you want to. But the last will be the hardest, and there will be no disgrace in riding again if the need arises."

Varlik nodded back, then took out his camera and recorded the resting T'swa, their shirts sweat-soaked, rings of whitish salts marking where it was most concentrated. *And they look as content as anyone I've ever seen,* he thought. The T'swa in Gorth Hasniker's novel couldn't touch the reality, at least in character. Briefly, he wondered what these men would be like in combat; he couldn't picture them cruel.

Then the command came whistling and he put the camera back inside his shirt as they formed ranks. Another whistle and they started off. They walked twice, then the second run continued until he realized they were to trot the rest of the way, and his heart sank. This was what Kusu meant by the last hour being the hardest. Only once more did they slow to a walk, just long enough to drink and let the water settle in their bellies before the whistle brought them to a trot again.

Just once he looked back over his shoulder, praying that the rain would arrive. It was nearer, in fact not terribly far, and he let that hearten him. Rain! Cooling rain! Thunder rolled. Then his attention was trapped again by the travail of running.

Topping a long low ridge, he saw the encampment ahead, no farther than half a mile, and for just a moment his heart leaped with exultation. Then a whistle shrilled, once and long, and the battalion broke into a gallop, almost a headlong run, so that he veered off to the side to keep from being trampled, speeding up as best he could, seeing black men in sweat-soaked mottled green run past him. He sucked wind into tortured lungs, felt his legs flagging, staggering, slowing to an unsteady shuffling jog. He was unaware of Kusu running backwards to keep watch on him, of the hovercar close behind, but kept doggedly on, gasping, half-blinded by stinging sweat, until he stumbled onto the mustering ground. The nearing thunder hadn't registered on him, nor had the puffs of cooling breeze. The T'swa had already been dismissed but had not dispersed. They were waiting more or less in ranks, grinning, all eyes on him, and somehow, as he staggered up, he did not collapse. And when he stopped before them, they applauded, big hard hands clapping, throats cheering. Those nearest stepped up to him, clapped his back, shook his hand.

And when they stopped, Varlik became aware of another sound, behind him, a soft murmur. He turned, stared, fumbled at his shirt. A wall of rain was sweeping from the southwest across the steppe, its murmur gaining force. Sudden wind whipped. A hammer of thunder smote the earth so that even the T'swa flinched, and the first fat drops splatted around them, the T'swa's white teeth flashing a choir of grins, then rain swept over them, a body of it, an assault of it, and instantly they were drenched, water streaming over black faces that beamed and gloried—desert people receiving the gift of storm. And Varlik's camera, in his right hand, sheltered by his field cap, was registering all of it on the molecules of its cube.

# 14

The rain would have been considered warm on Iryala, but on Kettle it cooled. They walked to their tents in it and stripped off their wet uniforms, draping them over the guy ropes where the rain continued to soak them. The T'swa had no body hair, not even pubic hair. Then Varlik followed the naked T'swa through the thunderstorm again, each carrying his soap and helmet, to the nearest hydrant. There they lathered themselves—Varlik had the advantage, his moderately hairy skin lathering more readily—then drew water and poured it over one another. Cleaned, they returned to their tents through the slackening rain, where they sat on the edges of their cots and used dirty undershirts to wipe the mud from their feet before putting on dry trousers and wet boots.

The slimmest T'swa in the squad loaned Varlik dry trousers which were only a little too large. Meanwhile, Varlik felt considerably recovered—tired, but not exhausted—again thanks to Voker's hard training, he told himself.

By the time they went to supper, the rain had stopped, and steam rose from the hot earth. The air was like a Turkish bath. Supper was another mixture, not very different from what he'd eaten at midday, but nonetheless more appetizing to Varlik now. The evening was growing dark when he strolled back to the tent with Kusu, his belt recorder operating as it generally was among the T'swa.

"What do you do when it gets dark here?" asked Varlik. "Go to bed?"

"That is a matter of individual preference. Some will reread favorite books. Others will talk with their friends, or do certain things— personal things we learn as children. They are not known to the Confederation Worlds; when you see someone kneeling quietly, perhaps on a small pad, he is doing one of those things. And some will no doubt wander out into the grassland—to the east, away from camp and our disturbances—to sense the life there." He looked at Varlik. "What will you do?"

"I need to go somewhere where I won't disturb anyone, and narrate on cube my impressions of today and the T'swa."

"Ah. Of course."

"You said some of you will read. Where do you have lights?" He gestured about him. "The only lights I've seen are in the mess tent."

"That is where they will read."

The mess tent as a place to read! It didn't really surprise Varlik. The T'swa were different in so many things, and he was getting used to them. "How much can they see of the local lifeforms at night? At least now, with no moonlight."

"It is more than seeing, although we T'swa see considerably better at night than you do."

"Really?"

"Yes. In the early generations on Tyss—for many generations, actually— our ancestors worked their fields by night. In fact, they lived much of their active lives at night, when it was not so hot. So far as possible, they spent the daytimes in holes dug into the north slopes of hills, to escape the worst of the heat. It is even hotter on Tyss than here, you know, and it was hotter then than now.

"Those were very hard years. Many died of heat and hunger— especially babies and pregnant women. In time, those genetic lines that continued saw better at night than their ancestors had, and tolerated greater heat. Even today, some field labor and other strenuous outdoor activities on Tyss are done at night, although the climate no longer seems cruel to us."

The two men, one black, one white, went into the tent. Only two other men were there, lying silent on their cots. Kusu lay down on his, and

Varlik also. "Is it all right to talk here," Varlik asked softly, "or will it disturb the others?"

"They will not be disturbed."

"How do you know about those early times? I've assumed that Tyss was settled before the historical era."

The T'swa sergeant nodded. "It was. Our knowledge of history reaches further back than your own."

"By how much?"

"By rather a long time."

Varlik wasn't sure he should ask his next question, but so far the T'swi had seemed very open, and he was curious. "We've assumed that the resource worlds, and probably some of the trade worlds, were colonized by dumping convicts there in early times. Was that how Tyss was settled, do you know?"

The T'swi smiled. "One could say so."

For a moment Varlik was silent. Then he asked, "Did I offend you with that question?"

Kusu chuckled softly, a sound which Varlik thought might have been echoed by the other two at the edge of audibility.

"No, Varlik Lormagen, you have not offended. You are a considerate and courteous man. I am glad to answer your questions, so far as I can; I consider you my friend."

Then Kusu stretched out on his cot, and Varlik sensed the withdrawal that meant their conversation was ended. Quietly he took his recorder and wandered out to the tiny vehicle park, to sit in the unmuddy privacy of a T'swa hovercar and record his still-fresh thoughts and impressions. Briefly, when he had finished, he watched the moon Gamma, barely large enough to show a demi-disk, like an overlarge star low in the east, then started back to his tent in the steamy, star-vivid night. Tomorrow, if he could find a ride, he would go to the base camp, pick up his other things, share his audio and video recordings with Bertol and Konni, and send off a report to Iryala via the message pod. And a letter cube to Mauen.

# 15

Excerpts from *Briefing on T'swa Mercenary Forces*, Department of Armed Forces; Document 711.5 290 196.

## Introduction

All T'swa military units are light infantry.

The T'swa rarely, perhaps never, fight with war machines. This is practical because they do not accept assignments where they anticipate facing war machines or needing them. To date, at least during recorded history, they have been employed only on trade worlds and resource worlds, where the multiplicity of national states and the frequency of foreign rule and Confederation trade prerogatives bring about wars and revolts.

Occasionally, regionally entrenched revolutionary movements on trade worlds have been able to hire T'swa. Only the wealthiest revolutionaries are able to afford them, however.

T'swa mercenaries are very highly regarded as units and as individual soldiers by those who have employed them. They are especially valued in wildland fighting and for clearing hostile towns, actions in which superlative individual and small-unit skills are most advantageous.

## T'swa Military Organization

The foundation of T'swa military organization is the "lodge," of which there are five, each located in a different region of Tyss. Physically, each lodge is said to consist of a ring of barracks and training facilities around a central administrative installation and school.

The regiment is the largest military unit used, supposedly without exception. The lodges form, recruit, and train the regiments. The lodges are also the contracting agents with whom prospective employers must deal. (There is no planetary government nor any national governments on Tyss. Trade and transportation remain primitive enough and the population orderly enough that local governments, trade associations, lodge councils, etc., suffice.)

The lodges select and recruit children, reputedly of ages five and six, and their training begins at that age. At age 11-12, the trainees are formed into proto-regiments, and from that point, regimental personnel continue to serve together as a unit. After seven years, the proto-regiment graduates as a combat regiment, at which time it becomes available for service, and usually will go into combat within the year. The first contract of a virgin regiment is often part of a multi-regimental operation, in partnership with a seasoned unit, but this is by no means always the case.

One of the advantages of the long T'swa training is the degree of cross-training possible. Every man is able to function in every post with every weapon used by the T'swa. The officers are of the same age and experience as the enlisted ranks, apparently being selected on the basis of demonstrated superior ability during the training years. But every man is supposedly capable of leading his platoon or company, or even regiment.

As in standard armies, the basic T'swa unit is the *squad;* however, the T'swa squad contains only 10 men. The *platoon* is made up of four squads, a platoon leader (lieutenant), a platoon sergeant, and two medical specialists, or 44 men. The *company* consists of four platoons and a command staff of eight: the company commander (captain), an executive officer (senior lieutenant), first sergeant, two communications specialists, and a three-man medical team, or 184 personnel. The *battalion* consists of 560 personnel; the *regiment* 1,720, all ranks. That does not include a variable number of *base personnel* who do not accompany the regiment into the field. Except in virgin regiments, where kitchen and clerical duties rotate among the ranks, base personnel are men with physical impairments, apparently resulting from combat or training injuries.

You will have noticed several peculiarities which will be gone into later. First, however, we will look at what we will term the "shrinking regiment."

The strength cited above—1,720 effectives, all ranks—is the *initial* strength. As casualties reduce squads to six men or fewer, decimated squads are consolidated within the platoon or company. As platoons lose personnel below some variable level, usually about 30, platoons are consolidated within the company. Higher level units are also consolidated as necessary.

The process of consolidation may, for example, result in platoons with only three short squads, a company with only three short platoons, and a battalion with only two short companies.

Of course, none of that is unusual in combat. What is unusual is that afterward, *the units are not brought back to their full complements. Casualties are never replaced.*

All of the consolidations described above will be made before the regiment is reduced below three battalions, but in time the regiment will inevitably be reduced to two battalions. As time passes and the attrition of personnel continues further, the regiment will be transformed to a single battalion, redistributing remaining personnel within it. However, the regiment still carries its original designation—the Blue Tiger Regiment, for example—even though it operates only as a battalion. If a contract continues long enough, casualties may reduce a regiment to company size or smaller.

The unit of hire is always the regiment, but the fee charged varies with the regiment's effective strength. Not infrequently, two or three battalion-strength "regiments" may be sent. They will function as a single regiment under a senior colonel, but will continue to carry their separate "regimental" identities.

Apparently there have never been T'swa units larger than regiments, and they never function as ordinary regiments belonging to a division. They operate simply as assault forces or hunter-killer groups. This is written into their contracts. They will refuse to fight on any other basis, standing on their contractual prerogatives. . . .

## T'swa Relations With Employers

T'swa mercenaries are invariably loyal. We have been unable to find any verifiable report of T'swa mercenaries having broken a contract. But if a contract with them is broken by their employer, they will invariably extricate themselves from the fighting as promptly as practical, and will usually depart the planet. They have been known, however, to take punitive action against the contract breaker on the authority of the regimental commander. The T'swa mercenary lodges, which commonly operate their own (leased) troopships (!), have even been known to make a punitive strike against particularly treacherous contract breakers, at a time and place of particular inconvenience to the contract breaker. This attitude of the T'swa has become especially well known among the governments of trade worlds, from whom come most of their employment, and a contracting authority seldom breaks a contract with T'swa mercenaries.

The T'swa warrior lodges never contract to undertake punitive expeditions against populations. They will, however, put down uprisings, and they are in fact most renowned for their exceptional value in breaking guerrilla insurgencies. Their approach to this kind of action, interestingly enough, is restricted to recognized guerrillas. They claim the ability to identify combatants through the recognition of what they term "auras." An aura (if it actually exists) is presumably an electromagnetic field around the individual human being.

## Weapons

### Procurement

With one exception, all T'swa weapons are standard, and since Y.P. 461, the T'swa have purchased their weapons from the Royal Armory on Iryala. (Previously they had been purchased from various worlds, based on the most favorable delivery price available.) The single nonstandard weapon is the *bayonet,* also produced by the Royal Armory, exclusively for the T'swa. The routine *issue* of standard weapons within a T'swa regiment is nonstandard, however. And as they commonly operate without the service of major ordnance depots, the weapons they take with them on a contract substantially exceed the standard complement. Those carried in any particular action vary depending on the nature of the action.

**Bayonet**

The bayonet is a form of short sword, appropriate to personnel from primitive worlds. The blade length is 18 inches. It can also be attached to a rifle barrel for use as a clumsy thrusting weapon. Apparently the bayonet is routine issue for all T'swa ranks, including officers, whether or not they carry rifles. The T'swa are said to be well drilled in their use. Bayonets are reputed to be effective psychological weapons when used by well-drilled troops against irregular forces.

**Individual Firearms**

Enlisted ranks normally carry the M-1 rifle, and by all reports, every T'swi military personnel is trained to a high level of skill in its use. Commissioned ranks normally carry the M-1 sidearm, but reportedly, platoon leaders may also carry the M-1 rifle in combat situations. . . .

# 16

The air-cooled staff car was approaching the T'swa encampment in the second hour of daylight when it passed the open-topped T'swa vehicle. Voker saw young Lormagen riding with two T'swa, and wondered how the journalist's first day had been.

The young man was naive, but he had persistence and at least a modicum of guts. And more importantly, he had luck. He'd need it, Voker told himself, he'd need it.

A few minutes later Voker's car crossed a low ridge, from which he could see the T'swa camp. When he'd first visited it, the day before, Voker had been astonished. It seemed impossible that Lamons could have read the briefing and a T'swa contract—any T'swa contract—and then tried to palm off a place like that on them, especially with a lumbering operation and cement plant in the Aromanis District, and a supply depot set up for major base expansion.

*Standardness, with a large S or a small one, is a two-edged knife,* he told himself, *and we keep cutting ourselves with it.* There were too many minds that couldn't function in the face of something nonstandard. They went idiot. Not that he'd voice that observation out loud.

*At least the rain had settled the dust here,* he told himself as they pulled up outside the headquarters tent of the Night Adder Regiment, and the soil wasn't a kind that made problem mud. As he stepped out of the staff car, the morning heat blanketed him. The waiting captain offered a handshake; the T'swa didn't seem to salute except ceremonially. The captain's hard palm didn't startle Voker. He'd gotten over that the day before, had concluded that the thick calluses protected the hand from hot surfaces, which on Tyss was probably almost any surface. It might be a genetic adaptation or simply have developed in childhood and youth in connection with some aspect of training.

Colonel Biltong and Colonel Koda were waiting in the tent for him; they stood up and shook his hand perfunctorily with hands as hard as the captain's, then invited him to sit. He did.

"Gentlemen," said Voker, "I gave our rough plans and specifications to the base engineer, Major Krinder. He and his staff worked up a materials list last night and they'll start work on your new camp today, two miles southeast of the army's base camp."

The T'swa nodded almost in unison. There'd been room for them inside the base perimeter, with the security and convenience that would provide, but they'd insisted on being outside, as if they felt no concern about possible Bird attacks. Voker had found it hard to believe they'd be careless after all their years of war. Perhaps they'd welcome an attack.

"Today," he said, "it's time to look at possible actions for your regiments. What kind of briefing have you had on the situation and combat environment here?"

"We received copies of your army's Orlanthan briefing cube before we left Tyss," Biltong said. "And we have an action to suggest. We generally prefer to engage a new opponent briefly, and so far as possible on our own terms, before any major campaign. To learn what he is like, and what the field of operation is like. Therefore, we would like to stage a raid in force on the two mining sites, simultaneously. My regiment will hit the Kelikut site, and Colonel Koda's the Beregesh site, by night."

"You'll find both sites strongly defended," Voker replied. "How do you propose to go about it? How much preparatory aerial bombardment will you want?"

"None. No aerial bombardment of any kind. We propose an attack by stealth. Marauder squads will parachute in from 30,000 feet, from several miles away, and strike enemy installations by surprise. We will want to examine aerial holos of the sites in detail, to help in planning."

Voker was staring, incredulous. "From—30,000 feet? They'll be scattered all over the district!"

"Not at all. It is a technique we T'swa are trained in, and use rather frequently. We will choose a night when the greater moon is large. We see almost like cats at night. Our marauders will freefall to within a few hundred feet, each squad body-planing to remain in contact and reach the drop site.

"While the insurgents are being distracted by the marauder squads, the regiments proper will put down by armored troop carriers, different companies at different points, and attack enemy fortifications in force, doing as much damage as possible. We will then disengage, leaving the marauder squads behind briefly as a rear guard to provide covering fire and confusion while the major part of the assault force withdraws to pickup areas."

"How will you get your rear guard out?"

"Once evacuation of the main forces is well underway, the rear guard will disengage and make their way out of the area by stealth, so far as possible, to be picked up by light utility floaters well away from the insurgent camp. We'll be very interested in how the enemy responds, and how much difficulty the marauder squads have in disengaging and getting away."

Voker contemplated the two calm-seeming T'swa. Not calm-*seeming*, he told himself. These bastards *are* calm! "Frankly, gentlemen," he said, "I can visualize offhand about twenty things that could go wrong, resulting in your regiments being chopped up and your marauders wiped out."

"Of course," Biltong replied, "there is always that possibility. But the demands on your air crews should not be excessive, and our people are extremely competent. Your adjectives 'resourceful' and 'proficient' come to mind. And 'nimble-witted,' if I may coin a term using Standard roots. Each of our people has survived fourteen years of war."

*High-elevation parachute jumps? Body planing!* Voker had never heard of such things. *How nonstandard can they get?* he asked himself. Without noticing, he began to feel excited.

"Colonels," Voker said, "I suggest we all go to base headquarters. We can find there all the aerial holos you'll want, and a large-scale tank to project them in."

When they left Colonel Biltong's headquarters tent, Colonel Koda took with him the audio recorder that he'd transcribed the conference on. It might be useful to their new publicist to have a record.

Varlik quickly fell into a routine that combined his desire to live with and learn about the T'swa and his other responsibilities as a journalist/publicist. He would spend one day with the T'swa, the next at the main base, narrating his reports and editing his cubes. There was never any difficulty now with his coming and going, and he gave Bakkis and Konni access to his material.

Meanwhile, progress on the new T'swa camp was rapid, the sort of thing that can happen when an army puts its manpower resources to work on a project. The base construction battalion was turned loose on it, and on the seventh day the T'swa moved in. Now their tents had floors, there were showers and wash stands, and their jungle boots padded on board-walks when they went to meals.

And with the new camp, the video team was allowed to visit the T'swa, shooting their own pictures. One afternoon they even rode along behind Company A on a training run, their cube showing Varlik running with the T'swa. He'd begged them to record some other outfit, but they'd have none of it.

The T'swa would have twelve full days to enjoy their new facility before their first action on Kettle, because when Lamons had been informed of their projected raids, he at once decided to follow them up promptly with a full-scale invasion and takeover of Beregesh. General preparations for the invasion had already been planned and were well underway, but even so, his staff had insisted that sixteen days, around the clock, was the minimum time needed to complete preparations.

With alternate days to recover in, those parts of the T'swa training regime that Varlik took part in were not too hard for the young correspondent. Not quite. The close combat drills he didn't even attempt. Parts of the bayonet drills he did attempt, though his muscles screamed obscenities at him. The speed marches he survived, sometimes taking a break in the hovercar that was always at hand. And the holo-briefings on the Beregesh mining site he found exciting. His bowels found them uncomfortably exciting.

Then one evening Colonel Koda sent him to the airfield with B Company, which had been selected to provide the Beregesh marauder squads. The T'swa strapped on their freefall chutes and loaded into several small utility floaters for a practice jump, Varlik with the First and Second Squads of the First Platoon.

He wore no chute; he was along for the ride.

When they took off, the troops were as bland and cheerful as always. Varlik was nervous, even though he wasn't going to jump. Shortly, they put on their oxygen masks. At what he'd been told was 30,000 feet, the troop doors were retracted; the air that swirled in was shockingly cold. This time their drop zone was their old camp site in the prairie, from which they would jog the twenty-six miles to the new one. The T'swa lined up as casually as if for breakfast, but wearing gloves and encumbered with chutes, weapons, and the heavy coveralls that would protect them from scrub vegetation when they jumped at Beregesh. Their protective mesh face masks were tilted up to make room for oxygen masks; they'd clip them into position at a lower altitude.

The blackness snarled and whipped about the door as they waited, and Varlik, camera busy, hoped desperately that he wouldn't be sick in his oxygen mask. The red light beside the door changed to yellow, and the floater slowed, stopped. Then it flashed green, and five T'swa trotted out the door into icy nothingness, Varlik dutifully recording the process.

The floater made three small circles then, simulating flight to another drop site, and at the end of each circle, five more men jumped. The greater moon was early in its first quarter, its light not enough to do an Iryalan much good, but by it the T'swa were supposed to see and body plane to the old campsite, where a target had been bulldozed that they could see from high in the night.

When the second stick of jumpers stood up, Varlik crouched beside the door, grateful now for coveralls and heated gloves. Camera in hand, he followed their drifting fall in his monitor until the floater's circling put them out of sight.

And when the last stick had gone, an exhausted Varlik, chilled and shivering, slumped down on a bucket seat while one of the air crew closed the troop door. He visualized the T'swa falling spread-eagled, planing through quiet darkness, eyes on the drop site and sometimes on the altimeters at their chests. To an Iryalan, the very concept was outrageous. Yet despite that, and despite the bone-numbing fear he'd felt when they'd jumped, he wished he was with them, though it seemed to him he'd surely have soiled himself before stepping out the door.

# 17

In a time which your people have long forgotten, when the many nations of man spoke each its separate language, it was well known that children up to a certain age—about seven of your years—could learn to speak foreign languages quickly and with ease. Then, over the course of a few more years, it became much more difficult, the degree of difficulty varying markedly among individuals.

In part the same is true of learning the T'sel. But in learning the T'sel, the effect of age seems more marked, for we have been able to teach some of your people to speak Tyspi—all of the few who wished sufficiently to learn it—but we have never succeeded in leading one of them to the T'sel. Of course, only perhaps a dozen before you have asked to be taught. But if you really wish your people to know the T'sel, it would be advisable to send small children among us and let them live as T'swa until they are well grown. Send children of five of your years. Then they would come to know T'sel without effort. They would know it as do those born to it, but with an additional viewpoint, for even as little children they would have an initial affinity with their own world and culture, and a greater personal, nonverbal knowledge of them than you might suspect.

And once trained, it is they who would be best suited to bring the T'sel to your world.

But even then, unless new techniques were developed, I suspect that most interested adults on Iryala would, in the main, only learn *about* the T'sel, and that is not having it. They would no doubt have pieces of it, which would not be without value to them and to Iryala, but it would be exceptional for one to gain the entirety. Therefore, it would be most effective if those children, once grown, returned to Iryala and formed a small community of their own, where more children could learn. If nothing else, that would save others from suffering the heat of Tyss.

Meanwhile, you do not yourself have that option for learning. But you are here, and much of value can be accomplished, so let us begin. Perhaps you will find your stay with us sufficiently rewarding that you will decide to see to the other when you have returned to Iryala.

And if you wish to propagate on Iryala an interest in the T'sel, let me suggest further that you not propound it, or expound on it, or talk much about it at all. Say only a little, to this one and that, and very casually, as if you found it mildly interesting but not important. Those who wish to know will no doubt hear of it, and of you, without effort on your part, and if any seek you out and question you, perhaps you will wish to speak with them about it at greater length.

—Master Fen Dys-Gwang to Dr. Barden Ostrak, by the waterfall at Tashi Dok (unedited from the recorded comments).

The two T'swa regiments stood in the late afternoon heat, heavily laden with weapons and gear, waiting to board the armored troop carriers, while Varlik, sweating copiously, walked nearby with busy camera.

Around them on three sides of the broad landing field were acres of ordnance, other equipment, supplies, minutely organized, with an armada of tarp-covered cargo movers parked and ready, waiting for the intensive activity of the morrow and days after, when the invasion proper would take place. Varlik wouldn't try to cover that; for better or for worse, he was committing his time and efforts to covering the T'swa. Even Bertol and Konni were giving the T'swa raid their full attention today. With their deluxe Revax camera, they would go with the Night Adders to Kelikut to film the raid there.

Lieutenant Trevelos and his own small staff of cameramen and copywriters would cover the actions of the Confederation Army, and their material would be available to Central News and Iryala Video.

The T'swa marauder groups had already left, on utility floaters like they'd jumped from in practice, and Varlik had recorded their departure. Now he moved to the assault floater that would carry the first and second platoons of Company A, and stood beside the ramp. An order was whistled—he knew the code well now—and he recorded the approach and loading of the T'swa. They loaded quietly, showing no sign of nerves, only a clear and quiet sense of controlled exhilaration.

Even as he recorded, their exhilaration troubled Varlik. Not that he begrudged them, but it seemed unreal, scarcely conceivable, that men who had known battle so intimately and for so long, had seen so many of their fellows killed or maimed, could feel that way. He himself felt nothing remotely like exhilaration; he was grateful that he had his work to do, to hold his attention and keep down the intensity of his fear. When all the T'swa were aboard, he followed; his seat was waiting for him at the end of First Squad, First Platoon.

The assault carriers were not large. With floaters, because they could take off and land vertically and had a long range, there was little advantage in larger craft for combat landings. These, which carried only two platoons each, could put down on rough ground, in small openings, and relatively few men would be lost if a ship was destroyed by heavy rockets.

A row of padded bench seats ran down each side of the craft, and two more rows extended back to back down the middle, divided by a padded back rest, neck high. The result was two wide aisles with facing seats. Now the aisles were partly filled with gear, notably large petards, and pole charges fitted with shoulder straps, their poles telescoped. If a rocket should penetrate the hull, the result could be spectacular.

With the state of his nerves, Varlik was grateful there'd been so little delay in boarding. Once closed, the carriers were cooled somewhat, and when they lifted, pressurized. Now there would be the long haul to Beregesh, 1,900 miles south, where the climate would make Aromanis seem balmy. He was glad the attack would be by night, that they'd be back in the air before dawn, and these thoughts he recorded.

Out by dawn. That was assuming everything worked out more or less as planned. Colonel Koda seemed confident, but Koda—Koda was *Homo tyssiensis*, not *Homo sapiens*. That also he murmured into the voice pickup at his throat; he could edit it out later if he wanted to.

Varlik used his camera again, recording the T'swa troopers who sat facing each other along the sides, seemingly relaxed, though only a few were talking. It would be hours before they landed, and he wondered how he, at least, could survive the trip, commenting to the cube that there weren't even windows available to look out of.

The T'swi beside him was a man named Bin, not much older than himself but whom he thought of, as he thought of all the regiment, as considerably older.

"Bin, how do you feel about the possibility of dying?" Varlik asked quietly. As usual, he spoke in Standard when recording, knowing that the T'swi would answer in kind.

Bin looked at him and smiled mildly. "How do *you* feel?" Bin countered, not bothering to keep his voice especially low. "We're in the same squad. It seems to me that you are at greater risk than I, because I have experience of battles and surviving them. How do *you* feel about the possibility of dying?"

"But you're T'swa," Varlik persisted, "and it's the T'swa that people on Iryala want to read about and see and hear on video."

Bin only grinned at Varlik, his T'swa eyes failing to look ingenuous despite their size and roundness.

"Well, tell me this, then," Varlik said. "How many of us do you suppose will be alive at this hour tomorrow?"

"Hmm." Bin appeared to calculate in his mind, frowning soberly. "I'd say . . . There are eighty-nine of us on this floater now, not including the crew. While tomorrow . . . tomorrow there will be approximately that number minus the number killed. That is as close as I can tell you."

For just a moment Varlik felt miffed, then the T'swi chuckled, and after a moment's lag, Varlik joined him. Somehow the throaty sound of the T'swi's laughter not only removed any sense of offense, but added a facet to T'swa humanity. It was the first time Varlik had been joked with by one of them.

And now Bin surprised him. "You asked," he said, "how many I suppose will be alive tomorrow. Most of us, I suspect; perhaps almost all. But ask me how many will be alive at the end of this contract."

Casually as it was delivered, the question seemed to paralyze heart and lungs. "How many?" Varlik managed to ask.

"Very few; possibly none." He looked at Varlik with an expression the newsman could only think of as kindly. "In war there are winners and losers. And who are they? The question is irrelevant. I've been told that your people tend to think of us as the supreme warriors, against whom none can stand except sometimes with a strong advantage of numbers or position. And that is not far from true. Yet we of the Red Scorpion Regiment are not much more than half our original number.

Many of our brothers have lost their game pieces, their bodies, looking down at them bloody and lifeless in dust or mud or snow. Or have sat leaning against some wall or tree or rock, looking at a shattered limb, at some wound that takes away their warriorhood. The winner becomes a loser.

"Eventually the regiment will be so decimated that the lodge will deactivate it as too small for further contracts. Then the survivors will be finished as warriors. This war will do it for the Red Scorpions, I suspect: The conditions appear to be difficult, and the enemy reputedly quite competent." He peered quizzically at Varlik. "Wouldn't you say?"

Varlik didn't say anything. Despite the somber content of the T'swi's words, he still felt that the trooper was somehow playing with him. He was also aware now that the T'swa around them were listening and watching.

"Yes, the winner eventually becomes the loser," Bin continued, "in any activity in the real world. And if things don't balance out in this lifetime, there will always be other lifetimes to complete the equation."

The T'swi stopped there, but his eyes remained on Varlik's, as if he expected the journalist to reply. Varlik started tentatively.

"Then . . . It sounds as if you feel it's your *fate* to die. Or be maimed."

"Fate? I am aware of the term from my student days; we study something of your philosophy, you know. What you refer to here as 'fate,' we simply look at as one of the laws—a tertiary, not a primary or even secondary law—but one of the laws regulating the activities of man in this universe. One may sometimes win predominantly, or lose predominantly, through an entire lifetime or even a sequence of lifetimes, but the equation will eventually tend toward a balance. Or perhaps it is just then balancing from some earlier winning or losing sequence."

Varlik frowned. "But why do you fight then, if you feel doomed to lose eventually? Why would anyone go through the pain and exhaustion and danger, and see his friends killed or mangled, when he's only going to lose in the end?"

"Ah! But we have no doom, and it is not the end."

The T'swi looked at Varlik for several seconds without saying anything further, as if considering how to make his answer more meaningful. "Varlik, why do *you* live?" he asked at last.

"Why? Because I can't help myself. A person is born living, and with the instinct to survive. That's why I live."

"Um." The blue-black warrior nodded thoughtfully. "Yet if you stay with us, you will see us put ourselves repeatedly in great danger. How is it then that the instinct you speak of is inoperative in so many of us? Including you, it seems, for here you are, going to battle with us.

"What you call 'the instinct to survive' is simply an emotional attach-ment to a body, growing in part from the misapprehension that if it is destroyed, you cease to exist. But in fact, while bodies are notably destructible, you yourself cannot avoid survival.

"The challenge is to live with *interest*. Unless one's fear is too great, which seems to be rather common among the worlds of man, one nor-mally prefers that that existence be interesting."

A hint of smile touched the wide mouth. "And even then, consider the possibility that the person who is fearful, who perhaps is even in hiding, may at some hidden level enjoy the experience.

"As warriors, we find our greatest interest and pleasure in battle, and our next greatest in preparing for battle. Winning is preferred, but the preference is slight. We are not allowed to—ah, 'graduate' is your near-est word to it. We would not be allowed to graduate if we did not know deeply and truly that the fullest joy and reward of the warrior is in being a warrior, and performing the actions of a warrior, with artistry! And that winning is something to favor only very slightly. We do prefer to win, but it is not important to us. We do not allow the matter of win-ning or losing, surviving or dying, to interfere with our pleasure. We go into battle ready to enjoy the experience, without anxiety over the out-come."

Varlik didn't answer, but after a moment looked away. He could see a certain logic in what the T'swi had said, but it wasn't what he felt in his guts.

After a moment he turned off his recorder, buckled his seat belt, and closed his eyes. Maybe, he thought, he could go to sleep; sleeping was the best way to kill time in a situation like this.

But instead he sat there, more or less slumped, thoughts drifting through his mind on no particular theme. There were questions, specu-lations, things that were or might have been. He was relaxed now, and it occurred to him that this was not much inferior to sleep itself as a way to kill time. Then, after an hour or so, he slept.

Varlik awoke gradually, nagged into consciousness by the discomfort of prolonged, unrelieved sitting. It was night; the four windows, two flanking each troop door, told him that. The lights had been dimmed, and almost all the T'swa seemed asleep, some propped against one an-other. Sergeant Kusu's eyes were open, though; they moved to Varlik, and the T'swi smiled, nodding acknowledgement of Varlik's notice. Varlik looked at his watch; he had almost two hours to wait.

It struck him then that among the more than eighty men, most of them apparently asleep, not one was snoring, and he wondered if they'd somehow been trained not to. Perhaps men who'd slept so often where a prowling enemy might hear, somehow subconsciously didn't allow themselves to snore.

He stood and stretched, twisted his trunk, rotated his shoulders, then sat and closed his eyes once more. It seemed to him he hadn't really gone to sleep again, and that no more than twenty minutes could have passed, when Platoon Sergeant Tok's voice barked out. "Ten minutes to Beregesh! By squads! First Platoon, stand and stretch!" Behind him on the other aisle, Varlik heard a similar command to the Second Platoon.

The first squad, with Varlik, stood and stretched, raised their knees, squatted and straightened, touched toes, twisted trunks, some with a quiet comment or chuckle, then sat back down, giving the aisle to the second. Varlik began to feel tension again, and it occurred to him to wonder what the tension would be like if they all felt it, if it fed back from man to man, building.

The two platoon leaders, with their sergeants, had gone to the two windows flanking the portside door. Varlik wondered what they could see. Then it occurred to him that he was not a trooper here, but a journalist with a journalist's functions, and he went over also. The windows were large, from deck level to above the head and forty inches wide, to let officers examine the scene before landing and unloading. From their elevation of perhaps 15,000 feet, Varlik could see low mountains, fairly rugged, silvered softly with moonlight. The four T'swa were gazing intently at a forward angle, as if they knew where to look, but Varlik could see nothing significant there. He decided they must be getting information over the radio speaker each wore in an ear. His camera alternated between landscape and men.

A minute later he saw a bright spark—an explosion, he realized—seemingly on the surface miles ahead, followed seconds later by two more. His muscles tightened. The four T'swa seemed as relaxed as before, strong black presences waiting for something more. The troop carrier was rapidly drawing up on the site, and Varlik could feel their craft descending, contributing to the weakness of his jellied knees. He could see in abundance now the tiny flashes of what he assumed was gunfire, or perhaps the hits of rockets. His colon felt extremely nervous.

The sporadic firefights drew nearer as the floater lost altitude, and Varlik lost himself in watching. Suddenly he realized his fear was gone, replaced for the moment by something like the exhilaration the T'swa seemed to feel. Lieutenant Zimsu called the order to belt down and be ready. Varlik moved back to his own place as the troopers fastened buckles, his camera recording T'swa faces, powerful forms, then he too buckled down. Around them somewhere was an entire fleet of assault floaters, with someone coordinating their movements, and it occurred to him to hope that the someone was competent.

Twice in the last half minute, Varlik flinched at the loud frightening bangs of light rockets exploding against the armored hull, and the carrier touched down harder than he'd expected, as if the pilot had been caught unaware by the ground, or felt hurried. The T'swa were striking the instant-release buckles of their seat belts and getting quickly to their feet, he scarcely slower. The troop doors opened and the ranks of troopers double-timed out, their weapons in their hands, Varlik carrying his camera in front of him, recording what he could from within the hurrying ranks. He'd lowered his monitor, but now he peered beneath it for wider vision, to see where he was going, his camera continuing to record.

Then he was on the short ramp and into the night, the T'swa dispersing to the sides, Varlik trying to stay within a couple of steps of Bin as he'd been told to do. The sound of gunfire was loud, sharp, immediate, and Bin was shooting short bursts. It occurred to Varlik that they ought to hit the ground, take cover, but they didn't.

Then the T'swa almost stopped shooting, and he realized that the nearby gunfire had been theirs, that Bin had not been answering it but adding to it. Still they ran, not hard but steadily, a trot. The low dark humps ahead must be the bunkers they were to destroy. Suddenly they came to a shallow ditch, and there Bin hit the dirt, Varlik landing next to him, most of the others running on. Varlik lay panting, wondering what was happening, why they had stopped. It occurred to him that they'd been off the floater for no more than twenty seconds. He raised his camera above the ditch's shoulder, panning, using his monitor now, seeing what he was capturing on his cube.

Gunfire burst out ahead to their right, and the men who'd stopped at the ditch directed concentrated fire in that direction. Except for Bin and himself, the men who'd stopped in the ditch all seemed to carry blast hoses; their racket was terrific, shocking, stunning, and in seconds the enemy fire had stopped.

Then they simply lay there, waiting in what seemed like silence, although less intense gunfire continued, apparently directed elsewhere. He thought to question Bin; why had the two of them stayed here? But he knew without asking: Bin had been told to take care of him; keep him alive.

From somewhere well ahead a rocket rose, followed quickly by another, and another, and more. Varlik knew from night exercises in his army days that the enemy had lobbers. He followed their upward flight, realized they were aimed at this ditch and its hosemen. As they began to descend, he saw others arching overhead in answer from behind. He tucked his camera under an arm and pressed his body hard against the forward ditch slope, waiting, aware of increasing gunfire. Seconds later he heard and felt the exploding rockets, a string of five evenly spaced crashes that threw rocks and dirt on the men prone in the ditch, echoed by a series well ahead, a booming background to the racketing gunfire.

Opening his eyes, he raised to his knees on the hard stony dirt, camera ready again for whatever was offered. The enemy firing seemed directed mainly elsewhere now, but the T'swa in the ditch with him were triggering leisurely bursts in the direction the earlier enemy fire had come from, so he recorded that.

Then massive explosions sounded ahead, a series of them overlapping, and Bin jerked the shoulder of Varlik's shirt. They all leaped up and ran forward, apparently not coming under fire. There were more big explosions somewhere. The bunkers, when they got there, were collapsed. Varlik lay with the others on the sloping heaps that had been bunker walls, in a smell of explosions and settling dust, sweating hard. For the first time Varlik realized how hot it was.

The troops that had charged the bunkers were gone—he hadn't even seen a body—and it seemed for a while that he and the men he was with had been forgotten, overlooked, the gunfire unrelated to them. Bin's attention was to their original right; the T'swa had lined up facing that direction now. Varlik could see muzzle flashes ahead that must be enemy fire, and when this increased in intensity, the men he was with opened up with their blast hoses again, the sound shredding the night while still more heavy explosions sounded, preceded by big flashes that flared and were gone. When they paused, a minute later, Varlik wasn't sure whether it was truly that quiet or if perhaps he'd been deafened.

The next ten or fifteen minutes alternated between relatively quiet inaction, brief outbursts of firing, and sporadic heavy explosions. Twice they came under brief fire from lobbers, and several rounds landed very near. He could smell hot hose barrels. A number of times he wiped at the sweat pooling in his eyebrows, his wet hands gritty with the dirt he crouched on, converting the sweat of his face into mud. He was recording constantly now—even when the lobber rockets arced downward and struck—commenting frequently for the audio pickup.

Then he heard T'swa bugles well behind them, and shrill whistling from several directions: somewhere troops were pulling back, but not those he was with. Instead, the hosemen opened fire again, shooting without benefit of seen targets, spraying covering fire ahead and to their left. From the general direction of the carrier, lobber rockets left bright thin trails that threaded the sky, then stitched the blackness ahead with flashes.

Nearby whistling commanded, and he stood up with the T'swa around him, trotting back in the direction of the carrier, not coming under fire again so far as Varlik knew. There was gunfire, but no sounds of blast slugs striking near or rockets landing. Like the others, he jumped the little ditch, pleased that he was able to, and after a minute could see their floater ahead of them, no lights showing. They slowed to a near-walk, jogging up the ramp past the two platoon lieutenants and their sergeants, who stood by the foot of it peering past them.

Most of the T'swa were already on board, had returned ahead of those who'd stopped at the ditch, and even in the darkness, Varlik was aware of gaps in their seated ranks. The door to the rear compartment—the aid station—stood open, a blackout curtain blocking the light within, and Varlik felt a lump in his stomach.

But the carrier did not lift; the platoons' four leaders were still outside by the ramp. Three troopers were helped in, wounded. They pushed the curtain aside and disappeared into the aid station.

Still the floater sat. Four more T'swa entered, each pair carrying a wounded man, and also went into the aid station. The lieutenants followed, with the platoon sergeants, and the troop doors finally hissed softly shut.

Seconds later the floater began lifting rapidly, pivoting as it rose, then Varlik felt horizontal acceleration as they headed north toward Aromanis. No rockets struck them. When the acceleration had stopped, the compartment lights came on low. Varlik looked around; the gaps were not large or numerous. Soberly, camera in hand, he got up and headed for the aid station.

It was daylight when they landed, but not by much; the daytime heat was only starting to build. Thick-witted from dozing, Varlik went straight to his old media quarters, showered, then went to the officers' mess for whatever he could get. They were still serving breakfast. When he'd finished, he returned to the air-conditioned comfort of his room to begin editing and narrating. He'd been at it only briefly when someone knocked.

"Come in," he said.

It was Konni. She was sweaty, dirty, and he could see she'd been crying. He got to his feet. She simply stood there, her face writhing with the effort not to cry again. Once more Varlik's stomach knotted.

"What?" he asked simply.

"Bertol," she said. It was all she got out before she broke down and began to cry like a little girl, utterly despondent. *Oh shit,* Varlik thought, and feeling wretched, went to her, wet-eyed himself now, to stand holding her till she'd cried herself out.

# 18

Bertol Bakkis's body would never again pickle in ethanol; Graves Registration personnel had treated it with something more permanent. At least, though, it had been spared the indignity of being torn up by blast slugs; a fragment of lobber rocket had ripped through his sternum and right ventricle, killing him instantly.

Not that Bertol and Konni had tried anything as strenuous as accompanying a platoon into action; they'd stayed near the carrier, shooting what cubeage they could from there. Several lobber rockets had hit nearby, and he'd been one of the casualties.

It took Varlik and Konni most of the day to edit their cubes and narrative reports. After they'd delivered them to the communications center for the next day's pod, they'd gotten maudlin drunk together in honor of Bertol. Then Varlik had jogged, sweating, through the prairie night to the T'swa camp.

He could have stayed in the air-conditioned media quarters at base camp. But if he had, he'd have ended up in the sack with Konni—she'd seemed to be inviting it—and he wouldn't allow himself that. Mauen, he felt, deserved better than an adulterous husband.

The first mile of jogging had taken him in uncertain wavers along the travelway, but by the time he arrived, he was pretty much sober from the exertion and sweating. And had begun to wonder and worry. Had the T'swa held a memorial of some sort for their killed and he missed it? At the tent of the First Squad, all of whom had returned unscathed, Sergeant Kusu raised his head for a moment as Varlik entered.

"Can I talk with you?" Varlik whispered.

In answer, the T'swi had swung his legs out of bed, and together the two of them went outside.

"I had to work all day, on my reports," Varlik said. "And one of the video team was killed at Kelikut, so the other one and I—got drunk this evening, in his memory. I hope I didn't miss anything you guys did, any memorial you held, for your dead."

"You didn't," Kusu said. "We make our farewells privately, personally."

Varlik nodded and turned on his belt recorder. "At the communications center they told me the regiment had lost twenty-nine killed and sixty-one wounded, but they said there weren't any missing. How could anyone tell the killed from the missing in the dark like that, pulling out the way we did?"

In the moonlight, the black face seemed to smile very slightly. "We have our method."

"Is it—all right to tell me about it?"

"Certainly. But you might prefer not to know."

The answer froze Varlik's mind for a moment. Then, "I see," he said, not seeing at all. "I would like to know."

"The dead come to us as spirits, thus we know who they are. All the rest returned physically. Thus no prisoners, no missing."

*The dead tell them.* Varlik had nothing to reply and nothing more to ask; he simply nodded. Kusu stood for a moment as if waiting for possible further questions. When none were forthcoming, he said good night and went back to the tent.

Mind spinning in slow motion, Varlik got his towel and walked to the showers where, beneath the stars, he washed away the sweat of his run. Somewhere in the process his mind relaxed, and when he went to bed, he lay awake only briefly. *The dead came to them, and the farewells were personal and private.* The sort of things—superstitions—that you could expect from gooks. But these "gooks" weren't gooks. And if they said it, he would not gainsay them, even inwardly to himself. Even if he couldn't accept it as truth.

Then he slept, and dreamed, and when the whistles wakened him near dawn, he felt rested and revived, and surprised by it, ready for the day despite all he'd had to drink and his shortness of sleep.

That day he trained with the T'swa. The day after that he went to the base. There wasn't much to report, although he sent off a letter cube to Mauen, but he wanted to update himself on the Beregesh invasion. He ended up flying south again, in an armored staff floater with Information Office personnel, to see and record the battle site. He hadn't thought to get a cool-suit, and had had the choice of either going later or going without one. He was the only one on the plane who didn't have one bundled beside him.

At Beregesh, he found the battle over, with two full divisions, one Iryalan and one Romblit, securing the surrounding area. Cargo carriers were landing equipment and supplies in quantity, the area resembling some mad and disorderly quartermaster depot. Casualties had been moderate, and yes, a major told him, the T'swa had done a thorough job of neutralizing Bird fortifications.

Occasionally he heard distant firing; some of it couldn't have been much farther than a mile away.

He ran into Konni at the field HQ. She'd arrived the afternoon before, when there'd still been sporadic hard fighting close by. She'd spent one night sleeping in a cool-suit, and was going back to Aromanis later; she'd share her cube with him if he'd like.

Next he caught a ride on a hover truck hauling digging equipment to the perimeter, where fortifications were being built. The driver was a Romblit reservist, a tall ex-farmhand corporal who looked rawboned even in his cool-suit.

"Mate," the Romblit said, "I don't see how you can live without a cool-suit. It's bad enough here with one. I tried to sleep without mine for a while last night and liked to have died. How d'you do it?"

"Not very comfortably. But I thought I'd better give it a try."

The driver steered around a caved-in bunker, then nursed the rig through a shortcut, angling down into a shallow rocky draw and up the other side, to hurry jouncing along a rough track bulldozed through open scrub growth. Mostly the way was slightly downhill. Varlik kept his camera busy.

"You're that news guy that lives with the T'swa, ain't you?" the man asked.

"Right."

"I figured, what with no cool-suit and that funny-lookin' spotty uniform. How come they make 'em like that?"

"They're harder to see in the woods. They call them camouflage suits."

"Huh! I've heard you train with the gooks—run all day through the hot sun like a herd of buck." The man's tone was not disparaging; he sounded impressed.

Varlik understood how things could get exaggerated. What puzzled him was how this man, and presumably therefore many others, had even heard of him. He decided it wasn't worth puzzling over; he'd relax and enjoy his new reputation.

"Yes," he answered, "I train with them."

"How come would anyone do that 'less they had to? I'm glad I'm in the Engineers, so's I don't have to even drill."

Varlik recorded a file of troops trudging along in cool-suits, rifles slung, headed the same direction as the truck.

"I thought I'd like to get an idea of what it's like to be a T'swi," Varlik answered. "Besides, if I'm to go with them in combat, I'd better be able to keep up or the Birds could get me."

The construction site was just ahead along the upper edge of a long declivity. Men with beam saws were felling the larger scrub trees and cutting them into short timbers. Reaction dozers pushed dirt and rock, gouging a broad trench, pushing the spoil into piles. Soldiers manhandled timbers into place, shoveled and tamped dirt, all in cool-suits. It occurred to Varlik that someone had manufactured a lot of cool-suits in the last year or so.

The driver spat brown fluid out the door. "I wish we had time," he said. "I'd like to hear more about them T'swa. They're supposed to be some tough gooks. You with them here night before last?"

"Right."

"Without no cool-suit."

"Right again."

The Romblit shook his head as he stopped the rig by a group of soldiers. "Maybe I'll see you again sometime," he called as they dismounted out opposite sides. "Maybe when we get this place civilized. I'll buy the beer and you can tell me about it."

Varlik poked around the area, keeping out of the way of equipment, visiting fortifications in different stages of construction. Half an hour was enough. Beregesh would take some getting used to; despite taking mineral tablets and drinking heavily at one of the huge water bags slung from tripods, he felt ready to head back to field HQ, and caught a ride on another truck. Its driver was taciturn, repeatedly eyeing his lack of a cool-suit, or perhaps his T'swa uniform, but saying nothing. The officer in charge at the landing site chatted briefly, commenting on his lack of a cool-suit, then pointed out a staff floater he could board that would be northbound in minutes.

The floater soon was full, and when the last seat had been taken, took off. Excepting Varlik, all the passengers were officers. Most looked tired, and there wasn't much talk. He got some looks at first, or his sweat-soaked T'swa camouflage suit did, but he ignored them and napped much of the way back.

# 19

The staff car pulled up in front of Colonel Biltong's headquarters tent and Carlis Voker got out. The new camp boasted duckboard sidewalks, and the tent a lumber frame. Although Voker had called ahead, no one was outside to meet him—his visits were frequent and he knew his way— but the two T'swa colonels were waiting when he stepped inside. And Varlik Lormagen was there, sitting back out of the way, recording; that was different.

"Colonels," Voker said, "I have a new mission for you."

"We've been expecting one," Biltong replied.

Voker looked at the two black men. Their invariable equanimity—it could be read as smugness—sparked a flash of irritation that quickly passed. The T'swa, he told himself as he took a seat, were the only troops who could do what the general wanted done.

"We know the Birds have radios," Voker said, "and we can assume they've notified their headquarters, wherever that is, that we've taken Beregesh back. The last time we took the place back, or the Rombili did, the Birds sent up troops and drove them out, and there's no reason to believe they won't try to take it back again. If they were willing to let us have the place, they wouldn't have started this war to begin with."

*Wouldn't have started the war.* The statement offended Varlik, a reaction unexpected. It seemed to him that the Rombili had started the war when they'd started enslaving the Birds. It was just that the Birds had taken nearly three centuries to mount an offensive.

"We know they have floaters," Voker was saying, "but apparently only light gun floaters—for which, incidentally, we're prepared now. Every unit, even administrative and service outfits, has M-4 rocket launchers ready to hand. At any rate, the only way the Birds can bring up troops is overland on foot. And the only source of large numbers of them has got to be the equatorial forests. Farther north, our surveillance platforms would spot large encampments without fail.

"Likewise, the only routes they can move north on are through the mountain forests, and for the last three hundred miles or so even those aren't safe cover for large bodies of troops; they're too open to aerial observation and attack." Voker paused. "Do you see what I'm leading to?"

Biltong nodded. "You want us to interdict the trails—make it difficult for them to bring troops up."

"Exactly! And I'd like you to begin soon." Voker got to his feet. "Why don't you look the mission over and see me at base HQ tomorrow morning. We can start working out transportation and supply. Now, unless there's anything more we need to discuss at this time, gentlemen? Good."

He looked at Varlik. "Good to see you, Lormagen. I hear you were along on the Beregesh night raid and visited there again yesterday. I'm glad things are turning out well for you; I suspected they might when I saw how hard you worked preparing yourself."

Turning to the T'swa, he saluted. "Colonels!" he said, then turned and left. When they heard his staff car's engine hum, Biltong grinned.

"Koda," he said in Tyspi, "by Confederation standards that is an unusually adaptable officer. At heart he's not as Standard as he's supposed to be."

Koda chuckled. "Perhaps we should have told him we'd already foreseen his need."

"We'll do it obliquely," Biltong said, and turning, called to the sergeant major. "Wuu-Sad, bring the file on the interdiction plan. And have Dzokan bring the car; Koda and I are going to army headquarters at once."

Koda laughed out loud, then turned to Varlik.

"Colonel Biltong and I have listened to and watched some of your cubes. They were copied by our communications chief when you turned them over to him. Do you object?"

"Would it make any difference if I did?"

"It would not prevent us from doing it again, if we thought it necessary; we do have an interest. We were very impressed with what you've done. I hope your editor appreciates you properly."

"I won't object to your looking," Varlik replied, "as long as I don't have to tailor my reports to fit anyone else's ideas about what I've seen."

"Not at all. You know the people you write for far more intimately than we do. And you do a good job of describing us objectively."

Koda changed the subject then. "Sergeant Kusu tells me you've done remarkably well on training runs here, but we are not sure it is physically feasible for you to accompany the troops on an extended subtropical assignment. You've spent a few hours at Beregesh now; do you think you could tolerate field conditions there without a cool-suit? Cool-suits won't be practical on interdiction patrol."

"I'm not sure whether I can or not. I'd like to give it a try, though. At best, the cool-suits hamper a person's mobility, and all I heard at Beregesh were complaints about them."

They heard a hovercar pull up. "Good," Koda said as he and Biltong got to their feet. "We're leaving now. Do you want to go to army headquarters with us?"

Varlik shook his head. "I think I'd better spend the rest of the day with my squad, if I'm going to try the tropics without a cool-suit."

Voker had ridden out with the air conditioner off and the windows open, to the concealed unhappiness of his driver, who had dared, while Voker was in the T'swa tent, to close the windows and turn on the cooler. When the colonel appeared in the tent door, his attention still behind him, the corporal quickly lowered the windows and turned the cooler off.

Voker didn't even notice the residual coolness in the car. Something that had occurred to him before had captured his attention again: There was little question that the Birds had been manipulating them from their first offensive. They'd made their resources known gradually and profitably, with full use of surprise. Drawn Confederation forces into actions that optimized their own, still not fully known, strengths and advantages. The Birds couldn't have done those things without a thorough knowledge—a considerable knowledge, at least—of Confederation military resources, psychology, and practices.

Someone from off-planet had more than armed and trained them. Someone was undoubtedly also directing them. But who?

It was as if a clue was staring him in the face, but he couldn't see it. He'd have to ask himself the right question—whatever that was. The reason, maybe: why were they doing this? Or who'd be able to use the technite if the Birds controlled it?

He'd have to review the situation—program an analysis and see what he came up with. He wasn't well trained as a programmer, or very experienced, but he wanted to work on this by himself, for a while at least. And sometimes just playing with the factors, flowcharting, could give you the answer you were looking for.

# 20

By the time the T'swa headquarters was relocated there, five days later, the army's Beregesh base was beginning to look as organized as it actually was, and a newer, more permanent defensive perimeter was rapidly being built a mile outside the original, complete with mine fields and cleared fields of fire.

The new perimeter was more than fifteen miles long, with as many bunkers built or under construction as the army was prepared to man at the time. As more divisions arrived, more bunkers would be built. Crews were out with beam saws, clearing the ground for 200 yards out, saving the more useful lengths of wood for use in bunker construction. The rest was pushed into piles by dozers, sprayed with a high flammable, and ignited, sending columns of smoke high into the dry, previously transparent air.

When the piles had burned themselves out, the dozers returned to level the field, leaving no cover, no depression or hump to hide in or behind. After the dozers moved on, a wirelayer floated out, laying down coils of accordion wire near the clearing's outer edge, and after that, mines of different descriptions—string mines, jumpers, compression mines, radio mines, mines that would trigger at the hover field of a vehicle no larger than a scooter, just in case the Birds showed up with any.

According to rumor, more wire was on its way from Iryala and other worlds, and still more was on order.

Bird attacks did not seriously hamper construction. Patrols in cool-suits operated constantly outside the construction zone. Other patrols worked the bush inside, hunting any Birds who might have infiltrated. Gun ships also patrolled, occasionally coming under rocket fire. Their armor was resistant to M-3H rockets. About a dozen, hit, had returned with little or no damage, but two had been shot down.

A new construction battalion had arrived from Rombil, and base support troops had been assigned on rotation to help. Timber and cement in quantities were being flown in on arch trucks and pallet trucks from the sawmill and cement plant west of Aromanis. Four power receivers had been installed and were receiving transmissions from the new orbiting power station. Prefab cool-huts for the troops were going up rapidly and being covered with timbers and earth for protection. Twelve-hour shifts, including the frequent rest breaks necessary when laboring in cool-suits, were standard for both officers and men, and work went on around the clock. The troops were too busy, and off duty too tired, to complain much, and besides, they felt they were accomplishing something.

The sporadic Bird attacks had been mainly against construction crews, although several patrols outside the perimeter had been wiped out or dealt nasty casualties.

Meanwhile, the T'swa troopers had been flown directly from the Aromanis Base to interdiction operations some two hundred miles south of Beregesh. All that the T'swa had at Beregesh was a joint regimental field headquarters and an office at the Beregesh communications center.

Colonel Koda had kept Varlik at Beregesh to see how he managed in the subequatorial climate. It was supposedly hotter than the equatorial zone, though much less humid. Also, he said, he was waiting until the danger level could be evaluated for the new T'swa operation. "We have almost eighteen hundred warriors," Koda replied to Varlik's impatience, "but only one accomplished publicist."

At least Varlik couldn't complain about lack of information or sweat. He was privy to all reports from T'swa troops in the field, and exposed to air conditioning only at the comm center or when he accompanied Colonel Koda to the army's Beregesh HQ. He even slept in a T'swa tent instead of a cool-hut, and never so much as tried on a cool-suit. His exercise regimen wasn't what it had been up north, but he accompanied Koda on the colonel's almost daily runs, each about an hour long.

He also spent an hour every other day trying to duplicate the unusual strength and flexibility exercises that most T'swa base personnel did in pairs in lieu of the more time-consuming workouts the combat troops had done up north. At first he was sore from them—belly, shoulders, hamstrings, arms—but he survived. Not comfortably as the T'swa did, but he survived, without heat prostration or total exhaustion—and with pride.

Confederation personnel reacted variously to Varlik: A few looked away in resentful irritation, and a few others glared: surely his behavior reflected disrespect for Standardness and his own people. But mostly his activities spawned good-natured exaggerations of his toughness and prowess, told as truth and even believed by the tellers. He was the only white man at Beregesh who went without a cool-suit—or who was allowed to, for that matter.

The Confederation troops were never briefed on what the T'swa were doing, but rumors flowed, a military tradition as old as armies. They started with the pilots who'd dropped the T'swa as numerous individual squads far back in Bird Land, or had flown in to evacuate casualties or drop supplies. Imagination took it from there, the T'swa reputation never suffering in the telling. Varlik, in a fey mood one evening, circulated among the army hutments, interviewing troops on what they thought of the T'swa. Selected interviews and excerpts went to Iryala and Rombil aboard pods, along with video recordings from the evacuation center showing wounded, both white and black.

Whenever a call of T'swa wounded was received, a small evac floater was sent out, but such calls were not abundant. Reportedly, casualties weren't heavy, and the T'swa didn't call for a floater unless (1) the wound was incapacitating, and (2) the wounded could be gotten alive to a place reasonably safe for the floater. The Birds were known to post lookouts, some with night scanners, in occasional tall ridgetop trees, so a floater landing could endanger an entire squad.

Every day after breakfast, Varlik reported to regimental headquarters, until one morning, when they'd been at Beregesh a week, Colonel Koda made his decision.

"Lormagen," he said, "I have a question. Are you quite sure you want to join your squad in the bush?"

Varlik's pulse quickened. "Absolutely, sir. When?"

"Late tonight. They have called in that they will withdraw from the contact zone for a supply drop. Have you ever parachuted?"

Varlik's bowel spasmed. "No, sir."

"Are you willing to?"

"If it's the only way, sir."

"It's the safest way. The floater flies a confusion course low over the forest—about three hundred feet above the trees—and drops supplies to a signal beacon. If Birds are watching, hopefully they will not know at what point the drop occurred, but if the floater stopped to lower you . . . You see."

"I'll jump, sir."

"Fine." Without turning to the door, Koda called his orderly. "Makaat!"

Makaat came in; he'd left half his left hand on Emor Gadny's World. "Yes, colonel?"

"Get Varlik equipped with forest jump gear. He's going south tonight. Drill him in landing rolls and letdown procedure; there must be some suitable trees around here. Then go over everything he needs to know about jumping over forest at night, and make sure he gets it all, thoroughly. When you're satisfied he can handle himself without excessive risk of injury, let me know. When he's ready, get him equipped with a lapse release chute, drill him in its use, and take him to the landing field. Major Svelkander, in charge of supply and evacuation, will have a floater for him. Take Varlik up and have him jump from, oh, 800 feet local the first time, over the marshalling field.

"The second jump should be from 400. We'll consider two jumps enough."

"Yes, sir."

"One other thing. You will go with him tonight and be his jumpmaster."

"Thank you, sir."

Koda's attention went to some papers again. They'd been dismissed. Numb, Varlik left with Makaat.

The forest jump gear was more cumbersome and awkward than Varlik had imagined. After drilling on landing rolls for a few minutes from a standing position on the ground, Makaat had him practice off the bed of a parked truck. After several jumps from there, he graduated to jumping off the cab roof, all to the attention of a small but very interested group of soldiers. Varlik was glad the Orlanthan gravity was lighter than Iryala's, even though the difference wasn't large. When he'd jumped from the roof three times, Makaat raised the truck to its maximum of thirty inches above the ground, then drove it at a speed of about five miles per hour and called out to jump. The landing roll worked so well that Varlik began to feel there was nothing to this.

Letting himself down from a tree proved simple and relatively easy, but Makaat had him do it half a dozen times, the last three blindfolded to simulate doing it in the forest night. And if the tree, the largest available, was only 35 feet tall, the procedure, he told himself, would be no different for a tree of 80 or 120 feet.

The preliminaries took them through lunch time. It was early afternoon when they reached the landing field, where a small group of airmen, apparently having heard of his impending jump, were on hand to watch.

Varlik didn't start to get really nervous until they took off. The light floater went straight up, faster than seemed necessary, leaving his stomach behind, then stopped at what Varlik assumed must be 800 feet. Makaat opened the door and looked back at him.

"Are you ready?"

Varlik nodded. He would *not* disgrace himself. He *would* step out that door into sunlit nothingness, and he would not soil himself.

"Ready," he answered.

His mouth felt dry; he was surprised that the word came out sounding so natural. Did the T'swa feel this way the first time they jumped?

"All right. Stand in the door as I showed you, with your hands on the sides. When I slap your shoulder, you step out. Agreed?"

"Of course." Varlik shuffled to the door, awkward in coveralls and harness, eyeing the lapse release Makaat wore on his belt. When he got fifty feet out, it was supposed to open his chute automatically—"explode" it, in a sense, from its pack. He wondered if they ever failed.

Better than having to pull a release handle himself, the way the T'swa marauders had done in their freefall jumps. His body felt too numb to pull a handle.

He stood in the door, hands on the edge, looking out, his whole gut clenched. It didn't seem possible to . . .

The hand struck his shoulder and he jumped, plummeted, and felt the opening, without the jerk he'd expected. He swung, swooped beneath the flowering chute, then the oscillating stopped and he was floating suspended, with the most glorious sense of joy he could remember! He looked down past his feet, utterly without fear now, then to one side saw the cluster of troops pointing up at him.

Let's see now. Hands on guide lines. Pull right—that's the way. Hey! It works! Great! I'm heading right toward them. Let's make them scatter. Oops, going to overrun them. Pull right again and spiral. Wow! Look at that! Now! Right at them!

Then the ground seemed to accelerate, the airmen in their cool-suits scattering. At the last moment the ground jumped up at him and his feet struck, his knees striking the ground because his legs had been too relaxed. He rolled back to his feet, whooping. The airmen applauded. The floater was already halfway to the ground to pick him up.

The second jump was anticlimactic. As he addressed the door, his bowel felt the same as it had the first time, but now it was an objective phenomenon, belonging to the body, not to himself. This time as he stepped out, the floater had a forward speed of about seventy miles an hour, as it would that night.

He held a right spiral to the ground; it took only seconds to get there, and this time he kept proper tension in his legs. He could easily have kept his feet, but Makaat had told him not to.

As they rode back to the T'swa camp, he felt cockier than he'd ever felt before in his life.

# 21

This time there was no sun, just the scant pale light of the sickled major moon, and the second moon similarly slender, spread over the forest roof. For a long, beautiful moment the treetops appeared remote, then seemed to accelerate upward as he fell toward them, and for brief empty seconds, alarmed, he tried to withhold himself. One grabbed for him. Branches buffeted, submerging him in darkness; his descent half halted. Then suddenly nothing held him and he dropped precipitously, to be somehow stopped short, panting, disoriented.

He hung there in blackness, regathering his attention, wondering if his chute had lodged securely or would slip loose, wondering how far it was to the ground, wondering if it was safe to move.

He had no choice. Looking around, down, he could see nothing. His hands felt for the coil of slender rope clipped to his side, found an end, and with a minimum of body movement wove it through harness rings and made it fast. He then ran a bight below one foot, stirrup-like, gripped the line clamp in his right hand—harder than necessary— removed the snap, and struck the harness release with his left. For one sickening moment, as the harness let go, the chute gave slightly in the branches above, but only to lodge more firmly. Then he let himself down, never seeing the ground, finding it with his feet. He must have been, he decided, some twenty feet up.

On the ground he removed the heavy canvas coveralls, the masked crash helmet, and the steel-arched forest jump boots, then dug jungle boots from his pack and put them on, felt forth his holstered M-1 sidearm and attached it to grommets on his belt. Next he took out his video camera, its battery fresh, put it into a capacious breast pocket, and slipped the strap over his head. Then he donned his monitor visor, followed by a field cap. Finally, he closed the pack, put it on his shoulders, and lay back against it to wait for the T'swa.

He was beginning to sweat just sitting on the ground.

He couldn't see his hand inches in front of his face. He could have activated his monitor visor, of course, but it operated off his camera, and his camera cells were not inexhaustible. And he'd probably be there for a week or longer.

Somewhere, perhaps thirty or sixty or a hundred yards away, would be the supply bundle he'd followed out the door—a large, foam-padded box with a ribbon chute that should first have slowed it, then presumably slid from the branches to let the box fall to the ground. Like his dangling harness, it would emit a weak radio signal for about twenty minutes.

But they'd hardly come and get him right away; even a T'swi couldn't see in such darkness. They'd take a bearing, then wait till dawn, itself not much more than two hours away. They'd have picked up the two signals and be wondering what the second package was.

Briefly, he wondered if they'd be pleased to find it was him, or disappointed, or neutral, and then it occurred to him that he'd never seen a T'swi irritated! He wondered what an irritated T'swi would be like; or an angry T'swi! Would a T'swa warrior enraged be more dangerous in battle than one with the usual calm?

After a bit he allowed himself, there in the close hot dark, to play with the idea of a Bird patrol somewhere nearby, equipped with a directional instrument that could pick up the signal from his harness. But that was too farfetched. Next he played with a scenario in which he'd come down too far from the squad, their instrument failing to detect his signal. He imagined himself alone in the forest, waiting until it was obvious he'd been overlooked, then striking off northward to find his way back to Beregesh.

And which way was north?

The sound galvanized him, a low hard "s-s-st," repeated seconds later. It could be no farther than twenty feet away, probably less. He strained to hear, thought he detected a sound, very slight, from the same direction. Then, nearer, in Tyspi, a whispered "Khua?" (Who?)

With equal quiet he whispered: "Varlik."

The T'swa claimed the night vision of a cat, but he wouldn't have thought even a cat could see in such darkness.

The chuckle was even softer than usual, almost as soft as the whispers. "Good. Good. Are you all right?"

"I'm fine."

Then nothing more. Varlik lay back and let himself relax. There must be insects out here, he thought; the climate was wetter than at Beregesh or Aromanis. Makaat had given him a field-issue insect repeller, an inch and a half disk with a two-day battery—the same thing sportsmen sometimes used when fishing. It was attached to his field belt, and when the battery died he would throw the thing away, replace the whole unit from his pack.

He closed his eyes then, intending to sleep if he could. Could Birds see in the dark like the T'swa? It seemed to him that in such opaque darkness his eyes could come open without waking him up. The next thing he knew was the calling of forest birds, and his eyes opened to faint gray dawn. Quickly more birds joined in, building to a literal din of warbling, whistling, twittering, screeching—a chorus, a wild arboreal laud to encroaching day. The T'swi named Tisi-Kasi was kneeling near him, grinning. Varlik looked around: Six of the squad were in sight close by. Only six. His breath stuck in his chest for a moment; had they lost four? No, he told himself, they had lookouts posted. They must have.

Nothing happened though until, after three or four minutes, the dawn cacophony thinned to scattered cries and trills. Then Kusu stood, raised his face, and made a querulous cry not unlike some from the trees, repeating it three times. He was answered from a little distance. The answer seeming to come from higher, as if from a ridge.

Kusu looked at Varlik. "It's good to have you back with us, my friend. Now it's time to leave; we have Birds to find, and havoc to create."

They were not six, or ten either any longer, but eight—nine now, counting Varlik. They hiked through much of the morning, not jogging but moving hard and fast, pausing occasionally to drink from their canteens, lick salt, or snack on dried rations during breaks. Varlik recorded samples of it on video. They crossed several brooks, refilling their canteens at each, dropping in a tiny capsule and shaking briskly to kill possible parasites not protected against by their broad-spectrum immunization. The combination of heat and humidity was definitely worse than at Beregesh, yet it seemed to Varlik that he was going to handle it all right.

The forest wasn't as thick as he'd expected. On flats and benches and in the bottoms of ravines it could be almost jungle-like, like the place he'd landed, but on many sites the trees were scrubby, the canopy thin or broken, the forest floor patched and dappled with sunlight, green with forbs and graminoids. Occasionally there were old burns, not large, seemingly where lightning had struck dead snags, setting them afire to sew the ground around with burning brands. Here and there, storms had thinned or flattened the stand, and in some such places thickets, large or small, had sprung up. Birds called occasionally, and sometimes a furry arboreal animal swung or scampered, noisy or silent. Varlik saw a large snakelike thing, thicker than his arm and a dozen feet long, and slowed, pointing, but Bin, who walked behind him, only grinned and nodded.

Three times he glimpsed large ungulates trotting away, and twice, on muddy stream banks, he saw the prints of some large animal, presumably predatory, with retracted claws.

After three hours they encountered a tiny rivulet flowing from a dense stand of saplings in the saddle of a ridge. Kusu hissed a halt, and again they refilled their canteens. Then he led them up through the thicket to the saddle's crest. There the saplings stood less densely, and there they stopped.

Four men disappeared to scout the vicinity. The others watched and listened while Kusu explained briefly to Varlik how the squad operated. Unless the scouts decided it was too hazardous, this place would be the rendezvous for the next two days. Kusu, along with Shan, the squad medic, would stay here with the supplies and radio while the rest went out in two-man hit teams, armed with M-1s and grenades, to find and attack Birds.

The heart of the region was a narrow plateau, hundreds of miles long, dissected lengthwise by long narrow draws into longitudinal ridges. Near the edges of the plateau, the ridges were less high but more rugged and broken, the draws deeper, and the forest more open. Thus the fringes were much less suited as lines of march than the central ridges, and it was among the fringe ridges that rendezvous were established.

The Birds were moving north in small columns of platoon size, following or sometimes making small trails. In the heavier central forest, this made it virtually impossible to spot them from a surveillance platform or gun floaters. A hit team would find a column, usually avoiding its scouts, ambush it—empty their rifles into it and perhaps throw grenades. Then they'd get out as rapidly as possible—not back to the rendezvous, but always away from the trail and the central ridges. Usually the Birds would not pursue them for long; apparently their orders were to continue north. When they did pursue more persistently, it was usually possible to ambush them.

The biggest hazard was occasional Bird hunter patrols.

Late the second day, the teams would return to the rendezvous, using utmost care not to be followed. There Kusu and Shan would be waiting, and they'd all move. Bird hunter patrols made it dangerous to stay long in one location.

When Kusu had finished the briefing, he sized Varlik up thoughtfully. "You kept up well this morning. What have you been doing since we left Aromanis?"

Varlik told him. Kusu nodded.

"Good. Very good. Now, what we do—what the hit teams do—is quite dangerous. The Birds move well; they are forest wise and very tough. We have succeeded as well as we have because we move freely while they feel constrained to move northward. But this advantage will diminish; the Birds will undoubtedly form more and more hunter patrols. We expect our activities to become increasingly hazardous."

So far, Kusu had spoken almost blandly. Now his gaze intensified, just a little, and he gestured at Varlik's camera.

"Which brings us to you. Your function here is presumably to show us not merely living in the field but also in action. And that is more dangerous for you than for us, because we can run faster and farther than you—and so can the Birds. Also, we observe more than you, move with greater stealth, and if necessary, we can find our way by night. The Birds, incidentally, seem to have no better night vision than you do, or not much.

"Frankly, I would keep you here with me, except that apparently it is of some importance to Koda that you record us in action."

Varlik nodded, feeling uncomfortable—not because of the danger he was in, but because he was a problem to this man he admired.

"So I will send you out with a team," Kusu continued, "but not into action at first. Bin and Tisi-Kasi will spend two days teaching you to move as silently as possible, disturbing the ground as little as possible. It is desirable that Bird hunter patrols not notice if they come near or cross your trail.

"Do you see the desirability of that?"

Again Varlik nodded, determined that this would work out. In two days he might not learn to move like a T'swi, he told himself, but he could come decently close. He'd always been a quick study, in things physical as well as mental.

"Of course," he answered. "I don't want to get killed, or to get anyone else killed."

"Fine. You have done well in all other respects; I'm sure you will do well in this also."

The burly T'swi gripped Varlik's hand on it, then they relaxed on the ground and waited for the scouts to return.

It was among the fringe ridges that Bin and Tisi-Kasi tutored and drilled their student. Three times that day they heard flurries of distant gunfire, near the edge of hearing—twice to the northwest, and once to the southwest. Other squads, the T'swa told him. Varlik had practiced into midafternoon, learning to recognize the ground conditions that showed tracks plainly, and those where tracks were least noticeable; how to move slowly without a sound; and how to run with the least possible noise. Then the two T'swa had lain with their eyes closed, and he'd crept up on them, had touched Bin's foot without being heard. They had also followed him at a little distance while he ran, critiquing his noise and the tracks he left. He'd never before thought of running "lightly"—running had simply been running. No longer.

It was then they heard the noise of nearer fighting, brief but furious, westward perhaps a mile—an eruption of automatic rifle fire followed by what had to be a blast hose. Then there was silence, interrupted moments later by two short bursts of rifle fire.

All three men had stopped as if frozen, listening, then drawn together. "Probably one of ours making a hit," Bin said to Varlik.

"Do you think they got away afterward?"

"If one of our people were killed, I would ordinarily sense it. If one was wounded . . ." His gaze went out of focus for a moment, then returned. "I believe they are all right. The danger now is that the Birds will chase them and get clear shots, or possibly run them down."

"Can they do that? Run them down?"

"Yes, in the sense of following them until they come up on them somewhere, unaware. The Birds, as Kusu said, are forest wise, perhaps as much as we are. But now we have things of our own to . . ."

There was more firing—long bursts from several rifles, overlapping. This time Bin disregarded it, gesturing to Varlik. "Begin."

Varlik began trotting again along the side slope, as soft-footed as possible, swerving uphill to avoid a steep stretch of bare, loose, ash-dry soil where tracks would be conspicuous, then along the contour just below a crest, where the forest was thin and the ground covered with a low thick growth of vines that would rebound when he had passed. More firing sounded, seemingly an exchange of short bursts—two rifles answered by one, then quickly again two. Varlik stopped, saw Bin grin before the T'swa waved him on.

Varlik angled downslope through undergrowth to the bottom of a draw, where a brooklet trickled from a seep. There the three of them stopped to refill canteens and take a break. In the soft mud, Varlik saw the prints of numerous clawed paws, as of a pack of large canids. Bin drew his bayonet, and from his pack a sharpening steel, and began to touch up the blade.

Tisi-Kasi knelt down a little apart, back erect, hands resting loosely on his thighs, and closed his eyes—one of the things they learned to do as children, Kusu had said. Varlik had never before seen a T'swi in that posture by daylight, and after a minute he questioned Bin quietly.

"What is Tisi-Kasi doing? He looks like he's in a trance."

"He is regaining *t'suss.*"

"*T'suss?*"

The obsidian eyes moved from Tisi-Kasi to Varlik.

"*T'suss* is a condition similar to what your culture calls 'nonchalance,' and your scholars have so translated it. But translated as 'nonchalance,' *t'suss* is readily misunderstood, for often the term 'nonchalance' is applied to a state resulting from confidence in one's ability to prevail over whatever difficulty may exist in the situation at hand.

"Like nonchalance, *t'suss* is a casual calm, a lack of fear or worry, but the word does not apply to states growing out of either confidence or apathy. *T'suss* involves complete readiness to accept whatever outcome, regardless of the alignment of that outcome with, against, or across one's own intentions and efforts. Ability and prevailing are irrelevant to *t'suss*, and in a sense, confidence is subsumed in the higher attitude of *t'suss*."

"Well, how does kneeling like that help someone regain *t'suss?*"

"It is not the kneeling. Posture is a matter of preference and circumstance, although kneeling erect is most often used. Tisi-Kasi is creating images. He might be said to be dreaming, but as the knowing father of his dreams."

Varlik nodded. "I believe I understand," he said. "We do that too, some of us, though I've never practiced it. It's called image rehearsal. A person sits down and pictures victory in his mind, over and over again. It's supposed to help him win . . . But you said—you said that winning isn't the purpose."

"Correct. The images that Tisi-Kasi is creating include images of victory and also of defeat, of continuing to live and of being killed. Perhaps he found himself wishing too strongly for victory, or being partisan on the side of coming through alive, or of his friends doing so—which is all right, but it is not our way. It causes a reduction of pleasure in war, and also a reaction on the spirit—the being himself—in case his body is disrupted. And it commonly leads to an anxiety response in battle, which might result in inappropriate combat behavior."

Varlik contemplated Bin's words. "Our psychologists," he replied at last, "tell us that to rehearse defeat can cause defeat. The idea is that you get what you rehearse."

Bin smiled. "That would be a special case, depending on certain predisposing conditions that may be common among your people. But it is not the general case. If a person is oriented on a win-lose polarity, this image rehearsal of victory may help him win if he has experienced enough defeats that it is time for a reversal."

This meant little to Varlik. Meanwhile, the T'swi turned back to the bayonet's edge, and after peering as if at some faint vestige of a nick, stroked first one side and then the other with the sharpening steel.

"But in the long run," he said as if in afterthought, "the win/lose equation will tend to balance. And in the long run, pleasure of action is not controlled by outcome. Pleasure is increased by near neutrality of desire. One can enjoy battle more—or games or work or learning—if one is nearly indifferent toward the outcome.

"So the intention to win should not go beyond a slight preference. Tisi-Kasi is creating images to reattain that state, which is *t'suss*."

Bin examined the edge again, returned the sharpening steel to his pack, then got up and slid the weapon back into its scabbard. "And he will not only enjoy battle more—he will also perform war more perfectly." He grinned at Varlik. "We have sometimes been depicted as epitomal warriors, and that is not entirely inappropriate. But our ability does not result from some genetic difference; your own warriors would be comparable if they had the T'sel, of which *t'suss* is a part."

The next day Visto-Soka was wounded by a steel bullet. Otherwise, he'd have been killed. The Birds, like the T'swa, used steel bullets in the forest. Blast slugs had the disadvantage that they did not ricochet; at first strike they blew up. Thus in sapling thickets or brush they were likely to be exploded prematurely by striking a twig.

The bullet had hit Visto-Soka high in the chest. It had ripped through the left pectoralis major just inside the shoulder, holed the scapula without shattering it, and emerged. He continued to fire his rifle, however, and with his partner, Bik-Chan, killed or wounded their pursuers.

Varlik was not clear on what Bik-Chan, or perhaps Visto-Soka himself, did to control shock, but the two returned to the rendezvous together on foot. The wounded T'swi had what was left of that day, and the night that followed, to rest. At first light the next morning the squad moved again, about two hours south, a little slower than they might have, and established a new rendezvous in a grove of large old trees on a broad bench, in an area thick with saplings. There Shan became Bik-Chan's new partner, while the wounded Visto-Soka took over as medic!

And from there, Varlik went out with Bin and Tisi-Kasi on his first hit. As they set out, they again heard distant firing: Some other T'swa were in action.

It was midday when they made first contact, and not from a selected ambush. They were moving quietly along a bench through heavy timber when abruptly they glimpsed a Bird patrol not two hundred feet ahead. Each side saw the other simultaneously, and opened fire as they hit the ground behind trees. Between bursts, Tisi-Kasi, in the lead, barked a command that Varlik didn't catch. Bin, snapping an order for Varlik to follow him, began to crab rapidly backward. Varlik did the same, trying to keep a tree between himself and the Birds while bullets thudded, ricochets sang, grenades roared. Bin and Varlik rolled on their bellies over a large fallen trunk where the bench broke into the slope beneath, and doubling over, scuttled downhill away from the fight.

"Tisi-Kasi is back there!" Varlik gasped as they ran.

Bin didn't answer, simply careened through the trees. Varlik struggled to keep up. For a minute they almost sprinted, then Bin, looking back at Varlik's bulging eyes, slowed to a trot. They were in the draw by then, the trees thicker again. The firing had stopped. Varlik wanted to ask if that meant Tisi-Kasi was coming now, but he had too little breath for it, and besides, he knew that wasn't it. They'd abandoned Tisi-Kasi! Bin had abandoned his lifelong friend, left him badly outnumbered; Varlik was certain he'd seen at least half a dozen Birds! Now Tisi-Kasi was surely dead, and here they were, running like rabbits!

And he knew why. Bin was getting him away to safety, or trying to, by Tisi-Kasi's order.

The Birds were probably following them. Clearly Bin assumed it. After jogging long enough for Varlik to regain a little wind, the T'swi changed course, angling up the slope, the timber less dense here but still fairly heavy. After two hundred feet of running uphill, Varlik could run no more, but slowed to a driving uphill walk. Bin, seeing this, slowed, waving him on while he himself crouched behind a tree, looking backward with his rifle poised.

It occurred to Varlik that if Bin were killed, or stayed behind and lost him, he could never find the rendezvous. The T'swa always seemed to know where they were, relative to any other place, but he wasn't so gifted. So he slowed, preparing to stand with Bin to fight, but the T'swi, after a moment, turned and started up the slope again, suiting his own pace now to Varlik's.

"Is he . . . ?" Varlik asked between gulping breaths.

"Dead," Bin said. "He's with us."

Varlik's hair stiffened, even as his legs drove him up the ridgeside. Shortly they topped the ridge, put the crest behind them, then Bin turned north, running again, along the contour now.

"And the Birds . . . are following?"

"Right."

They kept running along the ridgeside for half a mile, sweat burning Varlik's eyes, then Bin crossed the crest again, slanting down the first side into the bottom, which here was a narrow strip of marshy meadow. It occurred to Varlik that the Birds would be slowed by having to follow their tracks. They'd be back there now, somewhere along their trail, eyes on the ground. Or probably just one or two would watch for tracks; the others would be watching ahead and to the sides.

Then it struck him: He hadn't gotten any of this on cube! He'd forgotten what he was there for. He glanced down at his left hip. At least the belt recorder was on; its tiny red light glowed.

Bin led him up the next ridge, and again they slowed to a driving uphill walk, through a dense young stand that gave excellent cover. Partway up was a bluff. They worked past it, then Bin stopped and crawled out on its top, Varlik close behind. From its brink they had a partial view of the wet meadow in the ravine, and Bin held his rifle ready to fire. Varlik peered downward, his camera raised.

He had only a minute to wait; two Birds came into view a few feet apart, rifles poised. Varlik watched them in his monitor, zooming the camera until he could see, besides lean limbs and loincloths, the pouches on their belts and harnesses, the bolos at their hips. A dozen feet behind the first two, two more appeared. Bin fired a long burst, and Varlik saw all four fall. Instantly Bin shoved back from the edge, rose to a crouch, and led him off again on a run, angling up the ridge in the direction of their first encounter. But not for long. Near the crest they leveled off again, along the contour, still trotting, Varlik gasping. A little farther and Bin slowed to a walk.

"Are there more of them?" Varlik asked. He prayed there weren't; he could hardly hope to run much longer.

"I caught sight of two more. They took cover when I fired."

"Only two? Do you think they'll follow us?"

"Only two that I saw. And yes, I think they will follow. But warily."

He didn't make Varlik run anymore right away. They passed by the next dense cover, but at the one after that, Bin led him running through it downslope, and through a tangle of blowdown in the bottom, then a little way up the other side. Varlik thought he saw Bin's plan: Shoot the Birds from above while they were climbing over blown-down trees. But instead of taking cover there, Bin doubled north along the contour a short distance, then into the bottom again, among trees not far from the blowdown.

It was there they took cover, Varlik wiping again at the sweat which threatened to blind him, trying to keep his gasping as quiet as possible. He saw now what Bin had in mind. The Birds would bypass the blowdown, foreseeing an ambush from above. If they bypassed it on this side, Bin would get another chance at them.

And they did. There were four of them, crouching and well separated. Bin let the first two pass nearly out of sight among the trees, then opened fire; the last two fell. Those ahead opened fire from cover, but Bin led Varlik scrambling backward, keeping trees in the line of sight, then turned and once more ran, Varlik behind.

But only two! Almost surely now only two of the Birds were left! Bin led him fleeing northward along the bottom a little distance, then angled up the east ridge again, until shortly they slowed to the hard-driving walk, almost as hard on the legs as running but easier on the wind. Varlik, puffing, rubber-kneed, sweat-blinded, had almost nothing left, and told Bin so.

"A little more," Bin answered. At the ridgetop they paused. Varlik dropped gasping to his knees. Bin looked him over, then looked northward where the crest sloped slightly up. "Can you hit anything with that sidearm?" he asked.

Varlik nodded.

"Good. Take cover up there, in that brush. I'll climb this tree. I should be able to kill them both from there, but if I can't, I will surely get one of them. The other one, if there is only one, will be up to you. Let them get close before you shoot; a sidearm is for short range only."

Then he pulled Varlik to his feet, clapped him on the shoulder, and began to climb a liana that partly hung, partly clung to the trunk. Varlik started along the crest but stopped well short of the thicket, to lie behind a buttress-rooted tree with his holster flap unsnapped and his camera in his hands, watching Bin crouched on a branch with the trunk between him and their backtrail.

It was several minutes before the Birds showed up at an easy half-trot, one looking at the ground, the other ahead and around. Varlik's eyes shifted to his monitor and he picked them up with his camera.

He recorded Bin in the tree. Obviously the T'swi couldn't see the Birds—he was keeping behind the trunk—but he seemed to hear them. Apparently he planned to let them pass and shoot them from behind.

They stopped at the tree's very foot, one examining the ground. They seemed to talk, then one moved around the tree, both scanning the area. Abruptly one spotted Varlik and hit the ground, firing a short burst that sent bark, splinters, and dirt flying around the newsman. There was the roar of a grenade, and the shooting stopped. Another grenade exploded. Varlik peered out again; both Birds sprawled dead, Bin was looking down at them. Then the T'swa grasped the liana and began to lower himself to the ground.

That was the moment when Varlik saw the third Bird. He'd come up the ridge about twenty yards north of the others, and now stood nearly forty yards from Varlik, raising his rifle in Bin's direction. Somehow Varlik's sidearm was in his right hand, and without taking time to aim, he squeezed the trigger. Four shots burst out before he could release it, and the Bird went down, his upper torso shredded by blast slugs. Bin let go of the liana and dropped the last ten feet, rolling, coming up with his rifle in his hands, but there was nothing left for him to shoot at. Still crouched, eyes downslope, he moved toward Varlik, who lay shaking on the ground.

"There are no more," Bin said. "I am sure of it."

*You were sure before, when you killed the two with grenades,* Varlik thought. But he didn't say it, because he too felt sure that was all, and because, except for him, Bin could easily have been well away from danger.

Then, reaching down a large blue-black hand, the T'swi helped him to his feet.

They didn't wait until the next day, but went cautiously back to the rendezvous, as if another patrol, attracted by the much repeated gunfire, might come checking and find them. Which could happen, Varlik told himself.

The next day Bik-Chan returned alone, Shan having been killed, while Jinto and Dzuk came back with Dzuk's right wrist bullet-broken. The squad was down to six T'swa, two of them wounded. Kusu moved them a few ridges farther east, where recent fire had swept away the undergrowth and killed the older trees. There, from an opening on the crest, he called on evac headquarters to pick up the wounded and Varlik.

Then they sat together in the ashes, waiting. It would be somewhat less than an hour before the floater could arrive. After the pickup, Kusu and his three effectives would move back toward the Bird trails, operating as a single hit team instead of by pairs.

The floater was actually in sight when Bin, one of the two lookouts, saw the Birds, and the shooting began at once, furiously. Varlik snatched up Dzuk's rifle and hit the ground with the T'swa. As he dropped, he felt the bullet slam his left hip, but somehow it didn't seem serious except that his vision was blurred. So he fired blind, a long burst and then another in the direction of the Birds; then the clip was empty. He tried to crawl to Dzuk, a few feet away, for another clip, but his leg wouldn't obey. And then there was heavy firing from overhead—surely a heavy caliber blaster—overriding the noise of rifles, its exploding slugs making a series of loud violent slaps farther along the crest, so closely spaced as to seem almost a single long sound.

It was followed by silence. Then a long burst from a Bird called forth another staccato roar from overhead, and the shooting was truly over. Apparently the Birds hadn't seen the floater until after the firefight started, and were caught exposed.

Dzuk and Visto-Soka were still alive; they'd been lying down to start with. Kusu's chin had been shot away and Jinto was both gutshot and lungshot; Bin was the only one unwounded. He and a profusely bleeding

Kusu helped the evac floater crew load the rest, and they all left together. Then the two Iryalan medics began work on the wounded.

Varlik had recorded none of the final fight on video, though its sounds were all on cube, but now, sitting weak and bleeding on the floater, he began to record the wounded and the busy medics. Then one of the medics knelt beside him with a syringe and shot him with it. That was the last thing Varlik recorded before he slept.

# PART THREE
## *Tyss*

PART THREE

# 22

When Varlik awoke from sedation, he was in a troop carrier fitted to move wounded from the Beregesh field hospital to the base hospital at Aromanis. He could remember nothing beyond the evac floater and the medic with the syringe. He'd known something was wrong with his hip, but now his guts hurt badly, too.

He moved his head, his eyes finding a doctor with a captain's collar lozenge. The doctor saw his movement and spoke to him.

"You're back with us, eh?"

"More or less," Varlik answered thickly.

Taking a syringe from a case, the doctor walked over. "The pilot tells me you're the famous white T'swi," he said. "You keep dangerous company. I'm going to give you a little sedative now. It's another hour to the base hospital, and it's best if you sleep your way there."

The way he hurt, it seemed a good idea, but he had a question first. "Wait, doc."

The doctor paused.

"How are the guys in my squad?"

"I have no idea. I don't know who was in your squad."

Varlik looked at him blankly. Some of them were probably aboard this craft, and if he asked by name . . . But he was having trouble thinking.

"What happened to me? Something hit me in the hip, and then I couldn't move. Now my belly hurts."

"You were hit in the ilium—part of the pelvis, the hip bone—and the left end of it was broken off. Then the bullet went through the abdominal cavity and some of its contents emerged through the obliquus externus on the right side. They opened you up at the field hospital at Beregesh and did a nice repair job. Now all you have to do is lie quietly in a nice cool ward at Aromanis and heal. Just like your buddies."

The doctor pressed the syringe against Varlik's bare shoulder and fired it. Somehow it seemed to Varlik that he had more questions, but he couldn't remember what they were. Then the sedative took him.

✧     ✧     ✧

It was one of the T'swa wards, a busy place well stocked with medical technicians and wounded. His Romblit doctor there told him with some amusement that reception had initially been unwilling to put him in a T'swa ward. True, he'd been brought in with T'swa wounded, and his tag said "Company A, T'swa Second Regiment," but clearly he was not T'swa. Then a big T'swa sergeant with his lower face heavily bandaged had gotten off his stretcher, backed the reception sergeant into a corner, gathered a fistful of shirt front, and in grunted, barely intelligible words, made it clear that all his squad went with him, Lormagen included.

Varlik wondered if this was another case of facts inflated and embroidered, but the story pleased him. And he was glad to be where he was, a feeling that increased with the days. T'swa wards had a reputation among hospital personnel as the most cheerful, and T'swa the patients who were easiest to work with and recovered most rapidly.

Meanwhile Varlik enjoyed a rich dream life, though he could never recall more than bits and pieces of his dreams. Long afterward, he'd remember his days in the T'swa ward as among the more pleasant of his life, even though it was there he learned that only four of the First Squad had survived, besides himself. Bik-Chan had been killed on the ridge, and Jinto had died on the evac floater of multiple wounds.

On his first day they took him into surgery, where they welded his pelvis and did a mesh job on some ligaments. His visceral and major vascular damage had been handled at Beregesh.

By the end of the third day he'd talked the hospital into giving him temporary use of a small examination room, and there, after recording a long and reassuring cube to Mauen, he narrated his report on the T'swa raiders and the last days of the First Squad, then edited cubes both for newsfacs and broadcasting. This took him two days—his energy level was low—but when he was done, the cube was the best facs feature he'd ever seen or heard.

Three days later General Lamons came through the ward, pinning medals on the wounded. Varlik, who'd been sitting in bed reading, was deeply surprised, but not too surprised to slip on his visor and pick up his camera. Lamons saw him with it, scowled only briefly, then continued. When he got to Varlik's bed, he stepped in beside it and looked down at him. Varlik set the camera aside, though the audio recorder was still running.

"Your T'swa have been doing a good job," said Lamons.

"Yes, sir."

"Your Colonel Koda showed me a copy of your reports on the T'swa interdiction teams. That was good work you did. Took guts."

"Thank you, sir."

The general grunted, then bent and pinned a medal on Varlik's pajama top. "Carry on," he said, then turned to the next bed.

By that time the hospital had begun to feed Varlik solid food—not whatever he wanted, but solid food. And he was allowed to wheel himself to the "library," where boxes of books had been spread unsorted on tables. Walking would have to wait a while.

It was in the library that he ran into Konni. Eight days earlier she'd been recording the hardening of perimeter defenses when a Bird lobber rocket had hit a hover truck less than twenty yards away. Pieces of truck had smashed her left humerus and cracked her left supraorbital ridge and four ribs, while small rocket fragments had struck her in the left arm and leg. The left side of her face was an interesting purplish-green.

"My Revax is all right, though," she said, "and I ought to be out of here in about three weeks. The home office is sure to be sending another team out, so I'll probably go back to Iryala then, although . . . it's a temptation to stay. How about you?"

How about him? He hadn't looked at that. And for the first time, it occurred to him that there was nothing here to report on the T'swa now except more of the same. Maybe later, if there was a later, if the T'swa were given a new assignment. But now . . .

"I'm going to Tyss," he said. The statement took him totally by surprise, but he continued from there. "To the world that produces the T'swa regiments. There are guys going there from my ward—guys disabled or requiring prolonged rehab and reconditioning. I should be able to talk my way into going with them."

Having said it, he felt a pang of guilt. He could, after all, go home to Mauen now if he wanted to, and they could start the family they'd been approved for. Central News wouldn't complain. After all, he'd almost been killed. Probably they'd treat him like a hero.

He kept the pang for about ten seconds, then his attention went to procedural matters. Legally, his status with the Red Scorpion Regiment didn't validate traveling to Tyss without a visa from the Iryalan Foreign Ministry. In fact, legally he'd probably had no right to work for a foreign military force. But he was sure that Colonel Koda would approve his request, and for practical purposes, that would settle that. As soon as he had approval from Koda, he'd send word to Fendel. He was supposed to be here covering the war of course, but his reports to date would have built up a lot of interest in Tyss, and he had to spend his rehabilitation somewhere.

Besides which, he'd be gone long before they could get any argument to him.

He and Konni talked a while longer, mostly about the T'swa and his experiences with them in Birdland. She told him how impressed both she and Bertol had been with the early cubes Varlik had let them copy, then

Varlik let her borrow his cubes of the Birdland mission. After that she'd gone back to her own ward, and he'd called Lieutenant Shao, the one-armed officer who'd been left in charge of the T'swa's Aromanis camp. He explained that he wanted to be evacuated to Tyss so he could record something of the planet and its people.

It was marvelous, Varlik thought, how casual the T'swa were about so many things. Without a moment's hesitation, Shao promised to add him to the roster on the evac ship which would arrive, and leave, later that week. And no, the lieutenant assured him, there'd be no problem; he had all the authority necessary.

It was late the next day that Konni reappeared, just after Varlik had sent off letter cubes to Mauen and Fendel telling them what he was going to do. It was a lot harder to tell Mauen than Fendel.

"Well," said Konni casually, "how's your plan coming along to be evacuated to Tyss?"

"I leave day after tomorrow," he said. "No problem. Lieutenant Shao has even issued me the clothes and stuff I'll need there."

Her eyes lit up. "Good!" she said. "Look at this." She handed him a sheet of stiff paper.

TO WHOM IT MAY CONCERN:
 KNOW YOU BY THIS CERTIFICATE THAT KONNI WENTER, BY VIRTUE OF HER PARTICIPATION IN THE 711. 10.01-02 NIGHT RAID ON KELIKUT, ORLANTHA, IS HEREBY APPOINTED AND RECOGNIZED AS AN HONOR-ARY MEMBER OF THE NIGHT ADDER REGIMENT, LODGE OF KOOTOSH-LAN, WITH ALL THE RIGHTS AND PRE-ROGATIVES PERTAINING THERETO.
(SIGNED)
BILTONG, COL., COMMANDING

When he'd finished reading, Varlik stared at it for a moment longer and then at Konni. An extraneous, non sequitur thought drifted into his mind—that T'swa apparently only had one name each.

"In the name of Pertunis!" he said. "How did you get this?"

"When I left you the other day, the first thing I did was listen to your Birdland report and look at your video cubes. And decided I wanted to go to Tyss, too. Actually, I wanted to as soon as you talked about it; that just hardened it. So I called Colonel Voker and asked him if he could think of any way to do it without my having to go through the Foreign Ministry back home. That might take a year. He said he'd see what he could do. And this afternoon, this came from Beregesh. I know Colonel

Voker's behind it. He had this made up in his office and sent it south for Colonel Biltong's signature, I'm sure of it."

She took the "certificate" back. "I'm going to call your T'swa lieutenant now and apply for evacuation."

"It's Lieutenant Shao," Varlik said, and she hurried from the ward.

She was right, Varlik thought—it must have been Voker. How non-standard—perhaps even non-Standard—they'd become, getting around regulations the way they were! And Voker most of all—that was flagrant! Konni's certificate was an even flimsier legal basis for bypassing the Foreign Ministry than his own position as regimental publicist. Back home, for something like that, a person could be charged with a misdemeanor, at the very least. For Voker, surely a felony.

But that didn't disturb Varlik at all, because the T'swa couldn't care less, and no one at the hospital was going to question it.

He realized he was grinning broadly.


# 23


Konni wiped sweat from her forehead. "Do you understand these people?" she asked. "The people themselves, I mean, not the language."

They were eight days out from Kettle, with thirteen more to go before they reached the Oven—Tyss. She had copied Colonel Voker's Tyspi cubes, and with Varlik's help had been doing a cram course on the language. The hyperspace ship *Hedanik* was Iryalan but leased by the T'swa, and her operations crew as well as medical and housekeeping staffs, plus thirty-seven of her thirty-nine casualties, were T'swa. So the temperature was kept at a constant, and to T'swa pleasant, 95 degrees Fahrenheit. Not that the T'swa required high temperatures: They simply had an easy physiological and psychological tolerance of them. T'swa regiments had more than once fought in snow and ice.

"Understand the T'swa?" Varlik looked at her question; he'd never explicitly thought about it before. "I guess I don't. But I don't think I really understand Iryalans, either; I'm just used to them. And I suppose I'm getting pretty used to the T'swa now. Why do you ask?"

"I've listened to all the cubes you've loaned me of your conversations with T'swa. The ones where you were speaking Standard, that is. And some of their attitudes and responses—I don't believe I could ever understand them. I wondered if it's the same for you."

"I suppose it is. I just don't notice it so much anymore—I take it for granted.

"I'll tell you something, though. When the T'swa talk Tyspi to me, I usually understand everything they say. I'm a quick study, with excellent recall. But sometimes when two of them talk to each other, I hardly understand anything at all. Sometimes too many of the words are unfamiliar, but at other times I know the words and still don't know what they're talking about. So I guess I *don't* understand the T'swa all that well. But it's never seemed very important; it's as if I understand them well enough."

Varlik got up stiffly. "I'm hurting. Let's go to physical therapy for a bit."

"You go," Konni said. "What I need is a nap."

They left the small reading room, Konni turning right toward her room, Varlik hobbling left toward the therapy section. As he passed an open office door, he glanced in and saw a T'swa medic named Usu. On an impulse he stopped.

"Usu, may I interrupt you?"

The T'swi looked up from his papers and nodded, gesturing to a chair. "How can I help you?"

Varlik entered and sat, groping for an answer. "It's nothing really important, I guess, but . . . Well, there are a lot of things I don't understand about the T'swa."

"Oh?" The T'swi said nothing more then, waiting.

"For example, sometimes two T'swa will be talking and I don't understand at all what they're saying—even when I understand the words."

Usu nodded, eyeing Varlik thoughtfully. "I can see the difficulty. Let me make a few comments that may help. In the Confederation, not only most of your activities but also much of your reality are deeply constrained by the compulsion for and environment of Standardness. Both your Standard Technology and your Standard Management spill over onto beliefs and attitudes that, strictly speaking, are neither technological nor pertain to management. In fact, Standard Technology and Standard Management are, to quite a large degree, specialized codifications of broad, long-standing attitudes and beliefs. A codification which then reinforces those beliefs and attitudes by particularizing, institutionalizing, and enforcing them.

"Those attitudes, constraints, and prohibitions have severely inhibited seeing, and even looking . . ."

"My vision is better than most people's," Varlik interrupted. "I see really well."

"I do not doubt that. But I was not referring to your eyes. I referred to the inability of your culture to put its attention on, or even to notice, things that do not fit its conceptual framework." The bright T'swa eyes peered mildly at Varlik as if watching for some glimmer of comprehension; then Usu continued.

"Thus, you lack the concepts necessary to understand T'swa life and reality broadly, and where you have no concepts, your language has no words.

"Now in learning our language—those few of you who have undertaken to—you learn many of our words. But at least at first, the meanings attached to a Tyspi word—the meanings *you are able* to attach to a Tyspi word—are concepts you already have in your own culture. For many words in Tyspi, your concepts are quite adequate to our meanings, but for numerous other words, they allow only a partial and frequently crude understanding. Which means you understand the word, or approximate its meaning, in some contexts but not in others.

"While there are numerous other words that are not translatable at all into Standard because they apply entirely to concepts that you do not have."

Varlik sat frustrated. If that was true, then it seemed to him he would never understand the T'swa, and somehow just now it seemed important to.

"However," Usu went on, "it is certainly possible to begin gaining those concepts and thus share more of the realities of the T'swa. Indeed, perhaps you have already begun. If you would like, I can undertake to help you."

Varlik looked at the T'swi, this one a man smaller than himself, with artist's hands. "I'd appreciate it." He paused. "You're not a warrior, are you?"

A grin flashed. "No. While I am employed by a war lodge, the Lodge of Kootosh-Lan, my way is the Way of Service, not of War. Do you know the Matrix of T'sel?"

"I've seen a chart; in fact, I ran off a copy. It had headings like play and fight. And work."

"That is it. I have tasks to complete now, but if you wish, I can meet with you here at 15.50 and we can look into this matter further. And bring your chart; it will be useful."

Varlik got up. "Can I bring Konni Wenter with me? She's interested, too. In fact, I wouldn't have brought this up if it hadn't been for her questions."

"That will be fine. I will procure a third chair and expect you here at 15.50."

At half-past fifteen, Varlik and Konni were there. Usu had brought with him a T'swa woman, strongly built, whom he introduced as Dzo-Dek, the lab director and his wife. Her hair too was straight and short. Varlik had already been told that T'swa didn't cut their hair, that it seldom grew as long as an inch. Apparently that was true for both sexes. It behaved more like coarse fur, Varlik told himself, than like human hair.

He handed Usu a printout, creased from having been folded. "Here's the chart."

## THE MATRIX OF T'SEL

| | FUN | WISDOM/ KNOWLEDGE | GAMES | JOBS | WAR |
|---|---|---|---|---|---|
| PLAY | Play just for fun | Study as play; learning unimportant | Games as play; winning unimportant | Job as play; reward unimportant | War as play; victory unimportant |
| STUDY | Study for fun; learning secondary | Study for wisdom &/or knowledge | Study for advantage | Study to enhance job accomplishment | Study for power |
| COMPETE | Compete for the fun of winning | Compete to be wisest or most learned | Compete to win | Job as a challenge | War as a contest |
| WORK | Work at playing | Work at learning | Work for advantage | Work for survival | Soldiering |
| FIGHT | Fight to control pleasure | Fight to control knowledge | Fight to subdue | Fight for monopoly | Fight to kill or destroy |

Usu scanned it and smiled. "Ah, yes. And here, the heading 'Jobs'— the Tyspi word is *R'bun*, which I translated as 'Service,' but 'Jobs' is also a reasonable approximation. *R'bun* partakes of both concepts."

Usu had returned his gaze to Varlik as he spoke. "You have had experience with T'swa warriors. Where in this matrix does the T'swa warrior fit? At what action level, in what activity?"

"Why, at *Fight*, I suppose. At the action of *Fight*, in the activity of *War*."

"Ah. And where do the Iryalan troops fit?"

"Hmmm. Most of them—most of them fit at the action of Work, in the activity of War."

"Very good. And in the activity of War, which action level do you suppose would be most successful in terms of victory?"

"Why, it would have to be Fight. Here." His finger touched the chart's lower right-hand intersect.

"And what would you say if I told you that T'swa warriors fit here instead?" A long black finger touched down at the intersect of Play and War.

Varlik peered, then looked up at Usu. "I guess I'd have to ask how that could be. It's my understanding that your warriors almost always win, although I've had a lecture by a trooper named Bin on the win/lose equation always tending to balance at unity—one."

Usu grinned. "Then your education in T'sel began before today. But I must tell you that the activity of the T'swa warrior is not Fight, but Play. And I must take the lesson given by your warrior friend another step: The T'swa warrior *neither wins nor loses,* because it is all the same to him. What transpires in his career will be interpreted as winning and losing by those who do not have the T'sel; therefore, to discuss it with you, he spoke of it as he did. The T'swa warrior, in fact, has no victory nor defeat, no enemy nor any rival. He is an artist creating in the play form called War, and what another might regard as his enemy, the T'swa regards as a playmate. Almost always, their playmates regard the T'swa warrior as an enemy, but our warriors regard themselves as no one's enemy, and no one as theirs."

Varlik recalled Tisi-Kasi kneeling on the forest ridge, regaining *t'suss,* a neutral attitude toward win/lose, and wondered if he still had *t'suss* when he was killed. Somehow he hoped so.

"Each T'swa warrior," Usu continued, "becomes a master at the art of war before his regiment is ever commissioned, and performs his art as perfectly as he is able, without distracting himself with concerns of victory or defeat, survival or death. The warrior at Fight will usually fall to him. And for just those reasons, our regiments enjoy great success."

Briefly, Usu's eyes caught Varlik's with a glint that Varlik had seen in other T'swa eyes. "But let me tell you something else about this," Usu went on. "If you play at War without skill—if you are not an accomplished artist—then this fellow"—his finger moved to the Fight/War intersect—"*is very likely to kill you.* Even if he is not particularly skilled, his intention and energy make him dangerous." Usu chuckled. "Of course, if you are truly at Play, death will not matter to you. But the person at Play will seldom opt for War without the intention of becoming an artist at it."

Varlik nodded. Conceptually he could see and accept this, though as a reality . . . "Usu," he said, "I hope I don't offend you by asking, but how can you be so sure of the warrior's state of mind?"

Usu's grin was broad. "That is a very good question, my friend, and perhaps my answer will not entirely satisfy you. On Tyss, our *training,* to use your word, is in whatever activity we have chosen for our life. But before that, and beginning in infancy, all children and youth receive the same basic *education,* which is education in the T'sel.

"Now I have used your Standard word 'education' because you have no word closer to *tengsil,* our word which encompasses that concept. But the actions which constitute *tengsil* include those that allow a person to see, to experience, to verify for himself, the very basis of T'sel. And *tengsil* is the same for he who plays at any of these." His finger moved across the row at Play, from Fun to War.

"I am a—your people have translated it 'physician,' though 'healer' might be closer. Those to whom I administer may either live or die. I may help them recover numerous times, but sooner or later they *will* die, and I am agreeable to their doing it. Truly! If my patient dies, he departs with my full willingness and best wishes. I will perform my art to the utmost of my not inconsiderable skill, but if he dies, I am neither distressed nor offended. I do have a certain preference, only slight, that he survives and regains health and facility, and I intend that he shall. But that preference has nothing in it of desire, and I do not even remotely insist on it."

Varlik blew lightly through pursed lips, then nodded slightly, not in agreement so much as acknowledgement. "So then . . ." He paused, looking at the chart. "Are all T'swa at Play? And if they are, why do you show these lower levels? How do you even know about them?"

"May I answer that?" Dzo-Dek asked, looking at Varlik.

"Of course."

"Not all T'swa are at Play," she said. "About two percent are at one of the other levels, and we regard them as somewhat retarded, which they are. But our enlightenment about the other levels did not grow out of studying them. It grew out of the study of other cultures. And the lower levels are part of the Matrix because they belong there; they exist."

"And in the Confederation, what percent are below the Play level?" Varlik asked.

"Among adults, approximately ninety-seven percent. It varies a little from world to world."

Varlik's lips had thinned slightly. "And how do you know that?" he asked.

Dzo-Dek reached past her husband to touch the intersect of Play and Wisdom/Knowledge. "Those who play here"—she tapped the chart— "have direct access to an immense—let us say an immense data base. And their training provides tools your culture is not yet familiar with. The rest of us—those at War or Service or Games or Fun—we learn the easier of those procedures in order to have direct access to the T'sel, but only those who specialize become able across the full gamut of them. They are our educators and— You have lost the concept: our *scientists;* our *researchers.*"

The last word meant nothing to Varlik; his head was beginning to hurt. "So apparently you lump us, the people of the Confederation, with your retarded." His voice and face were strained when he said it.

Dzo-Dek smiled slightly. "No, there are major differences. First, what you mean by 'retarded' is mentally retarded. What I referred to is emotionally handicapped, although that certainly hampers rational thinking. And secondly, the two percent on Tyss that I spoke of are the way they are *despite* being exposed to the T'sel from birth. The people of the Confederation have not had that opportunity."

Usu interposed, looking first at Varlik and then Konni, the largeness of his eyes accentuated by their lack of visible definition between pupil and iris. "I believe we have taxed your receptiveness on this subject," he said. "You are still patients, and it might be well if you went to your beds."

Varlik nodded. His brief antagonism had died but he did feel depressed, and a little groggy. Getting up, he left the room without a word, Konni following. He went to his ward and she to her tiny room, and both went to bed without taking time to shower. Varlik didn't even try to sort out what he'd been told, and sleep took him quickly.

Not for the first time among the T'swa, he dreamed richly, though ten seconds after waking in the morning he could recall none of it.

But it seemed to him that remembering the dreams was unimportant. They'd been enjoyable when they happened, and the new day felt great to him, even in this mole of a ship burrowing through space. Konni, too, when he met her at breakfast, looked relaxed and cheerful.

And neither of them approached Usu or Dzo-Dek for any further lectures on the T'swa or the T'sel.

# 24

Excerpt from "Tyss, the T'swa World," by Varlik Lormagen. *Central News Syndicate*, Landfall, Iryala, 712.09.05.

Tyss, with an equatorial diameter of 9,100 miles, is somewhat larger than Iryala, and its surface gravity is 22 percent greater. Its axial tilt is only 9 percent, which means that while it has a winter and summer, the two seasons are not as different as we are used to on much of Iryala.

While its gravity is higher than all but a very few inhabited planets, Tyss is most remarkable for two things. One, it is extremely hot. And two, it is extremely dry. How hot can be shown by looking at some representative temperatures for different latitudes at different seasons.

## REPRESENTATIVE DAILY HIGH AND
## LOW TEMPERATURES ON TYSS
### [degrees Fahrenheit]
## AT DIFFERENT LATITUDES

| | *midsummer* | | *midwinter* | |
|---|---|---|---|---|
| *Latitude* | *high* | *low* | *high* | *low* |
| 0 (Equator) | 140 | 110 | 140 | 110 |
| 30 | 140 | 105 | 135 | 100 |
| 50 | 125 | 100 | 110 | 85 |
| 80 | 110 | 80 | 85 | 55 |

Oldu Tez-Boag, the principal city of Tyss, is at 48.7° south latitude.

As for dryness, only 32 percent of Tyss's surface is sea, compared to 78.8 percent on Iryala. This means there is much less free water surface giving off moisture into the air. The combination of heat and dry air has resulted in a planet that is mostly desert.

Unfortunately, the coolest parts of Tyss are absolute desert on which virtually nothing grows. In places these polar deserts extend toward the equator as far as 55° latitude. Because of extreme polar and subequatorial deserts and particularly intense equatorial heat, most of Tyss's estimated 30 million people live at between 40° and 55° latitude, in whatever regions and locales have enough moisture to grow crops without being too hot for the heat-tolerant T'swa.

For all is not desert on Tyss. Almost without exception, there are belts of forest and marsh on the downwind sides of the several seas, and the marshes are sometimes drained for farming. And where mountain ranges don't intervene to block the flow of moist sea air, back of the forest belts are belts of savannah and grassland.

The air is a little thinner on Tyss than we are used to on Iryala, but you probably wouldn't notice it unless you were doing something strenuous. The atmospheric pressure is about the same as at Eagle Lake....

Mineral resources on Tyss have not been valuable enough to attract off-planet investment or development, nor have T'swa agriculture and fisheries been attractive to Confederation export interests. Until very recently, the only significant exports from Tyss have been her famous mercenary soldiers.

Most of the people on Tyss, however, are employed at growing and harvesting food. Transportation and manufacturing are quite primitive, and because there is no synthetics industry there, lumbering, quarrying, and mining play a much more prominent role in people's lives than on Confederation worlds....

# 25

The city of Oldu Tez-Boag was a metropolis by T'swa standards, with an estimated 30,000 people. It sat on a coastal plain, mostly on an ancient river terrace above the Lok-Sanu River, out of reach of the infrequent floodwaters. Viewed from the hospital, Oldu Tez-Boag had little to recommend it aesthetically except the abundance of ancient shade trees, particularly the gray-green tozut trees standing broad-crowned and tall in yards and along streets; and the thick-walled adobe houses, stuccoed over in pastels and "white, almost all their windows facing south—away from the sun in this southern hemisphere town."

Oldu Tez-Boag had taken shape some four miles upstream of the highly salty Toshi Sea, but even at that distance, when Varlik and Konni stepped onto the third-floor balcony, their noses could detect the sweltering beds of kelp on the tidal flats.

A T'swi on the hospital ship had told him that Tyss had not always been a desert world. Like Orlantha, it had had great oceans once, millions of years before man had come there. Varlik had been exposed to geology in school, so he hadn't wondered how the T'swa knew. What he had wondered was what had happened to all that water.

The hospital, occupying a modest prominence just outside the city, was run by the Lodge of Kootosh-Lan for its own warriors and those of the other four war lodges. It was one of the few multi-storied buildings in Oldu Tez-Boag—at four stories the tallest except for grain elevators along the river.

Kogi-Ta, one of only a handful of administrative personnel at the hospital, nodded pleasantly to the two Iryalans when they came to his desk. His short, stiff hair was white, but he looked strong nonetheless. Apparently he'd been a warrior once. A deep seam, a product not of age but youth, creased the left side of his face from jaw to hairline, interrupted by an eye patch. The combination gave him a dangerous appearance with which his good-natured smile was inconsistent.

"Good morning," Varlik said. "Our doctors told us we could take leave if we'd like. We want to visit the town and some of the countryside."

Kogi-Ta leaned a large hand on the desk to help himself to his feet; more than his face had been damaged.

"If you want to visit the town, then you will want money," he said, and turned to an ancient file cabinet. There was no computer or terminal to be seen.

He pulled two folders and looked into them. "No pay record! Have either of you ever been paid?"

Both indicated they hadn't. "But I'm afraid I'm only an honorary member of my regiment," Konni asked, "not a paid member."

Kogi-Ta looked up. "A technicality," he answered cheerfully. "You have been lodged in lodge facilities, as an employee and an honorary member, and someone in authority signed an order sending you here, so you both have allowances due you. Are you familiar with the lodge's disbursement system? No? It is based on the Standard calendar because the regiments serve on so many worlds."

From another drawer he took a leather bag and grinned at them. "You are about to learn how little a warrior is paid. But you will be surprised at how little things cost on Tyss." Quickly, his nimble fingers counted out small piles of silver coins, then he made entries on two pages in a ledger, glancing up as he did so. "We T'swa do keep *some* records, you know," he said, chuckling, and handed the coins to the Iryalans.

Varlik looked at them. "This is Confederation money," he said.

"Indeed. It's what the lodges usually require for their services, and it's as acceptable here as any. On Tyss the service co-ops mint their own, but they have long since used Confederation denominations and weight standards."

They already had some Confederation money in their wallets, but if this was theirs, it seemed as good a time as any to get it. "Do we have to sign anything to show we received it?" Varlik asked. "And to show that we left the hospital?"

Kogi-Ta's eyes glinted as if in amusement. "Not unless you insist on it. The lodge is satisfied as it is on both matters."

"When do we have to be back?" Konni asked. "Is there a set time?"

"Not unless your physician gave you one. No? It is preferred that Mr. Lormagen not come in after his ward is dark. If he does, I trust he will be as quiet as he can. But as you have a room to yourself, that consideration does not apply." He chuckled. "Do not be surprised if you are invited to spend the night in some residence, however. You are sure to arouse the interest of townspeople. If you wish, feel free to accept."

They thanked him and left, cameras slung, audio recorders as usual on their belts. The hospital, like the ship, was air-conditioned to 95°— the only air-conditioned building in the district. Yet outside, the heat that swirled around them was oven-hot as they began to walk, even though the autumnal equinox was well past and the winter solstice little more than a dek away. From a tree, something Varlik supposed might be an insect made a long keening sound at the upper edge of hearing, and the dirt street, though well shaded, was dusty. "I can hardly believe that Kogi-Ta," Konni said. "Or the hospital in general. Either no one cheats here, or they just don't care."

"I'll bet it's the first," said Varlik. "No cheats."

"How can that be?"

"I have no idea. That's just the way it feels to me, after the T'swa I've known."

She thought about it as they walked. "All we've been around are warriors and other professionals. Mostly warriors. Do you suppose other T'swa are like them?"

"I wouldn't be surprised. From what Usu said, they all get the same education; only the training is different."

"At home," Konni pointed out, "or in the whole Confederation for that matter, practically everyone does the same curriculum until they're fourteen. Yet while most people are at least fairly honest, some turn into criminals."

Varlik shrugged. "Education's got to be a lot different here. The men in my squad, common soldiers, all seemed like—no, they all *talked* like—professors. The kind of professor that really knows and can teach."

They both were beginning to sweat freely with the mild exertion of walking, but neither paid attention to that.

"They were different from one another in various ways," Varlik went on. "Their wit, how much they talked—that kind of thing. Some laughed out loud at things that others just smiled at. Some seemed a lot more interested than others in things like that strange white man living with them. And some played cards while others read, although none of the card players seemed to take their gaming seriously; they didn't even bet.

"But all of them seemed bright and—stable, I guess is the word. I never saw one of them upset or behave badly, although I heard a rumor that one of them got a little truculent once," he added, remembering the story of Kusu and the base hospital reception sergeant.

"Anyway, whatever they do with them in school seems to work."

They were in the town now, the dusty road passing between rows of homes and yards. There were few gaps in the shade of roadside trees, and all about were gardens, some remarkably lovely, others simply utilitarian vegetable patches with fruited vines clinging to poles and frames. Several dogs investigated the two Iryalans, and while they definitely seemed to be genus *Canis* rather than some canoid look-alike, they were neither hostile nor noisy. They were what you'd expect T'swa dogs to be like, Varlik thought: civilized.

There were children, too, peering from yards and the roadside. Now two of them, seeming perhaps five and seven years old, trotted barefoot onto the powdery dirt to keep pace alongside. The girl was smallest. Konni stopped and turned to them, Revax at her chest, its tiny light glinting as it recorded. Her visor was tilted up; for close work she could see well enough in the horizontal view frame atop the camera.

"Hello," said Konni in Tyspi.

Both children had stopped, not staring so much as simply gazing.

"Are you Ertwa?" asked the little girl.

"I don't know what 'Ertwa' means," Konni said.

"She still gets times mixed up," the boy put in. He turned to his sister. "They are Splennwa. Ertwa were very long ago."

The little girl studied them. "Splennwa?" she said, cocking her head critically. "I think not. They are abroad unprotected in the heat of day."

Varlik would have contributed to the conversation but could think of nothing to say in the face of such seeming precocity. Then the children turned and trotted tough-footed to a nearby yard, saving him from the risk of saying something inane.

A little farther on was a small building, smaller than the residences, with a sign that read "cool drinks." On the roof was a solar converter, the first they'd encountered here except for the large battery of them at the hospital. Varlik paused. They'd walked half a mile or more by then, his longest walk since Birdland, and while he felt no pain, his legs were tiring in the T'swa gravity. It might be best, he thought, to take it easy.

"Shall we?" he asked, beckoning.

"I like the sign," Konni answered, wiping away sweat. "Especially the first word: *cool.*"

Within the thick, insulating adobe walls it was some fifteen or twenty degrees cooler, and they closed the door behind them, shutting out the heat. The room was lit only by daylight, through three windows that penetrated the thick south wall. They stood for a minute, looking around while their eyes adjusted from the outside glare. Even then it seemed dim, reminding Varlik of the T'swa's catlike vision.

There were only two others present: a waitress—the slenderest T'swi they'd seen—and a man in a loose white shirt who sat alone with a drink, watching them interestedly. Konni and Varlik sat down by a window; the waitress was already coming over.

"What you would like?" Her voice was quiet, her school-Standard rusty, her manner poised.

"What do you have?" Varlik asked in Tyspi.

She recited a list, most of which meant nothing to either of them.

"We are not familiar with those," Konni said. "Bring us what you yourself like best. I'm sure we'll like it, too."

They did, even though "cool," in Tyss, was not "cold," as they'd expected. It seemed to be a fruit punch, rather thin and non-alcoholic. The glasses were about pint-size, and after sipping briefly, the two Iryalans carried them around the room, looking at the numerous pictures hung on the walls. The waitress, as if knowing the deficiencies of their twilight vision, turned on an electric ceiling lamp that added moderately to the light.

The walls were paneled with boards, varnished and burnished, and the paintings and drawings excellent. They seemed to be by numerous artists, and varied from landscapes to portraits, from work scenes to archaic battles, from families to children sitting in a circle on a nightbound hill. Most of the subjects seemed T'swa, but some clearly were not. The styles included realism and impressionism—the styles accepted in the Confederation—and several others, including one that particularly took Varlik's fancy: landscapes done seemingly in ink, with an economy of brush strokes, suggestive rather than explicit. Konni's camera and his own were busy.

The voice of the other customer interrupted them in easy Standard from half across the room. "My name is Ban-Shum," he said. "If you have questions, I would be happy to answer as far as I can."

So they sat with him, asking questions about the art and the city. The paintings were not by a number of artists at all, but by the proprietress and her husband, each having mastered a variety of techniques. No, there was no particular market for art here; there were many fine artists, most painting for pleasure.

Ban-Shum was a teacher, a teaching brother of the Order of Dys Jilgar, and he would enjoy being their guide to Oldu Tez-Boag. This was a holiday for the children—there were numerous school holidays. He took the two Iryalans to his nearby home, where he harnessed his ilkan and hitched it to a buggy, to take the two Iryalans around. The ilkan was an indigenous species—all T'swa livestock were, he said—an ungulate with long legs, long erect ears, and short, soft, mole-like fur.

They saw and recorded the small school at which Ban-Shum taught; visited the wharves, some with barges, river boats, and small seagoing steamers tied to them, and others for fishing boats; racks where fish, split lengthwise, dried in the sun; the water-treatment plant. They saw people at work—mostly men but also numerous young women with no children yet to care for, and older women whose children had grown up. There were shops and markets where produce was sold, and others with meat or dairy products. Much was primitive, but where refrigeration was needed, there it was, powered by solar converters.

By the time they felt they'd seen and recorded enough, Konni was enervated from the 120° heat. Ban-Shum took them back to the place they'd met him, where they talked quietly over cool drinks again. This time the drinks were a light and fruity wine.

"So we have regiments on Orlantha," Ban-Shum said. "Interesting." Then he added something in what was definitely not Standard but didn't seem to be Tyspi either.

"I'm afraid I didn't understand that," Varlik said.

"It is Orlanthan. One of the principal dialects."

"Orlanthan?!" Varlik was startled—almost shocked. "How did you learn Orlanthan?"

"A T'swa regiment was on Orlantha more than two hundred and fifty standard years ago, to help put down a revolt by tribes from which mine slaves had been conscripted. It was there for two years, and each company had two Orlanthan scout/interpreters assigned to it. Naturally, T'swa being T'swa, some of the warriors learned the language and brought it home with them.

"Since then it has been of interest to some of us because, besides Tyspi, it is the only language in this sector entirely distinct from Standard. Even the other resource worlds have languages at least recognizably similar to yours."

"Huh! I never knew that a T'swa regiment had been on Kettle before. I don't think the army knows, either. What was it again that you said in Orlanthan?"

"*Wisosuka seikomaril, sensumakono.*"

"What does it mean?"

"A straightforward translation is, 'If you understand me, tell me so, my friend.' The root *wiso* means 'to know,' *su* is the second person singular, and *ka* is the suffix for the conditional case, equivalent to the word 'if' . . ."

Ban-Shum stopped short, laughing. "Forgive me; you are not interested in a linguistic analysis."

"I'm surprised, somehow," Konni said. "It's such a lovely language; so musical."

"Yes. Certainly it is a more aesthetic speech than Tyspi—softer, and there is a scale of stresses that can be played to provide maximum beauty. The Orlanthans had—I trust still have—great bardic poets, and the use of meter and tones were their favorite techniques. Their most highly developed implement was not a weapon or tool, but a stringed instrument used by poets as accompaniment."

No one said anything for a long moment. If Varlik had examined his discomfort of the moment, he might have identified both grief and guilt. Ban-Shum sipped again at his wine before breaking the silence. "You said you'd like to see more of our planet. Right now you are within a mile of the greatest highway on this part of Tyss, the Lok-Sanu River. It can take you through a cross-section of landscapes from coastal plain to the Jubat Hills, then through the Kar-Suum basin, and finally to the Lok-Sanu Mountains—from forest, particularly in the Jubat Hills, to deadly desert in the west."

"How would we go about taking such a trip?" Konni asked.

"There are river boats that carry passengers. One leaves the wharf at the foot of Central Street every morning and makes numerous stops along the river. It takes five days to reach the end of navigable water, at Karu Lok-Sanit, where there is a steel mill in the desert foothills. Both iron ore and coal are dug near there, in the Lok-Sanu Mountains. You could get off at any stop you liked, stay a while if you'd care to, and catch a boat on a later day. The boats are owned and operated by the Rivermen's Co-op."

"When does the boat leave here?" asked Varlik.

"At approximately six o'clock, I believe. That used to be the time, and I know of no reason it would have changed. Surely no earlier than five-fifty.[8]

"And they'd accept Confederation money?"

"I'm sure they would. Meanwhile, my wife and I would be pleased to have you as our guests tonight. That will allow me to drive you to the wharf before I must go to school."

Varlik looked doubtful. "We'd like to, but we have to walk back to the hospital to get a few things and tell them what we're going to do. We can probably arrange a ride from there in the morning and not impose on you."

"It would be no imposition. Let me make a proposal," Ban-Shum countered. "I will drive you to the hospital. You can go inside, get what you need, and I will wait for you. My wife and youngest daughter will soon be home, and will truly be disappointed if I do not have you there for supper and an evening with us."

Varlik looked at Konni; she nodded.

"That sounds good, then, Ban-Shum," Varlik said. "Let's finish our drinks and do it that way."


# 26


The ilkan's hoofs raised puffs of dust as it trotted down the riverfront street. On the wharves, smoking engines chuffed, powering cargo booms that loaded or unloaded nets of cargo from holds or decks. Voices called directions and warnings. And over and around it all, the morning's sea breeze brought the odor of kelp beds, adulterated here by a smell of sooty smoke from dock engines and deck engines and ships' funnels.

"That is the passenger boat," Ban-Shum said, pointing. "The one with the tall slender smokestack and the long deckhouse aft."

Smokestack? Varlik didn't realize for a moment what was meant, then following Ban-Shum's gesture saw a riverboat, with a thin plume of smoke rising lazily from an erect cylinder amidships. The vessel was some hundred or more feet long with a beam of perhaps twenty-five feet, built to carry both deck cargo and humans. The ilkan trotted even with it and stopped, then Varlik and Konni climbed out with their packs.

Ban-Shum reached down and shook their hands. "May your trip be all you wish," he said.

"Thank you for your hospitality," Varlik answered. "And for bringing us out this morning."

"And thank Ling-Sii and Gon for the meals and for their company," Konni added. "You were all very kind."

Ban-Shum grinned, his teeth still strong and white. "It was our pleasure to host you."

He clucked to the ilkan then, turned the buggy in the street, and drove off without a wave. It was like a dismissal by Zusu or Colonel Koda, Varlik thought, watching him go, then turned to the river boat. It occurred to him that he didn't know where to buy tickets, but considering how things were done on Tyss, one probably simply bought them from the man standing at the foot of the gangplank. The man wore a loose white shirt, like Ban-Shum's, only unbleached—they were common among civilian T'swa—but his cap was the only one in sight, suggesting an official function.

Picking up his own and Konni's packs by the straps, Varlik headed for the gangplank, then realized he didn't know the Tyspi word for "ticket." So he slowed his steps to allow a tall, high-shouldered T'swi to get there ahead of him. He'd listen and watch—see how it was done.

To his surprise, all the man with the cap said was, "Going back to Tiiku-Moks?"

"Right." The tall man then handed him a coin or coins and went aboard; apparently no ticket was involved.

The capped man looked curiously at Varlik and Konni as they stepped up to him. "Where to?" he asked in Tyspi.

"Up the river," Varlik said. "We've never been there before—never been on Tyss before—and we don't know just where we'll want to get off."

The man looked them over with unconcealed interest. "All right," he said, waving them up the gangplank, "go aboard. I'll collect from you when you get off. If you have any questions, you can ask me—I'm the mate—and I'll answer them if I have time. But you might get answers quicker from other passengers."

Varlik grinned at Konni as they crossed the gangplank. "No tickets, pay when you leave . . . It may not be Standard, but I'll bet here it works just fine."

She nodded without speaking, camera busy. On Tyss, Varlik had been lax with his own; her big Revax was better and more versatile.

The tall T'swi who'd boarded just ahead of them was leaning against the rail in the shade of an awning, watching a fishing boat pull away downstream in the direction of the sea. Varlik walked over to him.

"Good morning," said Varlik in Tyspi.

"Good morning," the man answered, surprised. "Do you understand Tyspi?"

"Quite a bit; we both do. This is Konni and my name is Varlik." He reached out and they shook hands. Like Ban-Shum's, the man's palm, though somewhat hard, was not as callused as the warriors'.

"My name is Lin," the man replied. "I'd thought of speaking to you, but I hadn't anticipated your ability with our language."

He was a forester, employed on a forestry operation in the Jubat Hills, and had come to Oldu Tez-Boag to visit his parents and a sister. The Lok-Sanu River region had been his home all his life, and he enjoyed answering their questions about it.

They'd been aboard no more than a quarter hour when they felt the vibration of the ship's screw turning. Longshoremen cast the lines off, deckhands retrieved them, and slowly the riverboat pulled away from the wharf. The current pushed her nose as she angled into it, her screw biting water, and she shoved her way upstream.

There were more docks just above the city, where they could see wheeled engines, long and squat, attached to trains of wheeled wagons— the *railroad*, Lin told them. Cargos were transferred from ships and riverboats to the railroad trains, which then distributed the goods throughout this part of the coastal plain. There too were the grain elevators from which, in turn, ships and riverboats were loaded.

Soon, though, they left the dock area behind, and the shores became farmland, with frequent water uptake structures for irrigation. These too were powered by the chuffing, stationary, smoke-belching engines, or sometimes by solar converters, and in a few cases by livestock plodding around a capstan. There were rowboats with fisherman, and occasional downstream rafts with goods piled on them, guided by T'swa at long sweeps. Wooden barges with smokestacks also passed, some with lumber stacked on their decks, ricks of fuelwood, or piles of stony black soil mounded above hatch coamings. Once they passed a flatboat with a cargo of what seemed to be thick metal rods.

"Is that steel?" Varlik asked.

"Yes. The largest steel mill on Tyss is at the foot of the Lok-Sanu Mountains, up the river 480 miles."

Varlik remembered Ban-Shum mentioning the mill. "Where do they get technetium to make steel with?" he asked. He used the Standard word for technetium; he didn't know any other, and they'd probably borrowed it into Tyspi anyway.

"Technetium? I'm not familiar with that. But I know little about steel-making; actually nothing. If you go as far as Karu Lok-Sanit, the town where the mill is, I'm sure they can tell you."

Varlik nodded; he'd try to get his question answered before he left Tyss. There might be more technology here than he'd realized.

"Lin," he asked, "what powers these vessels? What makes them go?"

The forester's brows raised. "Come with me," he said, and led them to a broad door in the deckhouse. Inside, the room extended not only to the overhead but part of it well below the deck, seemingly to the bottom of the ship's shallow-draft hull. It was filled with sound and machinery, long piston shafts rising and falling amid the smell of steam and hot oil, all ministered to by a wiry engineer, the smallest adult male T'swi Varlik had seen. He held an oil can whose long spout dipped and pecked among moving parts like some depraved giant hummingbird.

"Khito!" Lin shouted; obviously he knew the man. The engineer paused amid the booming, turning to look.

Lin pointed at the two Iryalans, gesticulated, bent over and made motions with his arms. The engineer in turn grinned and nodded, dismissing them with a wave. They backed out onto the deck again.

"That is the engine room," said Lin. "The engines are driven by steam under pressure. Come. I'll show you where the steam is made."

They followed him a few yards farther aft, where a narrow door stood open to the deck. From it flowed a river of heat considerably hotter even than the outside air. A short steep companionway led down into the ship's bowels, from which came a ringing of steel striking steel. Lin paused only long enough to tell the Iryalans that Khito had said it was all right, then he started down the hellish companionway, Varlik and Konni trailing hesitantly behind.

It led into a chamber like something from a nightmare, weakly lit by two small tubes, one next to the companionway, the other above a gauge of some kind. The heat was terrific; outside was nothing by comparison. The ringing noises had stopped before they'd started down, but the pounding of the engine could be felt and heard, and somewhere a leaking steam valve hissed. A grizzled T'swi, short and stocky and a virtual anatomical chart in holo, stood stripped to the waist, amazingly sinewy, all fat long since boiled away. The man's jeans were so sweat-soggy they stuck to his thighs.

Shovel in hand, he was watching the gauge. To his right was what seemed a metal wall with two small metal doors, behind him a bulkhead with a barred opening from which had slid a pile of the stony soil, shiny black, that Varlik had seen on passing barges.

Varlik and Konni stood transfixed, sweating extravagantly, their cameras recording the motionless tableau. Shortly the stoker turned to the metal wall and threw open one of the doors; inside was intense fire, glaring whitely. With a single easy bending stride, he slid his shovel crunching beneath the pile of stony dirt, half straightened, pivoted, and slung the shovelful into the fire, a smooth swinging movement, the heel of the shovel ringing on the baseplate of the door. Then he turned, dug again, and threw again, his movements as if choreographed, until he'd cast half a dozen scoops of soil into the fire. Then he closed the door, grinned at his visitors, and returned his attention to the gauge.

Lin nodded to the Iryalans and led them back out onto the deck, where briefly it seemed cool.

"That is where the steam is made for the engine," Lin said, leading them aftward. "And back here is where the force is applied to the water to propel the boat."

On the fantail he leaned over the rail, pointing downward. "Down there is the propeller. It works on the principle of the screw to push against the water."

Varlik didn't understand all the words, but he got the general idea. Only one thing demanded explanation.

"But Lin," he said, "why was the man throwing dirt and stones into the fire?"

"Dirt?" Suddenly Lin realized, and laughed out loud. "You are right; that's what it is," he said. "Dirt and stones! It's just that we don't think of it that way. We call it 'coal,' and it is flammable, burning hotter than wood and requiring considerably less storage space and handling for a given value of energy."

He laughed again as they picked their way among crates on the freight deck to the ship's bow, where the breeze of its movement was unbroken, there to watch the shore and the water traffic. *Incredible*, thought Varlik, *that the T'swa could have done these things. How could they have learned, have been so clever?*

Then he remembered something Voker had said: Every Standard practice had been an innovation once. An unheard-of concept, yet now that he looked at it, compelling; it *had* to have been that way once! Vaguely Varlik got the concept of innovation growing upon innovation over time, leading perhaps from this, or something like it, to the technology of the Confederation. In some remote, long-forgotten past, his own people must have been clever too, must have thought new thoughts and tried things for the first time.

The realization made him feel slightly ill rather than excited, as old and hidden psychoconditioning was activated, and he pushed the thought away. Within moments he didn't remember it—didn't even remember there'd been a thought.

## 27

Tiiku-Moks, several hours upstream from Oldu Tez-Boag, was the biggest town they'd come to, with maybe three or four thousand people. Well before they got there, they'd left the coastal plain, the river flowing through a gap in a series of transverse ridges that got higher eastward.

The Lok-Sanu's current had continued smooth and unchanging, a third of a mile wide, and deep enough for shallow-draft traffic. No rivers of size had entered it, and it had occurred to Varlik to wonder where, on such a dry world, the Lok-Sanu got its water. The answer, Lin had explained, was the Lok-Sanu Mountains, Tyss's highest, with many ridge crests rising sixteen thousand feet above the basin at their feet, and peaks to more than twenty thousand. Precipitation was relatively abundant there—snow as well as rain; it was the wettest place on the planet.

On this particular mid-autumn day, Tiiku-Moks was hotter than Aromanis had usually been. For miles now the river's shores had mainly been forested, with here and there a hamlet fronted by its own wharf, and Tiiku-Moks had the feel of a lumbering town—one with shade trees. Except along the wharves, there were trees enough that the buildings seemed almost to have been fitted in among them.

As a river port, its principal function was clearly the shipping of lumber: There were long stacks of it piled along the wharves, as high as men could build them by hand, and numerous carloads were parked on railroad spurs. The Jubat Hills, Lin explained, were the major source of wood for this whole part of the planet—everything upstream as well as down, and the districts all around the Toshi Sea, especially the dry eastern side.

Lin led them to a low building with the welcome "cool drinks" sign. Like the one in Oldu Tez-Boag, it had wooden paneling inside a thick layer of stuccoed-over adobe bricks. This one, however, was near the docks, and much busier and noisier with conversation than the T'swa cantina the two Iryalans had experienced the day before. The forester told them he had to stay in town for a day of meetings. If they decided to visit the forestry operations, the railroad ran north from Tiiku-Moks through fifty miles of them, with a sawmill village every few miles. Lodging and meals could be found in any village by asking around.

When Lin had left them, Konni and Varlik discussed it and decided they'd go on up the river. They could take this side trip on the way back if they wanted to.

Meanwhile, they had another hour to wait before the boat left, so they wandered along the riverfront, slowly, so as not to soak their clothes with sweat. The railroad line, which headed away from the river, was flanked here by a side track with a long string of empty lumber cars waiting for return to the sawmills. But not all the cars were lumber cars, nor empty. There was a flatcar with machinery, perhaps for a sawmill, boxcars with goods, even refrigeration cars with small solar converters on top. Toward the head end were three passenger coaches.

There were also three gondola cars with long bundles of steel rods visible atop their loads. When Varlik saw them, he felt a momentary thrill of discomfort, went over and climbed the rungs of one to peer over the edge. There was raw steel in bars and bundled rods, on underlying sheets of rolled steel, obviously going away from the river.

Going away from the river. What would some sawmill village do with three carloads, or one carload, of untooled steel? All the peculiarities, the little incongruities associated with Kettle, the insurrection, the T'swa—the whole business—boiled up for a moment, and he dropped to the ground looking troubled.

"What's the matter?" Konni asked.

"I'm not sure. Maybe nothing. But I want to take the train after all. I want to see where these"—he indicated the three carloads of steel—"get left off, and if I can, see what they're used for. Come on. Let's find out when the train leaves."

"Now wait a minute!" Konni insisted as they walked. "Give! Something's bothering you, whether you're sure or not. What is it?"

He walked on a dozen paces before answering. "I'm really not sure. I haven't had time to think about it yet. But steel! Where do they get the technetium to make it with? Would the Rombili ship technetium to a gook world, considering the shortage of the past year?"

"What would following these cars tell you?" Konni asked.

Again he kept walking silently while thoughts formed. "Konni," he said at last, "what if the T'swa are making weapons? Suppose there's an arsenal off north here somewhere?"

"Who would they make weapons for?"

"For whoever is shipping them technetium. The T'swa export soldiers, why not weapons?"

She slowed him, holding his sleeve. "But that sounds like a lot of trouble for someone just to get weapons, when they could make them themselves or buy them from us. Especially if they got caught; then they'd really have trouble!"

"Exactly! Anyone who'd go to that much trouble and take that big a risk isn't only up to something illegal, but something big enough to make it seem worthwhile. Maybe they're trying to arm up secretly. Maybe it's a trade world that's buying them! Maybe the Splenn. Remember the little kids that talked to us in the street, back in Oldu Tez-Boag? They thought we were from Splenn. Why Splenn? Do quite a few Splenn come to Tyss? And besides being one of the few trade worlds with space ships, Splenn's supposedly a haven for smugglers."

They'd been approaching the railroad administrative office, not much more than an adobe shack near the head of the siding, and stopped talking as they went in. The cheerful T'swa manager told them they had almost an hour, and there would be someone at the coaches, probably himself, to receive fares.

So they returned to the cantina to wait, replenish their body fluids, and refill the water flasks they carried in their packs. Konni was thoughtful now; clearly Varlik's arguments had impressed her. Then they walked to the siding again, paid their fares, and boarded a coach.

The coach windows bore no glass. The presence of forest in such year-round heat attested that it rained here fairly often and fairly heavily, but apparently the T'swa didn't mind getting wet. Shortly the couplings jerked and the train began to move, picking up speed to about thirty miles an hour, clicking along a track that kept close to the contour. On left curves, Varlik could see the locomotive, even glimpse the fireman pitching long lengths of firewood into the furnace. The smokestack, topped by a large spark arrester, trailed a plume of white.

They stopped at every sawmill village to drop off flatcars and sometimes other cars, until only a few cars were left. By then the sun was low, and the cars with steel were still in the train, close behind the engine.

Then the train slowed again, finally stopping, but this time not at a village, only a short siding, where a spur track disappeared into the forest. On the siding was a gondola car, and a flat car with large crates strapped on it. The cars with the steel were uncoupled from the train, and a little switch engine shunted them onto the siding. Then the train recoupled and drew slowly away, leaving the steel cars behind. Varlik lowered his camera. When they rounded the next curve, they saw another sawmill village just ahead.

He nudged Konni. "Here's where we get off," he said in Standard. "We can visit the sawmill today, a logging operation tomorrow"—he paused— "and take a walk in the woods tonight."

Visit a sawmill they did, recording its yowling head-rig and squalling resaws, its snarling hogger and screeching planer. And above all, the energetic, sure, and strenuous activities of T'swa workers defying the heat. Afterward they found a home with two rooms they could rent for the night, and ate supper there. When they'd eaten, they walked the evening darkness of the village's main street, often pausing to use their cameras, planning their spying in quiet murmurs, finally stopping at the local watering place for the usual "cool drinks," avoiding anything alcoholic.

They talked little there; their attention was on what they were about to do, and they'd said all there was to say about it. By deliberately nursing their drinks, they took another half hour; then they left, to stroll along the unlit dirt street that paralleled the railroad track. At the edge of the village the street continued, became a forest lane, and they just kept strolling, accompanied on their right by the railroad and blessed by a moon that was, for all practical purposes, full. They rounded the curve, leaving the village out of sight behind them, the cars on the siding slowly taking form in the darkness ahead.

So far they could easily explain their presence as an evening walk. Now the question forced itself on them: Might the cars be guarded? Would some T'swi step out of the shadows when Varlik began to snoop?

When they got there, Varlik dug their monitor visors and cameras from his pack, and they put them on. Then he climbed onto the flatcar to examine the packing boxes, while Konni recorded. The boxes were nearly as tall as he was, and not only were they strapped to the car; each was also wrapped around with metal straps and strongly cross-spiked. "They must," he muttered to Konni, "be very heavy to require such strong packing."

Next they looked into the gondola cars. From the ground they looked empty, but actually they were decked with layers of flat wooden cases, each case as heavy as he cared to lift in the gravity of Tyss. He stood staring at them.

"What are you going to do?" whispered Konni, clinging to a rung and peering in. "Break one open?"

Varlik shook his head. "It would be too obvious. Someone would wonder what happened, and someone else would remember the two Confederatswa."

"We could take one back in the woods and break it open where no one would notice it. No one would ever know; it would be just one case less."

He thought about that, then shook his head. "Not yet, anyway. Let's follow the spur track back into the woods and see where it goes. This stuff must come from back there somewhere."

They climbed down.

"What if there's a guard?"

"I'm hoping there isn't. You know how trusting the T'swa are, and they probably don't get foreigners in this district once a decade."

*How trusting the T'swa are,* he repeated to himself. *As if they're so honest themselves that they overlook the possibility of criminality, at least at home.* And how did that fit his suspicions? He shook the question off; he'd see where this track led him.

Back among the trees it was darker, much of the moonlight being intercepted. But using camera and visor to find the way would be a greater nuisance here, so they set off down the spur-line track, stumbling occasionally on the ties. When they'd gone half a mile and found nothing, they almost gave up and turned back, then saw moonlight ahead through the trees.

It turned out to be a clearing, roughly square and a quarter mile across, and from beneath the eaves of the forest they stopped to look. In the middle was a building like a very large, tall shed, of metal instead of adobe, resembling the sawmill, and for a moment Varlik wondered if that's all it was. But there were no log piles. The sides were open for several feet above the ground, and again below the eaves, presumably for free air-flow. The ground around it had been plowed and harrowed, and at first he thought of a mine field. Then it occurred to him it might be a fire break, to protect the building in case of forest fire, or perhaps the opposite. At any rate it would show footprints conspicuously.

There was no sign of a light in or around the building, but he reminded himself of the T'swa night vision. A watchman might not use a light. He looked at Konni; she was looking at him.

"C'mon," he murmured, and started across the clearing on the well-trod path that they now could see accompanied the spur track, no doubt worn there by workers going to work.

The little steam engine used to shunt freight cars waited in solitary silence by a loading dock. No one and nothing challenged them—nothing but the darkness of inside. The place was full of heavy machinery, and their cameras recorded all of it. There were conveyors, furnaces, drop forges, steam hammers, forging presses, lathes. . . . He couldn't have named most of them, but he could recognize or guess what they did. Then he examined some dies, and that left no doubt: Weapons were made here.

This place must be as loud as the sawmill, Varlik thought. Maybe that's why they built it so far back in the forest.

On the long loading dock they found rifles ready for packing, along with sidearms, blast hoses, rocket launchers, lobbers—every light infantry weapon. The rifles lacked stocks, as if those were added elsewhere. At destination apparently; the crates and cases on the cars seemed built and secured for the whole trip. Varlik turned to Konni.

"I've seen enough," he said. "They're arming someone, or helping arm them. I'll bet it's Splenn, or someone the Splenn smugglers contract with. And that's the source of the technetium used to make this steel."

"Not necessarily," Konni said.

"What do you mean?"

"Maybe the T'swa manufacture weapons for themselves here."

Varlik shook his head. "I doubt it. Could they make them cheaper than they can buy them? This place can't be as efficient as the Royal Armory on Iryala."

"Maybe they're stockpiling," she suggested. "Maybe they're training and arming a secret army to conquer someone."

"Who? They can't have more than a few leased troop transports. The Confederation fleet would stop any transstellar invasion in a hurry."

"Maybe they plan to conquer another resource planet. That might not bring the fleet down on them."

He shook it off; conquest didn't fit the T'swa he knew, either in the regiment or here. *Or do I really* know *any T'swa?* That thought, too, he tried to banish. "Conquest plans wouldn't explain how they get the technetium," he said.

"They don't have to. They could still get it through smugglers, and maybe steel doesn't take very much. Maybe they even get it legally. Certainly the Confederation knows they make steel here."

"Maybe the Confederation *doesn't* know," he countered. "Remember how little there is in the library about Tyss and the T'swa? No one in the Confederation pays any attention to them except as a source of mercenaries. And with technetium as precious as it must be by now . . ."

Konni didn't respond at once, but her expression told him an idea was forming.

"Varlik?"

"Yes?"

"What if the T'swa have their own technite mine? It wouldn't have to be very big."

The T'swa with their own technite mine? How could you disprove something like that? After a moment he reached into a partly filled packing case and transferred a sidearm to his packsack. Konni watched soberly; to steal on Tyss seemed an enormity, despite their suspicions.

"Let's go," Varlik murmured. "Let's go back and sleep on this, or try to. I don't know what to think. Or what to do next."

But by the time they reached the village he knew: Their next step was to get back to Oldu Tez-Boag and off of Oven.

# PART FOUR
## *Death of a Regiment*

# 28

Their return to Orlantha was less comfortable than the trip out, for it was a troopship they rode, the aged but well-maintained IWS *Davin*. She carried the Ice Tiger Regiment, a virgin regiment newly contracted for. Varlik had a shelf-like bunk in a troop compartment, while Konni enjoyed the privacy of a four- by eight-foot gear locker temporarily converted to her use.

The *Davin* was hotter than the hospital ship had been, too. The temperature was around 110°F during the wake period, Varlik guessed, though cooled during the sleep period by a dozen or fifteen degrees.

According to a lieutenant he'd talked with, the new regiment had been contracted for by the Department of Armed Forces, not the Crown, and requested by General Lamons. Varlik accepted this as truth; the T'swa were given to openly briefing officers and men of all ranks, and rumors seemed to have little or no place or function among them.

Apparently Lamons's medal-bestowing visit to the T'swa hospital wards had been more than politics.

Varlik and Konni talked together a great deal while killing time playing cards in her "room." They agreed to say nothing about the arsenal or their suspicions until they'd both returned to Iryala, and then only jointly. To make it known on Orlantha could only upset operations there.

Also, together and separately, they talked with T'swa mercenaries. These troopers were eighteen and nineteen years old, but seemed scarcely less mature than the fourteen-year veterans Varlik had lived and served with. Varlik joined them in their exercises, which were restricted by lack of space but strenuous nonetheless, and by the time they raised Kettle, he felt strong again.

They landed at Aromanis, of course, and Varlik, per protocol, checked in with Trevelos—*Captain* Trevelos now. The information officer had been given a larger staff and office—the Kettle War was much bigger news at home than it had been. Inwardly, Trevelos credited Varlik with making it happen, or at least helping it happen, with his coverage of the T'swa.

In fact Trevelos, usually polite, now positively deferred to him. It made Varlik a bit uncomfortable, and he stayed for only a few minutes, making small talk about Tyss and the new regiment.

Then Varlik checked Voker's office, and to his surprise found the colonel there. Voker, grinning but sharp-eyed, got up and offered his hand when Varlik came in.

"Sit," said Voker, motioning to a chair, and Varlik sat. "How did you like Tyss?"

"Interesting. And friendly. Someday I'd like to go back and really explore. Visit a war lodge. Maybe a monastery." Varlik had surprised himself with the latter because he hadn't thought of it before. "There's a lot more to the T'swa than mercenaries," he added.

"So. And meanwhile, what next?"

"Next? First a shower in unrecycled water, then listen to my mail. Then I'm going to send off some letter cubes and a report on Tyss. And after that . . ." He shrugged. "I don't really know. I've been thinking of going straight home. But I'll probably go to the T'swa reconditioning camp, at least for a few days. Get a feel for what's going on now and see whether there's anything more I want to do here before I leave."

Voker leaned back, contemplating the younger man. "Just don't talk yourself into going south again. The T'swa aren't doing anything different, and you've already covered that. There's a good chance of getting yourself killed if you go back down there." He stroked the morning's regrowth on his chin. "You've done a damn fine job here and made a name for yourself on Iryala. Go home and enjoy it."

Somehow the colonel's pitch put Varlik off, just a little and for only a moment, but Voker's eyes didn't miss it.

"Maybe I will," Varlik said. "But right now I want to say something while I think of it. I want to thank you for working my ass off on the way out here. And for your tip that got me back with Colonel Koda." Varlik chuckled. "I thought I was going to die that first day out on the prairie with them."

"Just make sure you don't die on your last day with them," Voker said.

That killed the conversation, but neither had anything more to say anyway. They exchanged a few trivialities, then Varlik excused himself. The rest of the day, the question occupied at least the fringe of his mind while he did other things. Why *shouldn't* he go straight home? The wisdom in Voker's suggestion felt compelling, but somehow he couldn't decide to do it.

Voker, in turn, after Varlik left, still had him on his mind, if only briefly. He recognized a certain responsibility for Varlik's being with the T'swa, and for the young man's likely death if he continued with them.

But if Varlik decided to, that was his prerogative. He'd survived so far, and the ultimate responsibility belonged to the person himself. Voker sipped thoughtfully at his tepid joma, then dismissed Lormagen from his thoughts and turned back to the plan he'd been working on.

# 29

The T'swa colonels, three of them now, arrived together at Lamons's weekly command meeting, each with his aide. The nineteen-year-old Colonel Jil-Zat seemed as poised, as relaxed and sure of himself, as Biltong and Koda.

Lamons had his staff with him, and a personal aide to the Crown—Lord Kristal. Introducing Kristal was the first order of business; when that was over, the work of the meeting began.

Currently, problems of logistics, coordination, and authority were minor, and could be handled at lower levels. These were reviewed briefly. Finally, there was nothing left but the major situation review and discussion.

"And now," said Lamons, "we come back to our purpose in being on Orlantha. We need to reestablish the reliable mining and refining of technite on a scale adequate for the continuance of Confederation industry. We have a time frame to work within, dictated by the need for steel. Lord Kristal has something to say to us about that." He turned to the dapper aristocrat in his precise and correct civilian garb. "Your Lordship?" said Lamons, and sat down.

Kristal stood. "I will be brief, and what I say here must not be repeated—in whole, in part, or in substance—by any of you to anyone not currently present. It would be regarded as treasonous, and no extenuating circumstance would be considered. Is that understood?"

Sober nods around the table assured him that it was.

"Good. I said that not from any concern that one of you might be loose-tongued. I simply wanted to stress the importance of silence on this subject." He scanned the table with its seated officers. "Now. Technetium shipments to trade planets have been embargoed for more than seven deks. This has had a very severe impact on the manufacturing and economy of those worlds, and as a result, on their ability to purchase goods from Confederation worlds. A side effect has been a growing depression in substantial sectors of the Confederation economy. Furthermore, the shipment of steel outside the Confederation, already tightened, was discontinued entirely almost three deks ago, and that is exacerbating matters seriously.

"And here are the most sensitive data: At the present reduced levels of use, existing stocks of technetium will last less than eleven deks. However, use restrictions will be put into effect at the end of this dek which, at the cost of increasing economic problems, will stretch the supply by approximately five deks to, say, fifteen deks. The capacity to ration supplies more severely than that is closely limited by what the economy can stand."

His hard grey eyes scanned the assembled military. "That establishes your time frame, gentlemen. And we can't wait the full fifteen deks; a certain lag time is involved in the economy. His Majesty wants significant new technite shipments underway from Orlantha no later than a year from now. Therefore, you have ten deks."

He nodded at Lamons then and took his seat. The general stood up. "Thank you, Your Lordship. For the purpose of establishing the operational situation, let me say first that the Orlanthan insurgency clearly has considerably greater resources of men and ordnance than we had thought as recently as two deks ago. And they are very effective fighting men." He turned to an aide. "Major Emeril, give us the current data on insurgent attacks and on our progress toward renewed technite production."

Emeril stood. "Thank you, general. Gentlemen, my lord, in the week ending last midnight, lobber rockets landing within our defensive perimeter numbered 387, up from 209 the week before and 117 the week before that. Apparently the insurgents are not only continuing to get reinforcements through; they are now bringing up munitions in greater bulk, on pack animals.

"We have stepped up our combat patrols outside the perimeter, and our ground contacts with the insurgents increased from 17 to 42; that's 247 percent. Again, this was for the week ending last midnight. Also, the intensity of those contacts has increased: Our patrol casualties rose from 61 to 239, with 81 killed. Yesterday alone we had 20 killed on patrols.

"Enemy were increasingly sighted by reconnaissance flights and platform surveillance, indicating either enemy carelessness or, more probably, increased activity. Gunship attacks on seen enemy troops increased from sixteen to twenty-seven. On the other hand, gunship losses to enemy fire increased from three to eleven. Apparently the enemy has now brought M-4 rockets into use, and may in fact be baiting our gunships into what we might call ambushes."

At that point, Lamons interrupted. "Let me add here that the Romblit engineering teams have completed renovation of the technite mines with heavy concrete mineheads. Given our existing defense perimeter, both the refinery sites and mineheads continue susceptible to enemy lobber fire. We hit such lobber positions quickly and hard as soon as they show themselves, but rebuilding the refinery goes slowly for now. We have to construct it like a fortress. But if it was ready now, bulk carriers landing for ore would be subject to rocket attacks, and they're not built to stand that sort of thing. Arrival of the four new divisions will permit us to man a larger defense perimeter, but establishing and building it will cost us." He turned to Emeril. "Major, please continue."

Nodding, Emeril went on, his eyes on Lord Kristal. "Equipment recently received has enabled us to begin expanding the Beregesh secured site. Our attempts the past week to establish six key strongpoints outside the defense perimeter were successful. Casualties in so doing were high but not quite exorbitant: 103 killed and 307 wounded, not including patrol casualties but including men killed and injured by ground-to-air attack on floaters being used to land them, again evincing enemy use of M-4 rockets. Casualties also include operator losses from rocket attacks on armored dozers clearing fields of fire around the strongpoints.

"Our success in strong-point construction has been encouraging, but of course they remain six isolated strongpoints—only a beginning in a defensive perimeter that will be"—he paused meaningfully—"over twenty-five miles long.

"Today we have begun the establishment of six new strongpoints." He turned to General Lamons. "Sir, that's the end of my presentation."

Emeril sat down and Lamons stood up. "Thank you, major." He looked around the table. "You will have noticed a second new face among us: Colonel Jil-Zat of the Ice Tiger Regiment. This is a virgin regiment with a full complement of men, and the contracting authority assures us that they are fully combat competent, albeit without combat experience. The latter will be remedied shortly. Colonel, will you stand, please."

The T'swi stood, tall and with shoulders big even for a T'swi, but almost shockingly young-looking. Jil-Zat nodded without speaking and sat down. The Confederation officers around the long table could not entirely conceal their misgivings.

Lamons continued. "I should add that the contracting authority tells me it is the only additional T'swa regiment likely to be available to us in the near future. Colonel Biltong, please brief us on T'swa combat activities during the last week."

Biltong stood, impassive as always at these meetings. "General, Lord Kristal, gentlemen. To our specific knowledge, T'swa raiders made 474 attacks last week on insurgents and their pack animals. Casualties inflicted are not known, but presumably are fewer per action than in previous weeks because of the increased insurgent tendency to move in small groups—now commonly in twos and threes—and to disperse their travel over a broader zone.

"This tells us something of the dedication and discipline of insurgent troops, and their ability to find their way in wilderness not personally familiar to them.

"Our own casualties have also been lower, partly because such small groups of insurgents have less opportunity and ability to return fire, partly because there are fewer of us for the insurgent hunter-killer patrols to find, and partly because of adjustments we have made in our tactics.

"And to echo General Lamons's comment, it seems abundantly clear that insurgent numbers are far greater than originally thought, while our two regiments have been shrinking. The two engaged regiments, as of yesterday, numbered only 396 men active behind enemy lines. Actually, some of those may be casualties not yet reported. We also have 80 men on rest rotation, 92 more in rehabilitation training following hospitalization, and 77 in the hospital with wounds that should not prevent their reassignment within a reasonably short time. That is a total of 645 men."

Biltong sat down then, and Lamons stood again. "We are aware," Lamons said quietly, "that the T'swa have been operating under sustained, very hazardous conditions, and at heavy cost in blood. We also realize the extreme importance of what they've accomplished. Colonel Voker, you have a proposal to make with regard to the T'swa."

"Yes, sir." Voker got to his feet. "Not all the T'swa in insurgent territory have been raiding insurgent lines of reinforcement and supply. I've had several three-man teams on long-range reconnaissance, tracing insurgent trails farther south. The trails come from a particular region of jungle within which I strongly suspect the insurgent military command and supply centers can be found, and probably the insurgent government.

"A few weeks ago I also put down several small T'swa exploration teams in the equatorial jungle, to report on operating conditions there."

Voker looked around the table. "At the same time, we have analyzed aerial reconnaissance holos of the landforms in regions we thought might contain those centers. Considering that roofed supply depots are necessary in such a rainy climate, and that suitable buildings should be detectable from recon platforms but weren't, I assumed that caves are probably being used. These would have to be extensive, and because of drainage requirements would almost surely be found in hills with certain characteristics. I've made certain other assumptions as well, and come up with a limited number of candidate areas.

"What I propose doing next is to withdraw the existing T'swa hunter-killer squads to Aromanis for rest and refitting, replacing them with two battalions of the new regiment. I recommend that the other new battalion be used at Beregesh to disrupt and inhibit insurgent activities in the vicinity of our strongpoint construction.

"Meanwhile, veteran T'swa scout teams will be flown south to find, if possible, the central insurgent command area. Assuming they find it, the veteran T'swa regiments would be used to strike the area by surprise, with the sole purpose of capturing and bringing out insurgent headquarters officers who might be able to tell us who trained and supplied them, and how, as well as giving us locations of other strategic sites we can hit from the air."

Voker scanned the intent faces around the table, then continued. "For interrogation, incidentally, we have several psychiatric specialists being flown here from Iryala with their equipment.

"After withdrawing the T'swa and their prisoners, we can strike key coordinates from the air, and hopefully seriously impair the insurgent ability to continue, while turning over to the Crown any information on off-world supporters of the insurgency."

Again Voker looked the silent group over. "That is the outline of my proposal. It has the apparent potential to weaken seriously the insurgents' supply capacity and to end any future outside aid to them."

He sat down, and for a moment no one spoke. Lamons started to rise then, but before he said anything, Lord Kristal spoke. "General, I recommend that you recess this meeting, its members to remain available on short notice. I'd like to speak with Colonel Voker and yourself with regard to the colonel's proposal."

That evening, with the decisions made and detailed planning underway, and a coded message cube off to His Majesty, Lord Kristal let his thoughts wander. The standard military mind! Even Voker, easily the most imaginative of them all, wore a mental strait-jacket. With the proper innovative use of resources at hand or available in short order, ore could be shipped within a dek—two at most. *But of course, if they were up to that,* he said to himself, *this project wouldn't be necessary in the first place.*

# 30

Rehab Section C came in from its two-hour speed march in the typical wild closing gallop, with Varlik, as usual, bringing up the rear. *If there was just some way to market sweat,* he thought as he stood in ranks again, chest heaving, waiting for dismissal while wiping his forehead.

It wasn't until after they'd been dismissed that he noticed the Red Scorpions' regimental area had been reoccupied; the regiment was back.

Or what was left of it. Walking between the rows of squad tents to the showers, he found about one in three occupied. Subconsciously he'd known it would be like this, would have said so if asked in advance, but seeing it was like being slugged in the gut.

The troopers seemed not to feel that way. The returnees and the men of the rehab sections greeted each other cheerily, some even exuberantly, and asked about others who might simply be elsewhere at the moment or dead. And as Varlik soaked this in, it so disjointed his sense of the appropriate that his initial depression became something different—a low grade, ill-defined resentment.

"Varlik!"

It was Kusu; the big sergeant stepped from a tent as Varlik was returning from the showers. The surgeons hadn't returned his chin to its old profile, had rebuilt it more roundly than before, but he was easily recognizable.

"So you are back from Tyss!" He stood back and looked the Iryalan over, reading Varlik's discomfort, and in response toned down his own high cheer. "Fit again, too," he added. "Apparently the physical differences between Iryalan and T'swi are more complexion than constitution."

Somehow Varlik wasn't able to reply.

"May I walk along with you?" asked Kusu.

"If you want." Varlik's tone was almost surly.

"There aren't many of us left, are there?" Kusu said calmly. "There's been a lot of recycling going on. Recycling tends to come a lot earlier among warriors than among others." His chuckle was barely audible. "Newsmen, for instance. I suspect most newsmen grow old and gray and watch their grandchildren grow up."

Varlik said nothing.

"What rehab section are you in?" Kusu asked.

"C."

"Then you are almost ready to join a unit, if that is what you plan. You told me once that you have a wife, and intended to have children."

Varlik answered without expression. "That's right."

"Fine." The T'swi slowed. "Maybe we'll talk sometime. I would enjoy hearing what you thought of Tyss." Then he turned back the way they'd come, and Varlik walked the last hundred feet alone to his tent.

*What's the matter with you?* he asked himself. *He's a friend. He was glad to see you. And you acted like a complete and utter ass.*

He wondered if Kusu had been offended, then rejected the idea. The man, the T'swa in general, seemed immune to that kind of emotion. But that didn't make it all right to act offensively toward him, to reject his friendliness.

Varlik hung his towel over the foot-frame of his cot, put on his off-duty uniform and fresh boots, then looked at his watch. They wouldn't serve supper for ten minutes, but he might as well do his waiting at the mess hall.

As he left, the rifle rack at the end of the tent caught his eye. He'd checked, and the rifles all had serial numbers, as rifles should; it was the only way to tell yours from the others. And he realized what was bothering him, had been bothering him since they'd been dismissed after training and he'd found the regiment back from the south. It was not just that the regiment—his regiment—was being shot to pieces bit by bit. It was that tied together with his suspicion that some T'swa faction was the source of this war, was supporting the other side—the Birds—and that the regiments were being sacrificed to duplicity.

*But you don't know that,* he argued. *All you have is circumstantial evidence. There could be various other explanations that haven't occurred to you.*

*Yeah? Name one. Think of one.*

He shook off the spiral of questions and, walking slowly, put his attention outward, on the visual: actually seeing the tents, duckboards, black bodies striding tentward from the showers, green-trousered troopers ambling toward the mess hall; blue sky, fluffy white cumulus, a high-soaring hawk riding an updraft.

In this way, by the time he'd walked the hundred yards to the mess hall he'd banished his upset—for the time being: The roots still were there. The regiment was decimated, on Tyss he'd seen what he'd seen, and all the anomalies, ambiguities, strangenesses in the situation remained.

On the mustering ground, something over five hundred veteran T'swa stood in ranks, at ease, in faint morning steam as the newly risen sun evaporated a thunder shower of the night before. There were five hundred forty-six troopers—four under-strength companies—most of what was left of the two regiments. Their regimental commanders stood facing them, each flanked by his exec and his sergeant major. Somewhere out of sight of Varlik Lormagen, a bird trilled, some songster of the Orlanthan prairie, intruded upon but not far displaced by the black mercenaries. It or others like it, Varlik thought, would be here when the regiments, and the army, were long gone.

It was Biltong, as the "senior" colonel, who spoke, using only his big voice unamplified. His Tyspi was almost as easy for Varlik to follow now as Standard would have been.

"T'swa," said Biltong, "we have a new assignment: We are to strike the Orlanthan headquarters and take prisoners—assuming that we succeed in locating it. Several reconnaissance teams are in the candidate areas now, in the equatorial jungle, and we can presume they'll find it."

Biltong went on to describe the plans in some detail, and Varlik listened in near shock. It sounded suicidal. Finally, Biltong finished. "Ground-model briefings will be made when the area has been identified and the ground described. You all know the enemy and his fighting qualities, so you see the challenge we face. It will almost surely be a battle of highest quality, and may prove to be our final action. Colonel Koda and I will be there with you, of course."

He turned and said something quietly to Koda, who shook his head as he answered. Then Biltong turned again to the troopers.

"Regiments dismissed!"

The troopers broke ranks and began walking to breakfast, and it wasn't until then that Varlik became aware of a deep and powerful *something* that had risen in them. They weren't saying much, but there was a sense of anticipation; he could almost hear their deep psychic chuckling, and it made his hair stand up.

In the mess hall at breakfast, a regimental clerk announced that Varlik Lormagen should report to Colonel Koda at 06.00. He was there minutes early—right after breakfast—and the sergeant major motioned him into the colonel's office. Varlik entered and, for some reason unknown to him, saluted.

"Sit down, Lormagen."

He sat. Koda looked at him, seemingly into him, through large black eyes.

"I want to thank you for the excellent job you've done as publicist. I believe you'll find, when you arrive back on Iryala, that you've succeeded equally well for your other employer." He smiled. "The one that pays well."

Varlik nodded without smiling back.

"You were in ranks this morning," Koda continued, "so you know what our next action will be. And it seems to me that for you, the risks this time outweigh the benefits. Perhaps it would enhance your reputation to die in the jungle, but I question whether death in battle was part of your purpose when you entered this lifetime.

"So I called you in this morning for two reasons. One, the army wants this action kept secret until it happens. I want your word that you'll say nothing till it's over."

Again Varlik nodded.

"I have your word, then?"

"Yes, sir."

"Good. And secondly, I'd like you to give me your resignation as T'swa publicist."

Varlik stared at the colonel from a viewpoint at which time seemed to have stopped, seeing the face more clearly than he ever had before—the strong bone structure; heavy jaw muscles; wide thin-lipped mouth that somehow was not in the least severe, seemed just now actually kind; the steady eyes that were neither shallow nor deep, their dimension being outward.

Time restarted when Koda spoke again. "I'm not insisting on your resignation, you understand. I do not know your deepest purpose."

It occurred to Varlik that he didn't know it either. "What are the odds of your actually getting the prisoners you're after?" he asked. "And the information?"

"Perhaps five to one that our search teams will find and report the Orlanthan headquarters. If they don't, of course, the action cannot take place. If they do, I would guess the odds to be roughly even that we bring out useful prisoners."

"And the odds of bringing out most of your troops alive?"

The eyes never withdrew. Most men, Varlik would think afterward, could scarcely have discussed the weather with such total equanimity.

"Call it one to two," Koda answered. "Understand though that in war, one cannot know the script; that is part of its charm."

*Its charm.* Varlik could only stare.

"You don't have to decide now," the colonel said. Then he turn͏ picking up a folder, Varlik dismissed from his attention. The ͏ up and left.

That evening after supper, Varlik asked Kusu if ͏ where privately. Kusu suggested one of the emp͏ wanted more privacy than that, so they wal͏ ening prairie. Insects buzzed and chirp͏ overhead, like some feathered project͏ a piercing and protracted "keee͏ veil of stars had crept up the ͏ sending scouts after the horizon.

It occurred to Va͏ technite been foun͏ world? Why had t͏ weren't really pe͏ like their worl͏

*You'd think,* *refuse an assi͏* *gooks. Excep͏* *one did. G͏*

Kusu ͏ about?"

"Abou͏

"All rig͏

"You're be͏ left." He peere͏ die just in this a͏

"Quite probably.͏

"Is that the goal of

"The goal of a T'swa warrior is to play at war, skillfully and with joy. Death is a common accompaniment."

"But . . . it's such an *empty* life!"

"Is it?"

Varlik stopped. "Isn't it?"

"It would be for someone who wanted to raise a family, or paint fine pictures, or"—Varlik could see the eyes turn to him in the near night—"create with words."

"And you kill people!"

"True again."

"Even if they have a new life afterward, the way you believe, you take away from them what they want desperately to keep."

"That too is true, more often than not. But ask yourself who it is we kill."

"What do you mean?"

"We kill those who, knowingly or not, choose to put themselves into battle with us."

"These Birds didn't choose to put themselves into battle with you!" ...lik snapped. "They're just trying to end the slavery they've been ...cted to. I'm surprised you aren't helping them, instead of fighting ... That would be the ethical thing to do."

...ld it?"

...dn't it?"

...ould not solve their problem, and it would worsen the prob- ...federation faces here while putting Tyss at war with the Con-

...e T'swa do not fight. For us, war is a form of play, and ...illfully at it. And true play does not have problems, but ...pportunities.

...see, are a matter of attitude; one being's problem might ...er in the same situation as an opportunity, perhaps ... With the attitude of play, you may see a situation ...eate a different situation in its place, without any ... must succeed. What you think of as success has ...it for the doing.

...rney in which the place you have chosen to ...nt than the traveling."

...gnation, and somehow couldn't find it. At ...n had, snowed by sophistries he couldn't ...ad told him that solid wasn't solid, that ...how—somehow, he felt distinctly better ...go of the matter, and smiled at Kusu,

"You're something," Varlik said. "You know that? All of you are."

"Thank you, Varlik. You are something, too."

For just a moment that stopped Varlik. Then a chuckle welled up in him that grew to a laugh, long and hard. The powerful T'swi kept him company in a rumbling bass until they gripped hands and shook on it.

Varlik had been sitting at a table in the work room of the army's media quarters. Not that he had anything to send to Central News. After making another letter cube for Mauen, he waited for Konni, idly browsing, admiring old field cubes. After a bit it was lunch time, and Konni hadn't appeared. Iryala Video had sent two new teams to Kettle, both at Beregesh today, and she was scheduled to leave for home the next morning. Varlik wanted to talk to her before she left.

Surely she'd show for lunch, he told himself, and got up to leave for the officers' mess. He hadn't reached the door when it opened, and Konni came in.

"What's up?" she asked. "Did you finally make up your mind to go home?"

"Not home. Not yet. The T'swa, both veteran regiments, have a new assignment. The word came in this morning confirming it; we'll be going next Fourday."

She stared at him. "What kind of assignment?"

"They're going to hit the Birds down in the equatorial zone, then blast enough of a hole in the jungle that floaters can come in and take them out."

"And you're going along on *that?*" Her fists were on her hips. "Varlik, you had to be crazy to go out on the last operation. This sounds twice as bad."

"It's five times as important, and I want to be close to it."

"Important how? What's it about?"

"It's confidential. I've already said more than I should."

Her brows drew down angrily. "Are you saying you don't trust me? After the information we've both kept to ourselves?"

"I trust you. But I had to give my word," he added unhappily.

She looked at him, her anger dying.

"It shouldn't be as dangerous for me as the last one," he went on. "For one thing, it's a single quick raid—land, strike, and leave. And I'll be in the least dangerous part of the operation. But, of course, there's always that little chance. So I wanted to tell you that if I'm killed, you're free to do whatever you want with what we recorded on Tyss."

Briefly her eyes tried to pry him open. "You're going to get yourself killed," she said at last.

He didn't answer, just shook his head.

"I'd have propositioned you deks ago," she continued, "but you were married. The reason I didn't was my respect for your wife. But if you're not going to get back to her anyway . . ."

"No, I'll be back. I don't know why I feel so confident, but I'll be back here when it's over—not even wounded this time."

Konni backed off. "Maybe you're right. I hope so." She grinned then, unexpectedly. "Anything I *can* do for you?"

He grinned back. "Sure. You can have lunch with me."

"You've got a date," she said, and took his arm.

# 31

Only the least moon watched, low in the east, little more than a bright point of light and less vivid than a clouded planet.

The floaters settled slowly, dull black landers from the large troopship miles above, guiding vertically down lines of gravitic flux. Eyes could not have seen them, even if there had been sentries above the jungle's canopy—not even as occlusions against the star field overhead, because clouds moving up the bowl of sky were approaching the meridian, eclipsing more and more the view.

To the proper instruments, of course, the floaters would have been as visible as at midday. But such an instrument would have to stand above the forest roof, and would have been detected in advance by recon flights. It had been a radio antenna that brought special attention to the site— a slender steel structure rising inconspicuously a dozen yards above the layered jungle.

Seeing by instrument themselves, and holding formation by keeping each to its own gravitic ordinate, the stealthy floaters stopped their still descent half a hundred feet above the tallest trees, those shaggy giants emergent from the general canopy. Now would come the first real hazard: letting down the troops. If they alarmed the birds and arboreal animals, the general cacophony might draw the attention of unfeathered Birds.

Unlit hatches opened. Slender weighted cables slid out and down, into the foliage below. Only isolated brief complaints could be heard, no more than might happen in the random mini-dramas of an ordinary jungle night. Below some threshold of excitement, silence and concealment were favored over noisy alarm by the jungle galleries.

The creatures near the cables adjusted quickly to their dangling presence and, already alerted, less susceptible to being startled, made even fewer audible responses to the men who followed, despite the movements of cables as they descended, and the release of branches as heavy bodies first depressed and then slipped free of them.

After he'd passed through the dense crown of a canopy tree, Varlik squeezed the let-down control of the harness he rode, slightly speeding his descent. From there to the ground, he passed through the branches of only one frail, light-starved undertree. Then his feet touched down on a narrow twisting root a foot high, and his ankle turned, throwing him heavily to the ground.

At least he hadn't come down on an ant mound, he told himself. The scouts had radioed more than the locations of the military encampment and cave entrances; they'd described as well the ground conditions.

To Varlik it seemed too dark even for the T'swa to see. They'd anticipated that, and the T'swa had night goggles.

Varlik had rejected night goggles. Instead, he took off his battle helmet and put on his monitor visor, then scanned about with his camera. In such dense darkness, visibility was limited even so, and the quality of seeing was strange. Beyond fifty feet he saw only dimly, and beyond eighty nothing at all. Nor was there much undergrowth where he was; by day few plants could photosynthesize in such dense shade.

He could see four T'swa. Two of them were Kusu and Lieutenant Zimsu; he recognized their insignia. Kusu was the platoon sergeant now.

Varlik had been the last man down his cable. Now he heard it twitch, the prelude to its being drawn back up. Half a minute later he watched and recorded it snaking upward out of sight, heard faintly its dangling harnesses swish through branches, and with its passing felt a heavy finality.

Then, visor in place, he put his battle helmet back on his head and reached up to make sure his communicator was turned on.

This was a very different kind of operation from the earlier ones; high mobility wasn't needed here. They'd been put down in the position they were to hold, would make only small adjustments in their line till time to leave. Thus the T'swa here carried and wore equipment that would have been more burden than help up north—not only battle helmets and night goggles, but quantities of grenades, while every third man had a blast hose and a satchel of box magazines for it.

Every third man. They were the ones who would hold their positions if necessary to let the others get away. Abundant explosives had been lowered too, to clear a place for evac floaters when the time came.

Somewhere out in front of them, B Company of the Night Adders was less encumbered. Carrying only rifles, sidearms, and a few grenades, they'd been put down by squads at coordinates where they could cover the trails away from the Bird cave and headquarters area. The scouts were to have

met them there. When the air strike began, they were to pick up fleeing Bird officers, then move quickly with their prisoners toward the
defensive circle formed by the rest of the force, dropping off men as they
went—men who would fight any rearguard action necessary.

The defensive circle was nothing to fight a prolonged action from. There
were too few T'swa for that, and too much cover for attackers, and there'd
be little opportunity to clear fields of fire. They'd clear as much as time
allowed after the bombing began and the need for silence ended. But
ideally, the pickup squads would bring their prisoners while the Birds
were still confused, and the evac floaters would take them out quickly,
with little or no fighting necessary.

And it could happen that way. Or the Birds might respond quickly
and in force.

According to Kusu, this wouldn't have been an exceptionally hazardous action against enemy they'd faced on other worlds, but the Birds were
special. Even on trail interdiction, where the T'swa had been able to choose
the time and place of their hit-and-run ambushes, they'd quickly learned
the quality of the men they fought. Here, on the other hand, the T'swa
were committed to fixed but unfortified positions. It was a question of
speed—how quickly the Birds realized what was happening and responded.
Time would tell. Or as the T'swa said, time would expose the script.

And they would revise it as the cast and stage and props allowed, ad
libbing from moment to moment. That was how Kusu had described battle
to him the day before—an odd concept.

The T'swa had been in a strange, almost joyous calm. Varlik had gotten
used to this, adjusting to their reality, and had even found it rubbing
off on him to the extent that, at times, he'd been almost cheerful.

But not now. Now he had a prime case of nervous gut, even hidden
as he was by opaque and silent darkness. He didn't wonder if the T'swa
were nervous, too; they weren't.

After a time a sound began, a distant susurrus, increasing quickly to
an irregularly pulsing swash of heavy rain upon the jungle roof, rain that
soon began to penetrate the canopy above. Some of the T'swa, taking
advantage of the noise, moved out with their swordlike bayonets and
chopped away what undergrowth and saplings there were. This scarcely
provided a field of fire, but it would help. Somewhere behind them, in
the middle of their ring, two platoons were setting explosives. Some of
the men, with climbing irons, were setting charges well up the trunks
so the trees would come down in sections. Otherwise, many would lodge
crisscross, perhaps denying the floaters adequate landing space.

The men cutting undergrowth finished and returned to lie waiting with
the others. Photography done for the time, Varlik curled on his side and
dozed in semisleep, wakened now and then by water running in his ear

or by infrequent thunder. Before long he became aware that the rain had stopped, though dripping continued from above. Now he could see more and farther than before; dawn was breaking. The morning bird chorus began, and when it ended he slept.

And awoke with a start to the first crash of bombs. He'd expected them louder—the target zone was only a mile away—but the jungle vegetation absorbed and deadened sounds. It was full daylight, and raising his head to look around, he saw the T'swa peering steadily outward. Somewhere out there, not far, lookouts had been posted. His hand touched the holster of his sidearm, then went to his audio recorder and camera.

There was little enough to record—the constant thudding of bombs, the T'swa lying ready with rifles and blast hoses—for about half an hour. No pickup squads arrived with prisoners, but he told himself it was too soon; there hadn't been time for that. Or they might have come through somewhere else. Then rifle fire erupted well up front, spreading, developing into a firefight that went on sporadically for minutes before dying. There'd been blast hoses, and the pickup squads hadn't carried any.

He spoke his thoughts for the record, mentally tuning out the sound of bombing. Without the firefight it seemed almost quiet—an almost-quiet ruptured suddenly by great roaring explosions, almost stopping his heart; the T'swa were blasting their evacuation clearing, a stupendous sound of high explosives and trees crashing. After a moment, pieces of branchwood fell through the canopy to patter on the ground. And when that was over, a matter of seconds, it was truly quiet, because the bombing had stopped.

The silence was brief, a minute or two. Nearby to his left a blast hose ripped a long burst of bullets, to be answered by hose fire from outside the circle, brief but shockingly violent. And close. Then all the T'swa were firing. Rockets hissed and slammed, and Varlik heard insistent Tyspi in his helmet radio, asking the pickup squads to report. None did.

The command came to move back. He did, crawling backward on knees and elbows, pausing frequently to record with his camera. The T'swa withdrew slowly, taking advantage of cover, maintaining fire. The shooting was intense. Lieutenant Zimsu exploded, literally, hit by a rocket. Varlik had seen it in his monitor while scanning with his camera.

After that for a time he didn't know what was happening or what he was doing, until he found himself behind a section of blasted tree trunk near the edge of the evac clearing, which he could see through the fringe of tattered trees behind him. Kusu was kneeling beside him, and a little way off, Captain Tarku crouched.

Kusu was gripping Varlik's shoulder. "Varlik," he was saying in Standard, "go to the clearing. That's an order. Floaters are taking people out.

Sergeant Gis-Tor is in charge of loading, and he knows you're to have priority. I want you out of here."

Varlik nodded, numbly willing. "And keep low!" the T'swa reminded. "I don't want you killed." Kusu peered into Varlik's eyes as if looking for something, then grinned and thrust him on his way.

The Iryalan crawled through debris into the steamy sunlight of the clearing. It was perhaps three hundred feet across, littered with blasted trees. He could see three evac floaters loading personnel, half hidden by jumbled debris, and Varlik paused to use his camera. Another floater, settling in, was hit by a rocket as he watched, and pitched forward, downward, impacting heavily. A few Birds had obviously reached the edge and could see and shoot at the floaters.

The din of firing was continuous now. A floater raised under fire, its rate of lift like a leap, angling up and away. Still another came in, almost recklessly swift, braking abruptly only a few yards above the ground, then settling quickly among the debris to load.

Another popped upward, was hit by a rocket, circled momentarily out of control, was hit again, and fell sideways to the ground. Others, hanging or circling well above, were hidden by jungle and could only be glimpsed. One came in and landed unhit. It occurred to Varlik that the Birds might have let it land, to shoot it down later loaded with men. As if to verify that, another, popping swiftly up, was hit at least twice, to fall back slowly. Another raised. It too was hit, but continued upward and away, as if the round had failed to explode after penetrating. Still another landed, and another.

He realized he'd been crouching there with his camera in his hands, recording. He was supposed to load and leave; no one would ever see his cube if he died here. Cautiously he moved, crouching toward the floaters.

Another floater lifted, jumping as if on a spring, was hit some fifty feet above the ground and fell crashing on top of one still loading. Then Varlik heard a radioed command in Standard.

"Floaters, attention. Floaters, attention. This is Major Masu, acting commander on the ground. Move away. Repeat, move away. Evacuation is cancelled."

That they were to be left here was not what impacted Varlik's mind. Rather, it was that Major Masu was in charge. That meant Biltong and Koda were probably dead. He glimpsed floaters still circling; they hadn't left yet, and he felt a brief surge of pride, for their pilots were Iryalan, or maybe Rombili: Confederatswa.

Again the radio commanded; this time the voice wasn't Masu's. "T'swa, regroup," it said. "Take cover in the clearing."

Of course. The litter of fallen trees here gave better cover than they'd find elsewhere. But where was Kusu? Crouching, crawling over fallen trees, Varlik started back toward where he'd seen him last.

"Lormagen!"

He stopped, knelt. Captain Tarku was on his knees behind a massive fallen trunk, looking at him.

"Where are you going?" Tarku had shouted to be heard. Varlik realized he'd been heading out of the clearing.

"To find Kusu."

"Kusu is dead. Stay here by me."

Varlik scuttled toward the officer. Grief surged, and the thought came that that was silly. Kusu wasn't grieving. Kusu was alive somewhere, laughing at all this. And he . . . Varlik stared at his hands through brimming eyes. He'd lost his camera somewhere, or discarded it. His hands groped. No, it was on its strap, inside his shirt—he held his sidearm in its stead.

Then bullets struck a branch stub in front of him, throwing bark and wood, and he hit the dirt, clinging to it, heart pounding. Someone hurtled over the log to land beside him headlong, and Varlik found himself staring at a Bird, head bullet-shattered. Shoving his sidearm back in its holster, he picked up the Bird's rifle and peered over the log. All he could see on the other side was debris and a T'swa body. Then bullets struck the log inches away, and again he hit the ground, not too shocked to wonder why he wasn't dead.

Off to the west, the bombing had begun again.

Tarku raised up and peered over the log, holding his head sideways, looking awkwardly across his nose to see, exposing almost none of himself. For the moment the shooting had slackened, as if the Birds were preparing something. After a few seconds the captain lowered his head again and spoke calm Tyspi into his mike.

"This is Captain Tarku," he said. "Major Masu is dead and I am in command now. Scorpion A Company, report if you receive me. Over."

The firing had almost died, and Varlik wondered what that meant. "This is Sergeant Gow, in command of A Company. We're at the west edge of the clearing and seem to have twenty or thirty effectives. Over."

The captain ran down the roster of companies of both regiments. Two didn't reply at all. *So few!* Varlik thought. *We're finished; done for.* And wondered that he felt so calm now. He rolled the Bird over and lifted two ammo clips from the man's belt. *I might as well go out like a T'swa,* he told himself.

Then he heard Tarku's voice, both directly and in his radio. "All right, T'swa, on my signal we will charge the enemy. Each of you has my admiration."

He folded the mike away from his mouth and looked at Varlik. "Lormagen," he said, "I want you to stay where you are until the fighting is over. Then call out your surrender in Standard. The Birds will probably come and take you prisoner; you should find that interesting. And it will be safer to have them come and get you than to try to make your way to them."

Varlik simply stared. Then, surprisingly, the captain winked before speaking to his radio again.

"Do I have trumpeters?"

Varlik heard the radio answer "yes." Two yeses.

"Good," said Tarku. "Sound the dirge, then the attack."

Not far away, surprisingly close, a trumpet spoke clearly, its sound as precise as if at parade, joined in mid-phrase by another some distance off. Tarku gathered his legs beneath him, and Varlik noticed now that one trouser leg was soaked with blood. It had been out of sight till then.

The trumpet call was something Varlik had never heard before. Not mournful. Not even solemn. Not like any dirge he'd heard or imagined. More like a fanfare—a fanfare on two trumpets, an announcement of death without regret. Then abruptly it changed, became an exultant battlecry, quick-paced, and the T'swa nearby rose up, rifles in hand, bayonets fixed, the captain vaulting over the fallen tree. The trumpets were almost drowned out by the sudden shattering roar of gunfire.

Varlik clung to the ground. The roaring thinned, thinned, then after a couple of minutes stopped, leaving only sporadic shots and short bursts. It occurred to him that no T'swi was likely to be captured conscious; even down they'd fight to the death with grenades and sidearms.

*The Regiment is dead,* he thought. And felt no grief now despite the moisture that blurred his vision. With a grimy hand he wiped it clear. No grief, only numbness. He sensed—possibly heard—movement, and lay still, eyes slitted. Someone passed about seventy feet to his left, tall and slender, sinewy, wearing Bird loincloth and battle harness, and disappeared out of his small field of vision.

It occurred to Varlik to look at the Bird rifle in his hands, look for the serial number. There was none. As his camera recorded the absence, the unmarked receiver where the number should have been, he wondered if the army had noticed this, and what they'd made of it.

The shooting seemed to have stopped entirely.

*And here I am alive. What I have to do now is get back to Iryala and find out why the regiment had to die.*

At the moment he had no doubt he'd do it. And no doubt that Iryala was where the answer lay.

He rose to his knees, raised his head, and shouted in Standard as loudly as he could: "I surrender! I surrender to the Orlanthan Army!" Then he tossed the rifle away and his sidearm after it, sat back against the log, and waited for them to come get him.

# PART FIVE
## *Finding the Trail*

# 32

Sitting against the log waiting, Varlik sank into a mental and emotional fog. At some point he took off his battle helmet and left it on the ground. Later he roused enough to call out again, and later again, then wondered vaguely if they were interested or whether perhaps he'd be sitting there when it started to get dark.

He became aware that the sounds of bombing had stopped, though he wasn't sure how long before. Perhaps the army felt they'd destroyed everything worth destroying here. Maybe they had. He began to rouse himself mentally, took another of the mineral tablets he'd been issued for this tropical mission, and drank the last of his water. His watch told him it was after 06.40, and the day's heat was building. He began to consider hiking in the direction of Bird headquarters, then became aware of being watched. Slowly he raised both hands empty and open overhead.

"I surrender," he called.

There were three of the Birds. To him they said nothing, and among themselves spoke their own language. One of them took his bayonet, camera and belt recorder, and his light field pack. A second searched his person, not particularly roughly, while the third tied his hands behind his back. Then they took him to a broad, well-packed trail where they began to trot, though not so rapidly that he had trouble keeping up with his hands tied, and soon he could hear the sound of chopping. Before long they came to men working, cutting saplings and vines and carrying them westward—the same direction that Varlik was being taken.

He began to miss a major use of the hands on Kettle—wiping sweat from the eyebrows. By that time his mind had begun to function more normally, though emotionally he was still numb. The sight of dead T'swa didn't touch him.

Shortly his captors turned aside on a lesser trail, and here too were work parties, numerous now, carrying saplings, long poles, matting, and other material, at least some of which he supposed had been salvaged from the bombed area. They were, he decided, moving camp to a new location.

After perhaps a mile more, he could see concentrated activity ahead: the new campsite. Shortly one of the Birds said something, and they halted. One uncoiled a leather thong from his belt, looped it around Varlik's neck and knotted it, pulling hard on the knot. It would, Varlik thought, be difficult to remove without cutting. Not that that made any difference; he had no intention whatever of trying to escape.

The one who'd given orders looked him over, then drew a heavy-bladed knife and, stepping around Varlik, cut his hands free. After tying the other end of his neck tether to a liana, the man departed, leaving the other two with Varlik. Both the Birds sat down, eyes on their prisoner, and Varlik, after hesitating, also sat, wondering if they'd roust him to his feet again. It was encouraging that so far he hadn't been harmed or even directly threatened.

He looked the two over obliquely, not wanting to offend them, and could read nothing in their faces. But they talked calmly enough between themselves, with no indication that they might abuse him. Tall and slender, they were a little darker than himself. The Birds at Aromanis hadn't seemed like these; the physiques had been similar but the demeanors different. These people bore themselves with calm self-certainty. *Rather like T'swa,* he thought.

After a few minutes the third man returned, accompanied by a considerably older Bird whose breechclout was indigo, and who wore in addition an indigo headband. At their approach, the two guards got up, and Varlik also; the older man seemed clearly to be an officer.

He looked Varlik up and down from a distance of six feet, curious rather than hostile or gloating, then spoke in Standard. "Who are you?"

"My name is Varlik Lormagen."

"Why were you accompanying the T'swa?"

*The man knows what the T'swa are called,* Varlik told himself. *And he speaks Standard. He's no jungle savage. He knows; if he wanted to, he could tell me who's behind this insurrection.*

At that moment Varlik knew how he would get out of this place, and his mind cleared, became sharp and directed.

"I'm a news correspondent from the planet Iryala," Varlik answered. "I've been with the T'swa in order to tell the people of the Confederation how the T'swa train and fight."

While he spoke, he watched the man for any sign of confusion, blankness, irritation, which would suggest he hadn't understood; the words and concepts would be unfamiliar to a true gook. But instead the old Bird's face reflected thought, calculation.

"Perhaps," Varlik continued, "I could describe the life and training of your warriors for my people."

The Bird regarded him calmly. "I will discuss you with certain others. We will decide what to do with you. Meanwhile, if you have urgent needs and cannot make them understood, speak my name, Ramolu, to your guards. They will send for someone who knows your language. But do so only if the need is severe; do not presume upon our tolerance. You are, after all, our prisoner."

"Yes, sir. And General Ramolu, sir, I have a—what is called a camera. It captures pictures. And a recorder that captures sounds. Do you understand? They . . ."

"The corporal has shown me what he took from you."

Varlik nodded. "If you are interested in my suggestion, they will be helpful in letting my people know what your soldiers are like. I'd like to have them back."

Lips pursed, Ramolu studied Varlik for a long moment, then spoke rapid Orlanthan to the three guards. The corporal unslung the instruments and handed them to Varlik.

"And spare recorder cubes are in my field pack."

Ramolu took the pack, hunted through it, and finding nothing harmful, handed it also to Varlik. Then he turned and walked away, in a manner that reminded Varlik of a T'swa dismissal.

Apparently the Bird *was* a general. At least, Varlik told himself, he hadn't reacted visibly to being addressed as one. It was as if he was used to it.

Varlik recorded his surroundings and guards with his camera, then switched it off. Gradually his earlier detached, slow-motion feeling returned. One of his guards took the canteens, including Varlik's, and left, returning with them full. Then briefly it rained again, heavy and warm, steamy. Later a Bird arrived with gruel in a clay bowl, and meat wrapped in a leaf; they proved edible.

A notion occurred to Varlik, and he tried speaking Tyspi to his guards, to no avail.

Also he wondered about certain things: What had happened to queer the raid—it shouldn't have gone *that* badly. They'd been attacked almost as soon as the bombing began, as if the Birds had been expecting them. Of course, they could have been detected in the night, and the Birds could have found their positions by dawn light, but that seemed unlikely. It was more as if they'd known in advance.

And had Ramolu become as familiar with the Confederation, its language, its technology, as he seemed, without going off-planet? Varlik doubted it. He never wondered if Ramolu was an escaped slave, though; nothing about the man fitted that.

The guards were relieved by a new shift, and the new men understood no Tyspi either, nor Standard. Then a young officer came, who also spoke no Standard, and with the guards, took Varlik to a rude shelter, a roof without walls. Ramolu was there with five other Birds who, like Ramolu, wore indigo loincloths and headbands. They had no chairs, but waited squatting, not rising at Varlik's approach. That surprised Varlik. They should have moved to dominate him, stand over him. Instead they seemed content with the knowledge, on both sides, that they were the masters and he the prisoner.

When he entered, he too squatted. His guards remained standing. Once down, Varlik turned on his recorder. "I'd like to record this in both sound and pictures," he said. "With your approval."

Ramolu nodded, casually waving a hand. "You tolerate our heat," he said. "I am surprised."

"I've been living with the T'swa for months now, and training with them. One either comes to tolerate the heat or collapses from it. Only three weeks ago I returned to Orlantha from Tyss; it is very hot on Tyss, too."

Ramolu seemed to know what *Tyss* was, for again he showed no sign of blankness, confusion, or irritation. "And what were you doing on Tyss?"

"I'd been wounded, and spent part of my recovery time there, to better understand and describe the T'swa to my people."

Ramolu smiled slightly. "And did you? Come to understand the T'swa?"

"Somewhat, I hope. Certainly I've gotten used to them, learned to feel comfortable with them."

Ramolu didn't react facially. "What would you tell the people of the Confederation about us," he asked, "if we allowed you to return to them?"

For a moment, with the sudden realization that his ploy might work, Varlik actually stopped breathing. "I would report what I saw. I would show them the battle, in the pictures I have taken. And I would tell them what the T'swa said of you: that you are the best fighting men they'd faced. And these T'swa were veteran troops. They'd fought on one world and another for fourteen years."

"Ah, but the T'swa are gooks, are they not? Like us. Great warriors, of course, but gooks. We are more interested in what the people of the Confederation think of us. What *do* they think of us?"

"To them you are a faceless enemy who prevents them from getting technite."

Steady hazel eyes held Varlik's during a brief silence. Finally Ramolu spoke again. "And what do *you* think of us?"

The question took Varlik by surprise. "I hadn't thought about it. The T'swa said you are not an enemy—that you are simply someone with whom they shared a war. I have been somewhat influenced by their viewpoint."

"But the Confederation thinks of us as the enemy."

"Oh, yes. Very much so."

"And you do not."

"*Enemy* is a consideration from a viewpoint. I learned that from the

T'swa. From my viewpoint you are not my enemy. But from your view-point, you may be."

Ramolu eyed him as Koda might have. "Suppose you ruled the Con-federation. What would you do about us?"

"I would—I would ask to confer with your leader. I'd offer to buy the technite mines from you and pay you a duty on all technite removed. I would offer to hire your people to mine it, and if they didn't want to, I'd bring in miners of my own. There would be no more slavery."

"And what of Aromanis?"

"Aromanis would not be important to me."

"If you, as a teller of the war, made such a suggestion to your people, of what use would it be to us?"

"Some people would like the idea; maybe many would. I first heard it from a common soldier from Iryala—Corporal Duggan. What would you think of it as an Orlanthan?"

"I find it attractive." Ramolu eyed Varlik quizzically. "And what do you think of me, an Orlanthan who speaks your language with considerable facility and knows enough about other worlds to talk with you as I have? What does this mean to you?"

Varlik looked at the tallish, graying, loose-jointed Bird who squatted opposite him in a loincloth, speaking Standard more precisely than most Iryalans. Only a light, singsong tonality clearly marked his speech as foreign.

"A Confederation officer, Colonel Carlis Voker, has pointed out to me numerous anomalies regarding what is called the Orlanthan insur-gency. He felt they pointed to some Confederation world or faction cooperating with you." Varlik was talking ahead of his thoughts, winging it. "So I'm not astonished to find someone like you here. Colonel Voker wouldn't be either, or General Lamons. Or His Majesty, the King. They'd expect it.

"Whoever equipped and trained your army has reasons of their own for doing it. It might be they wouldn't like the Confederation to make an offer like the one I mentioned. But it's an offer whose time has come, and I speak to many, many people via pictures and words that travel widely by something like radio. And even the rulers listen."

*It had to be the T'swa, he told himself—the T'swa, who obviously have their own technite. It not only looks as if they'd armed and trained the Birds; they'd educated their senior officers, at least. Who else could produce a man like Ramolu?*

*And the T'swa had sacrificed their regiments as a cover!*

The Orlanthan was eyeing Varlik with one brow raised. "You are not a man greatly burdened with modesty," said Ramolu, "but perhaps modesty would be inappropriate."

He turned and began to speak musical Orlanthan to the five others who wore indigo, as if summarizing the interrogation. Three of them seemed already to have understood, for they were looking at the other two instead of at the speaker. When he had finished, they conferred for several minutes, then Ramolu turned back to Varlik.

"We have decided to send you back to your people with some T'swa wounded—those fit to travel."

It was as simple as that.

After that he was tethered in a shelter not far off, still under guard. It seemed clear that the six whom Varlik now thought of as "the general staff" were the leaders here, perhaps even the leaders of the whole insurgency, for they'd made the decision themselves, without further consultation.

And repeatedly he found himself wondering if he really would be sent home with what he knew, what he'd seen. It was as if they considered it unimportant. He was certain they were too alert and intelligent to have overlooked it.

# 33

Varlik waited tethered in his small, open-sided shelter while one day passed and then another. Ramolu didn't appear again, but guards saw that their prisoner was fed and his canteen refilled as needed, all without visible animosity.

Not that it was a pleasant interlude. His sleep stirred ugly with nightmares. He'd waken gasping and desperate, or desolate, the dream content slipping away even as he opened his eyes, leaving him with no more than the sense that it had been about the regiment, or the Birds, Voker or Mauen or Konni. And sweatier than even the hot Kettle night accounted for.

His most restful sleep was in naps by day, and he slept about a dozen hours out of the twenty. To occupy his waking time, he undertook to learn Orlanthan from his guards—there were two at almost all times— and they were casually agreeable to cooperating. In part they taught him nouns by pointing and naming. Fingers walked and ran and jumped. He learned to count, name trees and body parts, insects and food items. And he recorded all of it, interjecting Standard equivalents. Nor was there any sign that they were playing word jokes on him, and at any rate it passed the time.

Varlik realized that this decent treatment, this absence of abuse, was remarkable, given what he knew of the Birds' history. He did not appreciate, of course, how bad it might have been. He had no criteria for comparison, nor did his imagination stretch far in that direction.

Meanwhile, there was no further bombing.

He wondered how the Birds planned to return him north; by their long trails through the forest, no doubt. It had to be at least a thousand miles to Beregesh, and he didn't know how well he'd hold up, hiking day after day. He'd done well enough on the trail raids, but that had been only four days, and the humidity there hadn't been nearly as bad as here. The mineral tablets would help, as long as they lasted, but he only had about a week's worth. He stopped taking any while he waited; he'd save them for the trek. He was almost out of water-treatment capsules.

On the morning of the fourth day an elderly Bird appeared wearing a cross-slung rifle. He was unusually short, still sinewy beneath age-loosened skin; he leered almost toothlessly down at Varlik, who sat cross-legged on the ground.

"Me boss you fella," he said. "Me name Curly. Take you fella you people, give you back. Me talk good Standard, give orders, you and black fellas go along you."

Varlik doubted that the man was anybody's boss; he wore no armband or headband of rank. His function was probably to relay orders. Then the guard corporal spoke Orlanthan to the old man. "You stand up," the old man ordered Varlik. "Some fella sweat bird him cover you eyes."

Varlik stood up reluctantly. Did he have to walk a thousand miles blindfolded? What reason would they have for that? They tied his wrists in front of him, which at least would let him wipe away sweat. A hand grasped his arm, letting him know it was time to march, and blindly, hesitantly, he began walking. It wasn't as bad as he thought it might be. Once he relaxed and trusted his guide, it went almost without a stumble.

Curly! A Standard nickname. The man must be an actual escapee, an ex-slave from either Beregesh or Kelikut, probably born into slavery, Varlik decided. He seemed different from the other Birds here, at least those Varlik had seen much of, as if the jungle nation had evolved its own culture, different from that of the labor camps and no doubt from the original tribal cultures, too.

Varlik knew at once when they were joined by the T'swa. Not that they spoke. But they moved, walked, and already his ears were functioning more perceptively. And the wounded men slowed the pace markedly. At this rate, he told himself, it would take them two or three deks to walk to Beregesh. But the slower pace would be easier on the long, hot trail.

It would be ironic if they were killed by army gunfire when they got up there. And even more so if they were killed by T'swa hunter/killer teams, though that was less likely; T'swa raiders were much likelier to see who they were shooting at than the soldiers were.

The trail changed. The new one seemed to be the hovertruck trail the scouts had reported, that led beneath the trees from a small river to the storage caves. It seemed fairly smooth, and wide enough that some of their guards were several feet to each side. Here and there it went through shallow water, once halfway to his knees, the bottom soft and mucky but not treacherous.

After a while he smelled something besides jungle, recognized it as a river in high summer—everlasting high summer here. Shortly they slowed, stopped, and he could hear thumps—the sound of activity on small boats. Then someone led him out onto a mudbank, and uncertainly, with a bumped shin, he got into a narrow, unsteady boat, to be led along it crouching, then seated on the bottom by someone wading alongside. His legs were somewhat bent, his feet against someone ahead of him—a T'swi, he supposed.

From the sounds and delay, they were loading several boats, and perhaps some wounded T'swa were having to be manhandled in. Finally his boat was pushed free of the shore, and he heard the bump and scrape of paddles on gunwales, helping the current move them. They were headed downstream. And from what he remembered of maps he'd seen, downstream here meant south, not north. He wondered what that might mean; it worried him.

It was tiresome and eventually painful, sitting on the boat's uncushioned bottom with nothing to lean back against and his hands bound in front of him. He wondered how long it would be like this, and whether he'd become comfortable with it after a while. There were almost no distractions, only the smooth rhythmic sounds of paddling, and now and then a few words of musical Bird, unintelligible to him. Once there was a low tense call from another boat, a break in the paddling, a short burst of rifle shots. Then there came a few rapid syllables, more shooting, a brief spate of rapid Bird again, with laughter, the tension gone. Some animal, Varlik thought, something dangerous, perhaps a river creature, and they'd killed it. The blindfold and bonds exasperated him more than ever now: He'd like to have seen and recorded the event on video.

The river was narrow, he knew, because on the recon photos much of it was completely overhung with trees, showing only as discontinuous interruptions in the jungle roof. Of course, the giants along the banks would lean out over the water and reach with branches farther still, to take better advantage of the sunlight, but still the river could hardly be

much wider than seventy or eighty feet. And the occasional cries of birds
and tree animals were sometimes close at hand, even overhead.

Once he got thirsty and spoke the Orlanthan word for water. He
couldn't understand the reply, but after a bit someone handed him a
canteen cup and he drank, probably river water, he decided.

Thunder rumbled distantly, then nearer, then boomed not far away, and
rain began to pelt, then pour. Quickly he was sitting in water, but he had
no complaint because, warm though the rain was, it cooled. When it
stopped, however, after perhaps half an hour, the air was steamier than ever.

His physical discomfort, which had become acute in the second hour,
deadened, along with his mental functioning. Once they stopped to eat,
but he was not untied nor his blindfold removed. A Bird held the food
in what seemed to be a large leaf, and at Curly's instruction, Varlik ate
by putting his face to the food.

It was late in the day when they stopped and the bow was pulled up
on a shore. Someone took Varlik's blindfold off, and he blinked in the
daylight, looking around. The sun was low, and the river had widened
or, more likely, was a different stream, some hundred yards across.

He counted seventeen T'swa distributed in six canoes. Two other canoes
seemed to have carried an escort of guards. On the shore by the boats,
guards and paddlers sat or squatted or walked around. Varlik decided that
the guards were those who carried their rifles in their hands, the paddlers those who wore theirs cross-slung.

The canoes had been carefully hewed and hollowed from single logs,
their sides no thicker than a board. Clearly the Birds had been supplied
primarily with military necessities; beyond those, they apparently made
do with primitive resources.

Just ahead was a river greater yet, a quarter mile wide or more, into
which this river flowed. The shore they were on was the angle between
rivers. Varlik looked around and found the old ex-slave, who now sat by
a tree. "Curly," Varlik called, "what happens next?"

"You people they come sky, take away you. When little dark come. Me
people got far talker, they tell you people what place."

"Can we get out and walk around?"

The old man looked at him a long moment. "You anyway got to be
in *riilmo*. You people come down on water, take you out *riilmo*. No place
here"—he patted the shore beside him with one hand—"no place here
they come down. Not nuf room."

*Riilmo* must be Orlanthan for canoe, Varlik decided. A Beregesh slave
would never have been exposed to the Standard for it. And the old man
was right—there wasn't room on the shore for a floater.

"Can we get out and walk around now? Until 'little dark' comes?"

Curly's old eyes glittered but he only shrugged. Then a sergeant asked him something in Orlanthan, and the old man answered. The sergeant spoke again, again the ex-slave shrugged, then the sergeant called an order. Several Birds came down to the boats and began helping the prisoners to their feet, and over the gunwales into the shallow water.

For the next hour or so they lay around on the shore, the T'swa saying little. It was as if there was nothing to say, for they didn't seem depressed. Perhaps, Varlik decided, they were adjusting to their new condition as survivors being set free. Only one of them was anyone Varlik recognized, though in his own uniqueness he'd be known by all of them. It didn't seem appropriate yet to question them—ask how it had felt to see their lifelong friends killed around them, or what it was like to be without a regiment. There'd be time enough for interviews at Aromanis.

Then, in the fleeting equatorial twilight, a floater appeared. Three floaters actually: a large evac floater accompanied by two gunships that stood off a hundred yards or so. The prisoners were loaded into the canoes again, and stolid paddlers took them to midriver. Gently the evac floater settled almost to the water, nearly touching Varlik's canoe, and two paddlers grasped the edges of the wide door to steady their dugout. Cautiously Varlik half-stood and climbed in, helped by med techs and followed by the two T'swa.

Then the floater raised slightly and moved to the next canoe.

Inside was dark, and somehow unreal. A quiet medic asked if he was hurt or ill, and Varlik answered no, he was fine. The T'swa were helped to cotlike stretchers while Varlik walked forward to clear the door. When all seventeen T'swa had been loaded, a handful of Birds—exchange captives—were transferred to the canoes. Finally the doors were closed, and the floater rose smoothly and swung away. Through a window, Varlik watched the dugouts disappear in the thickening dusk, and with a dream-like objectivity noted that he felt no jubilation.

Then the cabin lights came on and the medics began to examine the wounded.

# 34

It was little short of dawn when the evac floater landed at the base hospital at Aromanis. Because he'd eaten native food and drunk untreated water, Varlik too was entered, to be checked for parasites. The first thing he did was get a letter cube off to Mauen telling her that he was safe.

As usual, the T'swa wards were well occupied, mostly with young troopers of the Ice Tiger Regiment. From the veteran regiments there'd been fewer than thirty until the seventeen arrived, and the word was that only some forty had been evacuated unwounded, or too slightly wounded to remain hospitalized. Along with a couple of hundred disabled or undergoing rehabilitation from earlier actions, they were all that remained alive of more than eighteen hundred who'd landed on Kettle scant deks ago—they and a handful still among the Birds, too badly injured to be moved.

The forty able-bodied, informed of the exchange, had been at the hospital to greet them. The greeting had been neither exuberant nor somber. There were wide grins, handshakes, soft laughter, and an incredible sense of spiritual togetherness that left Varlik feeling left out. Not that he was ignored or slighted; he simply could not share in the feeling that was part of it, and that depressed him. He kept busy through it with his camera.

The new media people had not been informed of their pending arrival, and none of them were there.

There'd been a letter cube waiting for him from Mauen—long and warm and carefully devoid of worries or problems. He hoped she wouldn't hear of his brief "missing" status before she got his letter.

His nights in the hospital weren't as bad as some in the jungle, but the days were worse; around him were bandaged reminders of the regiment and what had happened to it. After two days of tests, shots, and observation, he was discharged from the hospital. He went straight to army headquarters, where he was accosted by a newly arrived young man from Central News and a team from Iryala Video. They seemed ridiculously impressed with him—the "white T'swa," they said he was called back home.

Somehow they angered him, though he knew the feeling was unreasonable—a matter of his own condition, not theirs. He shook loose from them as quickly as he decently could and went hopefully to Voker's office. Voker was the only one at Aromanis that he wanted to see. But the colonel was at Beregesh, expected back that day. Finally, Varlik arranged to leave Kettle on the next ship to Iryala, the *Quaranth* again, two days hence.

Then he arranged with Trevelos for a place of his own to work; he wanted privacy from the new media people. Trevelos was friendlier than ever, eager to help; the brief barrier between them had left no scars. Varlik spent most of the day editing his material and preparing his report. He didn't show Ramolu, though, only talked about him, as if the man had refused to be recorded. His recordings of Ramolu weren't news; they were *evidence*.

When he was done, he found Voker in and played it for him—the battle in the jungle and what he'd been able to record of the Birds. Voker, in turn, told him of fierce firefights between Birds and T'swa around Beregesh. The Birds had also mounted more concentrated hunt-and-kill sweeps to cut down T'swa trail harassment, resulting in increased casualties on both sides. But meanwhile, progress on rebuilding the refinery had improved markedly.

It had been necessary, Voker said, to keep revising upward the estimated size of insurgent forces. The figure now was thirty to fifty thousand, with no confidence that further upward revisions wouldn't be necessary.

Over Voker's good Crodelan whiskey, they speculated on why the Birds had blindfolded him and the T'swa while taking them out for evacuation—what was it they didn't want them to see?—and came up with nothing compelling. Perhaps nothing was the answer. Again Varlik didn't mention the arsenal on Tyss, and withheld his belief in T'swa complicity. He agreed to play his report again for Lamons at the next day's staff meeting.

After supper Varlik went to the T'swa camp. The men of the two veteran regiments shared a single company area, with only a few men to a tent. The Ice Tiger Regiment had moved into the rest of the camp, but most of them were south now, fighting.

Varlik didn't feel right with the T'swa anymore. He felt an urgency, a compulsion, to get home to Iryala. There, he told himself, was the answer to the Kettle mystery. Not its roots, perhaps, but on Iryala he would learn what those roots were.

The general's staff meeting wasn't particularly interesting, what Varlik saw and heard of it. After a little, he was asked courteously to leave; what would follow was confidential. He seriously doubted that the confidential session would be very interesting either. *You people think* you *have secrets!* he said to himself as he left. Afterward, he talked to the other media people. The new man from Central News talked a good job, but that he was still at Aromanis instead of Beregesh suggested otherwise to Varlik.

Most of the rest of the day, Varlik hung around the T'swa wards where the wounded from the Red Scorpion and Night Adder Regiments were. He got their views on what the future held for them: Some would marry, have families. For a few there would be lodge-related jobs—scouting children who seemed to have the warrior purpose, or training recruits, or administrative jobs, or maintenance or other duties. Others would take outside jobs. Several would join a monastery and become masters of wisdom; some of the best-known masters had earlier been warriors.

For him there was Central News. It hit him then for the first time that he didn't want to work for Central News anymore. He told himself that maybe he'd feel different about it by the time he got back. Fendel would give him an interesting assignment and he'd be ready to go again. But he didn't really believe it.

That evening he bought a bottle of decent whiskey and got drunk by himself. The next day, hung over, he boarded his old friend, the IWS *Quaranth,* for the trip home.

# 35

On the trip home, Varlik was effectively a recluse. At first various ship's officers tried to strike up conversations, for he'd become more a celebrity than he'd realized, and they were eager to question him about the war. But Varlik's answers were brief and evasive, though by intrinsic courtesy he avoided rudeness. He took to finding an unoccupied table at meals, and after a few days only Mikal Brusin gave him any attention at all.

Brusin was an exception, of course—an old friend—and Varlik had accepted the mate's invitation to a drink and a visit the first day. But after half an hour of avoiding the enigmas that had trapped so much of his attention, it seemed to Varlik that he was repeating himself. Brusin was too perceptive to be offended when Varlik excused himself. He could see the man was troubled, and connected it with the death of so many friends. So he didn't push—merely repeated occasionally his offer of a drink, usually declined and never leading to much talk.

To pass the long trip, Varlik again borrowed a firefighter's suit, and worked out long and hard in the gym. It helped him sleep, which he did a lot of, although here too he was often beset by bad dreams. Unintentionally, it also added to his mystique as "the white T'swi."

On the first day he'd checked the computer for instructional material on the Orlanthan language, and found nothing. So he played and replayed the cube he'd made in the Bird camp, finding in Bird conversations many of the words they'd taught him the meanings of—these numbered more than forty. Then, with these to start with, he'd analyzed the possible meanings of words he'd recorded but hadn't been taught. In this way, and because the language was agglutinative, he increased his vocabulary to about sixty words whose meanings he felt fairly confident of, with about fifty more whose meanings he could reasonably guess at. Then, although he knew almost nothing of Orlanthan grammar, he used his small vocabulary—including words with guessed-at meanings—in every combination he could think of, giving him mastery of what he knew. Probably, he told himself, his skill with Bird resembled Curly's skill with Standard, though Curly's vocabulary was no doubt larger and more functional. But if he was ever again in Kettle's equatorial jungle, he'd have a basis for communicating.

Not that he ever expected or intended to be. His language studies and drills served briefly as a pastime—something to do besides work out, sleep, and sit reading in the ship's library.

Eventually, the day of landfall arrived. And conscious of his aloofness on the trip, Varlik made a point at breakfast of going around the officers' mess shaking the hand of every man there, thanking them for the voyage. The thank-you didn't make a great deal of sense, and had he delivered it coolly, might have been taken as hauteur. But it came across with a tinge of regret, almost as apology, which in a sense it was, and when they left the messroom, in almost every case it was with the opinion that the white T'swi was a good guy, if not very social.

At 07.77, ship's time, the *Quaranth* came out of warp, and Varlik went to the observation room to watch intently the brilliantly glinting point that was Iryala grow to a beautiful cobalt and white orb, then to a looming planetary ball that moved in on them until it blocked out the sky. Soon a planetscape formed beneath him and Landfall appeared, spreading to cover the view.

He could see the spaceport, watched it grow and spread until it was the ground. Service trucks stood or moved; workers watched upward or went about their work. The *Quaranth* settled, touched down almost imperceptibly. He was back on Iryala.

# 36

It was 09.63, nearly midday, in Landfall and by ship's time, too. With a long layover planned, ship's time had been gradually adjusted until it agreed with destination time, helping circadian rhythms into sync.

In the terminal, Mauen had come into the reception area from the glassed viewing deck. She'd been waiting for almost three hours, had been there early, not wanting to miss him if the *Quaranth* should arrive ahead of schedule. Space flights seldom missed schedule by more than minutes, but she was taking no chances.

She wore her prettiest—a new sheer yellow dress with white under-lining, of party quality but wearabout cut that showed quite a bit of pretty leg. Her hair was newly coifed, and she'd taken more than usual care with her makeup.

The first man in the door was Varlik—from his eagerness to see her, she was sure. But preoccupied, he almost didn't notice as she started toward him; he had other things on his mind, and somehow it hadn't occurred to him that she'd have gotten off work to meet him. He'd planned to take a cab to the office and report in, then ring Konni. But Mauen called his name as she ran, jerking his eyes to her. Then, after the merest lag, he was running too, to set down his bags and gather her in his arms, hugging her too tightly, his mission suddenly forgotten. They kissed avidly until they became aware that people were staring.

"I can't believe how much I missed you," he breathed.

She noticed neither the underlying profundity of his words nor their surface absurdity, hearing only the love they expressed. "It seemed like forever!" she murmured back. "Half a year."

He signaled a luggageman and, with his bags being carried, walked hand in hand with her through the building and out to the cab area, where the first cabbie in line stowed Varlik's bags, then held the door for them.

"Where to, sir?" he asked.

The sight of Mauen had banished office, report, and phone call from Varlik's mind. "Media Apartments Three," he said.

Varlik came out of the bathroom belting on his robe, poured a drink, then went out onto the canopied balcony where he sat down on a chair. The afternoon sun was warm, though the season was late. Many trees were already bare; on the rest the foliage had turned—yellow, bronze, red. He sipped his drink reflectively, and a minute later Mauen joined him. When she sat, a knee peeked out at him from her robe.

"Do you feel properly welcomed?" she asked.

"That was maximum welcome. More welcome than that I could hardly handle."

"You've always had a nice body," she said. "Now you're so hard and muscular it's almost unbelievable. But I like you this way." She touched his hand. "And I'll like you just as much if you gain weight again."

They touched glasses and drank. Then he held his up to the sun, eyeing thoughtfully the gleam through amber brandy. "I'd like to make a phone call," he said. "Invite a colleague to dinner with us, to talk business. My business and hers. Yours now." He saw Mauen's smile slip at the pronoun *hers*. "Her name is Konni Wenter. She was on Kettle for Iryala Video," he went on, "and we ran into some strange things—evidence of a criminal conspiracy against the Confederation. We agreed to hold back what we found out until we learned more."

Mauen said nothing, asked no questions, simply waited soberly for Varlik to continue.

He got up. "Come back in," he said. "I'll show you some pictures that I haven't made available for newsfacs or videocasts. We can talk about what they mean, or seem to mean."

She followed him in and closed the doors behind them, feeling chilly now, and dialed the heat control while he activated the wall viewer and inserted a cube. Then they sat down together, and he played first his talk with Ramolu, pointing out the anomalies not only of the man's fluency in Standard but his obvious knowledge of the Confederation and technology and his general sophistication.

"So how did he get like that?" Varlik asked. "Who trained the Birds? Or probably the more correct question is who trained and educated the leaders like Ramolu, because the common Bird soldier doesn't speak Standard—or Tyspi, the language of Tyss. Probably the people who trained them are the people who armed them. Here's one of their rifles." He moved the halted sequence to the image of the rifle he'd picked up in the jungle, and pointed out its lack of serial number.

"Konni and I, after being wounded, went to Tyss for rehabilitation, and walked into town from the hospital there. We recorded this." He sat quietly, letting Mauen watch and listen to the two children who'd talked with Konni and him. Varlik stopped the sequence after each line of dialog, to translate from the Tyspi. "Are you Ertwa?" asked the little girl, and from the audio, Konni's voice answered, "I don't know what 'Ertwa' means."

"They are Splennwa," the little boy corrected his sister. "Ertwa were very long ago."

Mauen interrupted, and Varlik touched the *pause* key again. "What are 'Ertwa?'" she asked.

"I have no idea. The point is that he responded as if he assumed we were from Splenn. That suggests that Splennites visit Tyss often enough that people are aware of them as frequent visitors—even little children."

Then he played the audio recording of the teaching brother, Ban-Shum, their host and guide in Oldu Tez-Boag, who could speak Orlanthan. Why would a teacher on Tyss know Orlanthan?

And finally, he showed his video recording of the arsenal in the Jubat Forest and the weapons without serial numbers, then removed from a bag the T'swa-made sidearm he'd taken, also without serial number.

"How does all of this seem to you?" he asked. And realized that his body was tense, trembling slightly at some undefined stress.

"It looks . . . it looks as if it might be the T'swa who armed and trained the Orlanthans. But . . . where does Splenn fit in?"

"Splennites could have smuggled the weapons from Tyss to Kettle. Splenn has space ships, and at least in adventure fiction the Splennites are supposed to be smugglers. But I haven't told you all of it yet." He explained his theory—Konni's actually—that the T'swa had a technite mine of their own.

"And—why do you want to ask Miss Wenter over?"

"To show her what I recorded in the jungle. And she'd planned to see what she could learn here; I want to know what she's found out."

Mauen nodded. "All right. Ask her." She paused. "Why do you think there's anything to learn about this, here on Iryala?"

"The T'swa colonels wanted their regiments publicized here. Why? And more than the colonels wanted it; they'd already arranged for publicity to be channeled through the T'swa ambassador here. Besides that, apparently someone had expected both Central News and Iryala Video to have the T'swa featured." *And got the king to contract personally for the regiments,* Varlik added to himself; he'd never looked at that angle before. "It's as if someone here, someone in a very high place, is involved."

Mauen got up and went to her desk in their activities room, then returned with an address book. "Perhaps I have something helpful," she said. Varlik looked at her, puzzled. "I got interested in the T'swa from your reports," she went on. "Lots of people did, but especially me because I'm your wife. So I called the Royal Library for anything they might have on them. I didn't find much. But I thought there might be material that I didn't know how to access, so I called the library's consulting office. When the supervisory consultant realized I was your wife, she gave me the name and number of an expert on Tyss and the T'swa philosophy—Melsa Ostrak Gouer."

Mauen handed him the address book, open to the Gs. The name Gouer didn't mean anything specific to him, though he recognized it vaguely as belonging to an aristocratic family. But Ostrak—the Ostraks were one of the better known aristocratic families, holding certain interstellar trading rights in fief from the crown.

"Have you called this Melsa Gouer?"

"No. I hesitated to bother someone of a family like that."

"I think I will," he said. "Tomorrow. It could be that you do have something helpful here."

At least it could provide a lead to highly placed families with a pre-war interest in the T'swa. He made his call to Konni and she accepted the dinner invitation. Then Varlik got dressed to report to the office. When he was ready to leave, he stopped to kiss Mauen.

"Varlik?"

"Yes?"

"Did you sleep with this Konni Wenter?"

The question startled him. "Sleep with her? No. Or anyone else since I met you. Not ever." He stepped back to arm's length. "I hope you haven't been worrying about that."

"Not until you asked to call her. And then said you'd traveled to Tyss together. Is she pretty?"

"No, she's fairly plain. Not homely, but . . ." He grinned. "She's nothing like you. Except that she's nice, too. I think you'll like her. And she'll like you. Have you ever wondered about things like that before when I've been gone?"

"Not really." She smiled a little. "A time or two, maybe. I know that women must put themselves in your way sometimes. But while you were talking, it occurred to me that you shared something with her out there that was important to you both, and that I had no part in—a mystery, a war, and friends killed."

His eyes rested on hers. "True. But now the mystery is yours, too. You've even given me a lead."

Varlik checked in with Fendel, who told him to take a week off; then he'd have a new assignment for him. Varlik told him he wasn't done with the T'swa assignment yet, that there were odds and ends of it to look into here, and that when he was finished he was going to take two weeks off.

When he left Fendel's office, Fendel stared after him. The young man had certainly changed. Independent! But he was worth a little temperament. Subscriptions had soared with his coverage of the T'swa.

Varlik stopped at his own desk before he left, to place a call to the T'swa embassy. He got an appointment with the ambassador for the next morning at 07.75.

Varlik had been right. As different as they were, Mauen and Konni hit it off.

Konni hadn't learned much of value. A week after returning to Iryala, she'd been back at work and busy. She'd read or scanned everything the library had on Splenn, though, giving special attention to Splenn's politics and interstellar trade. It had been interesting but not very helpful. But clearly the Splennites—the Splennwa, Varlik and Konni called them, using the Tyspi—had a penchant for intrigues, at least at home.

And there had been several smuggling convictions by the Confederation Tax Commission, though the Splennite reputation was worse than a few convictions would account for. Also, T'swa regiments had been hired more than once to help in power disputes on Splenn; the current dynasty of the leading state on Splenn owed its position to T'swa regiments.

Varlik in turn told them about his appointment with the T'swa ambassador. He'd call Konni afterward, he promised, and tell her what happened.

Konni left by midevening—at 17.20. It didn't seem to her like an evening to keep Varlik and Mauen up late.

# 37

It had not been a good night for Varlik, though it started exceedingly well. Near dawn he'd wakened from a seemingly unending dream in which he and his platoon had been walking through a landscape that sometimes was like the Jubat Hills, looking for—whatever. Perhaps the source of the war, of their deaths. For they were dead; Varlik, too. And their bodies had been decaying. Their biggest difficulty was that body parts kept sloughing off as they hiked. The T'swa had been in high spirits nonetheless, as if it were a holiday outing, but for Varlik it had been constant and desperate struggle.

When finally it had wakened him, he'd gotten up quietly, not to disturb Mauen, had had a drink and read a bit before going back to bed.

Nor was morning a success. Overnight a front had moved in with dirty gray clouds. Strong raw wind clawed the last leaves from the trees, sending them hurling and swirling through the parklike city, leaving skeletons behind to greet the coming winter. Varlik, waiting at the transit shelter, was glad to get aboard the hover bus, and gladder yet to get inside the government office building where the tiny T'swa embassy was tucked away.

Like all government buildings, this one was aesthetic, a fact he took for granted, not consciously appreciating it. The register in the lobby informed him that the T'swa Embassy was on the ninth floor. The silent lift, rising smoothly on its AG unit, gave a broadening view of the bleak morning, and Varlik turned his back on it to face the door. The trip was quick; the government work day had already begun, and he had the lift to himself. Its doors opened to floor nine, and another register faced him as he stepped out.

The door to Suite 912 bore a simple sign that read, appropriately, "T'swa Embassy." It was open, and he walked in. A white-haired T'swa woman sat behind a desk, and smiled at him when he entered.

"Mr. Lormagen!" she said. "It's so nice to see you in person. Just a moment. I'll tell the ambassador you're here."

*She's the ambassador's wife,* Varlik thought, *I'll bet anything.* How T'swa that felt! *We'll see how nice they think it is when I'm finished here.* Varlik himself felt ugly and somehow perverse, but neither analyzed nor resisted it. He merely nodded acknowledgement as she touched a key on her communicator.

"Mr. Lormagen to see you," she said. Varlik couldn't hear the ambassador's reply—it came through the earpiece she wore—but the woman smiled and beckoned as she stood up. He followed her to a door which she opened for him, and he went in.

The ambassador was standing, looking somewhat older than his secretary and a little hunched, the hunch seeming somehow the result of old injury instead of age. Yet hunched though he was, he was scarcely shorter than Varlik, and considerably heavier. His body looked solid, although his stubbly hair was white, his face wrinkled, and deeply creased knuckles gave his thick fingers a telescoped look.

His eyes still showed large, not hidden by folds of aged skin.

He reached a beefy right hand to Varlik and Varlik shook it, not surprised at its hard strength, then the old T'swi waved him to a chair. Varlik sat, putting his open shoulder bag on the floor beside him and surreptitiously pushing the "on" switch of the audio recorder it held.

"Mr. Lormagen," the ambassador said, "it is a pleasure to meet you personally. My name is Tar-Kliss. Before we address your business, let me say how very much I enjoyed your reports. I hadn't been prepared for someone of your unusual ability and dedication, with the willingness to learn our language. To train with a regiment and accompany it in combat—especially in the Orlanthan climate! And your professionalism was the highest, your affinity with your regiment remarkable."

*My affinity with my regiment!* Varlik's expression sharpened, his emotion hardening, focusing, targeting. What did this old diplomat, this player at intrigues, know about affinity with regiment!

"You think so!"

"Oh, yes. I am confident of it. You gave your readers, your listeners and viewers, a remarkably accurate feel of the Red Scorpions—of any regiment. I know. I was a battalion commander—for a time the regimental commander—of the Rimla-Dok Regiment, which was also of the Lodge of Kootosh-Lan. With it to the end, or within hours of the end. Deactivated forty-six years ago."

Varlik's hostility fractured and dissolved. "You were a T'swa mercenary?"

The old head nodded. "And later a monk-scholar and master of wisdom, for the last twenty-seven years ambassador to the Royal Court of Iryala."

He smiled, showing strong square teeth.

"And—how did *your* regiment die?" Varlik asked.

Tar-Kliss's smile became reminiscent, almost beatific. "In a war between pretenders to a throne, on the planet Grovald. Two princes, both quite corrupt. It was a lovely war. Each had very presentable fighting men, in quantities, and some nicely unpredictable allies. Qualities highly contributive."

Though the smile remained, the old man's expression became shrewd now, yet kindly, the eyes penetrating but not aggressive, and he shifted the conversation into Tyspi. "But you didn't come to hear about me," he went on, "nor to hear me appreciate you. You have something to tell me, or something to ask."

"Something to *show* you." With Tar-Kliss's invitation, Varlik's mouth had gone dry. It occurred to him that he could never have given his presentation—his accusation, for that's what it was—without visible hostility, even open anger, had not the old T'swi set the scene for him with his personal history, his little comments. Another T'swa colonel! Or major, in this case. How Biltong had handled the truculent Lamons that first meeting! In Lamons's own headquarters, surrounded by his staff, in the midst of his divisions! Using just the right words, the right tone, all spur of the moment. And Lamons, as arrogant and stiff-necked as any general, perhaps more than most, had backed down without apoplexy, in time coming to respect, even admire, the T'swa.

Varlik took the player from his shoulder bag and inserted the "case" cube he'd prepared for this meeting. "If you'll turn on your wall screen," he said.

As the old man did so, Varlik switched on the player, and they listened to his recorded résumé of the war according to Colonel Voker, then continued with his recorded talk with Ramolu. Next they listened to the children in Oldu Tez-Boag. Occasionally he halted it for comment, continuing through Ban-Shum speaking Orlanthan; barges on the Lok-Sanu River with their cargoes of steel; the three carloads of steel on the siding at Tiiku-Moks; the siding and arsenal in the Jubat Forest, its products without serial numbers; and finally, the unnumbered rifle he'd taken from the dead Bird.

Once the pictures had begun to move on the screen, a relative calm came over Varlik. He felt less tense than when he'd presented his "short cube" to Mauen the day before. And when his little show was over, he asked a seemingly non sequitur question, not what he'd planned at all.

"So you knew that Central News was going to send someone to report on the T'swa regiments."

"Oh yes. In fact, I suggested it to your Foreign Ministry. They in turn suggested it to your employer, and to Iryala Video."

Varlik nodded, saying nothing for a long moment, gathering himself. Now was the moment of truth, and again his mouth was flannel-dry. "It seems to me that the T'swa are behind the Kettle War; that they armed and trained the Orlanthans."

Tar-Kliss nodded gravely. "The evidence, such as it is, seems to point that way—at least as regards arming and training. But of course someone further would be required—some smuggler, as you pointed out, and also someone who provided the Orlanthans with the floaters they've used."

He paused while Varlik reacted to the last comment. He'd overlooked the Bird floaters. "The question that comes to me now," Tar-Kliss added mildly, "is why we T'swa would do that."

Varlik's mind shifted. The old man was playing a game with him, agreeing on details while preparing to throw up barriers. They'd see how well, or how poorly, it worked. "The Splennwa could smuggle the arms in for you," Varlik replied, "and provide the floaters, too. As for a motive—Tyss has a technite deposit. It must have, to make steel. The Confederation wouldn't ship technetium to Tyss—not now, anyway."

The obsidian eyes neither flinched nor hardened. "I can assure you," said Tar-Kliss, "that Tyss has no technite. All the technite worlds lie within a two-parsec-wide corridor, and Tyss is nowhere near it."

"Then where do you get your technetium? You make steel!"

"There is a very simple answer to that question. An answer very accessible, very open to you. Figuratively speaking, it is staring you in the face. I will let you recognize it for yourself, which you will when you are ready."

It seemed to Varlik that the conversation was slipping away from the real issue: T'swa responsibility for the insurrection, and the apparent involvement of some highly placed faction on Iryala, with their motives, whatever those might be. "Suppose I publicize what I found on Tyss, and on Kettle," he said slowly. "Or suppose one of the people I left cubes with does. People would pay attention. They're interested in the T'swa now, and the war, and they respect what I say."

The old T'swi didn't seem to change, but what he next said flustered Varlik. "How familiar are you," Tar-Kliss asked, "with the policies of Standard Management?"

"What do you mean? We learn Standard Management throughout our education, at whatever point the individual policies are pertinent. And in the fifth level we have a whole year's course on the principles. We have to. Standard Management isn't only relevant to government and business, it's relevant to the individual's management of his life! Especially the policies dealing with principles!"

Varlik realized he was tense again. Tar-Kliss by contrast was as relaxed, as casual, as—as a T'swi.

"And who," Tar-Kliss asked, "who in the Confederation is responsible for foreign affairs? Per Standard Management?"

"Why, ultimately the Administrator General, His Majesty, Marcus XXVII." Varlik began to recite from "General Principles of Responsibility": "Narrower responsibilities for specific areas and duties belong . . ."

Tar-Kliss interrupted. "That's right. And to simply publicize, indiscriminately, what you've found, with your suspicions therefrom, would be to ignore, to depart Standard Management by bypassing the proper posts. Let me quote from the same source, even if needlessly: 'To bypass any proper post is to degrade the authority and function of that post and endanger the area of its responsibility.' In this instance your king, His Foreign Ministry, and the Office of Intelligence within that ministry. Again to quote, or very nearly: 'Therefore, to bypass any official government post—whether local, district, regional, planetary, or Confederation, when that post is functioning viably, is a crime. It may be a misdemeanor or a felony, depending on the consequences. Within a business or family or in ordinary interpersonal relations, bypassing has no formal statutory standing, but has common law standing in civil suits dealing with those areas.'

"You see, of course, the point I'm making. What you were suggesting is not only seriously illegal; it is very basic."

Varlik sat chagrined.

"I am not trying to stonewall you," Tar-Kliss continued. "You simply need to take your story to the proper person in the Foreign Ministry, which for you would be the Filter Section in the Office of Incoming Communication, via commfac."

The lined black face was sympathetic. "I realize that you distrust me, but I'm quite interested in seeing where your investigation leads you. And I can help you get your information directly to a decision-making level at the Foreign Ministry without the danger of its being dismissed or backlogged by a lower-level functionary. If you will resume for a day or two the position of publicist for the T'swa, I can properly refer you as my agent directly to the Deputy Foreign Minister for Intelligence, Lord Beniker. I'm sure he will find your discoveries very interesting, and quite possibly he will have information of his own that this will fit with."

Varlik was staring, not knowing what to answer. Could Lord Beniker be an Iryalan conspirator? When he didn't answer the ambassador, Tar-Kliss reached to his communicator, his thick fingers tapping keys. After a short delay, a secretary appeared on the screen. "Lord Beniker's office," she said. "Oh! Good morning, ambassador."

"Good morning to you, Jaren. I'd appreciate speaking with the Deputy Foreign Minister, if you please."

"Just a moment. I'll see if he's available."

The comm screen went black. Varlik sat silent. If Beniker *was* a conspirator, seeing him was dangerous. But it was also an opening. In seconds the screen came to life again, and from some telecast Varlik recognized the long, strong face of Vikun Dor, Lord Beniker.

"Good morning, Tar," the image said. "What can I do for you?"

"Good morning, Vikun. I have a young man in my office, an agent of mine, whom I feel you'll want to see. At any rate, I'd like to send him over to talk with you personally. He has information that could prove considerably important to Iryala and the Confederation, and he can present it better than I." Tar-Kliss paused meaningfully. "His name is Varlik Lormagen."

"Varlik Lormagen! Excellent! I'd like to meet the young man, in any event." Lord Beniker turned away as if looking at something, probably a clock. "Send him over now. It's 08.15. He should be able to get here by 08.65 with no trouble at all; I'll inform the Routing Desk and they'll have someone waiting to escort him. Is that it for this time?"

"Yes, Vikun, that's all. Thank you. I appreciate your attention in this."

"I'm happy to oblige. Let me know if there's anything more."

The screen went blank and Tar-Kliss switched off the communicator. Varlik got to his feet.

"Why?" he asked. "Why are you doing this?"

"So that hopefully you can learn what lies behind your mystery."

For a moment longer Varlik looked at him, then turned and left. Tar-Kliss watched him out the door. When it had closed, the elderly T'swi reached to his communicator and again keyed Beniker's office code.

Lord Beniker watched and listened to the same cube that Varlik had played for the T'swa ambassador, and Varlik's comments were essentially the same. When he'd finished, the Deputy Foreign Minister, tall and rawboned, sat slouched, introspectively frowning. After a few moments he shook his head, as if to disperse like hovering flies whatever unfinished thoughts were buzzing there.

Beniker was a highly accomplished actor.

"Mr. Lormagen, that is the most intriguing, and may turn out to be the most important set of information I've had brought to my attention since I've been Deputy Foreign Minister. Admittedly, it is far from conclusive, but it certainly deserves investigation."

He stroked his jawline, one side, then the other. "The most interesting leads are on Tyss and in the Orlanthan jungle. In the latter case we have no effective access, while in the former, we have no jurisdiction—unless, of course, we decide it's essential to Confederation security. But there are things I can have looked into here on Iryala, and I'll ask friend Tar to see what can be learned on Tyss. I'll be surprised if he can't turn up something there."

Varlik frowned. "The ambassador? But if the T'swa government is part of the conspiracy . . ."

Beniker looked at Varlik as if surprised, then the surprise faded. "I see your difficulty," he said. "Few Iryalans are aware that the T'swa have no government."

"No government?"

"That's right. Tyss has no government, nor any nations in the sense of tribes or states like other resource worlds do. No other world I know of could get by that way. The various lodges, orders, and cooperatives are each to themselves a government without geographical boundaries, but without authority over anyone who chooses to stand outside them or remove himself from them. Remarkable place. The closest thing they have to an authority is the religious/philosophical order of Ka-Shok, and Ka-Shok exercises no power over anyone. It's the acknowledged parent order of the several religious/philosophical orders on Tyss, each of them independent, but so far as I know not differing significantly from the others, or worrying about it. They seem to have split off in some far past as geographic or administrative conveniences.

"So it's the Ka-Shok we deal with, in lieu of any government. You've heard of the T'sel? The Order of Ka-Shok originated the T'sel—discovered it, if you prefer—and the T'sel is the basis of human beliefs and custom for the entire planet. So we've accepted the Ka-Shok as the de facto representative of all Tyss, and old Tar-Kliss is actually the Ka-Shok's ambassador. He's also an emeritus member of the largest T'swa war lodge, incidentally, the Kootosh-Lan—biggest of five—although that means nothing compared to his membership in the Ka-Shok. At any rate, if he decides to initiate an investigation on Tyss, he'll get cooperation, I'm sure. Not through any Ka-Shok coercion, but simply from the attitude of respect."

The deputy minister straightened. "Meanwhile, there is something *you* can do." He tapped keys on his desk console; within the desk a silent printer pushed out paper which Beniker tore off and handed to Varlik. "The address and call number of Lord Durslan, an expert on Tyss, including T'swa psychology, and occasional consultant to the Foreign Ministry. He's actually spent considerable time on Tyss. Try your presentation on him and see if he comes up with anything. Agreed? You'll do a better job of it than I."

Varlik looked at the printout and nodded. He wasn't sure, but he thought it was the same address and number Mauen had gotten from the Royal Library.

"Good," said Beniker, and tapped out a code on his communicator. From his vantage, Varlik couldn't see the screen, but audio was from a desk speaker, not a privacy receiver. And obviously, Beniker was answered by a secretary. No, Lord Durslan was away just then, but she could set up an appointment; actually, his calendar was quite open. Mr. Varlik Lormagen? Lord Durslan would be delighted to meet the young man, she was sure. Would Mr. Lormagen consent to be Lord Durslan's house guest?

Beniker turned to Varlik, eyebrows raised. "Would you?"

Varlik was flabbergasted. "I—guess so," he said.

"He would indeed," Beniker answered.

"Would tomorrow noon be satisfactory to him?" the voice asked.

Varlik nodded, and Beniker forwarded this too, as if amused at his function of go-between. The secretary said a car would be waiting for Mr. Lormagen at the airport—that he should notify them of his expected arrival time—and gave the same comm number Varlik had already been given by Beniker. The two exchanged courtesies then, and Beniker disconnected.

"A relative of Durslan's," he commented. "Sister, as I recall. Obviously not hesitant to commit him to house guests.

"So. Is there anything more, Lormagen?"

"I don't believe so, sir."

"Fine."

Beniker turned to his papers in dismissal, just as Koda would have. Varlik got up and left, gooseflesh prickling.

And Beniker, too, when Varlik had left, reached again for his communicator.

Beniker wasn't the only one who had a call to make. On the ground floor, central corridor, were enclosed comm booths. Varlik called Konni's desk at Iryala Video. To his surprise she was in. He summarized for her what had happened that morning, without mentioning the feeling he'd gotten when Beniker had dismissed him. It bothered him, but it also seemed paranoid to make anything of it. Konni might think he was losing his grip.

Konni's desk being one of several in a common work room, her communicator, of course, had a handheld privacy receiver. When she'd hung up, she sat for a moment, assimilating the information Varlik had given her. He'd seemed confident enough, but she was worried. He was looking for the key person in what seemed a major conspiracy, a person almost surely in some high or at least highly influential position. If that person learned what Varlik was doing, Varlik would unquestionably be in danger.

Government crime, and organized crime in general, were little experienced on Iryala, or on most Confederation worlds, but everyone was well aware of the concepts from histories, and from news, novels, and holoplays about trade worlds. She could imagine Varlik dying in some carefully staged "accident."

It also occurred to her that she was not immune. If someone should do something to Varlik—it really did seem rather unreal to her—they might suspect that she too had dangerous information. She decided to put together a report from the cubes she had plus additional recorded comments, and leave them with someone—a friend who wasn't a close friend and wouldn't be suspect. She thought she knew who—Felsi Nisben. Felsi was imaginative, a romantic, who'd take her seriously and follow through if necessary. If something happened to Varlik, and then to her, Felsi was to turn the package over to—who?

The Justice Ministry, obviously. But what if . . . ? There ought to be a second person to send one to. She thought then of Colonel Voker, who'd helped her get to Tyss, and whom Varlik thought so highly of. Voker had recognized that something was wrong before either she or Varlik had. So she'd make two copies, one for Justice and one for Voker.

*I'll go home and make them right now,* she decided, *and talk to Felsi tonight.*

# 38

When he'd finished his call to Konni, Varlik went to the Planetary Media Center, to Central News and his desk console, and called first the Royal Library, then the Central News files, finding everything he could on the current Lord Durslan and the current Lord Beniker. There was quite a bit on Lord Beniker, rather little about Durslan, and in both cases nothing that seemed significant. All they had in common was their nobility and their attendance at the same private school. And at school they'd hardly overlapped, probably hadn't even known one another, for Durslan was nine years younger than Beniker—about ten years older than Varlik. After the national university, Beniker had gone into government service while Durslan had stayed at home to assist with the family enterprises.

Varlik turned off his terminal and called Mauen. "Hello, sweetheart," he murmured. "I'll be home in half an hour; seventy minutes at most. How'd you like to go to the conservatory? Shouldn't be crowded on a work day."

"I'd love to. And I have some exciting news for you when you get here."

"Tell me over the phone?"

"No, you'll have to wait. It's worth it, though; you'll love it."

"Hmm. If it's a disappointment, do I get to set reparations of my own choice?"

"On one condition," she answered playfully. "If it's as good as I know it is, you'll have to pay me any bonus I name."

"Bonus? All right, you're on. I'll see you."

The clouds had broken, forming fast-moving islands of cold sunshine that coursed like the raw and cutting wind through Landfall's pattern of subcommunities. Yet Varlik found himself humming as he strode toward Media Apartments Three. For the moment he had set tomorrow aside, and Lord Durslan, and the way Beniker had dismissed him.

She was waiting for him, grinning, wearing a house-dress in which she somehow managed to be extremely enticing. "What's your exciting news?" Varlik asked after kissing her.

"What's yours?" she countered.

"Mine? That I'm home again with you. Ready for anything."

"That's not news," she said with a mock pout. "I already knew that."

He stepped back, eyeing her. "Not fair," he said. "I asked first. Tell me, so that one of us can collect reparations. Or a bonus, as the case may be."

"All right. We're taking a trip together!"

His enthusiasm blinked out, replaced by guardedness. "A trip?"

"A trip. I phoned Melsa Ostrak Gouer, the expert on the T'swa. When I gave the secretary my name, she asked if I was related to you, and when I told her I was your wife, she connected me with Mrs. Gouer. We had a three-way conference and—I got an invitation, too!"

Mauen beamed expectantly; Varlik only stood puzzled. "Too?"

"Mrs. Gouer," Mauen nudged. "Mrs. Garlan Gouer . . . Lady Durslan!"

Varlik stepped backward and sat down. This wasn't at all all right, but he didn't know what to say, how to handle it. He'd felt at least somewhat endangered at the prospect of going there, to some large private estate out in the forested Lake District, putting himself in the hands of people who might wish to silence him. And now Mauen intended to go with him.

She was laughing delightedly. "I thought you'd be surprised, but not that surprised," she said. "After I told them what I wanted—to learn more about the T'swa, and Tyss—the secretary told Lady Durslan she'd just made an appointment for you to see Lord Durslan tomorrow. That you'd be flying in to Lake Loreen in the morning, and someone would pick you up there. Then Lady Durslan—she told me to call her Melsa; isn't that marvelous?—Melsa asked if I was free tomorrow, and when I told her I was, she invited me to come with you. They even have their own conservatory. And a heated, glass-enclosed natatorium, so we're to bring swimsuits! Isn't that incredible!" Mauen spun in delight, a movement learned in dance. "She said she'd love to have us both for two days, even if your business with Garlan—that's Lord Durslan—only takes an hour. She said she hoped you'd talk with her about your experiences with the mercenaries; they're a part of the T'swa culture she hadn't had direct contact with. And she'd be happy to give you background on the war lodges that you might find interesting."

Mauen sat down across from Varlik. "We must have talked for fifteen minutes! And Varlik, she's such a lovely person. In appearance, too. I've already started to pack."

She paused then, for the first time perceiving that Varlik's reaction might be more than surprise. "Is anything the matter?" she asked.

"The matter?" From somewhere he mustered a smile.

"Yes. I'm worried about what that bonus is you're going to ask for."

Later, when Mauen decided to go out and buy some things for the trip, Varlik begged off, claiming need for recovery time and a nap. She laughed, then left. Tying his robe, he poured himself a cup of joma and called Konni, catching her at her desk. He told her what had developed.

"It really does sound all right," he said. "Lady Durslan made a big hit with Mauen, and Mauen's pretty sensitive to people. We're invited for two days. But if you don't hear from me by Oneday, maybe you'd better pass our information on to someone."

"Such as?"

"Whoever you think best. The authorities. And it might be a good idea to send a copy to Colonel Voker, on Kettle. You could send it by way of Captain Brusin, the mate on the *Quaranth*. Remember him? Tell him it's from me; I'm sure he'll do it. The *Quaranth* is being refitted; he mentioned it would take about ten days. And put it in a sealed package; that way he won't be tempted to snoop. It's slower than a pod, but somehow I'd feel better about it."

"Why?"

"Hmm. I don't know. Uncertified pod contents *are* subject to inspection, but it probably seldom happens."

Varlik paused. *I'm rehearsing trouble,* he told himself. "Not that it'll be necessary," he went on. "I'll be awfully surprised if it is. But it seems worth it to cover the possibility."

Konni told him then what she had done the day before, including arranging with Felsi Nisben as a backup. She hadn't told Felsi the nature of the information or that Varlik was involved.

Then she paused, hesitating. Varlik waited, sensing that she wasn't finished.

"Varlik," she said after a moment, "I've got a question—a serious one. I like Mauen, I really like her a lot. And obviously you love her . . ."

"Yes?"

"So—why in the name of Pertunis are you letting her go with you!? Probably nothing will happen, but why take a chance?"

He looked at it. "I guess," he said slowly— "Okay. It's because she's so enthused about it. So pleased and delighted. If I tell her, she's not going to accept it. She's going to argue, and there'll be a big upset. And I'd have to make it really strong to support my refusal, make it seem really dangerous. Then she wouldn't want me to go, and if I insisted, then she'd insist on going with me. I know Mauen. She's little, and pretty, and sweet—and she just doesn't push around worth a darn.

"Like I said, the odds are good that everything there will be fine—that we'll have two of the nicest days of our lives."

Konni didn't answer at once. "Lormagen," she said at last, "I hate to say it, but I agree with you again. Have a nice trip. And tell Mauen I love her, okay?"

"I'll tell her. And thanks. Thanks a lot."

When they disconnected, a broody Varlik sipped his joma. He wondered if he'd just talked himself into something he'd regret.

# PART SIX
## *The School*

# 39

The T'swa ambassador looked up at the white-jacketed serving man. "I will have bacon, crisp, with four large poached eggs," he said, "and muffins with butter and norbal. The bacon and muffins should be in quantities appropriate to four eggs."

He poured cream in his joma then, followed by three heaping spoons of sugar, while Lord Beniker ordered. Beniker, when he'd finished ordering, put a hand on the serving man's sleeve. "And Kirt," he added, "the ambassador and I will need privacy; we have confidential business to discuss. We'll call if we need anything."

"Yes, my lord." The man left for the kitchen of Beniker's large and comfortable apartment.

"So," said Tar-Kliss, "what have you arranged? Assuming that Garlan and Wellem cannot defuse the situation."

"Well, it isn't the sort of thing I care for, but . . . First of all, we've had an interesting piece of serendipity, and you know what serendipity indicates about the dynamics of the situation. Lormagen is a professional newsperson, and his discoveries were of a delicate nature. And of course he is very newly arrived back on Iryala. So it may well be that he hasn't shared his information and analysis with others than ourselves. The likeliest for him to have talked with is his wife. Nonetheless, Garlan considered it unwise to call Lormagen and suggest he bring her along; he's already suspicious, and that could easily cause him to do something unfortunate.

"*And then she, Lormagen's wife, called Melsa!* It seems she'd gotten Melsa's name from a librarian several days ago, as an expert on the T'swa, and the young lady wanted references she could read. It provided a marvelous opportunity for Melsa to establish a personal relationship and then invite her, which she did."

Beniker paused to sip his joma, which he drank black and unsweetened.

"Now, I have dispatched a team of four agents in my intelligence branch, men I can trust not to be impetuous or become needlessly physical. They'll be standing by near Garlan's, and if Garlan isn't satisfied with Lormagen's progress, he'll let them know. Then he'll have the

Lormagens drugged and my men will pick them up with a light floater. They'll take them to the office of a psychiatrist in Loreen, who'll psychocondition them. He's been alerted, although of course he doesn't know yet who his subjects might be. It will take only a few hours, and when he's done, Lormagen won't remember ever having been suspicious, and he'll see nothing untoward in the information that right now has him so upset. He'll even have the idea that he spent the night asleep at Garlan's."

"I'd prefer, naturally, that none of that becomes necessary."

"Quite probably it won't," said Tar-Kliss. "I have great confidence in Wellem. But there remains the young woman journalist who was with him on Tyss. Presumably she knows at least some of what he knows. And there remains the possibility that he related his suspicions to someone else."

"Of course. I'm prepared to have the young woman abducted, if necessary. And regarding a hypothetical further person: in the process of conditioning, I'll have that looked into. If there actually is such a person, the odds are decent that we can have him picked up the following day or evening, certainly before he sees Lormagen and realizes something's amiss with him. We'll condition him and have him back at his job the next day, none the wiser."

"It would be preferable to have Wellem and Garlan work on them first," Tar-Kliss said. "Psychoconditioning is not, after all, beneficial to the mind, as witness the billions who've experienced the Sacrament."

Beniker nodded. "Agreed. But it may not be feasible for Garlan and Wellem to work on them."

As a commercial floatercraft it was small, seating thirty-two. But the season was late, and today it carried only eleven passengers besides Varlik and Mauen.

Varlik's dreams had been bad again; he'd wakened troubled and introverted, and was not a good traveling companion. He had not, of course, mentioned his worries to Mauen. She assumed that his mood simply reflected preoccupation with his mystery.

So they spoke little, watching the landscape over which they passed, an undulating countryside of farms and small towns. There were rectangular fields and pastured hills, with woods on steeper slopes, along the larger streams, and around some of the lakes. The lakes were marvelous— blue with reflected sky—for the day, if cold, had dawned clear and bright.

After a bit the land became rougher, though its hills were not high. Lakes were increasingly numerous; woods spread, became forest that held most of the ground, trees bare except where enclaves of evergreens stood, notably on lakeshores.

The panorama dispelled Varlik's grimness and left him merely grave.

The resort town of Loreen stood beside the large and vivid lake which had given it its name. Or perhaps they'd been named independently for the same lady; the details lay lost in antiquity. The floater settled on the airfield at town's edge, where a chauffeur met them at the small terminal. He introduced himself as Bren.

Bren's good-mannered cheerfulness further lightened Varlik's mood. He picked up both their bags before Varlik could put hand to them, then, commenting on the welcome sunshine, led them outside to a limousine that was luxurious without ostentation, and held the doors for them. Neither Varlik nor Mauen had ridden in a vehicle like it before.

The travelway he took them on was three lanes wide, smooth and green, its grass mown short for hay. They followed it through forest broken only infrequently by small farms, past lakes whose blue they might glimpse through trees or across an occasional meadowed glade. There were numerous fine homes here, Varlik knew, but they were not visible from the road, or seldom and barely. Here and there lanes disappeared into the forest, unidentified by signs. Most, Varlik assumed, were for removing the logs of trees afflicted or well past their prime. Other lanes neatly mowed, almost certainly led—privately, unobtrusively—to the leisure homes of titled and untitled rich.

It was, to Varlik, very beautiful, though he had no least desire to live here. His glance moved to Mauen; she seemed entranced.

Before long they turned off on one of the manicured lanes. It wound through forest and down a gentle hill to a crescent of lake shore, to grounds half groves, half sunny lawn, where a home stood—a literal mansion. It probably was not Lord Durslan's ancestral home, not out here, but it was a mansion nonetheless, with two wings that seemed much too large to be accounted for by family use and servants' apartments.

He got just a glimpse of an island close offshore, with a little stone causeway leading to it like a footbridge. There was a building on the island—a building too large, it seemed, to be merely for ornament or parties. Its architecture was something Varlik had not seen before. It was out of sight before he could sort out the curves of its graceful roof, the carved posts of its veranda, the sculpted trees and shrubs that framed and partly screened it. Then the hovercar pulled up before the house.

Bren let them out, and as he did, the large front door opened, a woman stepping onto the entry porch. By her bearing, Varlik decided, she was either Lady Durslan or Lord Durslan's sister. She met them smiling.

"Mauen!" she said, taking the young woman's hand, "I'm so pleased to meet you! I told Garlan—Lord Durslan, that is—that you were lovely, but you're lovelier still in person." She turned then to Varlik, and the hand she gave him was strong. "And you are Varlik, of course. I'm delighted to be your hostess." She examined his face. "Your picture has graced the cover of several newszines. Did you know that?"

Varlik's last misgiving expired in the light of her charm, while her uninhibited and seemingly genuine pleasure left him somehow surprisingly unembarrassed.

"My name is Melsa," she told him as she led them into the house, "and I hope you will call me that. I'm sure we all have a great deal to talk about. Right now Lord Durslan will want to meet you both. He's in his study, preparing a market analysis that he looks forward to laying aside."

A man waited just inside. He didn't fit Varlik's concept of a butler, but he took their jackets and disappeared with them into a side hall. "That's Elgen," said Lady Durslan, "a man who wears several hats here, all of them extremely well."

Varlik and Mauen walked behind her down a main hall, pausing at a well-appointed office. "This is where Rennore works, Lord Durslan's sister. She talked with you yesterday, Mauen, but she's left with her husband on holiday. Bren delivered them to the airport when he went in to get you."

A few doors farther brought them to a small, intimate parlor. Lady Durslan seated them, then went to tell her husband of their arrival. Mauen beamed at Varlik, then, remembering his earlier concern—his mission—tuned down her smile, keeping only a little of it. "I was right, wasn't I," she murmured. "She's a beautiful lady."

He smiled at her. "Not as beautiful as another one I know." They reached to each other, touching hands for a moment, and he wished they could have an hour of privacy then. *I haven't been as horny for years as I've been these past two days,* he told himself, and thought then, unbidden, of plants that produce large seed crops when dying—an impulse to reproduce before death. The thought irritated him: There'd been no threat here, nothing but the warmest welcome. Still, the notion of danger had resurfaced and would not go away by command. And interestingly, with it his ardor died.

Then he heard someone in the hall just outside, and got to his feet as Lord and Lady Durslan came in. Lord Durslan strode toward him, hand outstretched—a small-boned, slender man of less than middle height who nonetheless failed to seem small or delicate.

"Mr. Lormagen! A pleasure to meet you! And Mrs. Lormagen!" He half bowed, smiling. It struck Mauen then that these people actually were nobility, and for a moment she felt ill at ease. Not knowing quite what to do, she moved her hand to the chair arm as if to stand. Durslan raised one hand. "Please don't get up," he said to her. "We seldom stand on formality here."

He seated Lady Durslan opposite the Lormagens, and Varlik sat back down. Lord Durslan moved to a small desk with console at one side of the room. "I can turn the video screen on and off from here," he explained, "and access my own files if need be.

"I understand from Lord Beniker that you have something important to tell me, Varlik, and a video cube he'd like me to see, to do with the T'swa. I must tell you that he left me quite in mystery. But I'm always interested in anything new or unusual about the T'swa; they're a marvelous people, as you obviously know quite well."

"Yes sir, I do, and they are. The most traumatic experience I've ever had, the worst by far, was the death of the Red Scorpion Regiment. I've had nightmares ever since. But that's not what I'm here about. I do have a cube with me—partly about the T'swa, but also about other things."

"Do you mind if I record this," Durslan asked, "so I'll have copies of my own?"

"Not at all, sir; I hope you will."

Then Varlik played his cube for Durslan, commenting as appropriate. When he was done, all four of them sat soberly.

"Thank you," Durslan said. "I can see that this would trouble you." He got to his feet. "And I believe I can shed some light on it, but I'll need a little time to seek out data and prepare. I'll have cook fix an early lunch while we show you around. That will give me a chance to sort the data in my subconscious, so to speak, or my superconscious, if you prefer."

He gave instructions to the kitchen via intercom, took his guests to get their jackets, then led them through a patio door onto the grounds between building and lakeshore. The place was an utter surprise to both Varlik and Mauen. Not only was there a bathing beach and boathouse, but there was a stack of boat dock sections piled by the boathouse, and what appeared to be two conservatories. There was also playground equipment—a tall spiral tubular slide, swings, horizontal and parallel bars. . . . Varlik stopped for a moment, looking.

"There are young people here much of the time," Lord Durslan commented. "About forty of them currently. It's quite a lively place at times."

From there Varlik could see the islet again, a hundred feet offshore, with its causeway and intriguing building, and again Durslan, following his gaze, commented. "A T'sel *ghao*," he said, "a place where students can counsel with a T'sel master, initiates can begin advanced procedures, and adepts can pursue advanced studies under supervision, in preparation for their elevation to master. There is, of course, a master in residence here. Would you like to talk with him after lunch?"

"Oh, yes!" said Mauen.

Lord Durslan looked calmly at Varlik. "And you, Varlik?"

"Why, yes."

"Good. I'll let him know that you'll be out. He stays quite busy, actually, with several projects, and I like to warn him of impending visitors. Not that he minds, you understand; he enjoys people. We have a lot of them here much of the time, but they're gone just now, for the coming harvest festival."

As they'd talked, they'd strolled. "Would you like to visit our conservatory?" Durslan asked.

They did, spending half an hour in its fragrant, glass-enclosed galleries. The groundskeeper had just finished watering, and the air was as damp as the Orlanthan jungle, though much less hot. Some of the plants were from off world, and one tall chamber had several extraplanetary birds flying about among small trees and draped vines. The conservatory served several purposes; it was a place to walk among flowers in any season and to grow plants of many kinds. It was a source of flowers for the house, and in season, one wing produced flowering plants for transplanting around the grounds. Mauen was agog. She loved the public conservatories at Landfall, and it had never occurred to her that a household might have such a large one to itself.

They looked into the other glasshouse too—the natatorium, with its 100-foot pool and its passageway to the manor.

Like everything else, lunch was an experience. The food was light and the selection modest, but for Varlik and Mauen the quality was beyond any earlier experience. When that was done, Lady Durslan excused herself, and Lord Durslan took his guests to the *ghao*.

Both Varlik and Mauen were surprised and disappointed to find the master not a black man but white—a sinewy, middle-aged Iryalan in white duck shorts and a tee shirt, his brown hair cut army short, his blue eyes calm and direct, his smile friendly.

"Wellem," said Lord Durslan, "I'd like you to meet two friends of mine—Varlik and Mauen Lormagen. You know of Varlik, of course. Varlik, Mauen, this is our resident T'sel master, Wellem Bosler. He is one in a line of Iryalan masters originating from Master Dao of the Dys Hualuun monastery on Tyss."

Durslan stepped back. "I'll leave you to get acquainted. Varlik has brought a very interesting and seemingly drastic situation to my attention, and I need to spend some time at the computer, make a few calls—that sort of thing."

Durslan withdrew then. The T'sel master motioned to a settee, little more than a cushioned bench with back. "Have a seat," he said, and himself took a matching chair opposite.

"You'd expected a T'swi," he told Varlik in Tyspi. "I hope you aren't too disappointed." Then he turned to Mauen and repeated it in Standard. "I spoke Tyspi to let your husband know there's been continuity since Master Dao trained the first Iryalan children at Dys Hualuun more than four centuries ago. One of them was my grandmother, fifteen generations removed."

He paused, smiling, regarding the two. "So you see, this family's interest in Tyss and the T'swa is of very long standing."

Neither guest had adjusted yet to the unexpected situation. And neither thought to wonder what he meant by "this family," which could mean his, or Durslan's, or that he was kin to Durslan. Mauen had wanted to see and talk with a T'swi of whatever kind, though she'd have preferred a warrior like those Varlik had lived and fought beside. Varlik, as Wellem Bosler had perceived, had been anticipating a T'sel master from Tyss. To Varlik, somehow, Tar-Kliss didn't count; he was an ambassador.

"Have you ever been on Tyss?" Mauen asked; it was all she could come up with.

"Oh, yes. All adepts on Iryala, when they are ready for their master's recognition, go to Tyss for their. . . ." He used a T'swa term, then saw that Varlik no more understood it than Mauen did. "It means something like 'dialog while operating in the reality of bodies.' It's more or less equivalent to the oral examination a graduate student has to pass before a committee of professors."

"And you did that?" Varlik said. "Who taught you?"

"My master was Melsa's great uncle, Tamos Ostrak."

Varlik was beginning to put things together now. "And the children who are away on vacation—they're studying the T'sel, hoping to become masters."

Wellem Bosler laughed, a pleasant laugh. "Yes and no . . . Only eight of our present students have Wisdom and Knowledge as their chosen area and will become T'sel masters. Of the eight, three are currently initiates and three are adepts. They serve as lectors and do much of the instruction and supervision of others. Most of our forty-two students are at Games, that being the area most satisfyingly playable in the Confederation. The games of business, government, money. . . ." It was apparent from the way he ended that his list was not all-inclusive.

"But talking alone won't enlighten you appreciably on the subject. A touch of experience will be much more informative, and make the words more meaningful." He got up, went to a bookshelf, and took down a folio-sized volume. "A book of photographs from Tyss, annotated," he said, handing it to Mauen. "They're quite beautiful. Mauen, with your permission, and his, of course"—he glanced at Varlik—"I'll take your husband to another room for a bit; the experience works best in seclusion. Meanwhile, you can enjoy yourself with this."

Mauen nodded cheerfully. "If I can have a turn later," she said. Varlik's response was uncertainty, tinged with that low-intensity fear called *worry*.

"Varlik?" said Bosler.

Varlik nodded. "All right," he replied.

"Good."

They left her there with the book already open.

The T'sel master led Varlik down a hall to the opposite end of the *ghao*, where he opened a door, holding it for his guest. Varlik didn't notice the door's thickness or its insulated core. When Bosler closed it, the bottom scraped dense carpet; there'd been no carpet, no floor covering at all, in the waiting room or the corridor. The walls inside were figured wood, unpainted and unstained, hung with simple paintings that were aesthetic but most unstandard. That the walls were also effectively sound insulated was not visually apparent.

A person could howl in there without being heard outside; even the windows were double-paned, of material responding poorly to sound vibrations.

All Varlik knew was that the place felt very relaxing. As he looked around, taking in the pictures, his tension drained away. They reminded him a bit of the art he'd admired in the cantina in Oldu Tez-Boag.

There were two chairs, one a recliner. The other, by a small desk, was a kneeling chair, like those used at desks. Wellem Bosler waved Varlik to the recliner, then perched erect and straight on the other.

Their eyes met, and Varlik found nothing in the other man's to challenge, to flinch from, to avoid in any way. Bosler's gaze was comfortable— direct and comfortable. Varlik wondered whether a T'sel master, when he looked at someone, saw anything that others didn't—wondered and failed to notice how non-Standard the notion was.

Then Bosler spoke. "A T'sel master's functions include helping others to command their own lives more easily, and that's always a good place to start. So let me ask you a question: If there was one thing you could change in your life, what would it be?"

"Umm. I don't know. I guess—" He looked at the enigma of the Kettle insurrection, but when he opened his mouth again to answer, what came out was: "I've never been very able to laugh easily and feel really light about things. All my life I've known occasional people who seemed really cheerful and happy, as if they really enjoyed life. It's always seemed to me they had something important that I didn't; that I was missing something valuable."

Beneath his words were thoughts of those others. Mike Brusin was one. Brusin seemed to notice so much, enjoy others so much.

"All right," said Bosler. "What feeling goes with that inability?"

"Oh . . . seriousness, I guess. It's a feeling of seriousness."

"Fine. Give me an example, an incident, of something feeling serious to you as a child."

"Well . . . Once, when I was in the third level at school, we were assigned to make a little book. They passed out these little books of blank pages, and we were supposed to fill them up—draw a picture of an animal on the left-hand page and write about the species on the right. Only I did it the opposite, and didn't realize I had it backward till it was too late to do anything about it. When I did realize it, it really upset me."

"All right. Was there any emotion connected with that?"

Varlik looked back, feeling for it. "Yes. Fear. I was afraid."

"Okay. What were you afraid of?"

"I was afraid . . . I don't know. I was afraid the teacher would be angry. Or scornful. Maybe think I was stupid or something."

"Okay. So imagine, just imagine now, something that might have been done to you for getting the pages reversed. Something severe."

"Well, I could have been given a low grade—a failing grade." He blushed slightly. "Although I was only marked down one grade for it."

"Fine. All right, give me another thing that might have been done to you for getting the pages reversed. Some punishment."

"Uh, well—I could have been made to stay after school in the disciplinary office and do the whole book over."

"All right. Give me another."

"Huh! Those are about the only ones I can think of."

"Okay. Imagine a punishment. Make one up."

"Um . . . Well, the disciplinary officer could have caned me in his office, on the buttocks. That's done sometimes, you know, for flagrant misbehavior."

"Right. Remember now, we're imagining. It doesn't necessarily have to be something Standard, something actually done to children at school. Give me another thing you can imagine being done to you."

"Okay, I'll try. I could have been . . . I . . ." Varlik shook his head, looking apologetically at the master. "I can't think of anything else."

"All right. Imagine that this was on a world where they didn't know about Standard Management or Standard Technology, and people had to make up things as they went along. Imagine what might have been done to you for getting the pages reversed. Some severe punishment."

"Well, they could have . . . they could have . . . *they could have taken my recess privileges away for the rest of the dek!*" He said the last with distinct pride for having come up with it.

"Good! All right, another one."

Lag. "They could have . . . caned me in front of the class!"

"Very good! Another one."

"Uh . . . They could have caned me in front of the whole school, on a world like that!"

"All right! Another."

"They could have . . . They could have hung me, like they do on some resource worlds. They punish people by hanging them up by the neck so they can't breathe. After a few minutes they die."

"Excellent! You're doing great! Give me another."

"They could have tied me to a stake," he answered promptly, "and piled flammables around me—dry wood—and set fire to it."

"Barbaric! Another."

"They could have thrown me in the tiger yard at the zoo, after not feeding the tigers for five days!"

"Fantastic! Another."

Varlik was grinning now. "Thrown me into a pit of scorpions!"

"Horrible! Another."

"Put me in a kettle of water and brought it slowly to a boil!"

"Ghastly! Another."

Varlik's grin was ear to ear. "Cut *x*es on the ends of my toes and peeled my skin off them and right up my feet and on up my legs and body and off over my head!" Varlik laughed at that one.

"Good grief! Gruesome!" Bosler paused. "How do you feel about having reversed the pages on that third-level assignment?"

Varlik laughed again. "Not very serious, I'll tell you that." Actually, serious seemed a remote condition to him just then.

"Good." Wellem Bosler smiled broadly at Varlik. "All right, close your eyes. Now, with your eyes closed—*turn around and look at yourself!*"

Varlik's hair stood on end. He didn't know what was happening; all he saw with his eyes was the inside of his lids, unfocused, dark purplish, overlaid with vague afterimages. But something was happening, something within that he couldn't describe even for himself. Externally, it felt as if his skin had drawn tight, the goosebumps pointed and electric.

"Fine." Bosler's voice sounded casual and far away, though easily heard and understood, as if it spoke directly into his mind. "Now, *erase your on-site personal history.*"

The words were like a trigger. The electric feeling discharged in waves, Varlik's body twitching and jerking like a faint version of that unrememberable but always present time as a little boy when technicians had carried out the Sacrament on him, the conditioning ritual, with their strap-equipped table, their drugs and electrodes and chant. But this time, that and much else were being erased from mind and psyche. He cried out once, hoarsely, not so much in pain as in surprise and release. It was something like a series of electric shocks, though not severe, and somewhat like an immense, too intense, whole-body orgasm. The phenomenon continued for a long half minute as he twisted and jerked, then gradually it tapered off. When it was over, he opened his eyes.

"That," said Varlik, "was the most incredible thing that ever happened to me—whatever it was."

The T'sel master was smiling at him. "Congratulations!" Bosler said. "You handled it admirably." He got up, opened a small refrigerator in a corner, took out a tumbler and a jar of fruit juice, and poured some for Varlik. As Varlik drank, the T'sel master took paper and a pen from the desk. "I'm going to draw you a little diagram, and when you're done we'll continue."

When they entered the waiting room, Varlik was looking bemused but happy, his mind aswirl with strange unsorted experiences and concepts.

"Hello, Mauen," said Bosler. "I'm returning your husband, not too much the worse for wear." She had looked up, interested. "Varlik," he continued, "why don't you lie down on the couch for a bit. Let yourself sleep, and give old equations a chance to balance."

"A nap?" Varlik grinned. "Great idea."

"And Mauen, if you'll come with me . . ."

When she was settled on the recliner, Wellem Bosler addressed her. What, he wanted to know, was the principal barrier to satisfaction in her life. What would she most like changed?

"Lack of talent," she told him without hesitation. "I'd love to be a real artist, but I don't have much talent at all."

"All right. Tell me something bad that might happen if you had a great amount of talent. . . ."

# 40

Melsa Ostrak Gouer, Lady Durslan, led Varlik and Mauen to Lord Durslan's study and ushered them in. As they entered, Durslan stood and seated his guests, then sat down across from them, crossing his legs comfortably.

"Varlik, Mauen," he said, "you came here with evidence of a conspiracy. I can tell you that indeed there is one."

Varlik did not tense as he might have earlier, but he straightened slightly, alert. Durslan paused, seemed to change directions. "Tell me, what do you think of the Confederation as it now stands?"

"Well," Varlik said, "they taught us in school that we're in a 'golden age,' and when you compare recent centuries to history, I'd agree with that."

Durslan nodded. "A fair evaluation, speaking comparatively. Comparatively little strife or corruption, comparatively high living standards, government that is stable and, as governments go, rather efficient. To what would you attribute that?"

Varlik shrugged. "Standard Management, I suppose. As far as I know, Standard Technology was around during the crazy days before history, and during the Empire."

"And looking at history, when would you say this golden age began? Or at least approached its present level?"

"Hmm. I don't know. Probably during the last two or three hundred years. Since the abdication of Fenwis IV in—the Year of Pertunis 371, I think it was."

Durslan nodded. "More than three hundred years after Wilman IX declared Standard Management into law. Right?"

Varlik nodded, eyes intent on his host.

"Standard Management was a definite and major factor in our present stability and prosperity, true enough," Durslan went on, "but by itself it was by no means sufficient. Among the Confederated Worlds we have hereditary monarchies with a great deal of power vested in the sovereign, as here on Iryala. There are meritocracies, in which the ruling echelon rises from the bureaucracy; and electoral democracies, in which the leaders are chosen by popular vote—all using Standard Management. Standard Management simply defines, regulates, channels *the administrative activities of the management machinery*. In a sense, that computer tank of seemingly immutable policy directives that constitutes Standard Management, those long shelves of sacred books—they are the management machine.

"But the topmost level in government—king or premier or president or first council—that authority which sets goals and aims the machine— arrives at his or her or their position in a variety of ways. Some of those people have been highly corrupt and self-seeking, and others highly ethical; some have been wise and some foolish; but most have been somewhere in between. And Standard Management has served them all, providing each with relatively efficient service.

"As you may be aware, some Confederate Worlds are better places to live than others. Their people enjoy cleaner and more aesthetic environments, better economies, greater justice and social stability. Some of this, of course, is due to planetary resources, but some of the most prosperous worlds are rather poor in physical resources. In fact, much of the difference reflects the goals and decisions of rulers. And much of the rest depends on how well their governmental machinery operates: Standard Management is more efficiently applied, its policies better understood and more honestly followed, on some worlds."

Durslan paused, regarding his guests calmly, as if setting them up for what would follow. "Do you suppose the Confederation would be enjoying this 'golden age' if Rombil was at its hub, and Rombil's First Council its administrator general?"

Both Varlik and Mauen shook their heads.

"Exactly. The golden age derives from Iryala, and on Iryala it derives from an association of people who call themselves 'the Alumni'—persons who shared certain special training that goes beyond Standard Management."

*And this is their school,* Varlik thought. *That has to be the connection.*

Durslan continued. "By ability which reflects their training and experience, some of its members rose to levels immediately below the Sovereign and were able to see to it that the administrative machinery ran more efficiently, more ethically. And in time, beginning with Consar II, they recruited and trained the king. Every prince since then has been educated and trained by the Alumni in one of their schools."

"Some of them right here, I suppose?" Mauen asked.

Surprised, Varlik glanced at her. She never before would have interjected something like that into a conversation with a man of rank. The experience of the day was changing her as well as him.

Durslan smiled. "Actually, no. There is a less venerable school more suitably located. But both teach the T'sel. There are eight such schools on Iryala now, and several on other Confederation worlds."

Varlik's eyebrows rose.

Durslan unfolded his legs and steepled his fingers. "There is a flaw in this 'golden age,' however. If our environment was as unchanging and self-contained as is generally assumed, it might not be a major flaw. But our environment is neither unchanging nor self-contained. You see, we, the humankind of this region of the galaxy, are not all the humankind there is. Nor is humankind the only intelligent life form."

"I've read about the concept," Varlik put in. "Generally, it's ridiculed. Do you have actual evidence for it?"

"You can read the evidence for yourself when we're done talking here. I believe you'll find it interesting. Basically, though, there *is* history which predates what the Confederation knows about—a great deal of such history.

"Now, about this matter of not being alone in the galaxy: It poses a danger, one which the Confederation as it presently stands is seriously unsuited to deal with, should it present itself—as it surely will. The conspiracy you detected, and the insurrection on Kettle, are the beginnings of a program to correct that deficiency."

The hands steepled again. "That is only some background to what I'll tell you about the conspiracy. But the rest must wait until you've read the outline of that 'prehistoric' history, and talked with friend Wellem again. How does that seem to you?"

Varlik grinned. "I'll let you know when I've read the history and talked with Wellem."

"Good enough," said Durslan grinning back, and they all got up.

*Varlik's changing*, thought Mauen, *just like I am. He'd never have said anything like that to a nobleman before. It'll be interesting, getting used to each other again.* But she had no qualms.

For supper, Konni Wenter commonly used the meal service in her building, even though it was somewhat more expensive than preparing meals herself. She seldom felt much like cooking after a day's work anymore. Being a team leader was more demanding than being Bertol's assistant, especially with the green assistant they'd assigned her. Also, it paid somewhat more, making the meal service more affordable.

She was eating in front of the video—braised beef cooked with gondel pods, over steamed barley with a side dish of steamed vegetables. There was a pint of ice cream in her locker for dessert. But tonight she was out of sorts, wasn't enjoying the meal. She should have invited someone for supper, she told herself—either a chum or the new guy in the sports department who'd taken her to lunch yesterday.

Her communicator buzzed and she got up to answer it. The face on the screen was a grinning Varlik, with Mauen beaming over one shoulder.

"Are you free tomorrow?" Varlik asked.

Tomorrow was Sixday, and B-crew had the weekend duty. "Yes," Konni said, "I'm free."

"Great! We're calling from Lord Durslan's. And look, things have sorted out beautifully up here. Can you come up? You have an invitation from Lord and Lady Durslan to get a rundown on things. We both really hope you'll come."

Their faces seemed to peer out at her as if, she thought, the screen were a window. "Why, I suppose I can." Somehow she felt muzzy-headed, as if she'd just wakened from a nap.

"Good. Look, *Lakes Air Transit* flies up here. I'm not sure what their weekend schedule is, but call and make a reservation. I'll call you back in an hour and you can tell me your arrival time. There'll be a car waiting for you at the terminal." He paused. "You okay?"

"Yes, I'm okay. This is just kind of sudden."

He looked back over his shoulder, as if someone was saying something to him.

"Konni, Lady Durslan says forget calling for reservations. The flight is on her and Lord Durslan; she'll arrange your reservations from here, against her credit print. I'll call you back and tell you the flight and time. How's that?"

"Uh, fine. That's fine. I'll be here."

"Good. I'll talk to you again in a few minutes. Oh, and pack your swimsuit. They have a big natatorium here," he added, then switched off.

She stared at the blank receiver, then went back to her meal. *Something's strange about that,* she told herself. *That was Varlik, no doubt about it. And Mauen. And they both looked all right. But there was something different about them. Not as if they were being forced to call; there was no one off to the side pointing a gun at their heads.* She tried to consider possibilities. *Maybe they've been drugged.* She didn't find the notion convincing, though. Things like that only happened in novels or holo dramas.

She returned to her meal. They were all right, she told herself. They'd just taken her by surprise. Getting all that stuff explained and straightened out could easily affect Varlik like that, considering how it had troubled him all these deks.

She finished eating and had just disposed of the debris when the communicator buzzed again. It was Varlik, and he gave her the flight number. He seemed just fine, but his grin was still not entirely real to her. She supposed she'd seen him grin before—she was sure she had, she could think of instances—but not like that.

After he'd hung up, she tapped in Felsi's number. It took a moment; Felsi answered with tooth cleaner on her lips.

"Oh, it's you," Felsi said.

"Who'd you think it was going to be—Reev Stoner?"

"I should wish. What's going on? Anything about . . . ?" she asked suggestively.

"Sort of. Look, Varlik Lormagen and his wife are up in the Lake District, guests at the home of Lord Durslan. Lord and Lady Durslan are very interested in the Kettle insurrection, and the T'swa. And I'm invited to go up there; I'll fly up in the morning.

"Now, I have no reason to think anything will happen to me while I'm gone, but it's possible. So look. I expect to be back Sevenday evening; I'm supposed to be at work on Oneday. If I don't call you by Oneday night, something will be wrong, and you know what to do. Okay?"

Felsi nodded, big dark eyes staring out at Konni.

"Fine. Like I said, I'm about ninety-nine percent sure that nothing's going to happen to me while I'm gone. I just don't want to take any chances. And thanks."

When she'd hung up, Konni stared worriedly at the wall. She'd deliberately tried to put Felsi at ease. It seemed to her that in reality, the odds that nothing would happen to her while she was gone were more like sixty-nine percent than ninety-nine.

✧     ✧     ✧

After "visiting" again with Wellem and talking with Konni, Varlik and Mauen retired to their room, but not yet to sleep. Lord Durslan had given them books from a classroom—books the children studied there—on the history of the Confederation, of the T'swa, and of T'sel. Hours passed before they went to bed, and the world changed even more for them.

In his sleep, Varlik was once more with the regiment—the platoon, actually—and they were in the sawmill in the Jubat Hills. But it was too noisy there, almost impossible to talk (although afterward, remembering, Varlik could not recall any actual audio sensation; it was the concept of noise). So they were somewhere else—not *went* somewhere else but *were* somewhere else—in a beautiful, quiet landscape of neat lawns among wooded, storybook mountains. And the platoon—led now by Colonel Koda—examined him with questions. It was an incredibly warm and beautiful experience. And for every question they asked, he had the answer, an ideal answer, lucid and brilliant.

He awoke at last, sat up in the darkness of the room with tears running down his cheeks. There was no grief, though, only a joy of reunion which seemed no less real for having been experienced in dream.

Of the dream, he could remember nearly all, with images of the world where they had tested him, a world not Tyss or Iryala or anywhere he knew of. He could remember how good it had felt to be there with them. He remembered everything except the questions and the answers, and their absence didn't seem important at all.

Because somewhere, he told himself, he knew. Smiling, he lay back down, rolled over, and went to sleep again, this time dreamless.

# 41

The night had brought hard frost, and a thin ring of ice along the lake edge, not at all like a night on Kettle or Tyss. But by a little past midmorning, when Bren drove up in front, the sun had raised the air temperature to over fifty, and in the virtual absence of breeze it felt even warmer.

Mauen had ridden in to meet Konni at the landing field. By the time they arrived at the estate, Konni was feeling relaxed; it was obvious that Mauen was all right, so Varlik must be, too. Mauen had smoothly avoided saying anything of substance about what had happened, slipping questions, letting Konni think she hadn't been privy to Varlik's conversations with Lord Durslan.

Melsa and Varlik greeted them on the porch. And no, Konni admitted to Lady Durslan, she hadn't eaten. She'd slept too late for breakfast. So she had a late breakfast at the manor while Varlik, Mauen, Lady Durslan, and belatedly Lord Durslan, kept her company over joma. They'd already breakfasted.

Konni, of course, was unwilling to question Varlik while the Durslans were present.

When she'd finished eating, Lord Durslan suggested she get acquainted with the situation in the same order that Varlik and Mauen had, and they all trooped over the causeway to the *ghao*, where she met Wellem Bosler.

She'd taken Bosler a bit longer to open up than had Varlik or Mauen; her distrust had reactivated, a distrust more deeply rooted in personality than Varlik's had been, but a half hour later she'd emerged in much the same state that Varlik and Mauen had.

Then Melsa had shown her to her room and left her for a short nap. All three guests had spent the afternoon with books. Briefly, *The Story of the Confederation* had upset Konni, and Wellem had guided her into and through a brief, gentle procedure that had taken care of her problem with it. That evening, Lord Durslan had given her approximately the same rundown he'd given Varlik and Mauen the day before, with the others sitting in. Like Varlik, Konni came out defused.

The next morning, Durslan promised, he'd give them the full story of the conspiracy.

Felsi Nisben had had a date for that evening, but he'd called to say he had to work. So she'd had a solitary supper followed by a solitary drink. Then she thought about the mysterious package Konni had left with her, and the strange, danger-spiced instructions.

It seemed to Felsi that if Konni expected her to do something like that, she'd owed it to her to tell her what it was all about.

Actually, Felsi resisted temptation for more than an hour—until drought hit the video and she'd had another drink. Then swiftly, not to argue herself out of it, she unwrapped one of the two packages, fitted the cube into her player, and turned it on. A quarter hour later she told herself she wished she'd never thought of it, wished Konni had given it to someone else. Actually she was thrilled; Konni and her friends obviously were in very real danger. Why Konni hadn't taken it directly to the authorities was more than she could understand.

She took Konni's folded instructions out of her handbag. The business of taking a package to the spaceport and getting in touch with some

Captain Brusin sounded altogether too difficult and complicated. And this Colonel Voker, deks away on the planet Kettle, wouldn't be able to do anything in time anyway. But the Director of Enforcement in the Ministry of Justice—he was only minutes away.

Then she reminded herself that Konni had said to do nothing before Oneday night. If she hadn't heard by Oneday night, then she could do something. She also reminded herself that she'd broken faith with Konni by opening the package.

Again swiftly, not to change her mind, Felsi rewrapped the package and returned it to her closet shelf. Then she had a double drink and went to bed.

The sign said "Cool Drinks." It was in Bird, and that surprised Varlik, even if it was in the middle of the Orlanthan jungle. Sergeant Kusu, wearing camouflage fatigues and his original chin, stood in the cantina door beckoning to him, and Varlik went over.

The cantina was much bigger inside than out, not very wide, but long. And hazy. Lord and Lady Durslan were there, wearing only breechclouts. For a moment Varlik tried not to look at Lady Durslan's breasts, and realizing this, she laughed. They were much bigger than Varlik would have thought, jutting roundly. The sling on her rifle passed between them, and it seemed to Varlik that she'd have real trouble unslinging it in an emergency.

All six of them then—Mauen and Konni were with him too now—walked along inside the cantina looking at the artwork. One of the pictures was of the arsenal in the Jubat Forest, and in it he could see Konni and himself looking out of the picture at him from behind door posts; both were waving to him from the picture, which seemed to Varlik very unusual. Kusu also saw them waving and, winking, nudged Varlik. Kusu was wearing a breechclout too now. Varlik took a rifle from one of the cases and looked for the serial number. Instead of a number, the words *Made on Tyss* were engraved on it.

As they walked, it was no longer the cantina, but a long, greenly lit aisle through the jungle. Varlik was impressed because, as he reminded himself, he didn't usually dream in color. All along the aisle were small stone steles marking the places where men of the regiment had died. Kusu named them off as they passed. At each one, Lord Durslan saluted and laughed, and as he did, a holograph of the T'swi who'd died there rose out of the ground and laughed good-naturedly back. But they were only holographs, Varlik knew. He asked Tar-Kliss, who was with them now, why holographs? Tar-Kliss told him the bodies had decayed, so the T'swa were using holographs to greet visitors with.

At the end of the aisle were the lake and the causeway, but the lake looked like the Lok-Sanu River and the causeway was a bridge. A bargeload of steel was passing beneath it, and Varlik looked down at it. Then Wellem Bosler called from the *ghao,* and they all hurried across and went inside. The whole regiment was there waiting, their new bodies looking just like the old ones, and General Ramolu was with them.

Ramolu came up to Varlik, shook his hand, then told him good-naturedly that he'd screwed the whole thing up. No, Varlik answered, it will all work out. Wait and see. It will all work out. Kusu laughed. It always does, Kusu said. Either way, it always works out.

With that, Varlik awoke and sat up. The moon had risen, and the curtains glowed with it. Very briefly he remembered the whole dream as a panorama, then most of it slipped away. All that was left, beyond some general impressions, was himself telling Ramolu that it would all work out, and a laughing Kusu saying it always did; either way, it always worked out. Varlik chuckled and shook his head. He didn't know what it was all about, but it felt right. He went back to sleep hoping to dream some more, but if he did, he didn't remember it afterward.

# PART SEVEN
## *Resolution*

# 42

Felsi Nisben woke up knowing what she had to do. Hurriedly, she got ready and left for the transfer stop with one of the packages Konni had given her, not taking time for breakfast. She often skipped breakfast on Sevenday anyway, and besides, she might think as she ate, and she couldn't afford to think. Right was right, and it was not okay to sit around rationalizing the way she'd done last night.

It was a matter of withholding evidence, and delay could endanger Konni's life—if she wasn't already dead. The thought sent delicious shivers through Felsi.

She'd gotten off the bus outside the Tower of Justice before it occurred to her that there might be no one available to see her. This was Sevenday, after all; that's why she was here instead of at work. *Though this takes priority over work anyway,* she reminded herself. *It's a matter of—Planetary? Confederation?—Planetary security at least.* The concept was so exciting she had another rush of shivers. They'd *better* be open here on Sevenday— this Sevenday, at least.

The lobby was different from any she'd seen before: there was no receptionist, though a solitary security officer eyed her thoroughly and impersonally as she passed him. There was no place to sit, just a long hall with a row of elevator doors down each side, each door marked with a single floor number.

There was a register; the *Office of Enforcement* was on the sixth floor. She went to one of the elevators marked sixth floor and touched the decal. The door opened at once. The elevator had been waiting for her, she told herself. A good sign; she was doing the right thing. She hadn't had to wait for a bus, either. It had come within fifteen seconds, a minor miracle; usually it took at least a couple of minutes—as many as ten on a weekend.

She wasn't aware of the electronic units that scanned her for various materials as she rode up. Had one of them detected contraband, the elevator would have taken her not to the sixth floor but to building security in the basement. And had she known that—duty be damned: Clean though she was, she'd never have gotten on the elevator.

But she didn't know, and psychologically fortified by good omens, she exited the elevator confidently into a reception area. Here security, though not a dominating presence, could clearly be seen—three officers sitting in little corner booths. The receptionist wore civvies, and watched politely as Felsi came up to her.

"How can I help you?" the receptionist asked.

"I have a package I need to give to the Director of Enforcement."

"Fine. May I have your name and registry number?"

"Felsi, F,E,L,S,I, 686 Nisben, N,I,S,B,E,N, 2546—3129—3217 Iryala."

As Felsi spoke, fingers moved on a keyboard, then the woman looked up and reached out a hand. "I'll see that the director gets it."

Felsi's expression hardened with unwillingness. "I'm supposed to give it to him myself. It's very important."

"I'm sure it is, Miz Nisben. But there are Standard policies we have to follow. Otherwise, this place would be a madhouse and nothing would get done." She kept her hand out, expectantly.

Felsi shook her head stubbornly. "It's an emergency. And important."

The receptionist nodded. "Are you reporting a crime in progress? If so, we need to inform the local or district enforcement authorities."

"No, it's nothing like that. It's—special. Different."

"I see." The woman made a decision. "Let me show you something on my screen. I'm going to write something into the computer, and I want you to see the read-out."

She swiveled her screen enough that Felsi could see, then her fingers ran over the keyboard again. Suspiciously, Felsi watched words form on the screen:

SITUATION: IMPORTANT EMERGENCY, NOT A CRIME IN PROGRESS. PERSON REPORTING SITUATION WISHES TO REPORT IT TO THE HIGHEST PERMISSIBLE POST. WANTED: IDENTITY OF HIGHEST PERMISSIBLE POST.

The receptionist touched a final key and the words vanished, replaced by a short block of text. Her fingers moved again, isolating a line and enlarging it:

THE REPORTING PERSON MAY BE ALLOWED TO SEE THE EMERGENCY ALERT OFFICER ON DUTY.

"That's as far up as I can send you," the receptionist said with finality.

Felsi stared at the line. At least this would get her closer to the top, and she still wouldn't give up the package if she didn't want to. "All right," said Felsi, "I'll see the emergency alert officer."

The receptionist pressed a button. A moment later a young man arrived and led Felsi to an office door. He made no move to knock, only stood there by Felsi until a buzzer sounded. Then he opened the door and ushered her in without following her; the door closed. A sturdy, pleasant-looking woman was seated at a desk.

"Miz Nisben," she said, "how can I help you?"

Felsi repeated her request.

"Felsi—may I call you Felsi?"

Felsi nodded.

"Felsi, I'm not unsympathetic toward your feelings about this, but I'm required to follow policy; it's a matter of Standard Management. I'm simply not allowed to let you see the director except under very special circumstances. And at any rate, he's not in today. On weekends one of the assistant directors serves as acting director."

For a moment Felsi froze, didn't know what to do. "Will he be in tomorrow?" she asked.

"Almost certainly."

"Then I'll come back tomorrow."

"Wait a moment." The emergency alert officer regarded Felsi thoughtfully. "How important is this?"

"Extremely important. It could even mean life or death for a friend of mine."

For a moment the woman's eyes withdrew in thought, then returned to Felsi. "If your information is that important—for example, if someone dies because you withheld it, or if any major felony results—the act of withholding could constitute a felony on your part."

Her fingers too moved over a keyboard, and when she was done she swiveled her screen so Felsi could see the law she'd called up on it. The language was straightforward; Felsi read it.

"That's not a threat, dear," the woman went on kindly. "It's simply something that, under the circumstances, you need to know. Let me ask you another question: What is the nature of your information?"

"It's about—a conspiracy against the Confederation."

The emergency alert officer's expression didn't change. *She doesn't believe me,* Felsi thought. *If she did, she'd look shocked or something.*

After a moment the woman asked, "Where did you get the information?"

"It's from a friend of mine with Iryala Video, who worked with Varlik Lormagen on Kettle. Both of them were wounded there. He gave it to her because he thought something bad might happen to him, and she gave it to me because she thought something might happen to her; it's all on the cube."

This time the woman's lips pursed for a thoughtful moment, and she drummed her fingers. Then she reached to her communicator and held a privacy receiver to her ear. "Monti," she said, "I'm bringing a young lady down to see the assistant director. . . . Right now. Yes. . . . I'll let her tell you that."

She hung up then and stood. "Felsi," she said, "this had better be good, because I'm sticking my neck out for you. The assistant director for internal operations has the duty this weekend—he's the highest ranking person here today. I'm taking you to see his secretary."

Hand on Felsi's arm, the woman led her out the door. "I'm allowed to deviate from protocol if I consider a situation sufficiently urgent. Standard Management allows for it. But if this is bullshit, I could be busted down to the secretarial pool."

The woman's words numbed Felsi for a moment, but she regathered her certainty. On another hall they stopped before a door, and the emergency alert officer opened it without hesitation. A lean, dark, youngish man sat waiting, hard-eyed and skeptical.

"This is Felsi Nisben," the woman said.

"All right, Felsi," the man said, "what have you got for us that's too important for normal routing?"

Felsi repeated what she'd said before. The man glanced at the emergency alert officer, frowning, then back at Felsi.

"So I repeat: what is there about all this that can't go through normal routing? Why does the assistant director have to handle it?"

At that moment she got an inspiration. Of course! she thought. She'd known there was an important reason why Konni had addressed it to the director.

"Because it involves a foreign government and an Iryalan nobleman."

The man's eyes sharpened. After a moment he reached to the privacy receiver on his communicator. "Sir," he said, "the emergency alert officer has brought a young lady in. I think it best you see her."

Fifteen minutes later the assistant director, another lean and humorless man, was on his own communicator to the director, Lord Ponsamen, at his home. "And involving as it does a lord of the realm," he said, "perhaps two of them, I felt it best that you be informed . . . Personally? . . . I see your reasoning, sir. . . . Within the hour, sir; I'll bring a squad."

Twenty minutes after that, with Felsi in tow, the assistant director was on the roof of the tower with a squad of armed marshals, loading into an unmarked, armored hover van.

"To Lord Ponsamen's residence," he ordered, then said nothing more.

Lord Ponsamen was waiting, not willing to fly away without first seeing some evidence. So while the squad lounged on an enclosed veranda with the driver, Ponsamen, in his study, viewed and heard the cube with the assistant director and Felsi. Lord Ponsamen watched the screen while Felsi covertly watched Lord Ponsamen. Tallish, he verged on portly, a man blond and pink, with pink, beefy hands. He was immaculately manicured, Felsi noted; she'd been a manicurist once. She had no idea what he was thinking; he looked as if he found the cube fairly interesting but not very exciting.

Yet when it was over and he went to his study closet, she saw him don a shoulder holster before putting on a casual jacket. He paused briefly to draw the weapon and examine it, as if making sure it was ready for use, ejecting the clip to see if it was loaded. "Haven't carried this for, hmm, more than six years," he commented, holstering it, then redrew it three times more, swiftly, as if reinstalling old trained reflexes.

He looked at the assistant director and Felsi. "All right," he said, "let's go see what Lord Durslan has to say about all this."

To Felsi, he sounded as blasé as if he were going out to walk the dog.

# 43

The pool was cooler than Konni had expected, not something for lolling in. In middle and upper school she'd been on the swimming team, and now began to swim laps, smoothly, powerfully, enjoying the unaccustomed feel of her muscles pulling and stretching. But she tired rather quickly, and hands on curbing, hoisted herself out of the pool without using the ladder. Varlik and Mauen were splashing each other while Wellem Bosler swam strong easy laps along the opposite side.

*That Varlik's got almost a gymnast's physique,* Konni thought, *and Mauen looks like a dancer.* She'd have to get her own weight down, she decided.

The one that surprised her was the T'sel master. His face said forty-five but his body suggested a vigorous thirty-five. She wondered which was closer. The face, she supposed. *Konni,* she told herself cheerfully, *you need to get yourself a boyfriend and stop this secret ogling. Too bad Wellem doesn't live in Landfall.*

Bosler too climbed out of the pool, and walked around to sit down by her. "How do you like it here?" he asked.

"So far so good," she answered. "I know for sure I like what's happened to me so far; I expect I'll like it even better when it's had a chance to settle in more. It feels as if things are changing in me that I don't even know about."

"That's the way it works," he said with a chuckle. "It's especially noticeable with adults. I had one call me up to tell me he'd just realized he hadn't felt regret for at least a year."

The concept startled Konni. Regrets were part of her standard repertory of feelings, or had been. She wondered if she'd regretted for the last time.

They were interrupted by Melsa, who announced that if they'd had enough of the pool, Garlan was in his study, ready to give them a rundown on "the conspiracy." She said the last two words with an emphasis after a pause, then waited. Varlik and Mauen swam to the ladder and got out, too.

"I'm ready," Varlik said. "How about the rest of you?"

Konni had already gotten up. "Me, too," she said, and looked at Bosler, who grinned back at her.

"I'll sit in," he answered, "although I'm probably familiar with most of it."

They separated to the two dressing rooms, dried, groomed briefly, and dressed, then regathered in Durslan's study. They'd just sat down when Elgen, in his role as butler, looked in without knocking.

"Excuse me, sir, but a hover van has just landed in the yard and armed men have gotten out."

"Thank you, Elgen. I presume they'll be coming to the door. Let them into the entry hall and then call me. I'll pretend surprise."

Elgen departed. "Well," said Durslan, "something unexpected to spice the day. Why don't we postpone my little seminar until we see what this is about."

They waited. Varlik wondered if the armed men had anything to do with the conspiracy. It occurred to him that for most of his life, a situation like this would have made him tense, guts tight, perhaps feeling half suffocated. Now he simply felt alert.

Konni wondered accurately if it had anything to do with Felsi Nisben and the packages.

Distant door chimes sounded. A minute later Durslan's intercom buzzed, and he pressed the receiver switch. "What is it?"

Elgen's voice answered; Durslan was taking it on the speaker so his guests could hear. "A group of gentlemen from the Justice Ministry, sir," said Elgen. "Lord Ponsamen, a Mr. Jomsley, a Miz Nisben, and eight armed personnel."

*Shit!* thought Konni. *I blew it! How in the galaxy do we handle this?*

"Armed personnel? Indeed! I'm with guests just now, but I suppose— Make the armed personnel comfortable in the front sitting room. They're no doubt on duty and can't drink alcohol, but have edibles brought out for them, and joma. Is Lady Durslan at hand?"

"She just came into the entry hall, sir."

"Good. Ask her if she'd kindly bring Lord Ponsamen and the two other persons you named to my study. A Mr. somebody and a Miz somebody."

"Yes, sir."

They could hear Elgen talking briefly to someone. More faintly others spoke. "Madam will bring Lord Ponsamen, Mr. Jomsley, and Miz Nisben down at once, sir," Elgen reported.

The comm went still then. "Armed men," said Durslan. "Curious." He sounded utterly unperturbed. Again no one spoke, and in a minute Lady Durslan opened the door. At that point, the three men present stood up—Durslan, Varlik, and Bosler.

"My dear," Lady Durslan announced, "Lord Ponsamen, Miz Nisben, and Mr. Jomsley." She ushered them in, then left. Jomsley was dour and Ponsamen genially businesslike. Felsi looked at Konni and almost cringed; clearly, Konni was perfectly well after all, and so were her friends.

"Good morning, Durslan," said Ponsamen, and looked around. "Seems we're interrupting something. Can't be helped, though; I'm here in an official capacity, and I need to speak with you."

He eyed Varlik. "You're Varlik Lormagen, aren't you? And one of you must be Konni Wenter," he added, looking at the two young women.

"I'm Konni Wenter," Konni answered. "I'm afraid I don't know what your official capacity is, Lord Ponsamen."

"As well you might not; I'm not exactly renowned. Lord Durslan knows me; I'm the Director of Enforcement, in the Department of Justice."

He turned his attention to Durslan again. "I'd like Lormagen and Miz Wenter to stay. Feel free to dismiss the others if you'd like, though if they leave, I'll require that they join my men in your sitting room until we're done and I approve their further departure."

"Perhaps you'd care to tell me first what this concerns," Durslan answered.

"It concerns information on a certain cube made in part by Miz Wenter and in part, I believe, by Mr. Lormagen."

Durslan nodded. "I see. In that case I suggest they all stay. I believe they're familiar with the information you're referring to. There's no use their sitting in my parlor wondering what's being said about it in here."

So *dreams can be prophetic,* Varlik thought to himself. He remembered what Ramolu had said in his dream last night: "Lormagen, you screwed the whole thing up." *Funny that I picked Ramolu to say that in my dream. And Kusu said it would all work out.*

Varlik's chuckle was soft, yet every eye in the room turned to him.

"You've something to tell us, Mr. Lormagen?" asked Ponsamen.

"Not really. I was just looking at how this all came about."

One eyebrow raised, Ponsamen's gaze stayed on him for a moment, without any hostility that Varlik could sense. Then the director looked back to Durslan. "Please turn on your wall screen," he said, and Durslan complied. "Mr. Jomsley, prepare to play the cube."

Jomsley had brought a player from his office, a quality machine. For the next ten minutes or so they all viewed the by-now-familiar scenes, heard familiar words, with Konni's paraphrased summary of Varlik's suspicions and conclusions, and her concern about Varlik's safety here. When it was over, Ponsamen cleared his throat quietly.

"Now I believe you understand the presence of armed marshals. And while it appears that Mr. Lormagen and Miz Wenter are in fact quite well, that leaves unanswered the implications of the material recorded off-planet. Tell me, Lord Durslan, how do you account for what appears to be criminal conspiracy?"

Durslan leaned back in his chair, arms folded. "Let me begin," he said, "by stating that I serve as a consultant to the Foreign Ministry. And as we just heard, Lord Beniker referred Mr. Lormagen to me—not because Lord Beniker is unfamiliar with the facts, but because I am more fully conversant with the details. The Foreign Ministry has been aware of the enigmas described for some time now, as also in part the army has been. And you can see why the Ministry has given them a top-secret rating.

He gestured casually at Varlik. "Mr. Lormagen encountered certain peculiarities and, being particularly energetic, thorough, and persistent, took them to Lord Beniker, who found himself confronted with the distinct danger of someone knocking over the soup, so to speak.

"So Beniker arranged for Varlik to visit me here. I was to explain matters to him, and make him privy to whatever data and work in progress I saw fit—which is a good deal more than I am free to do for you, I might add. From me you'll have to settle for a summary.

"At any rate, as it occurred to me that Mr. Lormagen might have shared his information and suspicions with his wife, she too was invited. And when he learned the facts, he called Miz Wenter, who had shared both his investigations and suspicions. She arrived yesterday.

"And now here you are! Without your swimsuits, I'm afraid, though well equipped in other respects." Durslan smiled perfunctorily.

"The Foreign Ministry has activities in progress on several worlds, directed toward the solution of the enigmas pointed out. And as I've indicated, I'm not at liberty to discuss them. Perhaps Lord Beniker will be willing; certainly the authority is his. You might wish to ask him . . ."

"As I will," Ponsamen put in.

"One thing I am free to tell you about," Durslan continued, "is the matter of the T'swa arsenal, which is not, I hasten to add, to be talked about. It is, however, less sensitive information than the rest, being rather peripheral. Some centuries ago the Sovereign, in his role as Administrator General of the Confederation, agreed that the T'swa could manufacture steel for their domestic use, and allowed them to import small quantities of technetium for the purpose. Then, several years ago, our present Sovereign licensed them to manufacture their own light weapons—indeed, the only kinds of weapons they use—for their own use. Existing regiments, of course, still carried weapons of Iryalan manufacture, but new regiments were to be equipped with T'swa-made arms as available.

"About three years ago, the T'swa requested a rush shipment of Iryalan-made arms to Frey Marzanik's World. It seems that a supply of T'swa-made weapons had been shipped there for a T'swa regiment en route—a virgin regiment on contract to one of the warring states there. Unfortunately, the supply base was overrun before the T'swa arrived, and the weapons were lost—weapons which the T'swa themselves weren't prepared to replace quickly. Thus their urgent request for replacement arms."

Durslan shrugged slightly. "From there the T'swa-made arms obviously found their way into some as-yet-unidentified smuggling channel, and thence to Orlantha, a fact of which we were well aware prior to Mr. Lormagen's independent discovery in the jungle. Our own intelligence branch is sorting out possible trails, which quite conceivably may provide us the identity of whoever made possible the Orlanthan insurrection."

Durslan straightened. "And that, Lord Ponsamen, is the story in a nutshell. Meanwhile, let me point out that even had there been some details in this mishandled by our government, I, as a consultant, would scarcely be liable. And as you can see, the Lormagens and Miz Wenter are quite well, so I believe your business with me here is at an end. I regret that your weekend was disrupted by this misunderstanding, but as we know, this sort of thing happens in government service."

Durslan stood then, signaling the end of their audience. He'd completely taken charge. "I trust you will keep all of this scrupulously confidential. To leak it could seriously compromise our investigations, and your positions as well, no doubt. I'll also trust you not to copy the cube you played here; I recommend you give it personally to Lord Beniker."

Ponsamen raised his large body from the chair more easily than might have been expected. A sour-looking Jomsley and an embarrassed Felsi got up, too.

"Indeed!" Ponsamen spoke a little stiffly now. "I shall personally take these matters up with Lord Beniker this coming week." He turned and followed Durslan from the room, accompanied by Jomsley and Felsi Nisben.

When the study door had closed behind them, the Lormagens and Konni looked at each other, while Wellem Bosler sat back smiling. After a minute, Konni spoke quietly. "I told Felsi to do nothing before Oneday night. She must have gotten curious, opened a package, and played the cube. And got all excited and worried. She may also have delivered a package to Captain Brusin."

"The *Quaranth* won't leave before Threeday, at the soonest," Varlik replied. "You'll have time to get it back if she gave it to him."

Lord Durslan returned several minutes later. "Well," he said, "they're off the ground. Now. Where were we?"

"You were going to tell us about the conspiracy," said Mauen. "Or was that it? What you told Lord Ponsamen?"

Varlik grinned. "I thought I detected some fictions in your story, sir. For example, in my experience, admittedly limited, a T'swa regiment travels with its weapons. They're not shipped ahead."

Durslan nodded. "No doubt. I thought I did rather well for spur of the moment fabrication, though." He held up an audio recorder. "I have it all on here, incidentally. When one lies, it's well to have a record of what one said."

"Maybe you'd better get a copy to Lord Beniker," Konni commented. "It sounds as if Lord Ponsamen is going to question him."

"I will get a copy to Beniker. But Ponsamen won't question him—not in any official sense, certainly. What Ponsamen and I said here was to mislead Jomsley, let him think that all of this was being handled and that Ponsamen was going to verify it himself. So that Jomsley could dismiss it all from his mind as a good Standard bureaucrat should.

"Incidentally, Ponsamen's an excellent actor, wouldn't you say? He needs to be. You see, he's an alumnus of our school here, as I am, of course. A classmate of Beniker's, matter of fact, and knows a good deal more about the conspiracy than you do. Which, if you will all sit and listen, I will now remedy."

He looked them over, smiled, and began.

"First of all, let me say that the conspiracy grew out of the T'sel, the Way, but began here on Iryala, not on Tyss. The T'sel is the T'sel anywhere, but persons who know the T'sel will create different activities in different environments.

"Until 630 years ago, interest in the T'swa was simply in their value as mercenaries. Then a son of the Ostrak family, Harden, decided to travel to Tyss and see how T'swa mercenaries were trained; it seemed to him that something of value might be learned there. He'd heard about the T'swa climate, and had planned to stay only two or three weeks—less, if it was too oppressive. He ended up staying four deks, though it was summer, retreating to his lander for sleep, some of his meals, and at any other time when the heat threatened to overcome him.

"On his return, to his wife's dismay, he arranged to send their second son, age five, to Tyss to learn the T'sel. They supplied him with an air-conditioned sleeping chamber, which, incidentally, the lad outgrew the need for. Within three years there were three Iryalan children on Tyss, and by the time the eldest was ready to come home there were seven. They returned wiser than their parents, by criteria Iryalan or T'swa, had already recognized the need for thoroughgoing change in the Confederation, and had begun to develop the basic features of a plan.

"Of course, they mentioned none of this to their families. Instead, with the backing of Barden Ostrak, they established a school on the Ostrak estate, which was later moved to this more secluded and aesthetic location.

"The alumni of the school, and of other schools which were established later, came to refer to themselves collectively as 'the Alumni,' as I mentioned to you yesterday. We do not have a formal organization, but we collaborate and keep one another informed.

"Incidentally, it's extremely unlikely that any other such illegal, conspiratorial society could have existed unknown in the Confederation for six centuries, or even six decades. Perhaps not for six years. There'd be dissension, group suppression of dissenters, desertions, and dissident splinter groups, and secrecy would be lost. And of course we are very non-Standard, and therefore susceptible to psychiatric imprisonment.

"The keys to our continuation have been the effectiveness of the T'sel in unlocking human potential, and the fact that its truths are sufficiently basic and self-discoverable that we act with a very large degree of agreement, to which are added mutual trust and respect.

"We impose no truths, incidentally, require no Beliefs or Standard behavior, preach no Basic Premises. Each of us discovers his own truth for himself or herself, but these have a high commonality from one person to another, and at the least are compatible. The T'sel drills simply make it possible and more or less inevitable that we do discover them. One person may come up with a talent or cognition that most others do not— to each his own, we say—and there are different levels of attainment, especially for those who play in the field of Wisdom and Knowledge. But there does exist that large area of commonality, of mutual experience and wisdom."

Varlik interrupted. "You said drills. What about guidance by questions, the sort of thing Wellem did with us?"

"What Wellem used with you are mostly techniques developed by Iryalan masters to help non-T'swa adults or older children. When children grow up in the T'sel, few such procedures are necessary. Mostly they grow up open and knowing, with few barriers to be removed."

Durslan drew his thoughts back to his dissertation. "At any rate, the early Alumni soon began to assume prominent positions in government. Firstly, they were very largely of wealthy, or at least well-to-do families, well connected, as is commonly still the case today. Secondly, their T'sel education and training allowed them to excel both in learning and decision making, and of course they were emotionally very stable. So when they left our school for college or the universities, they invariably did exceedingly well. And thirdly, their understanding of human behavior and their ability to deal with human emotions allowed them to manage human activities with unusual skill."

He grinned then at his audience. "There's a fourthly, too, but I'll leave you to discover it for yourselves.

"Unfortunately, though, because of the Sacrament and the social strictures and laws that grew out of it, the Alumni have been unable to break Standard Technology, despite the various high posts held—including the Crown for these many years."

"You talk about breaking Standard Technology," Varlik said. "What about Standard Management?"

"Standard Management is remarkably viable; it needs relatively little change. The limitations lie in Standard Technology and the psychoconditioning that underlies it."

Durslan paused, as if shifting gears.

"You've read now that humankind exists elsewhere, in the home sector from which our ancestors came, and you've also read about the garthid. There are other races, too, some of them wanderers, which our seers and those of the T'swa have perceived. Some of those cultures, human and nonhuman, are predatory, with the ability to conquer or ravage worlds and peoples no better prepared than ours to cope with them. There is physical evidence, as well as observations one can make while in advanced T'sel states, that certain of them visited this sector of the galaxy before our ancestors came here, with power that dwarfs anything the Confederation has."

"Can you give us an example?" Mauen asked.

"Certainly. There once were much more extensive seas on Tyss. Millions of years ago they were removed, drawn off to about the present level, by a race which for some reason wanted and was able to take that remarkable quantity of water." He scanned the others. "Consider, if you please, the technology required to accomplish that!

"So far as we know, however, none of them has the T'sel. While we, having it, have the apparent potential to grow beyond their force and to raise a civilization like no other we know of. Yet as it stands now, we're cemented into technical and cultural immobility. So our first challenge has been to break the grip of Standard Technology on the Confederation.

"The conspiracy is the second step in that; the first was to quietly gain widespread positions of influence and power in the Confederation.

"It has been necessary to move carefully, which in this case has also meant slowly. Nearly three centuries ago, Orlantha became the new technite planet. Rombil was given it in fief, and decided to use slave labor, which was their legal right per policies on the exploitation of resource worlds. Foreign affairs, as you may not know, is a field rather largely outside the purview of Standard Management. The administrative *machinery* is Standard with a capital *S*, but the purposes of interplanetary relationships, and in part how they are carried out, are not covered by Standard Management.

"Early, there had been a trickle of slave escapes which the Rombili didn't take seriously because replacements were easily gotten, and the Rombili correctly considered the condition of the fugitives so desperate as to render them no threat.

"But the Alumni saw opportunity there. Standard Technology has it that steel cannot be made without technetium. We already knew this was false, but dared not say it. The falsity was attested by the tiny steel industry of the T'swa, which the Alumni knew of early and which for millennia had made steel without technetium.

"If this had become known in the Confederation two centuries earlier, it might have brought down aerial attacks on the T'swa, and the destruction of the material progress they had made, setting them back into primitivism and hunger—depending on who was sovereign here, and who his advisors. At the least, Tyss would have been embargoed—quarantined as unfit for human contact. While here, the knowledge of steel without technetium would have been encysted, walled off as a singularity, an unimportance not allowed to influence Standard Technology. Steel made without technetium would have been described falsely as very inferior, not fit for civilized use.

"But if the Confederation's supply of technetium were cut off, and the need for steel became serious enough, non-technetium steel might be accepted if properly introduced. The people who provided it would have to be considered as somehow outside of Standard Technology, and thus free of the stigma of apostasy. And if somehow they were already admired, they might even be regarded rather as *wizards,* a concept from antiquity meaning, loosely, those who operate beyond understood reality."

Durslan scanned his guests, noting their lack of conviction. "At any rate, that is the basis we've operated on—and with promising results. For example, Varlik, because of your very effective help, the T'swa are already admired in the Confederation, most particularly on Iryala and Rombil.

"As for acceptance of non-technetium steel, and of whatever other non-Standard introductions and innovations we may undertake, who do you suppose has controlled the Sacraments on Iryala the last twenty-three years? Indirectly, of course. Twenty-three years ago last Sixmonth we obtained a Crown decision, written but of course not publicized, that Standard Technology did not require the hypnotic drug to be prepared at the individual Sacrament Station by the station's High Technician. The rationale was that absolute Standardness was better served by preparation at a central laboratory—run by Alumni, as it happens. So a generation of children on Iryala, and increasingly on other worlds, has been treated not with the hypnotic drug but with a strong soporific that puts the person into a sleep too profound for hypnosis."

Durslan scanned his guests for any sign of difficulty with that knowledge. There was none.

"That small alteration of Standard Technology," he continued, "in its guise as a bolstering of it, seems to have been the first since at least the Amberian erasure.

"As a result, there are billions of young people in the Confederation today whose attitude toward Standard Technology is social only, not enforced by the Sacrament. The attitudes of most of them toward Standard Technology are presently pretty much like everyone else's, but they are much more susceptible to change.

"Incidentally, the Sacrament and other psychoconditioning is not irreversible. You lost yours, and a great deal of other burdensome mental baggage, in your first session with Wellem.

"But that is only groundwork. We also instigated the insurrection and its step-by-step escalation. Recently, technite production began again on a small scale at Beregesh; a pod arrived with the news late yesterday, and the jubilation has begun. In four or five days another pod will bring news that the refinery there has been destroyed again, along with the mine head, *by intense bombardment with superior lobber rockets of a design not known to Standard Technology,* launched from well outside the new Beregesh defense perimeter by Standard infantry lobbers whose range is supposedly somewhat too short.

"You can imagine what the effect of that reversal will be. The technetium shortage has already become desperate. Steel mills have shut down entirely on several worlds. Then, by a major and highly publicized effort, the situation seemed to have been brought under control. And suddenly the primitive gooks come up with an unexpected resource, this one beyond Standard, and the situation suddenly looks hopeless.

"One of the weaknesses of Standard Management, let alone of Standard Technology, is its severely limited ability to adjust to the needs of large-scale emergencies. Take my word for it, throughout much of prehistory in humanity's home sector, an insurrection like that would have been suppressed in far less time. Normal procedures would have been suspended and all necessary ingenuity and resources concentrated on handling it."

Durslan grinned wryly. "Consider. The resources of all twenty-seven member worlds could have been mobilized to handle the Orlanthan insurrection, and no doubt would have been if Standard Management allowed. While in the absence of Standard Technology, the resources of either Rombil or Iryala alone would have been enough, although in that case the situation would never have come up in the first place.

"But getting back to reality. A few days after public announcement that the refinery has been destroyed again, a T'swa metallurgist will arrive from Tyss, imported by the Crown. He'll bring with him the T'swa formula for making steel without technetium. And under the circumstances, he and his gift to the Confederation will be gratefully accepted and abundantly praised.

"Beyond that, our program is mostly rather loose and conditional, depending on events. But we Alumni are serendipitous, and accordingly optimistic. There will be an offer of autonomy to the Orlanthans—their technite will still be valuable, just not essential—and much rewriting of law concerning the rights of resource worlds in general. We'll continue to publicize the T'swa, expand our T'sel schools, and further defuse the Sacrament network. And we'll begin to introduce, little by little, the concept of *science*, which you encountered in your reading here and which will come to mean more to you, I'm sure."

Durslan spread his hands in front of him. "And that's about all there is to that, unless you have questions."

"You haven't told us how the weapons were smuggled to the Birds," Konni said.

"Ah! Of course! Sorry I overlooked that. Even on most trade worlds we have Alumni in at least a few positions of power or influence. On Splenn, for example, there is the large and wealthy Movrik family, which owns the planet's only interstellar merchant fleet—eleven ships. The other Splennite interstellar carriers are one- or two-ship operations, and it's those small carriers who've earned the Splennites their reputation as smugglers.

"But it's the honest and highly reputable Movrik family who hauled arms to Orlantha. Before the insurrection began, Rombil had no surveillance or security system on Orlantha. None was considered necessary. So smuggling was simple, and precautions rudimentary. The smugglers needed only to avoid encounters with the ore barges, which was easy because the barges followed very regular approach routines.

"Since the insurrection began, of course, smuggling has required extraordinary procedures and been restricted increasingly to ammunition and medical supplies. It has involved landings on an island safely outside the area monitored by surveillance platforms, and uses modified harvester submarines protected from detection by the high turbidity of the larger jungle rivers. On the lesser rivers they operate on the surface, under cover of bank forest."

Varlik nodded; the picture was developing for him. "And the T'swa trained the Birds?" he asked.

"Centuries ago the T'swa educated an Orlanthan cadre—educated them as children, on Tyss, in the T'sel. That cadre then went home and trained a larger cadre, the foundation for the new Orlanthan culture, the jungle culture. Much later, when the time came, a new Orlanthan cadre, a military cadre, was trained on Tyss."

"How did the Orlanthans become so numerous?" Varlik asked. "Our military command on Kettle was continually having to raise their enemy manpower estimates."

"That was a matter of smuggling, too. We've been working on this for a long time, you understand. It was T'swa who found early escapees and led them south to the jungle. Later, T'swa-trained recruiters from the tropics were flown north to recruit additional Orlanthans. On some coastal islands, far to the north, lived tribes driven there from the mainland by rival tribes. Island resources are limited, and population pressures can develop which can't be successfully alleviated by emigration because the neighboring shores and fisheries are occupied by stronger tribes. Some entire island tribes were transferred south two centuries ago—several thousand people. Most of the insurgents are descended from them."

"It sounds to me," Varlik said slowly, "as if a lot of people have been manipulated."

Durslan's calm eyes met Varlik's without challenging. "Oh, definitely. Since the first Sacrament was delivered on the refugee fleet, hundreds of billions have been manipulated by coercion of the most extreme sort, and in early childhood at that."

"Touché," Varlik answered. "But I'm talking about Orlanthans."

"Ah. Of course. Since the first slave roundup by the Rombili . . ." He grinned abruptly. "Yes, we've manipulated them, too, in a manner of speaking, but never coercively. It is axiomatic in the T'sel that persons be given the broadest self-determinism appropriate to their ethical level. The island tribes were given an alternative to oppression and chronic hunger, and accepting it, were brought south to serve our purposes. By other Orlanthans, let me add, acting on their own determinism. For by that time the Orlanthans had made the idea of insurrection their own.

"You see, you cannot successfully manipulate people, once they learn the T'sel, but you can collaborate with them on the basis of overlapping interests and mutually held reality."

Varlik didn't respond for a long moment. His attention was elsewhere. When he spoke again, it was slowly. "All right. I can see that." Again he focused on Durslan. "There's another question that bothers me though."

"What's that?"

"The regiment, or regiments—sacrifice of. Why?"

"From our point of view and the viewpoint of our program, the use of T'swa mercenaries permitted strong and favorable publicity of the T'swa. From the mercenaries' point of view, it provided a good war."

Durslan leaned toward Varlik, forearms on knees, a pose unexpected of a nobleman. "Tell me, Varlik, are you familiar with a chart known as *the Matrix of T'sel*?"

"In a general way. It's been explained to me, but I forget the details. I probably have a copy somewhere."

"Good." Durslan got up and stepped to his desk, where his slender fingers tapped keys on his keyboard. The wall screen lit up, and a moment later a chart appeared on it, the now-familiar Standard translation, with an arrow. The arrow moved to the top row, the right-hand column. "Does this entry fit your impression of the Way of the T'swa warrior?" Durslan asked.

Varlik nodded. "Right. 'War as play,'" he read aloud, "'Victory unimportant.'" Then the words of Usu, the T'swa medic on the hospital ship, came back to him, clearly, almost as if he were hearing them again. "'If you are truly at Play,'" Varlik quoted, "'death will not matter to you.' A T'swa told me that on the ship to Tyss. And I accepted it as a concept, but it wasn't really real to me. It still isn't."

It struck Varlik then what made it unreal. "How can the T'swa," he asked, "how can *anyone*, find satisfaction in a war without purpose? Without a purpose meaningful to them? On Kettle, did the T'swa know what was going on—that they were being used?" *Or would they have cared if they'd known?* he added to himself.

"They may have known," Durslan said, "but I rather doubt it."

He stroked his chin contemplatively. "You asked how they could find satisfaction in a war without a purpose meaningful to them. Recognize first that you asked that from a particular point of view. Now let me ask you a question—a very personal question. Do you have children?"

The seeming non sequitur stopped Varlik. "Not yet. We hope to, though. We've recently gotten clearance."

"Fine. What was the purpose of your sex life before you got clearance? Was it a source of joy and happiness? A form of pleasure without regard to production of offspring? Sex as play?" Durslan paused to smile. "And now that you have clearance for children, do you go to bed with the attitude of a worker going to his job?"

Varlik smiled back ruefully, then unexpectedly laughed. "Okay, I see what you're getting at. I've had several T'swa, two at least, talk about the matrix to me. But you're the first one to find an approach that worked. Or maybe I was just ready this time."

Durslan grinned. "Maybe you were. Now, one more thing while I have it on the screen: Where do you fit on this chart?"

"Huh! Well, when I first went to work I was at 'Work for Survival'— payday, the weekly credit transfer. Then I moved to 'Work for Advantage'— promotions and raises."

"Fine. And very valid, both of them. But right now, does it seem to you— Can you imagine yourself operating at the level of, say, Job as Play, with reward unimportant? Not 'no reward,' but 'reward unimportant.'"

"I can imagine it, but it's not entirely real to me."

He turned from the screen to look at Durslan again. "Where are you on the chart?"

Durslan moved the arrow. "Games as Play. So is Beniker. So are Tar-Kliss and Wellem, even though, as Masters of Wisdom, they were at Study as Play for years. They moved to Games as Play when they agreed to take part in the game of overhaul the Confederation. At any lower level—say, at Compete or Fight—they couldn't hope to succeed in a game like this one."

Varlik contemplated the chart, and the things that had been said to him by Durslan, Usu, Kusu, Bin. To T'swa mercenaries, war was an activity as pure as healthy sex, and apparently as satisfying. Eventually, through death or wounds, they lost the ability to play at war any longer. That would happen to him with sex someday, through death or age or whatever.

And the people that the T'swa fought and killed? They were people at War, too, participating in it at levels of Fight or Work, most of them, though apparently not the Birds. That's why the T'swa warred as they did—very personally, knowing who they shot at, not killing indiscriminately, but so far as feasible shooting or striking only those who'd chosen war or allowed themselves to be coerced into warring.

"Okay, I can see it intellectually," Varlik said, "and I'm beginning to feel it at a gut level."

Durslan reached and the screen went blank. "Fine," he said. "Can I interest you in employment?"

Varlik's brows rose. "What do you have in mind?"

"Formally, you'd be self-employed as a free-lance writer. But the Foreign Ministry would contract with you confidentially to write certain types of articles, scripts, and books that would help prepare the people of the Confederation for changes to come. And it would be best if you stayed here; you could have an apartment in our guest house. Information and consulting would be more readily available to you, and Wellem could work on your education. Mauen could be your secretary." He laughed again. "'Reward unimportant' wouldn't mean you couldn't afford to pay a secretary. You'd be well paid."

Varlik looked at Mauen; her eyes were bright and on his, expectantly.

"Garlan," Varlik said, "consider me your free-lance writer." *Job as Play! By Pertunis!* It was beginning to feel real to him.

Durslan turned to Konni. "And as for you, Miz Wenter, in the new phase the program is entering, we have need of a video photographer, director, and producer. I'm sure that we—you and Wellem and I—can develop some attractive projects."

She laughed. "If you hadn't offered, I'd have refused to budge until you did. This sounds like the best game around."

"Good. Then let's talk about terms and timetables. I'll want you available as soon as possible."

# 44

He was in a little two-seat floater, flying over steep, forest-covered, storybook mountains, and remembered seeing them before in a dream. *And I'm dreaming again,* he thought. *Even if this is in color.*

Below was a large fjordlike lake, richly blue, the mountains rising directly from its mostly beachless shores. Ahead, around the shoulder of a mountain, a broad park appeared, open and grassy, its green as rich as the lake's blue. Here and there were small colonnaded marble buildings with rounded roofs, and marble walks and benches. Not a typical dream setting—not a stage with props, so to speak. It was rich with detail.

The floater bent its course toward the lawn, where a large number of children were playing. *Some of them are T'swa,* Varlik told himself. *Some are black and some white.* The children stopped as the floater approached, watching calmly, not quite motionless. It seemed to Varlik that somehow they'd expected him.

*Strange dream,* he told himself. *But what dream isn't?* He knew who the children were, too. The regiment. Black or white, they were the regiment.

The floater was on the ground, on the lawn, and he got out. There was no sense of his feet impacting the ground, and he told himself that proved it was a dream, if proof was needed, or made any difference.

The place was holding remarkably stable for a dreamscape, though. As detailed and stable as reality.

Then the children began to play again. He got the impression of voices laughing and chattering, but without the normal playground shrieking.

*Of course not. They're the regiment,* he reminded himself. Several came walking up to him—his old squad, with Kusu. "We've been waiting for you," Kusu said, looking up at him.

A *marvelous dream,* Varlik thought again: *The impression of sound is almost real, almost sonic.*

And Kusu's face was Kusu's face, though he appeared to be perhaps nine years old. "Are these your new bodies?" Varlik asked. "You look half grown already, but you've been dead less than two deks."

Kusu grinned Kusu's grin. "Rules like those don't apply here," he said. "Time here is different. But that has nothing to do with how we look to you. We look like this *for* you."

A recollection came to Varlik then, of something he'd read as an adolescent in a book of myths from prehistory. *Is this heaven, then?* he wondered. He didn't want it to be. He wanted Kusu and the others to have recycled, to live again in bodies, back in the universe of reality.

But they were here and they were dead. And if *they* were dead . . . "Am I really here?" he wondered aloud.

Kusu laughed happily. "Of course. You're always here."

"Then—I'm dead," said Varlik slowly. The thought didn't upset him at all.

"No, you're dreaming."

*That's right. This is a dream. It's not supposed to make sense. This is my superconscious playing.*

"It doesn't feel like an ordinary dream. It's so detailed. And it doesn't shift around." Varlik tapped his foot on the ground, and this time felt the impacts. "Why am I dreaming this?"

"It's the clearest way for us to communicate with you. Look!"

He pointed, and Varlik turned around. Another child had walked up behind him, and Varlik stared, recognizing him at once: Himself, also about age nine.

Himself grinned at him. "We wanted you to know we're here," Himself said cheerfully. "You've—you and I have—taken on an interesting game, but don't expect everything to go smoothly."

"Know consciously," Varlik echoed. "Does that mean I'll remember this dream?"

It was Kusu who answered. "The parts you decide to. When you're ready for them."

"Will I come here again?"

"Probably. But like I said: Yourself is always here."

*Of course! Turn around and look at yourself!* Varlik nodded and changed the subject. "Some of the regiment is white now, but you're still blue-black. Are you going to be a mercenary again?"

"No. I'm going to play at Wisdom and Knowledge next time." Kusu laughed. "More knowledge than wisdom: I'm going to be a scientist. It'll be lots of fun, and open the doors to all kinds of neat games and jobs. Science is going to be the big thing to do in thirty or forty years, and I want to be in on the ground floor."

*Science.* Varlik recalled the term from some reading Lord Durslan had given him, but the meaning was vague yet.

"And will you remember after you recycle? Remember being a mercenary? Being Sergeant Kusu?"

"Possibly. But that isn't important. On this side I'll never forget. On the other—it depends on several factors."

"Will I ever see you again?" Varlik asked. He found he didn't want to lose touch with Kusu now that he'd found him again.

"Oh, yes. We'll see a lot of each other. I'm going to be Iryalan my next cycle. In about eight deks."

"Will we recognize each other?"

"On one level, certainly. But the life one is living is always the important one."

"I hope you get good parents."

"I will. I will. I've got my penalty slate quite clean; that allows me to choose."

The blue-black face grinned up at Varlik, the eyes friendly and touched with playfulness. Then the storybook world began to fade, the face fading with it, and as they disappeared, child Kusu's voice was saying, "Parents? I've picked the best, my friend, I've picked the best."

Then Varlik awoke. He knew he'd been dreaming, though he didn't remember what. Something good. Maybe it would come back to him.

He sat up in the dimness and looked at Mauen asleep beside him. She stirred restlessly; perhaps she was dreaming, too. He leaned over and softly kissed her, and her eyes opened. She smiled and reached for him.

# Notes

[1] From *A Child's First Book of T'sel,* by Brother Banh Dys-T'saben.

[2] Words marked with a star are defined and talked about in the glossary volume.

[3] The Standard year is divided into ten decimi, or "deks."

[4] The Standard clock is divided into twenty hours of one hundred minutes each. Thus 13.20 is midafternoon.

[5] The first known emperor, Amberus, had had public and private libraries and collections destroyed wholesale. Government and other computer banks, archives, and paper files had been ruthlessly culled of everything earlier except Standard Technical material and very limited current administrative records, on the psychotic consideration that all events prior to his reign were not only irrelevant but an insult. Writing or telling about history became a capital crime, and historians were executed wholesale. While there were numerous efforts to secret historical materials, over the course of his twenty-seven-year reign, and with considerable use of bounties and informers, these were generally rooted out. Only fragmentary materials have been recovered.

[6] The Standard twenty-hour day, with its hundred-minute hours, are used throughout the Confederation, the unit lengths varying according to the planetary diurnal cycles.

[7] For *torvard, sergeant* in Standard.

[8] Half past five by the hundred-minute clock.

# THE WHITE REGIMENT

This novel is dedicated to
*KRISTEN LYNN JONES*
*my favorite redhead*
*Born Dec 24, 1987*

---

## Acknowledgements

Jim Baen, for his encouragement.
Rod Martin, Elaine Martin, and Larry Martin for ideas and discussions
that were central in developing the philosophy of the T'sel. For example,
Larry came up with the insight that grew into the Matrix of T'sel.
In my infrequent visits to Arizona, some marvelous evenings
have been spent in the Martin living room.
Elizabeth Moon, for comments that have sharpened my writing skills.
Elizabeth is the author of the outstanding *Paksenarrion* trilogy and such
excellent shorts as "ABCs in Zero-G" and "Too Wet To Plow."
Bill Bailie, U.S. Navy (retired), for the benefit of his knowledge of
electronics, ordnance, and a great deal more; and for our yak sessions
that cover the spectrum and help ideas germinate and mature.
And again for his friendship.
Staff Sergeant Phil Yarbrough, U.S. Army, eight years a ranger, for
reviewing the manuscript and for the loan of material on
military strategy and tactics.
Also my respects to the elite forces, notably the U.S. Army Special
Forces, the Ranger battalions, and their equivalents in the other
services; and Air Force, Navy, and Marine fighter squadrons. These
organizations in particular provide roles for warriors; may their
careers be spent in training.
And finally my respects and appreciation to all branches of the
United States armed forces.

# Prologue

## Summer Solstice, the Year of Pertunis 736

Head tilted, Lotta Alsnor looked critically at herself in the mirror, yet hardly noticed the freckled face and carroty hair, the skinny arms and legs. She'd dressed herself in what she thought of as her prettiest dress, a yellow print with small white flowers, that Mrs. Bosler had given her for Equinox. She'd worn it almost every weekend since, at Sixday mixers where you got to visit with the staff and the older children. Mrs. Orbig had showed her how to clean it—it was a kind you sprayed with a special cleaner, then rinsed with water and blew dry. At home she hadn't cleaned her own clothes. Her mama hadn't taught her, probably had thought she was too little. Things were different here, a lot, and of course she was seven now.

Lotta frowned. The dress didn't have as much body as when it was new. Mrs. Orbig probably knew how to fix that too, she told herself. She'd ask her. Her eye noticed a small scuff on a white shoe, on the toe. Taking a tissue from her desk, she knelt and spit on the place, wiped it as shiny as it would get, then threw the tissue away.

With a final glance in the mirror, she hurried out of the room she shared with two other little girls and an older girl, then down the hall, the stairs, through the vestibule and onto the side veranda, where she stopped to wait.

Sunlight was hazy yellow on flowerbeds and lawn; insects floated among clustered blossoms. It was seldom this quiet. Summer Solstice was the first holiday since Equinox long enough for children from far away to go home. Lotta couldn't, of course. Pelstron was 1,600 miles[1] away, and her daddy didn't make enough money to buy the ticket. That didn't bother her though; she took it for granted. And her mother had written that they'd be able to fly her home for Harvest Festival.

A bee reconnoitered the bank of butterflowers at the veranda's edge, and Lotta wondered what it would be like to be a bee. Wisdom/Knowledge was her natural area; in a few years she'd be able to meld with a bee and find out. She gave the insect her full attention, intending that it happen now, that she suddenly slip inside it. Thus she didn't notice Mrs. Lormagen come out on the veranda.

Mauen Lormagen watched the rapt child for a minute or so without speaking. "Good morning, Lotta," she said at last, and the child turned and looked at her.

"Good morning, Mrs. Lormagen." The little girl's gaze was steady and direct. Mrs. Lormagen was old—forty-nine she'd heard someone say—but still pretty. She taught dancing as part of the T'sel. You knelt; meditated space, time, and motion; then practiced the forms; and finally you danced. Mrs. Lormagen could stand on one foot, put her leg out in front of her, her foot higher than her shoulder, and hold it there without falling down. Lotta could put her leg out like that too, either leg, but couldn't keep it there without holding on to the balance bar. She liked dance next best to meditation class, and Ostrak sessions with Mr. Bosler; actually she liked all her classes.

Mrs. Lormagen was going with them on the picnic, and Lotta realized now that the woman was wearing rough slacks, a plain shirt, and casual beach sandals. Of course. The boat's seats might not be clean, or the picnic benches. For just a moment the little girl considered running back upstairs to change, then dismissed the thought. She *liked* to wear her yellow dress.

Mr. Bosler came out then, and Mrs. Bosler. Each carried a large wicker basket covered with a towel. The Lormagens' grown son Kusu was with them. Lotta knew that Kusu was too old, twenty-two, for her ever to marry. Twenty-two was fifteen years older than seven, more than three times as old. Although . . . when he was thirty-five, she'd be twenty. But someone else would marry him by then. Kusu was beautiful: he was tall and had muscles, and blond hair with some red in it, but not nearly as much red as hers. And he laughed a lot. His area was Wisdom/Knowledge like hers, and he was home from the Royal University.

Kusu grinned at her, a flash of teeth, then hopped off the veranda and loped across the yard toward the boathouse, where the oars were kept. Mr. Bosler grinned at her too. He was sixty something, she'd heard, and didn't have much hair; none at all in front. He led them across the yard to the dock, where they got in one of the larger rowboats, and Kusu came down with two sets of oars, one for himself and one for Mr. Bosler. When everyone was seated, they pushed away from the dock and started rowing.

Lotta watched the oars push them through the water, making little whirlpools at the end of every stroke. Mr. Bosler was strong too, though not as strong as Kusu of course, and they rowed in perfect unison, as if they practiced together.

"How're you doing on the selection of your doctoral research?" Mr. Bosler asked over his shoulder.

"I've decided to open up the project I talked to you about," Kusu said, "and establish its feasibility. You and I are pretty sure it's feasible, but Fahnsmor and Dikstrel are positive it's not, so what I'm proposing is a study of the nature of hyperspace."

He laughed. "It's remarkable how long we've used hyperspace travel without anyone knowing or wondering about things like that. I'm sure that neither Fahnsmor nor Dikstrel got the real Sacrament when they were little, but they're at Work, on Jobs. And educated when they were, they don't have the faintest idea of what research is about. They want a study plan with no room for the unknown, so I'll give them what looks like one, and we can be surprised together."

Lotta wondered what Fahnsmor and Dikstrel were like. Fahnsmor she pictured as tall and lanky, Dikstrel as short and pudgy, and wondered if they really were. She knew the difference between imagination and reality, but she also knew that people sometimes knew things subliminally they didn't know they knew, and called what they knew imagination to account for it.

"You haven't been home for a few deks[2]," Mr. Bosler said to Kusu. "Have you heard the idea your dad's been playing with recently?"

"I guess not. Something in addition to translating the T'swa history of the old Home Sector?"

"Right. There's been a frequency increase, the last dozen years, in disorderly pupils in the public schools. It's not conspicuous, but teachers and school administrators have definitely noticed it. Varlik had a survey done on sample schools, and more than seventy percent of disorderly students belong in the same slot in the Matrix of T'sel."

Lotta saw Kusu's eyebrows arch. "Warriors," he said.

"Right. An unprecedented bunch of little warriors have gotten themselves born, with nowhere to fight." Mr. Bosler grinned, his mouth and eyes both.

Lotta knew a child at home like they'd been talking about: her older brother Jerym. He'd gotten in trouble at school for fighting. Once he'd told her he was going to be a T'swi when he grew up. She hadn't had the T'sel yet then, so she'd thought that was a dumb thing to say. The T'swa were born, not made; she'd already known that. Now she realized that T'swa meant different things to different people—a human species that lived on the planet Tyss, and the mercenary warriors from there. And that a long time ago, in the Kettle War, Mr. Lormagen, Kusu's father, was called "the White T'swi," which was wrong grammatically—T'swa was plural or an adjective—but that was how people said it on Iryala. Kusu was even named for a T'swa: Mr. Lormagen's sergeant on Kettle.

"What's Varlik's idea?" Mrs. Bosler asked. "Or was getting the statistics it?"

"Tell her, Mauen. He's talked to you since he has to me."

"He's proposed to Lord Kristal that regiments of children be formed and trained. Like the T'swa mercenary regiments: starting with six- and seven-year-olds."

Jerym's too old then, way too old, Lotta thought. Ten.

"Who'd train them? T'swa?" asked Mrs. Bosler.

"The first ones trained would be a cadre unit. T'swa would train them. Then the cadre unit would train the white regiments."

"Would they be mercenaries like the T'swa? If they were part of the Iryalan army, they could easily spend their entire career without fighting."

"He's thinking in terms of having them trained under the O.S.P. He doesn't think it would work to have the army do it; they'd want it done their way. Then, when an actual regiment finishes training, they'd become part of a special branch of the Defense Ministry. The Movement would hire them from Defense as a mercenary unit, and contract them out to warring factions on the trade worlds."

"Wouldn't they be competing with the T'swa?"

"Not really. The trade worlds would hire twice as many T'swa regiments if they were available."

They were just about to Gouer Island. Most of it was woods, but the end they were coming to was grassy, like a lawn with shade trees. The grass was even short like a lawn. Lotta could see two sets of outdoor picnic tables, far enough apart for privacy, and a big, open-sided shelter with tables of its own, in case it rained. Kusu had stopped rowing, and crouched ready to grab the dock. Mr. Bosler dabbed with his oars to guide them in. Lotta reached down, unbuckled her white shoes and took them off, along with her socks, so they wouldn't get dirty on the island. But her main attention was on the grownups talking.

"We can use the profits from the contracts to open more schools," Mrs. Lormagen was saying. "With the teeth taken out of the Sacrament, society needs a new and better glue. Or it will when the various centrifugal factors have been operating for a while."

Lotta understood almost all the words they'd been using, and being a Wisdom/Knowledge child, she knew pretty much what they'd been talking about, even what Mrs. Lormagen meant about glue: People who knew the T'sel liked other people more.

But Mr. Lormagen wouldn't have to worry about contracting his regiments out. They'd fight for the Confederation; she had a feeling about that.

The boat slid alongside the dock; Kusu grabbed one of the posts it was built on, and tied up to it. Lotta was the first one off, running barefoot up the dock to explore.

# 1

Excerpt from *Historical Abstract of the Home Sector,* translated from the Tyspi, with commentary by Sir Varlik Lormagen. Until otherwise authorized, distribution of this book is restricted to The Movement. The material summarized here was compiled and refined over several millennia by T'swa seers. An entire monastery of the Order of Ka-Shok was occupied with the task for more than a millennium, and the work is continually being updated.

> The ancient home of humankind was dubbed "the Home Sector" of the galaxy by early investigators. . . . This civilization, an empire consisting of fifty-three planets, was destroyed by a megawar more than 21,000 years ago, the principal source of destruction being His Imperial Majesty's ship *Retributor,* an immense warship designed to destroy planets.
>
> Rumors of the emperor's intention to build the *Retributor* undoubtedly caused the confrontation between the imperium and its antagonists. Otherwise the megawar might never have happened, for the imperium was decaying, and the opposition, usually factionalized, might well have resigned itself to awaiting the empire's self-generated dissolution. As it was, rebellion and mutinies, more or less coordinated, broke out on a number of worlds, involving powerful forces both loyal and in rebellion.
>
> When *Retributor* sallied forth under the command of its mad emperor, it did not spare worlds already ravaged. They too were "punished"—literally blown apart. And when the emperor blew himself up with his ship, only one subsector of his empire—eleven inhabited or previously inhabited worlds—remained intact. Of these, eight had been totally depopulated, or so nearly depopulated that humans did not long survive on them. What was left of the empire's population, once nearly 600 billion, was at most a few score million, probably fewer, scattered on three planets. And those millions diminished further before they began to increase.[3]
>
> Eventually they did increase, but they had lost every trace of civilization and history. After a long time, civilization re-emerged, and eventually, on the planet Varatos, a culture arose that reinvented science. In time there was hyperspace travel again. By 19,000 years after the megawar, the other ten surviving planets, two of them populated, had been rediscovered, and those without humans had been colonized.

The eleven worlds found themselves surrounded by a vast region of space without habitable planets. They didn't know why, of course. In fact, it seemed to them that they occupied an aberration—a region with habitable planets in a universe where there seemed to be no others. Science provided no convincing rationale; by that time it was in serious decline. . . .

In the year 742 Before Pertunis, the eleven worlds became a religious empire—the Karghanik Empire. The statutory structures within the empire are largely but not entirely uniform. Actually, the "empire" consists of eleven somewhat autonomous, single-system sultanates, mutually engaged in political and economic rivalries. Neither the empire nor its sultanates are true theocracies. In each, the religious hierarchy shares power with a secular aristocracy.

The imperial worlds are tied together by a complex network of political treaties and trade agreements administered largely through an artificial intelligence known as SUMBAA.[4] It is probably only through SUMBAA that the Karghanik empire has survived in the face of rivalries and especially of distance. Each planet has its SUMBAA; the SUMBAA for Varatos serves the imperial administration.

The empire has a fleet and army more than sufficient to its rather modest needs.[5] Its ships are manned by a mixed crew from all the worlds of the empire, the mixes and proportions being based on recommendations by SUMBAA. The higher command strata are filled largely by officers from Varatos, the Imperial Planet. Army and marine units, up to battalions, are each from a different world, each with its own officers, and no imperial battalion is stationed on its home world. Divisions never contain more than two battalions from the same world.

Each world has its own flag, and also its own several warships and planetary forces under its own command, partly for purposes of home-planet security and partly for reasons of prestige.[6]

The monastery named Dys Tolbash stood on a narrow side ridge that descended from a much higher ridge to the east. The building, long and proportionately narrow, was constructed in the form of three uneven steps, accommodating it to the sloping ridge crest. It seemed almost to have grown out of the ridge crest. The lower step stood on an outlook, below which the crest slanted down abruptly like the edge of some rough plowshare, to the boulder-cluttered valley at its foot.

A tower stood at each corner of each step, eight irregular towers in all, overlooking the desert valley two thousand feet below and the two ravines whose craggy walls formed the ridge sides.

It was summer, a season of furnace heat on Tyss, a heat scarcely moderated by the elevation of 3,400 feet. In the west, the evening sun squatted on the horizon, and the temperature had fallen a bit, to 121°F. Master Tso-Ban didn't know that—there was no thermometer at the monastery—and he'd have given it no importance if he had known. At the moment he was climbing the stone stairs that slanted up the outer north wall of a tower.

His tower was at an upper corner, and therefore one of the two highest. At the top step, he paused to scan the rhyolite outcrops and the bristly scrub that broke their starkness here and there. In the pale sky, a carrion bird rode an updraft, tilting, watching, silent. A lesser movement caught Tso-Ban's large, still-sharp eyes. A rock goat, male and solitary, stood browsing with careful tongue among the leaves of a fishhook bush.

The old T'swa monk turned then and entered the top of the tower, a small cell with thick stone walls on three sides, open to the north, away from the sun. On the others, wide eaves-shaded windows gave access to whatever breeze might come. The only furnishings were two pegs in the wall, and a stone platform a foot high, padded with a hide over which a straw mat was spread. On one peg he hung his waterbag, on the other his unbleached white robe. At his age, the skin he exposed was no longer the black of a blued gun barrel, but a flat, faintly grayish black. Seating himself on the platform, he arranged his legs in a full lotus.

In seconds his eyes lost focus; in seconds more they saw nothing, though they did not close. It took a moment to find his unwitting connection, a man who never imagined that someone like Tso-Ban existed, or the planet Tyss. Unfelt, Tso-Ban touched him, and in a sense, in that moment, was no longer on Tyss, in a tower in the Lok-Sanu foothills. His attention was on the bridge of a warship, the flagship of a small exploration flotilla, outward bound from a world named Klestron.

Tso-Ban was a player at Wisdom/Knowledge, and had taken the Home Sector world of Klestron as his psychic playground. For some time, the Sultan of Klestron had been his unknowing connection. The sultan, an ambitious man, had decided to gamble, to send out a flotilla of three ships, with orders not to return until they'd found a new, habitable world. This action was quite unprecedented, by imperial standards illogical and arguably illegal. So of course it attached Tso-Ban's interest.

The sultan had given command of the flotilla to a brevet admiral, Igsat Tarimenloku, making him its commodore. Tarimenloku wasn't brilliant, but he was loyal, a devout son of Kargh, and a friend of the sultan, insofar as the sultan had friends.

Tarimenloku had become the T'swa monk's new connection. Tso-Ban could have used the ship as his connection, but far more information was available this way. In trance he became almost one with Tarimenloku, perceiving through him and with him, sensing his emotions, his surface thoughts, and in a general way his underlying intentions. But always there was a certain separation, Tso-Ban remaining an observer.

It was ship's night in the command room, the light soft, free of glare. Others were there, but Tarimenloku's—and with it Tso-Ban's—attention went to them only now and then. Mostly the commodore watched his instruments, which after a bit told him that in real space there were a major and a minor nodus adjacent to his ship's equivalent location in hyperspace. If he emerged now, he'd find a previously unknown solar system near enough to examine.

It would be better though to be nearer. Tarimenloku tapped keys, changing course, moving "nearer" to the major nodus and "farther" from the minor. He touched a key, and a bell tone alerted all personnel of impending emergence—a standard courtesy and precaution—then touched two other keys. Together his three ships emerged into "real-space," Tso-Ban sharing the commodore's moment of mild disorientation. And there, only 1.8 billion miles away, was a system primary, as he'd known there'd be, at 277.016° course orientation, with a gas giant barely near enough to show a disk unmagnified, at 193.724°. His survey ship, small, totally automated, crewless except for a dozen maintenance personnel, began scanning to locate the system's planets and compute first approximations of their orbits, radioing its data to the flagship's computer as well as storing it in its own. The troop ship followed, its marine brigade inert, unconscious in their stasis lockers.

Tarimenloku's main screen showed the alien vessel almost as quickly as his instruments found it, showed it newly emerged at a distance of only twelve miles. Looking like a disorderly stack of scrap metal and rods welded together, it was presumably a patrol ship. The commodore stared, alarmed: Clearly it had perceived him in hyperspace with a most unusual precision, to have emerged so remarkably near and on a matched course: Clearly the alien had technology well beyond his own. The alternative explanation was coincidence, and the odds of that were too small to compute.

Suddenly, on the screen, he was looking into what seemed to be their bridge, the first of his species, so far as he knew, to see an intelligent alien life form. The screen showed creatures vaguely humanoid, with thick leathery skin and vestigial horns, and somehow it seemed to him they were larger than men.

If there'd been any doubt of their technical superiority before, this dispelled it. Their instruments and computer were sufficiently sophisticated that in seconds they'd remote-analyzed the flotilla's electronics sufficiently to beam video signals compatible with Klestronu[7] equipment.

Then a voice came out of his speaker, seemingly a computer simulation of human speech. But the words—they certainly sounded like words—meant nothing to Tarimenloku. There was about a sentence-worth of them; then they stopped. After a pause of two or three seconds they were repeated.

"I do not understand you," he answered, and repeated it three times.

DAAS, his computer, spoke to him. "Commodore, there is an alien electronic presence in my databank, scanning."

Tarimenloku's brows knotted and he set his exit controls. "Gunnery," he said quietly, "do you have a fix on the alien?"

"Yes, commodore."

"Have you identified his control structure?"

"Yes, commodore."

"Fire bee-pees one through four."

As soon as his systems screen told him the pulses had been fired, he touched the flotilla control key with one hand and the exit key with the other. His three ships flicked back into hyperspace.

Then he keyed his microphone to confidential. He'd better record right now his justification for what he'd done. (Second thoughts were already pressing his consciousness, and he pushed them away.) It wouldn't do to have the alien reading, and surely recording, the contents of his databank uninvited; simply to try could be considered a hostile act. (But there was a subliminal awareness that the alien might have had no hostile intention at all.)

He had no idea how much damage he'd done to the alien ship. It seemed possible he'd destroyed it. Hopefully he'd at least prevented it from pursuing him.

"DAAS," he said to the computer, "what was the nature of the data being scanned?"

"Sir, it first found my vocabulary. Then it began to read verbal data files indiscriminately."

Another thought occurred to Tarimenloku, a thought that left a moment of bleakness in its wake: After the alien's failed attempt to speak to him, it might have been taking data for a linguistic analysis, for communication. If so, his action might have made a dangerous enemy for the empire and humankind, of beings who initially had not been hostile. He hoped he'd destroyed them, and that their government would never know who'd done it.

One more thought occurred to him; he wasn't sure whether it was trivial or important: Who had they thought he was when they tried talking to him in that unfamiliar speech?

One thing was certain. He wouldn't return to real space for three imperial months at least—best make that four or five—regardless of any interesting-looking nodi that said "system."

## Solstice Eve, Y.P. 743

The day of graduation was clear but not hot. A breeze ruffled the flags, of Iryala and the Confederation, that flanked the temporary platform where the dignitaries sat.

There was a sizeable grandstand facing south—away from the sun in this southern hemisphere. On it sat more than two thousand people—mostly relatives of the cadets plus press representatives from their home districts. Photographers occupied the uppermost row. The broadcast media had not been invited, so of course had not come; the Crown wanted the event known but not to seem particularly important.

A sound began from the other side of the nearby classroom building, high-pitched voices calling cadence. In the grandstand, the susurrus of conversations thinned, almost stilled. The cadets began to appear, nearly six hundred preadolescent boys in parade uniforms marching around the corner of the building in a tight brisk column of sixes, all straight edges and sharp corners, to enter and bisect the exercise field. Approaching the platform, alternating companies peeled off left and right, diverging. Their cadet major's boy-alto voice called a command. They halted, and crisply, in perfect unison, turned to face the dignitaries. Six columns had become six rows, aligned so precisely they didn't need to dress ranks. Another command and they semi-relaxed at parade rest.

Now attention went to the platform.

The dignitaries numbered eight. In the center sat Emry Wanslo, Lord Kristal, who was personal aide to His Majesty, Marcus XXVIII, King of Iryala and Administrator General of the Confederation of Worlds; and Colonel Jil-Zat, a uniformed T'swi who could almost have been carved from obsidian. To Jil-Zat's left sat his three principal training officers, T'swa like himself. On Kristal's right were Varlik Lormagen and two officials from the Office of Special Projects.

With the boys at parade rest, Jil-Zat got to his feet and stepped to the microphone. "Cadets!" he said. His voice was a resonant bass. "Congratulations! You have my respect and joyous admiration, which is not news to you. We know and understand each other well, and we will be together for your advanced training on the other worlds.

"More than that I need not tell you." The black face, the large T'swa eyes, shifted to the grandstands. "So I shall direct my words to our guests. This ceremony is to honor 594 young warriors on the completion of their basic training. A very special training. For five and a half years they have been learning to live and fight in a very famous tradition, the tradition of Kootosh-Lan. A tradition which is the gift of Tyss to the Crown of Iryala, expressing our thanks for the Crown's recognition, thirty-one years ago, of Tyss as a trade world under royal protection."

Jil-Zat paused, shifting to another theme.

"What are these young warriors about? What are *we* about, their cadre? Why this training? This school? Any of the cadets could tell you, but I am on the program and hold the microphone, so I will.

"Every person is born with a purpose. These young men were born to be warriors. And they have had the good fortune to find a special place, a home, a small society of warriors. As warriors, their training is very unlike that of soldiers. Their basic training has taken far longer, been much broader, much deeper. They have learned to be a very special kind of human being."

While Jil-Zat talked, Varlik Lormagen's eyes had been examining the front rank, the mostly twelve-year-old faces. Boy faces, most of them tanned, a few fair and freckled. Very different from the black, combat-seasoned faces of his old Red Scorpion Regiment, long dead. But they were cousins now in philosophy.

"Each of them," Jil-Zat was saying, "has mastered all his lessons, and all the skills so far addressed—mastered them very thoroughly. There are no marginal graduates. You can be proud of every one of them, as I am.

"Those of you whose sons these are, I congratulate for agreeing to their enlistment. Many of you, I am sure, felt misgivings at all this. Misgivings which I trust have long since been relieved by your occasional visits here to witness your sons' physical and spiritual growth."

*Misgivings, yes,* thought Varlik Lormagen. *But relief, too.* In the conformist culture of Iryala and the Confederation worlds, there'd never been a decent niche for the would-be warrior, nor any good way of dealing with a warrior child whose innate drives had been aberrated by life there. These parents had been given a respectable, an honorable way of dealing with their intentive warrior by allowing him to enter early a subculture of his own.

"... Their training on Iryala," Jil-Zat went on, "is over now. But they have six more years elsewhere. Three on Terfreya—"

*Good,* Lormagen thought. *I'm glad he didn't use its nickname.*

"—and three on my own world, Tyss." The black face flashed teeth. "Where, I might add, they will live in the only cooled barracks ever built there. We value these young men, and will not waste them. We require a great deal of them, but we treat them well.

"I consider it a privilege to be their commanding officer. . . ."

When Jil-Zat had finished, Lord Kristal spoke to the boys, beginning with a message from the King. It was neither rhetorical nor in the least hortatory; these boys, Lormagen told himself, didn't need rhetoric or exhortation. The speech was shorter than the guests might have expected, but long enough.

When it was over, the cadet major threw back his head and yelled, "Dismissed!" The boys didn't break ranks as they usually did, like an air burst. Instead they turned toward the stands and sort of spread out, waving at parents and siblings, waiting for them to come down rather than storming the stands themselves. Lormagen wondered if that was per instructions or grew out of the boys' own wisdom. Increasingly, these boys had been living the T'sel since they'd come here, and it was counterproductive to instruct needlessly; let wisdom function.

Together, the dignitaries walked toward the central building, led by Jil-Zat. In the Kettle War, Lormagen remembered, Jil-Zat had been a nineteen-year-old commanding officer of mercenaries, of a virgin T'swa regiment, the Ice Tigers. He wondered what rough trade world or resource world that regiment had finally died on, and how Jil-Zat had come to survive its destruction.

Ice Tigers! An interesting name for a regiment from Tyss, nicknamed "Oven," where few had ever seen even artificial ice.

At the building, most of the dignitaries dispersed to rooms or duties. A courier had been waiting for Lord Kristal, and handed him a package presumably containing a message cube. Lormagen and Jil-Zat waited while His Majesty's representative opened it.

"Colonel, may I use your computer?" Kristal asked. "Privately? This is from His Majesty's staff chief."

Jil-Zat gestured at his office. "Be my guest."

Even in the T'sel, courtesy oils human relations, Lormagen thought to himself. As Marcus's representative, Lord Kristal hadn't needed to ask. Kristal closed the door behind him, and Lormagen turned to Jil-Zat. "I hadn't thought to ask before," he said. "What exactly became of the Ice Tigers?"

Jil-Zat smiled. "We took considerable casualties around Beregesh, as you will recall. From there we went to the planet Ice—appropriately enough, considering our name. We'd been hired by its government, which was dominated by the fur ranchers' cooperative. In effect, the co-op *was* the government. They had been trying to suppress the free trappers, whose response had escalated from lobbying to sabotage to guerrilla warfare.

"It became a very interesting and enjoyable campaign. The trappers had scraped enough money together to hire what was left of the Ba-Tok Regiment, a short battalion actually—we were two somewhat short battalions ourselves—and we had some very good combat before the trappers faced reality and agreed to bargain. By that time we'd cut the Ba-Tok down to barely company size, and the locals themselves, both sides, had taken severe casualties."

The colonel chuckled. "Actually, I claim some credit for the peace agreement coming as soon as it did. I had exerted such influence as I could on the co-op's executive board, and they decided it was time to ease their unreasonable position. While Major Tengu of the Ba-Tok was influencing the Union to modify their more extreme demands.

"To directly influence our employer's political positions is not our contractual function of course, but it's the sort of thing we often do, where it seems likely to shorten a conflict to an ethical result."

Lormagen nodded, remembering Kettle.

"From there, the lodge contracted us both out to a mercantile consortium on Carjath, that had joined forces with a dukedom in revolt against a king. Operating combined, we comprised an overstrength battalion. It turned out that the consortium had seriously underestimated the king's support and overestimated the duke's." Jil-Zat chuckled again. "Intelligence organizations are as apt to mislead as they are to enlighten, and that was an extreme example."

His office door opened, and Jil-Zat cut short his account as Lord Kristal stepped out. "Thank you, Colonel," Kristal said. "Varlik, we need to talk."

They excused themselves, and the two Iryalans went to Kristal's room.

"The T'swa ambassador carried a report to His Majesty from Tyss," Kristal said. "From the Order of Ka-Shok. One of their monks has been studying a world in the Karghanik Empire, an ambitious world called Klestron. Not long ago, Klestron's sultan sent an expedition out of the imperial sector. Not to explore immediately neighboring space, but to scout far inward for habitable worlds. An unprecedented act." Kristal paused meaningfully. "Recently they reached Garthid space, which means they may be headed more or less in our direction. The expedition consists of a flagship—a cruiser, well armed of course—plus a survey ship presumably heavily instrumented, and a troopship carrying a brigade of 8,000 Klestronu marines. The lodge master thought we'd want to know."

Lormagen pursed his lips thoughtfully. "The Garthids may send them home. They might not grant passage to a naval flotilla."

"They've already met, and the Klestronu flagship attacked the Garthid patrol vessel without warning; attacked, then fled into hyperspace. And its commodore doesn't plan to come out until hopefully he's beyond retaliation."

"The Garthids may have gotten message pods off," Lormagen pointed out.

"True. In which case the entire Garthid Sector could be waiting for the Klestroni[8] to come out of hyperspace.

"Meanwhile the Klestronu commodore doesn't realize how *vast* Garthid space is. At the time, he was thinking of staying in hyperspace for deks. It will have to be a lot of deks—probably more than a year. So he'll probably emerge still in Garthid space. If he does, he may well encounter another patrol ship, or several of them, and could be destroyed."

Beneath black brows out of sync with his white hair, Kristal's eyes were calm and steady. "But if—*if* he continues long enough, it's possible he'll reach our sector. Should that happen, it's hard to say what the result might be."

Lormagen nodded. He could think of several unfavorable scenarios. The Crown Council assumed that outside forces would discover the Confederation Sector sooner or later, perhaps posing a threat to the independence, even the safety, of the Confederation and its people. But large-scale upgrading of military technology required first that the Confederation be led out of the millennia-long "hypnotism" imposed on it by the deep psycho-conditioning of the Sacrament. A process which wouldn't be completed for at least another couple of generations and couldn't safely be rushed.

Neither man commented on that; it was understood.

"I'm going to recommend to His Majesty that should the Klestronu expedition actually land their marines on a Sector world, we rush elite troops there, troops whose quality they're unlikely to match, and hit them on the ground. We have no prospect of defeating them in space."

"We'll need to call on the T'swa then," Lormagen said. "They have the only troops that fit the requirement."

"True. And we won't hesitate to. But their regiments are scattered, engaged on various trade and resource worlds, on contracts they'll feel bound by. That is, after all, how Tyss gets almost all its exchange. And we don't know if, let alone where or when, we'll need them. The T'swa seer will be able to tell us if the Klestronu flotilla is destroyed or turns back. Or when they emerge from hyperspace safely away from the Garthids. But he can't tell us where. He hasn't the technical knowledge.

"The odds are, of course, that the Klestronu expedition will never reach the Confederation Sector. The Garthids will stop them, or they'll emerge from hyperspace somewhere away from us. But we need to prepare. We'll want elite troops on standby, with transport on hand and ready, as a quick response force."

Kristal's eyes, though calm as usual, held Lormagen's now. "Varlik, several years ago you suggested a test, of the suitability of raw adolescents with warrior profiles for an elite force, and His Majesty decided against it. That's what I'm looking at now. A regiment of teenaged would-be warriors; 'intentive warriors' as the T'swa say. Youths in their mid- and late-teens that we can train intensively for two or three years, or for one if that's all the time we have. Even at hyperspace speeds, it will be quite awhile before the Klestroni can arrive."

Lormagen frowned slightly, remembering why the Council had earlier recommended against such a regiment: *Most of the kids would be misfits, the youthful troublemakers of Iryala. With two or three, seldom more, in a school, they haven't been a serious problem. More in the nature of nuisances. But gather two thousand in one place. . . .* He looked at Kristal and nodded. "It can be done. But we'll need to hire T'swa as cadre; some battle-wise veterans, the survivors of retired regiments. There shouldn't be any shortage.

"And recruits will be a lot easier to identify as teenagers; we can start by winnowing through school and court records for youths with particular behavioral problems, then check their personality profiles. They won't train up to T'swa standards, but they should prove a lot more satisfactory than any army regiment we have. I'd want certain recent equipment designs put into manufacture for them."

Kristal smiled. "I doubt there'll be any problems with upgrading infantry equipment. I'll tell His Majesty what you've said. Sometime within the next several days you can expect a request to present preliminary plans to the Council. Agreed?"

"Agreed." Lormagen felt excitement growing in him. He already knew who he wanted as regimental commander.

Kristal glanced at a wall clock. "Well then, it's time for lunch. Let's go down to the dining room."

As they left, Lormagen felt ideas stirring not far beneath the surface of his consciousness. He'd stay over tonight, and try them out on Jil-Zat this evening.

# 3

Farmland had ended several minutes back. Now rolling forest passed beneath the troop transport, a patchwork of late summer yellows and reds interrupted by occasional meadows, fens and marshes, lakes and streams. Narrow ribbons of road showed here and there, still summer green and seemingly without traffic.

Jerym Alsnor sat twisted in his bench seat to watch, feeling uncomfortable at what he saw. It was utterly different from the tailored industrial city of Pelstron where he'd lived all his seventeen years, and he felt sure that this unpeopled backwoods was where he'd be unloaded.

The Blue Forest Military Reservation they'd called it, back at the assembly center. He didn't know about the *blue*, but *forest* certainly fitted.

When he'd signed up, it had seemed the solution to everything, and an opportunity for adventure. But he'd also signed away his options, his freedoms, shaky as they'd already become, and now he was afraid he'd done the wrong thing. Again.

Ahead, buildings appeared, not of a town. Small buildings, looking somehow institutional. He felt deceleration: This was it—the Blue Forest Reservation.

Others had been looking too. Until then the floater had been remarkably quiet. Now a murmur began, and the recruits on the middle banks of seats got up, coming over to look out the windows, elbowing each other. Jerym might have felt hostile at the crowding, the encroachment, but his attention was too much on the buildings and their grounds. They weren't a kind of buildings and grounds he understood.

The transport began settling, sinking faster than his stomach liked. Its crew, in blue-gray uniforms, came down the aisles with batons, ordering the youths back to their seats, those who'd gotten up to see, whacking a few who lingered. The recruits obeyed, much more docile than might have been expected; they were in unfamiliar circumstances, felt exposed and vulnerable, didn't know what to expect.

Besides that, they didn't know each other. Under the circumstances not many had struck up conversations. Almost all were loners, misfits, had hardly known others like themselves, maybe two or three, excepting those few who'd been in reformatory. Then, at the assembly center, they'd been hurried, crowded, told to shut up, keep the noise down.

As Jerym watched, things on the ground acquired detail. Most of the buildings were single-storied; some were shed-like, a few mere roofs without walls. Men stood by, seemingly waiting for them, men in green field uniforms. Black men. *T'swa!* Jerym realized with a start. He felt a gentle landing impact, and one of the crewmen shouted orders. He got up tense, feeling a wash of desperation, sure now that he'd done the wrong thing in signing up. He'd never make it in this place. He'd have to find out how you got out of here; there had to be a way.

Colonel Dak-So, a subcolonel actually, watched the recruits shuffle down the ramp, a hundred of them. He'd never seen anything quite like them till yesterday's batches. Their postures were bad, their auras gray and murky. His noncoms herded them into a crude semblance of ranks. Supposedly they were intentive warriors. *Suppressed* intentive warriors. He regarded them like a sculptor regarding a new medium. *It will be interesting,* he thought.

Colonel Carlis Voker watched from a window as the semi-column of recruits slouched by, herded by T'swa noncoms. He was keeping aloof till they were broken in a bit. They'd accept the alien T'swa more readily than they would an old white geezer like himself, he thought; be a lot more impressed by them. They'd had too many old geezers telling them what to do.

*They were born to be warriors for a reason,* he thought, *one we're beginning to see now.*

These were the fourth load in today. With the floaters from Vosinlak and Two Rivers due before supper, there'd be 1,200 of them by lights out. The rest would come in tomorrow, which would keep Supply humping. After all the recruits got boots that fit, he'd send most of his supply people home to the army, which they'd no doubt find a big relief.

Tonight would undoubtedly be as crazy as last night. Or maybe not quite. Last night the T'swa had discovered what kind of raw material they'd been presented with, and after their initial surprise, had handled things with quiet, nicely-gauged force.

If these young men were what their tests and interviews said they were, Voker did not doubt at all that they'd leave here the best fighting men the Confederation had ever produced. (He wasn't counting the cadets, who were still preadolescent, nor the T'swa, who were from a trade world.) But it would take some doing. He had no doubt of that either.

Jerym Alsnor was almost a good-looking kid, would have been handsome except for the cast of chronic resentment and evasiveness on his face. He was tall and still growing, shoulders wide but not yet well muscled. His features were strong and regular, his brown hair close cropped by an army barber at the assembly center in Farningum. Though measured in mere hours, that seemed quite a while ago. Now he stepped onto a small, glass-topped platform, feeling foolish in his green fatigues. He didn't need a mirror to know how poorly they fitted. And the paper slippers he'd been given looked even more ridiculous. He was glad no one he knew could see him like this.

An overweight, red-faced corporal scowled and snapped at him. "Pay attention, recruit! Put your heels against the rounded heel plates and stand still."

Jerym did, thinking where he'd really like to put his foot.

"Now keep your weight evenly on your soles and heels." The corporal eyed a blinking red light on the small instrument screen. "Didn't you hear me, recruit? I said *evenly!*"

The light stopped blinking.

"All right," grumped the corporal after a moment. "Go over to that bench and sit down by the last guy. Someone'll call off your name and number."

Walking to the bench, Jerym glanced again at the numbered tag hanging from his neck. *Jerym D. Alsnor, SR-0726-401, BVLN.* Oh-seven-two-six dash four-oh-one. Easy enough; the first four numbers were his birth year. He sat down.

"How'd you like that fat sack of shit?" asked the guy next to him, thumbing toward the supply corporal. The name label above the youth's left shirt pocket read *Esenrok.*

"Like?" Jerym said. "I'd like to kick the snot out of him."

Both of them spoke quietly. They'd seen one recruit sass a sergeant when they'd been getting their uniforms. A very large, calm T'swi had grabbed the poor sucker and frog-marched him pantless out the door, the guy's right arm up behind his back and a big black fist bunching his green field shirt at the collar. It happened so quickly and quietly, you could have been looking the other way for five seconds and missed the whole thing.

The recruit on the other side of Esenrok gazed at him and Jerym as if they were a pair of children. He was older than they, probably nineteen. "Be glad the boots'll fit better than these greens," he said.

"What makes you think they will?"

"They're who's going to train us, make fighting men out of us, and they don't care whether our uniforms fit good or not. Not now anyway. They probably like it this way; keeps us from acting too smart. But our boots? Our boots have to fit or our feet'll go bad."

Jerym eyed the guy's name label, *Carrmak*, and felt like asking what made him so damn smart. But it didn't seem like the time or place; a T'swa sergeant was standing by the door.

Army guys kept coming to a door and calling names and numbers, and guys would go through the door and out of sight. To get their boots, Jerym supposed. In a few minutes Carrmak went, then Esenrok. Finally they called his name, and Jerym too went through the door. Another army corporal looked at his dog tags to make sure, handed him a pair of boots with treaded soles, and told him to put them on and fasten them. Then prodded and pinched as a last check of their fit, as if he didn't totally trust the computerized fabricator that had just tailor-made them.

"Okay." He pointed. "Out that door and wait."

Jerym went, glad to be rid of his paper slippers, and stood around with the others, waiting for someone to tell them what to do next. Conversations began. A couple of guys—their labels read Warden and Klefma—took off, to find out what would happen. The rest of them speculated on the subject, then two more decided to try it. About three minutes later, two T'swa arrived, a corporal and a sergeant, and had them line up. Each T'swi had a clipboard.

"All right," said the corporal. "When I call your name, raise your hand and say 'Here, sir!'"

He began to read, alphabetically. Here and there, hands popped up and voices answered; a "here, sir" was shouted for every name. When the roll call was done, the sergeant, who'd simply watched, walked along the line of recruits, looking at the names above their shirt pockets. Then he stepped back and gave an order, his deep voice soft but easily heard.

"Barkum, Desterbi, Lonsalek, step forward."

The platoon stood silent, hardly breathing, sensing that something was wrong. The T'swa were large and powerful men from a high-gee world, and their expressions were unreadable, now at least. Uncertain, the three recruits stepped forward. The sergeant walked up to them, opened their shirts and looked at the dog tags dangling from their necks.

"Barkum, why did you answer for Mellis and Thelldon?"

"I don't know. To keep them out of trouble, I guess."

"You have been told how to address a sergeant. Answer my question again. Properly this time."

"Sir! To keep them out of trouble."

The T'swi turned to the next recruit. "Desterbi, you answered for Klefma. Why?"

"Sir, the same thing. To keep him out of trouble."

"Lonsalek? Why did you answer for Warden?"

"Sir, to see what would happen."

The T'swa sergeant nodded, and when he spoke, his voice was conversational. "In this regiment you should not lie to each other, and you very definitely do not lie to your officers." He pointed. "You three stand over there, with your noses touching the wall. Lonsalek wanted to see what would happen. You will find out."

Unexpectedly he whistled then, loud and shrill, one long blast and two short, the sound somehow intimidating. A moment later two more corporals came trotting up. Again the sergeant pointed. "Take these three to temporary detention." The two T'swa went to them, grasped their collars from behind, and shoving, marched them off. None of the three showed any inclination to resist or argue. The sergeant scanned the rest of them. "Corporal, take them to their barracks. They are to remain there till I give further orders."

The sergeant turned and left. "Platooon!" the corporal called. "Attention!" Each recruit came to his version of attention, all promptly, some sullenly. "Riiight face!" They responded appropriately to the unfamiliar command. "Forwaaard, march!"

They started off, stepping on each others' heels at first, muttering till they got the hang of it. *Column right* and later *column left* they managed more or less. *Platoon halt!* was no problem at all.

Then he herded them inside the long, one-story building, where they sat down on their new bunks. No one said anything till he was gone;

then Esenrok spoke. "If we'd of jumped the son of a bitch, we could have beat the snot out of him, T'swa or not."

Jerym looked at Esenrok, saying nothing, thinking to himself he wasn't having anything to do with a crazy idea like that.

Again it was Carrmak who answered. "I doubt it. The first three or four that reached him, he'd have broken their necks. And everyone else would have backed off."

"What makes you so damned expert?" Esenrok snarled, getting to his feet.

Carrmak grinned mockingly. He was one of the bigger recruits in the platoon, probably the hairiest, and looked the oldest. "You don't believe me, go call him in. When he comes in, try him and see, you and everyone else that wants to. I'll watch. Maybe I'm wrong."

Blond Esenrok, seventeen, stood perhaps a little short of medium height. He was stocky, still with some baby fat, and so far his pale hair hadn't spread to chin or upper lip. He sat back down, flushing darkly.

"When do they feed us?" someone asked after a minute.

"*What* do they feed us?" someone else threw in.

Another looked at the wall clock. "It's 1740. I'll bet we eat at 1800."

Mellis and Thelldon came in then, grinning. Mellis looked younger than almost anyone else in the platoon, though at sixteen he was as big as most. "Hi, guys!" he said. "So they finally sent someone to bring you home."

*Home!* Jerym thought. *He'd called this place home!*

Thelldon was looking around. "Where's Barkum?" he asked.

"In detention," someone answered. "For lying to a corporal. Him and a couple other guys. For answering up for guys that took off. Like you and him." He indicated Mellis.

Mellis looked worried, Thelldon upset. "Shit!" Thelldon swore.

"What are you guys going to do?" someone asked. "The T'swa are sure to be looking for you."

"Wait here, I guess," Thelldon answered. "See what happens."

"Not me," Mellis said. "I'm getting out of here. I'm finding a road and leaving."

He went to the door, paused to peer around outside, then left.

Jerym and several others got up and went to doors and windows to look out. He saw newcomers being marched to other barracks, still wearing their civilian clothes. It seemed like a long time ago that he'd stuffed his civvies into a bag, tied a tag on it, and given it to a white sergeant. He wondered if he'd ever see it again.

He wished he was back home, arguing with his father.

# 4

The autumnal equinox was nearing, and when the recruits had finished eating, it was nearly night. Stars had washed up the sky from the east, and some of the brighter spilled down the west into the final gray of sunset.

In the barracks, the young would-be warriors were getting to know one another, clustering, choosing buddies. Would-be leaders were making themselves known. Esenrok was one of them, trying to establish himself by his husky aggressiveness.

The recruits had been told to stay in barracks till otherwise ordered. Esenrok, with three others, huddled briefly in a corner, talking in undertones. When they'd finished, he walked to the middle of the floor. Most eyes moved to him, as if their owners knew that something was about to happen.

"Guys," Esenrok said quietly, "listen up. I've got an idea. We'll go raid the next barracks and start a fight." He turned and looked at Carrmak. "Anyone doesn't go is yellow."

Carrmak grinned at him. "Just call me butterflower," he said.

Esenrok didn't know how to reply to that, so he ignored it. "Who's game?" he asked.

About a dozen were on their feet instantly, eager. Others began to get up one by one, not willing to stay out of it, but not enthused. They were worried about what the T'swa might do.

"Come on, Alsnor," Esenrok said to Jerym, and Jerym got reluctantly to his feet. He'd sworn off fighting. He was very quick, and by Iryalan standards very good. He'd been in juvenile court twice for damaging guys; once more, in the civilian world, and he'd go to reformatory. He wasn't entirely sure that didn't apply here.

Within half a minute, everyone was standing except Carrmak and Thelldon; then Esenrok gave instructions. He and five others would run in the door, start dumping over bunks, and run out when the guys they were raiding started for them. The others would be waiting outside, ready.

When the last of Esenrok's raiders was out, headed for the neighboring barracks, Carrmak and Thelldon stood in the door watching. Carrmak leaned against a door post with his hands in his pockets and chuckled. "That Esenrok's a crazy little turd."

Thelldon shook his head, watching the platoon begin to bunch up by the corner of the next barracks in the row. He was bothered by his failure to go with them. "I'm already in trouble," he explained to Carrmak. "And Sergeant Dao told me to stay here till someone came for me. I'm not going to get in any more trouble till I find out what they do to you. I don't know what to expect from these T'swa; they're not like anybody else I ever knew."

He turned to Carrmak. "How come you didn't go?"

Carrmak laughed. "I'm the strategic reserve."

Thelldon looked at him, at his grin, not sure what he meant. Carrmak's hands were out of his pockets now, opening and closing. Yelling snatched their attention. Then fighting erupted at the other side of the massed platoon.

The first few of the other platoon galloped around the corner of the barracks after the raiders, and ran into the waiting enemy before they knew they were there. Jerym grabbed one of them by the shirt, punched him between the eyes and decked him. Someone else hit Jerym in the mouth with a long left, and he slugged the guy hard in the gut, then twice in the face. Someone barrelled into both of them, and Jerym lost contact. More guys were pouring, yelling, from the raided barracks, and briefly, with the advantage of momentum, they drove the raiders back.

For a minute the fighters were almost too packed to swing or fall down. Then the mass of brawlers began to open up a bit, and Jerym, engaged with a heavier, stronger youth, was thrown to the ground. The guy was on top of him, trying to punch him, but Jerym had hold of his sleeve, pushing on the guy's chin with his other hand while thrashing wildly, trying to buck him off. He lost his grip on the sleeve, and a fist slammed hard above his left eye. Then someone lifted the guy off and threw him aside. It was Carrmak, whooping, louder than any of the others. Jerym got to his knees, squinting one eye against a trickle of blood, transfixed by what he saw. Carrmak seemed incredibly strong, irresistible, throwing guys aside as if they were empty uniforms, and suddenly the opposition began to back away, those who weren't too tightly engaged. A boot struck Jerym's head a grazing blow.

Shrill T'swa whistling cut through the yelling, and disengagement became general, both platoons hurrying back to their barracks, some youths pausing to help the fallen. It was Thelldon who grabbed Jerym and jerked him to his feet. They ran.

Inside was an excited babble. Noses bled, and mouths; eyes had begun to swell. But most had no visible wounds, or at worst scuffs or scrapes. Almost all of them were exhilarated, flushed, bright-eyed. In a minute or so, Sergeant Dao came in alone, and the babble stilled. Esenrok made no move; the T'swa were legendary, and suddenly each recruit remembered what he'd heard or read of them.

Also Dao had presence, a kind of warrior presence that few men could match. Even, it seemed to the recruits just then, even more presence than most T'swa. If they'd never heard of the T'swa, they'd still have backed off from this man.

Dao said nothing for several long seconds, just smiled, a smile not unfriendly, even slightly amused. There was something unnerving about it. Then, mildly but loudly, he said, "*Atten*tion!"

Instantly backs straightened, arms dropped to sides, feet came together. "Outside for roll call!" They shuffled out the door and formed ragged rows. Their squad leaders were waiting, looking hard and untouchable. Dao took his place in front of the platoon, and in the darkness, without a light, called roll himself from his clipboard. Thelldon wasn't the only absentee who'd returned. Klefma and Warden were back too.

"Has anyone here seen Mellis?" Dao asked.

No one answered.

"I presume some of you would like to eat tomorrow," Dao said calmly. "Or if not tomorrow, hopefully the day after. I will ask again: Has anyone here seen Mellis?"

"Sir," said someone, "he said he was going to find a road and leave."

"Thank you."

A corporal trotted off in the darkness.

"Now. It is not acceptable that you fight among yourselves. Platoon, atten*tion!* Riiight face! Forwaaard march!" Again feet stepped on heels; youths muttered curses. The platoon moved. "Column left!" They turned onto a drill field.

Dao walked backward now, watching them. "When I say 'double time,'" he instructed, "you will begin to jog, following me and keeping up with me at all times. Now!" He turned, calling over his shoulder: "Double tiiime, march!"

They began to jog, crossed the drill field, turned onto a grassy road, passed the motor pool with its parked hover vehicles, came to a gate in the mesh fence that surrounded the camp, and continued down the road into the woods. Jerym became aware that his eyebrow wasn't bleeding anymore.

It was much darker on the forest road, and easy to stumble. A hover truck came up behind them on its silent AG drive, and a lamp on its cab shone a broad beam above them, reflecting off the tree crowns ahead, helping them see the road. Dao turned, running backward, facing them. "You are the Second Platoon, Company A, First Battalion," he called. "I am your platoon sergeant; I give orders and you obey them. I now order you to keep up with me. Any who do not will be dealt with appropriately."

He turned his back on them and speeded up, trotting briskly. After a few minutes, Jerym's legs were tiring badly. He wasn't used to running any distance. His lungs labored to get enough oxygen; his breath rasped in his throat. A few guys had slowed to a walk, falling back or peeling off to the sides. Dao did not ease up. The column, strung out a bit now, turned off on a lesser road, and it seemed to Jerym that they may have slowed, just a little.

But not enough. Soon his legs seemed too heavy to run farther. His strides slowed. He turned aside, one of the outer ranks breaking to let him through, and he stopped beside the road, bent forward, hands on thighs, mouth gaping as he gasped for breath. The truck pulled past, paused, and a T'swi reached out to him. Jerym reached back. The T'swi clamped onto his wrist and hoisted him onto the truck. The man's hand startled Jerym: The palm felt tough as a boot sole.

There were a dozen or so other recruits on board ahead of him; in the darkness Jerym couldn't make out who. He remembered Dao saying that those who didn't keep up would be dealt with, but just now he didn't care. He was sure he couldn't have run another step.

A minute later he decided he'd quit too early: Dao had slowed the platoon to a walk. Jerym moved to climb down, but the T'swi gripped his arm. "Stay," the T'swi said, and Jerym stayed. They followed the platoon, and three or four minutes later it began to jog again, but more slowly now, without any more dropouts. Twelve minutes more of jogging brought it back into the compound, headed toward the messhall, but the truck swung away with its cargo of stragglers and went to a shed.

"Everyone off," said the T'swi, and Jerym climbed down with the others, sure that he wasn't going to like what happened next, wishing fervently he'd hung on for another minute, out there in the woods. He could have, he thought, for one more minute or maybe even two.

The truck drove away.

A light came on in the shed, and two T'swa herded him and the others inside. Jerym saw that Esenrok was there. Stacked on the floor were crude packs, bulky and shapeless, simple sacks sewn shut at the top and strapped to a pack frame. "Each of you put one on," a T'swi ordered. "Help each other if you need to."

Jerym grabbed one and lifted. Heavy! As he struggled into the straps, he decided the bag was full of sand. "All right, outside!" the T'swi ordered, and fifteen recruits left the shed. The two T'swa had them form ranks and checked their packs, adjusting straps as needed. Then they began marching. They passed the messhall, lit up now; Jerym wanted to go over and see what was happening inside. Then they were through the gate again. *It's better than running,* he told himself, but it didn't reassure him.

His mouth had swollen where he'd gotten hit in the brawl, and he was pretty sure his split lip was going to canker if he didn't get some powder for it.

❖          ❖          ❖

Pitter Mellis was tired and hungry, and worse than either, he had to admit he was lost.

He'd hung around another barracks, another platoon, talking with the guys there, until a bell rang, brief but loud, shocking in its unexpectedness. Then a T'swi had called in that it was time to eat. Mellis had thought about going to the messhall with those guys, but was afraid that if he did, he'd be caught. So he'd hung out in the latrine. It had seemed a safe place. If anyone looked in on him, he'd say he had diarrhea.

But if he was still there when the guys who lived there came back from supper, it would look peculiar. So he'd watched out the window till he saw guys start to come out of the messhall. Then he'd left the barracks; it was getting somewhat dark.

He'd already noticed where the gate was, and that a guard was posted there, so he'd gone to the far side of the compound, scaled the eight-foot fence, and jumped off. His ankle turned when he'd landed, and at first it worried him, but it walked off in half a minute and didn't bother him anymore. To avoid getting lost, he'd circled the compound on the outside till he'd come to the side with the gate, then angled to hit the road that came out of it.

He'd begun to feel unsure of himself. Maybe he ought to go back in; it might be a long way to anywhere, and he was getting hungry. On the other hand, it might only be a few miles, and he'd told the guys in his barracks that he was leaving. What would they think of him if he came dragging back in, saying he was hungry?

So he'd started down the road. By then it was crowding full night, and moonless; soon he couldn't see much. Then, after a bit, there'd been light, like a distant floodlight, paling the tree crowns where they overhung the edges of the narrow roadway, and he'd heard a sound behind him like running feet. Startled, puzzled, he'd left the road, scuttling back into the woods where it was really dark. He'd gone sixty or eighty feet, groping in blackness, hands in front of his face to protect his eyes from brush. Once he'd stumbled and fallen. Then he turned and watched, but couldn't see enough to tell him much. Running men passed with a tramping of boots, followed by a floodlight on what seemed to be a truck. When they were past, he groped his way back to the road and went on.

Occasionally it curved. Several times there'd been crossroads, forks, junctions, with signs, but he'd had no way to read them. Finally the road had come to a large meadow and appeared to stop there. It had seemed to him, though, that it must continue on the other side, that it was simply too dark to recognize a grass road on a meadow. So doggedly he'd started across. If he didn't find where the road went into the woods on the other side, he'd told himself, he'd just follow the edge of the meadow back to where he'd entered it.

But it was hilly there, humpy rolling country, and the meadow seemed to go on quite a distance. Seeren, the major moon, had come up more than half full, making it easier not to stumble, but it didn't show him any sign of the road. The meadow had bent right, then pinched out, and when he'd tried to backtrack, it had pinched out that way too, ending at a marsh. Anxiety spasmed. *How could that be?* he asked himself. He'd backtracked still again, and again it had pinched out, where it had pinched out the first time, he suspected.

He stood confused and defeated, utterly forlorn. Finally he decided to lay down and sleep till daylight. By daylight things would look different, he told himself, and he'd find his way out of there.

He'd never tried to sleep on the ground before. It was lumpy and hard and cold. He wondered if he could sleep. Lying there, he was soon shivering, and after awhile wondered if it would get cold enough to freeze to death.

"S-s-s-st!"

He sat up, staring in the direction of the sound.

"Recruit!"

It was a T'swa voice, deep and furry. *Shit!* he thought, *how could that be?*

"It's time to go back. On your feet, recruit!"

Mellis got up. *I would have been all right here,* he told himself now. *And gotten unlost in the morning.* But he didn't try to run. He was too tired and too hungry, and mostly he was glad to be found. The T'swi led off as if he knew just where he was going, and it occurred to Mellis that the man must have followed him all the way from the compound, letting him go, letting him get lost.

Jerym didn't know how far they'd hiked. Walked and occasionally jogged with forty pounds of sand on their backs, following close behind a T'swi and followed by two others. He remembered reading that T'swa could see like cats in the dark. Their eyes were big enough, that was certain.

They climbed one long steep hill that he thought must be the highest around there. His legs felt utterly exhausted by the time they reached the top, and he heard someone call out, "I name you Drag-Ass Hill." Somehow Jerym knew they'd climb Drag-Ass Hill many times before they left this place.

It seemed to him they'd been on the road for at least a couple of hours. His shoulders were sore from the packstraps. Seeren had come up, and her light made it easier to see.

"Fuck this shit!" a loud voice said up front, and someone stepped out of ranks onto the roadside. Jerym recognized the voice. It belonged to a guy named Romlar, a big, heavy, round-faced kid.

"Here. Give me the pack." That was a T'swa voice. Then Jerym was past them. A minute later, Romlar caught up, packless. Five minutes later they came into the open, the moonlight unscreened by trees. The gate was just ahead. Somehow they'd circled; there must be a network of roads in the woods, Jerym decided, and the T'swa knew them.

He wondered what would happen to Romlar.

They walked to the shed and got rid of their packs. A T'swi told Romlar to come with him, and the two of them left. One of the other T'swa took the rest of them to the messhall. Inside, a single panel glowed in the ceiling, and there was a big electric urn, its red light bright, with cups stacked by it upside down.

"Hot thocal," said the T'swi. "It will help you sleep."

*The only thing I need to sleep is my bunk,* Jerym thought. The hot cup hurt his split lip. The thocal tasted good though; good enough that he had a second cup. Unless he lay on his stomach, even his sore mouth wouldn't keep him awake, he was sure of it.

He wondered what was happening to Romlar. It didn't seem like a good idea to quit on something the T'swa gave you to do.

# 5

Jerym woke up needing to go to the latrine, badly, and groaning softly, got out of bed. It was the two cups of thocal, he told himself. The wall clock glowed at him: 0320. His legs were stiff and sore, enough that he limped.

Mellis was there, on a commode, slumped with his head in his hands. He wasn't doing anything, just sitting there, his pants up.

"Anything the matter?" Jerym murmured.

The head raised, shook a negative.

Jerym went over to the long, trough-like urinal, thinking that Mellis looked as worn out as he'd been himself, four hours earlier. When he was done, Mellis was still sitting there, his head in his cupped hands again.

"Where've you been?" Jerym asked.

Briefly Mellis told him. "And now I'm so damn hungry!" He almost keened it. "I haven't eaten since before we got on the floater, back in Farningum, and the damn T'swi made me run half the way back. And then, when we got back, he gave me a shovel and told me to dig a hole. Six feet long, six feet wide, and six feet deep! I'd have told him to go fuck himself, but I was afraid what he might do."

He looked up at Jerym. "I found out. There was another guy there from our platoon, a big guy, already digging. Real slow. The guard called him 'Romlar,' and when Romlar got his hole about ass deep, he quit."

Mellis shook his head, remembering. "There's some posts there, with chains on them, and the T'swi said, all right, come here. And started to chain him to a post. So Romlar started to fight him."

Jerym listened, engrossed.

"The T'swi never hit him or anything," Mellis went on, "just kind of grappled him around, and the next thing I knew, Romlar was laying there chained to the post, all curled up, swearing and crying. Actually crying! My eyes must have been as big as a T'swi's. The T'swi told him to let him know when he was ready to start digging." Mellis shook his head. "He said it as friendly as could be, even after Romlar had been calling him all kinds of things and trying to punch him.

"It took me quite a while before I got my hole dug, and when I was done, the T'swi pulled me out and had me fill it back up again. That's all; just dig it and fill it back up. Romlar was sitting up with his arms wrapped around himself, and I could hear his teeth clattering. It must be close to freezing out there now. The T'swi brought me here, and then I suppose he went back to Romlar."

*Amber's balls!* Jerym thought. *They're ruthless!* "You ought to go to bed," he said. "No telling what they'll have us doing in the morning."

Mellis nodded and Jerym gave him a hand, hoisting him to his feet. At Mellis's bunk, the younger boy asked for a boost. He had an upper bunk, and said he was so tired, he didn't think he could make it himself. Then he peeled out of his pants and shirt, and Jerym helped him climb up. After that, Jerym went to his own bed and lay awake for several minutes, thinking about his night and Mellis's, before falling asleep again.

He woke up to wild ringing that jerked him to his feet. There were groans and scattered curses as guys got up. Or pulled their covers up, trying to drown out the noise. A door opened, and a T'swi yelled in that they had three minutes to get dressed and outside.

The clock above the door read 0600.

Three minutes didn't even give a guy time to go piss! Jerym grabbed his shirt from the floor where he'd dropped it, and put it on, then his pants, his socks, his boots. Six-oh-two. That's when he noticed Romlar still in bed, asleep, face dirty, mouth open. The arm that was out of the covers showed he hadn't taken off his shirt. A booted foot stuck out too. Carrmak walked over, grabbed the bed by an edge, and dumped Romlar out.

"Hey! Fat boy!" he called. "Rise and shine! You've got about one minute to get up and outside."

Romlar lay on the floor, half wrapped in sheet and blanket, not moving. Spittle had dried at the corners of his mouth. A sort of half snore, half snort, came from it.

*Tunis!* Jerym thought. *What he doesn't need is to get in more trouble.* "Let's help him," he said to Carrmak. Carrmak grinned and nodded. Together they hoisted Romlar up, and half walking him, half dragging him, took him out between them for morning muster.

# 6

The morning was not the physical ordeal Jerym had half expected. After reveille, they'd had almost half an hour to use the latrine, clean up, and make their beds before breakfast. They had another half hour to eat; after that they waited by their beds.

Then a T'swa corporal had them pull their bedding off and showed them how to make a bed in the military manner. After making their beds several times to train in the proper technique, they went to the drill field and learned to salute and do left, right, and about face; then practiced standing at ease, attention, and parade rest. After that they learned to march, both in close-order drill and on the road. Sergeant Dao told them that in this regiment, saluting and close-order marching would not often be done—they were primarily for ceremony—but they needed to do them well.

T'swa cadre, in platoon formation, gave a demonstration to show how close-order drill looked—sharp and precise—and that warriors didn't consider it beneath them.

They drilled these things till noon under the unrelenting eyes of T'swa, then ate dinner.

They were gone when the transports brought in the rest of the recruits. The T'swa had taken them out on a road march, nothing particularly strenuous—no running, no packs—a brisk three-hour hike on roads of grass, through the forests and meadows and smells of near-autumn. It wasn't at all bad, and much of the stiffness in Jerym's thighs wore off. The only ones in the second platoon who had difficulties that day were Mellis and Romlar, especially Romlar. Both kept falling asleep on break, and of course had to wake up brief minutes later.

That evening they watched recordings in the company messhall, of army and T'swa and "Birds," in the Kettle War. The real stuff. Dirt flew, and pieces of trees, and guys got killed—even blown up! Jerym got a nervous stomach watching, from pure excitement. Most of the best of it, Captain Gotasu told them, had been recorded by an Iryalan who'd been with the T'swa, a guy named Varlik Lormagen who'd been called the White T'swi.

"You," Captain Gotasu said—Gotasu was their company commander—"will be the new White T'swa. When we have finished training you. It will be harder for you than it was for us, because we began at age six or seven, and learned and trained for almost twelve standard years before we went to war. But we will help you. We will help you find out that you can do far more than most people would believe possible. We will push you nearly to your limits—sometimes you may think we've pushed you beyond them—and you, and we, will watch those limits grow."

He paused. "And when you have completed your training, you will know, and we will know, that you are warriors to be proud of."

When Gotasu finished, there was silence, but every recruit in the company had been affected by what he'd said. He dismissed them, and they returned to their barracks with only time to get ready for bed before lights out. There was no horseplay; lights out meant quiet. And they'd been warned that the next day would see their training begin in earnest. Orientation was over.

# 7

The young chauffeur opened the door for Lord Kristal, who got out easily despite his eighty-one years.

The Durslan estate at Lake Loreen was one of Kristal's favorite places, although he got there infrequently. And this was one of its pleasantest aspects—mellowed by late afternoon sunlight slanting soft through trees and autumn haze. The changes since he'd arrived there as a pupil, seventy-five years earlier, had been modest and graceful.

The greatest change was an addition. Despite some architectural innovations, the new building, the Research Building, might almost have stood there as long as the others, for generations, fitted as it was among great *peioks* that shaded the lawns and had begun to spill bronze leaves across them.

It was the Research Building where his interest lay today, but the limousine had delivered him to the Main Building. He took this for granted.

Even among the alumni, even—especially—for a representative of the Crown, there was protocol to observe. But it was simple, common courtesy really, and with friends a pleasure. He went up the steps to the veranda, where Laira Gouer Lormagen waited, with Kusu, to greet him.

When she'd embraced her guest, she took his hand and stepped back. "Emry," she said, "I'm the only Gouer family representative here today, the only one who hasn't flown off to Durslan Hall to help prepare for Harvest Festival. But it's my husband's research you've come to see"— she half turned and put her hand on Kusu's sleeve—"so I'll wait till dinner to claim you for a talk, if your schedule permits dinner with us."

She left them then—she'd seen the test already; it wasn't pleasant— and the two men walked the winding, eighty-yard sidewalk to the research building, exchanging pleasantries. Kristal knew in general terms what the test had shown, but he wanted to see for himself. In the actual presence of an event, a useful cognition might be triggered, if not then, perhaps later. Especially in someone of his training and experience. And a relevant cognition was needed here. Although he was at Service instead of Wisdom/Knowledge, over the years he'd shown occasional flashes of exceptional perceptivity.

Kusu did not defer to Kristal's elderly legs; he knew His Lordship better than that. Instead of the elevator, they climbed the curving main stairs to the second floor and walked to Kusu's lab. The equipment there was meaningless to Kristal. In his school days there'd been no science, no such thing as research, and hadn't been for a very long time. The Sacrament had seen to that, as it had seen to other things, and they'd lived off the genius of ages long past.[9]

To Kristal, the most nearly familiar thing in the lab was a cage containing five pale olive sorlex, the Iryalan mouse. They looked up at him with eyes like tiny black beads, their noses twitching.

"How are the others?" Kristal asked. "Did any survive?"

"The last two died while I was talking with you on the comm," Kusu answered. "This morning I tried it with three meadow soneys I live-trapped; something with substantially more body mass. They only lived about an hour. And a feral cat I caught last night. It was worse than the rodents; by that time I'd attached this microwave emitter"—he touched a black apparatus on the side of the box—"so I could put it out of its frenzy. That's what I'll do with these, too, assuming they respond like the earlier sets."

"And sedation doesn't help, you said."

"Depending on its strength, it eliminates or reduces the intensity of the frenzy, but so does exhaustion, and they die just as quickly. Even when I put them to sleep before teleporting them."

"Are you having post mortems done?"

"On the sorlex and the soneys; they weren't microwaved. I've gotten the results, and they're not very informative."

Kristal nodded. "Well, let's see it operate."

Kusu raised the cage lid and reached in. The sorlex investigated his hands. He took two of them out on one palm and stroked them reflectively for a moment with a finger. Then, kneeling, he put them in a glass box that sat on a waist-high platform, part of a much larger apparatus, set a timer, closed a switch, and took Kristal to a vacant table at the other end of the room. There was nothing on the table except an electrical cord plugged into a receptacle.

"It'll be a few seconds yet," Kusu said. Suddenly, after a moment, the glass box was there, and inside it a virtual blur of movement, the two sorlex racing frenziedly about. They caromed off the sides, off each other, launched themselves upward with remarkable leaps to bounce off the top. After ten seconds, Kusu plugged the electric cord into the microwave emitter on the side of the glass box, flicked a switch, and the sorlex stopped at once, to lie unmoving.

For a moment the two men stood looking silently at them, then Kusu spoke again. "The cultures I teleported—bacteria and yeast—are still growing normally, as if nothing had happened." He gestured at several potted plants on a window sill. "So did the saragol. And the horn worms. And finally the sand lizards. The lizards acted a little strangely afterwards, for a few minutes—scurried around enough more than usual to notice— but they gave us no reason to expect anything like this."

"If teleportation had killed the other life forms, too, I'd set this work aside and go back to theoretical studies. Maybe I will anyway. But . . ." He gestured. "Only the mammals."

"Hmh!" Nothing stirred in Kristal's mind, and obviously not in Kusu's either. "I suppose the box couldn't have anything to do with it?"

"It didn't harm the lizards. Besides, I didn't use the box when I teleported a set of heavily sedated sorlex. They were asleep when I sent them across, and they died anyway.

"And I can't teleport things *into* a box, because the nexus won't form on the other side of a solid wall. I couldn't teleport them into the next room, for example, except through line of sight, say through the open door."

Kristal's brows raised a millimeter. "I hadn't realized there was that limitation."

"I hadn't either, till I tried it. The teleport didn't grow out of well worked out physical theory. The possibility occurred to me in an intuitive leap while I was studying some topological ideas the ancients apparently had played with but not done much with. So the research has been heavy on intuition and trial. And without adequate theory, a result like this can be a major block."

"Hmm. So what's your next step?"

"I don't know yet. I had Wellem up here for this morning's tests. He's much more at Wisdom and much less at Knowledge than I am, which can be useful when you hit a barrier like this. But he had no cognitions either; not yet anyway."

Kristal looked again at the sorlex, then back at Kusu. "Well," he said, "this feels like a good time to look in on him. It's been some two years. And his work is invariably interesting. Even when there isn't language to describe it."

# 8

Newly turned fifteen, Lotta Alsnor was becoming a rather pretty young woman, her once-carroty hair now auburn red, her old freckles mostly gone, her complexion faintly tanned, with pink highlights. Small, fine-boned, she would have been slight, had it not been for ballet and gymnastics and the strong-slender muscles they'd given her.

She stepped into the mail room after lunch. She seldom received mail, seldom went in to look. When there was something for her, she usually knew it. Almost invariably it was a letter from her mother.

Today it wasn't. She looked at the return address and headed for the veranda to read it. At Lake Loreen, autumn was considerably less advanced than in the Blue Forest, and today was almost summery. Slim strong fingers tore the end of the envelope, withdrew and unfolded the paper inside. She read:

> Dear Little Sister,
>
> I hope that getting a letter from me doesn't give you heart failure. I wish you were here. I'd show you around and we could talk a lot. In fact, I'd send you a cube instead of this letter, but I put all my bonus in the bank, and I don't want to wait till we get paid. I've never sent you a letter before, unless you count the three-line notes at Winter Solstice that were all Mom could get me to write. But I never felt like I had anything to write about before. It's as if all my life I've been waiting for something to happen. Now it has, and you're the one I want to tell it to.
>
> It's funny how you've been my favorite person in the family, considering that since we were little kids, I only got to see you

once or twice a year for a few days, and we never spent much time together even then. But I always thought of us as being more alike than most brothers and sisters. Even when you were still at home, when we were really little, I could tell you stuff and you didn't go and tell Mom or Dad. You were different. And when you'd been away and came back, even that first time, you were more different than ever. You were still you, but you'd changed, and I was impressed. It was as if you'd outgrown the family somehow, but you were easier than ever to be around.

Now I've left home too, not for the reformatory like Mom and Dad worried I would, but for the <u>mercenaries</u>. Has Mom written and told you about that? It isn't the army, although the government is doing it. It's under something called the Office of Special Projects. I'm at a place in the Blue Forest, getting trained. And our cadre, the guys training us, are T'swa! Real genuine T'swa!

I got put out of school right after you were home last, and got in trouble on the job I got, which I didn't like anyway, because this guy gave me a hard time and I knocked three of his teeth out. I had to pay to get them fixed and had to borrow part of it from Dad. But I only got charged damages, no amends, because the judge said the guy had provoked it. Then a guy came to my apartment one evening and talked to me about joining the mercenaries. He told me I'd been selected because my school personality profile said I'd make a good one. The pay isn't too bad—it's the same as the army—and I get my meals and a place to live, and he offered me a signing bonus of DR300. When I agreed, he offered Dad 300 for his signature of approval because I'm not eighteen yet.

As far as I know, all the guys here, all the recruits that is, are pretty much like me. They always got in trouble at school and things like that. There's even a few guys who came here from reformatory.

So here I am. I've been here two weeks now, and you're not the only person that changed a lot being away from home. This isn't a bad place. It's way out in the country, in the forest. At first I thought I wasn't going to like it. You wouldn't believe all the stuff they make us do. Sometimes I can hardly crawl from the shower to my bunk at night. But most of the time I like it, and most of the time I like the T'swa. And sometimes I hate it all, for a few minutes, but when I'm hating it, I know I'll like it again pretty soon. Strange, huh?

They make us do stretching exercises for twenty minutes in the morning, right after our run. Next week they're going to give us rifles; so far we haven't even seen any, but in a few weeks we'll learn how to shoot them. My intestines get excited thinking about it! So far all they've given us to carry are packsacks with sand in them. To build our strength. We hike with them and do pushups with them on our backs. When we get stronger, we'll do our chinups with them too. A few guys do already. You start doing them with sand after you can do twenty without any. I'm up to twelve.

The T'swa say they're going to make White T'swa out of us. There was a guy named Varlik Lormagen that they called the White T'swi back in the Kettle War. But we'll be the first *regiment* of White T'swa.

I hope you'll answer this letter, Little Sister who's not little anymore. Actually, you're the only person outside the regiment I really want much to be connected with. Not that I don't appreciate all that Mom and Dad did, and put up with, but the guys here feel like my real family to me, except I don't have any sister here. You're my sister, and you're too far away to suit me.

I'll probably send you a cube when I've been paid. There's hardly anything around here to spend money on, and talking is faster than writing.

With love,
your brother
Jerym

# 9

Company A formed up its ranks wearing raincoats. Ponchos weren't needed: The rain was light, a thin cold drizzle with sporadic, half-hearted showers, and they'd already had their morning run with sandbag packs.

Jerym felt a beginning of wetness down the middle of his back, spreading. He suspected what was wrong, and who'd done it.

"Atten*tion!* Riiight face! Forwaaard march!"

They marched down the broad grassy gap between company areas and across their battalion drill field. There the platoons separated, 2nd Platoon going to the A Company gymnastics shed. The shed consisted of four walls, a stanchioned ceiling, and a wooden floor, with simple heating by matric converter panels in the side walls below the ceiling. Sets of parallel bars in rows alternated with rows of horizontal bars. The trainees hung their raincoats on hooks by files and positions, and stood at ease by them.

Jerym took the opportunity to look at his as he hung it up. A blade had slit the back beside the center seam for about eight inches. He was satisfied he knew who'd done it, and decided to be open in his revenge.

"First and third squads to parallel bars," called Sergeant Dao. "Second and fourth to horizontal bars."

The youths dispersed to their equipment, and under the eyes of their cadre, did several minutes of stretching exercises. They'd been there for more than four weeks; the general routine was familiar. Then, after drying and chalking their hands, they began their training routines on one apparatus or the other, boots and all, swinging at first, then doing kips; muscle-ups; kidney swings; planches if they could; handstands with help as needed. . . . Changing apparatus halfway through. They spent nearly an hour at it. Near the end, a number of them, with cadre permission, returned to handstands, working on stability, a few even doing handstand pushups. Two did them on the parallel bars.

They'd already done several sets of ordinary pushups beside the road, wearing the sandbags, during "breaks" on their morning run. Almost all of them exercised with zest, with an eagerness to move on to new and more difficult things, impatient with their own failures, and with T'swa restraints that actually were quite permissive.

Then Dao whistled piercing blasts in a now familiar signal. The trainees hurried to their raincoats and put them on. Another set of blasts sent them outdoors, where the rain had stopped for the time being, although the eaves still dripped. They formed ranks, and at Dao's command marched to the next shed, where they stretched some more, then practiced tumbling, again for nearly an hour. And again there was no complaining or timidity, no malingering, no holding back. By now their bodies all were very flexible, though not as flexible as they would be. But for reasons of size, coordination, and strength, some made slower progress than others on the exercise routines. Still, they all progressed more rapidly than typical Iryalan youths would have, for they'd been born on the stage of life to be warriors.

Because of the weather, mail call was in the messhall at noon, just before dinner. There was a letter for Jerym; he glanced at the return address, then tucked it in his shirt and got in the chow line. After eating, they had half an hour to lay around. Many of the trainees catnapped.

The rain seemed to be over. The clouds had thinned, and vague sunshine brightened the day a little. Jerym, in his field jacket, sat on one of the benches at the end of the barracks. With a finger he opened his letter, and read it grinning, shaking his head, chuckling.

"Your ma?" Romlar asked. He was standing on the stoop looking down at Jerym, had been waiting for him to finish. Jerym looked up and shook his head. Though scarcely taller than Jerym, and still the heaviest youth in the platoon, Romlar was no longer "fat boy."

"My sister," Jerym said.

"Huh. You got a letter before."

"Twice before. One from my ma, and one from my sister earlier."

Romlar didn't leave, but said nothing more for a moment. Then: "I'll never get a letter. Everyone in my family is mad at me. Ma used to be all right till I got sent to tronk—reformatory. She gave up on me then. Said I'd never be worth nothin'. Then the guy come to see me there, and told me I could come here, and I did."

"You like this better than reformatory?" Jerym asked. Romlar never looked happy.

"Yeah. No comparison. Reformatory wasn't much worse than school, for me, but this—ain't bad." He went quiet again, but still didn't leave. Jerym got up to go inside.

"What did your sister write about?"

Jerym took both of them by surprise with his reply: He held the letter out to Romlar. "Here. Read it if you want."

Romlar stared for a moment, then hesitantly took it and read, lips moving, commenting only once. "She talks about Varlik Lormagen, the White T'swi." He looked up at Jerym. "And his wife. How'd she get to know them?"

"Lotta goes to a special school. Mrs. Lormagen teaches dancing there."

"Special school. Your folks got money then."

"No. She got to go there kind of like we came here. Some guy came around when she was a little kid—six years old. He said her tests showed she was eligible. It doesn't cost my folks anything."

"Huh." Romlar stared at nothing. "If I wrote to your sister, do you think she'd write back to me?"

The question seemed strange to Jerym, and he almost said no. What he did say was, "The only way to find out is write to her. You want her address?"

"Not now. This evening maybe. I'll get a tablet and pen, and an envelope."

The big trainee turned and went back into the barracks. Jerym followed, wondering if Romlar really would write to Lotta. He also wondered if she'd be mad that he gave Romlar her address, then decided she wouldn't. Whether she'd write back was something else.

# 10

It was an evening without any kind of training, an evening off. In the 2nd Platoon barracks, several trainees were involved in a contest to see who could do the most handstand pushups. Two others were practicing stability by walking on their hands.

Jerym came in with a new raincoat under his arm, unfolded it and hung it in his "wardrobe"—his half of a fifty-inch rod by the head of his bunk. Then he walked to the middle of the long low building and spoke loudly. "Listen up, guys," he said. "We've got an asshole in the platoon. I just went and got a new raincoat because someone cut a slit in the back of my old one."

The place went quiet, a quiet no one broke for a few seconds. Guys lowered themselves from handstands to watch expectantly.

"Maybe the seam just split," Markooris said.

That was Markooris for you: *Don't think anything bad till you get shivved.* "Nope," Jerym answered. "It was cut. Right next to the seam. I showed it to the supply sergeant, and he agreed."

"Who do you think did it?" Esenrok asked, looking brightly interested.

"Well, you're the leading troublemaker, but it was too sneaky for you." Jerym looked around. "Who's the sneakiest guy in the platoon?"

Several of the trainees turned their eyes toward Mellis's bunk. He'd shown a penchant for practical jokes, till he'd put feces in Romlar's boots one morning just before reveille. He'd made the mistake of telling people in advance what he planned, and after it happened, someone told Romlar, who'd beaten him up for it. Badly. No one, not even Mellis, had told the T'swa who'd worked him over.

"Hey, Mellis," Jerym called, "why do you suppose everyone's looking at you?"

"I didn't cut your fucking raincoat!"

"What you mean is, you've gotten smart enough not to talk about the shit you do."

Mellis dropped from his bunk and confronted Jerym. "You can't prove I did it, because I didn't. So stop talking about me like that!"

Mellis's indignation seemed too convincing to be feigned. "Okay," Jerym said, mildly now, "maybe you didn't. But considering the stuff you have done, you shouldn't be surprised if people jump to conclusions."

Mellis glared. He was the youngest in the platoon, but nearly as tall as Jerym, though slimmer. "You're all mouth, Alsnor," he said. "You think you . . ."

That was all he got out. Jerym punched him in the face and knocked him down. Mellis rolled to his feet, and Carrmak and Bressnik got between them. "Back off, both of you! Remember the rules!"

"*He hit me in the mouth!*" Mellis almost screamed it. Blood ran down his chin.

"Mellis," Carrmak hissed, "if you want to get the platoon in real trouble, keep yelling that someone hit you!" For a moment he glared, then the glare faded and his voice became patient. "You're the one that got this platoon on probation. You're sixteen and you act like eight. Alsnor backed off on what he said, but you couldn't leave it at that.

"Now, we've got rules here that we all agreed to. After Romlar beat the snot out of you, what was it Sergeant Dao told us?"

Mellis only glared. Carrmak went on.

"He told us if we had any more fights, it'd be speed marches for us, running and walking alternate quarter miles from 2230 till midnight, rain or shine. That makes eight miles with sandbags." He paused, held Mellis's eyes for a moment and added, "Three nights for every fight."

He turned on Jerym. "Alsnor, I'm disappointed in you. You had no business jumping on Mellis the way you did, and with no evidence. You're usually smarter than that. If we get stuck with three midnighters, you're as much to blame as anyone. More!"

Carrmak blew noisily through pursed lips then. Jerym said nothing, holding knuckles that bled from Mellis's teeth, thinking that Carrmak was right.

"Okay," Carrmak said, "I don't suppose it'll work, but we'll try covering this up. Maybe the T'swa will appreciate the effort and let it go this time." He paused, frowning thoughtfully. "Alsnor, you hurt your knuckles uh . . . How *did* you hurt them?"

"Cleaning his rifle," Esenrok put in, then raised both hands as if to fend off the looks he got. "Really," he said. "He pulled the slide back and it slipped, and his knuckles were in the way!"

"Unh! It sounds about as likely as a blizzard on Kettle." Carrmak looked around. "Anyone here got a better idea . . . ? No?"

The faces around him were glum. "Okay." He turned to Jerym. "You cut your knuckles cleaning your rifle. Just now. We all heard you when you swore, and we saw your hand bleeding. And you—" he said, turning to Mellis, "you hurt your mouth taking a shower. Slipped, almost fell, and bit your lip. Desterbi, you and I saw it happen.

"Alsnor, go to the dispensary, right now."

Jerym nodded, and left at a trot. Carrmak turned back to Mellis. "You go over in ten minutes. If you go now, at the same time as him, there's no way the T'swa will let us get away with this. Go bleed on a towel. We've got to make this look good, or as good as we can. Desterbi, we'll all three have to wet our heads in the shower just before Mellis goes over."

He scanned the others, his eyes stopping at Esenrok. "Esenrok," he said, "you don't look as gleeful as you usually do when there's trouble. Anything you need to tell us?"

Esenrok's head jerked a sharp negative, but he didn't meet the older youth's eyes. Carrmak nodded. "Okay. We'll write this off to experience. We don't need to be geniuses, but we need to act halfway sensible." He raised his voice then. "These T'swa, and Colonel Voker, and whoever it was up the line that decided to set this place up, are giving us a chance to *be* something. Something I think we all want. And none of us ought to forget that.

"But it's up to us to make it work. Let's don't make 'em decide to give up on us and shut this place down."

The army medic on night C.Q. at the dispensary said nothing worrisome when he treated the lacerations on Jerym's hand, nor later when he treated Mellis's split lip. The platoon decided maybe—just possibly—they'd gotten away with it. Carrmak lay on his bunk, reading, when Romlar came over to him.

"Carrmak."

"Yeah?"

"I want to take you on again."

Carrmak looked at him exasperatedly.

"We'd do it according to the agreement," Romlar went on. "No hitting in the face. No marks for the T'swa to see." His voice was earnest. "You're the champion around here. You've got to give people a chance to challenge you. And I'm a lot stronger than I was. I think maybe I can take you now."

Carrmak shook his head, though not in refusal or negation. "When you're just fooling around," he said, "it's easy to not hit in the face. But when two guys are trying to prove something . . ."

Romlar shook his head stubbornly. "I promise I won't hit in the face if you don't. Even if you do, I won't."

The others had turned to them, watching, listening. Carrmak recognized a situation here. He was the leader because these guys respected him. If they began to question his character and didn't recognize a leader anymore, one that had more than a teaspoon of brains, they could end up in the kind of trouble 4th Platoon was in these days.

"Okay," Carrmak said. "On these conditions: Rassling only; no punching. And that gives you a better chance, because you outweigh me. Also we wait till tomorrow night. The T'swa seem to have bought our lies, but they could still roust us out tonight for a midnight dance with the sandbags. And if you and I had been fighting, we'd never know whether it was us to thank for our troubles, or Alsnor and—whoever."

Romlar saw the logic of Carrmak's conditions and agreed, serious as always.

At 2130 the light blinked in the barracks, and guys started getting ready for bed. At 2145 the lights went out. Jerym lay with his eyes open for a bit, thinking about the evening. Someone had told him what Carrmak had said to Esenrok, and how Esenrok couldn't face him. It looked as if he'd accused Mellis wrongly, all right. He wasn't going to accuse Esenrok of it though. *Carrmak was right,* he told himself. *I've run off at the mouth too much already tonight.*

He closed his eyes then, thinking about the fight tomorrow night between Carrmak and Romlar. Second Platoon got leaned on less by the T'swa than any other in the company, maybe in the regiment, and that was because of Carrmak. In 2nd Platoon, the toughest guy was also the smartest, the most sensible. He hoped Carrmak won.

Not that he didn't like Romlar; he did. There was something about the guy he both liked and respected, though he couldn't put his finger on it. It wasn't Romlar's brain, that was for sure. Maybe it was because he stood by his principles, right or wrong.

Jerym's thoughts turned to his scuffle with Mellis; that had been childish. Maybe he'd apologize to Mellis tomorrow. If he did, Mellis would probably act like an asshole and throw crap on him. If so, he'd take it. If he *had* accused Mellis wrongly, why, whatever shit the twerp might throw, he had coming.

It seemed to Jerym that he'd just gotten to sleep when the lights came on and Sergeant Dao's voice called out:

"All right, 2nd Platoon, everyone on your feet! I am a man of my word: You will make a speed march tonight. You have ten minutes to use the latrine, dress, and form ranks."

Jerym rolled out with tight lips. It was his own mouth, he told himself, that had brought this on.

At breakfast, Sublieutenant Dzo-Tar and Captain Gotasu sat across from each other, speaking Tyspi, while Gotasu's executive officer, Lieutenant Toma, listened with interest. Dzo-Tar was the leader of 2nd Platoon. "So," Gotasu said, "you have put 2nd Platoon on company punishment. It has been our best platoon; perhaps the best in the regiment. Has there been some change in dynamics there?"

Thoughtfully Dzo-Tar chewed a mouthful of eggs and bacon. *Company punishment.* Even the concept was foreign; they'd had to borrow it from the Confederatswa. "The dynamics appear to be unchanged," he answered. "The same trainee, Carrmak, remains dominant, but there are limits to what he can do. And at this point it would be harmful, I believe, to invest him with formal authority as trainee sergeant. It would set him apart, cut him off from them, perhaps even endanger him. Dao agrees."

He sipped his joma. "Among ourselves these problems never arise. Too many of these young men are not sane. There is great and admirable energy here, but it pulls and thrusts in every direction. In the absence of the T'sel among them, and with warrior appetites, they need policing. And we cannot depend on them to police themselves. Also," Dzo-Tar added pointedly, "it is time to begin teaching them the jokanru."

Gotasu nodded. "And we cannot, while they are like this. The regiment will never become T'sel warriors until they have the T'sel, and we have no means of bringing them to it, at their age." Thick black hands and blunt fingers dwarfed the table knife as he applied jam tidily to another slice of toast. *We are warriors, not the caretakers of delinquents,* he thought, then reminded himself that that was no longer true. They *had been* warriors. After the Daghiam Kel, Ssiss-Ka, and Shangkano Regiments had finally been decimated in the Long War on Marengabar, the lodge had offered their survivors this opportunity to teach Iryalan warriors. Most had accepted.

"Perhaps Voker will have a solution," Gotasu went on. "He has the T'sel now, but he gained it only after the Kettle War, when he was already in his middle years. So clearly, age is no prohibitant. I will bring up this matter of the T'sel in staff meeting this morning.

"Meanwhile, have you contemplated assigning a sergeant to live in the barracks with 2nd Platoon?"

"Not yet. I know the 1st and 4th have gone to that, and it has helped reduce the trouble there. But the 2nd is not that unsane, and such an assignment would largely eliminate Carrmak's influence." Dzo-Tars's voice and face were calm, matter-of-fact. "In the final analysis, the solution lies in the T'sel, not in repression. We would do the Confederation a disservice to train repressed savages in the warrior arts."

# 11

Second Platoon had completed their three midnight speed marches, and on top of that, no training was scheduled for the evening. This, Romlar claimed, made it a good night for Carrmak to meet his challenge.

Carrmak agreed.

These matters were settled outdoors; the barracks had too little unoccupied space, too many sharp corners and hard edges. At the same time, for an entire platoon to go out and watch the fight would bring attention and the T'swa, so by nomination and the drawing of koorsa straws, five members were selected as judges. Then the two principals and five judges slipped outside by twos and threes, across the drill field to a space behind one of the gymnastics sheds. Despite the fair breeze, it was a reasonable evening for fighting. It wasn't raining, and Seeren, nearly full, shone blurrily through the overcast, a lamp in the sky. The temperature was mild for deep autumn.

Romlar was exceptionally strong, and he made a contest of it, but Carrmak's skill and explosive quickness were too much for him. They fought to three pins, and when it was over, shook hands and headed back for the barracks, Romlar telling himself that Carrmak was a good guy. If Carrmak ever got in trouble, he wouldn't let him down.

Carrmak didn't notice that some of the platoon weren't there till after he'd showered. "Where's Alsnor?" he asked, looking around. "And Esenrok? And Warden and Thelldon?"

It was Bressnik that answered, uncomfortably. "They've been planning a footrace—Esenrok and Alsnor—and they decided to do it this evening. Esenrok said we needed something to replace fighting, something that wouldn't get us in trouble with the T'swa."

*He's got a point there,* Carrmak thought, and frowned. "*Planning* a footrace? How come I never heard about this? And Esenrok runs like a damn yansa; there aren't three guys in the platoon that can beat him. Alsnor can't. How'd he get talked into this?"

"He might win if the race was long enough," Bressnik said. "Esenrok's pretty shortlegged."

"How far?"

Bressnik said nothing. It was Desterbi who answered this time. "They're running down the main road to the reservation boundary and back. Since the T'swa quit posting a gate guard, there's no reason why not. And it's not even against the rules."

"To the boundary . . . How would anyone know it was fair? If Esenrok got out of sight ahead of Alsnor, he could turn back short of the line and say he'd been there. While Alsnor, being honest, would go all the way. And he knows what Esenrok's like." Carrmak glanced around at the others. "Okay. What aren't you telling me?"

"We don't have to tell you nothing," Mellis countered.

"Shut up Mellis, or I'll slap the snot out of you, even if it gets us six more nights of sandbagging. Bressnik, what's the story?"

"Thelldon and Warden figured to borrow a hover car from the motor pool. Warden knows how to drive."

Carrmak clapped a hand against his forehead. "Borrow? You don't *borrow* a hover car. Not legally. The word is *steal.*"

Bressnik talked doggedly on. "They'll drive out and wait at the boundary sign till both guys have gotten there. Then they'll come back and put the hover car right where they got it from. And if they'd had any trouble getting one, like they were locked or something, they'd have been back long before this; they left right after you guys went out to fight."

Bressnik paused, suddenly unsure. "Tunis, Carrmak," he said, "it'll be all right! The T'swa will never know. They don't post guards any more. It's not like the first few days, when there were guys wanting to run away."

Carrmak shook his head. Sometimes he wondered about the T'swa. "Let us hope. If they find out about this . . . How come I never heard about it?"

Mellis answered this time. "Esenrok said not to tell you. He said if you knew, you'd stop it."

"So you guys are taking orders from Esenrok now. That crazy son of a bitch. Second Platoon'll go from the best to the worst in the regiment."

"It's not that bad, Carrmak," Markooris put in. "It's going to keep us out of fights."

Carrmak had a strong feeling that it *was* that bad. *Tunis! Let's steal a car to keep from getting in trouble!* When Esenrok got back, he was really going to work him over. And Alsnor! Sometimes the guy seemed like the sanest one of the bunch, and sometimes he didn't have the brains of a weevil.

The road crossed the boundary in a meadow. A little half-ton utility truck sat parked by the sign, with Thelldon and Warden in the cab, waiting. The clouds had thickened, burying the moon, and the breeze had picked up. It was darker, and getting cold. Now and then Warden would start the propulsion unit and turn the heater on long enough to warm the cab. Thelldon fell asleep, and Warden was getting drowsy himself, but that was all right. When the runners came, they were supposed to slap the cab and yell their name.

Warden saw the first snowflake when he got out to urinate. Turning his back to the wind, he relieved himself, and was getting back in when he saw someone coming. "Thelldon!" he said sharply. "Wake up! One of 'em's here!"

He recognized the chesty figure. Esenrok loped up, yelled his name as he slapped the front of the cab, then turned and started back.

"Huh!" grunted Thelldon sleepily. "Didn't even take time to crow about getting here first."

"Maybe he just wants to get home as quick as he can. It's starting to snow."

"Snow?! Amberus! It was almost warm when we left."

"It's not now." Warden peered through the windshield and saw another couple of flakes drift past. *If it never comes down harder than that, there won't be any problem,* he told himself, but even as he thought it, they began to fall more thickly.

Jerym hadn't tried to keep up when Esenrok moved ahead of him at the start. For the first several miles though, the shorter youth was content to stay just a dozen or two yards ahead, seemingly as a matter of principle. Pacing himself to last the distance, Jerym realized. Pacing had to be Esenrok's biggest concern.

They knew the road well by now, day and dark, and at the five-mile crossing, Esenrok had speeded up, satisfied that he'd have no difficulty with the distance. Jerym saw him glance back, but made no attempt to keep pace. *Let him think I can't,* he told himself. Then, when he'd been unable to see Esenrok for a minute or so, Jerym too speeded up, to stay within striking distance, keeping a sharp eye ahead. Twice, in the next mile, he glimpsed Esenrok at the edge of visibility in the darkness ahead, and eased off just a bit. He was pleased at how well it went, how smooth his strides felt, and how fast.

It was getting darker; the clouds, he realized, were thickening.

When he reached the edge of the boundary meadow and hadn't met Esenrok on his return leg yet, he realized how close he'd stayed. Grinning, he wiped sweat from his eyebrows. He heard Esenrok's yell at the truck, and seconds later saw him coming back. They were about sixty yards apart, and he wasn't more then eighty yards from the boundary himself. Here was his chance to psych Esenrok.

The shorter youth didn't seem to notice him till he was twenty yards away. Then his head jerked up.

"You're looking tired, Esenrok!" Jerym called. "I'm gonna run you into the ground!" Then they were past each other.

Jerym didn't look back to see whether Esenrok speeded up or not. He knew without looking. Grinning, he yelled his name twenty yards before he slapped the truck, yelled it as loudly as he could.

The sight of Jerym startled Esenrok out of a reverie of what he'd taunt him with when they passed, perhaps a quarter mile ahead. Jerym's gibe stung him, and he speeded up, swearing mentally. The son of a bitch actually thought he could catch him! He'd show him! He hadn't begun to tap his reserves yet!

Jerym's voice reached him clearly when he shouted his name. Tunis but that had been quick! He'd have turned, be headed back strongly now. Esenrok speeded up just a little more. His legs might be short, he told himself, but they were strong and tough and fast. He felt the light impact of his boots, the smooth pull and thrust as he jerked the road past him more than four feet at a stride. *Let Alsnor match this pace!* he thought grimly.

Warden watched Jerym's form disappear in the darkness. "Well," he said, "we might as well head back."

"Just a minute. I've gotta take a leak."

Thelldon got out and stepped behind the truck, out of the wind. A minute passed. Warden opened his door. "What in Tunis' name is taking you so long?"

"It didn't want to come out in the cold for a minute. It's doin' all right now though." Seconds later, Thelldon came to the door on Warden's side. "You said you'd show me how to drive."

"Me and my mouth. Okay, c'mon." Warden slid over and Thelldon climbed in. When Thelldon was settled behind the wheel, Warden pointed. "That's the starter."

"I know. I watched you. And I push on it, right?"

"Right."

"And this is the heater switch?"

"You got it."

"And I push on this lever to make it go forward. What do I do to go backward? Pull it toward me?"

"You don't need to go backward. We're headed the right way."

"But suppose I did? If I'm learning to drive, I need to know."

"All right. Before you go any direction . . . Start it. I'll show you."

Thelldon started it, then turned the heater on all the way. "Set it at low," Warden told him, "or you'll cook us out of here."

He turned it down. Then Warden showed him the drive mode control. "The indicator's at neutral, see? That's where you want it before you shift into a drive mode. Next . . ."

Pointing, Warden gave him the instructions, which were simple enough, and Thelldon backed up a dozen feet. It was jerky and so was his stop, but not bad at all for the first time. Then Warden had him drive ahead slowly. There were lots of snowflakes now; in the headlights they seemed to slant into the windshield. When the truck approached the meadow's edge, Warden reached over and turned the power off. The AG let the vehicle down with a barely perceptible bump.

"What'd you do that for?" Thelldon asked.

"'Cause the road is narrow through the woods. I took responsibility for this thing when we stole it, and . . ."

Thelldon interrupted. "Borrowed it," he said.

"Whatever. Get out and change seats. I want to be sure I get it back in one piece, and before the T'swa know we took it, or they'll kill us both."

Thelldon got out and started around to the other side. *The T'swa wouldn't kill us,* he told himself. *Maybe work us to death, but they wouldn't kill us outright.* When he was in again, Warden restarted the vehicle and drove ahead into the forest.

With visibility limited, Warden took his time. It was several minutes before their headlights found a runner, loping down what looked like a white tunnel through the forest, while a suicide charge of snowflakes swooped headlong at their windshield. Without slowing, Jerym swerved to the edge of the roadway and they passed him. Eighty or a hundred yards beyond, Warden blew the horn, long and hard.

"What'd you do that for?" Thelldon asked.

Just ahead was a curve. Warden rounded it, and the headlights showed them Esenrok not more than forty yards ahead. He too swerved to let them by, and Warden, passing him, blared the horn again.

"He heard me blow before," he explained, "and he'll think it was when I passed Alsnor. He'll think Alsnor is right behind him. Shake the arrogant bastard up a little."

Thelldon nodded. Warden and Esenrok had fought a couple weeks earlier. Esenrok had won, and he'd crowed about it. A guy shouldn't crow like that. Not about a buddy.

As the truck passed, horn blowing, Esenrok felt a pang of anxiety. As much as he'd speeded up, Alsnor was gaining on him, or at least holding his own. Again he added speed; he was not going to let Alsnor beat him. Soon Esenrok was breathing heavily. Within a mile he was laboring, his legs tiring. Badly. Despite himself he slowed a little, and wondered how much he'd added to his lead.

The snow had begun to stick on the grass of the roadway, coating it with wet whiteness. He tried to ignore it, even though his boots weren't gripping the road as well anymore. Once he slipped, sprawled heavily, and lay there for ten or twelve seconds, chest heaving, melted snowflakes mingling with the sweat on his face. Then he got back up and began to run again. Slower, hobbling briefly. He was almost weeping with frustration, and after a minute speeded up once more, as much as he dared. Alsnor would be having trouble too, he told himself. If he hung tough and kept pushing hard, he'd still come in ahead.

Jerym wondered how far behind he was. The footing slowed him some—his boots didn't grip as well—but it wouldn't be any better for Esenrok. The snow was about three inches deep and falling more thickly than ever, when he saw Esenrok not more than thirty yards ahead, running with the choppy, labored stride of someone badly tired.

When he passed him, Jerym did not taunt. It didn't even occur to him. He loped on by without saying a thing, only glancing back briefly a few strides past. Esenrok's head was down; Jerym wondered if he'd even seen him. Surely he'd notice his tracks though; he was bound to.

On an impulse—the kind of impulse a T'swi does not ignore—Sergeant Dao put down his book and went to the door to look out. It was snowing, hard, and where there was grass, the ground was white. But it wasn't snow that had touched his psyche.

He put on his field jacket and left the neat hut he shared with the other noncoms assigned to 2nd Platoon. Left for the 2nd Platoon barracks. It was dark of course, except for the latrine windows. Quietly he opened the door and went in, and quietly walked down the long aisle between the rows of bunks. One, two, three, four bunks were empty. And Carrmak he sensed was still awake, despite the stillness of his blanketed form.

There was no sound from the latrine, and he did not bother to look in. It would have disrupted his night vision for the moment, and he did not question his ears, or the less standard, less precise sense that was similarly important to him.

He'd just turned when footsteps sounded on the stoop. The door opened and two youths came in, quietly they thought, starting toward their beds. Dao's soft voice stopped them in their tracks.

"Thelldon, Warden," he murmured, "come into the latrine. I want to talk with you. Carrmak, you come too."

Carrmak was on his feet and starting up the aisle before the other two, who stood frozen for a long moment. They had to pass Dao to enter the latrine, all but Carrmak keeping as far from him as the aisle allowed. Dao followed them through the door.

"Sit!" Dao said, gesturing at the row of commodes. They sat. Dao's eyes settled on the one he judged most vulnerable. "Thelldon," he murmured, "I want to hear your explanation." To Thelldon it sounded as if Dao already knew what they'd done.

"Sir, we were monitoring the race."

"Ah-h?"

"Yes sir. Esenrok thought that races could replace fighting."

"Umm."

"But Alsnor didn't trust Esenrok, so Warden and me, we went to monitor the race. And that's it. Really."

"I see. Where did you go to monitor it?"

"To the reservation boundary. We wouldn't ever have taken it otherwise."

Dao never blinked, never asked "taken what?"

"And we, Warden that is, parked it right where we got it from. In the exact spot. You can see for yourself."

"That won't be necessary. I'll take your word for it. Where are Esenrok and Alsnor?"

"They're still down the road, running. On their way back. We wanted to get the truck back as soon as we could. The last we saw of them was—" He turned to Warden. "Where? About a mile and a half, two miles from the boundary?"

Warden had been staring at Thelldon in shock. What in Tunis was making him run off at the mouth like that? At Thelldon's question, he shrugged. "Something like that," he answered.

Thelldon nodded. "About a mile and a half this side of the boundary. Esenrok was maybe a hundred, two hundred yards ahead. They've probably come another couple of miles since then."

Dao nodded calmly. "Thank you, Thelldon. You and Warden get ready and go to bed. I will talk with Carrmak now."

The two left. Dao looked at Carrmak without speaking for a moment. He could hear the sibilance of Warden's furious whispering to Thelldon in the sleeping quarters.

"So. Foot races to replace fighting? There is something to be said for that. Did you approve their taking a vehicle?"

Dao's face showed only curiosity, but Carrmak was sure that inwardly the sergeant was chuckling. "Sir, I didn't know about it," he said. "I was— out fighting."

"Fighting? Indeed. Put on some clothes, Carrmak, and come with me. I will trust Esenrok and Alsnor to arrive without my attention. They've gotten used to the roads after dark."

Glumly: "Yes sir."

Dao waited while Carrmak pulled on pants, shirt, and boots, pressed the boots shut, and slipped into his field jacket. They left together. Thelldon and Warden had shed boots and shirts. Now they headed back for the latrine. Barkum, whose bunk was next to the latrine door, joined them in the underwear he slept in.

"Tunis!" Barkum swore. "Carrmak's in real trouble now. And probably the rest of us." He paused. "I'm surprised Dao didn't take you guys along too."

"Where's he taking Carrmak?"

"I don't know. But he knows that Carrmak was in a fight tonight. I could hear 'em talking. I knew someone would see a vehicle was missing. Boy! I hope they don't do to us what they did to 4th Platoon."

The prospect seemed so grim, Warden forgot to continue reading Thelldon the riot act.

✧　　✧　　✧

Outside, Dao felt uneasy, as if there was something else that needed to be taken care of. But the feeling came without direction, so he led Carrmak through the slanting flakes toward A Company's messhall. There'd be privacy there, and they had things to talk about.

They were almost there when they saw the glow of flames inside it, through the windows. The door opened and two youths slipped out, not seeing Dao and Carrmak at first. Dao rushed. One turned aside and fled. The other hesitated for just a moment, rattled, and when he did run, Dao cut him off and tackled him, his big hard body slamming the trainee to the ground. Dao was on his feet in an instant with the young man under a thick arm, feet foremost, and ran with him into the messhall.

Benches had been piled against one wall; paper and boxes burned beneath them. Carrmak was already slinging benches away from the blaze, benches that hadn't caught fire yet. Dao thrust the arsonist stumbling, then sprawling, in the direction of the kitchen.

"Get a fire extinguisher!" he bellowed, then pitched in with Carrmak. In half a minute more, all the benches not already on fire had been removed from the pile, leaving several burning. Behind the benches the wall was aflame, but the fire was not yet large. The arsonist arrived with a ten-gallon pot half full of water which he slung at the wall. He hadn't known where the fire extinguishers were. Dao did, and in another minute the fire was out.

Then Dao and Carrmak turned to look at the arsonist. He did not return their gaze.

When a tired Jerym arrived through seven inches of snow, the barracks was as quiet as if nothing had happened. He closed the door behind him and announced his arrival and victory, as agreed. Heads raised in the darkness, and— Someone got off Jerym's bed, someone large and black.

"Congratulations on your victory," Dao said. There was nothing sardonic in his voice except in Jerym's imagination. The sergeant stepped into the middle of the aisle, his voice taking them all in now. "There will be no celebration. You will all go back to sleep. Alsnor, come with me."

Jerym followed Dao out the door feeling as if he'd been slugged in the stomach.

The snow was falling more thickly than ever, the carryall's headlights penetrating it less than thirty yards, a cloud of white pluming behind. A mile from the compound they saw Esenrok lying in the road, white with the wet snow that stuck to him.

He was conscious, saw the headlights and raised his head. The moment that Dao stopped, Jerym was out, helped Esenrok to his feet and into the carryall. Esenrok began talking as soon as he was in.

"I'm all right," he said. "I was just resting. I'd have made it." He turned to Jerym then, "You told!"

Somehow Jerym let it lay, not answering.

"No," said Dao. "I was waiting for Alsnor when he came in. I already knew the story, stolen vehicle and all. Now lie down on the seat and be quiet."

Esenrok subsided and Jerym got in front beside Dao, who restarted the vehicle and turned it back toward the compound. When he pulled up in front of the dispensary, Esenrok was already asleep, and only semi-wakened when they took him in. He was soaked with sweat and melted snow.

# 12

Colonel Carlis Voker had been away from Blue Forest for more than a week. His older sister, Meg, had been dying of *glioblastoma multiforme*. She'd served as surrogate mother to Voker after their mother had died; he'd been seven and she twelve. Now Meg was gone. He'd personally sprinkled her ashes in the Rivertown memorial garden, on a bed of candle flowers, as she'd once said she wanted.

From Rivertown he'd taken a commercial flight to Landfall the day before, and an OSP floater had brought him to the compound at Blue Forest after breakfast. He'd sensed that things had gone badly here, had noticed and identified the feeling while flying up, though what specifically had happened was not part of the perception.

His secretary, the only OSP civilian employee at the compound, gave him a cheery enough good morning, then told him Colonel Dak-So wanted to talk with him at his earliest convenience. Voker thanked the man and went into his freshly dusted office, scanned the originator/subject headings of the communications backlog on his terminal, and decided that whatever Dak-So wanted to talk about had priority.

He pressed a key on his commset. "Lemal," he said, "tell the colonel I'm ready to see him."

His joma maker was hot—he heard it chuckle—and he drew a cup, adding cream from the small refrigerator. Then he walked to the window and stood looking out at the snow—there'd been none at Landfall— wondering what the trainees thought of it. A minute later his secretary's voice spoke from the communicator: "Colonel Dak-So to see you, colonel."

"Send him in."

Dak-So entered, half a head taller and a hundred pounds heavier than Voker. In the T'swa manner, he did not salute. Although Voker was retired army, the relationship between these two was far more T'swa than army. Voker waved at a chair, and while Dak-So sat down, took one himself. "So," he said, "tell me about it."

"Carlis, trainee behavior has deteriorated since you left. I should say has continued to deteriorate." He catalogued some of the more extreme examples, beginning with a gang attack on Lieutenant Ghaz of 3rd Platoon, F Company,[10] and ending with the attempted arson of A Company's messhall by two members of C Company.

Voker nodded, lips pursed. "And the training: How is it going?"

Dak-So chuckled. "The *training* continues to go very well. We are developing a regiment of tough, increasingly self-confident savages who tend to do to each other what should be reserved for opponents. They are not the sort of person we recommend training in jokanru, for example."

Voker sat with eyes steady on Dak-So, saying nothing, listening.

"I remember," Dak-So continued, "when my regiment was virgin, newly shipped out, and I a nineteen-year-old battalion commander. I was amused at the large number of administrative staff in the military forces on Carjath. I could see the reason, of course: They did not know the T'sel. Like most armies, they consisted largely of personnel at the level of Work. A level at which there is a tendency to be orderly. But even so, they were sufficiently aberrated that a large staff—record keepers, guards, military police and the rest—were necessary. You are thoroughly familiar with that sort of thing, of course.

"By contrast, rather few of your intentive warriors are at Work. Most of them alternate between Fight and Compete. And become unruly and self-destructive when brought together like this. Fortunately, under the duress of discipline, they are at Contests much of the time, instead of Battle."

Dak-So stopped, giving Voker a chance to speak. The colonel only nodded, an invitation to continue.

"I wish to review some things for you," Dak-So went on. "Most of it you already know, but itemizing will connect it and establish its relevance."

"Go ahead."

"On Tyss we grow up with the T'sel, from nurselings. Each of us is born with an intended area of activity, with its own natural rules and rights, so to speak. As you are here, of course. On Tyss it is infrequent, and thus rather quickly conspicuous, when someones tries despoiling others of those rights. When one knows the T'sel, respect for rights and for reasonable rules is natural and does not have to be enforced. Thus guards are not necessary, nor military police. While far fewer records are required when people behave reasonably and have no impulses to cheat or steal."

Voker nodded and sipped his joma.

"Those of us born to be warriors are trained by our war lodges to high competence. We develop not only the skills of combat but the wisdom of combat, including what a warrior may do without the universe penalizing him. Thus pleasure in war is possible for us throughout our careers.

"Do you know our service history? Those of us training your regiment?"

"The basics," Voker answered. "You're remnants of three regiments. In the recent war on Marengabar, you were contracted to opposing sides and fought each other. You're old 'enemies,' in a manner of speaking. And you fought long and bloodily. But of course, you were never really enemies at all."

"Exactly! The T'swa warrior has no enemy. He only has those against whom he makes war. Opponents, in a sense. Also, your term 'playmates' applies."

It occurred to Voker that most people would consider that impossible. Or insane.

"We were contracted to train warriors for you," Dak-So went on. "And of course we will honor that contract. But unless your young trainees can be brought to know the T'sel, it seems that heavier and heavier discipline will be needed. And when they have been trained, you will have something dangerous on your hands, which can only be destructive to you."

Voker said nothing, sipped joma, listened.

"Unless, as I said, they can be brought to know the T'sel. And I do not know how that can be done, with youths their age. Perhaps you do. On Tyss we grow up with the T'sel, and learn simple personal procedures to stay attuned to it. Among your people, the T'sel is relatively new. Relatively very few know it, or even know of it. Some of you—you are one—come to know it as adults."

"I was in my forties."

"And the procedures by which that was done—can they not be applied to your trainees?"

Voker nodded. "We looked at that. And foresaw problems. Our procedures require talented, very skilled operators who know the T'sel. People in very short supply, compared to the overall need. And the procedures were designed for use in a calm, controlled environment, not among a disorderly concentration of troublemakers. So we decided to go at it the way we have, and see what we could accomplish.

"It's been my experience that in any large number of people, there are some who respond well to hard challenges. And I knew that a few leaders would arise within the ranks who'd try instilling sanity from inside. But apparently they're not enough, with the overall dynamics so aberrated.

"I've considered giving the natural leaders authority—make them trainee sergeants. We'll need to do that sooner or later anyway. But with these kids—it's not time for that yet. The leaders would lose the kind of influence we need them to have, inside influence on viewpoints and attitudes. And anyway, part of what they need is a willingness to behave rationally without coercion."

He paused thoughtfully. "So it's time to try something further. Including Ostrak Procedures."

He smiled ruefully at Dak-So. "You people have the better system. It's more effective and much easier to start people from birth in a T'sel society. For example, I'm not as wise in the T'sel as you are, who grew up with it. But Ostrak Procedures, used on adults, make dramatic changes in just about anyone they're used on. When delivered by masters working in reasonable environments. We do our best by starting with selected small children, like the cadets we shipped to Backbreak last summer. Generally you don't need to use the procedures as much when you start with six-year-olds.

"So I'll see what can be done about getting these yahoos introduced to the T'sel.

"I'm optimistic that something can be arranged; it's a matter of the wise investment of resources. The Crown has a long-term program to bring all Confederation worlds to the T'sel, and our qualified Ostrak operators are fully committed to projects that are part of it. Is the regiment important enough to pull some of them out and assign them to a project here? Considering the uncertainties in it? Including the uncertainty that this regiment will ever be needed?

"The decision is His Majesty's to make. I'll discuss it with Lord Kristal." Voker got up. "Meanwhile I'll see what else we can do." He grinned. "I've had to deal with yahoos most of my life, and I've got forty years of army experience. Experience that I can look at now from the viewpoint of the T'sel. Let's assume we'll get some kind of help from the Crown.

"Meanwhile you and I are going to provide a groundwork. This afternoon. . . ."

# 13

After the noon meal, the entire regiment crowded into the assembly hall, the first time they'd been there. The first time they'd all been inside anywhere together. Their cadre was with them—more than four hundred commissioned and noncommissioned T'swa officers. (But not administrative and service personnel—clerks, cooks, mechanics etc.— almost all of whom were Iryalan army people on detached service to the Office of Special Projects.) When the trainees were seated, a man white like themselves walked out on the podium, an old man of scarcely medium height and compact build, his gray hair thin and as short as their own, his face lined and leathery. He appeared to be in his sixties.

The chatter thinned to murmuring.

He ignored the lectern, which had been left at one side, and positioned himself front and center, where he stood for a minute without speaking, as if examining his audience.

Then: "*At ease!*" he bellowed, and the room went silent till he spoke again. His voice seemed quiet now, but it filled the hall. "I am Colonel Voker. I am your commanding officer."

He paused, then bellowed once more: "Who likes it here?"

There was a brief lag followed by a few tentative *me*'s, then the hall erupted with cheers. He'd expected them, but their vehemence surprised him, though he didn't let it show. He gave them half a minute, then bellowed again, this time using the microphone in his hand in order to be heard over their cheering. "AT EASE!!!"

It took several seconds before he had quiet.

"Good!" He looked them over again. "Each of you is a would-be warrior. We knew that from your personality profiles. So I expected you to like it here. There's no other place in the Confederation that's worth a damn for warriors."

He paused then. "And I want you to like it here." Again he paused, then raised an admonishing finger. "But on my terms! T'swa terms! It will have to be on my terms!"

It seemed as if somehow Voker looked at every one of them at once. And spoke to each of them, not simply all:

"You've come a long way since you got here. You've come a long way— and you've still got a *long* way to go. I have no doubt you can make it . . . Most of you. But I will not hesitate to kick any one of you out, or any one hundred of you."

Abruptly he switched modes, from genial to hard. "Third Platoon, Company F, answer 'Here Sir!' "

Forty trainees, standing in ranks in the back of the hall, shouted "Here Sir!" in response. They were clothed in stockade uniforms, faded and patched. Their heads were covered by bags with eye-holes, and they wore handcuffs to assembly. In addition to their regular training schedule, they'd been sleeping on the ground in squad tents and doing two-hour midnighters nightly, all on beans, rice, bread and water, supplemented with raw cabbage and poor quality apples.

"Third Platoon, Company F, you are very lucky. Tell me you're lucky."

Their answer boomed: "Sir, we're lucky!"

"Right." Voker's voice was casual now. "And here's the reason you're lucky: If anything like what you did happens again, the people involved will be out of here the next day. In an army prison. That is not a threat. It is a *promise!* We are sparing you that."

The hall was very quiet. He left it that way for several seconds before he spoke again. "We are not trying to break you. We want to *make* you. Or more accurately, we want to help you make yourselves. Into White T'swa." He paused for emphasis. "And T'swa—*would never, do, the kind, of stupid shit that many of you have been doing!* They have too much pride to act like a bunch of savages.

"Last night two men from First Platoon, C Company, tried to burn down A Company's messhall. 'For something interesting to do,' they told us. One of them is no longer with us. He's on his way to Ballibud Prison. The other one helped put the fire out. He is here with us now. Tonight, immediately after supper, he will begin to repair the damage done to the messhall. When he has finished repairing his damage, he will make amends to the Regiment by starting a swimming pool. With a shovel. His contribution to it will be a three-yard span across the shallow end, a span 200 feet long and four feet deep. He will dig from 2300 hours to 0100 hours each night, or longer if his guard feels he hasn't worked hard enough.

"After I told him the conditions of his remaining, he thanked me for letting him stay. Because he is not basically stupid. I doubt that any of you are. He simply did a seriously stupid, destructive thing."

Voker paused again and pursed his mouth. "Now. I am going to ask you a question, a question for each of you. And I want you to answer honestly to yourself. If the answer is yes, I want you to stand up and remain standing. Don't think honesty might make you look bad. It won't."

He could feel the silence, the uncertainty. The tension.

"Would you, any one of you, like to leave here? And return to civilian life? If you do, we'll arrange it."

No voice spoke. No one stood. Not Pitter Mellis, not anyone.

"Good.

"In a few minutes, Colonel Dak-So will speak to you, and when he's done, you'll begin to realize a lot of things. But that'll be in a few minutes; I've got a few things to tell you myself yet. And show you.

"Your training has just begun. You've learned to do some of the basics. Among other things, you've learned to follow orders and to do some things as part of a unit. You've begun to toughen physically; you've begun to develop the needed strength. Soon you'll begin weapons training.

"But there are a lot of things you haven't begun to learn, that make the key difference between a unit of soldiers and a unit of T'swa warriors. I was a soldier for years myself, and proud of it, but a warrior— a warrior is something else."

He paused. "Trainees Coyn Carrmak and Varky Graymar, come to the front of the hall."

Neither man froze for more than a second, then each pushed his way to the aisle and walked to the foot of the podium, where they stood side by side, seemingly calm.

"Your first sergeants consider you the best fighters in your companies." He turned to the regimental sergeant major. "Sergeant Kuto, do you have the straws?"

A stocky T'swi answered. "Yes sir!"

"Fine. Bring them to me."

The T'swi did. Voker arranged them in one fist and turned to the trainees. "Each of you draw a straw. The short straw wins. Carrmak, you first. Step up here."

Carrmak stepped onto the podium and faced the colonel.

"Draw."

He did.

"Graymar, your turn."

Graymar, a bit taller and slimmer than Carrmak, also drew.

"Show your straws to Colonel Dak-So."

They did. "Colonel Voker," Dak-So said, "Carrmak's straw is shortest." He held them up.

"Fine. Carrmak, over here." He stepped to the center of the podium, Carrmak following. Then Voker spoke to him so all could hear. "You and I are going to fight," he said.

Carrmak looked carefully at the old colonel, a lot smaller and so much older than he. Voker took a jokanru stance.

"Are you ready?" Voker asked.

Carrmak flexed his knees, raised his fists. "Sir, I am ready."

Voker's left fist jabbed out, and the youth moved to counter. Carrmak wasn't sure what happened next—none of the recruits were—but in a second he was on his belly on the floor, left arm angled upward and twisted back, his wrist in Voker's grasp, Voker's knee on his kidneys.

The colonel spoke without getting up or letting go, still lecturing. "This is a warrior skill," he said. "In combat, I would have done it a little differently: I would have dislocated my opponent's shoulder and followed with a death blow."

Then he let go and stepped back. Carrmak got to his feet. "Thank you Carrmak, Graymar," Voker said. "Your cadre say you're both more than just tough. You have the making of outstanding warriors. Return to your seats now."

They did. The silence of the trainees had changed. It was swollen with attentiveness.

"How did I do that?" Voker asked. "What do I have that you don't? Besides long training and experience? Obviously it's not youth. Nor strength. Nor superior quickness. Those I lost years ago; I'm seventy-six now. For one thing, I have jokanru, the close combat techniques developed by the T'swa. You just saw one of those. They are more than physical; they are mental and spiritual. And they are very useful to a warrior.

"But they are far less important than something else the T'swa developed. Something called—the T'sel." Voker's voice shifted, still casual but louder. "*Remember that word! T'sel!*" He spelled it for them.

His voice softened then, though it was heard clearly in back. "It is the T'sel that makes the T'swa what they are. With the T'sel, much becomes possible that otherwise would not be.

"You have met challenges here already. Successfully. Challenges of the body, challenges of tenacity and endurance. You are *beginning* to discover, *beginning* to realize, how good you can become. Now we have a new challenge for you, a challenge of the mind and spirit, the attainment of the T'sel.

"It is not a challenge that requires great effort, only a willingness to look at things in a new way. It is a challenge that I expect each of you to meet. Without the T'sel, you will never be T'swa."

Voker turned then and looked at Dak-So. "Colonel, talk to them about it," he said, and joined the other regimental and battalion headquarters officers in a short row of chairs on one side of the podium. Dak-So got up and stepped to the center. A large screen lowered behind him. The lights went out.

# 14

Light filled the screen, and a chart appeared. At the top, Jerym read the words: MATRIX OF T'SEL; below that was a bunch of stuff. He hoped it wasn't going to be like school.

"This," Dak-So said, gesturing with a light pointer, "is not the T'sel. It is an introduction to it." His eyes were faintly luminous as he scanned the room. "Trainee Alsnor!"

Having the regimental executive officer call his name hit Jerym like a jolt of electricity, knocking the breath out of him. After a moment he managed to answer. "Yes Sir!"

"Trainee Alsnor, when you were a child, what did you dream of being? Some day."

A picture flashed in Jerym's mind, one he hadn't remembered in years. He'd been about seven years old, sitting in the living room watching a story about a war. Probably some fictional war set on a trade world somewhere—he couldn't remember much about it. But it had had T'swa in it; actors made up like T'swa, they had to be, and he'd thought it was really great. He'd told Lotta—she was watching it with him—he'd told her that when he was big, he was going to be a T'swa!

"A mercenary, sir!" he answered.

"When did you first dream about being a mercenary?"

"When I was—" He flashed to an earlier time. When he was really little. Could he have been only two or three? It seemed like it. His parents had been watching— Watching reruns of some of the same cubeage Captain Gotasu had shown them in the messhall, the second day he'd been here! He'd been playing with something—what it was didn't come to him now—but much of his attention had been on the screen. And he'd known then what he would someday be.

"—two or three years old, sir!" And hadn't recalled it since! He'd been into playing "soldier" after that, by himself and with other kids in the park, which older people didn't like. Some parents hadn't liked their children playing with him at all, because they usually ended up playing war. And he'd played warrior in his mind when the weather was bad or before he went to sleep. He'd never been someone else in his dreaming, either. He'd always been himself, grown.

"Thank you, Alsnor." Jerym realized then that he'd stood up when his name was called, and sat back down. Dak-So continued.

"Did any of the rest of you dream of being a warrior or mercenary or soldier a lot when you were children?" A general assent arose, not loud and boisterous, but thoughtful, contemplative. It occurred to Jerym that the others, or most of them, were recalling as he had.

"Then perhaps it is real to you that a person, every person, begins life with an intention, a purpose to be something more or less specific. Be it athlete, dancer, warrior, farmer . . . Something.

"Now look at the screen."

Jerym had forgotten the screen. He gave it his attention.

## THE MATRIX OF T'SEL

| | FUN | WISDOM/ KNOWLEDGE | GAMES (CONTESTS) | JOBS (SERVICE) | WAR (BATTLE) |
|---|---|---|---|---|---|
| PLAY | Play just for fun | Study as play; learning unimportant | Games as play; winning unimportant | Job as play; reward unimportant | War as play; victory unimportant |
| STUDY | Study for fun; learning secondary | Study for wisdom &/or knowledge | Study for advantage | Study to enhance job accomplishment | Study for power |
| COMPETE | Compete for the fun of winning | Compete to be wisest or most learned | Compete to win | Job as a challenge | War as a contest |
| WORK | Work at playing | Work at learning | Work for advantage | Work for survival | Soldiering |
| FIGHT | Fight to control pleasure | Fight to control wisdom and knowledge | Fight to subdue | Fight for monopoly | Fight to kill or destroy |

"There is a row across the top, in capital letters, defining categories of *purposes* from Fun to War. The words here, of course, are in your own language, Standard. The originals are in Tyspi, my language, and the translations, being restricted largely to one-word headings, are not precise. In fact, they differ slightly in different translations. But they provide a useful approximation.

"Any human activity can be fitted into one of these categories.

"So. In which of them does Warrior fit?"

A number of voices answered: "War."

"And a farmer?"

"Job."

"What of a dancer?"

There was less unanimity on dancer; some said Job and a few Games, but more, after hesitation, said Fun. *Of course it's Fun,* Jerym thought. *If we're talking about purposes.*

"Very good. And on the left we have a capitalized series from Play to Fight. Now consider a possibility. Consider the possibility that a person is *born* to follow one of these purposes, from Fun through War. Depending on his environment and personal history, he will pursue that purpose if possible, at one of the levels from Play to Fight. Though he may also Work at Job, in order to survive. In many cultures, as a small child, he will be at the top, at Play. Often to move downward over the years until, usually from the level of Work, sometimes from that of Fight, he falls off the chart with his purpose abandoned."

Dak-So paused. "Look the matrix over. At what intersection of columns and rows do T'swa warriors fit?"

Answers started popping almost at once, building toward a consensus for War at Fight. Jerym felt an elbow nudge his arm, and Carrmak, grinning next to him, murmured "War and Play."

Jerym's eyes found the intersect of War and Play, and was irritated with Carrmak. Victory unimportant? Tell that to the T'swa!

"Tell me," Dak-So said, "when you have had fights lately, what are called 'fights,' how many of you tried to kill or destroy your opponent?"

No one spoke up.

"We have here a confusion because of words," Dak-So said. "This chart, this translation, has a column headed War, but with a subheading Battle, to better cover the full meaning in Tyspi. So for the sake of discussion, consider what you were doing as 'battling.' Did you battle to kill, or did you battle for pleasure? Or as a contest?"

The answers began quickly, divided between pleasure and contest. Jerym couldn't see much difference.

"Excellent! I will not tell you why the T'swa battle. Not now. I will point out, though, that when we have asked you why you have started fights, or done other destructive acts, no one has said to injure or destroy. Mostly the answers have been something like 'for fun,' or 'to see if I could take him.' Or 'to see what would happen.' Injury and destruction occurred, but they were not the purpose of the acts."

"Sir!" someone called. "Can I ask a question?"

"Ask."

"I read once that you guys, you T'swa, fight for money. That it costs a lot of money to hire a T'swa regiment. Wouldn't that put you at Work on the chart? Or at Job?"

"We do not make War to get money, although we receive money for it. Money is not our purpose, it is only a means. Most of it goes to our lodge, to finance the training of other boys such as we were, helping them fulfill their purpose. To make possible our way of life—the more than eleven years of training, the warring on various and interesting worlds with various and interesting conditions. And to care for us when we are unable.

"Let me mention that what you are doing, training as warriors, falls under the concept labeled here as War. A warrior delights in good, intelligent training. You may wish to examine whether you enjoy yours or not.

"Now, are there other questions?"

There were; more than thirty minutes' worth. Then Dak-So cut them off and they left the hall by companies, for more training.

From the assembly, Voker went with Dak-So to the T'swa colonel's office. There Dak-So poured them each a glass of cold watered fruit juice, the favorite T'swa drink.

"Carlis," Dak-So said, "despite your rather limited contact with the trainees, I must say you know them very well. Our presentations to them took hold better than I'd expected."

Voker grinned. "They're my people, Dak. I've dealt with them—coped with them, handled them, what have you—all my life. For most of that time, forty-one years, I was one of them. Lived as one of them, thought like they do, and had the Sacrament like all my generation, though in me it somehow didn't take the way it normally did.

"But you were right this morning. We do need to deliver the T'sel. If we can. What we did this afternoon was a start. It set things up, and I expect it to reduce the disorders considerably. But there's a lot of aberration there."

After they left the assembly hall, Jerym was too busy to think any more about the Matrix of T'sel or what it might mean to his life. When they finished training that evening and went to their barracks, each bunk had a printout of the Matrix of T'sel on it.

He put his on his shelf. He'd look at it when he wasn't so tired.

After showering he went to his bed. Next to Carrmak's. The lights were still on, and Carrmak was lying on top of the covers, looking at his copy. Jerym, before he lay down, saw Carrmak purse his lips and nod at whatever he'd just read, his eyebrows arched. Tomorrow, Jerym decided, he'd look his over during dinner break.

# 15

The novice, Itsu-Ta, stood in the darkness outside the little tower room, looking at the marvelously star-rich desert sky, admiring it. Itsu-Ta was *Homo tyssiensis* of course, and to his large T'swa eyes, night was somewhat less dark than it might have been to a man from, say, Iryala. He was from the Jubat Hills, from Tiiku-Moks, where the sky was to some extent obscured or closed in by trees, and not infrequently cloudy. The monastery of Dys Tolbash, on the other hand, was on a ridge crest, and he on a tower of the monastery, with the night sky a vast, bottomless, scintillant bowl.

It might almost have drawn him into it—his full attention or even his soul—but he was on the tower for a purpose, and not free just then for wandering in the spirit. So he satisfied himself with looking, and enjoying the gentle winter breeze on his nearly naked body. (The temperature had slipped to about 85°F.)

He stepped back into the tower room; there was no wall on the north side, where the sun struck briefly only in summer, near sunrise and sunset. Master Tso-Ban sat there with his legs folded, had sat for sixteen hours unmoving, scarcely breathing, his heartbeat only sufficient for the tonus necessary to an upright posture.

Yet his attention was fully occupied.

Itsu-Ta could have eavesdropped; he had the ability. Although he was only a novice, he had been born to Wisdom/Knowledge, had been nurtured in it, had drilled its techniques for most of his eighteen years. But to eavesdrop on a master uninvited would have been discourteous, and more, it might have distracted Tso-Ban. Itsu-Ta's function this night was simply to give Tso-Ban's passive body a little water from time to time, water spiked with fruit juice as sustenance.

Tso-Ban's spirit was in a ship in hyperspace, on its bridge, with Tarimenloku's watch navigator. (The commodore himself was sleeping.) It seemed that the Confederatswa were very interested in whether the ship might emerge in Confederation Space. Which had provided Tso-Ban with a very interesting challenge, and, incidentally, Tyss and the Order with useful Confederation gold dronas.

So from the monastery library, Master Tso-Ban had memorized, imprinted, the galactic coordinates of a number of reference points in Confederation Space. Then by long and patient monitoring of ship's data, and its subliminal analysis, *he'd gradually managed to visualize as a chart the ship's—the computer's—galactic model, with its coordinates!* He'd had no one to instruct him, even unwittingly: Tarimenloku and his officers operated by long-conditioned automaticities, and relied heavily on the ship's computer. Tso-Ban's feat had been one of the outstanding accomplishments of millennia of Dys Tolbash's monks.

Then, after fixing his purpose, he'd meditated long, until the two sets of coordinates finally had reconciled for him. The project had kept him thoroughly engrossed for a number of deks. Now, with the coordinate models reconciled, he was monitoring in order to get a fix on the ship's course in hyperspace, as related to the Confederation's galactic chart.

Because the night was cool, Itsu-Ta did not attempt to give Tso-Ban another sip just then. Instead he assumed his own lotus posture on a mat on the stone floor, and re-entered a sort of reverie, monitoring the condition of Tso-Ban's body.

Dawn was still an hour away when Tso-Ban roused, and with him Itsu-Ta. The master yawned, stretched hugely, took a swig from the water bottle, bowed slightly to Itsu-Ta who bowed back, then began to descend the steep outside stairs that zigzagged down the side of the tower.

Tso-Ban had completed the challenge. The course the Klestronu flo-tilla was on would not take them into Confederation Space or even very near it. And with that knowledge, his interest in the flotilla faded. He'd had enough for now of a ship in hyperspace. A ship that had been in hyperspace for months and promised to be there for another year or more, if it didn't emerge prematurely to destruction by Garthid weapons.

Perhaps he would return to his off-and-on interest in the sapient sauroid hunters on another world he'd encountered. There were humans there, too, unknown to the Confederatswa or the Karghanik Empire, and sapient ocean life forms as well, but the sauroids interested him most.

# 16

The enemy leaped from behind the tree, blast hose raising, and Jerym half turned, crouching, rifle at hip, squeezing off a burst as he pivoted, then threw himself prone onto the wet leaves (the snow had melted) while his "assailant" fired a crashing burst of sound before evaporating into its constituent photons.

From behind them, a T'swa voice announced, "Trainee Alsnor: you expended most of your burst before your line of fire reached the enemy. Your last round scored a superficial wound, right pelvis, insufficiently severe to prevent enemy from firing effectively. Enemy blast hose caused severe casualties to your squad."

Scowling, Jerym got to his feet and turned the point over to Esenrok, wishing he knew where the projectors were. Esenrok bagged the next holo and gave way to Romlar, who got off his burst on target but too late.

When they reached the end of the course, Esenrok clapped Jerym on the shoulder in mock friendliness. "Remind me to get transferred to another squad, Alsnor. Before we get into combat somewhere and you really get your squad wiped out."

Jerym turned to him, eyes blazing. "Off my back, asshole! Yours was right in front of you. Mine was around to the side."

"'Mine was around to the side,'" Esenrok said in a mocking falsetto. "Come off it, Alsnor. You're a fucking crybaby..."

Jerym was on him then, a hard punch catching Esenrok full on the nose, blood splatting. For a moment they grappled furiously, heels striving to trip, before Jerym got Esenrok's feet off the ground and threw him, crashing on top of him.

That's when it ended. Their squad leader, Sergeant Bahn, grabbed Jerym by the shoulder, sending a wave of numbness through him, and then, by his jacket collar, jerked him backward to his feet. Esenrok scrambled to his, attempting to get at Jerym, but Bahn caught the swinging fist with his free hand, Esenrok dropping to his knees at the pressure.

"Alsnor," Bahn said, "go to the stand and sit down. I will speak with you later."

Jerym, shaking with emotion but saying nothing, picked up his rifle and left with the squad, all of it but Esenrok, all equally silent, walking toward the small stand where they'd receive a critique of their performance.

Bahn gripped the stocky Esenrok by the shoulder and started walking him toward the company's aid man, another T'swa sergeant, leaving Esenrok's rifle where it lay.

"My rifle!" Esenrok objected.

"It will be seen to," Bahn replied equably. "And you will receive company punishment for taunting a squad mate."

Esenrok, whose nose was bleeding copiously, squealed with indignation. "Me? Company punishment? He slugged me! Sucker-punched me!"

"He did not sucker-punch you. He will receive company punishment too, but it will be less severe than yours. Had you not taunted him, he would not have struck you."

Esenrok shook loose from the burly T'swi's grip on his shoulder, screaming, "Next time I'll shoot the sonofabitch!" With startling suddenness, shocking power, a T'swa fist grabbed Esenrok's jacket front and jerked him close, disregarding the blood. Esenrok went limp with the wave of fear that washed through him.

Bahn replied almost gently. "Trainee Esenrok, let me clarify some things for you. You started the fight with Alsnor, with your mouth. Thus you will receive the more severe punishment. Now, with that same uncontrolled mouth, you have earned something more severe, perhaps expulsion, for threatening to shoot a squad mate."

In a state of shock, Esenrok said nothing more, stumbling numbly to the aid man, propelled by Bahn's thick hand. A T'swa corporal, one of the cadre not assigned to a specific platoon, trotted over, picked up Esenrok's rifle, and put the partially expended clip into one of the large pockets in his field pants.

Lieutenant Dzo-Tar and Sergeant Dao, waiting near the stand, had heard Esenrok's screamed threat, and watched Bahn handle him.

Dzo-Tar turned to his platoon sergeant and spoke in Tyspi. "In your view," he said, "should we get rid of that trainee?"

Dao shook his head, eyes still on Bahn and Esenrok, who were with the aid man now. "I recommend that at this time we do not. True he is

2nd Platoon's principal troublemaker, but if the Confederatswa procedures the colonel has spoken of prove efficacious, Esenrok should become an excellent warrior. He has valuable leadership qualities."

He looked at his lieutenant then. "Interesting how Voker's and DakSo's lectures ended almost entirely the challenge fights and vandalism, while fighting in anger has increased. Has the captain heard anything further about when the procedures will begin?"

Dzo-Tar's eyes moved to the trainees seating themselves on the stand. "He mentioned nothing further this morning. Apparently it is still scheduled for sometime this week."

That evening before dismissal for supper, Dao addressed the platoon in ranks. Jerym was there, and Esenrok, the latter with a bandage on his face and no rifle.

"There was a fight in 2nd Platoon today," Dao said. "But there will not be a midnighter tonight. We'll save them for you, for later. The captain has learned this afternoon that visitors will arrive tomorrow. They will interview certain of you, and we have been asked to see that you get a full night's sleep in preparation.

"Alsnor, Esenrok, I want to talk with you. The rest of you are dismissed."

The platoon broke ranks and hurried into the barracks. Jerym and Esenrok still stood there, not looking at each other, Jerym's expression morose, introverted, Esenrok's sulky, defiant. Dao, on the other hand, seemed genial despite what he was about to say. "Alsnor, I have not yet decided what the penalty will be for your behavior today."

He turned to Esenrok then. "Esenrok, Lieutenant Dzo-Tar will discuss your case with Captain Gotasu. You will be informed of the captain's decision at second muster tomorrow morning. I have spoken for you incidentally. Like Alsnor, you have certain admirable qualities that particularly commend you as a warrior-to-be. Unfortunately you have shown a severe propensity for causing trouble, not only for yourself but for others." The large T'swa eyes had drawn Esenrok's to them. "Therefore the captain may decide you are not worth it. Or he may decide to give you another chance.

"Meanwhile there is tonight." Dao looked them both over. "I am going to handcuff you two together, left wrist to left wrist. Very awkward, I know. At supper you will eat with me at a separate table, handcuffed, and— you will not feed yourselves. You will feed each other. If you do not work out an effective, cooperative system, you will go hungry. Tonight you will put your mattresses together on the floor of the dayroom and sleep there, again with your chains on. I shall sleep there too. And if you fight, at any time, I will handcuff you together, all four wrists, on the opposite sides of a tree, and you will spend the night there in your greatcoats.

"This is a test of you both, but especially, Esenrok, of you." He looked at them with an almost kindly expression. "Are there any questions?"

Both youths stared wordless at the ground.

"Very well. Go and clean up now. And remember that tree."

Company A's dayroom was a small building lined with bookshelves. Beyond that it had a drinking fountain, chairs, small tables, and at one end a latrine. Nothing more. Jerym and Esenrok, manacled together, had managed jointly to lay their mattresses side by side with their blankets spread over them, and to get their boots off. But there had been no hint of reconciliation. Dao eyed them speculatively.

"Before you lie down to sleep," he said, "there is something I require of you. First, place two chairs facing each other, four feet apart."

Sullenly they did. Then Dao removed their handcuffs. "Sit down," he said, and still sullen, they sat.

"Now I will give you instructions, and the sooner you carry them out to my satisfaction, the sooner you lie down to sleep. Also, do not forget the tree. Alsnor, I will ask you to tell Esenrok something you like about him. It must be genuine, neither untrue nor sarcastic."

Jerym sulked.

"Esenrok, I will ask you to do the same to Alsnor. You must look at each other while you do this, and the one who is complimented must thank the other." He looked from one to the other. "Alsnor, begin!"

Jerym took a deep breath and let it out. "Esenrok, you— You're the best sprinter in the platoon."

Esenrok could scarcely grind the words out: "Thank you."

"Another," said Dao.

Jerym grimaced. "You are . . . You fired the fifth highest score on the target range."

"Thank you."

"Another."

Jerym shot a scowl at Dao, then turned back to Esenrok, saying nothing for several seconds, as if he couldn't think of anything. Then: "You had a good idea about running races instead of fighting. If we'd done that earlier, we wouldn't have had all those midnighters."

Again Esenrok thanked him, and again Dao called for another.

"You can do more chinups with a sandbag than I can."

"Thank you."

"You— Got more guts than sense." Jerym turned quickly to Dao. "That's a compliment! Around the barracks that's a compliment!"

Esenrok's blush was visible beyond the tape on his face, but gradually he grinned. "Thank you."

"Very good," Dao said. "Now it is time for Esenrok to have a turn. Esenrok?"

His first took only a few seconds. "Uh . . . You beat me in the race."

"Thank you."

"Again."

"You . . . You never snore."

"Thank you."

"Again."

"For a long-armed guy, you can do a lot of pushups."

"Thank you."

"Again."

"And you . . ." Once more Esenrok grinned. "You got an awful good straight right."

Jerym blushed. "Thank you," he answered, then a grin began to creep onto his face too.

Dao added his own grin. "I have one more instruction for you." They looked at him. "Take your mattresses back to the barracks, and go to bed there. I will return the handcuffs to the master-at-arms."

No one said anything when Jerym and Esenrok came into the barracks, jointly carrying their mattresses one atop the other with their bedding on top. They made up their beds, then went outside together.

"They gonna fight, you think?" Romlar asked.

Carrmak shook his head. "For one thing," he said, and fingered his nose, "when your nose is broken, you don't want anyone bumping it. And Captain Gotasu is likely to ship them both home if they get into it again. Very soon anyway. Neither one of them wants that."

Outside, Jerym and Esenrok strolled toward the dayroom, which normally would have been dark by then, but Sergeant Dao hadn't turned the lights out yet.

"Esenrok," Jerym said, "I never should have slugged you like that. I'm—sorry."

Esenrok stopped. "Sorry doesn't fix this," he answered, touching his nose gingerly. "But look. I've always had a big mouth. I know that. And a lousy temper. And I've told myself more than once that I was going to quit mouthing off." He shrugged. "But it seems like I don't remember it when I need it."

Jerym nodded. "My mouth hasn't been my problem, but slugging someone has. The last time, the judge told me, 'Once more and you go to the reformatory.'"

Esenrok nodded. "They told me that when I was fifteen. So I quit slugging guys, pretty much. After that's when my mouth got really bad."

He spread his hands to Jerym, as if to say, what's to do? "You know, there's a lot of us here like you and me."

"Yeah. Shit!" Jerym's mind went to the Matrix of T'sel, and wondered where he was on it. "This is the first place I ever knew of for guys like me. And you. I mean, you know, a place for us. For warriors I mean . . ."

"I know what you mean. And you're right." Esenrok looked worried now.

The lights went off in the dayroom, and the door opened. "Just a minute," Jerym said. "I got to say something to Dao." He loped off. Esenrok waited, curious, till he came back.

"What was that about?"

"I told him . . ." This time it was Jerym who spread his hands. "I told him you hadn't really meant it when you said you'd kill me, and that he should tell the captain that. I told him it was just a way of talking. A way of saying how mad you were. I told him that's the way we are here." He shrugged. "Maybe when we're T'swa it'll be different."

They turned and strolled together toward the barracks. "You know," Esenrok said, "maybe I did mean it when I said I'd kill you. I was crazy. You know?"

Jerym nodded. "I know. But maybe the captain doesn't. And anyway you didn't shoot me. And when I—hit you—you had your gun."

Esenrok stopped walking, stared at nothing. "Huh! I guess I did, didn't I. Well." He turned to Jerym and grinned ruefully. "I'm not as bad as I thought I was!"

He put out his hand and they shook, making it a contest of strength. When, after half a minute, neither had won, they both laughed, let go, and went on to the barracks.

Dao had paused beside a tree and watched the scenario between the two trainees. When he went on, it was not to the rows of neat huts that comprised non-coms' country. Instead he went to officers' country, a hutment scarcely different from that of the noncoms. (For they all were T'swa.) Lieutenant Dzo-Tar would be interested in the reconciliation of Alsnor and Esenrok, and what it said about the young men.

These Iryalans still surprised him from time to time, refining his knowledge of them.

# 17

Youths in field uniforms hustled out the door to form ranks in the freezing gray morning. Briefly Sergeant Dao regarded his watch, then looked up. "Atten*tion!*" he called, and the ranks stiffened. "Report!"

The T'swa squad sergeants didn't need to take roll. A glance had served. "First squad all present, Sir!" snapped Sergeant Bahn, and the sergeants of the second, third, and fourth squads followed suit. Dao about-faced easily but crisply, and saluted Lieutenant Dzo-Tar. "Second Platoon all present, Sir!"

For the purpose of training these Confederatswa, the T'swa had adopted army-style protocol, a major but easy adjustment for them. In T'swa units, roll call might be taken if there'd been casualties or if personnel had been dispersed, but otherwise never. "Sir" was seldom used except in the presence of foreigners who expected it. And when they did salute, it was in the Confederation style, because they lacked a salute of their own.

Similarly, in most situations, Sergeant Dao spoke for Lieutenant Dzo-Tar because Voker considered it good tactics with these trainees. Let the platoon sergeants be the immediate authority; let the platoon *leaders,* the lieutenants, be a step remote, each ruling through his sergeant, with whom the trainees would then feel more rapport.

The T'swa had no problem with this; they accepted Voker's experience and judgement.

But at morning roll call, the platoon got its day's orders from on high, from Lieutenant Dzo-Tar. They'd come to expect this. During the day, Sergeant Dao would enforce, interpret, and modify those orders as circumstances required.

"Men," Dzo-Tar said, "the uniform of the day will be winter field. The following men will remain in barracks after breakfast and receive specific orders later. Alsnor, Bressnik, Carrmak, Darrmiker . . ." He read off a dozen names including Romlar's. Then Dao dismissed the platoon, and they went in and washed up for breakfast. Jerym was optimistic that whatever this special duty was, it would prove to be good. Because the others named were all trainees in good standing with the cadre. He was the only one of them currently on a shit-list.

After breakfast, the rest of the platoon went off on their morning run. According to Markooris, who'd passed by the drill field where the company had been forming up, it looked as if 2nd Platoon was the only one with men held out. None of the twelve waiting in the barracks even speculated out loud what this might be about, but they remembered what Dao had said the day before about visitors and interviews. They hung around, read, played cards, practiced walking on their hands, even managed not to scuffle or get into other trouble. After a little, Carrmak and Jerym got into a situps contest, but they'd only gotten up to 517, with the others loudly chanting the count, when a T'swa corporal came in and called six names, including theirs. It was cold out, about ten or fifteen degrees, Jerym thought, with a breeze, so they put on field jackets before they left.

The six of them were led to the Main Building, the administration building. There'd been a lot going on there lately, buses pulling up with civilian workers, trucks with building supplies, and Jerym wondered now if that had anything to do with them. The corporal left them in a room with chairs and sofas, and a bunch of books spread on a table. All the books seemed to be about the planet Oven—Tyss—or the T'swa or the T'sel, and there was a big Matrix of T'sel on a wall, with a lot more writing in the boxes than there'd been in the version he was familiar with. Jerym went over to look at it, but was too fidgety to do more than scan.

After five or ten minutes a civilian came in with the T'swa corporal and took the six of them on a tour, showing them where they'd be going, describing briefly what to expect. They'd be led individually to one of a number of small rooms along a hall—a hall that smelled like fresh lumber—where someone would interview each of them privately. The civilian used the terms *interview* and *interviewer,* instead of the unfamiliar *session* and *operator* which might worry the trainees.

Even so, Jerym wasn't sure he liked the sound of this. He'd been interviewed by psychologists at school and before going to court, and while nothing bad had happened, he'd felt exposed, endangered by their questions.

The civilian told them that when they came back out of the interview rooms, someone would lead them to a room where they'd be given a snack. The snack room seemed small to Jerym, with six tiny tables, each having a single chair. If, their civilian guide said, there was more than one of them in the snack room at the same time, they were not to talk about what had happened in the interview. From the snack room they'd be led to a room with a bunk in it, where they were to lie down and rest—sleep if they felt like it. Afterward they could go back to their barracks. They were to say nothing about any of this to the others. They could say they'd been to the administration building and been interviewed, but that was all.

That was the end of the tour. They went back to the waiting room curious and apprehensive. They didn't wait long though, any of them. The civilian came back to lead them, one by one, to the hall with the fresh lumber smell, where he'd knock at the assigned door, then leave them there.

✧        ✧        ✧

After Carrmak, Jerym, and the other four had been led from the barracks, Romlar napped in his bunk. He hadn't even watched out the window in hopes of seeing where they were being taken; he'd know soon enough. That had been 0730; it was 0930 when the corporal came in again and took the rest of them. They saw the same waiting room as the earlier six, the same everything. Bressnik was in the snack room when they passed, with a glass of something and a sandwich.

Romlar felt good about it. It wasn't anything he could put his finger on; he just felt good. He didn't even feel restless about not being out training, though he, like the others, had developed a strong appetite for it. (Physically he was a very different Romlar than had fallen out on the run and on the sandbag hike, that first night at Blue Forest.)

The civilian made sure he knew not to talk about what happened to him. He wondered what that would be. He wasn't nervous about it though, or not much anyway. He was pretty sure he could wad the civilian up in a ball, if it came to that. Or just about anyone except the T'swa and Carrmak. And that gray-haired little colonel!

Back in the waiting room he browsed a book by Varlik Lormagen, about the T'swa. He remembered the name, Varlik Lormagen. The White T'swi. Alsnor's sister knew Varlik Lormagen. It occurred to him that he'd never written to her, never even gotten her address from Alsnor.

The book was mostly about T'swa warriors on Kettle, in the war, but there was also stuff about their home world, Tyss, and what it was like. There were lots of pictures to help make it seem real. While he was looking at it, the civilian came in and led Lonsalek away, and Markooris, and then Presnola. The next time he came in, he called: "Romlar!"

Romlar got up, and now his stomach was nervous after all. He wished he'd had a chance to talk to Carrmak and find out what they did to you here. But Carrmak wouldn't have told him, because they made such a big deal out of not telling.

The civilian led him down the hall to one of the doors, and knocked firmly.

"Send him in," a voice answered. It sounded like a female voice, and came from a little grill. The civilian opened the door and motioned Romlar through. Romlar stepped in, ducking his head a bit as if he thought he was too large, too tall for it, and the door closed behind him with a firm click. Romlar didn't notice the thickness of the door, or of the carpet, and couldn't know about the sound insulation between the wall panels. What he did notice was—the girl. Just a young girl! Fourteen or fifteen, he thought, on the skinny side, with red hair and a pretty face. And green eyes! He had a sudden impulse to turn and leave, run out. He'd always been afraid of girls. At school, girls had made fun of him, and if you ever hit one of them, forget it! You'd be put away.

She smiled at him. "Artus Romlar?"

"Uh, yeah." Even at home, not many people called him Artus: his mom and dad, his teachers— That was all. Here the guys didn't even know that was his name; here people called you by the name above your pocket, your last name.

"My name is Lotta," the girl said. "Sit down please, Artus." Across the desk from her was a chair with a cushioned seat. He sat down on it.

She was still smiling. Her teeth were pretty—small and even. "Do you like it here at the Blue Forest Reservation?" she asked.

"Yeah."

Her green eyes were direct, steady, comfortable. "Good. What do you like best about it?"

"Uh, I don't know . . . I like the T'swa pretty good. They work our tails off. And they never get mad at us."

"Okay. Is there anything else here you like a lot?"

"Uh, yeah, I guess so. I like the guys really good. And the training. I really like the training."

"Sounds good. How do you feel about yourself these days?"

The question startled him, and for several seconds he didn't know what to answer. "Uh— Oh, pretty good I guess." It seemed to him that that was true. And that it hadn't been true before he'd come to Blue Forest.

"All right." She paused, drawing his attention out of himself, to her next words. "Now if you could change one thing about yourself," she said, "what would you most like to change?"

The question snapped his attention back inward. He couldn't think, couldn't possibly answer. Then he heard his own voice saying, "I'd like to not be stupid."

"All right," she answered. "Tell me about a time you felt stupid."

Romlar nodded slowly. "My first night here. A T'swi told me to dig a big hole. Because I fell out on the run, and then I quit on the sandbagger—the sandbag march—and told them they could go *F* theirself. And after I dug awhile, I quit digging and told him that again. And the T'swi was going to chain me to a post until I would dig some more, so I tried to fight him but he was so strong I could hardly believe it, and he knew just what to do. And it was cold and I was sweaty, and all I could do was lay on the ground and shiver, because I was cold. And I— I cried. And I felt so damn stupid, because all I needed to do was run a little farther, or hike a little farther, or dig a little farther, and I wouldn't have been laying there on the cold ground, chained to a post."

A six-inch-high shield sat on the desk, and behind it from time to time her fingers moved on a flat keypad, silently and unobtrusively. Her gaze, however, never left Romlar's face. It was as if her hand operated on an independent circuit from her eyes and tongue. "Okay," she said. "Was there an earlier time when you felt stupid?"

It came to him at once, but he wasn't sure he ought to tell her. Then he heard himself saying: "I was— I asked this girl in school to go to a music program with me. I asked her because she'd always talked nice to me and she wasn't too pretty. She said she couldn't because she was supposed to go somewhere with her family that night. But somebody told me later that he'd heard her laugh about my asking her. She said she wouldn't go out with somebody as stupid as me; that I'd probably try to rape her."

Romlar looked at the redheaded girl to see what she thought. She was just gazing at him, quietly and steadily. "I got that," she said. "What's the earliest time you can remember feeling stupid?"

The question stopped him. The earliest time. He sat dumbly, shaking his head. Nothing came to him. "The time with your father," she prompted. "When he held you up by the ankles."

Her words were like an unexpected blow. His buttocks began to burn, and the back of his legs, to sting, to hurt. He didn't want to remember, wanted to get up and run out of the room, but his body wouldn't move. "I was . . ." he heard himself start. "I was—just a little kid. Maybe two." He had no idea what this was going to be, but a feeling of dread had crept through him. "And—" He paused. The images were slow to form, the events conceptual at first. "I guess I must have broke something. Something valuable. My father came in and he was really mad. And I was scared. Scared! He grabbed me by my feet, my ankles, and held me up with one hand and started beating on my ass and legs as hard as he could."

Romlar had begun weeping, tears overflowing, spilling down his cheeks. "And he yelled at me and he yelled at me and yelled, 'You damn stupid little animal! You stupid little animal! Look what you did! Look what you did! You stupid little animal!' And he kept on hitting me and hitting me and yelling like that, a big strong man, and I was just a little tiny kid and he kept hitting me and hitting me!"

By the time he'd finished the account, Romlar was blubbering the words brokenly, and when he was done, lapsed into violent, bitter sobs. Not only were tears rivering down his cheeks; his nose was running, and he was slobbering. The girl sat there and didn't say anything till he tapered off and looked across at her. Her gaze was as steady as before, and she handed him a box of tissues. "Thanks for telling me about it," she said quietly. "And it's all right for you to cry in here. We kind of expect it, and it's all right. This is all just between you and me."

He nodded, mopped his face, blew his nose. This girl wouldn't talk about him to people and say he was stupid, or that he'd cried. He knew that. He was sure of it.

She had other questions, and there was more weeping. It seemed as if, when she asked about something, it came to him. When she needed to, she prompted him, as if seeing his memories before he was able to. And Romlar didn't think of it as weird, didn't wonder how she knew those things.

After each time he cried, he felt better, as if he'd never have that grief again. Finally she asked him about a time he'd been happy, and he told her about rassling Carrmak. And the time when Esenrok slapped his shoulder and told him he was okay. And some other times, on the playground, and when he was little. Even a couple of times when his father took care of him and dished them up ice cream, and told him stories about being a boy on the farm.

By that time Romlar could laugh, not something he did very often, and the girl laughed with him.

"Well," she said when he was done. "Thanks for coming in. We'll talk together again soon." She must have pushed a button because someone knocked on the door—it didn't sound very loud—and she talked into a little microphone, telling them to come in.

The civilian at the snack room gave him juice and a sandwich and the first ice cream he'd had at the compound. Then another civilian took him to a little room with a cot—he was starting to feel drowsy already—and when he lay down, he fell right to sleep.

# 18

Eight imperial months previously, Commodore Igsat Tarimenloku had awakened with a decision: to reenter real space. It was a reasonable mistake; so many mistakes are. It happened like this:

He'd long since convinced himself that his spur-of-the-moment attack on the strange patrol ship had been imperative, the only justifiable action. Still it had no doubt put himself and his flotilla at serious risk, so to be safe, he'd remained in hyperspace for six standard months, long enough to clear any conceivable politically unified sector.

With this decision in mind, he'd spent a few minutes in his shower, then went to his private dining room. After a disinteresting breakfast, he went to the bridge and informed the crew on watch there of what he was going to do.

This emergence was not done carelessly. After activating security systems—emergence wave detector, command room alarm, automatic shield and targeting responses—*he entered real space at a point where their instruments showed no nodi, no sign of a planetary system.* There should be no patrol there.

When they'd emerged, though, there was a system in the vicinity, if you consider the vicinity to extend more than 85 billion miles, more than five light days, from the primary. Still, it was surely far enough.

They'd been recording in real-space for less than two minutes (DAAS, the flagship's computer, gave him the figures later: one minute, 29.27 seconds) when the alarm began to beep its response to an emergence wave.

Instantly, or as close to it as human reflexes allow, Tarimenloku touched the flotilla control and exit keys. And at the moment of disorientation heard/felt the shrieking of what had to be a ruptured matric tap. Not the flagship's, or he'd never have heard it, would have ceased to exist. As it was, his head rang with it.

The monitor screen showed the hyperspace blip of only one other ship, the troopship. Clearly it was the survey ship that had been destroyed. Fortunately, he told himself, it had been manned by only a handful of maintenance people. Thank Kargh for all blessings! But actually he didn't feel fortunate at all. He felt shock, and loss, and threat. And being a senior commanding officer, did not let any of these interfere markedly with his functioning.

It was after the ringing in his head had moderated that Tarimenloku conferred with his executive officer, Commander Dimsikaloku, and they'd sorted it out.

Their reconstruction of the situation, admittedly conjectural, had it that the hostile patrol ship had been stationed in real-space at some distance outside the system, detected them from there, and shifted at once into hyperspace for the "short" jump (in terms of hyperspace "distances"). That would account for its quick arrival. To have detected the flotilla's emergence wave, the patrol ship had almost surely been on the near side of the system and outside the Oort Belt, which might have been coincidence, or ... Or maybe the system was ringed with patrol ships! *Maybe it was the aliens' home system!* That would explain the prompt hostility and the distance from the primary! They wanted strong security at the maximum practical separation from the home world!

And it had emerged at a separation of twelve miles again, like the patrol ship in the earlier system. Interesting.

But this one had begun shooting virtually on emergence; there'd been time (milliseconds at most) for only the briefest identity scan. And it appeared that they'd known the intruder was himself, the one who'd attacked a patrol ship eight months and some eighty parsecs back. Message pods must have preceded their arrival here, and patrol ships were on orders to attack without further attempt at communication.

Dimsikaloku had favored turning back then, taking home the information that an alien civilization existed here, the probable location of the aliens' home system, and what they'd inferred about alien technology. But the commodore had decided against it, a position easy to disagree with. He'd justified his stance—more to himself than to Dimsikaloku, because the rank was his—by pointing out their mission orders: The sultan had sent out this expedition—a politically risky decision—because he was intensely interested in the possibility of worlds to expand to. And as yet they had found none. Furthermore, the danger here could be minimized by remaining in hyperspace long enough to *ensure* they were out of the hostile sector.

All that had been more than eight imperial months earlier, and even now, Tarimenloku had every intention of staying in hyperspace for another three. Though it was hard to conceive of a politically unified sector even approaching that volume of space; the problems of communication, administration, and control would be impossible.

Just now though his attention was on a most unusual major nodus. The apparency was of quadruple primaries near enough for a four-way tidal sharing of plasma, a situation which seemed physically impossible. He slowed, tempted to emerge long enough for a quick data recording. Not nearly what his survey ship might have given him, but enough to excite the astronomers back home.

It was that slowing that exposed their pursuer and stunned Tarimenloku. A second hyperspace blip showed briefly on the monitor, very briefly, but unmistakably. They were being followed! Then the pursuer reacted to their slowing by slowing himself and disappearing from the monitor.

And suddenly all the rationalizations for the prompt, close appearance of the alien ship in real-space, eight months earlier, came into doubt. It could well be the same ship they'd fired at fourteen months earlier!

And obviously the aliens' instruments could perceive farther in hyperspace than theirs could. Which had allowed the alien to follow without being noticed.

The commodore did something then that he'd never heard of before; something his chief science officer agreed theoretically might work. He sent a distortion bomb in the hyperspace "direction" of their shadow, their follower. Then, having given the two time to approximately coincide, he changed course by fifty degrees in the plane of the ecliptic, and briefly, seconds later, by thirty *from* the plane of the ecliptic.[11] The purpose was to lose their pursuer. Several times during the watch, Tarimenloku slowed sharply again, and several times changed course. There was no further sign of pursuit, which was somewhat reassuring but by no means proof of anything.

Meanwhile they were well off the course they'd been on, the one prescribed by admiralty staff. (And the one described by Master Tso-Ban, who was no longer monitoring.) But this seemed substantially safer. It could not be extrapolated by their ex-pursuer, if in fact they'd rid themselves of him, and it was consistent with mission orders as drafted by the sultan, which included the line "with due regard to a successful return."

Of course, they had no locational objective anyway.

# 19

Rifles slung, A Company double-timed down the road, carrying the almost ever-present and now even heavier sandbags. They trotted through a cloud of fog—their breath—and nine inches of new snow. It was the coldest day they'd seen here, for some the coldest they'd ever seen.

Still, the gills of their winter field uniforms were open, the earflaps of their helmet liners were tucked up, and some had stuffed their finger mittens into their waist pockets. Standing in ranks that morning, they'd felt glum about the subzero cold, but exertion had soon warmed them.

"How cold d'you think it is, Carrmak?" Jerym asked.

"Ask Bahn. Maybe he's heard."

"Bahn," someone else called, "how cold is it?"

"It is exactly as cold as it is," Bahn answered cheerfully. There were groans.

"I think my nostrils may have frozen," Markooris called out. "They feel funny."

"That feeling in your nostrils is the hairs." Bahn said it without puffing. "When it is cold enough, the moisture on them freezes and they stiffen, tugging on the membrane."

"Where did you learn that?" Jerym asked. "Not on Oven, I'll bet."

"On Hemblin's World we fought in very cold conditions. And I never heard of anyone's nostrils freezing, although all of us froze the outside of our noses."

"Does it hurt? To freeze your nose?" someone asked.

"You do not even notice when your nose freezes. The ears though, and fingers and toes, you definitely notice."

"How do you know when it happens then?"

"Others tell you. It is visible; your nose turns gray. After it thaws, the skin splits, and a scab forms."

Lieutenant Toma, who was leading A Company this morning, speeded the pace a little, as if to say that having breath enough to talk so much, they had breath enough to trot faster.

Jerym thought of the T'swa, from such a hot world, having to fight in polarlike weather. He couldn't imagine them complaining though. Which made him think of Mellis, who complained a lot. Mellis wasn't with them today; he was getting interviewed—one of the last in the platoon. Maybe now he wouldn't hassle people to tell him what went on there. Some of the guys had been interviewed twice already—Romlar for example, and himself—and Esenrok was having his second this morning.

He wondered if Mellis would still be a whiner when he came out. Interviews changed you. You could feel it in yourself and see it in other guys. In Romlar more than any of them. Romlar still seemed a little stupid—that hadn't much changed—but he was cheerful now, talked more, seemed less introverted. He even talked differently—more grammatically.

Ahead someone farted, loud and long, to a mixture of groans and laughter. "Bressnik!" someone yelled, "back to the end of the line with you!" "Gentle Tunis," said someone else, "it's making my eyes water! They'll freeze on a morning like this!"

First Platoon turned off on a side road. After half a mile more, Sergeant Dao led 2nd Platoon off on another, a road Jerym was sure they'd never been on before. It crossed an easy hill, then sloped gradually down until, after a mile or so, it ended in a small opening, where they halted. Around the opening was sparsely wooded swamp, dense with underbrush.

Dao ordered them at ease, and they all stopped talking. "Now," he said, "you will apply your lessons in reading maps and compasses, to find your way over unfamiliar ground. You will travel by fire teams. Your squad sergeants will give each team a map. A course is marked on it, with bearings you will follow. Each course has five or six legs. All but the last leg end at a marked and numbered point where you will find an instruction to follow. The last leg will end at a point on a road, where you will be picked up and transported by vehicle to the compound for dinner. Do not be late, or you will go hungry."

Their squad sergeants took command then, instructing. Each man was to be the compassman on at least one leg. Then they left, group by group on different bearings, disappearing into the thick brush. There were only four in Jerym's team; Esenrok was getting interviewed that morning. As team leader, Carrmak led the first leg.

The damn brush was not only thick; it was about seven or eight feet tall and loaded with snow. But in the subzero cold, it didn't melt on your clothes, didn't even stick on them. Jerym quickly discovered why the trees were so sparse: A forest fire had killed most of the old stand, and in time most of the killed trees had fallen over, lying at different angles to the ground. Their snow-covered trunks had to be climbed over, crawled under, or bypassed, their uptilted root disks gone around. Jerym couldn't see more than fifty feet through it, which was about as far as they got before Carrmak called a halt.

"I need something or someone to guide on." He pointed. "Alsnor, you'll be the next compassman, and the next compassman will always be the guide-on." He pointed. "Go through there till I tell you to stop."

Jerym went, wearing his mittens now, parting the snowy brush with them, until Carrmak called for him to halt. He did, turning to look back. Carrmak was peering down the compass sight. "A couple steps that way," Carrmak said gesturing. "There! Right on!" Then he came with the others to where Jerym stood.

"Tunis!" Jerym swore. "This is slow going! I hope this course isn't very long, or we won't get anything to eat."

Carrmak shrugged. "Takes as long as it takes," he muttered, raising the compass. "And according to the map, the legs are only a quarter to a half mile long." He pointed. "Through there," he said, "and this time I'm not going to do any yelling. We'll do it right—pretend we're sneaking through enemy territory. So go about fifty, sixty feet and stop. If you can't see me then, backtrack till you can."

Thinking that if the T'swa wanted them to keep quiet, they'd have said so, Jerym led off again. And again. It was tricky climbing over blowdowns with a bag of sand on his back; it kept overbalancing him, wanting to dump him on his face.

It was a slow quarter mile before they hit the first check point, hit it right on—a post with a small, snowcapped box, and a small sign hung on it. Carrmak read the instructions aloud and took a coded tag from the box, evidence that they'd found the checkpoint. Then they went on, Jerym with the compass now, and Romlar as his guide-on. He almost missed the next checkpoint; they were only about fifteen feet off line, but on the wrong side of an uptilted root disk. It was Romlar that spotted it.

Romlar turned out more than just lucky, Jerym decided. He turned out weird! It was his turn next as compassman. And instead of sending Markooris out as guide-on, Romlar flicked a glance at the compass, shoved it in a pocket, and bulled off through the brush. He couldn't possibly have picked out a useable mark to go to. Jerym looked at Carrmak, who opened his mouth to call to Romlar, then changed his mind and followed him. Romlar never slowed, never took the compass out of his pocket, just kept going.

Halfway through his leg, which was a somewhat longer one, they came out of the swamp, the brush now replaced by sapling growth. The saplings weren't *that* thick, and they were vertical, not a tangle, while here the fire-killed older trees were mostly still standing. So the visibility was better and the walking easier; Romlar speeded almost to a jog. And hit his checkpoint dead on, grinning, pleased with himself. It was at the margin of unburned forest, into which they could see a lot farther. So Markooris didn't need a guide-on, either, though he used his compass. Here there was always a visible tree on line ahead, or near enough on line to correct course by eyeball.

Each time Markooris took his next shot, they'd jog to the guide-on he'd chosen, usually a hundred feet or more. It was a half mile leg, and at the check point they found a snow-covered stack of slender logs—big posts, really, nine or ten feet long and about eight inches thick—roughly 120 to 150 pounds each. The instructions said each man was to carry one of these logs to the final checkpoint. Added to sixty pounds of sand, that was a lot.

This was the kind of difficulty most trainees enjoyed best, even reveled in. They tipped the logs up, Carrmak helping the others get theirs balanced on the shoulder which didn't have the rifle slung on it. Then he shouldered his own. This last leg was Carrmak's again. They lumbered off with their burdens, Carrmak pausing as infrequently and briefly as possible for compass shots. At each pause, each trainee lowered one end of his log to the ground, resting for a few seconds while Carrmak found another guide-on.

Before long they came out of the woods into a meadow, and saw the final post eighty yards ahead, with a T'swi waiting nearby on the road. Carrmak began to run with his cumbersome burden, the others galloping after. Jerym almost whooped, then remembered Carrmak's injunction against noise. When they reached the post and the grinning Sergeant Bahn, they let the logs roll off their now-sore shoulders, panting, sweating copiously. Breath and sweat had frozen crusty on their eyebrows, collars, and the rim of their helmets.

"I radioed when I saw you coming," Bahn said. "A bus will be here soon."

They stood waiting in the cold sunlight, and for a minute or so, no one spoke. Then Carrmak said to Bahn, "If you T'swa had to go from there to here, through all that brush, and you'd never been here before, how would you do it?"

Bahn's eyebrows rose. "We would walk or run. As you did."

"Would you use the compass?"

"If necessary."

Carrmak looked intently at the sergeant. " 'If necessary' isn't the kind of answer I'm looking for. *Would* you use the compass?"

Bahn smiled slightly. "No, we would not. We would simply—go from there to here. Walking or running."

Carrmak thumbed toward Romlar. "That's what he did, on his stretch: just barrelled off through the brush. I thought you ought to know he can do that."

Jerym looked at Romlar, whose face was flushed but grinning.

Then the bus came and picked them up. After awhile it had a load of guys and took them back to the compound.

Jerym made a point of walking with Carrmak from the barracks to the messhall. "What in Tunis's name," he asked, "made you ask Bahn how they'd have done that course?"

"Read Lormagen's book on the T'swa," Carrmak answered, "or just look at his cubes. On Kettle, the army set the T'swa down in the jungle, jungle they'd never seen before. And there weren't any maps or roads or anything. But the T'swa ran around all over the place, zigzagging and circling, hunting Birds and fighting them, and always got back to their rendezvous, their rally point. Never got lost. When Romlar started off like he did, I was going to stop him, but then I thought, no, I'll let him go. If the T'swa can do it, then probably some other people can too. Let him try."

"But if he'd gotten us lost," Jerym objected, "we would've missed dinner."

"Big deal. We've learned something—that Romlar can do it. And now the T'swa know. And Romlar feels good, the kind of feeling good that'll stay with him."

Jerym nodded silently. He'd learned something just now, too: A way of looking at things, of considering importances. And a little more about the kind of guy that Carrmak was.

Second Platoon's noncoms had their own table. It was round, but wherever Dao sat was the head. Bahn sat down next to him and mentioned what Romlar had done. When Dao had finished eating, he went to the officers' table and told Lieutenant Dzo-Tar, while Captain Gotasu listened. From the A Company orderly room, Captain Gotasu phoned Colonel Dak-So, who told Colonel Voker, who phoned the civilian in charge of scheduling interviews. All in all it was no big deal, but it was the sort of thing they were watching for, expecting to see from some of their intentive warriors.

When the company fell in for its afternoon training, Dao ordered Romlar to stay at the barracks. Someone would come to take him to an interview.

# 20

Romlar settled himself on the chair, glad it was the red-headed girl again who would interview him. He suspected that was how they did things—always gave you the same interviewer. And he didn't think of her as "just a girl" any more.

"Cold out there," she said, glancing up as she arranged her notebook. "Did you train outdoors this morning?"

"Yep."

"What did you do?"

Grinning he told her, including how he'd done his leg of the course. Mentally, psychically, he was far lighter than when she'd first seen him, much happier, far more confident.

She grinned back at him. "Marvelous," she said. "I love it!" Then she moved to another subject. "We got a lot taken care of in our first two sessions. Now at the end of our last one, I asked if you still thought of yourself as stupid. And you said—" She paused as if inviting him to finish for her.

"I said yeah, I guess I was, but it didn't bother me anymore."

"Right. How do you feel about that now?"

"The same. I know I'm not as smart as most of the other guys, but that's all right. I'm me. I do some things better than most of them."

"Good. So tell me a use for stupidity."

"Huh! Well— I can't think of any."

"Okay. Then imagine a use for stupidity."

"Imagine? Well, uhh— If you're stupid, you don't get asked to do some stuff."

"All right. Now give me something more specific than that."

"Uhh . . . Well— People don't ask you to figure stuff out. They know you can't do it very good."

"Good. Tell me something else you don't get asked to do if you're stupid."

"You— You don't get asked to do some things that are really important."

"Okay. Another."

"You don't . . ." He stopped, eyes suddenly blank, face expressionless, mouth slightly open, and sat like that for a long minute.

"Um-hm?" she nudged.

He'd begun visibly to sweat. "You don't get asked— You don't get asked to decide things that other people's lives depend on." He'd said it in an undertone, little more than a whisper.

"All right," she replied calmly. "What else don't you get asked to do?"

For a moment he trembled, vibrated might be a better word, then began to jerk, then rock back and forth, rotating from the hips in utter silence. She watched him quietly for a minute, not nudging him with what she saw. Instead she simply repeated the question: "What else don't you get asked to do?"

He croaked the words: "To lead."

And with that her serious work began. Per instructions, ordinarily she tried to keep sessions to about an hour, two at most. This time it took nearly three before she had him through all of it, alert again and in good spirits. Actually very good spirits. And ravenous! She wrote him a chit to give to the cook at the project's small dining room; the snack room wouldn't be adequate to his needs. After that he went to one of the nap rooms and slept for more than an hour, dreaming swift eventful dreams he couldn't afterward remember.

After the session, Lotta Alsnor went to a small office at the end of the hall, and knocked.

"Who is it?"

"Lotta."

Wellem Bosler was in charge of the project. Because of the shortage of fully qualified people, he'd selected the best of his advanced students, his and others', and had coached them intensively for a week before bringing them here. And because their experience was limited and some of the cases promised to be especially demanding, he'd come with them to supervise, and to bail them out when necessary. One of the things he did was call up and look over each session record before any further session was scheduled with that particular case. So far everything had gone remarkably well, and his operators had quickly gained confidence in their ability to do the job here.

Lotta was the second youngest, and the most gifted if not the most skilled.

"Come in, Lotta," Bosler said.

She did. "Wellem," she said, "I'd like you to check out the session I just gave Artus Romlar."

He called it up, and his eyebrows raised as he scanned. When he'd finished, he looked up at her with a grin. "Marvelous, Lotta. I'm proud of you. Talk about the unanticipated! If I'd had any misgivings about your readiness for this job, and I didn't, this would lay them to rest." He paused then before adding, "You need to get him back after supper, you know."

She nodded. "I thought—you might take him after supper. I'm afraid I might get in over my head."

"Ah. But I want *you* to take him, and if you do get in over your head, *then* I'll take over. Okay?"

She nodded. "If you think it's safe for him that way."

Wellem Bosler grinned. "Even if you screw up to the maximum, we'll have him in good shape before morning."

Then he outlined briefly the approach he wanted her to use.

# 21

Wellem Bosler's office was tiny but adequate. Much of its space was occupied by a work table on which sat a computer, the repository of session reports. With Voker and Dak-So there, seated on folding chairs, the room was crowded.

"So you've got a preliminary evaluation for us," Voker said.

"And a very positive one." Bosler paused to sip carefully the scalding joma that one of his runners had brought for the meeting. Usually he was too busy, too preoccupied, to have joma, or to remember to drink it when he had it.

"We're getting very good results, even though my team is green. Or was green. By working with one platoon at a time, and by starting with its dominant trainee and the people closest to him, we're largely avoiding the problems of the individual's barracks mates getting on his case before he stabilizes. For a day or so after a session, and particularly during the first few hours, the individual is susceptible to being sharply introverted and invalidating what happened to him."

He grinned. "It's a little like a new painting: You need to let the paint cure before you handle it much. Then, once a person's stabilized, he's pretty much immune to self-doubts. The nap helps with that, the nap and the dreams."

"Will they know the T'sel when you've finished with them?" Voker asked. "Or is this treatment too abbreviated?"

"Let's just say they're more sane, and stably sane, than the great majority of humankind. That's the bottom-line result; a regiment of sane warriors. Some will know the T'sel. All will have considerable T'sel wisdom,[12] and this will increase bit by bit after we're done with them. They'll cognite on things, and grow, in the process of living."

His eyes shifted to Dak-So. "As for the ancillary abilities that are general among your own warriors—useful degrees of psychic awareness, like the ability to orienteer without a compass, that sort of thing—they've already begun to crop up. I don't know how frequent they'll be. Don't look for them to be general though. Just take what develops."

"When do you expect to finish here?" Voker asked. "Or is it too soon to predict?"

"In about a dek and a half. It depends somewhat on how well the two new teams do; they'll carry out their first sessions here this afternoon. I didn't train them—one team's from the school at Kromby Bay and the other's from Ernoman—but I know the people who did train them; know them well. I anticipate that they'll do as well as my team. Six to eight more weeks should finish our work here."

"Ah." Dak-So turned to Voker. "I would like your decision on whether to train our young warriors in jokanru, and if so, when. I have had thoughts on the matter."

"Let's hear them." Voker looked at Bosler. "We'll take our discussion somewhere else—get out of your way."

"Fine. Today's interview reports won't start coming in for another hour, but I need to review administrative procedures with the new teams."

The two officers left, talking as they walked down the corridor. "Are you satisfied with the kind of results Wellem described?" Voker asked.

Dak-So nodded. "Yes. They're not what we might prefer, but combined with their warrior intentions and their young strength and level of training, they will be superior to any troops I foresee them facing, given comparable equipment. Unless of course, as mercenaries they face my people."

"Good," said Voker. Apparently the Klestroni were going to miss Confederation space after all, but presumably someday they would meet. Then there'd be the matter of equipment. T'swa seers had assured the Crown that the Karghanik level of military technology was not inordinately superior to their own, for planetary warfare. In fact, the empire had stagnated technologically, not as badly as the Confederation had under the Sacrament, but badly nonetheless.

As for Iryalan regiments fighting T'swa regiments, that could be addressed in contracts or treaties—Kristal would work it out.

"Okay," Voker said. "Let's hear your plans."

"I have prepared a limited menu of close combat skills and drills," Dak-So said, "that young men like these can master quickly at an effective level. They do not constitute jokanru, but they are based on it. They emphasize aggressiveness and force, with less reliance on refined technique. The practitioner would be no match for someone trained in jokanru, someone reasonably well conditioned. But with their strong, flexible, gymnast bodies, these young warriors would quickly destroy ordinary soldiers in unarmed combat.

"And jokanru is less a combat tool than a matter of developing the complete warrior, mentally and spiritually as well as physically. The time required for it would be difficult to justify, when we have only three years to complete their training.

"What I propose can be completed in far far less time than full training in jokanru. I recommend we train the entire regiment simultaneously, during mud season. By then the trainees will have completed their basic training in other skills, and also the Ostrak operators will be done with them, even if they progress more slowly than Wellem envisions. Further, the more advanced gymnastics training they'll have had by then will have increased their flexibility."

Voker nodded. "Not to mention their strength. And frankly, what you've described is the sort of thing I'd envisioned for them anyway. How long will this training take?"

"I foresee three weeks of very intensive full-time training. If necessary, we can add a week to it. Then, when they're done, we'll begin their training in battalion and regimental actions."

"Fine," Voker said. "That'll give us time to get the necessary equipment made: bags, dummies, whatever. I want a list as soon as possible."

By that time they were standing at Dak-So's office door. "Can I see what techniques you have in mind for them?" Voker asked.

"Of course. I made photocopies."

They went in. A minute later Voker came out, examining a thin sheaf of papers, nodding as he scanned. These kids would love it. They were going to be a hell of a regiment.

# 22

The evening of Winter Solstice was clear and still, moonless and moderately cold, but inside the main building were warmth, light, and noise. Most of the benches had been removed from the big assembly hall, stacked in an adjacent storeroom. Scattered tables, surrounded by slowly eddying trainees and T'swa, held food in quantity, delicacies, mostly prepared by the regiment's cooks but partly flown in. Here and there, mingling with the military, were young civilians about the age of the trainees—the Ostrak people—and army personnel on detached service there.

"You were right," Esenrok was saying to Jerym. "No liquor. I suppose they were worried about the guys that haven't been defused yet, getting drunk."

Jerym chuckled. "I'm pretty sure they weren't worried about the T'swa. I wonder what a T'swa would be like, drunk."

"Huh! I can't imagine one ever getting that way. But if one did, I suppose he'd be as mild as if he were sober. Just not as well coordinated."

"Yeah, I expect you're . . ." Jerym stopped. A slim, red-haired girl had walked up to him on his right, looking at him; he turned and stared.

"Lotta!"

"Hello, Jerym. You've changed. And grown."

He reached out unbelievingly, and they held each others' hands between them. "It's been a year last Harvest Festival," he said. Then, "What are you doing here?"

"I'm an interviewer."

"An inter. . . . You must be one of the new ones."

"Nope. I've been here for three weeks, working seven days a week from eight in the morning till 21 or 2200 in the evening—more than half around the clock. Otherwise I'd have looked you up."

He stared, then recovered and turned to Esenrok, who stood watching and curious. "Esenrok, this is my sister, Lotta. She's— Well, you know as much about that as I do. Lotta, this is a buddy of mine, Esenrok. Eldren Esenrok, isn't it?"

"You've got it." The blond trainee and the red-haired girl saluted each other formally, but grinning, hands raised to the sides, shoulders high, palms forward. "Jerym never told me he had a good-looking sister."

"I do though," Jerym said. "And right now I've got first claim on her time. We've got some catching up to do."

Esenrok shook his head. "And I thought we were friends. Ah well. Glad to meet you, Lotta."

Jerym led her away toward a bench that had been left down, then spotted someone and steered her off in that direction. "There's someone else I want you to meet," he murmured to her. "I showed him one of your letters, and he said he wanted to write to you. But he never did. Too shy."

Romlar's back was to them. He turned at Jerym's touch. "Hi, Alsnor. Oh! Hi, Lotta! I see you found him."

"Hi, Artus. Yes, he brought me over to introduce us."

Jerym's jaw had dropped, then he turned to Lotta. "You interviewed Romlar?"

"That's right. We're good friends."

Jerym looked from one to the other. "Well, then, let's you and I go sit somewhere and talk. You two have had hours to talk lately!"

"Go ahead," Romlar said. "But, Lotta, when you're done, I want a chance to ask *you* some questions. So far it's been all one way."

"Sure," she said, then left with her brother, stepping into the corridor to escape interruptions.

"I guess you know Medreth," Jerym said. "My interviewer."

"Medreth was yours? We've been at Lake Loreen together since she was eight and I was six."

"You guys don't—" Jerym's grin was lopsided. "No, I guess you wouldn't. Share confidences about interviews."

Lotta laughed. "Wellem would skin us alive if we did. No, it's never done."

"When you're at home, why haven't you ever done for Mom and Dad what you guys have done for us?"

Her eyebrows rose. "Consider the questions," she said, "the kinds of questions we ask, the things we ask you to do. Can you picture Dad or Mom sitting still for them? Especially from one of their kids!"

He laughed, imagining.

"Actually I have done some," she said, "in a sneaky way. Nothing ambitious, nothing formal, but it helps."

They talked, about home, parents, life in the regiment, for about twenty minutes before Voker's voice overrode the lively hubub of hundreds of conversations. "*At ease, men! At ease!*" The noise level dropped abruptly. "*At ease and face the podium!*"

The brother and sister stepped inside to watch and listen. Then His Majesty, Marcus XXVIII, strode out from the wings without the customary fanfare and attendants, a tall, lean, vigorous man of sixty-seven in a white dress uniform. The final murmurs of conversation stilled instantly. The trainees hardly noticed the man a step behind His Majesty on his right.

The king stopped just back from the podium's front edge and looked the silent audience over. "Good evening, gentlemen!" he boomed, without electronic augmentation, and they responded instantly, almost in unison, as if drilled in it.

"Good evening, Your Majesty!"

He waited three or four seconds, then continued. "I had several other invitations for this evening. The most tempting was to spend it with my grandchildren. But I understand you don't have too many evenings off, so I decided to take this opportunity to see you instead."

There were a few tentative hurrahs that grew into somewhat ragged, audience-wide cheering. The trainees were in a state of low-grade shock.

"You men, you trainees, are a first in the Confederation—a regiment of warriors. You will not be the last such regiment, but you are the trailbreakers. It has not been easy for you, in more ways than one, but you are proceeding very well, and as you continue, you will do better and better."

He paused, once more scanned them deliberately, then boomed again: "What do you think of your T'swa cadre?"

The question released them from their awed bemusement, and they began cheering at the top of their lungs, the cheer shifting gradually to a chant of "T'swa, T'swa, T'swa!" This went on for the better part of a minute, until Voker's voice came over the loudspeakers: "That's it, men. At ease." The chant stumbled and stopped. "Thank you," Voker said.

"And now—" His Majesty went on, "now I want to introduce someone to you—the man who first proposed we form such a regiment." He half-turned to the man who'd followed him onto the podium, and gestured at him with a white-gloved hand. "The man who told people what the T'swa truly were like, the man who was called 'the White T'swi,' Sir Varlik Lormagen."

Again the crowd erupted with sound as a grinning Lormagen stepped up beside the king. After half a minute, Lormagen raised his hands overhead, so that the cheers faded. He too was a man in his sixties, taller than average and husky, recognizably the same man they'd seen on the old cubes from the Kettle War. When they were quiet enough, Lormagen spoke, using a microphone clipped to his collar.

"I want to tell you just one thing," he said. "I'm proud of you, every last one of you."

Again they cheered. Voker might have interrupted them, but the king looked toward him as if anticipating that, and still grinning, shook his head, then waved to his audience and left the podium with Lormagen. Cheers followed them into the wings and out of sight.

After that the crowd began to eddy again around the tables, bemused at first. But soon their conversations were even livelier than before.

When the cheering was over, Pitter Mellis worked his way to a door and walked down the corridor to a latrine. It was crowded, the commodes occupied, the urinal lined with men, with others waiting. He turned and left, going to an exit and out into the cold. It was only 200 yards to the barracks; jogging would be better than waiting.

No one was at the barracks when he got there, and he went quickly to the latrine, seating himself on a commode. After a minute he heard the barracks door open, heard footsteps coming his way, several sets of them. Others, he thought, had gotten the same idea he had.

But the men that peered in at him were strangers.

"What are you guys doing in this barracks?" he demanded.

They looked at Mellis, then at each other, and came into the latrine, two, and then four more. When he started to get up, reaching to pull up his pants, they rushed him, grabbed him. He opened his mouth to yell, and a hard blow to the gut drove the wind out of him. One arm was free, and he swung it wildly, cursing. Someone hit him hard on the nose, breaking it, another slugged him in the kidneys. His head snapped back at that, so that a blow at his chin struck his throat instead. Then, pants around his ankles, he was dragged bleeding and choking through the barracks. At the door their leader stopped them, measured his victim and hit him a heavy blow to the point of the chin, slamming Mellis backward off the stoop, unconscious. They left him lying there in the snow.

After the king had left the podium and the cheering had stopped, Lotta promised Jerym to see him again when she had a chance, and began to circulate, talking with other trainees. Jerym headed for a table, where he put hors d'oeu'vres of several kinds on a plate. A moment later he spotted Romlar again and worked his way to him.

"So you know my sister."

"Yep."

"How'd you know she was my sister? By the name?"

"I didn't know her last name. At first, to me, she was just a girl named Lotta. But the last interview I got, it came to me: 'This is the Lotta that's Alsnor's sister.' So I asked her, and she said she was.

"But she asked me not to say anything. She said she'd surprise you at Solstice.

"You know," he added, "the King made us out pretty special, and maybe we are. But without the T'swa training us, we'd be nothing, and what those interviewers are doing is as important to this regiment as the T'swa are. We need the training, but we need the Ostrak Project just as much."

Jerym nodded, thinking that the changes in Romlar might be bigger than anyone else's in the platoon. And Lotta had been Romlar's interviewer.

Esenrok, with one of the hot, non-alcoholic drinks in his hand, saw Sergeant Dao standing beside the main entrance to the assembly hall, and went over to him. "What do you think of that?" Esenrok said. "The king came to see us." He peered at the big black man curiously. "Does the king know the T'sel, do you suppose?"

"I have heard that he does. And perceiving him as I did, I am sure of it."

*Perceiving him as you did.* Esenrok wondered what the T'swa might perceive that he didn't. "How old are you T'swa when you get the Ostrak Procedures?"

"We do not get the Ostrak Procedures. They are something originated on Iryala, I believe, for persons who did not grow up with the T'sel in a T'sel environment. "He gazed at Esenrok for a moment before continuing. "It was a man named Ostrak who brought knowledge of the T'sel to Iryala, you know."

Esenrok hadn't known, and it occurred to him to wonder why. He was about to ask Dao—the sergeant knew so much else, he might know the

answer to that too—when a hoarse croak interrupted them from behind,
from the door they stood beside. He turned and stared; Dao reached and
grabbed the form there as it teetered.

"Mellis!" Esenrok said, staring. "What in Tunis happened to you?"
Mellis's cheeks, nose, and ears were waxy gray from frostbite. Blood
smeared his lower face and shirt, frozen blood granulated with snow.

Others nearby, having heard Esenrok's exclamation, were turning to
look.

"They trashed the barracks." Mellis barely mumbled it; his jaw didn't
move.

"Bahn!" Dao bellowed. "Here!"

The crowd nearby began to form a vortex through which Bahn pushed
from not far off. "Take Mellis to the infirmary," Dao called to him, then
started off himself with Esenrok at his heels. A few others followed till
Dao told them to go back.

The barracks was a mess. Mattresses and bedding were on the floor,
slashed and torn. In the latrine, washrags had been flushed, and the
overflowing commodes had flooded the place. Windows had been
broken. Glow panels, dislodged from the ceiling, lay trampled and bent.
Esenrok felt rage begin to swell, then saw Dao's calm, and felt the rage
ebb.

*First Platoon,* occurred to Esenrok; it was the 1st on whose barracks
he'd led the raid that first night. But he rejected the thought immediately. First platoon had been interviewed too, most or all of it; it wouldn't
have been them.

These thoughts flashed while he followed Dao, striding back through
the barracks and onto the stoop, where the big T'swi looked around. The
latest snow had been a week earlier, and was trampled beyond tracking.
Beside the stoop, it was stained red where Mellis had lain bleeding. Dao
stood unmoving for a moment, frowning, lips pursed, then started for
the main building at a lope, Esenrok close behind.

Within five minutes, groups of T'swa were fanning through the compound. Two barracks and several T'swa cabins had been vandalized. Six
men were busy vandalizing another barracks. They'd left two sentries
outside. These yelled, then fled at the T'swa's approach. Two T'swa peeled
off in pursuit, and surprisingly ran them down.

The culprits were manhandled off to the main building, into the
assembly hall, and up front. The regiment had been formed up as units,
and stood waiting. The Ostrak teams and army service personnel stood
curious in the rear of the room. Voker and Dak-So stood at the front
of the podium, with the king and Lormagen to one side, observing, faces
unreadable.

Mounting the podium, Dao reported quietly to Voker and Dak-So.

Bahn had already reported on Mellis's condition: A broken nose, bruised larynx, dislocated jaw, concussion, frostbite. And hypothermia; it was surprising and fortunate that he'd regained consciousness.

Voker questioned the six captives then. They denied knowing anything about Mellis. While they were denying it, some T'swa frog-marched four more captives in. Sergeant Major Kuto informed Voker that all ten were from 3rd Platoon, F Company. And that only four regimental personnel remained unaccounted for, also from 3rd Platoon, F Company. He'd hardly said it when two more culprits were brought in, one unconscious across a T'swa shoulder.

Voker gazed coldly down at the second group of captives. "Trainee Mellis is in the infirmary," he said, "with multiple injuries, hypothermia, and frost bite. Who did it?"

One of the second group straightened and looked up at the colonel with glittering eyes. "Sir, we did! We couldn't let him spread an alarm."

Voker's gaze turned thoughtful. "I see. What is your name?"

"Trainee Jillard Brossling, sir!"

"Brossling." Voker seemed to taste the name. "And why did you vandalize barracks, Brossling?"

"Sir! This was our opportunity. Everyone—almost everyone—was here in the main building."

"Ah. And why did you wish to vandalize barracks at all?"

"Sir! It was something warriorlike to do. And we chose platoons the T'swa favored—their pet dog platoons!"

"Mmm." Voker turned to Sergeant Major Kuto. "Sergeant major," he said mildly, "have the criminals, under T'swa guard, erect a squad tent to live in. Have them do it barefoot, so they won't take too long. The rest of 3rd Platoon, F Company, will erect a barbed wire enclosure on X-posts around the tent. When the tent has been erected, the criminals will be given their boots and sleeping bags and will sleep in the tent on the ground, manacled. The rest of 3rd Platoon, F Company, will stand sentry shifts around the fence. Between sentry shifts, the remaining members of 3rd Platoon will also repair and clean up the vandalized huts and barracks tonight. The building engineers will supervise the work and see that 3rd Platoon has the materials for the job.

"The platoons which were vandalized will occupy 3rd Platoon's barracks tonight, and the overflow will move into other F Company barracks. While there, they will carefully abstain from doing any damage whatever."

He turned his gaze back to the culprits. "We'll decide in the morning what to do with you. But know now that you will be required to make up the damage, make heavy amends, and petition the rest of the regiment to be accepted back into it when the amends have been satisfactorily

completed. You are responsible for what you did, and it is a responsibility you cannot avoid. If we send you to Ballibud, it will not be before
you have met that responsibility."

# 23

All his adult life, Wellem Bosler had made a point of getting enough
exercise to keep his body functioning well. Here, for several weeks, he'd
let it slip. Now he'd begun jogging and walking about the compound in
the dark of pre-dawn morning. Sometimes it was snowing; more often
the sky was clear, starlit, and cold.

The detention section—sixteen youths from 3rd Platoon, F Company—
had been digging on the intended swimming pool at night, breaking the
hard-frozen earth with sledge hammers and long-handled chisels, throwing
the larger chunks out by hand, the smaller with shovels. But they'd be
sleeping exhausted in their squad tent, their jail—*tronk* was their slang
for it—well before he came out.

Not much, good or bad, surprised him about human beings, but the
tenacity and morale of the detention section had. They trained hard
all day, then dug till past midnight, yet the few times he'd made a point
of strolling out to watch them dig, before he retired in the evening,
they seemed to be in good spirits, vying to see what pair could move
the most dirt.

Third Platoon, F Company, had been the most aberrated in the regiment, the result of two dominant individuals who were reasoning
psychotics. Second and 3rd Squads were the most aberrated in the platoon. Third would be the last platoon to undergo the Ostrak Procedures,
and the fourteen men in the detention section, all from 2nd and 3rd
Squads, would be the last individuals.

Yet Voker had left Brossling with them—Brossling, their ringleader and
chief troublemaker. The wise, tough old ex-soldier and the tough but crazy
intentive warrior, had come to an understanding: Brossling would ram-
rod the amends project and maintain discipline, and Voker would grant
them the privilege of not having a pair of T'swa corporals bossing the
job, would let them do it on their own.

Usually, when T'swa whistles rousted the trainees out of bed, Bosler
jogged back to the Main Building for a hot shower and breakfast. This
morning though, he stopped to watch, from a little distance, one of the

platoons go through reveille, heard its squad sergeants reporting in their mellow T'swa voices. And recognized one of the trainees, even at forty yards in the predawn: Artus Romlar. Bosler himself had done the last two interviews on Romlar; the procedures needed were beyond Lotta's training and experience.

That had been a week earlier. Romlar needed a few weeks to settle out before they did anything further with him. Then perhaps . . . Bosler turned and jogged toward the Main Building. Romlar had received three times the attention of any other trainee, but he had a potential unique in the regiment. He'd been born to a particular role, one they understood only vaguely. Which didn't necessarily mean he'd get to play it, or that he'd succeed if he did.

The trainees had eaten dinner—the midday meal—and had a half hour to loaf around before forming up for training. Jerym lay on his bunk, booted feet on the floor, looking at his hands. Before signing up, he'd never even seen hands like them, their palms and fingers callused like boot leather, with hard ridges and pads on the pressure points.

"I never thought I'd be doing what I did this morning," he said, to no one in particular.

"You mean giant swings?" Esenrok asked. "I knew you were ready. What impressed me was Romlar doing 'em. Remember when he was 'fat boy'? Less than four deks ago, for Tunis' sake!"

Romlar had entered the barracks just in time to hear Esenrok's comment, and paused to raise the foot of Esenrok's bunk with one big paw, lifting it chest high, Esenrok on it, before setting it gently back down.

Jerym had watched the little interplay. He really didn't feel that much changed himself, but Esenrok and Romlar now . . . Romlar especially; he still didn't say a lot, but somehow or other he was definitely no longer stupid.

He explored his calluses with a finger, remembering the hard T'swa palm that had hauled him onto the straggler truck, that first, late summer night when he'd fallen out on the run. Give him another dek or so and he'd be able to juggle hot coals.

Giant swings for Tunis' sake!

At 2000 hours, Artus Romlar stopped at the Charge of Quarters desk in the Main Building. CQ was an Iryalan soldier on detached service, good at obeying orders and not bad at thinking for himself.

"What's your purpose here?" the man asked. Seated as he was, Romlar loomed above him, not threatening but impressive, almost T'swa-like in his size, his physical hardness, his sense of calm strength.

"I've come to see the civilian interviewer, Lotta Alsnor."

The CQ touched keys at his console, his eyes on the display. "Do you have an appointment?"

"No. She'll see me."

The soldier, a buck sergeant, looked Romlar over. "What's your name?" he asked, and Romlar told him. For brief seconds the sergeant hesitated. He knew how little free time these project people had, and this request was irregular. But then somehow he shrugged, and keyed the console again. The button in his right ear told him her room comm was buzzing. After three or four seconds he spoke to his collar mike. "Lotta Alsnor? This is Charge of Quarters. There's a trainee Romlar here to speak with you. Do you want to see him?"

After a few seconds he touched a couple of keys, looking up at Romlar again. "She'll be down," he said, and gestured with his head. "Have a seat over there."

Romlar did. A few minutes later Lotta came down the stairs, wearing coat, mittens, and fur cap. Romlar got up and met her at the door.

"This is a surprise," she said as they stepped out into the cold.

"I didn't know whether it would be or not. The way you looked into my mind in interviews."

She grinned. "Those were special situations. A special environment, and the stuff I was helping you pull out to look at was pretty powerful, easy to see."

They began to walk, nowhere in particular, beneath bare shade trees, stars glinting through the branches. "What brought you over?" she asked.

"I wanted to say goodbye. Now, when we had an evening without training."

"Goodbye?"

"Yes. You're leaving, you know. Within the next day or two. Maybe three or four."

She didn't ask how he knew. "For where?"

He shrugged big shoulders. "That's not part of it—part of what I know. Where you came here from, I suppose. Lake Loreen, you said at Solstice."

A move was news to her—they were extremely busy here—but she didn't challenge him. If he was wrong, it didn't matter. If he was right . . . He might be; she wouldn't be astonished at it. "It was nice of you to want to tell me goodbye," she said.

He grinned, shrugged. "I'm not sure why I did, really." His tone changed then, became softer. "That's not true. It's because I've got a crush on you. I suppose everyone does that you interview. And I wanted you to know how I feel.

"When you've gone, you're not likely to be coming back, and next fall we're supposed to go to Terfreya for a year, and then to Tyss for another one." He chuckled. "That'll be something, training on Tyss. No frostbite there! Tomorrow we'll be out in twenty inches of snow and probably below zero, with explosives and fire jets, learning how to clear fortifications.

"From Tyss I'll go somewhere to fight, to some trade world or gook world." Again he chuckled. "And never see you again. It's the sort of thing that, on the cube, they'd make out to be sad, and me heartbroken. But somehow or other . . ."

He shrugged, grinned, and with a hand on her arm, turned her, facing him. "Anyway I need to let you go now. I imagine you need rest as much as we do." Her face was clear, her features fine-boned, her eyes shadowed but somehow penetrating in the night, looking into him. "And thank you," he said, "for what you did. I feel as if I'm on the track now. Whatever that is, and wherever I'm going on it."

"It seems that way to me too, Artus. That you're on the track."

He walked her back to the Main Building—they hadn't gone a hundred yards—and said goodbye to her inside the door. From there he walked to the barracks and got ready for bed. It wasn't lights out yet, but near enough, and someone had turned the light intensity way down.

Before he closed his eyes, it occurred to him that he really didn't know why he'd gone to see Lotta. He did have a crush on her, true enough, but that was only part of it.

Then it struck him: *I was demonstrating,* he thought, *showing off my precognition.*

He wondered, as he drifted toward sleep, if this precognition would prove an isolated occurrence. It seemed to him that for a warrior to get precognitions useful in battle would take the joy out of combat.

It also seemed to him that the universe wouldn't be wired that way.

# 24

"Come in," said Wellem Bosler, and Lotta Alsnor entered.

"Unless there's something you don't like in the session record," she said, "I've just completed Forey Benster. I'm ready to start three new cases tomorrow."

*Which makes this the ideal time for it to happen,* she added silently, *if Artus was right. It's unusual to turn over a full slate of operants on the same day.*

Bosler nodded and gestured her to a seat. "Tomorrow I've got a different kind of assignment for you."

He looked at her curiously then, as if he'd picked up on her inner reaction. Which, she thought, he no doubt had. "You've always been good at melding with nonhuman life," he said, "mammals, birds, insects, plants. You've done more of it than anyone else I've known, of any age."

He leaned his elbows on his desk, fingers interlaced beneath his chin. "I suppose you know what Kusu's been working on, and what he's run into."

"You're referring to the teleport, and what's happened to the mammals he's tried to put through it."

"Right. Theoretically there shouldn't have been any problem, but the theory was pretty sketchy, pretty incomplete. So when the mammals came out insane, at first he tried to tinker his way through it. When that got him nowhere, he went back to the theory, to expand and strengthen it. Which he did, appreciably. But when all's said and done, it made no difference in the apparatus or the results, and it didn't give him any leads."

Bosler straightened. "Today he called me. He's decided he needs a study on what, subjectively, happens with a mammal's mind when it teleports. And asked me who I'd recommend to work with him. I told him you. He wasn't surprised."

Lotta's look was steady and direct. "I can already see some procedural problems."

He nodded. She didn't elaborate.

"You wouldn't be offering me this assignment," she said, "if you didn't think it was important enough to cut your staff here by one. But what makes it urgent? Is there something I'm overlooking? He *could* wait till we're done here."

"True, he could. And I can't specify why it seems urgent. The initial sense of urgency was his, and he can't rationalize it either. But the feeling I get is that he's right; it is urgent." He paused. "Although not so urgent that it calls for reckless action."

She made a face at Bosler, then nodded once in decision. "I'll do it. It does sound really interesting. Is there anything more you and I need to say about it before I leave?"

Bosler shook his head. "Anything out of the ordinary in the session?"

Lotta laughed. "Most people would say so. Actually it was pretty routine."

"Good. I'll call Lemal and have one of the OSP floaters ready for you tomorrow after breakfast. Say 0800. You'll be at Lake Loreen for lunch."

"Right." She got up. "I'll see if Jerym is still up. We've only visited once since I've been here." She stopped with a hand on the door. "Oh! There's something you should know." Then she ran down for him her brief conversation with Romlar the evening before. "And that was before Kusu called you," she added.

"Hmh! Interesting." Bosler grinned. "I'm not too surprised, considering. But it's good to know."

When she'd gone, he shook his head. The T'sel certainly saved a lot of teenaged anxieties. That fifteen-year-old girl—woman—was more mature and stable and intelligent than ninety-nine point nine nine percent of the middle-aged population on Iryala, and bringing the population at large to anything approaching Lotta Alsnor's level wasn't going to happen overnight. Or in a generation, or even several.

# 25

Wearing white winter field uniforms, A Company worked quickly in the bitter, midwinter dawn. They'd eaten breakfast—cold field rations—in their sleeping bags. Afterward each man stuffed his bag in the small sack provided for it, and each pair struck their tough if fragile-looking two-man winter tent, separating its velcroed halves and stowing them in their packsacks. They did more with their mittens on than looked possible, taking them off almost not at all. Their winter equipment, of recent issue, was designed with mittens in mind.

When their packs were ready and their snowshoes clamped on, they donned their new helmets. The optical visors, face shields were pivoted into the *up* position, headphones snug over ears, microphone tucked out of the way. Every man could hear his platoon leader and sergeant, and talk to them if necessary. Sounds from the environment—squad mates, wind, the hiss and occasional clack of snowshoes—were also mediated electronically, could be amplified by a simple finger adjustment or reduced in the din of combat. But they took some getting used to, and some of the trainees still felt cut off by them. The visors none of them much liked yet. They weren't supposed to ice up or fog, but on days like this they did when they were down, even if lowered only to the end of the nose.

They'd just spent their second night in the field; this would be their third day on this exercise, in thirty-two inches of snow. The first two days had been on the march, on snowshoes, at first making as much speed as conditions allowed. It was undesirable to sweat heavily; there was a limit to what the gills in their winter uniforms could vent.

On most of the second day they'd kept to the most difficult and unlikely terrain: a series of steep, timbered recessional moraines;

burned-off swamp forest, thickly brushy; fens where the snow, supported by sedge and heath, had not settled but lay more than forty inches deep, so that even wearing snowshoes, the scouts and lead men sank to their knees.

(Covert troop movement was often feasible for mercenaries. A substantial part of the mercenary market was on resource worlds, the so-called "gook worlds," where off-surface equipment, including reconnaissance aircraft, were generally prohibited for military use by the Confederation. This was true even when the combatants were, or more often had the support of, rival Confederation commercial interests. It was one of the strictures installed more than seven centuries earlier by Pertunis, in the Charter of Confederation, to reduce the ravages of war. While on the trade worlds, the national governments had planetary compacts, though they were not always strictly adhered to, which prohibited the use of aircraft in one or more military roles.)

The T'swa had begun assigning trainees as acting officers and noncoms, with the cadre observing and coaching. Mostly Carrmak had served as A Company commander, although others had worn the hat. On this exercise it was Romlar, who no longer feared to lead, and who, as acting squad leader and platoon leader, had discovered both taste and talent for leadership.

The exercise was to attack an enemy encampment, hopefully by surprise. Of course, there was no assurance that the camp would still be where the map showed it, nor that the enemy wouldn't have learned of their coming and have an ambush set. Enemy patrols could be expected. Certainly pickets would be posted, and presumably fields of fire would have been cleared.

The map was in part a fiction: It showed things that weren't there in reality, but for the sake of the exercise must be treated as if they were. The first two days the company had followed a marked route with no other rationale than to give them a variety of difficult terrains. However, for this third day the map showed no marked route; the commander was to find his own. Using his map, and information from his scouts, Romlar moved his company out. The men were free to talk as they went, but softly, and there wasn't much talking. They'd done plenty of drills on scouting, picket duty, and reconnaissance, training each man to stay highly aware of his surroundings, so their attention was mostly outward.

Romlar's orders were to be in position to attack by midday. Supposedly another company was to approach by a different route and attack at the same time: 1200 hours. Romlar suspected it was an imaginary company, pretended for the purpose of the exercise. If it wasn't there, A Company was to attack by itself. After the enemy was destroyed, Romlar was to march his company to a rendezvous by 1530 hours.

For the most part he followed the crest of a broad ridge that ran for miles, generally about fifty or sixty feet above the country flanking it. Which on the map was marked liberally with wetland symbols, much of it with the subsymbol for brush, and also with occasional small round ponds that suggested fen pools, roofed thickly with ice in this season.

It seemed apparent to Romlar that the planners intended him to stay on the ridge crest. The required time of arrival seemed to demand it. The side slopes would be much more difficult, and slower, to snowshoe on, and on them he'd have been more vulnerable to attack, though less to detection. While if he traveled through the adjacent brushy flats, with their real and imaginary fens, he'd arrive too late to make the attack.

It was a design for ambush, and on a hunch, he marched the company faster than he might have, sweat or not.

After more than two hours, the point radioed back that they'd come to a stringlike fen not shown on their map. All the map showed was the creek that flowed through it. Romlar ordered the company to stay put, and with Jerym, his trainee first sergeant, moved up to see for himself. Lieutenant Toma followed, observing, saying nothing.

The scouts lay back a bit from the fen, close enough to observe it but keeping back among the trees and behind the sapling fringe. They were nearly invisible in the snow, white hoods hiding their helmets; even their rifles were white. Romlar took off his snowshoes, then crawling, slipped slowly forward between his scouts and down to the edge of the fen, where he could see better. Jerym followed, and Lieutenant Toma.

Jerym judged the fen to be 250 to 300 yards across, with no visual cover except for isolated patches of tattered cane grass, head tall, dead leaves fluttering and rustling in a light breeze. The nearest way around was a mile to their right, where the fen ended in evergreen forest. He watched Romlar scan the woods on the opposite side with white binoculars.

Toma spoke while Romlar scanned. "What will you do?"

Romlar didn't answer till he'd put his binoculars away. "Go around," he said.

"How near are you to the enemy encampment?"

"According to the map, two and a half miles plus a little bit, if we cross here."

"Going around will add considerable distance and take additional time. Consider whether you'll be in position to attack by midday."

Romlar didn't even glance at Toma. He's not interested in advice, Jerym told himself.

"I allowed for the time," Romlar said. "There's no cover in the fen, and if we were attacked there, we couldn't move fast in the loose snow. We'll go around."

The T'swi said no more, and the three of them backed away into the woods, to their snowshoes. Back with the company, Romlar changed its course. In something less than half an hour they'd flanked the fen and were at the creek. There was sag ice on it, something they'd run into before and learned about the hard way. It had frozen over in autumn, then the ice had gotten snow-covered. Afterward the creek had fallen, leaving an air space beneath the ice, which had sagged. Insulated by the thick snow atop the ice, the new water surface had probably not frozen thickly enough to carry a man. It looked like a good place to fall through and soak your feet, maybe even lose a snowshoe—serious incidents on a day of minus fifteen or twenty Fahrenheit and with snow up to your ass.

Romlar had scouts cross, moving carefully. When they'd checked the forest on the other side, he had the company advance, spread out, a few at a time, not crossing in bunches. It slowed them, but not critically.

After they'd crossed, Romlar had them form a column of twos again, Toma not questioning, letting him function, and they moved out once more, angling now to regain their old line of travel.

Romlar spoke quietly into his throat mike. "Rear guard, be alert and keep well back. Flankers on the left, stay wide. I suspect there was an ambush laid at the fen, across our old line of march."

"Yes sir."

He moved them fast. Thirty minutes later they hit snowshoe tracks headed from the encampment toward the fen, and Romlar adjusted their direction of march, following the trail toward the encampment. After a bit they heard rifle fire not far ahead. His scouts reported contact with pickets. Romlar ordered 1st and 2nd Platoons into a skirmish line and sent them forward, leaving immediate tactics to their platoon leaders. Shortly the volume of fire increased, now including blast hoses. The T'swi with the enemy pickets reported that the pickets all were casualties. The T'swi with Romlar's scouts reported light casualties. First Platoon reported sighting the encampment in a meadow. A minute later, 4th Platoon's lobbers could be heard thumping. The rocket launchers weren't loud enough to hear.

Romlar had ordered 3rd Platoon to backtrack down their trail aways, to form a crescent facing their would-be ambushers from the fen, who'd probably be coming at a run. Ahead, an imaginary force at the encampment was counterattacking 1st and 2nd Platoons, and the T'swa informed him that the company which should have been helping in the attack on the encampment seemed not to have arrived. Romlar wasn't surprised. He had 4th Platoon concentrate their fire, lobbers and rockets both, on "the counterattack" instead of on the encampment. Minutes later the T'swa reported the counterattack broken, with heavy enemy casualties. Fourth Platoon then began bombarding the encampment again.

Romlar then called 2nd Platoon back and ordered them to join 3rd

Platoon, to move toward the fen in a broad crescent, horns forward. The T'swa with 2nd Platoon had tagged twelve of its people dead or disabled, including Carrmak as platoon leader. Esenrok, as platoon sergeant, was unwounded and took command. Overall command of the two platoons fell to 3rd Platoon's leader, a trainee named Kurlmar.

About nine hundred yards back, Kurlmar stopped his advance at the top of a mild slope, the steepest locally available. The assumption was that the enemy, pressed for time, would follow his old, straight-line snowshoe trails, rather than detour and break new ones. Nonetheless, Kurlmar separated two squads from each end of his line, half his force, and sent them well to the sides, with orders to send scouts out farther, just in case.

Six minutes later he saw enemy movement in the forest to his front, and gave the order to fire. The enemy began to advance, moving from tree to tree as much as possible. Blank ammunition from rifles and blast hoses ripped the forest with their racket.

It was quickly apparent that the force they faced was a full company. Kurlmar's outlying squads too began firing; enemy troops were moving to flank him. He was tempted to withdraw, but instead called for reinforcements.

By the time Romlar arrived with 1st Platoon, most of the 2nd and 3rd had been tagged by their T'swa as casualties, but the enemy had suffered substantial casualties too. (Fourth Platoon had been left to watch for an attack by whatever [imaginary] enemy might have survived at the encampment.) A few minutes later the T'swa called the fighting off, and everyone, dead, disabled, and operational, mushed to the enemy encampment. There the cadre took command and led them all on a forced snowshoe march back toward the compound, fifteen miles away on snowburied roads.

# 26

It was midafternoon at Lake Loreen, but dark enough that Kusu Lormagen had the lights on in the lab. Thunder muttered, and sleet rattled on the windows. He sat at his desk reading a thin sheaf of papers, while Lotta Alsnor watched from a tall lab stool. When he'd finished, he looked up at her.

"You're convinced then," he said.

"Right. A ported mammal goes berserk because teleportation reactivates every terror, every pain, every rage it ever felt. Or inherited, so to speak. Its whole case turns on, all at once, full force and out of context."

Kusu grunted. "Even those that were sedated and unconscious . . ."

"Right. Beneath that unconsciousness, an absolute mental frenzy broke out.

"Since then you've exposed mammals to each of the constituent fields, separately and in partial combinations, without severe effects. Mostly they didn't even notice. The most logical conclusion is that it's the actual *transfer* that activates their cases."

She paused for emphasis. "The point is, that if you teleported a mammal without a significant case, it would come through sane and safe."

He smiled at her. "Can you provide me with a mammal like that?"

She nodded. "As near as need be, yes. Me."

Kusu laughed. "Serves me right for asking." Then, more seriously: "You haven't proved your thesis though. The evidence is highly suggestive, but by no means conclusive." She said nothing. "I know," he went on. "You're volunteering to be the proof.

"But consider: It's not vital that we teleport humans. Or any mammals. Teleporting manufactured goods, foodstuffs, mail, almost anything else you want to name, will make this far and away the biggest technical advance since the invention of hyperdrive."

Lotta shook her head. "Human teleportation is where the biggest potential lies," she said. "And you've got a made-to-order experimental subject: me. Use it."

" 'No significant case,' " he said. "How do you know what the level of significance is?"

She shrugged. "The evaluation is subjective, obviously. But it's the only informed evaluation you're likely to get."

"Why shouldn't we test it with someone else who knows the T'sel? Me for example."

"Why don't you answer that?"

"Sure. Because you feel significant uncertainty about your evaluation. You don't want someone else to risk their life on it, or at least their sanity."

Lotta nodded. "Certainly not *your* life. It might take quite awhile before someone else could digest your logbooks and interim write-ups and figure out what to do next."

Kusu laughed again. "What makes you think I know what to do next?"

"You know several things you could do next. You're just not sure which to choose."

"True. Well. To paraphrase a famous Pertunian principle: When you don't know what to do, grab an option, at random if you have to, and do it. So. Supposing we subject you to some constituent fields, one at a time, and you can evaluate subjectively what each of them feels like. To a human, not a sorlex or soney. A human that knows the T'sel. And after light tranquilization, just to hedge our bet."

She shook her head. "We know tranks don't help. The rest of it I'll go with."

Kusu smiled. "It's a deal. It'll take some time to build a port big enough for a human. We have the design and some of the components, but others are still being built. You draw up a set of safety precautions for my approval, and meanwhile I'll expedite the hardware."

She nodded. "I'll have a draft of the safety proposals for you in the morning."

"Good. Oh! And one thing more: Be sure they include having Wellem standing by. If you come through like the sorlex did, maybe he can bail you out."

# 27

Kusu watched while Wellem Bosler and the Institute's physician fastened Lotta to the table with a rubber body sheet. *When she agreed to draw up a set of safety proposals,* Kusu thought, *she went all the way.*

The jury-rigged teleport was not a single unit. Made of metal tubing, the gate itself resembled a door frame without a wall, with a ramp to accommodate the gurney. Modules sat on a lab bench and on a small wheeled work table, with cables to the gate. But it had passed a series of tests without problems of any kind—a series that ended with the successful teleportation of horn worms and sand lizards.

Lotta lay patiently while the fastenings were secured. She hadn't expected to be uneasy, but she was. And so, she sensed, was the student technician who stood at her head, waiting to push the gurney.

When they'd finished with the fastenings, it was Bosler who spoke. "Are you ready?" he asked her.

"Ready," she said. Her speech was thick; she wore a rubber mouthpiece to protect her tongue and cheeks from her teeth, a mouthpiece too big to spit out.

With the physician, Bosler walked a dozen feet past the gate, to stand beside the target site. He could *feel* Lotta's unease, and the physician's, and the student's. And Kusu's most of all. Each had its own flavor, distinguishing it from the others, including his own. None was severe, but the tension was there, and as sensitized as he was just now, it was palpable to Bosler.

He looked at Kusu and nodded.

Kusu threw a switch. A red light came on beside the gate. Bosler turned his gaze to Lotta. Hers too was on the light. Her face was calm but the tension remained. The red light switched off, and the green one beside it flashed on. He saw her eyes close as the technician rolled the gurney up the ramp, onto the platform—

And into the gate.

It was the length of the gurney that made it conspicuous: The foot end began to appear in front of Bosler while the rest was still on the runway. The effect was startling and disorienting: Lotta's feet and legs were a dozen feet from her torso. Then all of her was there. Her eyes still were closed, her face relaxed as before.

His nerves settled. "You made it," he said quietly.

"I know," she answered, and her eyes opened, her face turning to him. "Now if you'll let me loose . . ."

# 28

Equinox was well past, and the snow, still twenty inches deep, had been settling wetly beneath the springtime sun. That noon, A Company had reached a "village"—a set of buildings crudely framed—only to find signs informing them that it had been "burnt" by "the enemy" when he'd left. Then, by snowshoeing hard all afternoon, they'd reached a meadow with supposedly an "enemy camp," arriving between sundown and dark. The "enemy" wasn't there, and when "he'd left," of course, he'd "destroyed his camp and taken his supplies with him."

It had been a tough bivouac. They'd been out for five days and four nights, breaking camp each morning and carrying it with them. Once a radioed message from regiment had routed them out at midnight, and they'd moved in darkness. On top of that they hadn't gotten their scheduled resupply, and had been on half rations. They'd been drizzled on and snowed on, and definitely preferred the snow. One morning they'd been ambushed, and one night their camp had been assaulted. In turn they'd ambushed or assaulted other companies twice, once in the night.

In general they'd enjoyed themselves enormously.

Of course, while the T'swa had set things up to seem as real as readily feasible, the casualties had been assigned by umpires, not bullets, and after each encounter were reinstated as alive, combat-effective, and ready to march.

They had cadre with them, but the T'swa had kept apart, saying nothing except as umpires when the company encountered a real or imaginary enemy force.

Carrmak set pickets out, and the company pitched their winter shelter tents in the adjacent woods. (The trainee company commander now was always either Carrmak or Romlar.) The command tent was somewhat larger than the standard two-man size—made with four panels, longer and differently shaped, sheltering Carrmak; Jerym as his EO, his executive officer; and the trainee first sergeant, Orkuth, from 3rd Platoon. They'd carried the panels and framing in their own packs, T'swa style, rather than having someone else carry them.

It was dark in the tent, but not utterly dark. The only artificial light was the tiny red dot of the power light on the command radio, on the floor by where Carrmak would sleep. But Seeren was at the end of her first quarter, wouldn't go down till around midnight, and the thin fine fabric of the tent roof glowed faintly with her light. *Like daylight for the T'swa's big cateyes,* Jerym supposed. He spread his insulating ground pad beside his rifle, unrolled his sleeping bag on top of it, opened the bag and laid down on it. His clothing was warm enough for now; he could crawl in the sack later, when it got colder.

They'd spoken very little in the tent. There wasn't a lot to say. Jerym lay with his eyes open for a little and heard someone's stomach growl. His own answered. They'd eaten the last of their field rations that morning, and his attention kept returning to his hunger. His last conscious thought was to wonder if it would keep him awake.

The moon was still up, the tent faintly lit by it, when he was awakened by the command radio: "Able Company, this is regiment, over. Able Company, this is regiment, over." It rolled Jerym onto his knees, instantly intent. Stripping off his mittens, he fumbled the orders recorder out of a pocket on his officer's pack. The voice had been Gotasu's. Carrmak, kneeling, picked the radio up. "This is Carrmak commanding Able Company, over."

"Able Company, I have map coordinates for you."

Jerym thumbed the *record* switch on his recorder.

"In quadrangle J-2-7-M-5-3. Coordinates are: X:2113, Y:1797. Again, X:2213, Y:1797. Over."

The pale oblong of Carrmak's face turned to Jerym. "It's recorded," Jerym murmured.

"Recorded," Carrmak said into the radio. "That's in our present quadrangle, coordinates X:2213, Y:1797. Over."

"That's right, Carrmak. Take Able Company and proceed to those coordinates at once. You will find vacant defensive positions dug in there—bunkers and trenches. You will occupy them by not later than 2400 hours, midnight. And wait for further orders, prepared to defend them if attacked. Over."

*"If attacked,"* Jerym thought to himself. *"Further orders."* *They're apt to leave us sitting there for a day without food, or have us get ambushed on the way. Or the defensive positions might have enemy in them when we get there.* A real enemy could hardly be more unpredictable, a fact in which he found much satisfaction.

"Got that," Carrmak said to Gotasu. "Able Company will occupy dug-in defensive positions at X:2213, Y:1797, not later than midnight, prepared to defend against possible attack. Over."

"That is correct, Able Company. Regiment out."

"Able Company out."

Jerym looked at the time glowing green on his recorder, then thumbed it off: 2141 hours and seven seconds—they had just less than two hours and twenty minutes to get there. How far, and what was the terrain like? He took out the mapbook,[13] switched it on, called up the quadrangle, and tapped in the coordinates as the display lit up.

A tiny white square appeared, with a hard white center dot, defining the exact coordinate point and the limits of coordinate precision. They fell within a pale yellow square, a field, surrounded on the holomap by the pale green of forest. This was a part of the reservation they weren't familiar with. But the terrain was gentle, which was encouraging, given the time limit. Jerym called up a distance scale with its two ends on their destination and their present position, then held the map board so Carrmak could see it.

"There's a crossroad within the square," he said. "The dug-in positions are probably to defend it. It's 7.12 straight-line miles from here."

"Good," Carrmak said. "Orkuth, roust out the company. Tell them they've got till 2150, eight minutes, to break camp and be formed up for the road. Alsnor, decide on a route and show it to me."

Deciding the route was easy. One of the roads that crossed the coordinates crossed the meadow they were in, a nearly straight shot. Call it seven and a quarter miles, allowing for the few curves in it. The only alternative was to go through the woods, which would slow them to no advantage unless they swung far enough from the road to avoid possible ambush. That would add distance, and time they didn't have. On snowshoes they'd have to push hard as it was, after having hiked all day, almost without food and only an hour and a half's sleep; no sleep at all for the guys on picket duty.

He showed Carrmak the route. Carrmak agreed, and they struck their tent, assembled their packs. Around them was activity, crisp and meaningful, with acting sergeants giving quiet orders.

It was a beautiful night. Seeren, seeming perfectly cut in half, was partway down the western sky. The air was absolutely calm, and still felt somewhat above freezing; the snow was doomed, Jerym thought. His mittens were in his parka pockets; the parka itself was open and the hood thrown back. The snow seemed to give off light of its own; visibility was no problem at all. It seemed to him that, outdoors, the T'swa could hardly see better than he could on a night like this.

When Carrmak sent the point out, and the flankers, Jerym's wristwatch read 2149:49. Two minutes later, Carrmak gave the order to march. They had almost exactly two hours and eight minutes.

The snow on the road was undisturbed, except for a slight hollowing caused by wind swirl from some hover truck before the thaw had started. But the warm weather had settled it so much, their snowshoes didn't sink in at all. They'd have no trouble reaching the crossroad by midnight, Jerym told himself, unless there was an ambush waiting for them.

Within the first hundred yards, the swinging stride, the soft crunch of snowshoes on spring snow, the moonlit snowscape, combined to produce a dreamlike clarity in Jerym's mind. His thoughts, what there were of them, seemed remote and out of time. He'd become a mobile observing unit; any computing was subliminal. Along the road, the forest canopy was mostly of deciduous trees that let the moonlight through, with here and there tall evergreens, their thick tops variously oval or pyramidal or ragged blacknesses. Occasionally he saw the small round blobs of yarpu roosting asleep in the treetops. And twice smelled urine and excrement somewhere nearby, beneath some evergreen, some koorsa tree whose top had been homesteaded by a burly, twenty-pound stinkpig who'd spent days or even weeks there feeding on buds, needles, and inner bark, relieving itself repeatedly onto the snow beneath.

Time did not pass for Jerym. He floated through it without effort, neither tiring nor hungering. Yet at any point he could have told you without looking what time it was and how far they'd gone and how far they had to go. He saw the ethereal tracery of branches against the night sky, the glint of stronger stars between them, those that could override the moonlight.

The condition lasted until, at 2341, they reached the crossroad. The defensive positions were a circular series of six-foot-deep foxholes with firing steps on both sides, connected by narrow, four-foot-deep crawl trenches. All dug by machinery in some past summer.

But snow-filled, they weren't evident, would have been hard to find except for the mounds of four snow-covered bunkers spaced along the circle. Carrmak had pickets posted, then set the men to digging out the snow with their trenching tools. They worked furiously; it was to be finished by midnight.

They'd cleared the foxholes and were working on the crawl-trenches when, without warning, the first explosions occurred in the middle of the circle, sending dirt and snow flying. The ground jarred with them, and the sound, unexpected, was stunning. The explosions went on, one after another and several at once, within and outside the circle. Between the explosions, Jerym could hear the violent hammering of blast hoses spraying the area. Their tracers seemed to float lazily, yet their blast slugs, slamming into the parapets, ripped them, throwing chunks of frozen dirt into the foxholes and onto the men that crouched in them. The noise, the violence, were shocking.

Yet after half a minute, the trainees crouched less low, gripped their rifles less tightly, checked to make sure there was a round in the chamber. When the barrage ended, an assault seemed likely.

A minute later it did stop, and they got onto their firing steps, ready. Though still somewhat deafened, they could hear the sounds of other, similar barrages miles away, before those too ceased. Then a bull horn sounded from a silent floater overhead, and they recognized Gotasu's voice:

"That's it, gentlemen, end of exercise!"

None of them got out of their holes though; they hadn't gotten it from their acting company commander yet. Then Carrmak crawled out of the bunker and gave them the word: "Able Company, fall in!"

They scrambled out and formed up ranks while the floater landed, unloaded Captain Gotasu and Lieutenant Toma, and left. The field was humps and craters now, brown mixed with white. Jerym wondered if the "shells" they'd been bombarded with had been explosive charges buried in the field long in advance. Or if the T'swa had such confidence in their own marksmanship that they'd used actual lobber rounds, dropping them safely, near but not too near. Most of the churned-up ground was toward the center of the circle or outside it by at least fifteen yards.

Gotasu looked them over. "A Company," he said, "you've done very well on this bivouac. Your trainee officers and noncoms have done very well. We are now twenty-one miles from the compound. We will march there tonight." He paused. "And the cooks will serve you a very good breakfast. Meanwhile, if the platoon sergeants will come to the vehicle, there is a carton of hardtack, with a packet for each man."

Gotasu waited while the hardtack was distributed and devoured. A packet held three ounces; it took about a minute to eat it. He looked at Carrmak then. "Commander, consider the war over, the enemy vanquished. You need not put out scouts nor fear attack. Move your troops out."

# 29

Company A, still hungry and almost without sleep, hiked hard and fast, marching into the compound soon after sunup. It was the first night in nearly four deks that it hadn't frozen, and they arrived sweating. Breakfast was toast and jam, baked omelets, juice, and buttermilk. Delicious, and enough but not enough. They got only one large serving each, to avoid the risk of getting sick. The mess sergeant, a somewhat overweight Iryalan, announced that at dinner they could eat all they wanted. And here, dinner was at noon.

After showering, the trainees crashed. It was the first time in more than five deks of training that they'd been allowed to sleep during normal training hours after a night exercise.

The alarm bells were used to waken them at 1145, the first time the alarms had sounded since their first week. It gave them fifteen minutes to get ready for dinner. The meal was steaks and baked potato, with mixed vegetables barely cooked, and corn fritters. There were seconds, even thirds. Dessert was hot fruit cobbler with ice cream. Then they were ordered to the assembly hall.

While the trainees filed into the rows of benches, Voker and Dak-So came onto the podium and stood waiting. When the regiment was seated, Voker grinned and spoke:

"Good afternoon, warriors!"

The response was deafening. "Good afternoon, sir!"

"I'm up here to say I'm proud of you. When you came here, I knew you were going to be good. As I watched you, those first rough deks, I never doubted, in spite of all the trouble you made for yourselves. All I had to see was the way you trained, the spirit you put into things, to know you were going to be as good or better than I'd originally expected."

He paused, looked them over, then continued. "Now, though you've been here for less than six deks, you're already better, as individuals, platoons, and companies, than any other light infantry in the Confederation. Unless you count the T'swa, and they're determined to make you as nearly their equal as possible in three years. T'swa pride doesn't let them do anything less than their best, and I know yours won't either.

"You've all just come in from a tough, wild five days. Your companies have reconnoitered each other, ambushed each other, assaulted each other. And last night we exploded a whole lot of takite and other good stuff, giving all of you the sound and feel of gunnery, and plowed up a lot of dirt doing it. Then marched you back in on almost empty stomachs, for distances of fifteen to twenty-three miles. In the last five days and nights you hiked about a hundred and seventy miles on snowshoes and short rations, most of it with full winter packs, and some of it in tough terrain. That would have killed a lot of troops, and had most of the rest of them bitching their heads off."

Again the old man looked them over, then nodded emphatically as if approving what he saw. "You've completed a phase of your training," he went on, "the phase in which you've operated solely as platoons and companies. This spring and summer you'll be working as battalions and as a regiment. And between now and then . . . We'll talk about that later— before we're done here today. I think you'll like it.

"Now I'm going to turn this meeting over to Colonel Dak-So. He's the man in charge of delivering the training, and he's got things to talk to you about. Colonel," he said turning, "they're yours," and took a seat to one side.

"Thank you, Colonel Voker." Dak-So flashed a quick grin at the regiment. "You *are* good," he said. "You are tough, enduring, strong, and growing smarter. Even wiser! And wiser is very important to a warrior. We have given a number of you responsibilities as acting officers and noncoms, and you have shown growth and skill in carrying these out. I have no doubt that the rest of you could function in those posts, too, because all of you are warriors. But some men have a special, innate talent to lead, and we will take full advantage of that."

He stood silent for a moment then, drawing their attention more strongly. "I mentioned wisdom. Your company commanders have, on occasion, discussed further with you the Matrix of T'sel. You have shown by your responses and questions that you have rather largely absorbed its principles and made them yours. That is very reassuring, because without them, a warrior is not complete. I now want to look at some principles with you which heretofore you have been introduced to only casually."

Again Dak-So paused, his eyes settling on Artus Romlar. "Trainee Romlar," he said. "What is the most important thing a warrior must be able to do?"

Romlar stood. "Sir, a warrior has to do the right thing at the right time."

"Good! And Trainee Brossling, how does a warrior know what the right thing is?"

Brossling got easily to his feet. "He just knows. He either knows or he doesn't."

"Good. Now Brossling, both you and Romlar got in trouble early on, doing the wrong things at the wrong times—" He paused, grinned, went on. "Although you exceeded Romlar in that. What made the difference in your early performances and your recent performances?" He cocked an eyebrow at the trainee C.O. of F Company, earlier the regiment's number one troublemaker.

"Sir," Brossling answered, "most of the difference comes from getting our heads straightened out. The colonel made us see our responsibility and make it up to the regiment. You T'swa never let us run over you. And the Ostrak Procedures took it from there."

Dak-So raised an eyebrow again and nodded. "Excellent. You may sit down now . . . All right. A wise warrior knows correctly. An unwise warrior knows incorrectly. You might say there is a state of knowingness and a state of false knowingness.

"And the difference is what the Ostrak teams call one's 'case.' When you, with their help, unloaded the heavier and more active parts of your cases, you became far more able to know correctly.

"Incidentally, some might say there is also a state of *un*knowingness. Such a state only seems to exist. Knowingness and false knowingness are very often at a level below awareness, hence the appearance of unknowingness. Even so, our knowingness or false knowingness drives our decisions."

His eyes sought again. "Klarister, how many times have you been killed since you've been here?"

Klarister rose. "Twice sir," he said. "Twice that I got tagged for. Last night they weren't tagging us, but if that had been a real barrage, intended to hit us instead of miss, it might have been three times. Seems likely."

"Ah. And how many cadre are we here?"

"T'swa? Uh, probably three or four hundred I'd guess, sir."

"Four hundred twelve. We are almost the totality of the able-bodied survivors of three regiments—of nearly fifty-four hundred men originally on our rosters. Thank you, Klarister." His gaze took in the entire assembly then. "You do know, I trust, that most warriors die violent deaths, mostly while still more or less young."

His eyes stopped on another trainee. "Benster, doesn't that worry you?"

Benster stood. "Not particularly, sir. I'm a warrior. Because I want to be. The danger is part of it; you can't have the game without the risk."

"But getting killed!? . . ."

Benster grinned. "Call it recycled, sir. Lotta, my interviewer, helped me see lots of times I got killed, died in bed, what have you. Old and young, what have you. Seems like I keep coming back."

"Ah! Seems! And suppose that what you saw during your interviews was all hallucination, somehow an outgrowth of suggestion."

Benster shrugged, the grin undimmed. "I suppose that possibility has occurred to most of us. But what it comes down to, sir, is that if we recycle, death isn't that big a deal. And if, when we die, that's the end of it for us, then we won't miss it, because we'll be dead. So we might as well live the life we're here for, and enjoy it."

"Thank you, Benster, for a good exposition." Benster sat down, and Dak-So's eyes moved again, stopped.

"Trainee Alsnor, Benster mentioned his interviewer, his Ostrak operator, Lotta. As I recall, she is still a young girl, perhaps fifteen or sixteen. Suppose she was in danger, Alsnor. In immediate danger of being murdered. How would you respond?"

Jerym's face was stiff. "Sir, I'd do anything in my power to keep it from happening."

"I'm sure you would, Alsnor, I'm sure you would. Be seated please, and thank you." Dak-So scanned the assembly again. "The operator we talked about, as some of you know, is Alsnor's sister. I did not ask him that question to make him uncomfortable. I wanted to make something real to all of you: That there are circumstances which tend to carry strong polarity with them. Even when a warrior is neutral about his own survival, prepared to accept death, there may be matters about which he has strong preferences. Things he wants and rejects, must have and must not have.

"As a warrior or a workman, a father, an athlete—whatever roles one plays in life, one can be appraised by the excellence of his performance. Aside from whether he wins or loses. And the excellence of that performance is a reflection of his decisions.

"T'swa warriors for millennia have been humankind's most successful warriors, but sometimes we lose engagements, even wars, and the great majority of us die in battle. We always intend to win, we always intend to survive and see our friends survive, and most often our actions are such as to bring about victory and survival. But these actions are not compulsive. They are not burdened with a sense of 'must have' or 'must not have.' We are perfectly willing to lose, or to die, or to see our friends die, if that is what transpires."

The T'swa major paused. "I do not insist that you agree with me on this. If you do, that is fine. If you don't, that is fine too. And in either case it is all right to change your mind. But I will tell you that to the extent you have strong preferences and strong aversions, to that degree you will make decisions which do not conduce to high performance as a warrior.

"In fact, strong preferences and aversions are likely to result in losing that which one strongly wishes to keep. And in experiencing that which one despises.

"Feel free to disagree with me. I've told you these things not with insistence, but because I want you to be aware that T'swa warriors hold such a philosophy. Nonpolarity is a key to what we are like."

Again Dak-So paused to scan them. "Very well, enough of that." He turned to Voker. "Colonel, your regiment."

Voker stood, stepped forward, grinned. "Feel the floor with your feet!" he ordered. Genially. The wooden floor resounded with the clomping of field boots, the room changing auras with the release of tension.

"Was the floor there? Did you feel it?"

"*Yes!*" came an answering roar.

"Good. Look at the person on your right! If you're on the extreme right, look at someone else . . . Good! Now tell that person hello! . . . Good! Now stand up! . . . Good! Now stretch! Hard! . . . Good! Now sit down again, and I'll tell you something I believe you'll like to hear."

They sat.

"Tomorrow you will begin to learn unarmed combat. You have three weeks to learn it. You will train at it all morning and all afternoon. In the evening you will study various other things, many things. But during the daytime you will learn to fight with your hands and feet.

"For a week after that, you'll receive training with and against the knife, and improve your skill with the bayonet."

He felt their incipient cheer, and held up a hand, postponing it a moment. "Do you like that idea?" he asked.

Their enthusiasm came bellowing out, the most deafening cheers yet. He let it continue till it started to weaken, then cut it off with a single motion. "Good. The people who analyzed your civilian records and tests told us you were intentive warriors. It's obvious they knew what they were talking about.

"This afternoon, however, you will clean your barracks to the satisfaction of your company commanders, and they will be hard to satisfy. This evening—" He grinned again. "This evening there will be a holo show here from 1915 to approximately 2100. How would you like to see, um . . . 'For Love of Thora'? I understand it's a good cube."

There was applause.

"Or would you rather see 'A Crown Prince on Ice,' a cube about a T'swa campaign?"

Hands beat, feet drummed, throats roared. After some seconds he cut them off. " 'A Crown Prince' it will be then. But I warn you, it's an old cube from before the Kettle War, and the T'swa in it are figments of an uninformed imagination. Considering your experience, you'll no doubt look at it as comedy.

"Now, when I dismiss you, leave the building in an orderly manner. You are free till 1430. At 1430, you will start cleaning your barracks. Dismissed!"

Voker and Dak-So watched the trainees file out, talking as they went. *They are good young warriors, progressing very well,* Dak-So told himself. *Given three years training, they will be very good indeed.*

# 30

Commodore Igsat Tarimenloku took the bit in his teeth and pressed the two keys. His Reverence's ship *Blessed Flenyaagor* emerged into real-space with its troopship companion. Everyone was at his battle station, but nothing happened except that they continued at emergence speed in the now star-bannered blackness.

He hadn't really expected an attack. For the last two hours in hyper-space, he'd stopped, speeded, stopped again, with no sign of a bogey. And it was inconceivable that they were still inside the hostile sector they'd been in before. But as the first minutes passed, he felt the gradual ebbing of tension, leaving him slack, letting him know how tense he'd actually been.

He'd emerged in a system whose primary was a singlet, a Type F main sequence star, visually a small disk blazing intensely some 800 million miles away. His flagship couldn't evaluate the system for a habitable planet nearly as quickly as the lost survey ship would have, but if any planet had parameters promising enough to call for close examination, he'd know it within the hour and close on it within a day or so. And depending on the outcome of each subsequent phase of observations, he'd determine its critical habitability parameters within a few days more, at most.

# 31

Lord Kristal walked a trifle carefully; his arthritis was flaring up a bit. "We could have done this by cube or beam of course, and saved me the trip," he said. "But I like to see things live when I can. The touch of reality can make a difference."

The new peiok leaves were out and half expanded, sheltering the lawns with springtime's delicate green. The last time he'd been to Lake Loreen had been— That long ago? Early autumn—more than half a year. Then the leaves had shown the first touches of autumn color: yellow, bronze, scarlet.

"I'm glad you came down," Kusu answered, and grinned. "For a milestone of sorts."

They entered the Research Building, and Kusu turned right at the foot of the stairs, stopping at the elevators where he pushed a button. *Hmh!*

thought Kristal. *He noticed the knees. Otherwise we'd have walked up. Not much gets by this young man.* The doors opened and they stepped on.

"Is Wellem around?" Kristal asked. "And your parents?"

"All three, and Laira and Konni. I'm under orders to bring you to lunch if at all possible. If you want to get with any of them singly, I don't suppose there'll be any difficulty with that either."

The elevator stopped and opened, and it was the roof they stepped out onto, which did not surprise His Lordship. It would have to be the roof; the thing didn't work through walls. A girl was there, a young lady with red hair, standing by the parapet. She turned toward them as they stepped out, as if she'd been watching something and heard the elevator doors open. The "something" had no doubt been the *oroval* which now was running up a branch of a peiok tree, its long tail undulating behind.

And there, sitting on an AG sled, was one of the three teleports Kusu had built.

Kristal returned his attention to the girl. "You must be Lotta Alsnor," he said. "The first person to teleport."

"Yes sir," she answered. "You're right, as usual."

He bowed slightly. "I understand you have other talents—qualities and skills that go beyond boldness. Please accept my admiration."

He turned to Kusu then. "Ernoman you said. There's an ocean between here and there. A horizon and— What? A hundred degrees of curvature? You said it only works on line of sight."

"I was wrong. And I hope you don't ask me to explain it. One of the problems with inventions that grow out of an intuitive leap is that you may not really understand how they work. And draw wrong conclusions from incomplete observations. Besides that, weak understanding can make things pretty tough to explain, let alone debug and modify. I can teleport objects to Offside Base on Seeren if I hit a limb at a tangent, more or less. It's as if it slides around the circumference then. But if I just aim as if to teleport something on a straight line with Seeren's mass in between, nothing happens. It just sits here; it doesn't go to the intervening mass or anywhere else. It either goes to the coordinate destination, or else it stays.

"On the other hand, something like a tree trunk is no obstacle."

Kusu raised a hand slightly, shaking his head. "None of which makes sense, I know, any more than the exclosure limitation does. Theoretically and apparently the object being teleported doesn't traverse the intervening space. It simply ceases to be at one set of coordinates in real space, and instead and instantaneously it's at the other, through their intersection on the back side of reality, so to speak. No physical movement seems to be involved, and hyperspace isn't generated.

"Sense or not though, it works the way it works. And we seem to be making progress on theory; some, anyway. I've had two grad students working on it for several deks now; they're each taking a different approach, and I'm taking a third. We brainstorm usually once a week. But how long it'll be before we understand it remains to be seen."

Lord Kristal's eyes left Kusu, moving to Lotta. "And you, I understand, are to make a real trip, the first long jump, so to speak."

He turned to Kusu. "To Ernoman. Hmh! I'd like to go with her. A step behind, so she'll have the honor of being first. Will you send me?"

The request took Kusu completely by surprise. Lord Kristal had been brought up in the T'sel, but even so . . . "If Your Lordship wishes. There may still be a risk though."

Kristal ignored the warning. " 'Your Lordship?' " he parroted. "When did I stop being Emry to you, Kusu Lormagen?"

Kusu laughed. "Never. But at the same time, you've always been Your Lordship to me, too. Considering all the things you've done and how long you've done them, and how well." *Personal aide to the king,* he added silently, *and to the king before that. The man who sees to things, all kinds of things, takes care of things, without arrogance, upsets, or unwanted notice.*

Kristal had turned to Lotta and spread his hands. "What can I say to someone who butters me up like that?" He grinned, showing still sound teeth. "Lotta, will you accept my company on a brief but long trip?"

Entering his playful mood, she curtsied. "Your Lordship, I'd be honored."

"Hmmph! 'Your Lordship' again!" He looked at Kusu. "I believe I'm being put in my place. Are any preparations needed, or can we go now?"

"I'll power up and we'll give it half a minute." Kusu stepped to the teleport, pressed a switch, and they waited without speaking. Kristal felt his stomach knot a bit, and was mildly surprised at it. After perhaps twenty seconds, a green light came on. "It's ready," Kusu said.

The nobleman and the girl went to the ankle-high platform, then Kristal gestured. Lotta stepped onto it. "Ready," she said. Kusu pressed another switch and she was gone. In her place was what seemed a rectangular hole in the local reality, a door with the gate for its frame. Through it, seeming both in and beyond it, they could see Lotta's back. Then she stepped aside, disappearing, and Kristal found himself looking onto another roof. Farther off he could see a blurry section of parapet and, blurrier still, what seemed to be an evergreen tree. Obviously the teleport was not much good for tele*viewing*.

Then Kusu looked at Kristal. "If you're ready," Kusu said, and gestured. "Just step through."

His Lordship stepped onto the platform too, and through the gate. He hadn't known what to expect, hadn't thought about it. For him, it was like a mild twitch, a whole-body twitch. Then he was on another roof, and it was evening. Lotta Alsnor was standing five feet away, beside a young man His Lordship had never met. Beyond the roof, the trees were not peioks, and in the distance, a row of mountains stretched with snowy upper slopes. It was early evening instead of late morning.

"Well. I seem to have arrived." He gave his attention to the young man. "I don't suppose you expected me. I'm Lord Kristal."

"I'm Rinly Barrlis," the young man said. "You know my father, I believe."

"So I do. So I do." He looked at the nearby teleport, an apparent duplicate of the one he'd just used, and then at Lotta. "I seem to have no business here, beyond arriving, and I do have people to talk with at Lake Loreen. Is there any reason I shouldn't go back directly?"

"No sir. I should go right back too."

He turned to young Barrlis. "Will you do the honors, Rinly?"

"Of course, Your Lordship." He powered up the teleport, and in less than a minute, Kristal was back with Kusu. Lotta followed a few seconds later, and handed Kusu an envelope which he put in a pocket. The test was over. And somehow it all seemed quite natural to His Lordship, not epochal at all.

It was a half hour short of lunch, and Kristal saw no point in interrupting the mornings of busy people, so he and Kusu sat on a sunlit bench, looking out across the lake. A light breeze blew, cool enough to make the old man glad of his jacket. Wavelets chuckled against rowboats tied to a dock.

"You've teleported objects to Seeren," Kristal said. "What seems to be the feasibility of sending persons to other systems? Persons without a burden of case, of course. Is there any possibility they'd arrive frozen or asphyxiated?"

"There shouldn't be. The last thing I sent to Seeren was an airtight box with three sand lizards. They arrived there alive and well, which says something about temperature, at least. There's a problem though, in sending anything to other *systems*. Actually we key a set of conventional coordinates into the teleport's computer. The computer converts those to operational, topological coordinates, using an equation."

He paused. "Are you familiar with mail-pod astrogation?"

"Not really."

"Well, to teleport outsystem, the math we use is analogous to that used in mail-pod astrogation. It guides the pod to an imprecisely predictable location within the target system, where it emerges from hyperspace. From there, the pod homes on a beacon off the target world, normally mounted on the local Postal Outsystem Processing Center, which is parked on a gravitic coordinate outside the radiation belt.

"But there's always an error of location, an inaccuracy, in the point where the pod actually emerges from hyperspace. A targeting error. At distances like, say, from here to Rombil or Splenn, a typical error is around a hundred thousand miles; an extremely minute error over a distance of several parsecs. But in teleportation we'd like accuracy within yards—close enough that we can correct by eye to as near as need be, which could be at the entrance of a specific building.

"That's the ideal, of course. At the very least we'd want to land things safely on the planet's land surface."

Lord Kristal's expression was thoughtful. "What needs to be done to attain that accuracy?"

"The most basic approach would be to develop a new math that better fits the topological problems involved. The *quickest* approach though, and the one we can be surest of, is probably to refine the targeting equation. I've started a pair of astrophysicists working on it—members of the Movement of course. They fly down from L.U. on weekends and use the teleport to get data."

"Hmm. Can someone see the roof and the teleport here from the other side? The destination side?"

"No. It's a one-way gate and a one-way view."

"What do you think are the short-term prospects of succeeding?"

"Assuming that 'short term' isn't too short, the prospect of putting things down on a land surface on the target planet seems fairly good. From there, for a while, we may have to settle for providing our passengers with a beacon, so a shuttle can find them and take them by air to where they want to go."

Kristal nodded thoughtfully. "Good. Because now that we have this"—he thumbed back toward the Research Building, where the teleport stood—"I have a feeling we're going to need it."


# 32


The reality generators, in a coincidence of factors, had brought forth against the Lok-Sanu Range a desert storm, a rain of rains to rend the night, drowning and nurturing, carving and smoothing. It boomed and banged, lightning pulsing, stabbing mountain ridges, punctuating a darkness otherwise absolute. Wind whoomed. Rain slashed in sheets against thick walls and stubby towers. Torrents, rock-laden, snarled and rumbled down deep ravines.

Inside his tower-top cell, Master Tso-Ban sat in trance, unaware of the misted spray, the ruptured rain which swirling gusts brought in beneath the eaves and through the open side to wet his skin with unaccustomed coolness.

His awareness was elsewhere—much farther even than Iryala. In fact, he lay as a sellsu, in a cool ocean current, on a world as wet as his own was (usually) dry. Rose and fell gently, slowly, on oil-smooth swells fathered by some distant storm, his flippers gently stroking to hold him in place. Floated among his pack listening to a poem, a favorite ode among the sullsi, told this night by a master bard who phrased the well-known tale in words and meter of his own. A human maiden, Juliassa, daughter of a chief, had found a sullsit chieftain, Sleekit, left by the tide sick and dying on a beach. She'd cared for him, brought fish to him, protected him from saarkas. Had even learned to speak the sullsit air speech, so they could share stories, until he was well and strong enough to fish and fight again and travel with his own.

And how, with the help of the far-listening serpents who call themselves Vrronnkiess, the sullsi, people of the waves, had gone to war to save Juliassa's people from the big-ship humans who'd come to enslave them. (Two verses were given to explain enslavement, and another for war.)

The bard was describing the gathering of the packs, when Tso-Ban felt himself drawing out of the sellsu he'd melded with, a sellsu who'd been aware of him as a psychic presence, a visitor silent and benign, and by now was used to him. For just a moment, Tso-Ban was aware of his tiny tower room. Then, unexpectedly, he was with—

*Tarimenloku! Nearby!* Quickly but gently he melded, and found himself looking at a screen, the bridge's version of a window, looking at a world, his own world, Tyss, a tan ball with a visible area of blue flecked with white. The Klestronu flotilla was parked 50,000 miles out, beyond the radiation belt.

Tso-Ban stayed unnoticed with Tarimenloku for hours—till after sunup. Because Tyss was technologically so backward, at 50,000 miles the ship's instruments failed to perceive that it held people. Instead, from those instruments he reluctantly decided that this planet was not habitable. Most of its surface he judged too hot for human life, while in the polar regions it was utter desert. Closer examination would not be worthwhile.

Although it was the most nearly habitable world that Tarimenloku had found in the systems he'd examined. In a sour mood he moved his two ships away from Tyss, accelerating in a warp field toward a point far enough from any gravitic nodus that he could generate hyperspace safely. Meanwhile his astrogator was taking data on the nearest other stars, deciding which to visit next.

Gently Master Tso-Ban disengaged, woke his body from its trance, then stood and stretched, and stepped outside. Desert rocks steamed beneath the newly risen sun. He would go and notify Master Deng before his exercises. This unexpected visit by the Klestroni was something the Confederatswa would want to know about.

# 33

It was a lovely late-spring day—one might say presolstice summer— when Lord Kristal called Wellem Bosler. Bosler didn't answer. Reception referred the call to Laira Gouer Lormagen, who wore the coordinator's hat at Lake Loreen. She paged Bosler while Kristal waited, and when there still was no response, told His Lordship that Bosler must be at the *ghao*, a small, rather Pagoda-like building on the islet in Gouer Cove. The ghao had no commset. She'd go herself and see if he was available.

There was a wooden causeway to the islet, giving quick access. She found the red light glowing on the door of Bosler's inner sanctum, warning her away.

Kristal knew that much of what went on at the ghao was not to be interrupted short of serious emergency. And while his business, which was the Crown's business, was extremely important, it was not immediately urgent. He told Laira this, and asked her to have Bosler call him back at his earliest opportunity. And that Kusu was to sit in on the call if at all possible.

Within The Movement there was a large amount of mutual respect. That, not rank, was the basis of their operation, for all of them knew the T'sel. Although there was rank, and one gave orders as needful. But usually it was only necessary to make known what was wanted, what needed to be done.

It was the better part of an hour before Kristal's commset chirped. When he switched it on, his screen was split, showing both Bosler's face and Kusu's.

"Ah, good!" Kristal said. "Wellem, this is mainly for you, but Kusu needs to be in on it too." Then he read them a message to His Majesty, a message that had just come by pod from Tyss, from the Grand Master of Ka-Shok. One of their seers had discovered the Klestronu flotilla in the Confederation Sector, parked off Tyss. It was looking for habitable worlds, and decided that "Oven" didn't meet their criteria of habitability.

"That was twenty-eight days ago. It could already have landed on some other world, and it might not be known on Iryala for weeks."

"But the Ka-Shok are monitoring it again?"

"Right. But there's still that twenty-eight-day communication lag. That's one reason I'm calling you. Can you meld with their monitor? You or anyone else you know of on Iryala?"

Bosler frowned. "I've never melded with anyone as far away as the next room. Very few can meld without eye contact, and of the few who can, it's generally with someone they know and have strong affinity with." He paused thoughtfully. "When we're done with this conference, I'll see what I can come up with. I have an advanced student who might, just conceivably, work out. Meanwhile I recommend you check with the other institutes."

Kusu spoke then. "Why didn't the Ka-Shok have one of their seers connect with you, Emry? Or with Bosler? That'd take care of the lag."

"They recognize the situation. But they're communicating by message pod, so there may be technical reasons. On the other hand they may simply have chosen not to. I don't try to understand the Ka-Shok; I believe the word is 'inscrutable.' Wellem?"

Bosler shook his head. "They have reasons, I'm sure. Which can be as trivial as curiosity about how we'll handle the situation, or as profound as"—He gestured. "As curiosity about how we'll handle the situation."

Kusu grunted. "Did the Ka-Shok alert the warrior lodges?"

"It wasn't mentioned," Kristal answered. "They may have, of course, but they may not have. The war lodges are rather like the Ka-Shok in that respect: They look at things in their own way, with their own sense of importances.

"But even if they had alerted the lodges, it could easily take a dek or more to get a troopship from Tyss to wherever it was needed. Assuming they had a regiment available at the time. Or a fledgling regiment they were willing to send short of graduation, which seems very unlikely. But then, this is not the sort of thing that's come up before.

"And Kusu, that brings up what I need to talk with you about. How ready is the teleport for the interstellar transfer of humans?"

"Umh!" Kusu's response was a grunt, almost as if he'd been elbowed in the stomach. "You're talking about people who've been through Ostrak Procedures of course. We're not nearly ready. Haven't been looking at the problem as urgent. The people working on it didn't even come down last weekend. Family activities."

"When *can* it be ready?" Kristal asked.

"I don't even have a respectable guess for you; I haven't been following their progress very closely lately. I'll get in touch with them today, get a status report for you, and tell them we have an urgent need. That's the best I can do. That and start an independent analysis of the problem myself, when I have their report."

"Hmm." Frowning, Kristal pursed his lips. "If you had to guess, are we looking at a dek, two deks? A year?"

"Possibly as soon as a couple of deks. If all we have to do is get people onto a planet's surface. Getting them on the right continent is something else."

"Is there any reason I can't have the teleport from Ernoman?" Kristal asked. "For Blue Forest? How long would it take to build another?"

"You're welcome to the one at Ernoman. And I can have another one ready within about a week. Meanwhile if you can get some qualified people sent here from L.U., we can start building a large one for teleporting smaller teleports to places. Along with small floaters—things like that."

"Good. You asked for qualified people. Give me some names and I'll see what I can do."

Kristal's fingers quick-stepped on his keyboard while Kusu named. There weren't many. *We've got too few scientists in The Movement,* Kristal told himself. *And in the culture at large. And too few highly qualified technicians.*

The long-term job was to transform the Confederation from a calm but stagnant, firmly aberrated order to a sane one, from quasi-religiously imposed conformity under the Sacrament to consensus under the T'sel. The recognized priority need, toward that goal, had been for human services—the delivery of Ostrak Procedures on twenty-five Confederation worlds and two key trade worlds. All of it very quietly, covertly.

The job had been more dangerous when virtually the entire population was under the Sacrament, although caution was still important. But so was acceleration now, because with the Sacrament defused, the problems of slow but accelerating centrifugal forces in society would surely assert themselves. And strain the fabric of a confederation that had long depended on the Sacrament, the canons of Standard Practices, common origin, and basic cultural similarities to compensate for vast distances, slow communication, and little personal contact. The first signs of strain were evident already, small but unmistakable. So The Movement, under Crown leadership, was trying to shorten the job from centuries to hopefully not more than three generations, with the hump to be crossed within fifty years.

Now the Klestronu expedition was complicating and crowding the timetable.

Bosler spoke when Kristal had finished writing the names he'd been given. "If you're considering teleporting the regiment from Blue Forest," he said, "we need to run them through more Ostrak Procedures. Some might arrive safely, but I've examined Lotta's analysis of the experimental animals, and I can almost guarantee a dangerous fiasco if we send our young warriors as they are."

Kristal bobbed a nod. "Right. Which leads to my next question: Can you get them all processed in, say, a dek?"

"It's barely conceivable. Two or three deks seems more likely. It depends on how much need we'll have for advanced procedures. There aren't many operators qualified to use them; not on Iryala. They're scattered all over the sector."

His Lordship's gaze was steady. "Do what's necessary. I'll back you. But don't disrupt other work more than you need to. Kusu, I'll get you the people you need to make the larger teleport.

"Meanwhile I'll have the teleport at Ernoman flown to Blue Forest. Wellem, I suppose you'll have to establish the hard way what case levels can be teleported safely. If you want to, use trainees for your tests."

His Lordship straightened. "We'll talk again at 2000 hours, or sooner if necessary. Any questions you need to ask right now?"

There weren't.

"Good. At 2000 then."

Kristal cut the connection. Each of the others began at once to jot down a working plan.

# 34

When she stepped into the Main Building, Lotta smelled fresh lumber again. Of course. The Blue Forest Reservation was on loan from the Army, which had used it at intervals over the centuries. The Main Building had been built not only as reservation headquarters, but as an officers' dormitory, and the new interview rooms, like the old, would have been made by subdividing offices and sleeping rooms.

Her team got brief instructions in the lobby, then went to find their sleeping rooms.

The one she'd been assigned was a virtual duplicate of the one she'd been in before, but instead of two beds, it now had two double bunks and two large dressers, and the couch was gone. A narrow metal cabinet had been added in the bathroom. She unpacked and put her things away, then the four of them found their supervisor's office, knocked, and were let in. Eight empty folding chairs were crowded in front of a desk.

Two people were there ahead of them, both middle-aged: a woman behind the desk, and a man standing. Lotta had never seen either of them before. "You're from Lake Loreen?" the woman asked.

As senior in operating qualifications, Lotta answered for her team. "Yes ma'am."

"Good. We'll start when the others arrive." Gray eyes examined them briefly. "You're Lotta Alsnor?"

"Yes ma'am."

"Were all of you in the previous project here?"

"We four were. Two of the other Lake Loreen team weren't; they're brand new Intern-Twos."

There was a knock. The other four entered and took seats.

"All right," the woman said. "We'll get started. I'm Meteen Voranis Kron, your supervisor." She gestured at the man. "This is Jomar Kron, my husband and your bail-out operator." She grinned. "The ideal is not to need him. We were here in Iryala, vacationing from Rombil, and Wellem tabbed us for this emergency project; we're old students of his. Which of you are the new I-Twos?"

A boy and girl of fourteen or fifteen raised hands.

"Congratulations." Her eyes took in the rest of them then. "I suppose you all got a technical briefing before you left Lake Loreen."

"Yes," Lotta said, "from Wellem over the comm. But it was short and pretty general."

"I'll give you another. You can ask questions afterward.

"There'll be eight teams of us—fifty-three operators plus eight bail-outs. Wellem is in overall charge, of course. Jomar and I are Masters. We've spent the last five days here with Wellem, setting things up.

"We selected a sample of twenty trainees, stratified by case level, to send through the teleport. Ran them through 'a space-time loop,' as Kusu calls it, bringing them back to the same place and same time they'd left. The level 5s weren't fazed by it. Which was expected, but we had to know for sure. They knew something had happened, but that was all. The 4s were disoriented and more or less spooked, but they weren't a serious problem. We snapped them out of it with two or three minutes of 'Look at That.'

"The 3s came out either scared stiff or semi-comatose, but at least we could get through to them. Took a little while though to get them back to normal. Had to give them each a session."

Meteen smiled slightly. "We almost didn't send a 2 through; we could assume he'd be worse. But would he be manageable? It was worse than we'd thought. He came out totally berserk—it was a good thing we had a couple of T'swa on hand to control him—and for a little bit we thought we might even lose him, it was that bad.

"And of course, we don't have any 1s or zeros here. The earlier project took them all at least to 2s."

Again she smiled. "We sent a T'swi through too, just for the record. All he had to say was, 'Interesting.'"

"So—" She paused and looked them over again. "We have a lot for you to do. The 5s don't require any processing, but there are only three of them in the regiment. We need the whole 2,000 at 5. That's our job, ours and the other five teams. Sixty-eight percent are 2s, which any operator in the project can upgrade to 3s. Another twenty-seven percent are 3s, which most of you can handle. Roughly five percent, a total of ninety-one, are 4s. They'll require Experts, which we're short of." She scanned them. "Lotta and Bart— Which one of you is Bart?"

He raised his hand.

"I presume you're aware that Wellem has raised you to provisional E-Ones. Congratulations. He says you can handle it, and if he says so, you can.

"Granted it usually takes only one session—seldom more than two— to take a 4 to Level 5. But we've got nearly 2,000 men here who'll need a session or two from an Expert or higher. And aside from supervisors and bail-outs, we've only got eleven E's or higher in the project.

"And we can't have the bail-outs doing routine sessions. They have to be available when an emergency comes up. While the supervisors will have their hands more than full, supervising.

"Wellem's gotten agreement from a number of E's to come and help out when the 4s start to pile up on us. You may not appreciate how few Es and Ms there are on Iryala, planet-wide, or on any world; not nearly as many as there'll be ten years from now. For too long the need for lower-level operators has had the institutes sending most of us out when we'd reached journeyman."

She scanned them again, grinning now. "So you journeymen—that's Feelis and Norla and Rob, right?—as much as we need you to process Level 2s and 3s, in the evenings you'll be training instead, under Jomar. We plan to make provisional E-Ones out of you, to help with the 4s. It'll be a crash course, but we're depending on you.

"Any questions?"

There weren't.

"Fine. The exception to that is tonight. All of you will be giving sessions this evening." Meteen got up and gestured. "You'll find the summary and instruction for your next trainee on a shelf in the ready room, above your name. Now I'll show you what session rooms are yours. You'll be there no later than 1845 this evening, and familiarize yourself with the case summary. A page will bring your trainee to you at 1900.

You'll get another one at 2100, unless the first one gets into something that takes unusually long to lead him through."

They left the small office then. To Lotta's surprise, she had the same session room as before. She still had time to look up Bosler, if he was available.

Bosler was tied up, so she waited till supper and caught him on his way to the dining hall. They got their food and sat down side by side; their conversation was casual until they'd finished eating.

"So," he said then. "What is it you need from me?" Lotta's gaze, as always, was direct. "I'd like to give a session, sort of, to Artus Romlar. Tomorrow evening would be a good time."

Bosler's eyebrows raised slightly. "Romlar's a 5. In fact, he's already been through the teleport. Unfazed. I have no session lined up for him at all."

She nodded. "Right. I'd like to give him one anyway."

" 'Sort of a session,' you said. What do you have in mind? An Expert-One is pretty limited in what they're qualified to do with a 5."

"I know. I want to do a meld with him."

Wellem Bosler wasn't often surprised. He was now. "Before I ask you why," he said, "let me remind you that that's tricky business with a 5. For an E-One certainly; especially a provisional. If he was a Level 3 or 2, it would be pretty safe; most 2s wouldn't even be aware of a meld, and most 3s probably wouldn't know what was going on—feel a bit spooky perhaps, or exhilarated. While a 7 and probably most 6s have enough stability to deal with it easily. But a 5's got a lot of power freed up, Romlar especially. The meld could easily get out of control. Then we'd have to bail you both out, and it could take awhile." He eyed her curiously. "What do you hope to accomplish?"

"I'm not sure. But you know what he is, what his potential is. And you said you wanted to get him in session again before he left Iryala."

"Hmh! I did, didn't I. I've had so much to do, I'd lost track of that. But—" He smiled slightly. "I was talking about me, not you. Supposing that's what we do? I'll give him a session—get him up to a 6—and maybe you can meld with him then. Will you settle for that?"

"I'd like to have you give him a session. But meanwhile, I'm asking to do a meld with him myself. As he is."

"Hmm." Bosler frowned, contemplating the suggestion. Ordinarily he'd have said no, out of hand. But ordinarily the matter would never have come up. And Lotta Alsnor had more native talent than perhaps any student he'd ever had. Including Meteen Voranis. Someone like that needed as free a rein as possible, when their intuition spurred them.

And when someone as sane and talented as Lotta asked to do something crazy-sounding, he couldn't help but wonder if she was giving birth to a breakthrough of some sort.

Although he still couldn't see what a meld would accomplish. Melds were not in themselves therapeutic.

"All right," he said after a slow minute. "I'll speak with Meteen about it. If she's willing to spare you, you can have him tomorrow evening. I'll have her alert Jomar, in case you get into trouble. And you be sure your monitor is on before you start, so he can keep half an eye on you."

She nodded soberly. "Thanks," she said. She got up and took her tray to the wash belt, then left, wondering if she really had any business doing what she'd proposed. She caught herself half hoping Meteen would refuse.

# 35

Romlar came in and closed the door behind him. "Hi, Lotta," he said cheerfully, and sat down. "I hadn't expected to see you again."

She smiled. "I hadn't expected to be here again. How have things been going?"

"We're doing battalion exercises now. And good old 2nd Platoon's been hogging the command posts. Coyn Carrmak and I have been switching off as battalion commander and battalion EO. And Jerym is A Company exec under Eldren Esenrok, when it's not the other way around."

"Well! Congratulations! Did you have a good supper this evening?"

"Always. Almost always."

"Good. Did you get enough sleep last night?"

"Yep."

His aura reflected good health and good spirit. "All right. We'll start the formal interview then. I want you to sit back and relax. Get nice and loose. You can close your eyes if you'd like."

He did.

"All right. Now just let your mind relax too. Let it drift if it wants to. And if you feel anything strange happening, it'll be all right. Just let it happen and ride along with it. It'll be no big deal."

He didn't nod, didn't move, just let himself go. For almost all his life, it would not have been possible except while falling asleep; resentments, worries, and thoughts had tended to crowd his mind. Now letting go was easy. An idea drifted through and he watched it pass, was aware of watching it, then aware of its absence, all very relaxed and unimportant.

Then something else was there that for a moment he couldn't identify. His awareness sharpened a little with curiosity. Of course! [Hello,
Lotta! What are you doing?]

[It's called a meld. Our minds join.]

[What do we do next?]

[Relax and let things happen. Or not happen.]

His awareness softened again. Another thought came to him. His
thought? Or hers? He decided it didn't matter. After that, for a while,
nothing seemed to be happening, and he lost track of time. There was
time, but he had no real notion of how much was passing. His main
awareness was of a sense of intimacy and dormant power, power that
was his and that he hadn't recognized before.

Then he saw his own face, as through Lotta's eyes, and the thought
was there, her thought, that it was time to separate. [All right,] he thought
back to her. And felt her withdraw slowly, gently, till his mind was alone.

Alone but not the same. He was aware of himself at a depth beyond
anything he'd experienced or suspected. In spite of so little having
happened.

He opened his eyes. "Thank you," he said. "Thank you very much."
And when he left the room, it seemed to him he was bigger, had expanded,
was seeing the floor from a foot higher than before.

Wellem Bosler awoke gradually, uneasy in the dark of his small room.
It struck him then why. [Who,] he asked, [is in my mind?]

[Lotta, Wellem.]

[Huh! Where are you Lotta? Physically I mean?]

[In my room.]

[You can meld at a distance then.]

[I thought I could. After I melded with Artus. I felt such power when
we were together, he and I. So did he. Wellem, you need to have a session
with him. To know where he's at. At what level. He's not just a 5; not now
anyway.]

[All right. And I need to do an eval on you, to find out what level
you're at now. You've changed too, I'm sure of it. Huh! I've melded with
Konni, and with others a few times, and never got any personal change
out of it. Never before heard of anyone getting any.]

She didn't respond, seemed relaxed. After what might have been a
minute or two, her mind stirred. [I'm going to leave and go to sleep now,]
she thought to him, and he felt her disengage.

When she was gone, he lay awake for a while. Remarkable, he thought.
He'd heard of a few Iryalans—Masters like himself, and Experts—who
could contact friends at a distance, perhaps on another continent, and
might even meld with them. The T'swa of course had a long history of

producing seers who could meld at a distance with almost anyone, as if distance didn't exist for them. But the entire population of Tyss knew the T'sel—or ninety-nine percent did, something like that—and had for millennia. They'd long since needed no procedures to gain it. And every T'swi who was born to Wisdom/Knowledge was trained as a seer. It wasn't terribly remarkable that some, a few of them, could find and meld with someone hundreds of parsecs away.

And now— His psyche quickened. Could Lotta learn to? Learn to find the T'swa seer? Or even the Klestronu flagship and its captain? He'd have to look into this, even if it required slighting his work a bit as project leader.

# 36

Voker's commset chirped. He touched a key. "Yes?"

"Sir, Lord Kristal wants to speak with you."

"Thanks." He touched another key and the screen lit up. Kristal was sitting at a desk which, by Voker's criteria, was cluttered. "Good morning, Your Lordship."

"Good morning, Carlis. His Majesty and I have a plan. I want to run it by you before we decide on the details and implement it."

"Okay."

"We want to publicize the regiment. Judiciously of course. And later the Klestronu intrusion—and the teleport. The Klestroni will be used to make the teleport necessary and acceptable. It's touchy business of course. Some thirty percent of our population on Iryala, more than fifty percent in the Confederation as a whole, underwent a real Sacrament as children. And a lot of the rest are about as conservative, if less compulsively so. But circumstances seem to be forcing our hand. And if we handle it well, it will broaden the public tolerance of change.

"Varlik Lormagen's publicizing of the T'swa did wonders for us thirty-two years ago. So we've been screening feature journalists. Women, mainly."

"Emry," Voker interrupted, "a suggestion. Whoever it is should be in excellent physical condition. If she or he's going to follow these young men around effectively enough to get to know what they do."

Kristal nodded. "Good point."

*And chances are, you've already considered it,* Voker told himself.

"Another thing," he added: "Any such person around here just now, or for the next two or three weeks, can't help but be aware of the Ostrak Procedures, and wondering what it is that involves so much time and activity. Are you willing for that to become public?"

"Obliquely, yes. Wellem suggested we call it 'special psychological drills to provide the trainees with T'swa calmness of mind. Very useful for fighting men.' Which is the truth, presented from a particular point of view. But we won't send her to you till the larger part of the activity is over with, and all the men have been processed to 3 and higher. Quite a few will be 5s by then, and done with."

"Umm." Voker cleared his mind for a moment, to let anything else come up that needed to. "And you're going to publicize the teleport too, you say."

"Yes. Assuming the Klestroni land in this sector in other than a properly peaceful, ambassadorial manner."

*Which makes disclosure close to a certainty,* Voker told himself. "What cautions shall I give the trainees? What shouldn't they say?"

"Wait till we've selected the young lady. I'll let you know."

Kristal shifted subjects. "Meanwhile Kusu's people are assembling a teleport for shipment to Tyss. We're sending it on a fleet supply ship, with a pair of technicians to operate it. They'll leave in four days if no complications arise, and it'll take fifty-one days to get there by hyperspace. Including a quick stop at Terfreya to deliver some new-model equipment to the cadets there."

"Why not send the teleport directly to Tyss, and send the cadets their equipment separately?"

"We'd only save four days that way. Iryala, Terfreya, and Tyss are as nearly aligned as any three inhabited worlds in this sector." Kristal paused. "Do you have some thoughts on that?"

The colonel looked at it, frowning. "I guess not. What time of year is it on Tyss?"

"What? Ah, I see your point. We've looked at that. At Kootosh Moks it's early winter." Kristal chuckled. "If I may use the term."

"How large are the vehicles it can teleport?"

"Small; almost the smallest. Light utility vehicles and armed scout floaters. It had to be something we could construct with components on hand or easy to make. Kusu's still designing the big one, the one we'll send the regiment's vehicles with. Although he has men fabricating parts already. It's quite a project."

Voker nodded. It would be, when most of the components couldn't be bought off the shelf anywhere.

"Oh, and Carlis," Kristal said, "your floater crews should arrive next Oneday morning. All with warrior profiles, you'll be glad to hear, and cross-trained for maintenance. And the eight-man regimental medical team you asked for. They'll all need Ostrak Procedures of course. Do you want me to tell Wellem?"

"No, I'll tell him. I'll be seeing him in a few minutes at lunch."

Having said everything necessary, they ended the conversation and disconnected. *A full contingent of floater crews with warrior profiles!* Voker thought. *Hmh!* He hadn't thought the army had that many warriors in its air branch. Not that six scouts, eight combat personnel carriers, and four gunships required a lot of personnel; mental arithmetic made it 120, with two crews per aircraft.

The sad thing was, their senior officers would be glad to see most of them go. Well, he'd be glad to see them arrive.

He was very glad there'd be a teleport on Tyss. Although he still felt a little—uncomfortable about sending it by way of Terfreya. But a four-day delay wasn't going to mean anything when the war lodges wouldn't be graduating new regiments until equinox there, still a couple of deks away.

# 37

Spring was on the verge of summer, even at Blue Forest, in the Subaustral Zone. The night smelled of things growing, and it was warm enough that Lotta carried her jacket as she walked through the gate into the compound. The new leaves were fully expanded, and the woods behind her sounded with the stridulations of small courting creatures, both insects and amphibians.

She'd found a place in the woods to be away from human busyness, physical and mental, a dry place where she could sit on the ground. She'd been going there at night after her last session. From there she contacted people she knew, people all over Iryala. Melded with them if they were sufficiently advanced and agreed to it, and occasionally if they were unaware and wouldn't be harmed by it. She was becoming adept at this by now, could have done it in her room with others present, but she liked getting away.

Entering the Main Building, she switched off her insect repellent field and walked briskly to the project dining room, where snacks were available for those who worked late. Meteen Kron was there; she'd finished reviewing the evening session reports. After drawing a cup of thocal,

Lotta went to the table where Meteen was sipping joma, and sat down across from her.

"Been practicing?" Meteen asked.

Lotta nodded. "In the woods."

"Have you tried reaching anyone off planet?"

"I'm not sure I know anyone off planet. I suppose I do, but I don't know who they are."

"Did you know Kari Frensler? You were probably at Lake Loreen when she was still there."

Kari Frensler. Lotta recalled a tall, rather gangly teenager who'd graduated and left years ago, when she herself had been—nine; newly nine. "Is she off planet?"

"Nine parsecs off planet. She's on Sandhill's staff on Rombil, with Jomar and me. Teaches history. It would be interesting to see if you could reach her."

Lotta felt a small surge of excitement. "Yes it would," she said. "Especially since I hardly knew her. We may have spoken all of three times. It would be a good test."

She and Meteen exchanged small talk then, briefly, and Lotta finished her thocal more quickly than usual. She'd go outside and sit on one of the benches—it would be quiet there, this late—and try the contact before she went to bed.

# 38

It was the most promising-looking world yet—blue and white, blue-green and tan—ocean and clouds, forest and steppe, and no doubt desert. At higher latitudes, some of the white clearly was snow or ice, even in the summer hemisphere. In fact, the instruments insisted on it. They'd already reported temperatures in the habitable range, though the mid-latitude summer was rather cooler than one might wish. Nothing serious.

And the atmosphere promised to be breathable.

There was a complication though, of course: it had an obviously sapient life form. Broad-band monitoring had long-since found an object bearing a beacon, parked outside the planet's radiation belt. Commodore Tarimenloku examined the object on the viewscreen. Considering its location 55,000 miles above the planet, he told himself, it could be a processor for incoming mail pods, a processor with a homing beacon. It was assuming a lot to think that a race out in this Kargh-forsaken sector would have mail pods, but if they had hyperspace generators, mail pods would no doubt have to be invented.

There *was* radio here, there was no question about that, though only one broadcast source had reached the *Blessed Flenyaagor*. The voice even sounded human, and while that could be coincidence, the commodore was not addicted to coincidence as an explanation for anything. The words, of course, meant nothing to a son of Kargh.

That this object was here at all indicated a reasonably advanced civilization. If it was a pod processor, it indicated a multi-system civilization. And it was already clear that this was not a world with cities or the extensive use of powerful electronics—not a major planet. It would seem then to be a very minor world. Very minor.

Tarimenloku gave an order to pick up the pod processor or whatever it was; it should tell them something worth knowing about the technology here. He also gave an order to be alert for and destroy any missile sent up from the surface. These beings might detect them and send out either a war missile, or a message pod programmed to go to the nearest naval base, reporting an intruder.

# 39

The sides of the tent were rolled up for light, and cadet Varlik Krellzo sat on a folding camp chair, at a folding table, figuring a food supply order the hard way, with stylus and writing board. His rolled-up sleeves exposed arms that were still slender but very sinewy. Varlik was nearly thirteen years old.

A command radio sat on the table, with a long-life power slug. It beeped a standard warning, and Varlik touched the record key, just in case.

After a moment, a voice spoke from it. "Attention! Attention! This is the Confederation Ministry at Lonyer City, with information to whomever it may concern." A sense of suppressed panic in the voice sharpened Varlik's attention. "This morning, at Lonyer City 0746:22, our systems monitor informed us that the pod processor's homing beacon had ceased to signal. At 0829:09, a shuttle lifted from the Lonyer City port to repair the processor. At approximately 0846:43, the shuttle crew reported two nonstandard ships—*repeat, nonstandard ships!*—one of them extremely large, parked in the vicinity of the processor's gravitic coordinates. The processor seemed to be absent. The shuttle crew undertook to return to the Lonyer City port and abruptly went off the air. It may have been destroyed by the nonstandard ships.

"We recommend that you leave your radio on for possible further information."

Varlik Krellzo was on his feet by that time, grinning. When the broadcast ended he tipped his head back. "*YEEEE-haaah!*" he whooped, then got on the radio to Colonel Jil-Zat. Young Krellzo had a definite feeling that he was going to be in a for-real war very soon.

# 40

Excerpts from "Terfreya," article in the *Standard Encyclopedia*, YP 748, Landfall, Iryala.

Terfreya, or Karnovir 02, is a trade planet. Local tradition has it colonized early in the prehistoric era, in the 15th millennium before Pertunis. There is abundant evidence that mining was extensive there for centuries and possibly millennia.

By the historical era, however, mining had ceased. A native spice, *kressera,* had become almost the sole export. It was popular throughout the sector, and Terfreya became or remained a prosperous world. However, in the 2nd century before Pertunis, a substitute "kressera," growable on many worlds, preempted much of the market. . . .

During the prehistoric era, probably in the early years of human settlement, Terfreya was nicknamed "Backbreak." This nickname is sometimes used in the literature, and was the vernacular usage both on Terfreya and Confederation worlds. Presumably it derived from the rigors of hard labor in Terfreya's gravity of 1.19 gee. . . .

The Terfreyan year contains 434.471 Terfreyan days, each day being 26.551 standard hours long, making the Terfreyan year 1.316 times as long as the Standard year. The orbit is somewhat eccentric, the maximum radius being 134 million miles and the minimum 118 million miles. . . . The axial tilt is 24.19, making the swing of the seasons almost as great as on Iryala, but as virtually the entire human population of recent millennia lives in the equatorial zone, axial tilt does not directly impact the lives of Terfreyans. . . . The relatively low solar constant makes Terfreya, overall, somewhat cold, but the temperature regime of the equatorial zone is comfortable year-round, if one disregards occasional chilly periods of winter rain. . . .

In YP 741, the planetary population was restricted almost entirely to a single region, and numbered only 87,911. It consists largely of farm families scattered in locales especially favorable for the cultivation of kressera. There are few villages. The administrative seat, Lonyer City, serves as the center for trade and services. . . .

General Kartoozh Saadhrambacoora[14] had been awake and mostly on his feet since landing on the planet with two of his four regiments at approximately 0830 local time. He'd gotten them bivouacked on farmland near the ridiculously small town which seemed to be the capital of this world. And harangued his officers with the importance of strict discipline. Troops were to stay within the hastily fenced base except as otherwise ordered, keep away from the local females, and in general avoid incidents.

A small crowd had approached the base to stare. And from the way the troops had ogled the women, you'd think they'd been conscious and dreaming of copulation the whole two years, instead of unconscious in stasis chambers. Or did they dream in stasis? He hadn't, but it was hard to be sure about peasants.

The women here *were* attractive, many of them: light-skinned, and either they had little hair on their arms and legs, or they shaved.

With a guard company, he'd personally marched to the most important-seeming buildings, taken the prisoners the commodore wanted, and sent them on a shuttle to the *Blessed Flenyaagor,* where DAAS would develop a translation program for their language and they could be properly interrogated.

At least he hoped DAAS would. The language here sounded more foreign than anything in the empire.

Now he sat down heavily in a camp chair, had his orderly pull his boots off, and his stockings. He wiggled his toes and regarded them with a certain glumness. It was easy for the commodore to say "no incidents." With 4,000 men on the ground, most of them peasants, it was something else to ensure it. But he would try. And Kargh take the soul of the man who caused one, for his head belonged to his general.

# 41

The stadium at Lonyer City had stands along both sides, and its benches, the general had been told, would seat more than ten thousand. Using the now-functional translation program, Saadhrambacoora had ordered a public assembly, requiring attendance by all male adults of the town and district, telling the local authorities to see to it. He'd helped compliance by telling them that the offending marines would be publicly executed there. And that if the stands were not full, hostages would be killed.

Standing with his guard detail at one end of the field, he eyed the now-packed stands. Hundreds more people, perhaps two thousand, stood behind the stands. And many of those attending were females; a strange people, these. The general did not doubt that there were concealed weapons among the crowd, but he did doubt they'd be used. There was a chance they would, of course—a chance that he would not live to eat supper, or pray again to Kargh. But the gunships circling overhead with beam guns and rockets—weapons he'd had demonstrated for the local authorities—militated against an uprising. He was sure the gunships were far more intimidating than the two companies of armed marines on the field, a company along each sideline, facing the stands.

He let the crowd wait a bit, then spoke into his throat mike. Seconds later, two hovertrucks moved through one of the stadium's open ends—the far end—accompanied by two squads of military police on hovercycles, and stopped at what appeared to be the goal line. From his end, Saadhrambacoora now marched onto the playing field. He was flanked by aides, and by a hovercycle on which a translator was mounted. His guard section followed on foot.

The stands were remarkably quiet, and the general's hair crawled a bit, exposed as he was. But to keep the situation in hand, short of nuclear punishment, which the commodore would never consider, something like this was necessary. Almost at mid-field he stopped. From one of the hovertrucks, seven men were removed, seven marines, and marched in chains to the mid-field stripe, each accompanied by a pair of guards. When they were lined up along the stripe, they were ordered to kneel and bow their heads. In his Klestronu dialect of Imperial, Saadhrambacoora urged the seven to pray to Kargh.

After a minute he had one of his aides turn on the translator. Then he spoke to the crowd, the volume high so all could hear. "Inhabitants of the town named Lonyer," it boomed out, "and of its rural vicinity. The seven marines who kneel here are those who forcibly copulated with a young woman of your people. That was an act abominable in the eyes of Kargh, and a breach of military discipline. I will now punish them for it."

He stepped away from the translator, drew his large sword, ceremonial but scalpel-sharp, and walked to one end of the line of kneeling men. Peasants, each of them, except for the sergeant he now stood above. Saadhrambacoora raised the sword with both hands. His eyes were open, almost bulging, fixed upon the nape, then he brought the blade down with all his strength. With a spray of blood, the sergeant's head fell free, his body toppling, and a collective sigh came from the stands as if from some giant who'd been holding his breath.

Grim-faced, the burly general went down the line. The seven had been treated with an obedience drug, but the dose had not been heavy. It had been necessary that they be alert enough to pray. Thus two of the men tried to avoid the stroke. One jerked his head up and back, so that the blade took him across the face, then split his rib cage. He clove the other's skull, adding crumbs of brain to the blood which by then had soaked the front of his own uniform. Of the other five, only three were beheaded cleanly, but all were very dead.

Beneath a moderate layer of fat, Kartoozh Saadhrambacoora was a physically powerful man. But when, sweat covered, he'd killed the seventh, he felt drained, his thick arms suddenly weak. The truck that had brought the prisoners came out onto the field, and bodies and heads were thrown into it. Then it left. Saadhrambacoora pulled himself together and walked to the translator.

"Yesterday," he said huskily, "five marines were murdered and nine wounded, by a cowardly ambush. We do not know what persons are guilty, but some of you do. Thus I declare that it is *your* responsibility to punish them, and the punishment must be death. The dead guilty people must be delivered at the gate of the military compound by midday the day after tomorrow. That is 1200 hours on Fiveday.

"We have hostages from you. If you are late with the delivery of those dead guilty ones, on the first day of lateness there shall be fourteen hostages executed, one for each of my casualties. And fourteen more on each further day of lateness. I have executed my guilty persons; I expect you to execute yours.

"This meeting is now finished. You will now leave."

Saadhrambacoora stayed where he was, watching the crowd move slowly down the aisles and out of the stands. He'd thought of mentioning that while they'd been there, marines had visited a school and taken 100 children hostage. But it had not seemed like the time and place to let them learn of it.

# 42

General Saadhrambacoora crouched beside his dressing table in officers' white pajamas, listening, confused, to gun fire from the south and east, seemingly near the southeast corner of camp. He was suffering one of the nightmares of a general officer; that is, his troops were under attack and he had no idea at all what was going on.

First there'd been explosions, then gunfire—light automatic projectile weapons—then more explosions, different this time, as of mortar rounds. Right after that the gunfire had intensified strongly. Enemy gunfire, because his standard infantry weapons were beam guns, not projectile weapons. Someone had attacked his camp. And as the intensity of the racket seemed now to be lessening, presumably his people were either driving them off or subduing them.

With automatic weapons and mortars, it could hardly be locals unless they had a militia. Which seemed highly unlikely. The commodore would have learned of such a thing from his captive officials.

The bodies of six young men, locals, had been deposited with his officer of the guard at the gate, two days since. In recognition of the act, he'd released half his child hostages. It seemed to the general he had the beginnings of an amicable arrangement with local officials, and with the people here. They were commoners of course, but they did not seem to be peasants, so one might hope for rationality from them.

Going to a door, he pushed a flap aside to look out. His guards were there, guns ready. The projectile weapons *were* quieting; only sporadic racketing could be heard from them now.

A tall figure was trotting among tents toward him—Major Raspilaseetos, his aide. When the major saw his commander, he called to him. "General!" His voice was urgent, with an undertone of relief. Saadhrambacoora beckoned him in, letting the flap fall behind them.

"What is it?"

"Children!"

The general stared uncomprehendingly.

"The attackers! They are children!"

"Children!?"

"Those who saw them say so, and we have three bodies. They are children!"

Gooseflesh crawled. "What—kind of children?"

"Boys. Armed boys in uniform. They seem to be about twelve or thirteen years old. They attacked by stealth, moving about in the camp with knives, killing people silently!"

The general realized with a start that Raspilaseetos was trembling with emotion, which somehow calmed his own nerves.

"And—I'm told they killed men within a hundred feet of your pavilion! They must have seen it but not come to it."

Inside the officers' area then, despite the fence and guards.

"And the shooting?"

"Some were discovered in the Third Battalion area, but before anyone could do anything, they had disappeared. The tower guards heard the shouting though, and began to play their lights around. Then someone outside began to shoot at the towers with rockets, and put them all out of action. Right after that, some sort of high trajectory weapons lobbed explosives into camp, and projectile rifles began firing."

"How did they get access?"

"I don't know sir. I haven't had time to find out."

"How many casualties did we take? Approximately."

"Not known. I've seen several myself. It seems these children—" He paused, unnerved. "They preferred to kill two in a tent, then go on to the next. But I have no idea how many tents they visited. Or how many of our men were killed by the shelling and rifle fire."

While they'd talked, the general had put on his field uniform. Now he buckled on his side arms and strode from the tent, his guards falling in behind him, headed for his prefab command center. He'd send men outside the perimeter to hunt for enemy wounded they might take captive. And send for local officials, to learn what they knew. He needed information.

# 43

As its senior officer, Tarimenloku was authorized to have alcoholic beverages aboard ship, but he didn't often use them. It was his observation that to drink more or less frequently meant to drink more and more frequently, which was not compatible with his responsibilities. This evening though—this ship's evening—he was having a *dharvag*, and would probably have another when it was gone.

His cabin was twice as large as any other on board, except for His Reverence's cabin; there was one of those, never occupied, or almost never, on every naval ship. Tarimenloku's cabin also had a window, more than a yard square and very expensive. Through it he could see Terfreya without electronic mediation. A beautiful world. Why in Hell did it have to be difficult down there? Cadets! If those were cadets, what must their soldiers be like?

Sooner or later the Confederation would learn he was here, though apparently no pod had gotten away. The prisoners who should know insisted that only one pod had been sent, and he'd destroyed that one outbound before destroying the rest on the ground. His Chief Intelligence Officer had assured him the prisoners had told the truth; his instruments insisted they had.

He couldn't occupy Terfreya indefinitely. Didn't want to, didn't intend to. His role was reconnaissance, not conquest; he'd landed to get knowledge. The two marine regiments, the first two, he'd sent down for security, and to establish a posture suitable for an embassy of the Sultan and of Kargh. He'd known it was risky when he did it, but it had been necessary.

Now he'd learned enough that he could justifiably go home, and he would if it weren't for those damned cadets. They'd attacked his marines and continued to harass them, thereby insulting Klestron and the Empire. If he ran away from the situation, His Reverence the Sultan would have him impaled atop the palace wall. While the emperor, the Kalif, when he heard, would demand his bones and commit further indignities on them.

Nor was nuking a solution. Kargh would never forgive nuking a planet in other than defense of the Faith. While on another level, nuking might easily bring about a hatred of the Empire that would make the conversion and rule of this sector very difficult.

No, nuking was another way to earn a place on the palace wall, decorating a long iron stake.

Responsibility!

As insurance, he'd sent off seven small pods of his own, carrying the requisite reports to Klestron. It was a hellish long way, and the standard error of arrival location accordingly large. DAAS had computed that five should be sent, to be substantially certain of one arriving within beacon range of Klestron. He'd hedged his bet with two extra.

Tarimenloku raised the glass to his lips again, sipped, and gloomed down at the serene-looking world below, visualizing jungle, and in the jungle, children. Boys with sharp knives, boys too young to know a woman yet, let alone shave. Children slipping among the trees with projectile weapons in their hands and killing on their minds.

It would help to know how many there were. His prisoners knew little about them, their estimates ranging from five hundred to a thousand. The cadets didn't seem to mind taking casualties, though they'd left few enough behind. Their wounded fought to the death. They might lay seemingly unconscious, but with an armed grenade concealed, or a sidearm, then kill the marines who came up to them. So now his marines shot to rags any fallen cadet who wasn't conspicuously dead, orders be damned, and prisoners for questioning had so far been nonexistent.

Probably the salvation of the situation would be supply. The cadets had shown themselves frugal in their use of ammunition, a clear sign that their supply was limited. In time they'd run out, and landing the rest of the brigade had no doubt speeded the day.

He hadn't intended to, but Tarimenloku fell asleep over his drink, waking with a start, half an hour later, to the comm-buzzer on his wall. He reached, touched the acknowledge key. "Sir," a voice said, "we just registered emergence waves."

"Thank you. I will be on the bridge directly."

One damn thing after another! He sighed heavily. It was probably a merchant ship. He'd expect the matric disturbance of a mere pod emerging to be dissipated beyond the *Flenyaagor's* ability to detect it. And there was no reason to anticipate a naval vessel. His information was that Terfreya received one regularly every ten Confederation years, and that the next one expected was four years away. Even the cadets, it seemed, had arrived on a merchantman.

The emergence waves traveled at light speed, but even so, the ship that had made them would be well on its way by now. And surely its captain had noticed that the homing beacon was missing. Would he be suspicious? Were merchantmen armed here? And there was always the possibility that it was, after all, a warship.

Tarimenloku went to the door and out into the corridor. He'd prepare as if it was naval, he decided, and wished that even one of his prisoners was informed on naval armament. He was confident that his own was superior to theirs, in general, but who knew what they might have, what one weapon, that he'd never heard of and wasn't prepared for.

How quickly would it know he was alien? Did they have a class of ships that resembled his? And the troop carrier? Would their instruments discern him before his discerned them?

Then a terrible thought occurred to him: *What if it was a warship from the hostile sector that had somehow tracked him down?* Irritated, he shook the notion off. The odds of it were zero, or nearly enough as to make no difference.

He'd be as ready as he could, and see what, in fact, happened.

Hours later his instruments picked up the approaching vessel. It showed no awareness of him, perhaps because it wasn't looking for him.

Meanwhile DAAS, in its role as gunnery computer, tracked it. He weighed the relative risks of firing at too long a range, thus warning it, against waiting till it saw him, in either case giving it time to generate a shield. It was a computation DAAS couldn't make for him. Finally he fired, at a longer range than he'd have liked, and moments later the screen showed a vivid flash, an explosion. The strange ship came on, haloed by a cloud that disappeared almost at once. He fired again, and its forward end disintegrated. Again, and there was a massive explosion. Then there was no ship there; his instruments registered only debris.

He had his gunnery officer generate a shield, on the off chance that some piece of the debris might collide with the *Flenyaagor*, then ordered the stand-down from battle stations. He wasn't happy to have destroyed a merchant ship unwarned, but he'd seen no acceptable alternative. Kargh did not admire such acts, although he did not actually condemn them. And the Confederation ship could not have been allowed to land, or attack him, or return to hyperspace to notify the Confederation.

# 44

Someone stepped through the door, and Voker's secretary looked up from his computer screen. The woman who'd entered was younger than he'd expected. In her early or mid-twenties, she was tall, honey blonde, and athletic looking—overall quite attractive. Her gaze was direct without being aggressive.

He stood up.

"I'm Tain Faronya," she said. "From Central News."

"Of course, Ms. Faronya. I'll tell Colonel Voker you're here." He bent, touched a key on his communicator. "Colonel, Ms. Tain Faronya is here to see you."

Voker's voice answered through his ear piece. "He'll see you now," the man said, and stepping to Voker's door, opened it. The young woman walked past him, smelling faintly of bath soap.

Tain heard the door close quietly behind her. Her gaze took in the colonel's office without conspicuously scanning. It was orderly in the military manner, but more personal than she'd expected. Shelves held books, some with bright covers, and on a small table, a fringed cloth was spread. Indigo flowers bushed out of a joma mug on his desk.

The uniformed colonel had gotten to his feet. He was a bit less than average height. His stubbly hair was gray, his face abundantly but not harshly lined. He was older, a lot older, than she'd expected, but he stood straight, his gray eyes calm and intelligent.

"Colonel Voker?" she said.

*She's athletic all right,* Voker thought. Somehow though, he hadn't expected her to be so good looking. "That's right. I saw you cross from the floater pad. What did you think of our reservation, flying over it?"

"If it started where the pilot told me," she said drily, "it's *very* big."

His use of *our* had offended, Voker realized, and her tone of voice suggested that the place was too big, a misuse of land. One of the new generation of journalists, he decided, that sometimes felt critical of government; sometimes even expressed that criticism. "It has to be big," he said, also drily. "It's an important field location for training officers, or was till we got it. They held major maneuvers here."

"Where are your soldiers?"

"They're out on a regimental exercise under their trainee officers, an exercise covering about thirty square miles of woods. They need experience in coordinated large-unit movements in forest, where the companies can't see each other and their regimental officers can't see any of them. Coordination is by radio and mapbooks."

"Why aren't you with them?"

"I'm a planner and administrator, Ms. Faronya. Their field training is supervised by a T'swa cadre under Colonel Dak-So. The main reason I'm here at all is that the T'swa aren't used to training young men of cultures and customs other than their own. And they're not familiar with our government and law. I am, and I'm also familiar with the T'swa; I was the army's liaison with them during the Kettle War. Beyond that, for a long time I was an advocate of this type of military unit, when almost no one else was. All of which the Crown knew. So when this job came up, they called me out of retirement and gave it to me."

He'd mentioned the Crown not only for effect, but also because the Crown was a central part of the truth behind the regiment. "Let me show you around the compound," he offered. "A barracks, a kitchen . . . These young men train extremely hard, and eat accordingly."

So he's a *changer,* she thought as they left his office, and realized then that her initial disapproval of him was really disapproval of his generation— a generation like hundreds before it which had refused change. She didn't, of course, know the reason for that.

She'd done an article on the army the previous summer for the Central News weekly magazine, spending two or three days at each of three army bases. Which she supposed had something to do with her getting this assignment. She'd never experienced anything more conservative than the army command there, nor had so little cooperation. Her interest in coming here had grown out of her editor's comment that this regiment was supposedly something quite different.

They talked as they walked, and her skepticism lost its edge. Voker seemed genuinely interested in her assignment, and answered her questions openly, or seemed to. These youths had been misfits, he told her, misfits in their schools and communities, in trouble for poor concentration in class, and for fighting. Here their behavior had become exemplary, their learning ability high.

"Colonel," she said, "you sound like a public relations officer. I'm afraid I'll need to observe them myself before I'll believe it."

Voker laughed. "Of course. That's why you're here, I presume. Otherwise you could have prepared your article by interviewing me over the comm."

Until evening though, the only trainees she saw were a few walking from their barracks to the Main Building. Colonel Voker said they were on their way to do psychological drills, to develop the calmness of the T'swa. She recorded his saying it, of course, but it didn't interest her. She'd been poorly impressed with the psychology courses she'd had at the university. To her, psychologists had too often been apologists for the status quo.

The messhall she looked in on did impress her. Three cheerful, well-fed cooks on loan from the army were beginning preparations for supper, helped by four flunkies also on loan. The flunkies, Voker told her, were misfits of a different kind, out here to separate them from liquor. They kept trying to make their own, but their various fermenting mashes kept getting found and confiscated.

The barracks were—barracks, orderly and clean.

She got Voker's written permission to eat with the troops, and that evening was taken to A Company's messhall. The first sergeant spoke with the mess sergeant, who set out tableware for her at the table assigned to 1st Squad, 2nd Platoon. Somewhere outside a klaxon sounded. Trainees started filing in, took sectioned trays, and were served by the kitchen crew. The mess sergeant inserted her into the line, and she went with the flow, startled at the size of the servings she was given—that all were given. The trainees looked too lean and hard to have been eating so much, and she wondered if the quantity of food was a ploy to impress her.

There was little talking at table; the trainees ate with dedication and apparent enjoyment. The one on her right was the best-looking youth she thought she'd ever seen: tall, tan, and muscular, his cropped brown hair showing the beginnings of curls. The name above his shirt pocket was *Alsnor,* obviously a last name, but it would have to do. "Excuse me, Alsnor," she said. "Is there a rule against talking at the table?"

He'd deliberately not been looking at her; he hadn't wanted to make her ill at ease. Now he did look. "Against talking needlessly, yes. If you want the salt though, or some joma, just ask."

She smiled. She wasn't above using her looks to get cooperation. "I'm with Central News. May I interview you after supper?"

"Me?" For just a moment he looked flustered, then grinned, showing strong white teeth. "Sure. I'll meet you outside after supper." Then he returned his attention to the food. Others at the table glanced at her now, also grinning, and suddenly she was self-conscious. Possibly even blushing; she hoped not.

She left first. Alsnor had emptied his tray before she had, but had gone for seconds. When he came out, he smiled without grinning. "Would you like to walk?" he asked.

"After a meal like that," she answered, "I need to walk."

He led off, sauntering across thick grass, through the long shade of frequent stately trees. Tain had her recorder on. "Where are you from?" she asked.

He told her, and as they talked, his troubled childhood and troublesome adolescence came out. She was surprised to learn that he was only eighteen. They passed the large swimming pool where a dozen trainees already cavorted, lean and muscular, ignoring the ancient warning to wait an hour, or two hours, after eating. The pool, she judged, was about two hundred feet long and half as wide.

"I'm surprised the army built such a nice pool here. Or was it intended for officer trainees?"

Jerym laughed. "Would you like to know how we got it?"

Eyebrows raised at his tone, she said she would, and he told her the story of 3rd Platoon, F Company: of the mugging of Pitter Mellis, the arson, the vandalism, and the hard core troublemakers of the detention section, who'd dug the pool with sledge hammers and chisels in the middle of bitter winter nights.

She stopped, looked hard at him. "You're joking."

Jerym shook his head. "See this?" he said, and pointed. His left eyebrow was bisected lengthways by a scar. "Our first night here, 2nd Platoon had a big brawl with 1st Platoon. That's where I got it." He laughed. "Anyone but the T'swa, the T'swa and Voker, would have sent us all back where we came from. Prison fodder, that's what we were. But they had faith in us, faith and patience, besides which they could whip any of us. Our 400 T'swa could have whipped all 2,000 of us at once, no problem. Colonel Voker fought the guy with the reputation of being the toughest in the regiment, Coyn Carrmak, and beat him easily."

"Colonel Voker did?!"

Jerym nodded. "That was last fall. He couldn't do it now of course, considering what we've learned."

That finished the interview; she excused herself and left. Despite the qualifications Jerym had added to his story about Voker, it seemed to Tain that he'd been lying to her all along. And she resented being made a fool of.

But afterward, alone in bed, she imaged his face, his smile, his keen friendly eyes and pleasant voice. His large strong hands . . . And decided that the rest of what he'd told her had probably been true—the part before the story about Voker. She'd get a better idea when she interviewed more of the trainees.

Jerym Alsnor had spent most of the evening at lectures: one on the use of diversions, the other on the dangers of bypassing subordinate commanders. He'd hardly thought of the woman journalist.

But that night he dreamed of her, her violet-blue eyes, her lips—her long legs. And woke up with heart thuttering, face hot . . .

*Tunis but she was pretty! Even beautiful.* He wondered if she'd dreamt of him. He hoped so.

# 45

The squad had been lying in the woods, waiting. Then the word came and they got to their feet, Tain Faronya with them, and began trotting easily. She was as tall as several of them, her legs as long, and her pack much lighter. Her helmet camera was light too, its focus following the direction she was looking, its pictures approximating closely what she saw in the square on her visor. She was well-drilled in its use; her head movements showed it.

Through the trees she could see the opening where they were to show themselves. Though why they'd do that she didn't know, except that Brossling had ordered it; Brossling, the teenaged battalion commander. She'd heard it on her radio, through the descrambler she'd been issued. Now it was time. Someone in some other unit had reported an enemy gunship headed this way.

It seemed crazy to her, even if the gunship would be firing blanks. It made no sense to do things in maneuvers that you wouldn't do in combat, and ordinarily they'd been keeping carefully to cover thick enough to hide them from aerial observation. Now they were supposed to show themselves to a gunship!

In half a minute they were trotting down a short mild slope and into the opening. It was a wet meadow, about a hundred yards across, she decided, seemingly boggy near the middle. Quickly the ground turned springy underfoot—a little strange to run on. Someone called out and she looked around, saw the silent gunship overflying one end of the meadow, and ran faster. It swung their way. The trainees had begun to sprint, dispersing, and runner though she'd been, fit and lightly laden though she was, she fell behind. She heard the floater's heavy blast hoses, a sound shocking and harsh, making her heart speed wildly, and her legs. Her feet encountered bog, splashed water and muck; one foot hit a soft spot and she fell heavily, jarringly headlong.

Prone, she saw a trainee, Venerbos, with a rocket launcher at his shoulder. The sound of it was lost beneath the coarse frenzied roar of hoses firing out of synch, but she saw the flash when the rocket was fired. It startled her; the rocket was real! Which reminded her that the blast hoses were firing blanks. Abruptly they stopped firing, and the floater, rising, swung away and left. She got to her feet and jogged into the woods, reflexively wiping wet hands on wet shirt.

Her radio was tuned just now to F Company, to which this squad belonged. She could hear Third Platoon's two umpires talking to Mollary, the squad leader, and wondered how many casualties they'd charge them with—how they'd decide. They hadn't been with the squad. The decision would have to be arbitrary, which irritated her, but she supposed there was no alternative.

And there'd been a real rocket, which apparently had hit the gunship!

Several minutes later the umpires arrived, a big-framed T'swa corporal and a lanky army lieutenant. Tain wondered how they worked together, with such disparate ranks. Ground rules, she supposed, but even so . . . They painted each casualty with a red substance, sleeves, helmet, and face. Red for blood, but this blood would wash off and leave no scars. Both sleeves and both sides of the face meant dead; one sleeve and one side, wounded and unable to continue. There were no other casualty categories from this encounter. The squad had been "destroyed": seven dead, one WOA—wounded, out of action. Heavy blast slugs rarely produced light wounds.

"What about her?" the lieutenant said, looking at Tain. "Should she get off free?"

"She is not part of the maneuvers," the T'swi answered, then spoke to her. "Would you like to be a casualty?"

She stared at him, not sure what he was suggesting.

"It would have no practical significance," he added. "You would be free to continue. But if it would make you feel more a part of it . . ."

*Part of it!* She shook her head. Through her earplug she heard Third

Platoon's leader telling the two able-bodied survivors to join the platoon when the umpires released them. The umpires in turn told the unwounded they could leave when ready. Venerbos said he'd stay to give aid to the wounded man, and catch them later.

Tain stared, hardly believing, feeling the growth of anger. They'd abandon their wounded as well as their dead! The other unwounded trainee was already trotting off through the trees, not crossing the meadow again. It was the T'swa corporal who answered her unspoken accusation, his large dark eyes holding hers.

"The regiment is in enemy territory," he said, "isolated, on the move, without means of evacuation. That is the predicated situation of this exercise.

"The casualties will, of course, be picked up by a floater, but not as a combat evacuation of dead and wounded. Simply because they're done with this exercise. They are out of the game now."

Then, without saying more, he trotted off with his army counterpart.

*Out of the game now?* What kind of game was this, where men practiced being killed and wounded? What kind of people were these? She wanted to ask the umpires that, the T'swi, actually. But somehow, just now, she didn't have the will to follow them. Instead she went over and squatted down to watch Venerbos treat the "wounded" man. As if the wound were real. He'd already cut away a trouser leg, applied a tourniquet around the thigh, sprayed something on a hairy calf. He'd even snugged up the tourniquet.

"You fired a rocket!" she said.

Venerbos answered without turning to her, continuing to bandage. "Right. Scored, too. If that had been a live round, I'd probably have crippled the bugger, at least. The umpires on board must have agreed with me; anyway it quit shooting and left."

So the rocket had been an uncharged round, hitting without explosion. "Could it have damaged the floater?" she asked.

"Naw. These practice rounds are dummies and collapse on impact. It left a patch of orange though, to show where it hit. When the floater gets back to base, the umpires can decide whether it's a kill or not."

*A kill.*

She'd come to Blue Forest guardedly pleased at the assignment. It had sounded potentially interesting, and it could help build her career. For five days she'd mixed with the young men—more than kids despite their youth. Watched them train, hiked with them, even ran with them, though she'd run without pack or weapon. Had been awed at their fitness, and gained their respect, it seemed to her, by her ability and willingness to keep up.

Now her enthusiasm was gone. Entirely. This war game with the army's

8th Heavy Infantry Brigade was real enough that she suddenly realized what the regiment was all about. Its function wasn't hypothetical anymore, was no longer something less than real. It was the gunship attack that had done it, made her see it—that and the umpires painting the casualties. She'd heard shooting off and on all day. Once, quite a ways off, it had been heavy, insistent, tapering off only after half an hour or so. But this— This had been immediate and personal.

From Blue Forest, the regiment would go to Backbreak and train for a year in its jungle, probably its tundra-prairie too, and maybe its cold rainforest, in a gravity of 1.19 gees. After Backbreak there'd be a year on Tyss, with its terrible heat and its 1.22 gees. Then they'd go to some trade world or resource world, to die in a war that was meaningless, or get limbs torn off.

She'd thought about going to Backbreak with them for a few weeks, had planned to talk to Colonel Voker about it. Now, suddenly, the attraction had died of acute reality.

She squatted, attention obscured by her thoughts, then realized that Venerbos, his bandaging done, was reassembling his aid kit.

"And now we wait," she said.

"Not him. Us." It was Mollary who answered. "Dead" Mollary. "You can go with him or stay here with us casualties."

She sat groping for what she wanted to say, how she wanted to say it. "And if this had been real," she pronounced slowly, "real bullets, some of you'd be really dead by now!"

"Right. Maybe all of us." Mollary looked at her without his usual grin. Not, she thought, because the enormity of it had gotten through to him. It hadn't; she was somehow sure of that. But because he read her mood and realized that a grin would offend her. "And the gunship," he went on, "might be lying out there in the grass, smoking. Unless Venerbos had been one of the casualties too, hit before he could get his rocket off. The umpires decided he wasn't, probably the ones in the gunship."

Tain looked hard at him. "Do you know what you're really doing here?"

His eyes met hers calmly. "Maybe not. I thought I did."

"You're practicing dying."

"Not really. Dying is incidental. We're practicing war."

"*You're practicing dying! And dying is not incidental!*"

"Okay. I understand."

She stared, partly deflated by his reply. "Do you? Really?" Her words were part challenge, part question.

"I think so. You consider death the end of existence. That when someone gets killed, that's it. And that bothers you, pretty badly."

Her gaze, her perception, seemed to change, become dreamlike, as if her eyes had photographed him and she was looking at the print, a print with definition sharper, colors more vivid, than reality: sandy hair, blue eyes, his cheeks tan where the paint didn't cover them. "And you don't think so?" she heard herself ask.

"That's right," he said quietly. "I don't." Quietly as if, again, to soften the impact on her.

She remembered some of the trainees going to the Main Building in the evenings. When she'd asked about it, asked to accompany one of them, she'd been refused, almost the only refusal she'd received with the regiment. The drills, what the trainees did there, she was told, were personal and confidential. She'd gone to Voker then, hoping he'd overrule the refusal, but he hadn't. They were doing psychological drills, he'd repeated, to develop T'swa calm. *There's another way of putting that,* she told herself now. *They've been psycho-conditioning these kids with some technique they didn't tell us about in Psych A and B. Something T'swa that they probably don't even know about at school.*

A chill ran over her. "So," she said, also quietly. "What *do* you think happens when you die?"

"What are the possibilities? It's either the end or it's not. To me—I recycle. Maybe take a vacation first."

"And if you're wrong? If you don't?"

He shrugged. "If I don't, I won't know the difference because I won't exist anymore. But that's not real to me."

*What do you say to something like that?* she asked herself, and getting to her feet, walked toward the opening, the meadow.

"Tain," Mollary said from behind her, "don't show yourself in the opening. A gunship might see you and waste his time strafing here when we're already dead. It wouldn't be fair."

*Fair!* His warning seemed to her an accusation, and she glared back at him without answering, then sat down a little ways within the forest edge, absently switching her recorder from *on* to *wait.* It would turn itself back on in response to any voice. Taking out her mapbook, she played angrily with it, hardly noticing what she did. Another matter surfaced in her consciousness: Why had they shown themselves to the gunship? To get an open shot at it? Would they sacrifice a squad for that? She couldn't think of any other reason, and the thought added to her anger.

She remembered the girl she'd met the evening before, on a late walk. Lotta. They'd strolled together, talking, and Tain realized now that while Lotta had learned a lot about her, she'd learned nothing about Lotta. The girl looked no more than fifteen or sixteen, but had to be in her twenties. They'd said goodnight at the reception desk—perhaps guard station was a better word—she turning off toward the guest section, Lotta turning in the direction the trainees went for their drills.

It occurred to Tain now that Lotta might know something about those "drills," and she determined to find and ask her.

Less than twenty minutes later, a floater landed. She boarded it with the casualties and it took off for the compound. By then her mood had recovered somewhat, to mildly aggravated.

The dispatcher wouldn't send a floater to take her back to the platoon. That would tell the "enemy" where troops were. Tain wasn't really disappointed. It was nearly supper time, and she'd been with Third Platoon, F Company, since daybreak. So she was tired, despite her hobbies, recent and not so recent—dance and gymnastics in lower and middle school, track in upper school and college, and since then, backpacking, orienteering, mountain climbing, ski touring. And the workouts she did semi-regularly to stay fit for the other four.

She'd eat and take a nap, she decided, then look up Lotta and see what she might know about the "psychological drills."

If Lotta would talk. And she would. Tain considered herself a good interviewer—one reason, she supposed, that she'd gotten the assignment. This was only her third year on the job, but she'd demonstrated more than once an ability to get people to open up to her.

# 46

Tain's after-supper nap was deeper than she'd anticipated. It was nearly midnight when she woke up, woke just enough to take off her clothes, stumble to the bathroom, and crawl back into bed. She never even thought of Lotta. And when she got up in the morning, it was to shower hastily, eat hastily, and get shuttled to the headquarters of the 8th Heavy Infantry Brigade, "the real army," where she expected to experience the maneuvers from the other side.

It was not a good day. Brigadier Shiller seemed irritated that she was there, and assigned a youthful officer, Lieutenant Bertol Gremmon, to be her escort. Obviously with instructions to keep her out of the way. Politely and perhaps even regretfully, he refused her request to visit "the combat zone," and to ride a gunship on a sweep. It was, she was told, too dangerous; "accidents were possible." Both arguments she considered asinine.

Instead she spent the day around the fringes of brigade headquarters, a meadow with enough tents and command modules to house a battalion, it seemed to her. She saw officers coming and going, saw them consult, but was allowed to hear none of it. She was also refused permission to interview the brigadier or his executive officer, or any of their aides. They were "too busy."

She kept her pocket radio on at all times however, listening to it through her helmet receiver. The radio itself she carried in a shoulder bag. Voker, a referee and hence a neutral in this wargame, had given it to her that morning with two comments: it would access the brigade's command channel for her; and it would be best not to mention it to them. She kept the volume barely loud enough to hear and understand, and when something on it sounded particularly interesting, she reached inside the shoulder bag, adjusted the volume, and brought out a tissue to dab sweat from her face.

Much of what she heard was too cryptic to be very informative. There were too many shorthand terms, jargon she didn't understand, and an absence of contexts. She gathered impressions from it, but only a limited and fragmentary picture.

Gremmon didn't help much, evading or refusing any question that dealt directly with the maneuvers, till it seemed plain that Shiller didn't trust her not to tell everything she knew to the other side—the "mercenaries" as they called them, or "mercs." Gremmon ("call me Bertol, please") did answer more general questions though, and volunteered some background comments. For instance, the brigade was not at full strength. There were two regiments of mobile infantry, each with its scouts and utility floaters, gunship squadron, and squadron of combat personnel carriers. But the third regiment was armored-remote, and an armored-remote regiment was inappropriate to both the forest and the predicated "scenario" here. So its personnel, numbering about half that of a mobile infantry regiment, were being used as an over-strength infantry battalion, so the army's force here was more like a light infantry brigade.

But a single mobile infantry regiment, the lieutenant assured her, would be more than adequate. For one thing, the mercs were "undisciplined adolescent hoodlums." (Questioning brought out that they'd gotten this reputation within the army from the administrative and supply personnel who'd processed them in.) And secondly, the army's umpires would see to it that the T'swa did not direct the merc's actions.

The army would show those kids how professionals did it.

Tain was smart enough not to waste her time telling Gremmon that (1) the central purpose of the maneuvers was to exercise and test the "adolescent hoodlum" commanders, few of whom were as old as twenty and none of whom had as much as a year's service; and (2) that the "adolescent hoodlums" she'd just spent six days with had been open, poised, friendly, and intelligent. Albeit with some strange viewpoints.

By early afternoon, she and Gremmon were thoroughly tired of each other. She asked if there was material she could read on the brigade, and he was overjoyed to take her to a tent where several clerks sat at computers, writing into them occasionally, watching their screens, and monitoring something or other on headsets. Before he left her there, Gremmon provided her with a chair, a small table, and several manuals and handbooks, putting her on her honor not to leave farther than the nearby sanitary facility they'd set up just for her. He also told a corporal "not to let her get lost," and to see that she got whatever she needed.

The corporal kept her joma cup filled and hot all afternoon. If she'd tried drinking any large percentage of it, she told herself wryly, she'd have come through it bloated and waterlogged. Meanwhile she browsed the material Gremmon had given her, listened covertly to the brigade's command traffic, and thought how glad she'd be when the day was over. She wouldn't give Shiller the satisfaction of asking to leave early though.

On her radio she overheard an interesting butt-chewing. It seemed part of a conference at brigade headquarters, rather than intended radio traffic, as if a microphone was open which shouldn't have been. Tain inferred from things she'd already overheard that the brigade's plan was to catch the mercs, or the bulk of them, in the smallest block possible surrounded by roads. Then locate armored mobile gun batteries at frequent intervals, with troops dug in between them; clear fields of fire; sweep the area with gunships, hosing anything that moved; lay artillery and lobber fire into areas where merc concentrations were thought to be; and in general to pound on the merc while keeping him at arm's length. Meanwhile the merc would be living out of his pack, and had only the ammunition he carried on his person.

It made sense.

The butt-chewing occurred when someone suggested to Shiller that they airlift troops to engage the enemy in the forest, causing him to expend his ammunition much faster. Shiller exploded. Couldn't "the damn fool" remember twenty-four hours? From the content of the lacing Shiller gave the man, Tain gathered that they'd airlifted a rifle company in the day before to test the enemy in the forest, and within thirty minutes, umpires had counted the entire company killed. The [unprintable young hoodlums] had taken no prisoners.

She remembered the prolonged firefight she'd heard the day before, and supposed that was it. She also caught herself justifying the refusal to take prisoners: The regiment was operating in enemy territory as more or less separated units, without air or any other support services, and keeping to cover, with high mobility their only tactical advantage.

Through it all, her little audio recorder was power up, keyed on by every human voice and strong sound that reached it, either live or on the radio.

In late afternoon, at about 1620 hours, Gremmon returned to tell her that a floater was standing by to take her to the compound whenever she was ready. That, she told herself, would give her time for a relaxing shower before supper at 1800, and she accepted. On the short flight to the compound, she thought how odd it was, after yesterday, to be pulling so strongly for the regiment to win this war game.

After supper she went to Voker's office. Ford, his secretary, told her that Voker was gone, standing a shift as referee. She already knew that a team of four referees was over the maneuver area at all times, in a specially equipped floater, monitoring and evaluating the maneuvers and available to decide any disputes between umpires, the referees being senior. On each shift, two of the referees were ranking T'swa, or Voker and a T'swa, and two were senior army officers.

No, Ford told her, there weren't many disputes. Major General Thromlek, Lord Carns, had been selected by the Crown to assign the army's umpires. Thromlek had been a friend of Colonel Voker's, and was known in the service for his efforts to improve training and organization. His selections would be fair. The Crown itself had assigned the army's referees—younger officers from the general staff's staff. Colonel Voker was quite satisfied that both the umpiring and the refereeing were as impartial as could reasonably be hoped.

After supper she went to the Main Building and asked for Lotta, but was told that Lotta was busy and couldn't be disturbed. She'd probably be available around 2230. Briefly Tain wondered if the confidential services the girl performed might be sexual, then irritatedly rejected the thought. Out of curiosity though, she hung around the entrance to the Main Building for half an hour. Only a few trainees came in for drills— "casualties" home from maneuvers, she supposed. Then, in her room, she printed out and edited her recordings so far, adding commentary. She didn't try to contact Lotta again that night. She needed to go early to bed. Tomorrow would start at daybreak.

# 47

Outside her open window, black night had scarcely been tinged by dawn when Tain pulled on her field uniform. It was a strange-feeling morning, as if she'd awakened in a different time, in a world where the things that happened, and how they felt, were subtly different than she was used to. The birds sounded tentative, chirped instead of sang, as if unsure of the coming day.

Dressed, she went downstairs to a quick breakfast with the referee teams that would stand the day shift together: two T'swa Majors, Duk and Git-Ran, and two army colonels, Vornkabel and Dorsee. They did not speak to her; their name patches were all the introduction she received. Nor did the teams exchange greetings. The two T'swa murmured occasional quiet Tyspi; the two white colonels spoke to each other even less—quietly, tersely, the content obscure.

She did not look forward to her day.

After breakfast, they walked to the floater pad through an overcast dawn that was chill and breezy, like autumn ahead of time. She was glad to climb inside the referees' floater.

She found it surprisingly comfortable. There were three large window bulges on each side, for 180° observation; six swivel seats, contoured and padded; monitor screens that just now were black except for cryptic combinations of letters and numbers glowing patiently blue; and a small stainless steel restroom, sparklingly clean, which nonetheless she did not look forward to using. There was also a kitchenette, and two army orderlies, one for each team, to use it.

One of the orderlies had been assigned to orient her, which he did quietly and concisely. Each seat had a terminal; she was not to use hers. And there was a speaker over which relevant umpire traffic would be received; also a headset for each referee and one for her, that made them privy to the command traffic of both forces.

They took seats and the floater lifted. Apparently someone called for a situation update. The monitors lit up, rolling for them the events of an evening and night which had had little to report. As if, she thought, the opposing forces had recessed for darkness and gone home to bed.

In minutes their floater parked over the approximate center of the maneuver area, then the floater with the nightshift bobbed a salute and left for the compound. Somewhere down there, she told herself, was F Company, and what was left of 3rd Platoon. Taking out her mapbook, she called up the largest-scale quadrangle she was sure applied, locating landmarks she could see on the ground—ponds, a stream, small scattered bogs, a grove of dark and particularly lofty koorsas towering above the canopy of broad-leafed trees—and from these approximated her present position. From her window she could see two army recon floaters some distance off, parked at a similar altitude, no doubt with instruments and possibly eyes watching for movement below. She suspected that two more were visible from the windows on the opposite side.

There wasn't a lot of command traffic yet from either force, and what there was was mostly army. The regiment's command channel had traffic only now and then. The army's dealt mainly with troops moving on the road, and gunship reports. As best she could, Tain related these to her map and to what she could see from her window, and with her electronic pocket stylus, began to add to the map the army's designations for different roads. Before long the radio traffic began to make more sense to her.

Something else began to take shape as the morning and the traffic went on. "Little A" was regimental headquarters, Artus Romlar commanding. "Big C" was 1st Battalion headquarters under Coyn Carrmak, "Big J" was 2nd Battalion under Jillard Brossling, and "Big K" was the 3rd. These she knew from her pre-maneuver briefing by Colonel Voker's secretary. But though there was occasional command traffic to Big C, Big C neither replied nor acknowledged. While Big K not only didn't send anything, regiment never sent anything to it! Tain found that exceedingly interesting. She knew that transmittal locations could be read by instrument, and it seemed to her they must be keeping radio silence to prevent brigade from determining where they were. Big J, on the other hand, did broadcast occasionally, presumably on the move to avoid the resulting gunship attacks on its points of transmittal.

Brigade headquarters plotted the two sources of merc command traffic and found them moving on more or less parallel courses. The major source baffled them. It tended to stay in one place till attacked by gunships. Then somehow it would show up somewhere else. After a bit, and to Tain inexplicably, an order came from brigade headquarters to discontinue gunship attacks on sources of merc command traffic.

Except for the early gunship attacks on regimental transmitter locations, almost the only action was attacks by "mercs" on hover trucks—hit and run affairs by platoons of 2nd Battalion—and gunship attacks *on* 2nd Battalion. Gunships responded rather quickly to ambushes on road traffic, hosing the woods in the vicinity. But having spent a day with F Company, she suspected the gunship responses weren't very productive; after a brief strike, the squads would have separated, loping off like wolves, and been well away from the ambush sites before the gunships arrived.

By 0820, vehicles on certain roads were being convoyed by gunships.

Ambushes diminished, and what there were produced fewer casualties, as if made by squads or fire teams—half squads. At the same time, the ambushes having tied up gunships, gunship attacks on targets of opportunity were fewer than they'd been.

The more serious gunship attacks, more productive of merc casualties, were on targets of opportunity—mercs sighted from the air. The sightings were brief but the responses immediate; invariably they were followed by radio traffic between umpires on the gunships and those with the trainees on the ground, deciding on casualties. Twice it was decided that a gunship had been shot down, and twice more that one had been damaged. There was an appeal to the referees concerning one claimed "shot down." The referees compromised. It was badly damaged, they decided, but not shot down. It returned to its base and was henceforth out of action.

On Tain's map, and on the army's too she supposed, the sightings and ambushes built a clear picture of mercs moving westward. The line of march, or more properly the broad avenue of march, was centered on a creek and bounded by parallel roads two miles apart. But judging from the mercs' occasional, descrambled radio calls, this movement was apparently all by 2nd Battalion, something the army of course would not be aware of.

It occurred to her to wonder if squads of 2nd Battalion were letting themselves be seen, the way 2nd Squad, 3rd Platoon had that first day.

On the holographic photomap, she thought she could see where the regiment—2nd Battalion anyway—was headed: If it kept going—big if—by evening it would come to an extensive swamp forest, much of it fairly dense, some of it sparsely timbered but thick with tall brush. Here and there were pools and small round ponds, looking black and bottomless on the map, though she suspected the water was shallow and only the muck beneath it bottomless. Frequent densely wooded humps marked low islands in the swamp, and there were no roads at all. It seemed to her that a woods-wise force would be almost impossible to root out.

But they'd have to cross two roads to get there. The first road was narrow, minimal, a straight, twenty-foot-wide track through the trees. They'd reach it in early afternoon, say 1300 hours, at their present rate of movement, which seemed to her uncharacteristically slow and cautious. The army would no doubt make a crossing expensive. The second road they might reach that evening. It was somewhat wider, and bordered almost continuously by the bare sites of old log decks, making it much more exposed.

About the time she'd put the picture together for herself, army radio traffic began to increase. Armored assault vehicles—hover vehicles—were being dispatched. Troops began clearing fields of fire along the two roads the mercs would have to cross. Tain began to have nervous stomach; emotionally she was definitely committed to the regiment.

At the same time, attacks of opportunity ceased entirely, and so did ambushes along the flanking roads. Second Battalion's radio traffic ceased too. Army command, concerned now that the mercs might change direction and break out across one of the flanking roads, intensified gunship patrols along them. It seemed to Tain, though, that her mercs would hardly make such a move. It would only put them in a different box. The obvious move, the one with most promise, was across the narrow road ahead of it to the west.

Under the circumstances, she forgot all about 1st and 3rd Battalions.

At 1215, hopefully with many of the army's people sitting or squatting with mess gear on their laps, eating lunch, 2nd Battalion made its move to break across the narrow road. The attack was abrupt and intense, the racket of blank ammunition audible even in the referee floater a mile from the firefight. Umpire traffic was just as intense. Gunships swooped and circled like angry hornets. The major merc force—initially it was thought to be the entire force—was attacking one short segment of the road, but minutes later there were swift thrusts at two other points almost at the flanking roads, thrusts so quick, and by that time unexpected, that gunships didn't get there in time to play a role.

By 1235 it was over; 2nd Battalion was across at a cost of "201 killed and 42 wounded, out of action," including those "hit" by gunships after crossing. Tain found herself relieved that the cost wasn't greater, though 243 seemed a lot from one battalion. If it *was* just one battalion. Two hundred and forty-three "dead," really, assuming the WOAs would be abandoned. The army had lost 48 killed and 71 WOA on the ground, plus three gunships destroyed with their crews, and four severely damaged. All in all it clearly suggested that elite training did not balance off fire power, air support, and position.

She wondered how she'd feel if the losses had been real instead of hypothetical. Or if she'd been on the ground with F Company. Things seemed different, sitting in a referees' floater 4,000 feet above the ground.

Her thoughts went on to 1st Battalion. And 3rd. First had at least gotten some cryptic orders, even if it hadn't replied to them. Third had gotten none, at least by radio. Could the 3rd be operating with the 2nd, to make it more convincing in its apparent role as the entire regiment? Perhaps they'd both crossed the road. Or was it with the 1st, wherever the 1st was?

As far as she could see, the army had no way of knowing that Big C and Big K weren't on the air, unless they'd broken the merc's scrambler system. And it seemed to her that Little A must be using 2nd Battalion to mislead the enemy and occupy his attention, *while the rest of his force escaped, perhaps dispersed, trying to sneak free under cover.* Second

Battalion would have to fight its way free, or try to. The regiment's objective definitely seemed to be escape. In fact, it seemed all they could hope to accomplish.

Not long afterward, Shiller himself was on the radio, demanding faster progress. *Progress on what?* Tain wondered. Probably on fortifying the final road, and maybe the flanking roads.

The referees' floater moved, circling at 2,000 feet the road-framed block of forest where 2nd Battalion was now. This block differed from the previous one. Not only was it quite a bit smaller; the land rose gradually from east to west, and the creek occupied a deeper valley, with side slopes that grew higher and steeper farther west.

The north road ran along the top of the slope, and near its west end was what seemed to be an army field command center. A dozen hover modules were parked along the road there, with trucks and armored assault vehicles. For half a mile, in the strip between road and rim, men and reaction dozers were finishing defensive positions overlooking the slope. Behind it were truck-mounted heavy lobbers, and many light lobbers. Flanking this line were lesser defensive positions all along the road. Shiller had something specific in mind for all this, Tain was sure, and had to remind herself that these were maneuvers, the ammunition blank.

After circling the block, the floater parked over the middle of it at 4,000 feet—centering itself among the four army recon floaters parked at the same altitude. Tain was glad to see them there. If she was right about Little A's plans, this meant they'd succeeded to the extent that Shiller was investing his full attention on Big J. Or seemed to be.

Brigadier Barnell "Barney" Shiller sat in his command module, his field operations center, which his troops referred to wryly as "the brain case." He was watching a battery of monitors. And not seeing much—mostly treetops from 4,000 feet, the input of his recon floaters. *Damn mercs aren't bad,* he admitted grimly. What sightings there were were momentary, and scattered widely enough that it seemed the mercs must have dispersed across almost the width of the block. Damn poor targets.

He was also impressed at how little the mercs used their radios. Their main transmittal source, presumably their regimental headquarters, obviously used narrow beam signals, hitting relays that converted them to 360 degrees. That took foresight, and superb performance by whoever was placing the relays. Their regimental commander could be sitting miles away if he wanted.

It was the accurate relay placement that most impressed Shiller and gained his grudging admiration.

And at the breakout, merc point men had worked their way between hose outposts almost to the road itself without being seen. They were only discovered when they began shooting up the outposts from behind. He'd expected a lot higher bag than the umpires' tally of 240. Five hundred would have been a lot harder on merc morale, and made it less likely that a significant number would break out of the sack he had them in now.

He cheered himself, though, with the thought that the final road they'd have to cross was wider, and his people more fully prepared there. He'd *wanted* the mercs to get across the first one; he'd simply intended that they pay a higher price for it. And they would have if he'd known when and where they'd attack.

Actually he'd rather expected them to wait till dark and try infiltrating across. His people had pretty much finished digging in by lunch, but they'd been less than ready mentally. Which was why the outposts had been hit from behind, he told himself.

But that was all water over the dam; he had them in his sack. Work was far along on clearing fields of fire along the west road. A mine layer was busy there, and the electronics were already being emplaced—a bit thinly perhaps, but Storker had assured him they'd do the job. And Storker was clever. Not smart, but clever. Setting a security field was the sort of thing you could trust him to do very well.

Things could always go wrong, of course. If he hadn't learned anything else in his fifty-seven years, he'd learned that. But you did your best, kept options open when you could, and moved with due speed once you'd made a decision. When it was clear that the mercs intended to try for the wild country, he'd known at once what to do.

And had left them with damned poor options. To try crossing any road would cost them. All his gunships were assigned now to road coverage. The least costly road to cross would be the flanking road on the south. But if the mercs decided to cross it, which would cost them, they'd be in a strip only three-quarters of a mile wide, backed up against the reservation's boundary with the Blue Forest Wildlife Preserve. Which was strictly off limits to them, a restriction the umpires would enforce adamantly. And westward on that narrow strip they'd be hemmed in by open bog impossible to cross without being chewed up from the air. As for crossing the north road— His eyes narrowed. He hoped they'd try. That would be the quickest and most satisfying.

Mentally he rehearsed scenarios. The mercs would scout the west road and discover his preparations. They'd probably try infiltrating it first, at night; then, after taking enough casualties, give up on it and try an assault. If they pressed it long enough, he'd butcher them. If they backed off, he still had them in his sack. If they tried the north road, they'd find out what real trouble was. Crossing the south road would be practical but costly, and then where were they? Between the hammer and the anvil.

And if they stayed inside his sack, they'd soon be hungry. Any time they let themselves be seen, his recon floaters and scouts would give the coordinates, and he'd lay lobber fire on them. Sooner or later they'd either surrender or commit themselves to a west road crossing. A few would probably make it into the wild district, but they wouldn't be a regiment or even a battalion any longer. The referees would call the game finished, and he'd have shown the Crown that T'swa-type forces were no match for well-led regulars, that they'd built their reputation on fringe planets—trade worlds and gook worlds—fighting ducal armies, militias, and untrained rebels.

And the general staff would notice who'd demonstrated it. When he retired, in two and a half years, maybe it would be as a major general instead of a brigadier.

"Corporal," said Tain Faronya, "how can I talk to Colonel Voker at the compound?"

"Ma'am?"

"From here, that is. He's a referee on the next shift."

"Yes ma'am, I know." The orderly stepped to the back wall of the compartment and touched a small grid. There was a small screen above it and a slanted keypad below. "Right here. I'll key it for you, if you'd like."

He tapped keys as she stepped over, and when the screen lit up, she found herself looking at another army corporal, presumably at the compound. He put her through to Voker's secretary, who, after a short wait, connected her to Voker.

"Colonel," she said, "I'd like to be out here with the next shift of referees. This afternoon that is. But— Is there any way I can? I suppose you'll be on station up here before we leave."

"Yes, there's a way." He paused, examining her. "Why do you want to put in a sixteen-hour day?"

The question took her off guard. "Sir, I don't know. It just . . ." She shrugged. "How can I do it?"

Voker smiled slightly. "Each referee floater has a hatch in the top and one in the floor, in the utility locker. When we've picked a gee coordinate and parked there, if your pilot will let down to a foot or two above us, I'll have the top hatch open. You can climb out onto the top of our floater and get inside through the hatch."

He observed her expression. "It's safe enough, if you're not overly afraid of heights and if the wind's not blowing too hard."

She didn't answer for a half dozen seconds. "It sounds—scary, but if you'll have that top hatch open . . ."

"Fine. I'll see you in about an hour. Is that all?"

She nodded. "Yes sir."

"Good," Voker said, and disconnected.

She stood there for a minute, composing herself. Maybe the pilot would be unwilling, and she wouldn't have to do it. But she knew that if he refused, she'd give him an argument.

Jillard Brossling lay on his belly, peering through the branches of a fallen tree at the hill sloping up in front of him. He believed in looking things over personally when he could. The trees on it had been painted with orange rings at chest height, in lieu of actually cutting them down. Those of any size were marked with double rings, indicating they'd been dragged away as well. Standard war games procedure. Farther up the slope he glimpsed reaction dozers maneuvering their way uphill, pretending to drag away imaginary logs.

The army was thorough, or tried to be, Brossling told himself. That was for sure. Carefully he began working his way backward to rejoin his troops, half of whom should be napping.

It was dusk, edging into twilight. In charge of 2nd Platoon, A Company, Jerym Alsnor crouched in the woods, waiting. He'd never in his life felt this much responsibility.

The overcast had broken that afternoon, the liberated sun expelling remnant clouds. Seeren, more than half full, would light the first part of the night, which would help, even given the enhanced night vision provided by their helmet visors.

Jerym ignored the mosquitoes. Several times in early summer, the T'swa had left the trainees out all night without repellent fields. Repellent fields ran down in time, and while the trainees had been injected with anti-venin so they wouldn't swell, they'd needed to develop a psychological indifference to being hummed around and bitten.

The T'swa had interesting ideas about psychological toughness. Once the regiment had been flown in to a slaughterhouse, company by company, and had had to crawl around in guts, roll in them, smear blood and slime on their faces. They wouldn't need that tonight of course, but if this were for real . . .

Jerym heard leaves rustle overhead—a bird perhaps, or an *oroval*. Now and then an evening *rast* trilled, like whistling down a tube with a pea in it, but somehow with a delicious sweetness. At school they'd said bird calls were challenges; this sounded like an invitation.

Pretty soon there'd be plenty of noise; enough to cover any sounds they'd make moving up. Even with all the practice the regiment had had that summer, it was hard to move around in the woods with no noise at all, especially after dark.

The dusk thickened. Then he heard the first shots from the enemy positions ahead, shots that quickly escalated into a racket of rifle and hose fire that drowned out the thumps of small caliber lobbers. Supposedly aimed the other way. To 2nd Platoon it was the signal to move forward, alert for pickets whom they needed to get past without disturbance.

Jerym started forward through the twilight, half crouched. Covering the hundred or so yards took several minutes that seemed longer, but finally, through the tress, he saw an opening. There were vehicles parked there. Apparently he'd hit close to their target; the vehicle park was supposed to be opposite the command center. Not half a mile ahead, the army poured gunfire down the hill in the direction of 2nd Battalion. Jerym turned down the exterior sensitivity of his headset and kept moving.

He didn't know if they'd bypassed any pickets or whether there simply were none. Romlar had said there might not be, a statement that had left Jerym skeptical. Reconnaissance had been sketchy, a walk-through by two guys in army uniforms stripped from soldiers jumped the day before. The soldiers still were held handcuffed—the only prisoners the regiment had taken, though technically they were dead.

To Jerym, the most impressive thing was that Romlar had known in advance what the enemy would do. Seemingly before the enemy himself could have known. It had been convincing enough when Romlar had gone over it two evenings earlier, giving the rationale, but to stake so much on it . . .

Standing, Jerym walked among the vehicles to the road. From there he could see no sign of defenses facing north, which fitted the report by the two scouts.

He scanned the other side of the road. There were several command modules down off their AGs, apparently resting on timbers to keep them level. One, the operations control center, was his personal target, but from where he stood, it was hard to tell which module that was. The scouts had said it was approximately in the middle, which would make it a hundred feet or so to his left.

They'd navigated it nicely, with Warden's guidance. Warden had come up with Romlar's talent for intuitive orienteering—for "going without knowing," as Esenrok had dubbed it. To Warden's amusement, Jerym had kept track of their progress on his mapbook, using compass and landmarks, just in case.

He hadn't broken radio silence for two days, nor did he now. After pivoting his visor to the top of his helmet, he stepped into the road and began walking eastward till he was opposite his target. There he stopped. The roar of gunfire was extreme, even damped by the headset control.

A guard stood outside the operations control center, watching him, an anomaly in the scene. Jerym took out a pocket lamp, lit it, and waved its light conspicuously, signalling his men. Then he repocketed the lamp and began walking briskly toward the module.

The guard watched him approach through the twilight. Jerym seemed innocuous: He wore only side arms—knife and pistol—and behaved as if he belonged there. He was within five feet of the guard before the man began a double take, perhaps waking to the camouflage pattern on his field clothes, or the different, visored helmet. Abruptly Jerym's right fist struck him in the breastbone, the trauma paralyzing him, then struck him hard on the neck with a side hand. As the man slumped, Jerym supported him to the ground, then rolled him under the module.

No one had seen. Drawing his pistol, Jerym opened the door and stepped inside. Shiller, who'd been watching his monitors, pivoted on his chair to see who had entered. He started to rise, opening his mouth to yell, and the heel of Jerym's hand slammed him between the eyes. The chair went over backward, the brigadier hitting the floor like a bag of sand. His aide, a captain, grabbed for his own pistol, then froze his hand as Jerym's pointed at his face.

"I don't know what yours is loaded with," Jerym said, "but the blanks in mine would give you a bad burn. Might even blind you."

The army's umpire stared in consternation. The T'swi raised his eyebrows slightly. "Consider that I just shot them both to death," Jerym added, then gestured at the unconscious Shiller. "I couldn't have him raising an alarm. Just a minute; I've got another dead one outside." He stepped out and dragged the sentry in.

"This one we'll say I knifed," he told them. "Quieter that way." *Not,* he added to himself, *that it would make any difference out there in all that racket.*

"Very well," said the T'swi, "all three are dead. But—" he pointed at the radio. "The microphone is open. The shots might have been heard."

"Got it." Jerym was skeptical that they would have, but he raised his pistol and fired two blank rounds at the ceiling, then took an object from his thigh pocket. "This is a blast grenade. I'm about to cripple this place." He shut off the power to the computer-communication central, armed the dummy grenade, pushed its plunger, and laid it on the console, then ducked back out the door and under the module. *The grenade should be going 'pop' about now,* he thought, *and to the umpires that's as good as a boom.* He swiveled his mike to his mouth, then reached into a pocket and switched his radio to the regimental command channel; the need for radio silence was over.

"Little A, Little A," he said, "this is 2nd Platoon, A Company, Alsnor commanding. The enemy's commanding brigadier and his aide are dead. Their operations control center is crippled; I've destroyed their computer and comm central. Oh, and we encountered no pickets."

Acknowledgement was prompt. Then feet ran up to the center, hesitated for a minute outside the door. Someone opened it and stepped in, the other one following. Jerym rolled out and to his feet, and went in after them, gun in hand again, firing more blanks at the ceiling. "Two more dead!" he snapped, and turning, was gone again. One of the last two had been a full colonel; and he suspected he'd "killed" the brigade exec. Now it was time to steal some armored assault vehicles.

First Battalion, with G Company of the 3rd, moved through the woods as fast as feasible in the dark, toward the rear of the hilltop containment line. Shiller had taken no precautions at all against such a possibility. And in the noise and flash of their own gunfire, it never occurred to the brigade to look backward.

Meanwhile men from 2nd Platoon started a number of armored assault vehicles and sped down the north road a mile to its end, their two umpires following in a borrowed command car. The assault vehicles turned onto the west road, their heavy caliber hoses spewing blast slugs. They'd gone half a mile before the troops dug in there realized what was happening and began to shoot back. When finally they did though, their fire was heavy. The umpire channels were alive with traffic.

The augmented 1st Battalion didn't start shooting till they hit the north road, striking the brigade's forces from behind, "shooting hell out of 'em and taking no prisoners." Then some of them too started assault vehicles and headed west.

In the woods below the hill, 2nd Battalion's attack had never been more than a diversion. One company, thinly spread but guns blazing, had made a feint, then drawn back with heavy casualties. It had been enough to start Shiller's entire line firing downhill into the woods. Whenever the brigade's gunnery slackened a bit, a few remnant merc squads would start firing again, showing their muzzle blasts, and brigade gunnery took new life.

Then Little A informed 2nd Battalion that 1st Battalion had begun its attack, and also that the west road line had been shot up and disorganized near the northwest corner. With that, Brossling pulled his men back, and they started westward at a lope to make their breakout.

In the referees' floater, Tain Faronya, switching between command traffic and a buffet of umpire traffic, found it hard to keep from cheering.

# 48

It had been a long but jubilant night-march from the maneuvers area to the compound. Most of the brigade's personnel were picked up by big TTMs at their headquarters area and flown out, but now and then a convoy of army cargo trucks had passed on the road. Each time the hum of their approach was heard at the rear of the column, the word went by radio to Romlar, up front, and he gave the order to double-time. To the army drivers, it seemed that the mercs ran the whole twenty-odd miles back. Their reputation would not suffer from it, and in the soldiers' tellings, the distance grew to forty.

At the barracks, the previously evacuated "dead and disabled" had already been notified of the victory. They'd decorated the barracks with what they had on hand—toilet paper twisted and strung about. The cooks, army though they were, had gotten out more colorful paper to decorate the messhalls, and a feast was ready for the stoves and ovens when the word came of the approximate meal time.

The trainees arrived tired but happy. Shower rooms filled with steam and laughter. Evacuees, some of them, got dragged in with their clothes on. Then everyone dressed in clean field uniforms and trooped to the messhalls for a four-in-the-morning breakfast—a breakfast like none of them had seen before: sugar-cured ham, potatoes and gravy, buttered goldroot, green vegetables, hot rolls with butter, tart *rilgon* jelly, pie and ice cream. There were impromptu speeches, especially in A Company mess, which after all held the trainee regimental commander, the 1st Battalion's trainee C.O., and the man who'd killed the enemy general.

Afterward everyone went to their barracks and collapsed, being allowed to sleep almost till muster, which wasn't till 1300 hours. For most, the afternoon was dedicated to laundry and cleaning the barracks. After supper, they knew, there'd be assembly.

Each trainee officer and noncom, though, got a mini-debriefing by his T'swa counterpart. At 1600, the T'swa met with Voker to give him anything particularly noteworthy that they'd been told.

Tain Faronya had returned well ahead of them, in the referees' floater with Voker and Dak-So. She was tired too, but the stress had been nervous, not muscular, and she wasn't sleepy. She'd looked up Lotta Alsnor, who it turned out was busy with one of the evacuees. So with her repellent field on, Tain went out for a long, solitary run on familiar forest roads, till she was physically tired. Then she showered and went to bed, her alarm set for the normal hour.

As usual she ate breakfast with Voker, his staff, and the battalion staffs, in the command dining room. The T'swa were amiable as always, but there was an added spark, a certain ebullience even, that she hadn't seen before among these scarred veterans of various wars.

She spent her day editing the hours of recordings—audio and video—that she'd compiled during the exercise; dictating draft commentary; and outlining a plan to get the additional material she deemed necessary.

Coming back in the floater, the night before, Voker had let her know there'd be an assembly in the evening, to review the maneuvers with the trainees. She was there a few minutes in advance, on her feet in the rear, a fresh power slug in both recorders, audio and video, her camera helmet conspicuous. At 2003 hours, the trainees began filing in, and while they were entering, she saw a number of civilians, two dozen at least, come in through a side door, the girl Lotta among them. They took seats in a separate row at the rear of the hall, seeming as happy as the trainees.

When everyone was seated, Colonel Voker got up from his chair on the podium, stepping front and center. "Good evening, men," he called out.

"*Good evening, sir!*" the regiment boomed back. The roar kicked in the volume modulator in Tain's audio recorder. It also kicked in a distrust of broad and enthusiastic consonance. The thought returned to her, from days earlier, of "drills" and psychoconditioning. Irritated, she shook it off. She knew these youths, and Voker, and liked them all very much. As she did the T'swa, foreign though they were.

"This won't take a lot of time," Voker went on, "and when we're done, you can stow the benches for a party. But first I want to congratulate you all for the great job you did in maneuvers. Give yourselves a hand!"

The place erupted with cheers, whistles, and the sound of strong, callused palms beating together in what quickly became a rhythmic unison. Voker let it go on for a minute or longer before he cut them off.

"And I especially want to congratulate—" He paused, let them wait a few seconds. "I particularly want to congratulate your regimental commander, Artus Romlar, for his ingenious, and more importantly his successful, strategy. Artus, stand up!"

Romlar did, and the place erupted again. After fifteen seconds, Voker, grinning broadly, once more waved them quiet. "Artus," he called, "come up here."

The big trainee, also grinning, hopped up onto the podium, ignoring the steps, faced Voker and saluted. Voker held something in one hand. He stepped up to Romlar, pinned it on the young man's collar, and stepped back. "The bronze fist of a subcolonel," he said. "Colonel Romlar is now your official regimental commander. Ranks and insignia will be presented to others at ceremonies later in the week." He shook hands with Romlar. "But the cadre and I still rank you, young fellow. Till your training is over. Take a seat now."

"Thank you sir," Romlar answered, and taking the steps down, returned to his bench.

"All right. Now for a brief review. I won't go into details, but starting with less than forty percent of your opponent's manpower and less than a tenth his firepower, lacking any support services, and threatened and harassed by his air support, you maneuvered him into an exposed position with his forces spread out and dispersed. And without his getting the least notion that he was being manipulated. You destroyed his operations control center, killed his commander and part of his command staff, took control of much of his hover stock, totally disrupted his operation, and inflicted substantial casualties—casualties somewhat heavier than your own. In the eyes of the army's own referees, you performed more than creditably; you won the game brilliantly and decisively.

"In fact, Major General Thromlek, Lord Carns, was in the referees' floater during the final shift, and he sends his personal 'very well done' to all of you. He was extremely impressed not only with Colonel Romlar's strategy, but with your mobility, your endurance, and your initiative and resourcefulness as individual units and fighting men. As well as your coordination as separated, sometimes widely separated units, mostly with only one-way communication. He plans to recommend that the army's infantry and officer training be reexamined in the light of what you accomplished out there."

Voker paused and looked his audience over. "Although the army doesn't have warriors to work with in any large numbers. On the Matrix of T'sel, most soldiers are at Work, not Play, and training and tactics have to recognize that. But on the other hand, units of soldiers well trained and led can be very effective. In the Kettle War, for example, a majority of the Orlanthan army was not warriors, but determined soldiers."

He paused and looked them over again. "You've noticed I didn't refer to the 8th Brigade as 'the enemy.' And I suspect that many of you could tell me why. They were your playmates, not your enemy. Just as Colonel Dak-So's old Lightning Regiment and Captain Tuk's Ro-Sok Regiment were playmates when they warred against each other on Gwalsey."

In the back of the hall, Tain Faronya stared, a numbness creeping along her spine as she absorbed what Voker had said about the T'swa. They'd killed each other for pleasure!

"Brigadier Shiller, killed in action at his operations control center, had no comments for us, even after being returned from the dead. For one thing, he was suffering from a concussion. I'm afraid that Trainee Alsnor, the warrior who killed him, slightly miscalculated the impact necessary to prevent the newly dead brigadier from raising an alarm before the umpires could make his death official."

The colonel paused, looked them over. "Incidentally, the umpires who witnessed the event agreed that striking the brigadier, while startling and unprecedented, was not unreasonable under the circumstances.

"Which brings me to another matter. The umpires and referees assigned from the army did a generally fair and unprejudiced job—and a competent job—in their part of the exercise. Although the army in general has not been friendly to the concept of elite forces like yours."

Voker glanced back at the T'swi sitting to one side. "Now I'll turn this meeting over to Colonel Dak-So, who'll look at the overall results with you and give them some perspective. Colonel?"

Dak-So stepped front and center. "Let me add my voice to Colonel Voker's," he said. "You all did very well indeed. I speak for your entire cadre in saying that; we are all very proud of you."

Dak-So's words, in his deep resonant T'swa voice, nudged Tain partly out of her numbness. Pride was something she empathized with, and she did not doubt the black colonel's sincerity. It occurred to her that the drills might actually have been just what Voker had said—something to develop in the trainees a T'swa emotional stability. Something had.

"You performed splendidly," Dak-So went on. "And consider the stated scenario of the game! You were a regiment without support, caught within hostile territory. The opposition sent a brigade to destroy you. You broke that brigade.

"But meanwhile—" He paused for emphasis. "Meanwhile you were running out of food. Your ammunition was seriously depleted, although you might have replenished it with captured supplies. You had lost more than twenty percent killed, and left wounded scattered over many square miles of forest. And you were still within hostile territory.

"The maneuvers were over, but in a sense the game was not. It was simply well begun. Very *successfully* begun, but just begun. You had reached, or were approaching, a time when your strategy and tactics would need to change. What changes you might have decided on would reflect circumstances not described in the scenario provided you."

He scanned the regiment. "I want you to play with these thoughts, and someday soon we will discuss what you might have done next.

"And now—" He stopped, grinned. "We T'swa have watched you grow and develop as warriors. At the beginning, we thought of you as 'the recruits.' Soon that changed, and we thought of you as 'the trainees.' Now, with this experience, this victory under your belts, to us you are more than trainees, though there is still a great deal you will learn. To us you have become 'the troopers.'"

He paused, then continued more slowly, to stress what he would say next. "It is the custom, in the Lodge of Kootosh-Lan, for the novice warriors to name their own regiment. Occasionally they change their minds later, and rename it when they've graduated. You may conclude that it is time to name yours. But until you do, your cadre has decided to call you by an informal name of their own selection. One we feel fits you." He paused again. "After your performance of the last three days, to us you are—" Once more he paused. "*You are now The White T'swa.*"

Tain wasn't sure what she expected. A concerted cheer, or possibly a palpable sense of embarrassment. What she got was a long moment of silence, and a sense of sudden sobriety that seemed could not be hers, must be theirs. Then Artus Romlar stood up. "Sir," he said, "we are honored." His big voice was tight with emotion. "And on behalf of the troopers of the White T'swa Regiment, I thank you for all you've done to help us become what we are—to help us fulfill our purpose."

Romlar stopped and looked around. His voice had been on the verge of breaking, and when he continued, it had lowered in both pitch and volume. "I also thank the Ostrak Project for all they've done. Project personnel, those of you still here, please stand up." He waited while they did, then turned to Dak-So. "Without them you could have made us warriors, but you'd never have decided to call us 'White T'swa.' "

Turning again, he raised both hands overhead, fisted, and his voice became a sudden trumpet. "Regiment! On your feet!"

They stood, and Tain, covered with chill bumps, could feel something building.

"Let's let our cadre and the project both know what we think of them!"

It wasn't instantaneous, but when it came, it was abrupt. The cheering that arose was wild and elemental, more emotional then anything Tain Faronya had ever felt or witnessed. Then the regiment left their places, stepping over benches, some headed for the T'swa, some for the civilians near her in the back. There were embraces, handshakes. The grins were unbelievable, many mixed with exuberant tears, and she stood apart confused, almost in shock, getting it all with her helmet camera, not understanding nor fully trusting, but deeply moved by what she saw and how it felt.

For just a moment their emotion shook Voker almost to tears of his own, and it troubled him not at all that the assembly had come apart as it had. This was needed. So much had happened in nine deks. Nearly two thousand young men whose dreams, whose drives, had been frustrated, had had their purpose validated here, had found themselves and felt their lives salvaged.

Several of them jumped grinning onto the podium, converging on himself and Dak-So. His hand was being pumped. He was hugged.

After a moment the first troopers were off the podium again, but more were coming. Voker stepped quickly to the microphone—he'd need it to be heard—and spoke.

"Men, the assembly is over. When you've finished doing what you're doing, stack the benches and we'll bring the goodies in and continue from there."

Then he turned his attention to another round of embraces and handshakes.

# 49

The music was on cube, by the Garyan Quintet. Tain arrowed to Jerym, shaking off invitations as she went. His back was to her when she got there. "Want to dance, soldier?" she said to him suggestively. His head snapped around, and she laughed. He echoed it, reached out, and they clasped in the daring new style in which the couple dances close together.

"I have an apology to make," she said. "I've been staying away from you. I shouldn't have."

He tilted his head back, eyebrows raised. "Tell me about that."

"That evening we walked together," she said, "you told me some pretty wild stories, and I believed them all. Until you told the one about Colonel Voker beating some trainee, some kind of trainee champion, in a fight. And that sounded so far-fetched that it suddenly seemed to me you'd been lying all along, to see how much I'd believe."

"Ah!"

"I liked you at once, you know. Maybe more than I'd ever liked a guy before on first acquaintance, so it really stung me." She paused, holding his gaze, wondering how he'd take such bold frankness. "Well, I just congratulated Artus Romlar on getting his subcolonel's bronze fist. And I said something like, 'How does it feel to replace Colonel Voker at age nineteen?'

"He said no one replaces Colonel Voker, and told me the same story you did. And that you—the regiment that is—owed Colonel Voker for everything you've become."

Jerym nodded soberly.

"He said you owed the T'swa, too, and the Ostrak Project, that you'd never have made it without all three, but that Voker was the one who guided it all. Is that how you see it?"

Again Jerym nodded. "Voker is our father, the father of the regiment.

The T'swa are our teachers, and the project our— The ones who got us acting sane."

She nodded. "Anyway I'm sorry I doubted you. And stayed away from you."

She paused, started to ask him about the Ostrak Project, then didn't. It might sound as if her apology was a way of getting him to talk, which in fact was what she'd started out to do. Instead she danced closer, felt the warmth and hardness of his body. Reminded herself that he was eighteen and she was twenty-four, and that they had no future together. The music stopped, they stepped apart, then abruptly she stepped close again and kissed his cheek.

It startled her as much as it did him, and she almost fled, then got a grip on herself. "I'll only be here three more days," she said. "And I know you'll be busy. But I'll write to you when you go to Terfreya to train, and I hope you'll write back."

Then she turned and left, left Jerym, left the assembly hall, wondering what had gotten into her. Jerym was scarcely out of adolescence, and she'd only talked to him twice in her life, for only minutes each time; it made no sense at all. She couldn't possibly love him.

But she would write to him, she was sure about that.

She went to her room, wondering what Jerym thought about it. Had she seemed like a fool? Or had he been attracted to her the way she had to him? Was he downstairs at the party wondering? Feeling confused? Frustrated?

Perhaps she should go back down, find him, and take him to the woods or—to her room. The thought troubled her even as it attracted her. It would be cheap, degrading. Not to him perhaps—men were different— but to her.

She stayed for a while; tried to read, but couldn't keep her mind on the book. Perhaps she could go down and dance with others. Finally she got up from the bed and left her room, unsure of her motives or what she might do when she saw Jerym again.

From the hall outside her door, she heard trooper voices filling the main-floor corridor, spilling out into the night, as if the party was over. She went to the stairway and most of the way down, watching them leave. The girl Lotta flowed with them, Lotta who was part of the mysterious Ostrak Project.

Lotta moved out of the current, stepping onto the first step up, out of the troopers' way, as if waiting for them to pass. Tain went down and stood beside her.

"Waiting to take a walk?" Tain asked.

Lotta looked at her and smiled. "Yes, as a matter of fact. Want to come along?"

The place emptied quickly, and they left together. Seeren bulged lop-sidedly white, and the breeze and chill of two nights earlier had been replaced by mellow stillness. The two young women strolled down the main road, its grass newly mown and blown from the right of way, its fragrance sweet around them.

"I'm afraid I'm not a party creature," Tain said.

Lotta nodded. "Me either. I enjoy them, but they're nothing I feel much attracted to. I generally prefer the company of a friend or two—or maybe half a dozen."

Dak-So had announced to the troopers that tomorrow they'd begin parachute training, Lotta said, and that was all it had taken to wind down the party. The troopers had been looking forward to parachute training. On less Standard worlds than Iryala, parachuting had long held a certain minor interest as a sport, but as a military technique, it was unique to the T'swa, who used it for covert infiltration, jumping from high elevations and at some distance from the drop zone, then body-planing in.

Tain decided it was time to turn the conversation to the psychologi-cal drills. "How old are you?" she asked.

"Sixteen."

"Sixteen?!" She peered at Lotta, honestly surprised. "I thought— You look about sixteen, but somehow you seem older."

"I suppose I do."

The road forked. They kept to the wider one, where more moonlight got through to light their way.

"What is it you do here?" Tain asked. "At age sixteen."

"I interview the trainees, the troopers that is, and take them through psychological drills. To improve their emotional stability."

Tain glanced sideways at her. "To give them the emotional stability of the T'swa. That's what Colonel Voker said. Tell me about the drills."

Lotta was tempted to *show* her. Find a good initial button, jump her into whatever opened up, and take her through it. That would really give her reality on it. But the journalist was not to know what the Ostrak Procedures really did. That was the word from Wellem—from Emry, actually. Besides, there were journalists, prominent ones, who'd grown up in The Movement and knew the T'sel. The Crown had brought in Tain Faronya instead, because they wanted an outsider who'd write from a viewpoint closer to the public's. To open her up, even just once, would alter that.

"There's really not much to tell," Lotta said shrugging. "We lead the trainee around"—mentally that is, she added to herself—"get him to look at things." Just don't expect me to tell you what kind of things. "I'm afraid it's not very interesting. It's a lot of repetition; quite time consuming."

Tain frowned. It didn't sound like much. It didn't sound like something that would do any good. "And these are drills the T'swa do?" she asked.

"No no. The T'swa are the way they are because of how they grow up. The philosophy they grow up with. Have you read Varlik Lormagen's book on Tyss?"

"I'm afraid not. But I've read his *With the T'swa on Kettle*. How do the drills make the troopers like the T'swa? Frankly, they don't seem much like T'swa to me, except as soldiers."

"They aren't. The T'swa are from another culture, a very different culture. They're even a different species. Their life experience has been a lot different, and these T'swa are twice as old as the troopers."

Tain nodded. *Three or four wars older!* she thought grimacing. "I spent the first day of maneuvers in the forest with 3rd Platoon of F Company," she said. "And heard some weird things there. Like, death is only incidental, and dead isn't really dead. Does that attitude grow out of the drills?"

Lotta laughed aloud, not only to mislead Tain but to reduce her seriousness. "It does sound weird, doesn't it? But you need to expect a different viewpoint from them. There's one way they're very much like the T'swa: They're inherently warriors. Their psych profiles show it—profiles of their innate personality. That's why they were recruited."

She changed the subject then. "We'd better go back now. I have to work in the morning. Want to run?"

They ran. When they reached the Compound, Lotta was much the more winded. At Main Building reception they said goodbye, each going to her own room.

As Lotta showered, she told herself that this had been her last conversation with Tain Faronya. The woman was too persistently inquisitive.

Interesting though that Tain had read *With the T'swa on Kettle,* and still had the questions she had about dying and death. Apparently what the T'swa had said to Varlik had seemed so unreal to Tain, when she'd read it, that it simply hadn't registered.

Tain lay down and turned off the light. As she composed herself for sleep, it occurred to her that she'd never really gotten an answer, a real answer to her question about the drills. Or had she? Perhaps they were nothing more than Lotta had said. Perhaps she was making too much of it. Apparently the psychs had identified these kids as warriors—or inherent warriors, whatever that really meant—and that could account for their peculiar views.

Interesting that the psych courses she'd taken at the university had never mentioned innate personality.

And if her talk with Lotta hadn't been very enlightening, at least she hadn't run into Jerym again, perhaps truly to make a fool of herself.

# 50

It had taken twenty-eight days for the first report to reach Iryala about the arrival of the Klestroni at Terfreya. Twenty-eight days by mail pod from Tyss. After that they got a new report almost daily.

Master Tso-Ban didn't learn everything that went on with the Klestroni there, although he was spending as much as fourteen hours a day monitoring. For instance, he'd been out of touch when Tarimenloku destroyed the Confederation ship, and subsequently the encounter hadn't entered the commodore's conscious mind while Tso-Ban was melded with him. So the monk didn't know about it. But Tso-Ban sent word of the Klestroni landing, and later the capture and questioning of prisoners, the executions, and the attack by the cadets.

Nor had it occurred to Kristal that the supply ship might have been destroyed. Tso-Ban had said nothing about it, and the elapsed time made it easy to assume uncritically that the supply ship had already left Terfreya, continuing on toward Tyss, before the Klestroni arrived. A simple check of its scheduled arrival time would have corrected the assumption, but nothing happened that caused Kristal to look.

Originally it had been planned that the regiment would travel by ship to Terfreya, after the equinox, for a year of training there. Now the training plan and the transportation plan both were obsolete. For one thing, travel by ship was slow. And it seemed quite possible that the Klestronu flagship by itself was too strong for anything the Confederation could send to protect the regiment's troopship. Earlier, in the Garthid Sector, Tso-Ban had said something about the Klestronu ship having a force shield; the Confederation had nothing like that.

So clearly, the most promising way to get the regiment to Terfreya was to teleport it, with its equipment, as soon as the large teleport was ready. Assuming Kusu had developed adequate targeting procedures by then.

Meanwhile the assumption was that they'd soon have a teleport, with its technicians, on Tyss. The ship would leave a shuttle there as a suitable power source. And when the targeting procedures were adequate, a Crown representative would be ported there to expedite the hiring of a T'swa regiment.

Of course, if the war lodges had contracts for their graduating regiments in advance, as they usually did, they might very well refuse to bump one of the contract holders and give the Confederation priority. On the other hand, they might do it without being asked. Or they might put together a regiment or battalion of demobilized veterans.

*We'll just have to wait and see,* Kristal thought, and reached for his comm set to make his daily check on Kusu's progress.

# 51

"Lotta Alsnor to see you, Colonel," said the voice from the commset.

Voker's eyebrows arched. "Send her in," he answered, then sat back in his chair. A moment later Lotta stepped into his office, and without asking, sat down facing him.

"We're done with the floater crews," she said, "but I hope you're not done with me."

"Wellem told me last night that you'd finished. What do you have in mind?"

"I want to go to Terfreya with the regiment."

"Oh?"

"As part of Headquarters Company. Intelligence Section. I have no doubt at all that I can meld with the Klestronu commander on the ground. And probably their commodore."

Voker was instantly interested. "Wellem told me what you were working on. I didn't know you'd made such progress." He looked her over. Five feet two, he thought, and ninety-five pounds. But then, she wasn't asking to be a lobber man. "What makes you so sure you can meld with him?"

"I've gotten so I can find people I've never met, if I know of them and have some idea where they are. And if I can find them, I can meld with them. I've done it, to make sure."

"Can you reach him from here?"

"Not yet. I should be able to—theoretically the distance shouldn't make any difference. But for some reason I haven't succeeded with anyone outsystem, except for a couple of people I know personally."

"What about language?"

"That shouldn't be any problem. One of the things I learned as a little kid, melding with animals, is that their minds deal with a surprising lot of images and even concepts. They don't verbalize them, but you can read them quite completely. Even people only verbalize some of their mental activity."

She laughed then. "I've been practicing on your cadre. They know it, of course; you can't slip into a T'swi's mind in secret. So I touch one of them psychically, and if it's all right with him, I meld. He can be reading or talking or meditating. And even when he's talking Tyspi, which I don't understand at all, the verbalization's no problem. I ignore it."

"Hmh! Headquarters Company may move around a lot on Backbreak. The way it did on maneuvers. Possibly on foot for security. Do you know the gravitational constant on Backbreak?"

"One point one-nine gee."

"And how much do you weigh? Here."

"A hundred and two."

"That much! Is that with boots on?"

She grinned. "That's wearing a smile and nothing more. I'm heavier than I look; my body's hard. I've done gymnastics and ballet most of my life, and I've made time to run and work out lately."

"That's a lot short of what these troopers have been doing for next to a year now," Voker replied. "As you well know. And on Backbreak, a hundred and two pounds of mass will weigh a hundred and twenty-one."

"Right. And Artus's 210 will be 250."

Voker laughed, shaking his head in appreciation. "Since the beginning of warfare, military commanders have been wanting intelligence officers that can do what you can. So I'll accept your offer on one condition: that Artus agrees."

"Thanks," she said, and got up.

"Does Wellem know about this?" Voker asked.

"He's known for deks that I've had it in mind. And he's got his students working on melding. It's good experience, even if they never go very far with it. Maybe you'll have more intelligence people like me in a while."

"If Colonel Romlar agrees"—*and I have no doubt he will,* Voker added mentally—"tell Captain Esenrok I want you running and hiking with A Company as much as you can, until you're ready to leave. With 2nd Platoon; you can buddy up with your brother."

She nodded, turned and left. Voker sat thoughtfully motionless for a few seconds, contemplating what the girl expected to do, then swiveled his chair to his terminal and began scanning reports again.

# 52

In the twilight, the big teleport gate seemed to loom above the instrument van, and Carlis Voker, standing by it, grunted softly at the strangeness he felt. Kusu Lormagen unlocked the van's rear door and opened it, a light coming on automatically inside. He motioned the other two men in—Voker and a middle-aged civilian—then followed them, leaving the door open.

The portly civilian, a one-time Iryalan trade official on Terfreya, exuded tension. Though he hadn't received the true Sacrament, to be in the presence of anything as utterly non-Standard as this, anything so conspicuously, technologically new made him distinctly uneasy.

While Voker watched, Kusu keyed the power on, then called up and briefly checked several subsystem status reports. Satisfied, he called up a holomap, a globe, showing Terfreya's inhabited hemisphere, rotated it thirty degrees, moved the cursor to a point in the equatorial region, and called up a map of the district it covered.

It looked like a high altitude aerial holo. A black thread of river crossed it, and locating the cursor on it, Kusu called for another enlargement. Now, near the top, Voker could distinguish an irregular, light-colored strip—open ground—with the river a slender ribbon curving through it. Kusu moved the cursor, the map recentering as he did. "This one looked good to me," he said, and called up another enlargement.

The open ground showed now as a valley bottom more than half a mile wide; a white line in the upper left corner provided scale. The bordering ridges were jungle clad and fairly steep. Voker guessed them at perhaps three hundred feet high; Kusu didn't call for contour lines.

Again Kusu recentered the cursor and called for maximum enlargement. Now they were looking "down" at tall grass—a variable stand ranging, he guessed, from waist high to taller than a man, and mostly sparse, with scattered denser clumps and patches.

Kusu looked at the third man, whose face was the color of bread dough in the artificial light. "What can you tell us about that?" Kusu asked. "As a site to put a regiment down on."

"That's tiger grass," the man answered. "It means the valley floods briefly now and then, during heavy winter rains and maybe after exceptional summer storms."

"Winter?" Voker said. "That's near the equator there."

"They call it winter. Things cool down planetwide in the long arm of her orbit. The solar constant gets down to point-seven-eight about midway between the winter solstice and spring equinox. It gets chilly, even at Lonyer City."

*Of course. I should have realized,* Voker thought. "What makes the tiger grass so sparse?" he asked. "Is the ground mucky?"

The ex-trade official shook his head with tight little movements, over-controlled. "No. It's probably covered with a layer of stones. Flat rounded stones about an inch or two across. That's what you find when the grass is thin like that. And tiger grass never grows on mucky ground. Or so I've heard."

Kusu looked at Voker. "Okay as the transfer site?"

Voker nodded. The year was halfway into Sixdek on Terfreya;[15] a flood was highly unlikely. "Considering the time factor," he said, "and what's likely to be happening to the cadets, let's get on with it."

He watched Kusu back off the magnification, move the cursor to where the grass was relatively sparse, and touch a key. Planetary surface coordinates appeared top-center, and Kusu touched another key, presumably entering them into the targeting equation.

"Now," said Kusu, getting up, "we tinker the equation and cut the error."

It was near midnight at the outgate site on Terfreya when the LUF—light utility floater—ported through well above the jungle's roof. It had two men aboard—a pilot and a T'swa corporal. The pilot parked the floater at 500 feet. All they could see below was forest; there was no sign of an open valley. After raising the roof hatch, he folded down a ladder from the overhead, climbed it, and took instrument readings on the sky. Then he climbed back down and fed them to the computer.

Their location within the planetary coordinate grid popped onto the screen. *Not bad,* he thought. *We're less than eighty miles off target.*

In Tyspi, the T'swi sent an open message pulse across the radio wavebands, a message which included their coordinates. Within seconds he had a narrow beam reply in unaccented Tyspi, from the cadet night CQ, getting the status of the war and all they knew about the locations of enemy forces and cadet units.

The boy's voice broke a couple of times, but from puberty, not emotion. They were operating as short platoons, he said, had lost a third of their personnel. Their walking wounded—what there'd been of them—had been gotten to local farms, where the farm families were hiding them.

The T'swi told the cadet what to expect, approximately where, and how they'd arrive. A couple of deks earlier the cadet might have cheered wildly at such a scenario. Now he simply grinned. "All right!" he said in Tyspi. "Tell them our T'swa say it's as good a war as any they've seen since Kettle."

After that the LUF landed in a little glade, and the T'swi guided a small,

AG-mounted teleport out the door. The pilot set the teleport controls on a reverse vector. The T'swi peered through, signaling till the pilot had gotten the outgate site on the ground. Then he stepped back onto Iryala, with a radio to let Kusu know the correction and Voker the war situation. And to get himself picked up, of course.

The second LUF arrived less than seven miles off target and flew to the open valley, where it examined the target site first hand before porting a second T'swa corporal back to Iryala for a final correction.

When Kusu had entered the second error report, he left the teleport site to its guards, troopers from the regiment, and drove back to the Lake Loreen Institute with Voker and the ex-trade official. He left the official with Wellem Bosler. The man had become visibly upset when the first LUF had ported out. Wellem would get him out of it.

# 53

The season seemed later than it was, with the peiok trees around the hayfield tinged purplish bronze by early frost.

It was obvious to Lord Kristal why Kusu had chosen this place. It was a level open field, secluded, and less than a mile from the Lake Loreen Institute.

Although it was none too large. He could see why Voker didn't have the whole regiment there at once; the place was already on the verge of being crowded. First Battalion was there, and Headquarters Company with its 158 personnel including floater crews and medical section. The regiment's floaters were parked at one end: four gunships, six scouts, and eight CPCs—combat personnel carriers that could haul two squads each with gear. Not much compared to army regiments, but for a T'swa-type regiment, unprecedented.

Kristal eyed the quiet troopers standing relaxed in ranks and wondered idly what it would be like to step from this rural, mellow, somewhat sylvan late summer landscape into equatorial jungle. What would the weather be like there today?

The focus of attention here was the teleport, looking much different than the small apparatus he'd stepped through on the roof of the Research Building, not so many deks earlier. It was wide enough for the

floaters and seemed needlessly tall, a gate-like structure on a low platform. No doubt, thought Kristal, there was good reason for its height.
On one side was a metal housing resembling a narrow shed or overgrown
cabinet, presumably holding whatever made the teleport function. This
in turn was connected by cables to an instrument van with the door open.
He'd seen Kusu go inside. An assistant knelt on the platform, comm set
in hand, seemingly waiting for something.

A small media contingent had been invited, had arrived with an
eagerness grown in part from sharp public interest in the Central News
series. In fact, they were the busiest-seeming people there, those from
Iryala Video shifting around with Revax cameras on their shoulders. Two
small camera floaters positioned and repositioned themselves, like
hoverbirds over a flowerbed. The young woman from Central News had
dressed in the camouflage uniform she'd been given by the regiment,
wearing it like a badge as she walked quietly around, talking to one and
another of the troopers.

Kristal himself didn't really need to be there, had no function there.
But this was an important event, the climax of an activity that had held
more than a little of his attention for over a year. He'd developed a
considerable affinity with its young men, even though his knowledge of
them was largely indirect. Very soon now—perhaps before this day was
over—some of them would die. Probably many would over the next weeks,
perhaps most of them. Presumably none with regret. For not only were
they warriors; they knew the T'sel now.

He would not regret either, of course. Though he would miss Lotta
Alsnor, should she die. To him she was a symbol of the future, and he'd
been tempted to veto her accompanying the regiment to Terfreya. But
he'd rejected the thought at once. One did not interfere with the self-
chosen role of someone like her.

And in a few more generations, perhaps no more than six or eight,
the people of Iryala and the Confederation as a whole would know the
T'sel. They'd be comparable to the people of Tyss then, their children
wise and playful.

Assuming there was no serious invasion from the empire. Conquest
could not kill the T'sel, but it would doubtless throw the timetable out,
and change the nature of the playing field, perhaps for a long time.

Carlis Voker rarely fidgeted, but he did now. And noticing, stilled it
with a T'sel order to himself: "Turn around and look at you." In response
he felt a brief wave of chills and a sense of unfocused amusement.

He scanned the assembled troopers again. This was incomparably the
best regiment he'd ever been part of, and now it had a new commander—
a commander still short of twenty years old. *And with more talent,* Voker

told himself, *than I ever dreamed of having*. Too, the floater crews, a late addition to the Table of Organization, had fitted in beautifully. There was good reason to hope that the regiment would accomplish its objective: Chew up the enemy ground forces, and send the imperial ships home convinced that the Confederation sector was not a promising place to invade.

He was sending no T'swa advisors with the regiment, a decision that hadn't been easy to make. Dak-So had agreed though, without reservation. The regiment was good, very good, from top to bottom, and Dak-So said that, even by T'swa standards, Romlar was a tactical genius.

Besides, 2,000 new recruits would be arriving at Blue Forest at week's end, needing cadre to train them. This batch would average less troublesome than the first. The recruiters had used a much slower screening system to identify candidates—winnowing through many thousands of innate personality profiles, rather than starting with a preliminary selection by behavior records. For not all, or even most intentive warriors on Iryala were troublemakers.

A command on the bullhorn broke Voker's thoughts, and his gaze sharpened, focusing on the port. One of the gunships had begun to move toward it.

Tain Faronya had found a good angle, where she could see the gunship float into the gate. And disappear! She'd been briefed on arrival, she and the video people—had been told what would happen. And she'd believed; it seemed to her some hadn't. But seeing it happen excited her in a way she'd never imagined. She felt suddenly eager, and at the same time queasy, her knees momentarily weak.

A slow-moving column of troopers followed the gunship, stepping onto the platform in two files, and she recorded the first few pairs disappearing. Then she took her eyes from them, looking around as if for another vantage or another shot. Climbing down off the hood of the hovercar where she'd been standing, she moved back along a column of waiting troopers, her helmet camera on their tan young faces as if to document their fearlessness, their eagerness.

When she came to the rear, she stopped behind them and looked around again. Her excitement manifested as a seeming need to relieve herself. As best she could, she ignored it. Here the personnel carriers were parked, loaded not with troopers but supplies. Their pilots were visible in their cockpits; other crewmembers were standing on top, where they could better see the troopers disappearing.

As casually as possible, and certain that everyone's eyes were turning to her, Tain went to one of the rearmost carriers, stepped up the ramp and inside.

The cockpit door was open, and she could see the pilot's right arm and shoulder. In the troop cum cargo compartment, there was hardly any room at all except for a narrow aisle between stacks of cases. The cases were of different sizes, and in several places there was room enough for a person to lay down on top of them.

She stepped quickly to one such place, grabbed a tie strap and pulled herself up, then squirmed sideways as far back as she could, all the way to the side of the floater. From there, all she could see were the ceiling and the tops of boxes.

Only then did she feel her heart thudding. She'd committed herself! Tunis only knew what they'd say when they found her, somewhere on Terfreya—wherever they arrived there. But they couldn't send her back, not through the teleport. The briefing had made clear that a teleport was a one-way gate.

Her wait seemed long; long enough that her heart slowed to something like normal, and she had time to imagine discovery scenarios—exposure scenarios, actually, with her coming out of hiding. Then the rest of the crew was boarding; it must be time! She had no doubt she'd know when they arrived: She'd feel the craft sit down, hear the crew talking.

It lifted. She felt it, barely, but she was sure. Felt it move forward, shift direction slightly, accelerate a little. She realized she was holding her breath. And then . . .

# 54

The scream so startled Flight Sergeant Barniss that his hands twitched on the control wheel, causing the floater to jerk forward, almost bumping the craft in front of it. He recovered instantly, though the screaming continued—repeated shrieks, inhuman and shockingly harsh. In the troop compartment, he heard Kortalno swearing loudly.

"What the fuck's happening back there?" he called over his shoulder.

"Sergeant, we've got a stowaway! A woman on top of the cargo, back against the side of the aircraft! She's coming unglued up there!"

"Oh shit," Barniss muttered. "Arlefer, go back there and help him get her down. And be careful. I don't want her hurting herself, and I damn well don't want her hurting either of you."

His copilot got out of his seat and was gone, while Barniss swung the floater out of line and to one side, looking for the nearest place to set her down. "Little A, Little A, emergency on CPC 4. Emergency on CPC 4. We've got a stowaway having a screaming fit on top of the cargo, a stowaway gone psycho on top of the cargo. Get us a medic right away."

Troopers were getting out of his way, and he put down between two platoons. The shrieking hadn't changed; it was raucous, blood-curdling, and utterly mindless. *Already a damned emergency,* he thought, *and I haven't even had a chance to see what this world looks like.* When he felt the floater touch down, he hit the AG switch, swung out of his seat, and started back to help Kortalno and Arlefer.

Lotta was standing within eight feet of Romlar when CPC 4's emergency call sounded from the command radio, and she *knew*—knew who it was, though she hadn't seen her at the field, hadn't known she'd be there. She moved a stride behind the medics, running through coarse sparse grass as high as her chest. Troopers dodged out of their way.

As they approached the floater, she saw one of its crew standing disheveled at the head of the ramp, waving them on. The shrieks sounded as if they'd rupture the lining of the screamer's throat. On board, the crew had gotten Tain down from the cargo stack. One of them, angry scratches across a cheek, lay on her, arms around her hips, more or less pinning her legs with his body. Another, with a bloody lip, held her arms with his knees and hands. Dr. Orleskis had arrived with his belt kit open. Now he knelt, held her head still between his knees, and triggered a syringe against her cheek.

It took a few seconds before she stopped jerking, her movements reduced to feeble shudders.

"Is she unconscious?" Lotta asked.

"No more than she was. I gave her a tranquilizer; in large subcutaneous doses it's very effective for psycho-motor convulsions. Is this the teleport shock I was told about?"

Lotta nodded, remembering the sorlexes. Sedation had controlled their convulsions but they'd died anyway. "Get her on her feet," she ordered.

Orleskis frowned. "On her feet?"

"Support her; carry her upright."

The crewmen were already disengaging themselves from their stowaway. She stank; both excretory openings had let go. Two medics hoisted her to her feet. "Outside," Lotta said, and one under each arm, they carried the stowaway, her toes dragging, following Lotta down the ramp and into the tiger grass, here considerably trampled.

Lotta stopped them and took Tain's right wrist. "Tain!" she ordered, "lift your right hand!" then raised it for her to shoulder height. "Thank you," Lotta said, then lowered it, shifted to the left wrist and repeated the action. Next she turned the woman's face left, then right, always after

the appropriate command, always thanking her for the enforced completion. Had her "go over to" the floater, the medics toting her, and providing both guidance and impetus, had her touch the side of it with one
hand, then the other. All on command, all in a regular, unvarying for-
mat. After a bit, troopers relieved the two aid-men and carried Tain to
the nearby forest, out of the way, where Lotta continued the procedure,
using trees. Later other troopers replaced the first two. Within an hour,
Tain was moving her legs a bit, as if trying to walk, and Lotta could
feel her feeble effort to raise her arms for herself, though her eyes still
were glazed.

Orleskis had left briefly to see to other things. Now he'd returned.
"Want me to take over?" he asked.

Lotta shook her head. "It's working. Best not to change."

The doctor nodded and watched. After another twenty minutes, Tain
was largely supporting her own weight, moving her own head, directing her attention as ordered. Her eyes weren't glazed any longer, though
they were vague and she did not try to speak. After another ten minutes,
her head was drooping as if she was starting to doze.

"Can we get her to bed somewhere?" Lotta asked.

Orleskis nodded, and turned to one of his aid-men. "Get ready to clean
her up," he ordered. "In the aid tent." The man trotted off. The rest
followed slowly, two of them supporting Tain.

"She's going to make it," Orleskis said. "No doubt about it. Where did
you learn to do that?"

"I've been inside the minds of experimental animals when they were
teleported, and got a sense of what they were feeling: incredible panic,
and utter disorientation; not the most enjoyable thing I've ever experienced. The first time it bounced me right out.

"Later I read the reports of teleportation tests on trainees with insufficient processing. They'd described a feeling of having no control, of
either body or environment." Lotta shrugged. "What I did back there just
came to me—reestablish her control, even if only by proxy at first. It
seemed appropriate."

Orleskis nodded. *Inside their minds!* he thought. *What a diagnostic tool!*
If he got back to Iryala alive, he told himself, he'd see about learning
to do some of these things, including the Ostrak Procedures.

Tain slept heavily without sedation. The medics, with Lotta standing by, had cleaned her up, then dressed her in army hospital pajamas.
Orleskis had said that when she woke up, she'd be stiff and sore from
the convulsions.

It occurred to Lotta that now she'd have a tentmate. And that she'd
probably need to run some Ostrak Procedures on Tain, regardless of what

the Crown might prefer. Such drastic teleport shock was bound to have severe mental after-effects. As far as that was concerned, the Crown had already gotten the main story it wanted from her, while the departure story had been covered by Iryala Video.

She wouldn't try anything ambitious with her, Lotta told herself; her intelligence duties wouldn't leave time for it. Just handle her through the zone that had been agitated and sensitized.

# 55

After Tain had fallen asleep, Lotta had taken time to find her way around Headquarters Company. Their outgate site was fifteen miles from the nearest farming district and probably somewhat farther from any area patrolled by Klestronu ground forces. But there seemed a risk of discovery by Klestronu aircraft, so the regiment was bivouacked in the forest. Even the combat personnel carriers had been maneuvered back among the trees.

It seemed important now that she find the Klestronu ground forces commander, meld with him, and learn whether he was aware of anything unusual happening. But camp held a lot of people and a lot of activity, some of it hectic. She'd learned back on Iryala that to make a first contact with someone she only knew *about,* and not much about, she needed freedom from distraction.

So she left camp and hiked far enough into the jungle that none of the activity intruded on her attention. Two troopers went with her as bodyguards; there were tigers, blue trolls, and other dangerous wildlife in these equatorial forests.

It took a few minutes to still her mind, after a day so eventful, but it was no real problem. There were a few seconds during which her body seemed to resonate like a harp chord—an occasional personal symptom of readiness. Then, eyes closed, she reached.

She was surprised at how easy it was. She was with him at once, and the meld was effortless. But not terribly informative. She stayed with Saadhrambacoora for half an hour. He was working intently on administrative matters, and apparently was not much given to ruminating on things other than business while working. But it seemed obvious that he hadn't an inkling of a new enemy force on Terfreya. If he had, it would have been apparent to her, even if his conscious mind had been engaged with other matters. It would have been just below consciousness, with a discernible unit of attention stuck to it unavoidably.

So Lotta had pulled her attention back and returned to Romlar's command tent to let him know that so far their secrecy hadn't been compromised.

That done, it was supper time—field rations—and by the time she'd eaten, it was getting dark. The troopers were retiring to their tents, and stillness was settling over the bivouac. She wore a visored helmet to find her way in the darkness. Romlar offered her a parked scout-craft, a small three-man floater, as a private place to sit while she sought and melded with the enemy commodore in his flagship.

The scout sat not many yards from the command tent, just within the jungle's edge. She chose the pilot's seat. From there she could see between trees into the open, starlit valley bottom. From somewhere came a distant, keening howl; perhaps a Terfreyan wolf, she thought. She felt very relaxed now, and the trance came easily. *Commodore!* she thought softly, and reached outward with her attention. *Commodore!*

There was brief darkness, a familiar sense of otherness, then of beingness that was not her own. The beingness ignored her; that was good—

Terfreya nearly filled the commodore's window, blue and white, blue-green and tan. The half that wasn't night-dark, for the terminator was creeping westward toward the ocean. Tarimenloku sat in his lounging pajamas, gazing out at it. He'd have liked a dharvag, but denied himself; he'd been drinking more than he should lately, and it was time, he'd decided, to assert his self-control.

By ship's time it was late evening. And so it was at the marine base, 55,000 miles out. Or down. The terminator had passed Lonyer City, leaving it in darkness, or twilight at least. Darkness didn't mean relaxation and inactivity for the marines down there, he knew. Stealth was the enemy's ally, and the child warriors, the cadets, were often active at night.

He'd gotten brigade's daily casualty report shortly before retiring: sixty-three—fifty-two dead plus eleven wounded and unfit for service. A bad day. More and more the cadets were using captured beam guns, which usually killed what they hit. Although the killed-to-wounded ratio had been surprisingly high from the beginning, reflecting the enemy's excellent marksmanship.

The day's reported enemy body count was 115, 113 of them cadets, and 2 large black men. Tarimenloku knew from his informants that the black men were the cadets' training cadre, and renowned fighting men. He also knew that they were mercenaries, and not numerous anywhere.

*A body count of 115! If the body counts I'm given are correct,* he thought wryly, *then we've killed a total of more than 3,000 cadets and cadre. And all from a beginning number estimated at 500 to 1,000! Remarkable!*

He thought about having just one drink, and pushed the thought away, focusing his eyes again on the world outside his window, a world on which Klestronu colonists could prosper and multiply. One of dozens of such worlds in this sector. Again he thought of disengaging—of going home with what he'd learned. But there'd be an evaluation, legal and military, and any claim that he'd been driven away by greater military forces would be uncovered as a lie. He was fighting a small force, a single battalion, mostly of children!

Considering the value of what he'd discovered, it was possible, though not likely, that he wouldn't be executed. But if death were all he'd have to face at home, he told himself, he might well start back tomorrow, or as soon as he could bring his people off that world out there. *Disgrace* was what he feared most, and disgrace there would be, for himself and his family, whether he was impaled or not. If he allowed himself to be driven away by forces less than clearly superior in numbers or armament.

The commodore realized he was sagging in his chair, and stiffened, straightening. Getting old, he thought sourly, old and pessimistic. With the entire brigade on the ground, and far better armed, surely his marines would outlast the cadets, who might in truth be nearing extermination. It seemed likely that, in a week or two, the opposition would melt, the ambushes and raids dwindle to nearly nothing. Then he could go home with honor.

Lotta Alsnor opened her eyes and stared out through the night forest toward the star-lit valley. She felt depression and shook it off; it wasn't hers.

She felt something else, too, and realized it was the T'swa seer who'd been melded with Tarimenloku when she had. Now, for a moment, he was with her, an amused but friendly presence. Inwardly she saluted him, felt a glow at his acknowledgement, and realized that now she could find and touch him at will—meld with him if she wished.

She opened herself to deep perception. At least that was what she intended; neither experience nor education had anything to say about the possibility of deep perception. But it seemed to her it was possible, and she wanted the T'swa seer to know as much and as quickly as he could.

Then the T'swa presence was gone, and it seemed to her that it wouldn't be back, that it was leaving surveillance in her hands. She got up and stretched. She'd report to Artus, then check on Tain. And then go to bed. It had been a long day.

# 56

Flight Sergeant Faron Gosweller sat in his LUF, LUF 1, wishing his computer had something interesting to read. He was parked at the edge of a half-acre glade, backed between two trees and concealed by the eaves of the forest. The last twilight had faded from what little he could see of the sky, and it was dark indeed.

It had been a long day, and he still hadn't gotten a call.

As far as Gosweller knew, the enemy wasn't aware of him. Even if they'd picked up his 360° call to the cadet force, the night before, that had been from two miles away and above the trees. The only investigation he knew of had been by local wildlife. Twice large herds of tiny deerlike animals had entered the glade to browse, stopping frequently in their feeding to look toward the floater. The herds had numbered twenty and thirty-odd; exact counts had been impossible because the animals moved around too much. There'd also been a band of much larger deer—an even dozen of them. Of these, the larger had three horns each—a central pike flanked by two lesser, out-curved horns. The smaller wore only the central pike, a matter of sexual dimorphism he suspected.

Once a band of small piglike animals had entered the glade, where they seemed to be rooting up tubers or mushrooms. Then something like a big cat, black dappled with tan or gray, had rushed out and killed one of them. After momentary panic, the pigs had rallied, swarming at the predator, and the cat had escaped into a tree. After a little the pigs left, and the cat jumped down to reclaim its kill.

The cat looked big enough to kill a man, it seemed to Gosweller, and he'd decided not to go out unarmed. Or at night.

*Too bad I couldn't have downloaded a book on Terfreyan wildlife before I left Iryala,* he thought. Instead, everything not essential to his mission had been erased from his computer's memory, on the off-chance that the enemy might capture the craft.

But what they really didn't want the enemy to capture was the teleport, tricked up though it was. Sitting power-up a few yards outside his floater, and connected to it by a power cable, it was Gosweller's escape hatch. If the enemy threatened to find him, he was to run to it and press three switches in order: The first targeted the port on Iryala on a reverse vector; the second activated a destruct mechanism with a one-minute delay; and the third opened the gate for a single passage, after which the targeting program would revert to the default target, which was the teleport platform itself. If anyone tried to follow him before it destructed, they'd enter a loop and arrive at the same place and time as they'd "left." But in teleport shock, unless they'd been defused.

A tiny light began flashing on Gosweller's console, accompanied by a soft beeping. He reached, opening a switch, knowing who it had to be. His computer screen told him it was a scrambled message via a fifteen-degree beam pulse transmission; the regiment knew, of course, approximately where he was.

"LUF 1, LUF 1, this is Little A, this is Little A. Bring your teleport to the accompanying coordinates. Repeat: Bring your teleport to the accompanying coordinates."

His computer copied the coordinates and he had it read them into his navigator. Then he acknowledged the message. And even as he pressed the *acknowledge* key, he realized he'd screwed up. He was a civilian pilot with warrior tendencies, who'd been called up from the reserve for this project, and he'd brought some civilian habits with him. He'd sent 360°; he should have sent a narrow beam aimed at the coordinates. Or not acknowledged at all.

He swore under his breath. Well, he'd hustle—load the teleport and get away from there quickly.

The slowly cruising Klestronu gunship was alone and it wasn't; a narrow carrier beam from brigade's comm central was locked on it. The badly bored pilot, Flight Sergeant Sarkath Veglossu, was expecting an order to return to base; nothing had been heard of the enemy radio source since the night before.

Instead he received a set of coordinates for a new enemy radio source less than three miles away, and an order to attack it at once. His computer gave the coordinates to its navigation program, and the gunship swung around.

The teleport was on an AG dolly, which made it easy to raise off the ground. Its mass and inertia were considerable for one man to handle though; otherwise Gosweller might have had the rig inside the LUF before the gunship got there. As it was, one end was in the door. He might even have gotten off the ground with it—perhaps even gotten away. As it was, Veglossu's high-intensity floodlight caught the Iryalan by surprise, blinding him for brief seconds. Long enough that he wasn't able to find any switches, let alone press them, before the gunship fired a concussion pulse that struck the side of the floater less than four feet from him.

Veglossu saw him fall, and put a crewman down to investigate. Sweating, heart thudding, the Klestronu private made his way to LUF 1 and the teleport by a series of short sprints, hitting the dirt after each of them. He had no notion that he'd make it alive. When he did, he found Gosweller dead.

Using his belt radio, the private let Veglossu know. Veglossu then radioed base to send out a floater and pick up the loot, whatever that consisted of.

# 57

The tree stood some thirty yards back within the jungle's edge, but rose well above any others around it. Hensi Kaberfar, age thirteen, had climbed the lianas that laced it, and lay on an ascending branch thick enough to obscure him from the road nearly half a mile away.

The 300-acre piece of jungle he was in, he and his platoon, occupied a low bulge of quartzite, its soil shallow and infertile, bordered on two sides with fields and on the third, a road backed by scrub. On the same three sides it was surrounded by Klestronu marines. On the fourth, the north side, flowed the Spice River, eighty yards across, with extensive jungle on its opposite side. Gunships watched its brown current from a distance deemed relatively safe from cadet rockets. If the cadets tried to cross it, the gunships were to move in quickly and chop them up.

Hensi's tree was on the south side however, and from its height he watched the marine company deployed along the road. There'd be other companies on the east and west sides, he knew. Sooner or later the Klestroni would have to make a decision. Send a company into the jungle—maybe two companies—or sit around behind their electronic sentry fields and try to starve their quarry out. Starve them out or root them out. Odds were, Hensi thought, they'd called for armored missile trucks, each carrying a battery of launchers that could pour scores of ground-to-air rockets into an area in a hurry.

All for an understrength platoon—twenty-one cadets.

Just now Hensi's sniper-scoped rifle was cross-slung on his back, and binoculars occupied his hands. He wore no helmet, but a throat mike was clamped to his collar. The artillery would come up the road from the west, if it came, and he was to report when it appeared. The Klestroni were a light brigade, without any real artillery, and their missile trucks were not heavily armored. They tended to use them sparingly, in favorable situations. The idea was for this to seem like a favorable situation.

The plan had been for two platoons to ambush a company of marines on a road, by daylight, pour fire into them for half a minute, then take to "the bush," a district of mostly overgrown, abandoned farmland.

The Klestroni didn't have an endless supply of gunships either, so troops on the road usually rode unescorted in armored assault vehicles. A gunship, or more than one, could be sent in a hurry if called for.

The ambush had been a success. They'd holed some AAVs and killed maybe twenty or thirty Klestroni, then all but three guys had taken off into the young forest. The three who stayed were well separated and carried surface-to-air rocket launchers. A gunship was armored but not invulnerable, and given enough hits—a single hit if you were lucky— you could bring one down.

They'd hit the bugger all right, and although they hadn't brought him down, they'd sent him veering off, clearly hurt and no doubt radioing for reinforcements.

Klestronu scout floaters and two more gunships had arrived minutes later. And gotten glimpses now and then of a cadet or cadets moving through the scrub, glimpses most often deliberately allowed. One platoon had laid low, as planned, then slipped away unnoticed. It made no sense to expose both.

Hensi's platoon had been larger when the ambush was made; they'd numbered thirty-one then. When someone exposes himself to a gunship, there's a good chance he'll get his ass shot off, along with assorted other body parts.

Now Hensi saw dust. It was the missile trucks coming, he had no doubt, but he waited to make certain. When he was, he radioed. When they'd parked, gravitically locked to firing positions along the road, he radioed again. When they began to fire, he didn't need to radio; missiles slammed into the jungle with a ragged roar heard for miles. Hensi could easily have been killed then, but as usual he was lucky. And instead of scrambling back down, he sat tight; he wanted to see what happened next.

The launchers themselves were noisy enough that the Klestroni ignored the two gunships at first, even when they'd begun strafing. And when they became aware of what was happening, it was with disbelief, because gunships were their own—had to be. The cadets had none. So the response, briefly, was shock and indignation instead of returned fire.

The gunships passed over two hundred feet apart, the first giving its attention to the emplaced troops, the other to the missile trucks. They didn't make a second pass. Then lobber fire began to land on the emplaced marines from behind, lots of it, accurately. Someone had established the range in advance.

The missile trucks stilled.

Hensi slid to the first crotch below him, then went hand over hand down the lianas toward the ground. If the Klestroni reacted as expected, their gunships were already responding, leaving the river unguarded. The platoon would be concealed along the riverbank, watching for their chance, ready to drag their boats to the water, boats that locals had stashed for them. He'd have to run all the way or be left behind.

When the Klestronu artillery had begun firing from the south road, the two companies along the east road had been grimly pleased. Their rifle platoons lay ready and alert, watching mainly the jungle in front of them, into which their mortar platoons began to throw their own high explosives.

There were two companies on the east side because there was no longer any open field there, only the road, with forest in front of them and an abandoned field, more or less overgrown with scrub, behind. This was the side the cadets had come from, and these two companies were part of the force that had pursued them, "driven" them. Its marines had been nervous till now. The cadets had long since established their capacity for tricks, surprise, unpredictability.

But not from the air; the cadets had no air support.

The regiment's gunships, having shot up the artillery along the south road, rounded the corner and surprised the two companies along the east. The result was more than casualties, though there were lots of those. It was also shock and utter confusion. Thus when 1st and 2nd Platoons, A Company, came out of the scrub to the rear, hoses and rifles blazing, the surviving marines, most of them clinging to the ground, hardly reacted. Grenades arced, roared.

Then Jerym Alsnor, the assault team leader, saw another gunship line up with the road. The regiment's were gone by then. He barked an order into his helmet mike, and barreled back into the scrub, Tain Faronya beside him. She'd recorded the assault. A dozen seconds later, energy beams—butcher beams, the cadets called them—slashed angrily through the regrowth, severing fronds and young stems. Then, for the moment, it was past.

Another hundred yards of running took them into older regrowth, dense young woods sixty to eighty feet tall. There they pulled up, breathing hard, beside the streamlet that bordered it. There were more sounds of falling fronds and branches, as if the gunship was ranging over the scrub and forest shooting blindly.

Jerym had allowed for the gunship response. His assault line had been thin, its men initially a dozen yards apart. Thus fleeing through the scrub, they'd been mostly unseen and very scattered targets.

Again he spoke into his helmet radio, ordering the two platoons to their rendezvous. Fourteen minutes later he arrived at a cutbank above the Spice River with Tain beside him. There were stragglers—able-bodied troopers helping three wounded. After an hour, twelve of Jerym's eighty-plus troopers had not arrived and could not be raised by radio.

Hopefully 4th Platoon A Company had gotten away unscathed; it had been they who'd shelled the south road with lobbers.

Jerym moved his men out then, hiking through forest, upstream along the river. He'd given, and received, his first casualties—given a lot more than he'd taken. But now the excitement and exhilaration were past, and he lacked both the perceptivity of the T'swa and their deep calm. Thus he felt the deaths as personal losses. After all, the casualties were men he'd lived and trained with for more than a year.

Tain sensed his feeling and said nothing, felt it herself, though not as sharply as she would have expected. Nor was she angry or indignant. Her two sessions with Lotta had done more than help her over the lingering effects of teleport shock, and this was war. Fought at least on this side by warriors, men who warred by choice and did not fear dying.

# 58

Igsat Tarimenloku frowned at the structure sitting in his conference room. It had been put there instead of in the Intelligence Section because the conference room door had been large enough to accommodate it. The thing looked a bit like a tubular metal doorframe without a wall, a doorway that went nowhere. A nearly square-topped metal arch, it stood on a base that reminded him just a little of a large platform scale. At one side, against one of the vertical tubes, was something like a cabinet or locker.

Strange looking. No function suggested itself, but presumably it had one. "And DAAS has no suggestion?" the commodore said to his chief science officer.

"None, sir. DAAS says its computer was wiped by the concussion pulse that killed the man with it.

"Hmh!" He scowled as if considering how he might coerce it, then turned to his CIO, his chief intelligence officer. "And the man was an adult white, you say, but in uniform. With a floater."

"Yes sir. And the floater has markings on it—numerals and letters— that could have been a military designation. Although it was unarmed.

I'm told they had a different pattern than those observed on civilian equipment."

The commodore searched his mind for anything in the weeks of warfare that seemed to relate to a cadet use of floaters, or of reports of floaters, but nothing came to him. There were things that might be explained by air support services, but it seemed extremely unlikely that there'd been any. They'd surely have been detected.

Still, there was, or had been a floater in presumably enemy hands. Floaters had been few on Terfreya, but there may have been some, or one, not on the tax records, and thus missed during the impoundment sweep. As for a uniform—private clothing could resemble a uniform, or even . . .

A thought struck him then which seemed almost likely. Certainly it fitted experience on Klestron and probably every other empire world: smugglers and sometimes brigands. On a world as loosely managed as this one, there were sure to be some, and the dead pilot might very well have been one. He'd have his captives interrogated about the . . .

The security comm beeped, and the CIO flipped its switch. "Commander Ralankoor here," he said.

"Commander, I have a class one message for the commodore, from the general."

*Class one!* "Let's have it, Yilkat," the commodore barked.

The message shook him. Hostile gunships had hit a marine battalion surrounding a company of cadets in an outlying block of forest. The battalion hadn't been prepared for gunship attack, hadn't even realized at once what was happening. Then a strong enemy ground force had attacked the battalion and been driven off. Casualties had been heavy. A full casualty list and the enemy body count were not available yet, but the enemy casualties had been white adults.

*Not cadets. White adults.* Tarimenloku's skin crawled. *Uncanny!* "How large was this enemy force?" he demanded.

"Sir, I was not told."

"Well damn it, you should have asked! Find out! Right now!" *Kargh damn people who take no Kargh-damned responsibility! You'd expect better than that of a senior lieutenant, especially of the Yilkatanaara family.*

He looked around at the others there: his EO, chief science officer, chief intelligence officer. "Gentlemen, I'm going to the command room." He gestured at the foreign machine. "Bavi," he said to his CIO, "I'm leaving this enigma to you. You will interrogate our captives about it, of course, and about this new enemy force. Let me know at once of anything you learn."

Tarimenloku stomped out into the corridor then. How big was this new force? he asked himself. Where had it come from? Why hadn't they run into it before?

His instruments and sentry craft hadn't reported any ships entering real-space, nor approaching this world from elsewhere in the system. And it was hard to believe anything could have gotten through undetected.

He shook his head, an angry, impatient gesture. Somehow he had no doubt at all that his captives would know nothing about it.

He decided he was no longer seriously concerned about the enemy machine. Not now anyway. But he'd *demand* some live military prisoners from Saadhrambacoora; they might know what it was. If they didn't, SUMBAA would have to work it out when they got home.

When they got home. Tarimenloku brightened a bit. *Maybe this new enemy force is big enough to justify leaving,* he told himself, *justify heading home to Klestron!*

Lotta's daytime "office" was a quiet place on top of a ridge, some hundred and fifty feet from camp, where she could sit alone, except for two bodyguards, and plug into the minds of the enemy commanders. Occasional spots of sunlight dappled the ground around her. She'd been sitting in trance most of the time since breakfast, with a short break for lunch.

Now her eyes opened. She stood and stretched. It had been a good day and a bad one: Earlier, word had come of the successful assault on the enemy force surrounding the cadets, and of the cadets' successful escape without further casualties. First and Second Platoon's casualties had been moderate, and Fourth's zero. But both of the regimental gunships involved had been lost; the Klestronu gunships were faster, and their weapons more effective.

And now—now she knew why only one LUF had come when called last night. She started jogging along the ridge to Romlar's headquarters tent. She'd tell him what she'd learned, then come back and look in on Saadhrambacoora again.

# 59

Once the battalions had moved into contact zones, regimental headquarters had moved too, to a safer location. A series of relay transmitters had been set up on high points, to which headquarters could radio its messages on a tight beam. The selected relay transmitter in turn sent them outward on a more or less narrow beam—from five to sixty degrees—toward the intended recipient unit or units.

Only 1st and 2nd Platoons of A Company were located with head-quarters, as an air-mobile strike force. The rest of the regiment had no home; its battalions lived separated and on the move, supplied at night by floaters from one of several supply dumps.

The hills in which Headquarters Company now hid were the remains of an old plateau, not high but dissected by numerous ravines, mostly narrow and steep, all heavily forested. Just now it was located next to one of those ravines.

From a nearby patch of marsh, floaters could sneak up the ravine under cover, and park beside the creek in its bottom, cut off from the sky by overarching trees. Just now, two scouts sat parked below headquarters on their AGs; most of the others were parked not far away.

It was preferred that the floaters travel by night. When they did travel by day, they moved largely in ravines, flying above the treetops but, where possible, below the hilltops. The headquarters, however, they approached only beneath the forest roof. The camp itself was on the broad and fairly level hilltop.

The CPCs carrying 1st and 2nd Platoons slipped up the ravine bottom, moving a few feet above the creek. The sun was newly down, daylight weakening, when they arrived below camp, parked on their AGs, and disembarked their troopers. The two platoon leaders climbed the hill to the headquarters tent. After a debrief, Jerym went to his own tent, stashing rifle and pack, keeping his sidearms with him, and his helmet, then walked to the larger tent assigned to his sister, and stood by the closed flaps. It was a little apart from any others, for privacy.

"Hello," he said quietly. "Anyone at home?"

"Come in." He recognized Tain's voice, and opening the flaps, ducked in, leaving his helmet on the ground outside. It was darker in than out, but he could see Tain half reclining, leaning on an elbow. He knelt beside her on the tent floor.

"I hoped you'd be here," he said, and realized it was true. "I—want to tell you how well you did today. That wasn't the safest place in the world."

"It wasn't, was it. It—I'm amazed I wasn't terrified. Nervous, yes. My stomach was in knots, and my pulse must have been going a hundred and twenty a minute. But it wasn't fear; at least it didn't feel like it." She paused, put her hand on his arm. "How about you?"

"Huh! I don't know. About my pulse, I mean. I don't think my stomach was all that nervous. My attention was on other things, I guess."

Neither of them said anything for a few seconds, then Jerym reached, put a hand on her shoulder. "Right now my pulse is going pretty darned fast though," he murmured. "If you want me to leave, tell me."

Tain's grip tightened. "I don't want you to leave, Jerym. I want you to stay here. Tomorrow you may be dead, or I may, or both of us may, and I want very much for you to stay."

He nodded, not thinking whether she could see the nod or not. "Lotta may come back," he said.

"Lotta left three minutes before you came. She was going to one of the scout floaters to—do whatever it is she does there. Spy on the Klestronu commanders."

She leaned toward him then and kissed his lips, brushing her hand down his arm to rest on a muscular thigh. When the kiss ended, she laid back. He kissed her again, fumbling at the buttons on her field shirt with a hand that, embarrassingly, trembled. A minute of tugging and twisting left both of them naked. He thought of telling her it was his first time, then decided it was best not to. They embraced, kissing, and it seemed to Jerym he couldn't breathe at all. Hands explored, caressed and fondled, but only briefly. Then she squirmed, got beneath him, helped him. His orgasm began at once, and he was done in seconds.

But Tain was not inexperienced, and he was young, his desire and recuperative powers strong. They made love over most of an hour.

When he'd pulled his outer clothes back on, he kissed her once more, tenderly. "I—think I love you, Tain," he murmured. "I really think so. And I know I'm the luckiest guy on Terfreya."

She nodded, eyes welling. *I hope you're lucky,* she thought. *So lucky, you'll come through this war alive.*

He didn't see the nod nor hear the thought, but he never questioned whether she felt the way he did. He touched her cheek gently, felt the moisture of her tears and was awed by them. He left his fingers there for a moment, then kissed her again and backed out of the tent.

He wasn't ready to go to his own yet though. Instead, putting on his helmet and lowering the visor for night vision, he found his way down the hillside toward where the scouts were parked. A trooper squatted by one of them.

"Who goes there?" the man asked quietly.

"Lieutenant Alsnor, A Company. I'm Lotta's brother; I want to talk to her. Figured I'd wait here till she came out."

The trooper chuckled. "Pull up some ground and sit. I don't know how long she'll be. I guess you guys had some fun today, eh?"

It took a moment for Jerym to realize that the guard had the firefight in mind. His own attention was stuck on Tain and himself, and what it might mean. "Uh, yeah. It was good. I wish Sergeant Dao could have seen his old platoon. He'd have been all grin."

It had been good. His senses had never been so sharp, he thought, his reflexes so tuned. It occurred to Jerym that the guard might like to hear about it. But it also seemed that, talked about, it might not sound like all that much, so he said nothing more. And the guard didn't ask; they squatted there without talking further.

Jerym wondered if Romlar planned to rotate his headquarters personnel into fighting platoons so guys like this guard could see some combat. They might see combat anyway, of course. The Klestroni might locate Headquarters Company and come with gunships and a force of marines. But it seemed unlikely. The Klestroni had never been able to pin the cadets down, and Romlar seemed to operate out of a level of subliminal wisdom that hopefully would keep him outguessing his enemy.

*Romlar!* The one-time dumb fatboy! And that's what he'd have stayed, except for the regiment. Except for Varlik Lormagen and Colonel Voker, and the T'swa and the Project.

And himself? He'd probably have become a jailbird.

He dozed off then, squatting near the scout, and woke up to Lotta's voice. "Jerym?" She wore a helmet too, to help her walk in the jungle darkness.

He grunted awake and got up. "Can we talk?" he asked.

She turned and gestured. "Will the scout do?"

"That'll be fine."

They got in, Lotta sliding the door closed behind them, and sat in the pilot's and copilot's seats. "What did you want to talk about?"

"I'm in love with Tain."

He paused. "I suppose that sounds strange. I mean, Tain and I don't know each other all that well, haven't talked to each other very much. But . . . We're attracted to each other. Pretty strongly. And I'm afraid I'll get polarized, lose my neutrality about living or dying. I've sure as Tunis lost my neutrality about Tain living or dying.

"And it could affect my performance as a trooper. Which is not okay, especially for a platoon leader."

"Ah. All right. In this life and others, how many times have you been in love before?"

The question took him by surprise, and for a moment he didn't answer. Then he grinned, the grin widening. "Huh! All right. Many times. Many many times."

"Care to say a number?"

He chuckled. "Not necessary."

"Okay. How many times have you been separated from a lover by death? Your death, your lover's death, someone else's death."

Chill bumps flowed; Jerym laughed. "Okay. Your point is made."

"Good. Now tonight you'll dream about dying, and about Tain dying, and it'll be all right. You'll also dream about both of you living a long time together."

"Can you do that? Make me dream that?"

"No. You'll do it. Although I might help a little."

They got out and hiked up the hill together with the bodyguard following. At the top they separated, Jerym going to his tent, Lotta to hers.

When she crawled inside, she could smell what had happened there. It made her a little horny herself. For Romlar. It wasn't the first time she'd felt that way. But she'd given him no sign, and wouldn't. He was doing very well. To complicate his situation would be unwise. Tain was asleep, her breathing slow and shallow. Lotta decided to help her dream too.

# 60

Looking like some neoclassical sculpture come to life, Artus Romlar stood nude in the creek, washing off sweat. The sun was newly up, the air cool, but he'd just finished thirty minutes of stretching and gymnastics, and fifteen more of close combat drill forms.

Romlar's belt radio chirped at him, and he went to where it lay atop his neatly folded clothes beside the creek. "This is Romlar."

"Artus, this is Jorrie. We just got the pulse from today's supply drop. Bressenhem's on his way to his scout to go check it out."

"Good. Thanks."

The daily supply shipment from Iryala usually outgated at about sunup, on a hover truck. The general area used had numerous glades and small meadows to outgate into. When he was down, the driver moved his truck under cover, then took directional reads on regular Klestronu and Lonyer City radio sources to triangulate his location, and set his radio for a two-degree transmission beam in the direction of a relay. The relay location had been specified in the previous evening's regimental report, teleported to Iryala via LUF 2's gate. The regiment's comm center, part of the regimental computer, would receive the truck driver's message pulse and extrude the outgate's coordinates on several navigation tabs. One for the navcomp in a scout and the others for combat personnel (cum cargo) carriers.

A scout would go check out the location and any possible dangers. Assuming all was clear, the carriers would follow, to pick up cargo and driver. The truck would be abandoned and its driver ported back to Iryala.

Romlar brushed water from his body, dressed, and hiked up the hill to his command tent. His executive officer, Jorrie Renhaus, and their sergeant major were eating breakfast out of ration cartons, using a crate as a table. "The female reporter left some cubes off to port back," said Renhaus. "Showing the assault yesterday. We played the video cube on the computer. Very good stuff. I'm glad you decided she could stay; it'll be good publicity."

Romlar opened a ration carton. "If she wants to stay, why not. She went through hell getting here. And we couldn't port her back without Lotta spending a lot of time working on her first."

Renhaus grinned. "Which reminds me: I've got an idea about the teleport the Klestroni captured. Leak word to them what it really is, and how to use it. Teleport someone into their base camp, so they'll take it seriously. And give them the coordinates for Iryala, for Landfall. Then they'll teleport a regiment there, figuring to capture the government, and the marines will land helpless and dying from teleport shock."

Romlar looked up from the fruit juice he was mixing, and cocked an eyebrow. "Jorrie, are you serious?"

Renhaus laughed. "No. But it's a funny thing to imagine. Actually, let the Klestroni know what the teleport is, and they'll take it and run for home. If they have any sense at all, which they must have."

Romlar nodded absently. Renhaus's weird humor had reminded him of a problem they'd talked about earlier; the risk of a cadet or trooper being taken alive and giving up the information that the regiment had been teleported. Then the Klestroni'd probably suspect what the thing was that they'd captured.

Apparently it also reminded Renhaus of the problem. "What if the troopers were told to say they'd arrived by ship?" he said. "Say a ship with some sort of invisibility device; call it a cloak. Landed in the prairie tundra and they'd flown north in combat personnel carriers? Or if it was a cadet, he could say the troopers had come by personnel carrier, he didn't know where from. And they could say that the teleport is a device sent for the execution of any high-ranking Klestronu prisoners we might take. They're considered 'criminals responsible for the invasion of a Confederation resource world.'

"Presumably the port's on the default setting, right? So if they try it on someone, it'll execute him sure enough, very unpleasantly. Unless they try it on the prisoner, in which case it won't appear to have done anything."

Romlar looked thoughtfully at his EO. "Jorrie, write up that idea in the form of an order to be read to the regiment. And one for the cadets. I don't know whether one of them could get away with lying under instrumented interrogation—they probably couldn't—but if someone gets caught, he can try."

# 61

Tain had been in on D Company's raid from the beginning—had been in the headquarters tent when the idea came up.

First and Second Platoons had been out on several raids since the one she'd been on, but Romlar hadn't let her go along. Too dangerous, he'd told her.

Jerym had been on each of them. It hadn't been easy, waiting, and when he'd returned safely, they'd had each other in the tent, or off in the forest away from camp.

Then this situation had come up. Romlar had heard about it via a cadet radio message; the cadets had learned it from a local, a kressera broker. A marine battalion was bivouacked in a large open area. Their headquarters seemed to be in an armored floater marked by abundant electronic bric-a-brac.

It was obviously intended as a very temporary bivouac: The marines had dug in, but just foxholes, nothing elaborate, and they hadn't fenced the area. There were two antiaircraft trucks on each side, in case of gunship attack, and they were sure to have electronic detection measures— sentry fields. It was the sort of display the Klestroni made from time to time, showing themselves in settled districts, conspicuously and in force. Presumably the idea was to keep the locals properly impressed and intimidated.

It was the sort of setup you couldn't approach undetected. But port in two men in black with satchel charges, next to the AA trucks on one side, and poke a pole charge through next to the armored head-quarters floater, then blow all three, and the place would go frantic. Blow the HQ first, as a signal, and immediately afterward the trucks. The electronic detection measures would be centered on the headquarters floater of course, so that knocking out the HQ should knock out the sentry field. Then send in a company to raise hell in the confusion— hit, shoot the place up, then get out before the Klestroni could get gunships there. After which a lobber platoon could drop high explosives on the place.

It wouldn't be much better than a suicide mission for the guys with the satchel charges, but they'd make it possible to blow the AA trucks, which would save lives.

Second Battalion was nearest the Klestronu bivouac—only six miles from it.

Of necessity, the planning was thin; the opportunity would be brief. Romlar talked it over with Renhaus and his sergeant major, then by radio with Brossling, commanding 2nd Battalion. Brossling talked it over with the CO of D Company. They were all for it. Romlar began to give orders. . . .

Tain had talked Romlar into letting her go along, not as part of the assault, but to observe and video-record from a little distance. Now, watching from the scout in the moonless night, she had nervous stomach. Nervous colon, actually. A small ravine issued onto the open area, and the scout, the command post for the raid, was parked a little back from its mouth, nestled in the treetops. Given half a chance, a scout could outrun Klestronu gunships; they'd learned that the exciting way.

She stood peering out the open top hatch, camera recording everything she saw. With the cam's state of the art night viewer, it was surprising how much she could see. Just now she was looking at the Klestronu camp nearly half a mile away. D Company, sheltered within the edge of the woods, was keeping back, out of her sight. No one knew how far out the Klestronu sentry field was set to operate. The troopers would move fast when the fireworks blew. Swiftly and quietly.

Then the first explosion roared, powerful enough, it seemed to Tain, to have turned the Klestronu headquarters into shrapnel. The two AA trucks blew almost simultaneously a few seconds later. This was the cue. The scout moved out of the ravine and over open ground at perhaps thirty feet, staying low to keep the hills as a background, instead of open sky. And now she could see D Company jogging along in a line on both sides of her, falling a bit behind.

Some kind of alarm horn was howling in the Klestronu camp.

Halfway to the camp, the scout stopped abruptly as a dozen, a score, a hundred sharp lines of visible light began lancing outward toward D Company. The sentry field was still operational, had to be! The scout began to lift, veering away, and a bigger beam, thick as Tain's wrist, sliced into its nose. The scout staggered, throwing her off her feet, off the small platform she was standing on. She screamed, smelled hot metal and burned flesh, felt the scout slipping downward, sideways, felt its heavy impact with the ground, and briefly knew nothing more.

She regained her senses gradually, vaguely aware of explosions that seemed to go on for a while, then of no more explosions. Her next awareness was of someone trying to open the scout's door, which wouldn't function. Someone from D Company, she thought blurrily, someone come to get her out. "I'm all right," she called—croaked—and got unsteadily to her feet. Her helmet was gone—she'd disliked wearing the chinstrap when she didn't have to. She staggered, although the scout was almost level, stepped back onto the platform, pulled herself up through the hatch and slid down to the ground. There were men around her.

"Tah rinkluta koh! Drassnama veer!"

The words froze her. Someone grabbed her from behind. Another stepped close, peering into her face from beneath brows bushier than any trooper's. His hands gripped her shirt and ripped.

"Hah! Rinkluta koh, dhestika!"

They began to laugh then, loud, ugly, a sound more frightening than anything she'd ever heard. She began to kick wildly, then a fist hit her hard in the stomach, driving the wind out of her. The man who held her threw her down. Other hands were on her, pulling at her belt, her waistband, her legs.

Suddenly there was a roar of command, an angry roar, a scream, and the hands were gone. She stared up from where she lay, at a man holding a sword, pointing with it, barking orders, another beside him with a ready gun. The other men were backing away, then reluctantly, growling, began jogging off into the darkness. One man lay across her feet, her lower legs, not moving, and she knew he was dead.

Watching them depart, the man with the sword blew a gust of relief, almost a snort, then looked down at her. She realized her shirt was off, except that one hand and wrist were still in a sleeve, and her brassiere was gone. Her field pants were down to her knees, along with her torn underpants. Her skin crawled beneath his gaze.

He stared long, gave an order. The man with him holstered his gun, bent, and dragged the corpse off her feet. She could see now that the dead man's head had been cleft like a melon.

The man with the sword reached down. She found herself reaching up, and he pulled her to her feet. She crouched, pulled up her field pants, rethreaded the half-jerked-out belt through the loops and fastened it, then pulled her shirt back on.

When she was done, the officer spoke sharply to her, pointing with the sword again. The other man grabbed her roughly by an arm, shoved, and they began to follow the men who'd run off, toward the Klestronu camp.

She was still somewhat in shock when they got there. They walked her between foxholes, shell holes, and shelter tents to a large tent, a line of weak light showing faintly beneath overlapped flaps. Inside were men's voices. The officer called quietly. The light was killed; the flaps drew back and he entered. She heard him talking. There was a pause, then a peremptory order in another voice. The other man shoved her in ahead of him. The light came on again, not brightly, a battle lamp.

There were several men there, mostly officers she thought, some seated at a folding table, others standing. They stared as she was pushed toward them. One, a heavyset man, was clearly in charge, and he spoke to her. She shook her head, not knowing how else to respond. He gave an order and one of the men left. The rest began to talk, their glances lascivious but not threatening. They were more relaxed now, even laughed. In about a minute, the man who'd left was back with handcuffs, and her wrists were manacled in front of her.

The man who'd brought the manacles turned her around, then walked out into the night ahead of her while another pushed her after him. They walked her among some tents and past a crater—where the headquarters had been, she supposed—to a small hover van with barred windows, where the first man opened the door, stepped in, and flashed a handlamp around inside. The other pushed her in after him.

Four thin narrow mattresses had been leaned against a wall on their sides; a pail and jug sat in a corner. The man with the light flipped one of the mattresses down onto the floor with his foot, looked at her, and opened her shirt to stare at her breasts from beneath hairy brows. The other, behind her, unfastened her belt and shoved a rough hand inside her field trousers. Then the first man snapped an order and the hand was removed. Pointing, he ordered her down on the mattress, and she obeyed, cringing.

But they did not molest her further, simply fitted a set of irons on her ankles, over her boots. That done, they left, closing the steel door behind them. She lay there and shook violently. It was several minutes before the shaking stopped.

Then she stretched out on her back, staring at the dim ceiling, wondering what was going to happen to her. And what had happened to D Company. She remembered the explosions she'd heard while semiconscious; 4th Platoon, the weapons platoon, must have been laying in covering fire from the edge of the forest, she decided. Maybe they'd gotten away, some of them, most of them.

She heard a key, heard the latch turn, and faint star light came in through the door. A man stepped in, gave an order, and the door closed behind him. A lamp flashed on in his hand, settled on her exposed breasts, and she saw the heavyset commander looking down at her. She lay stiff as a board.

He spoke to her in his own language, not harshly, a question. She shook her head. "No. Leave me alone." The words came out quiet but intense. He looked a long minute longer, then left, switching the handlamp off before he opened the door.

With some difficulty she snapped her blouse shut. After a time she slept.

# 62

Tain awoke to faint dawnlight through the window. It seemed to her she'd dreamed continuously, dreams in part violent but not nightmarish. She couldn't remember their content. Crablike, she worked her way across the floor to the pail, after some difficulty relieved herself, then refastened her field pants and crept back to her mattress to sink immediately again into dream-filled sleep. When next she awoke, it was daylight, and someone was unlocking her door. As it opened, she raised her head to look.

A hard-faced man peered in at her, like the others bushy browed, his close-shaved jaw and cheeks blue against brown. He snapped an order over his shoulder in a voice as sharp as a laser knife, as hard as steel. Another man she hadn't seen before scuttled in to remove her ankle irons; her day jailor, apparently. When he'd put the irons in a pocket, he reached down, grabbed her wrist, and jerked her roughly to her feet, only to be lashed by the tongue behind him. Hand flinching away from her, he yelped his reply, then motioned her to the door.

She went, confused but not just now feeling threatened, feeling much better in fact than she would have imagined when she'd been brought there. The dreams had helped, she thought. She couldn't remember what they were, but she was sure they'd helped. She stepped outside into early-morning chill, though the sun was up. The hard-faced officer's uniform was tailored, its creases as sharp as his voice. He had an aide with him, his uniform less elegant but also sharply pressed. Low on both dark foreheads was a small laser tattoo, a tiny star artistic and precise, distinct by daylight even on their dark skins.

The officer spoke to her in Standard that was accented but easily understood, his voice brusque but not harsh. "I am here to take you to General Saadhrambacoora. You will there have an opportunity to bathe and eat." He examined her not quite insolently, his eyes taking in her long legs. "You will also inform the general if you were forced to copulate with anyone here."

She nodded, then shivered, this time from cold, and he turned to the man who'd freed her feet, his voice once more a whiplash. Again the man yelped a reply, and left at a run.

The officer led off toward a small floater parked in a nearby opening, surrounded by shelter tents that, from their size and appearance, seemed to be for officers. The aide steered her by an arm, firmly but not roughly. Before they reached the aircraft, the jailor had caught them with a jacket, which the aide draped over Tain's shoulders.

She found herself saying "thank you," and wondered why. The aide helped her into the staff floater, seated her, and moments later the craft took off.

When the radio message ended, Saadhrambacoora sat back in his chair with a grunt of relief. The prisoner was alive and seemingly sound, even though a woman. Or perhaps because she was a woman. He turned to a lieutenant who stood white-faced by the door.

"You realize, I trust, that if anything had happened to her, if she'd been killed or rescued, I'd have broken you to private, had you flogged, and assigned you to a penal platoon."

The general's words had been delivered quietly, coldly. The young officer felt faint. Penal platoons were used in the most dangerous situations, their men to be shot on the spot for any failure, or even slowness, to obey orders.

"As it is," Saadhrambacoora went on, "I am transferring you to the 1st Rifle Battalion for assignment as a platoon leader. Perhaps you will learn something about good sense there. If you don't, one of those little boys may cut your throat. Tell Sergeant Major Davingtor to prepare the transfer form. I will read and sign it."

He watched the man leave the room. *Idiot,* he thought after him, and turned to his computer with its accumulation of messages and reports. *After all the emphasis I put on obtaining a prisoner—with all the emphasis the commodore has put on it—to leave her overnight in the field where she'd be subject to murder, even conceivably to rescue . . . And all on the idiotic grounds that my sleep should not be disturbed!*

He shook his head. Families who raised sons to such uselessness, then used their influence to get them staff positions, were no longer noble, and should be stripped of title and land. But in this day and age . . .

He focused his attention on the screen, on the work awaiting him. It would be a few minutes before she arrived; then allow an hour for her to bathe and eat. A prisoner of such rarity and value, of such interest to the commodore, must be delivered in good physical and mental condition—as good as possible. But he had no doubt at all that Major Thoglakaveera was handling things properly.

He'd keep his own questioning brief, and find out what if any punishments to battalion personnel were called for. And what *rewards* were appropriate; she was, after all, alive and ambulatory.

Lotta sat in the jungle with her legs folded in a full lotus; she'd been like that for hours.

She'd awakened from sleep abruptly, the night before, aware that something had happened to Tain, and had found and melded with her without leaving the tent. Then, when Tain had gone to sleep, Lotta had withdrawn and gone back to sleep too. She had to be asleep herself to help someone dream; so far as she knew, there was no other way of doing it. The next time she woke up, she remembered little about the dreams, any more than if they'd been hers. She only knew she'd been there, guiding.

Briefly she'd melded with Tain again, then with Saadhrambacoora. Now she was with Tain once more, accompanying her outward 55,000 miles.

As reflected by his three-syllable surname, Bavi Ralankoor's family were gentry, not aristocrats. An exceptional record in secondary school had gotten him into a professional college. Where, given the conservatism of some professors and academic administrators, he'd had to be very good to pass, much better than if he'd been noble. And his opportunities for advancement in the fleet had ended at lieutenant commander. He was proud of what he'd accomplished though, and seldom troubled by the limits which birth had laid on him.

Still it made him a bit nervous to have the commodore watch while he worked, particularly with this prisoner, from whom much was hoped for. Strapped to the interrogation seat, she'd said nothing at all out loud, though she'd given him some interesting monitor reads. He could always, of course, apply a drug. And while neither responses nor readings were reliable under the drugs, they could provide valuable leads for further questioning, and in the long run rather exact information. To get explicit answers, pain or the threat of pain, with punishment for lying and rewards for the truth, were often quicker. Or so the manual said. But an occasional subject became tenaciously recalcitrant under such treatment. While a few were said to show an impressive ability to lose consciousness under pain or even the threat of it, a sort of escape mechanism.

He'd probably end up using a drug on her, he decided, but there were a few more questions he wanted to ask first.

He turned to the commodore. "Sir, I'd like to take her to the conference room and question her about the apparatus there."

The commodore nodded without speaking, his broad face expressionless, and they all left together, a mixed procession. Ralankoor led, his two assistants wheeling the interrogation chair with the prisoner still strapped into it, the two marine guards walking alongside. The commodore, his aide and orderly brought up the rear. An elevator took them two levels up.

When Tain saw the teleport, the monitor betrayed her reaction. Ralankoor turned to Tarimenloku. "She's afraid of it," he said, then looking at her again, keyed on the translator and pointed. "Are you afraid of that?" he asked; the terminal spoke the question in Standard, in a decent facsimile of Ralankoor's own voice.

Again she said nothing, but the monitor screen did.

"Do you know what it is?" he asked.

She shook her head, her first voluntary response.

"My instruments tell me you do," he said, and the reading of fear became stronger.

Fear. Of what, specifically? Deviating from standard interrogation procedure, Ralankoor took a shortcut, a shot in the dark. If it didn't work, no harm would be done; if it did, it could save considerable time. "If you do not tell me everything we want to know," he said drily, "I will have you wheeled onto it, and turn it on."

Again the monitor responded strongly. Tain turned to the man and for the first time answered him, her words issuing from the terminal in Klestronik. "You're playing with me," she said. "You know if you put me on it, you'll learn everything anyway."

He looked thoughtfully at her, then at the teleport. "Of course we will. But it is painful. I give you an opportunity to tell us without it."

His attention was on her face now, instead of on his instruments. Her expression showed distrust. "Painful?" she said. "Why do you play with me like that? What can you gain from it? The truth machine is not painful."

"Commander," Tarimenloku interrupted, and turning to look at him, Ralankoor put the translator on hold. "Can you operate it?" the commodore asked.

"I have read the labels—those that are complete words: *Power. Activate.* That's all."

"Put her on it!"

"Yes sir." Ralankoor felt vaguely ill at ease, and thought of trying it on a crewman first. But the commodore did not tolerate having his orders questioned. He eyed the mysterious "truth machine"; the cumbersome interrogation chair was clearly too wide for the platform, so after activating the translator again, he took a small, palm-sized instrument from his belt and held it in front of her.

"Do you know what this is?" he asked.

She shook her head.

"It is a neural whip." He thumbed the setting, pointed it at her, and squeezed the trigger. She yelled, recoiling at the pain. "And now," he said, "you know what a neural whip is. At its lowest setting. It can be much worse. My assistants are going to release you and place you on the truth machine. If you do not cooperate, I will show you what a high setting is like, and then we will tie you and you will go on the truth machine anyway."

He released her restraints himself, then his men helped her to her feet and walked her to the apparatus, gripping her arms. She stepped onto the platform, holding back a bit, her face ashen. At the control panel, Ralankoor pressed *power*. A small red light came on. He wasn't sure what it meant; sometimes apparatus required time to reach full operational status, and often this was indicated by a light coming on, or changing color. After some seconds the red light went off and a green light came on. He looked at the prisoner; she was staring at it, trembling visibly. He pressed the *activate* switch, and the red light began to flash. She started to moan, to shake more strongly. Admirable! Clearly she had a very strong ethic not to tell what she knew.

"She is holding back, sir," said one of his assistants. "She doesn't want to go."

"Force her!"

They pushed, and suddenly, taking them by surprise, she lunged forward into the gate.

*And went berserk, bounding from the platform with a wild coarse howl, crashed blindly into the commodore's aide, sending the man sprawling, then charged into the conference table, rebounded, still howling, staggered, lunged, and fell over a chair onto the deck, where she lay thrashing and kicking.* Ralankoor, recovering partly from his shock, ordered the security detail to hold her there, then strode to the comm to call the chief medical officer.

Holding her wasn't easy; his assistants had to help the two marines. Tense, avoiding the commodore's eyes, Ralankoor could only wait helplessly for the doctor to get there. The howling had changed to shrieks, which were worse. The prisoner's body arched and writhed, her limbs jerking in the grasp of the men who held her; they had all they could do to control them. The reek of her made Ralankoor ill.

It occurred to him to shut the apparatus off, but when he turned to the control panel, its lights were dark. He pressed the switch anyway, his hand shaking a bit. In the three minutes it took the chief medical officer to arrive, the prisoner's violence hardly slackened. The CMO administered a sedative, and when the prisoner had gone slack, looked at Ralankoor as if to ask what in Kargh's name he'd done to her.

Then the commodore stalked out without a word, followed by his shaken aide. Ralankoor wondered what this would mean to his career.

An hour later, in the clinic, the CMO stood observing the prisoner's vital signs on his monitor panel. She would probably survive, he decided; he'd been uncertain for a while. He wasn't at all sure what she'd be like when she regained consciousness though.

It was evening. The sides of Romlar's command tent were rolled down, and a field lamp was on low, lighting it dimly.

For Lotta it had been a long day, a long night and day, and she'd given her report slumped in a canvas folding chair. "Apparently something went wrong with the teleport after they used it," she said. "Even its power tap seems to be dead."

Romlar nodded. "You mentioned the flashing red light. That's a warning—of what I can't even guess. Maybe not to use it without a program cube; something like that."

She nodded. "I disconnected from her when she decided to do it; being melded when she looped through was not something I wanted to experience. Then I melded with the intelligence officer. Didn't think about it, just did it. I'd never realized I could switch like that without coming back to my body between times."

She stood up and rotated her shoulders. "After they sedated her, I melded with the commodore for a while. He's scared to death of the teleport now, though he'd never admit it, even to himself. He's glad it's out of order—had it hauled to a storage compartment where they keep a lot of broken down components of this and that. Told his chief engineer not to touch it, that SUMBAA would take care of it. SUMBAA's a computer on Klestron; apparently some kind of master computer."

Her eyes focused on Romlar again. "Next I melded with the doctor. He thinks she's going to come through it. Then I melded with her, and I think he's right. Probably it's partly having recovered from it once before, and partly the work I did with her afterward, the sessions we had."

Lotta got up. "I'm going to go check on her again. Then I'm going to catch some sleep."

Romlar got up too. "Sounds good. Give me another report in the morning."

In the clinic on board HRS *Blessed Flenyaagor*, Tain Faronya awoke from nearly eighteen hours of unconsciousness. Awoke stiff, sore, and hungry, but surprisingly cheerful, as if something good had happened. She didn't remember that she was Tain Faronya, or where she was or how she'd gotten there. Wasn't even aware that anything was missing. It was almost as if she were a clean slate. Even quite a bit of her vocabulary was gone, although she hadn't missed it.

Lotta stayed in her mind for a time. Then, with a sense of loss, she withdrew and went to bed.

# 63

Lotta no longer had bodyguards. No predators at all had been seen in the vicinity, or their tracks or scat. They seemed to be staying well away. Thus she was alone by the creek, washing her clothes—soaping them, then beating them with a stout stick, the sound of it dull and soggy.

"Sis."

She looked up. "Yes?"

"I'd like your help."

"Can it wait till I've rinsed these and wrung them out? Rinsed them anyway. I'm about done."

"Better yet," Jerym said, squatting beside her, "I'll help."

He began rinsing and wringing while she finished washing, his powerful hands and wrists squeezing things drier than she could have. When they were done, they stood, she coming about to her brother's chin. Together they climbed the hill and draped the wet things on saplings near her tent.

"I guess you miss your tent-mate," Jerym said.

"Yes, I miss her. But not as much as you do."

"That's what I've come to you about. I've got this feeling of vengefulness, and I'm afraid it'll warp my judgement—endanger my missions and men. We've lost thirty-four in 1st and 2nd Platoons, with me coolheaded. It's been a couple days since we've been out now, and Romlar's bound to give us another mission tonight or tomorrow."

"Okay," Lotta said. "Let's find us a log and sit." Not far from the last tent, her tent, lay a log, mossy and mouldering, too far gone for the local equivalent of ants. "Sit," she said pointing to it, and he sat. Then she sat on the ground in front of him, in the lotus posture, back straight, head up.

"Okay. This isn't going to be an Ostrak Procedure. It's just you and me, talking like brother and sister." Her eyes had settled on his face. "So. You want to revenge yourself."

"No. I want to avenge Tain."

"Okay. For what?"

"For— Their taking her away."

"Ah. How do you suppose she's taking it? Being away?"

He frowned thoughtfully. "Well, you say she doesn't remember anything. So I suppose she could be taking it all right."

"Actually, more than all right. She's happy. She remembers how to talk and take care of herself, and she's learning about the world around her, the only world she knows. The Klestroni aren't mistreating her at all; they plan to take her home with them—see if their medics there can get her memory back for her—and find out what she knows, of course. They've even assigned a female crew member as an attendant. So I'd say vengeance isn't needed; not by her."

Jerym frowned. "It's as if she's dead, not remembering like that, not knowing."

"True. It's a little as if she'd committed suicide to save the secret of the teleport. But instead of being reborn as an infant, she's been reborn as an adult." She shifted focus a bit. "Do you feel as if you need to avenge Bressnik? Or any of the other guys you've lost?"

He shook his head. "They were warriors."

"And?"

"Warriors expect to die. It's as if you're already dead but the timing hasn't been settled yet."

"That's true of everyone, Jerym. Everyone dies, over and over. Warriors just tend to die younger. Do you worry about dying, when you go out?"

"No. But I've had the Ostrak Procedures. I know it's not the end. Just a change."

"Okay. Tain didn't worry about dying, either—not then. Even if she hadn't remembered dying before, and living again. I was with her, remember, experiencing her thoughts with her. She was intent on what she was doing, and she carried it off. Took a lot of guts; a *lot*. In a way she was a warrior just then."

Lotta studied Jerym. His focus was elsewhere. "What are you thinking about?" she asked.

He half grinned. "Don't you know?"

"I could. But I'm asking, instead."

"What you just said reminded me of—things. Tain and I loved each other. And when I'd come back off a mission, we'd—we'd get together. You know. Make love."

She nodded.

"So I had something special to look forward to, and you'd think I'd have had attention on getting back alive. Not just to see Tain, but to make love with her. But— When I was out there, all I had on my mind was the mission. I'd start to think about Tain again when we were flying home from the rendezvous."

Lotta laughed. "Okay! That's a warrior! A warrior will sometimes give up his warriorhood if things happen just right. Or just wrong. But you didn't.

"It probably helped that you were T'swa-trained and had the Ostrak Procedures. They'd both give you a sense of perspective on Confederation-type cultural beliefs, beliefs that are fine for people at Job and Compete, and to some extent even Fun. But not so good yet for Wisdom/Knowledge, unless you get picked up by one of the Institutes. And it's not good at all for Warriors."

Jerym nodded thoughtfully.

"With these things looked at, d'you suppose, on your next mission, you'll have attention on vengeance?"

"Umm, probably not. I'm not sure, but probably not."

"Good. Medreth would have showed you a diagram before one of your sessions with her, probably not long before she went back to Lake Loreen. Remember? It was called the parts of man."

"Yeah. I sort of remember."

"Tell me about them."

"Well, a person—not the body, but the part that survives—has parts that do different things, like body parts do different things. And most of them come as a set, like bodies have a set of arms, a set of legs . . . Pairs. One pair deals with the role, like the warrior role or dancer role, or what *you* do, for example. I suppose they have to do with keeping you defined. And another pair has to do with the script, you could say." Jerym frowned slightly. "I kind of pictured it starting out with a script, and then revising it to current situations, trying to keep its integrity at the same time, keeping it in line with the role as far as possible. And that's as far as I can go, talking about it. That's as far as I understood it."

Lotta smiled. "Those are the basics. So Tain has all those too, right? Had them and still has them."

Jerym nodded, sensing now where Lotta was taking this.

She eyed him knowingly. "Anything you want to say about that?"

He grinned at his sister. "You know I do. Tain came out here to Terfreya in spite of the fact that stowing away wasn't the kind of thing you'd imagine her doing. And she talked Romlar into letting her go with D Company, when he started out saying no." He paused, his expression changing. "Although I'm not ready to say she scripted being captured by the Klestroni."

"Okay. Anything else?"

"Well— I suspect her script people have done a lot of rewriting the last couple of days."

Lotta's laugh was a light arpeggio. "Big brother," she said getting up, "I hereby declare this discussion at an end. Unless there's something more you've just got to say to me."

He stood too. "Just one thing. I'm sure as Tunis glad you're my sister."

She laughed again. "I am too, Jerym, I am too."

# 64

Lotta was at the command tent and the sun newly risen when Romlar walked in, his hair still wet. He grinned at her. "How's my favorite intelligence specialist?"

She stuck her tongue out at him. "Big praise! I'm your only intelligence specialist. The rest of your information comes from scout flights and cadets, and the locals the cadets keep in touch with."

He laughed. "Don't knock praise. Especially from the regimental CO. What've you got for me today?"

"The general's worried about his diminished supply of gunships. Your guys wrecked another of them yesterday, beyond repair, which leaves him with only eight. And the nearest replacements are more parsecs away than he cares to think about."

"Mmm."

"That's right. You might want to think about reducing them further. With your replacements, that could give you a huge advantage."

Romlar nodded thoughtfully. "I wouldn't bring in more gunships; I don't want air superiority that way. I want to drive them off with inferior numbers and inferior weapons; that'll stamp us with the mystique we want them to remember the Confederation by. But it would save us a lot of trouble and lives if we could wreck *their* gunships; gunships have given us probably eighty percent of our casualties. They're hard to kill though. They're better armored than ours, and even when we shoot one of them down, they usually haul them away afterward. To repair, or cannibalize for parts." He paused, lips pursed. "Tell you what. You've made me relook at the situation. It's going to cost some guys, but I think I see a way to thin them out. I mean *really* thin them out!"

When Lotta left the tent, she hadn't fully recovered from Romlar's reaction to her report. She'd long known, intellectually, what warriors were all about, and hadn't questioned it. She understood the function of war and warriors in the real world of acquisitive rulers and merchant princes, of grudges and greed, threats and responses, rivalries and hatreds. And for the better part of a standard year now, she'd lived and worked among warriors, been around their activities, seen their mental images, even been inside their minds.

But when he'd said, "It's going to cost some guys, but I think I see a way . . ."—and with enthusiasm!—it had struck her as something totally foreign. Those "guys," after all, were his friends, even if they were warriors.

As she walked to the supply tent for her day's rations, she contemplated the matter. Then it struck her—the side of the matter she'd overlooked, obvious though it was: Every gunship destroyed now meant lives not lost later.

She regarded herself with wry amusement, this sixteen-year-old woman, seer, spy, and mental therapist. *My wits,* she thought, *where were you hiding? In war, a commander, when he has a choice, invests his resources. Some perhaps in actions that promise modest payoffs at low risks, and maybe others in higher risks for bigger payoffs.*

*Maybe,* she thought, *I need to find my big brother and have him repeat what he told me. And this time listen for my own self.*

It was the zone between afternoon and evening, still full daylight but with the sun lowering in the west. Standing back within the edge of a dense second-growth forest, Jerym looked out between trees and across nearly half a mile of open pasture and field to where the Spice River flowed. The weather had been dry, the river relatively low, the banks consequently high.

On the other side of the river was forest.

Four miles west, a Klestronu battalion was setting up bivouac in open ground between the river and a road, a bivouac designed to look assaultable. In fact, the Klestronu general intended it as bait in an enticing deathtrap.

It had taken several days of waiting to get a set of factors this favorable.

The Klestroni, Lotta had said, would have a scout overflying the area constantly, watching hopefully unnoticed from two miles up for indications of cadets or troopers. If it spotted any, the bivouacked battalion would be warned. If it spotted a large enough concentration of them sufficiently vulnerable, a flight of four gunships was standing by, six miles west, ready to fly immediately. They could be over the field in front of him within three or four minutes.

Jerym peered out again at the sun. The boats, he thought, should be putting in the water within minutes, a little way upstream—carrying the whole of H Company, sweating in camouflage ponchos. Not that they'd be trying to hide themselves; they wanted to be seen. The ponchos were to cover what they were carrying.

Getting the boats had been easily the most difficult and dangerous part of the mission so far. At the request of a cadet—the Terfreyans loved the pint-sized warriors—the boats had been gathered by locals twenty miles and more upstream the day before. And been transported by floater at night along the river—as much as possible under the sheltering eaves of the bordering forest. The risk of detection and destruction had been considerable.

The cadets had been in position since dawn, one platoon in the woods across the river, another under the dense brush that overhung the bank on this side. Each cadet had a stubby surface-to-air missile launcher and five small, wicked rockets. Under their ponchos, each of H Company's troopers had the same. As did several of the twenty-eight troopers in 2nd Platoon.

Timing was important but not absolutely critical. When the boats launched, they'd let him know. When they approached a point opposite him, they'd let him know that, too.

Lotta had learned of the Klestronu plan the day before, in the morning, but that had simply provided the details of where and exactly how. Romlar's general plan had been made six days before, and the request for additional rockets and launchers sent to Iryala. When Lotta's mind-spying had provided a specific situation, Romlar had had a hurried day and a half to set things up. The cadets had timed the current, clocking floating wood over a quarter-mile section of river. If everything went more or less as planned, Jerym thought, they'd have a real coup. Otherwise— That would depend on what went wrong.

So far the regiment had had only one disaster, a semi-disaster actually, when D Company had lost 62 troopers, two scout crewmen, the company commander—and Tain.

Jerym waited calmly, looked for the sun again, saw it squatting red and swollen on the horizon. A moment later he got the radio pulse that told him the boats were in the water. He called to his platoon directly, maintaining radio silence. Each man knew they had about six minutes: Romlar's best guess-timate of how long it would be before the boats were observed by Klestronu aerial surveillance, plus time for the gunships to arrive. If the gunships arrived later, things would be awkward; sooner, and things could go very badly. If the gunships didn't arrive at all, which was possible, the mission would be scrubbed.

So far, with that one exception, Romlar's judgement had been very good, and as far as Jerym was concerned, that had been more than chance.

They waited, Jerym at last feeling tension. The second radio pulse beeped with no sign of gunships, and he moved the platoon westward, out of sight within the forest's edge, moving at a rate intended to match the boats' speed. They hiked for several minutes before he heard a rocket explode, then quickly another, and 2nd Platoon moved closer to the forest's edge, to see.

There were four gunships over the river. Three were rising and presumably also firing, their silent gun beams invisible in the daylight. The fourth described tight, climbing circles, tail up. Two more rockets struck it, and it began to fall slowly, spiraling now, while rockets exploded against two other craft without apparent effect.

The crippled ship disappeared behind the high bank while the others continued to fire from higher up. For a moment there were no further hits, then another was struck three times within as many seconds. It staggered and began to settle slowly, moving toward the open bank. It was hit again, twice more, but its rate of fall remained the same till it was over land. Then it set down heavily in a kressera field.

During all this, 2nd Platoon crouched motionless, as if frozen by the sight.

Of the remaining two gunships, one was hit again and began to climb sharply as if damaged and trying to get away. That concentrated the rocketeers' fire, and quickly it was hit twice more. It slid down and to one side, then plummeted, the splash visible above the bank when it hit.

Jerym wouldn't have been surprised to see the other run then. Instead it seemed to intensify its attack, diving, swooping, its guns surely slashing at targets. Rockets struck it without apparent effect, and it doubled back as if determined to wipe out the boats and men below. Almost it disappeared behind the bank, then rose abruptly, seeming to labor, swerved, took another hit, and came down in the same kressera field, plowing dirt.

"Now!" Jerym bellowed, and 2nd Platoon ran out into the field. The rocketeers led off, and at closer range fired rockets into the motionless targets. Then the hosemen took over the lead, firing short bursts at the gunports, in case anyone aboard still lived and tried to man their guns.

They didn't. While everyone else stayed back a hundred yards, two troopers ran up to each of the two craft, planted satchel charges, then trotted back, and the charges were detonated. High explosives roared, gutting the armored gunships.

Jerym led the platoon to the riverbank. From there he saw no sign of the other two floaters, nor of any boats beached. What he did see was some floating boat wreckage not yet out of sight downstream. There were no floating bodies; they'd been too loaded with equipment. A few troopers stood or lay on the far bank, some being administered to by cadets and other troopers—perhaps twenty troopers in all—but it seemed to Jerym that H Company was no more.

Other cadets were trotting downriver on his side, from their bypassed ambush upstream, and Jerym went to meet them. They'd have seen where the two other gunships went down, and he'd have men dive to find them. They could plant charges and blow them under water, so there'd be no chance of salvage.

The Klestroni were down to four gunships now, apparently, but at the moment he didn't feel like rejoicing.

# 65

They never did blow up the sunken gunships. Even before Jerym had a chance to question the cadets, hover vehicles came into sight down the road: a column of armored assault vehicles loaded with marines from the Klestronu bivouac—apparently two companies of them.

Second Platoon and the cadets, totalling fifty-four men and boys, went over the rim of the riverbank, fired their remaining STA missiles at the enemy, then threw weapons, equipment, helmets, and their remaining satchel charges into the river in order to swim for it. They were neither situated nor equipped for a serious fight with a force like that. The unexpected intensity of their brief rocket attack, though, plus Klestronu caution, allowed them to get across the river without being closed on. Then they separated again, cadets from troopers, into the jungle, into the evening, the troopers to find their way to places where floaters could pick them up.

One cadet went with 2nd Platoon. Their mapbooks and radios were at the bottom of the Spice; his radio and local knowledge would help them get picked up. Also with 2nd Platoon went H Company's thirty-two survivors; five of them, wounded, were carried on makeshift stretchers. The early part of the night they slept in the jungle; without their visors, it was too dark beneath the forest roof to travel. Later, when a moon came up, they pushed on, along the river bank where visibility, if poor, was not impossible. Jerym wished he had eyes like a T'swi's.

It was close to dawn when they reached another farming district. Two CPCs waited at the back edge of a pasture, and the troopers crowded aboard. The cadet left them then, to trot to one of the farmsteads where he could get a meal and a few hours' sleep in the hay.

On their return to Headquarters Company, 2nd Platoon slept much of the day. When they got up, they mustered beneath the trees with 1st Platoon, along with H Company's unwounded survivors. The wounded had been ported back to Iryala already. Romlar assigned thirteen H Company troopers to 2nd Platoon, bringing it to full strength, and the other fourteen to bolster 1st Platoon.

Then he dismissed them, except for the two platoon leaders. Romlar took them to the command tent, where Jorrie Renhaus and a T'swa major were waiting, the T'swi being Colonel Jil-Zat's EO from the constantly moving cadet HQ. Major Dho-Kat had arrived the night before in a scout floater.

"Jarnol, Alsnor," Romlar said to the platoon leaders, "something's come up, and we're planning a major action. The Klestroni aren't what you'd call innovative, but their flagship's engineering section is modifying a pair of shuttles for ground attack purposes. Lotta found out last night. Their idea is to instrument one of them as a stratospheric observation platform. And to modify both of them for dropping bombs.

"If we let them pull this off, we'll be up against a weapon we can't get at. This whole region will be under constant surveillance, and it'll be a lot harder to conceal our movements and positions."

The teenaged colonel looked over his people, his friends, then went on as calmly and casually as if he were talking about a proposed ball game.

"I expected that if we reduced their gunships enough, we could move around more openly, maybe get them to bring troops into the jungle after us, where we could whip them good. I also thought it just might break their commodore's will to persist. But according to Lotta, he's developed a kind of grim resolution to leave Terfreya only on a victory. Which is just the opposite of our purpose.

"They seem to think the modifications won't take long—a week, maybe two or three if they have problems—and they've already flown marine ordnance officers back up to help design the bombs and get them built.

"So now's the time to do something decisive. To run them off. Here's what I've got in mind. . . ."

Six days later, his strike teams were ready. His plan was three-faceted but not intricate. Any one of its three operations could shock and hurt the Klestroni, regardless of the success or failure of the others. If all were successful, they'd hurt him critically.

Preparation had required considerable floater traffic, and with less than usual caution, for supply hauls to headquarters from the outgate sites. More combat personnel carriers were ported in.

Now it was night in the jungle. Handlamps, pointed more or less groundward and on low intensity, moved here and there to light the final preparations. There were several troopers with pole charges, and seventy cadets who'd been flown in to Romlar's headquarters. Fourteen cadets, selected for prepuberty voices and features, were dressed as girls, in party clothes provided by farm families. Their wigs, customized in Landfall on one-day's notice and teleported, were held to fresh-shaved scalps by a theatrical adhesive.

Preparation had been as careful as time allowed. The fourteen had had very little opportunity to observe teenaged females, so Coyn Carrmak had been flown in from 1st Battalion to help Lotta inspect and coach them. According to a couple of troopers who'd known Carrmak in their days "outside," he'd been somewhat of a ladies' man. He and Lotta drilled the pretenders in appropriate walks and mannerisms.

The other skills they'd need on their mission they already possessed, very highly developed.

In their shoulder bags, beneath cosmetics, mirrors, and tissues, they carried automatic pistols and spare clips, with blast slugs. And one fragmentation grenade each, in case capture was imminent. Two carried additional grenades.

The other fifty-six cadets wore black uniforms especially dyed and ported in for this night mission. A number of them carried rocket launchers and rockets, and several had blast hoses. The rest carried rifles.

When the cadets were ready, Romlar went into his command tent, where a photomap at maximum scale already occupied his computer screen. At such a short distance, teleport targeting was highly accurate, but in this case the target had been built after the map photography was done, and was shown on the map only in a pen approximation. So Renhaus knelt on the platform of the small teleport, peering through, ready to coach Romlar's targeting.

Romlar hit it almost at once, then gave the word, and the "girls" went through the gate. When the last had stepped through, he retargeted and sent the other cadets through.

Again he retargeted, one of the troopers signalling as if greater precision was needed. The trooper raised a hand to halt him; then they waited, Romlar's eyes on his watch, for several minutes. Finally, "Now!" he said. The trooper activated the fuse on his pole charge and shoved it through the gate. On the headquarters side they couldn't hear the explosion.

Over the next several minutes they repeated this with several more pole charges. Then Romlar got up and rotated his shoulders, swung his arms. Uncharacteristically he'd gotten tense. There'd been a lot of details to handle, and he'd been hurried.

Now the first two teams were committed, the first operation well underway, and all he had to wait for was the rising of the lesser moon to start the next.

In the darkness, twelve combat personnel carriers sat hidden by trees in creek beds, waiting for orders to take off. Each held two squads of troopers, fully manned up and wearing parachutes and arm webbing.

Shortly after the White T'swa arrived on Terfreya, the Klestroni had established two regimental field bases about twenty miles from their main base near Lonyer City. One northeast, one southeast. Miles from any sizeable jungle as well, these were fenced and had sentry fields, bunkers, minefields, and anti-aircraft batteries. One of the four remaining Klestronu gunships was stationed at each; the other two were at the main base.

Romlar had assigned three manned-up platoons to attack each

compound. When the order came, the troopers would jump, body-glide over the compounds, and open their chutes at low elevations. Every second man carried a blast hose, the others rifles, all supplied with blast slugs instead of the solid rounds preferred in jungle righting. Every man's grenade pocket held fragmentation grenades.

Waiting, they didn't talk much.

The men of 2nd Platoon sat or lay around near Romlar's command tent, waiting for the word. With their H Company survivors, they numbered forty-two, including Jerym and his platoon sergeant, Warden. The T'swa major who'd arrived with the cadets was squatting in the darkness outside the tent, and Jerym squatted down next to him.

"Do you T'swa ever get nervous?" Jerym asked.

The major chuckled. "Occasionally. When neutrality slips a bit. There are things we do then to calm ourselves."

"Such as?"

"A momentary transfer of attention to the 'I' outside this universe usually provides the necessary perspective."

"Outside the universe. The Ostrak people call it the balcony," Jerym said.

The T'swi chuckled. "That is a suitable way of talking about it."

"They taught us to do that too," Jerym said thoughtfully. "Look at the 'I' in the balcony. 'Turn around and look at yourself,' they say. But it's easy to forget—for me, anyway. Till about a year ago I usually felt lousy— mad, resentful, guilty, hopeless—take your choice. What I feel now, when I'm not feeling good, is only a shadow of how it used to be, so I don't always remember to do something about it."

He paused. "We were supposed to get a lot more training when we got to Tyss—training in the T'sel, including meditation, as well as in military know-how. Maybe we will yet, when we're done here."

Dho-Kat gazed mildly at the teenaged Iryalan. "May I evaluate your troopers for you?"

"Sure. Go ahead."

"You do very well indeed, both as warriors and as human beings. I have associated closely with the people of several worlds—allies and adversaries belonging to various cultures and subcultures. With the exception of the cadets, none of them were your equals, or even approached you, as warriors or with regard to sanity. Or general happiness."

Jerym contemplated that for a few seconds, then asked, "How far are we from being T'swa? Really?"

Jerym felt more than saw the smile. "Speaking strictly," Dho-Kat said, "*T'swa* is a word used to describe human beings of a particular planet with a particular history and culture. But the beings in this universe who are being T'swa, who are playing the role of T'swa, are of precisely the same nature as those who have taken the role of Iryalans. Or of Klestroni. Those who, by intention or default, play the role of victim, do not differ in their nature from those who have taken the role of hero.

"You are Iryalans, the *new* Iryalans. At last the Iryalan culture is changing, and that change is accelerating. I suspect it approaches the point beyond which it cannot be defeated by internal factors. And if The Movement succeeds, as seems probable, the result will be beyond even that which Kristal visualizes."

It seemed to Jerym that the T'swi was talking as much to himself now as to his listener, examining his perspectives as he voiced them.

"Culture on Iryala and in the Confederation as a whole will take forms which ours on Tyss cannot. It will grow a new richness and splendor. In future lives, if you choose, you will take part in that, as I may." He laughed softly. "Or you may decide to spend a quiet life in a monastery on the backwater world of Tyss. That could be pleasant."

He squatted silent for a few seconds while Jerym waited. "By the circumstance of birth, you will never be T'swa in this lifetime," Dho-Kat finished. "But you have no need to be. You are truly exceptional warriors, tested and proven in combat. Think of yourself, if you wish, as 'honorary T'swa'; those of us here on Terfreya would agree without hesitation."

Jerym peered at the powerful black man squatting in the jungle night, and shook his head admiringly. "Major," he said, "you are something."

"As are you, Lieutenant."

"But suppose—even if we send the Klestroni home with a bloody nose and his tail between his legs—suppose they lead an imperial fleet back here in eight or ten years. A fleet that can destroy ours thirty times over. What then?"

"What indeed? If that should happen, perhaps they will land on Iryala and conquer it, and from there rule the Confederation. But the T'sel would not die, not on Tyss and not on Iryala. Eventually it would conquer the conqueror. Meanwhile for a time, perhaps a long time, lives would be less comfortable, their roles perhaps less free. But they would be very interesting."

Someone stepped into the door of the tent, and Dho-Kat got to his feet. "But that is at most a future script which may never be played," he went on. "Meanwhile you have the now, the present to enjoy—this night, this war, this world. Within the hour you will go into battle leading men who know well how to fight and take joy in it, against opponents who are better than many you might encounter.

"Go into combat with the thought that you are already dead, that it simply has not happened yet, and enjoy the battle."

The man in the door stepped outside then, and with a handlamp started off down the hill toward the scouts, Dho-Kat following. Jerym too got up, limbered his knees and joined his troopers, digesting what the T'swi had said.

One part especially had stayed with him— "Go into battle with the thought that you are already dead. . . ." Considering 2nd Platoon's assignment for the night, it seemed a realistic assumption.

# 66

The cadet sergeant in charge of the "party girls" gated into the Klestronu officers' recreation compound and promptly stepped out of the way, looking around as he did so. He saw no one except the next two cadets, the third, the fourth, and at last the fourteenth. It was night, but not very dark there. The cadets were in shadow behind a squad-size tent with a raised floor, one of a large circle of them, their sides rolled down for privacy. In the center of the compound, unseen from where they were, the dance pavilion sent lanes of soft light between the tents. And music, foreign and rollicking.

They knew the layout, from a diagram and from a crude scale mockup on the Regimental Headquarters hill. Lotta had visited the recreation compound in the mind of young officers three times in the preceding days. She'd come to know them through her meld with their general.

When all fourteen cadets had gated in, eleven followed their sergeant between two of the lesser tents, remembering to walk like teenaged girls. The other two began to circle the tent ring from behind.

The brightly lit dance pavilion was centered in a space of grassy ground, and its sides were rolled up, giving a sense of openness and a free flow of air. Inside, the twelve could see couples dancing. Four of the cadets would stay outside. They separated from the others, moving in pairs to two opposite corners of the pavilion. The pair at the front corner stood as if talking, looking past each other, hands in their shoulder bags. Those at the back corner knelt as if hunting for something dropped, to keep out of the line of fire.

Meanwhile the others, regardless of the open sides, walked to the front entrance of the pavilion. A couple passed them, headed for one of the encircling tents—a Klestronu officer and a local girl who might have been sixteen. She was giggling. Her skirt was hiked up to her waist in back, and the officer had his hand in the rear of her underpants. Neither of them paid any attention to the newcomers.

Two guards stood casually at the front entrance, the only guards in sight. They gave the new "girls" little more than perfunctory glances as they filed in; obviously the recreation section had found more who were interested in a good time and a wad of requisitioned local money.

The cadets didn't worry about the guards. The two at the left front corner would take them out. The eight who went in sized up the situation as they distributed themselves across the front: The pavilion was crowded, girls in short supply, and a number of officers danced with each other while waiting.

The cadets wasted no time. Their hands came out of their shoulder bags with guns in them, and they began at once to shoot, first at the officers who already had started eagerly toward them. The flat blasts of their shots were mixed with the uglier sound of blast slugs exploding in flesh.

After the briefest moment, the screaming began, and the stampede. The cadets kept shooting, pausing only to eject an empty clip and slap in a fresh one. Bodies littered the dance floor. Several Klestroni tried to reach them and died. Most fled, scores of them ducking under the rolled-up sides; many of these fell to gunfire from the corners.

Except for the two door guards, the gate detachment and tower guards, the compound's security troops were posted in two large tents, side by side, from which they were to issue if called upon by whistles. So far they'd never been called on. Their shift lieutenant had arranged to be visited by one of the "hostesses," and had gone with her to one of the "rest" tents. Whereupon his men had brought forth a pair of bottles, passing them around to help shorten the shift.

When the firing began, there was a moment of stunned bewilderment. Then they dropped bottles, scrambling for their guns. At that moment, at each tent, a "girl" stepped into the entrance, threw a grenade, then another, and hit the dirt outside, below the floor level. The first grenades exploded almost at once, the second a long moment later. The cadets reappeared then, and darted in to pour blast slugs into the sprawled bodies. One wounded Klestroni managed to draw his own weapon, and one of the cadets died, but no guard escaped either tent.

The other fifty-six cadets, those uniformed in black, lay dispersed but ready along both sides of the road between the rec compound and the headquarters compound. But much nearer the rec compound: some one hundred yards outside its high barbed wire fence, and somewhat farther outside its fifteen-foot concrete wall. They felt exposed, lying there, and in fact they were. Harrowed every week, the field was smooth and bare of growth, while near the fence, floodlights bathed it, their light spilling farther, diffusing and thinning.

The fifty-six heard small caliber pistols begin to fire. So far, so good; their turn would come. The gunfire thickened. About a minute later there was a roar as the armored cab on one of the guard towers blew apart—one of the towers in front. The other blew a minute later.

The floodlights and spotlights had been mounted on the towers, and their destruction had left the cadets cloaked in darkness. Now, like furious badgers, the boys began to dig quick shallow holes, something to lie in. Meanwhile a gunship appeared from the direction of the headquarters compound, and circled the rec compound well above the wall. Its spotlights walked about inside, but its beam guns did not fire. This continued for a minute, then a tower cab blew on the back wall, and the gunship climbed higher, not knowing what had caused the explosion.

The cadets gave the gunship little attention. They too wore the new helmets now, visors down, watching as a column of twenty armored assault vehicles moved down the road from the headquarters compound. The fourth and final tower burst; they heard its roar. As the column approached, the cadets on the north side of the road opened fire on it with rockets. The AAVs stopped, turrets pivoting. Beam guns came to life, lancing across the field, firing mostly too high at first. More rockets hissed, slashed, exploded. Marines piled out the hatches on the off side, the south side, and as they did, rockets hissed from that side too, into the open hatches, while blast hoses and automatic rifles poured blast slugs into the marines. Fire from most of the turret guns ceased, but marine rifles sent scores of wire-thin beams sweeping and crisscrossing toward the cadet muzzle blasts in a deadly, well-drilled pattern.

Meanwhile the gunship, unsure at first what to do, sallied out to hit the cadets in the field. Two rockets exploded on its armored bow, and its pilot swung away to fire from a distance, as if not wanting to risk his craft.

Another powerful roar blew the gate and gatehouse, and the cadet riflemen, those who were able, began to pull back, leaving the blast hoses to hold the marines' attention. The marines advanced on bellies, knees and elbows, stopping only to shoot or die. Grenades roared. The hose fire thinned, stopped.

The combat personnel carrier slowed almost to a walk. "Visors down!" the jump master ordered quietly, and twenty grins dimmed behind face shields curved and tinted.

"Gloves on!" They pulled on warm gloves; it would be cold outside.

"Stand up!"

They got to their feet, the two rows of men dovetailing to form a single line. They wore no reserve chutes and no field packs. Their rifles were snapped diagonally across their harness in front; their magazine pouches were full.

The right-side door slid open to the night and cold.

"Stand in the door!"

The front men shuffled forward, spreading the line a bit. Their platoon leader stood with the toes of his boots over the edge, looking at the Klestronu field base, recalling Romlar's orders: "Aim for the middle—the muster field." Headquarters and officers' country—the primary killing zone—were immediately east of it. "Kill the head, and the body's in trouble," he'd said. For an outfit like the Klestroni especially.

And these troopers knew the base well, from aerial holos provided by a high overflight two nights earlier, had "drilled" their platoon and squad assignments on a crude scale mockup.

The jump master watched the computer screen beside the door. It showed the Klestronu field base 12,000 feet down and 2,300 feet east of their line of flight. The red blip on the screen was their floaters; white blips were the others. The red blip led.

The CPC's computer integrated atmospheric pressure, air movement, the lateral momentum that would be imparted to the jumpers by the floater's slow forward speed . . . A light above the screen lit green, and the jump master slapped Varns on the shoulder. The lieutenant dove, the line of men behind him following quickly out into nothingness. The jump master followed the last of them, leaving the troop compartment empty.

Jerym stood at the head of 2nd Platoon, watching as Renhaus and Romlar targeted the teleport.

"There!" said Renhaus. "Looks good!"

Romlar went and looked briefly for himself, then turned to Jerym and his men. "Okay. You'll gate into the exec messroom, as planned. Right now, as far as I can tell, there's no one there to see your mode of arrival, but don't depend on it. And remember, when you gate out, the entrance you'll be facing is at the south end, toward the operations area."

Lotta had provided a lot of "eye witness" information for them, including sketches, from "personal" observation during melds. And they'd "drilled" repeatedly their individual and unit actions on a crude scale model, mocked up on the ground outside Romlar's headquarters tent.

There were a dozen last minute advices Romlar could have given, but they weren't needed, and he knew it. "Any questions?"

No one said anything. Teeth showed. Eyes gleamed.

"All right. Alsnor, lead off."

Jerym jogged through the gate . . .

✧   ✧   ✧

. . . and into the Klestronu exec messroom. He moved to one side and turned to face the rear, the kitchen area, while the rest of his platoon gated in trotting, running softly. He saw no bogeys, and speaking quietly, sent two men to check the staff officers' messroom on the far side of the kitchen area. Then he moved quickly to a window by the door, where Warden, his platoon sergeant, was already peering out.

He'd barely had time to look when there was a shot from the other messroom. The platoon, already distributed around the walls, turned; one fire team slipped into the kitchen, rifles ready. Seconds later, a trooper came back in to report there'd been a messman there, apparently checking an urn and platter of cakes for staff officers who might come in, perhaps after or before a shift. He'd run for the door and been shot.

Jerym nodded curtly, reminded by this that they might have very little undisturbed time here. He looked at his watch and pressed a button on it. "Team leaders here!" he said quietly, and they moved to him. "That shot's been heard, must have been, but they're not likely to nail down the direction of an isolated shot like that. And with all the emergency radio traffic they must be getting now, they don't have much attention for anything else. If they don't hear any more shooting right away, they'll likely assume it was an accidental discharge by some security detail. Remember, their internal security uses projectile firearms too.

"So we're going to sit quiet till I order otherwise—two minutes—and let their attention get back fully to what it was on before. Then you'll move out and hit your targets. Now take positions by the doors you'll move out of."

He turned back to his window then. The area was lit by lights on poles, not brightly, but sufficiently for seeing. A hundred feet away, by the door of the Klestronu command center, a guard stood on the small porch. Before, his rifle had been slung on a shoulder; now he held it in his hands as he scanned the neighborhood, though overall his demeanor still seemed casual.

Jerym looked at his watch. Most of a minute had passed since he'd set his timer. He waited half a minute longer, then swiveled his mike. His radio was set to transmit at minimum power. "Platoon listen up," he said. "The signal to move out will be a single shot from just outside the east door. Klefma!"

"Yes sir."

"Have Barkum go out the east side door and take cover behind the porch. There's a door guard at the entrance to the command center. I want Barkum to kill him with one round. And I don't want the guy to yell. Bang and he's dead. Then we move out. Barkum will join you when you leave. Questions?"

Barkum's voice answered: "Bang and he's dead. Then I go with my team."

Jerym grinned. "You got it. Start."

He watched then, eyes intent. Seconds passed quietly, ten, fifteen. The shot sounded and the guard fell at the same moment. "Go," Jerym barked, this time not using his mike, and men began moving out the doors. The team assigned to destroy the command center itself moved past him out the south door, followed by the teams assigned to the other prefab buildings of the operations area: the communications center, the briefing center, and the dispatcher's center.

Warden, the platoon sergeant, with Desterbi an interval behind, trotted toward the command center, slowly enough to mistake for marines going to report. They mounted the steps, then paused to let the strike men of the other hit teams—two from each—trot to their own targets. Their buddies stayed behind to give them fire support if needed. Warden bent and shoved the dead guard off the porch, while Desterbi put the basket bomb down, out of the way to one side.

*So far,* Jerym told himself, *so good.*

He'd hardly thought it when automatic weapons fire burst out north of the messhall, where four of the sweep teams should have been waiting for their cue to begin their kill sweep of officers' country. Across the way, Warden pushed open the command center door and stepped in, Desterbi right after him. Jerym could hear the racket of their rifles on automatic, and bare seconds later Desterbi was outside again, his back against the wall, waiting for Warden. From the nearby communications center, a basket bomb roared, followed a second later by another from the dispatcher's center, and almost at once by a third from the briefing center. With the particular explosive used, anything that might have survived the blasts would have been seared by heat flash.

The nearer yard lights had been shot out, and Jerym lowered his visor to see better.

The nearby gunfire was gaining intensity as the sweep teams spread into officers' country. Four or five long seconds passed before Warden backed out the command center door, dragging an inert body that had to be the Klestronu general. As Warden backed down the steps, Desterbi picked up the basket bomb, but before he could throw it through the open door, he fell, shot. For an instant Jerym held his breath, turning away to protect his night vision from the expected blast, waiting for the bomb to go off, to wipe out Desterbi, Warden, and the general.

There was no blast; Desterbi had been shot before he could flip the time fuse. Warden was crouched beside the porch. When nothing happened, he raised up enough to see, and there was Desterbi, motionless, and the bomb. Warden sprang up beside him, snatched the bomb, and jumped down again. Gunfire yammered, and from somewhere, a Klestronit swept a rifle beam across the area. Warden fell. Still the bomb didn't go off.

"First and 2nd squads!" Jerym snapped into his mike, "do whatever's necessary to suppress that enemy fire. Move out if you have to."

"First squad moving out."

"Second moving out."

"Mellis!"

"Yes sir!"

"When I say 'go,' get over there and throw that Ambers-damned bomb in the door. Then take care of the enemy CO."

"Got it!"

Jerym waited. Gunfire erupted seemingly at the other end of the messhall. "Go!" he ordered.

He watched Mellis dash in a low crouch, hit the ground, roll, scramble, dash, hit the ground . . . In short seconds he was beside the porch and the body of Warden. He bent, straightened, threw, hit the ground again. Again Jerym averted his eyes. Three seconds later the bomb roared, and he looked. There was a glow inside the open door as things flammable began to burn. Mellis was pulling off the general's shirt. It came free, and he crouched over the form again, working furiously, fell, got back to his knees, then pitched forward on his face. The automatic weapons fire increased.

"Shit!" Jerym swore, and went out the door. There was no one else to send. He ran as Mellis had, dash, hit the dirt, roll, scramble, dash . . . He rolled Mellis off the general and quickly finished removing the general's trousers and shorts. *Hairier than a bear,* he thought. *Three times hairier than Carrmak.*

Then, still oblivious to the gunfire, Jerym slipped off his light combat pack, drew out a small spool of det cord, and in what shelter the porch offered, he hog-tied the general.

Done, he crouched beside the porch, looking around. In close, the shooting was only sporadic now, but it was furious nearby in officers' country. Three troopers ran toward the messhall from the direction of the ruined briefing and communications centers. The floaters would land at the muster ground north of the messhall, if they were lucky enough to get through. Jerym bent, grabbed the general under the arms, and dragged him into the open, away from the building. Then he turned and sprinted for the cover of the messhall.

Not far from Lonyer City, three combat personnel carriers, widely separated, held back as if spectators. They carried no troops, only their pilots and copilots, who watched three gunships exchange fire a mile away.

The fight was brief, the two that fought with rockets and hoses shooting down the one that fought back with beam guns. By that time, one of the victors was losing altitude, angling off toward the city as if its pilot hoped to take refuge there.

When the Klestronu gunship went down, anti-aircraft guns began at once to fire, beams slicing the sky, seeking the enemy craft that remained. Instead of trying to escape, the gunship challenged them, thinning them, its descending tracers a delicate, hypnotic stitchery in the darkness, before it fell abruptly in a flurry of coruscating lights.

The sky went quiet, and the three CPCs moved in low and fast, at first undetected, drawing no fire. Then small-arms fire stormed first at one, then at a second. Their flight paths converged toward the center of the enclosed base, and the muster ground there. They slowed abruptly, pressing their pilots against their straps, then landed. Their doors shot open.

Men sprinted for one of them, several falling as they ran. Others, in a cluster, sprinted toward a second. The first group clambered in, and the floater launched while her door was still closing. She accelerated sharply, keeping low, barely clearing the tents in front of her, and with scarce feet to spare passed over one fence, another, beams slashing at her, then sped off across a field pursued by only random fire. Behind her, the second took a different though similar course. But the men who'd boarded her were marines. One threw a grenade into the cockpit. It roared, and skidding, the craft took out a row of tents, hit an antiaircraft emplacement and somersaulted. The third had risen last and without boarders, climbing vertically to decoy attention and fire. It was hit, staggered. More antiaircraft beams stabbed and sliced, till it plummeted, hit the ground heavily and broke in two.

In the first floater, Jerym got to his knees, then to his feet. Hot metal reeked. Around him in the rear of the troop compartment, other men picked themselves up. There'd been no time to belt down or even sit, and abrupt acceleration had sent them sprawling.

He counted heads. Eleven including himself. Eleven out of forty-two. Not enough to feel like celebrating, but eleven more than he'd had any right to expect. And the platoon had ravaged the Klestronu ground command structure—officers and equipment.

Crouching apelike against possible maneuvers, he went forward and congratulated the pilots. The copilot grunted the only acknowledgement; their attention was fully occupied, intent on monitors, instruments, and what was visible in the night through the scorched and spalled armorglass windshield.

Appreciation delivered, Jerym went aft and belted himself into a seat. He was alive. *How many of the original 2nd can say that?* he thought.

*Romlar and Carrmak, but they haven't been exposed to combat. And probably Esenrok; company commanders don't get exposed all that much either. But of the guys who've been in the thick of it, there's Presnola and Markooris, wounded and ported back to Iryala; and maybe half a dozen more. Add the H Company survivors and we've maybe got a squad and a half.*

*Why me?*

He'd almost given himself up, back when the Klestroni had rushed them. Well, maybe not almost, but for an instant he'd felt an impulse to crawl beneath one of the tent floors, then turn himself in when the fighting had stopped.

It had been brief, like a sort of mental hiccup.

It seemed to him that he must have known then what had caused it, though he'd had no time to look at it. Beneath that impulse had been the hidden idea: *Get taken prisoner, taken up to the flagship, and be with Tain. Somehow be with Tain and help her remember, help her be Tain again. Go to Klestron with her.*

Crazy! They'd have questioned him and learned about the teleport, and how they'd been beaten—the tricks and tactics and technology used. Guys had died to keep those things secret. Tain had, in a way.

He hadn't come close to doing it, of course. But he'd had the impulse. And it had soiled him. *I'll talk with Lotta,* he thought, *have her clean me up.*

Or am I making too much of this? Everyone's flawed in some way.

Then a question struck him, one she might well ask: What good is a flaw? What can you do with it?

He didn't have the answer, not consciously, but for some reason—some strange, but welcome reason—asking the question lightened him and brought an unexpected chuckle to his throat.

The trooper next to him looked at him curiously. "What's funny, Lieutenant?" he asked.

"I was just thinking how weird it is that here I am, still alive."

It wasn't a true answer, but it had the ring of truth, it could have been true, and it served. The trooper grinned at him. "Yeah. Some of us seem to be wired to duck at the right time. I don't know whether it's our script writer or maybe our props man."

There were other chuckles around them, and Jerym realized that he was feeling a *lot* better, extroverted again. He'd tell Lotta what he'd felt, he decided, but he wouldn't ask her help. Tunis! He hadn't even exercised what he knew to do, hadn't turned around and looked at himself yet!

Romlar sat in the dark at his radio. Beneath the jungle roof, the night was black as tar. All he could see were the tiny red power lights of radio and computer.

He could have pulled his visor down to see, of course, but just now the dark was comforting. The evacuation floaters should be headed back, he thought, those that could, but they were keeping radio silence. Apparently at least one of the Klestronu gunships was still alive, possibly two.

But of the survival and evacuation *status*, he knew nothing except for the cadet operation. Three of the "girls" had gotten out of the rec compound and reached the evacuation site, along with seventeen of those who'd made their escape possible by ambushing and engaging the relief column. That made twenty of seventy. There weren't many cadets left— a hundred maybe, and half as many cadre. He was prepared for even heavier casualties among B and C Companies, who'd dropped into the Klestronu field bases.

As for 2nd Platoon—if any got out alive, that would make it a really special coup. But then, the version of 2nd Platoon that went out tonight held nothing but survivors. The remaining originals had been through more tough missions than perhaps any other platoon in the regiment, while the guys who'd been assigned from H Company . . .

It was a regiment to be proud of, and he was proud. But at the moment he was depressed. *Sure it's unreasonable,* he told himself, *and sure the T'swa wouldn't feel like this. But it's how I feel.*

He'd talk with Lotta about it after she made her report. Whenever that was. It seemed to him she could handle his mood with two or three questions.

Just now, thinking of her, he felt horny, which surprised him, and he pulled his thoughts to the operational situation, so far as he knew it. The regiment was still formidable. And the Klestroni had so few gunships left— probably one, maybe two—that even if they got their new surveillance ship up, their responses would be badly limited. He—he and the regiment and the cadets—had hurt them badly. The question was whether they'd hurt them badly enough to drive them back to Klestron.

# 67

Igsat Tarimenloku's back was straight but his morale had slumped. The bridge crew stayed as quiet as possible, moving as little as possible, as if someone in the room was dying. He'd come there from the chapel, where he'd prayed first to Flenyaagor for His guidance. And when, with that guidance, he'd made his decision, he'd asked Flenyaagor for His support with Kargh. Finally he'd prayed to Kargh himself, something he hadn't had the courage to do since his over-bold youth. And it seemed to him that when he'd finished, Flenyaagor had breathed His Divine Breath upon him, as if telling him to be of good faith.

He had not asked Kargh for mercy. Only for His blessing on what he must now do.

Back in his command seat, Tarimenloku had called onto the screen a holo of the marine base, magnified to look as if seen from 10,000 feet. It wouldn't look much different now, from 10,000 feet. No heavy weapons had been engaged. It hadn't been devastated. One could easily miss that a disaster, even a calamity, had struck there.

Would it have been different if he'd had a heavy brigade, with its tanks? He didn't think so.

Things had seemed so simple when they'd set it up. This was a backward world, seemingly without an army, its population scant and scattered. Control the small capital, learn about them, milk them of their information about the rest of the sector, and then leave. It was a Karghsent opportunity involving no apparent major risk, requiring no great haste. Eight thousand marines had seemed more than enough; the initial 4,000 he'd sent down had seemed ample.

Even now, nearly 5,500 officers and men were still alive, more than 5,000 fit for duty. But of the 615 marine *officers* who'd landed, only 283 were alive, only 241 fit for duty! Almost no senior officers were still alive: one colonel and three majors! And Saadhrambacoora of course, but more than his leg had been broken. Almost no one left down there had ever commanded a unit larger than a company, and even at the company and platoon levels, the officer shortage was severe.

You could not operate a brigade without qualified officers. To raise company commanders to battalion commands invited worse disasters than they'd already suffered, and who then would command the companies, the platoons? Peasants lacked the self-discipline, nor would they accept other peasants as their officers. It took more than insignia.

Even the remaining officers had lost authority. He knew it without being there, had heard it in Saadhrambacoora's voice. What a diabolical thing to have spared the man, thought Tarimenloku, deliberately leaving him alive among the dead, like the drunken Thilraxakootha on the Eve of the Battle of Klarwath. Even peasants would see the parallel; the man could never command effectively again.

Tarimenloku shook his head. *How could they know us so well?*

The commodore didn't ask himself another question: how the enemy might have done what he'd done. It never occurred to him; defeat gripped him too tightly. In a voice as hard as ever but somehow flavored with apathy, he gave the order he'd decided upon in prayer: He ordered Saadhrambacoora to prepare his marines for withdrawal. It was time to return to Klestron.

When Lotta emerged from her trance, she did not at once get up. A unit of her attention was stuck on one of Tarimenloku's thoughts: *How could they know us so well?*

In a meld she knew the other's conscious thoughts, and felt—got the taste of, the sense of—the layer of active unconsciousness just beneath them. But she didn't go deeper. Couldn't, as far as she knew. So she'd never gotten the insights, personal and cultural, that Artus seemed to have, the insights implied in the actions he'd ordered.

How *had* he known?

She was reasonably sure that he couldn't have voiced those insights, but at some level he knew. The wisdom was there.

She thought she'd seen what Artus was, and almost certainly who he'd been—one of the whos—even though he hadn't recognized it himself. And Wellem had agreed with her appraisal. But that was no explanation for what Artus had done here, or it didn't seem to be. There was something deeper, but she was *not* going to poke around hunting for it. And she doubted that Wellem would either, when they got back to Iryala. It could throw Artus into something not even Wellem was prepared to handle.

She got to her feet. Time to report what the commodore had ordered.

Again Romlar sat in the inky dark alone. Lotta had reported to him, and when she'd left, he'd wanted to go with her, to spend what was left of the night with her, if she'd have him.

*Artus,* he'd told himself instead, *don't be a jerk. You want to use her to help you hide.*

So. Hide from what? Tonight he'd sent 411 personnel on what amounted to suicide missions. Ninety-two had come back; only 92, though that was more than he'd thought there might be. But deaths weren't what was bothering him. Tonight had broken the Klestroni, and if lives were the issue, tonight may well have ended the killing here. Tonight had saved lives, both Iryalan and Klestronu.

He grunted. It was true. And recognizing it hadn't helped at all. So something else was the problem.

Who'd died? Guys he'd known and guys he hadn't. On his side almost all of them warriors. All but some of the floater crews; the replacement crews hadn't been warriors. But they'd had the Ostrak Procedures, and not one of them had tried to weasel out of a mission. They were at Work, at Service. They couldn't truly be warriors but they could be soldiers, and they'd been good ones, laying their lives on the line and being effective.

*Which shows me something,* he told himself. *The operational difference between warriors and soldiers isn't necessarily courage or will. Soldiers, some of them, a lot of them, have all the courage and will you could want. The operational difference is talent—the kit that comes with being born a warrior, especially a cleaned-up warrior: the inherent attitudes, the inherent responses, the luck. And in most cases the reflexes and strength.*

Lotta reached her tent and ducked inside. Artus had had a cloud hanging around him, but it felt like something he wasn't ready to have handled. *If I went to sleep and he went to sleep, we could probably cook up some dreams to ease it,* she told herself, *maybe lay it to rest awhile, but the big oaf won't go to bed.*

She skinned out of her clothes and lay down on top of her sleeping bag. Maybe *he* wasn't going to sleep, she told herself, but she was.

But when she closed her eyes, it seemed to her that she was feeling what he was. Opening them, she sat up irritatedly, not used to being affected by things like that. Then, without a conscious decision, she reached. [Artus!]

[Yes?]

To that she had no answer, didn't know why she'd reached. All she could think of was that a meld might help, and she had no reason to suppose it actually would. She hadn't been melding with him on Backbreak. He might be in conference, or on the radio, and going in person to headquarters was less intrusive than touching his mind.

[The meld sounds good,] he thought to her. [Let's try it.]

For a minute they sat, she in her tent, he in a canvas folding chair in front of his computer, while nothing happened. Then, [why don't I come over there?] he asked.

She didn't have an answer to that either, in words, but felt her body quicken. She was with him every step of the way, electric, and three minutes later he was outside her tent flaps, taking off his boots. Belatedly it occurred to her that she was naked, and somehow, for a moment, the realization alarmed her.

She heard as well as felt his chuckle. [I suspect,] he thought to her, [that for a couple of virgins, we won't do too badly.]

Lotta was breathing quietly, asleep; Romlar had been right. Just now he lay beside her with his hands behind his head, not sleepy a bit, feeling very good indeed. He had a semi-erection again but felt no need to do anything about it. Somewhere up above, in the top of the forest roof, he heard a bird chirp. Seconds later it was answered.

*They must be seeing dawnlight,* he thought. *Better get out of here before people start moving around.*

Carefully he felt about him, found his shorts, pulled them on, his undershirt, shirt, field pants. He was glad he'd issued the women a four-panel tent; it made dressing a lot easier. Then, sitting on the ground in front of it, he put on his boots. Already a little dawnlight was penetrating the leafy roof, so that the darkness beneath was no longer absolute. The bird calls had changed from tentative chirps to phrases, snatches of songs. *In a minute or two they'll be a chorus,* he told himself, and got to his feet.

*And today— Maybe today we'll organize an evacuation of our own. We'll see.*

# 68

It was an overdue rain, a badly needed rain, and it had been coming down hard for half an hour. At first almost none of it had penetrated the forest roof; now drip from the leaves pattered arhythmically, abundantly on Lotta's tent. But where her attention lay, it would never rain. She was with Commodore Tarimenloku in his office adjacent to the bridge of HRS *Blessed Flenyaagor.* It was a facility he didn't use a lot, but just now he wanted privacy on duty.

The marines were back aboard the troopship, and in stasis except for a few who needed medical treatment first.

The commodore sat watching his comm screen. He'd just ordered his chief intelligence officer to prepare the prisoners from Lonyer City for their return to the planet. The man's acknowledgement lagged for three or four seconds.

"Yes sir," he said at last. "Does that include the female soldier who was captured?"

"*The prisoners from Lonyer City,*" the commodore repeated testily, then with a held breath calmed his temper. "The female soldier we will retain. She is a prisoner of war, and the war is not over."

"Yes sir." The CIO's expression was troubled as he said it.

The commodore noticed, and touched the *record* key. In the empire, even in this time of infrequent wars, the repatriation of prisoners was a subject stressed at the academy. A sensitive subject wrapped in imprecise legalities, with significances cultural and religious as well as political and military. And while nothing he might do now was likely to save his life and honor, he would not abandon propriety or integrity. "Commander," he said, "would you care to speak for the record as the Conscience of the Prophet?"

"If you please, sir."

"A moment then. I will have the chaplain witness." He tapped other keys. After several seconds his screen split, a middle-aged face and shaven head sharing it now with the chief intelligence officer. Briefly the commodore explained the situation to the chaplain, then returned his attention to the lieutenant commander.

"So. As the Conscience of the Prophet, speak."

The younger man's face was even more serious than usual. "I have spoken with the chief medical officer about the female prisoner. She remains deeply amnesic. So profoundly so that he feels she will never recover her past while she is with us. Therefore . . ."

"I am aware of the chief medical officer's *opinion*," Tarimenloku interrupted, then wished he hadn't. "Continue."

"Yes sir. Assuming the chief medical officer's opinion is correct, and it *is* the most informed opinion available to us, she will never be of value as an intelligence source. He also thinks that she probably would recover, in time, if she were back among her people."

The commodore's expression did not change. "I have discussed this with the chief medical officer myself, with regard to her potential for successful interrogation. He admitted to me that he has only opinions. Amnesia, he tells me, is little understood."

He glanced at the chaplain, then looked back to his CIO. "For your personal information and for the record, I will point out that I too have considered, briefly, the matter of her repatriation. There would be some grounds for it if she were noble, but she does not bear the mark."

"Sir, as you know, I have interrogated the civilian prisoners extensively, to develop a picture of Confederation government, society, customs, and values, as well as their technology. The Confederation, at least its principal worlds, has its nobility. But—" the CIO chose his words carefully now—"they stress its importance less than we, thus noble families do not mark their children. The female prisoner, while bearing no mark of it, could easily be noble."

Tarimenloku grunted, a hand moving inadvertently as if to rise and touch the time-dulled, polychrome star on his forehead, a mark less than half an inch long. *A strange nobility,* he thought silently, *without sufficient pride to mark their offspring.*

"What evidence have you seen, if any, that suggests she might be noble?"

"Her action, sir. She saw a means of avoiding interrogation, and she was willing to die a gruesome death to keep it from us."

"Hmm. True. Well certainly she's no peasant. But she lacked not only the mark but the demeanor of nobility. The apparency is that she's gentry.

"And what is more relevant, Commander Ralankoor—sometimes even nobles are not repatriated until after a treaty is made. Usually there is at least a formal truce."

Tarimenloku's gaze had intensified, and when he paused, Bavi Ralankoor knew that, one, this refusal would not be reversed; and two, his superior was not done talking.

"Now. What do you suppose she feared we might learn from her? When we are back on Klestron, it is possible that SUMBAA will find out for us. And the information may be highly important to Klestron and the Empire. Therefore I have no choice but to take her with us."

He turned his eyes to the chaplain. "Unless Pastor Poorajarutha finds something seriously amiss with my reasoning."

The chaplain's expression betrayed no emotion. "Not at all," he said.

The commodore went on. "Nonetheless, Commander Ralankoor, as the Conscience of the Prophet you have made a case, albeit not a strong one, for her possible nobility. Therefore, have her moved to a cabin appropriate to noble rank. And see that she learns our language fluently.

"But before you do that—before you do anything else—have the civilian prisoners prepared for departure. Which will be at 0815; that gives you less than thirty minutes. They're to be delivered safely at the square in Lonyer City. Have Ensign Sooskabenloku accompany them in the shuttle. He's to be back aboard ship at not later than 1150 hours; make sure he knows that.

"We will leave these parking coordinates at 1200."

The chief intelligence officer voiced a rather subdued "yes sir; by your leave sir," and his face disappeared, allowing the chaplain's to occupy the entire screen for just a second before he too disconnected.

The cleric had had nothing further to say. They'd known one another for twenty years, he and the commodore. And he knew what Tarimenloku faced on Klestron. He knew also that any sympathy he might show, even silently, would only trouble the commodore's soul.

Tarimenloku looked at the clock. *In four hours and seven minutes I will turn my back on this accursed world. Kargh forgive me, I wish I could leave it in smoke and mourning, but I will not.*

His lips thinned, tightened. *But we'll be back. Not I, nor any fleet the sultan could send. And maybe not soon. But we will be back.*

*And it will be an imperial fleet. With an imperial army, armed not merely to control uprisings, or repel unlikely incursions by other sultanates. A real army, unconstrained in its armaments. Then we will see how this confederation fares!*

# 69

The regiment's 1,178 troopers, along with the 106 surviving cadets and their remaining 47 T'swa cadre, had been gathered at several locations to be sent back to Iryala through the small teleport. Equipment larger than man-carried was stored at the Lonyer City landing field for later pickup. A single light utility floater stayed with the regiment, moving the teleport from one departure location to the next.

Headquarters Company would be the last to port home— Headquarters Company and what was left of its two attached rifle platoons. It hadn't yet struck its tents; its hour of departure wasn't certain, and neither was the weather, which had changed from persistently dry to sporadically showery. Lotta, after withdrawing from a trance a little earlier, had found Jerym. Now, together, they explored the creekbed above camp, mainly for something to do while they talked. Both carried sidearms. Neither wanted to be killed by some tiger or blue troll—certainly not on the day, the eve at least, of going home to Iryala.

The creek had swollen somewhat but was still small, bridged here and there by fallen trees in various stages of decay. Its pale amber water, still clear, ran mostly knee-deep now, or deeper, and four to eight-feet wide, in places striped with green water plants waving sinuously in the current. Mostly though it showed gravel bottom. Small fish swam in place, or disturbed, darted for cover under bank or log.

"If Tain was still with us," Lotta was saying, "what would you two do now?"

"I don't know. Why do you ask? She's probably half a parsec gone from here and getting farther fast. The chance of our ever seeing each other again is exactly zero."

Lotta bellied over a fallen log overgrown with what resembled a fine-leaved turf or coarse moss. "Right," she said. "But it might be useful to look at it with someone."

Jerym shrugged. "If Tain was still here . . ." He examined the question. "Romlar says we'll probably be sent back here in a week or two to continue our training. Not here in the jungle probably—I think we know jungle fighting pretty well now—but to the steppe, or the tundra prairie. Or maybe the coastal rainforest; I hear that's a lot different from this. Meanwhile Tain would be sitting here waiting for a ship." He turned and looked at his sister. "Unless you stayed and ran Ostrak Procedures on her so she could port back."

Again he shrugged; the matter was moot. "If we decided to be together, either she'd have to be with us here somehow, on some basis, and then go with us to Oven, or I'd have to leave the regiment."

"So what do you think you'd decide, the two of you?"

He shook his head. "It wouldn't be much of a life for her, with the regiment. I think she'd be too smart to try it. To be honest, I'm not sure she actually loved me; she might have just thought she did. It might have been a matter of the danger, of my going out every day or two to maybe get killed.

"No, if we were going to be together, I'd have to leave the regiment."

"Could you have done that?"

He stopped, looking thoughtfully at his sister. "I think so. One of the things the Ostrak Procedures do is make a person less compulsive. Right? You get more control over your decisions and actions. And look at the T'swa: When one of their regiments finally gets so shot up that it's down to a company or so, maybe understrength at that, the survivors get shipped back to Oven to do other things." He turned and led off again. "They stop being warriors," he added over his shoulder. "Our cadre weren't being warriors. They were being teachers.

"Maybe I could have become part of a training cadre. We're going to need cadres. The Klestroni might not come back, but I wouldn't bet on it, and His Majesty won't either."

"So," Lotta said, "as it is, what are you going to do?"

"No question. I'm staying with the regiment. It'll have to be my family." He used the word for marital family—spouse and children—then stopped again to look at Lotta.

"How about you? And Romlar? Anything developing there? I know he was interested in you, back on Iryala."

"We've had a strong mutual affinity from early on," Lotta answered. "I think it's scripted. Whatever; it'll have to wait. I'm going to tell Wellem I want to develop a program for training seers. Seers like the T'swa have. I intend to port to Tyss and train at the monastery of Dys Tolbash. Artus and I can get together later, when the regiment's disbanded."

Jerym's gaze was direct. "If Artus comes through alive."

"Right. If he comes through alive." *And I'd bet on it,* she added silently. *I am betting on it.*

# HISTORICAL CHART
## of the Human Species during and after the Great Annihilation

This chart outlines the histories of two of the three known human sectors. In different places and at different times, different calendar systems have been used. In this chart, year lengths are Confederation Standard years, but numbered from the emperor's decision to launch the Great Annihilation.

The historys of the different human sectors are sketched in separate columns in the chart.

### The Home Sector

**Year 0**—In the Kron Empire of 53 worlds, which would later be termed "the Home Sector," the Congress of Constitutional Government meets to protest the Imperium's prolonged disregard of the constitution. They issue a position paper that includes a virtual ultimatum to the Imperium: Align your policies with the constitution or face rebellion.

The emperor orders construction of the HIMS *Retributor.*

**Year 3**—Plans approved for the *Retributor,* a gigantic, highly automated warship reputedly with the power to destroy planets. Actual construction begins.

**Year 4**—Coordinated rebellions break out on 17 worlds.

**Year 6**—Rebellions have spread to most worlds. Imperial fleet forced to concentrate on a limited number of worlds at one time. Two squadrons of the Imperial fleet mutiny, join the rebels.

**Year 7**—The *Retributor* is launched with the mad emperor as her master and with a psychoconditioned crew of fanatics. It reduces two rebellious worlds to orbiting rubble.

Further units of the Imperial Fleet declare for the rebels.

**Year 8**—Some worlds have fought themselves into collapse. The *Retributor* continues to "punish" (destroy) worlds for their rebelliousness.

**Year 9**—The surviving planets of the empire are devastated and in utter chaos. The emperor continues to destroy planets.

**Year 10**—Civilization has collapsed within the empire. More planets destroyed.

**Year 12**—The emperor suicides by destroying his ship. Of the 53 worlds previously inhabited, only 11 remain intact. The human species is nearly extinct.

**Years 12 to roughly 100**—On 8 of the 11 planets, the remaining humans, if any, succumb to severe conditions. On the remaining 3, one or more groups survive in extreme primitivism.

**Years 100 to roughly 10,000**—Hampered by the inaccessibility of fossil fuels and certain minerals, sulfur for example, and tin, the human advance out of primitivism is very slow.

**Year 12,000**—The sailboat has appeared on the seas of the planet Varatos.

**Year 16,114**—The calculus is invented on Varatos.

**Year 18,349**—First space flight to the moon of Varatos.

**Year 18,517**—Interstellar exploration ship from Varatos discovers the nearest other inhabited planet, Klestron. Exploration accelerates.

**Year 18,619**—The last of the 11 surviving habitable worlds is discovered. Within a century, further exploration ends with no further habitable worlds found.

The sciences begin a decline that will be broken only occasionally and briefly.

**Year 20,008**—The Varatosu Empire becomes a religious empire, the "Karghanik Empire," with 10 semi-autonomous planets, sultanates, under the rule of Varatos and its Kalif.

**Year 21,491**—The Sultan of Klestron sends a flotilla to seek habitable worlds at whatever distance. The objective is eventual colonization.

**Year 21,492**—The Klestronu flotilla encounters a Garthid patrol ship, engages it, then escapes into hyperspace.

In a later encounter with a Garthid patrol, the exploration flotilla loses a ship to enemy fire.

**Year 21,493**—The flotilla successfully emerges from Garthid space and begins to reconnoiter systems adjacent to the Confederation sector.

**Year 21,494**—Chodrisei Biilathkamoro becomes Kalif of the Karghanik Empire.

The Klestronu exploration flotilla lands marines on the Confederation trade world Terfreya (Karnovir 02) and captures Lonyer City, its capital. They are soon engaged in jungle warfare.

The marines are driven from Terfreya. The Klestronu flotilla leaves the Karnovir system for home without victory but with much information.

Year 21,498—The Klestronu flotilla arrives back in the Karghanik Empire and reports on the habitable world it found, part of a sector with many habitable worlds. The evidence is that the Confederation fleet is smaller and technologically inferior to that of the empire.

Year 21,500—A Karghanik invasion of the Confederation of Worlds sets out, with conquest in mind. [See *The Three-Cornered War*.]

Year 21,502—A powerful Garthid invasion of the Confederation is launched, its intention the destruction of human civilization. [See *The Three-Cornered War*.]

## The Confederation of Worlds

Year 4—Fleeing the impending megawar, a convoy of eight large merchant vessels refitted as refugee ships quietly departs the planet Renyala. Its ruling committee intends to look for a new home well outside known space.

Year 5—The refugee convoy from Renyala enters the previously unknown Garthid Sector and encounters a Garthid patrol ship. It is allowed to proceed through the sector but warned not to stop again within it.

Year 6—Psychiatrists with the refugee convoy develop "the Sacrament," a psychoconditioning procedure designed to prevent megawars in the new civilization they hope to found. The basic premises used in developing the Sacrament are (1) that men will fight each other; and (2) that research and highly advanced science are necessary for the development of megawar technology. Thus the Sacrament suppresses the type of mind which might otherwise pursue scientific enquiry. An additional effect is a tendency not to question authority.

Five subcultures (septs) among the refugees refuse the Sacrament and are segregated from the rest and from each other. The rest of the refugees are psychoconditioned, and the Sacrament will be delivered to all their children as they come along.

The refugee convoy leaves the Garthid Sector and finds a marginally habitable world deemed unsuitable to the unassisted development of technological civilization. Three of the five septs which had refused the Sacrament are offloaded onto it.

Year 7—The refugee convoy finds several further habitable worlds. It offloads the remaining recalcitrant septs on one of the most marginal.

Year 8—The refugee convoy lands on a highly suitable world, names it Iryala, and begins the work of making it home.

Year 117—One of the refugee ships leaves Iryala to explore the sector.

Year 798—The Ruling Council on Iryala, concerned over what they regard as dangerously innovative technology, passes the Standard

Technology Act, which severely restricts the right to employ technological elements in new configurations. This virtually freezes technology in its existing form.

**Year 892**—The first new emigrant ship is sent out from Iryala to colonize another planet. This begins nearly fifteen thousand years of sporadic colonization.

**Years 900 to 14,824**—Thirty-six planets are colonized.

**Year 14,916**—Amberus is crowned emperor of what had been the Confederation of Human Worlds. A shrewd megalomaniac of remarkable charisma, Amberus regards history as a personal insult, and prohibits teaching it. He has the calendar years numbered from his coronation. After careful, covert planning, he has all historical libraries, collections, and archives destroyed, public and private, and all historical matter erased from computer banks except for administrative data directly necessary to government. Historians, professional and amateur, are hunted down and killed. This continues throughout the 27 years of Amberus's reign, ending with his assassination.

Currently, history prior to Amberus is known very largely from later reconstructions by seers on the trade world Tyss.

**Years 14,944 to 15,690**—Period of additional exploration and colonization. The planets Orlantha and Tyss, colonized long since by the off-loaded recalcitrants, are rediscovered. The manner of their settlement is not known.

**Year 15,697**—A decree prohibits further colonization, on the grounds that a larger empire will be impossible to administer. The empire continues in more or less efficient stagnation under the force of the Sacrament and Standard Technology, reasonably safe as long as no major perturbation occurs.

**Year 20,750**—After a brief revolt overthrows a later, so-called Thomsid Empire, the Iryalan general staff crowns Pertunis of Ordunak King of Iryala and Emperor of the Worlds. Pertunis promptly declares the empire dissolved, formalizing the actual state of affairs. He then proceeds to build a loose economic and administrative network of worlds with Iryala (as always) the central world.

**Year 20,787**—The Confederation of Worlds is ratified by 27 planets, with Pertunis as Administrator General. He then delegates most of his administrative duties and spends much of his remaining life developing a theory and structure of Management intended to rationalize and stabilize government, business, and personal life. At his death, this compilation of principles and policies is proclaimed "Standard Management." It provides a new level of understanding and efficiency, but also further calcifies human thought and action in the Confederation, leaving little room for innovation of any sort.

The love and respect accorded Pertunis results in the calendar years being numbered from his coronation.

**Year 20,832**—Harden Ostrak, Lord Heriston, becomes the first Iryalan to investigate the T'sel, the philosophy of Tyss, one of the two marginally habitable worlds on which the recalcitrant septs were offloaded. The Sacrament is not given on Tyss.

**Year 20,834**—Merlan Ostrak, age seven, becomes the first Iryalan child to live and train on Tyss under T'sel masters. He is joined within three years by two more Iryalan children. Being reared in the T'sel overrides the Sacrament.

**Year 20,851**—First covert T'sel academy founded on Iryala, on the Ostrak country estate. It appears to be an ordinary private academy.

**Year 20,878**—The so-called "Movement" is established by alumni of the Ostrak academy. A second academy is opened, the beginning of an expansion.

**Year 20,913**—Prince Jerym enrolls at the Green Plains Academy.

**Year 20,949**—Prince Jerym is crowned King of Iryala and Administrator General of the Confederation of Worlds, as Consar II. From that point, all Iryalan princes are covertly trained in the T'sel.

**Year 21,439**—Covert disarming of the Sacrament is begun on Iryala to break the Confederation free from the long technological stagnation.

**Year 21,460**—The Kettle War starts. [See *The Regiment.*]

**Year 21,462**—The Kettle War ends. The role played by nonstandard T'swa metallurgists and mercenary regiments is used by The Movement to crack Standard Technology. [See *The Regiment.*]

**Year 21,487**—Training of selected Iryalan children as warriors begins with the "cadets."

**Year 21,493**—An experimental regiment of adolescent Iryalans, "intentive warriors," begins training under T'swa veterans.

**Year 21,494**—A teleport is successfully tested with human subjects. The personal attributes for survival of teleportation are defined.

The Karghanik exploration flotilla lands marines on the Confederation Trade World Terfreya (Karnovir 02), and captures Lonyer City, its capital. The marines are soon engaged in jungle warfare by the twelve-year-old cadets in training there.

Their black T'swa cadre dub the Iryalan regiment-in-training "the White T'swa," following its highly successful graduation maneuvers.

The white regiment is teleported to Terfreya, and in company with the preadolescent cadets, drives the Klestronu marines off of Terfreya.

**Year 21,498**—The Klestronu flotilla arrives back in the Karghanik Empire and reports on the habitable world it found, part of a sector with many habitable worlds. The evidence is that the Confederation fleet is smaller and technologically inferior to that of the empire.

# Notes

[1] In this book, customary units of measurement, as well as the twenty-four-hour clock, are used for convenience in visualization. However, Confederation calendar units are used here instead of months.

[2] In the Confederation Sector, the year is divided into ten parts, known as deks. Each world has its own calendar based on its orbital period. The *Standard Year* and *Standard Deks*, used in interplanetary records, commerce, and Confederation government, are the year and deks of the principal planet, Iryala.

[3] Of course, there were the survivors—refugees, our ancestors—who fled early in the rebellion in a fleet of eight large merchant ships, and came to the sector we live in now. But they are not the subject of this work. [Translator]

[4] SUMBAA is our Iryalan acronym for Sentient, Universal, Multiterminal Bank, Analyzer, and Advisor—our translation of their name for it. They have their own acronym. We do not know very much about SUMBAA. It was designed to program itself, with the potential for self-expansion, and has grown beyond, perhaps far beyond, the understanding of the people who designed it. And their ability was considerably above that of the empire's present-day computer scientists, let alone our own. [Translator]

[5] It seems probable that any one of its fleet combat teams—three vessels working together—could defeat the entire Confederation fleet as now constituted. [Translator]

[6] Their weapons too seem generally superior to our own, and apparently their naval armament is far superior. We can expect it to take two to three generations before we will have caught up in the technology of space warfare. If we decide to. First our culture will need to adjust sufficiently to the changes we are leading it through. [Translator]

[7] Klestronu *adj.* Of, pertaining to, or derived from Klestron or its inhabitants.

⁸ Klestroni noun, plural; singular Klestronit. Persons native to or inhabiting Klestron.

⁹ Even at the time of this story, the Sacrament constrained them, though in practice it had become an empty ritual. Roughly thirty percent of the people on Iryala, an aging thirty percent, had received the ungelded Sacrament, and in the Confederation sector overall, the percentage was considerably higher. Thus many things could not be said or done openly. Science and research could not be publicly discussed except in the most carefully oblique way. For example, what might more accurately have been called the Bureau of Research and Development was named simply the Office of Special Projects.

To have done otherwise would have been to trigger widespread psychosis and disorder.

¹⁰ Made not with intent to kill or maim, but "just to see what would happen." Twelve trainees plus Lieutenant Ghaz and Corporal Toka-Ghit were treated in the infirmary; three trainees were flown to the army hospital at Granite River. All in all a remarkable demonstration of the value of T'swa training.

¹¹ Hyperspace is not actually a space. It is a field enclosing a ship, generated by the ship's hyperspace generator and fully occupied by the ship. In this limited sense, hyperspace is analogous to the warp field enwrapping a ship at sublight speeds, with the additional similarity that in either case the ship has no momentum as gauged against external fields. However, a ship riding its warp field travels through space, while a ship in hyperspace is in a sort of limbo: It can be said to be nowhere. Its field can be said to move, taking the ship with it, but in a sense they aren't moving through anything.

Yet in an equally valid sense it is moving, with a movement that can be quantified and perhaps actually measured—a matter of dispute— through a sort of quasi-topological "reverse side" of real-space. Thus different ships separately "in hyperspace" (more properly in separate hyperspaces) can communicate with each other by simple radio, with the transmission times a complex function of their "hyperspace positions" relative to each other.

Suffice it to be aware that a ship in hyperspace can stop abruptly or turn without inertial effects, though gauged within the specific hyperspace field, inertia is normal.

¹² Wisdom, as defined by T'sel masters, is appropriate action, and knowledge of appropriate action.

¹³ So-called. The new "mapbook" is a computerized holographic atlas 12 X 10 X 1 inches—about the size of the standard army field mapbook. Based on high elevation, computer-enhanced holography, it gives a realistic display of the topography and, at the largest scales, of tree heights. The

computer adds contour lines. The broadest vegetation categories are differentiated by color. At larger scales, the classification becomes progressively more detailed, the finer types being outlined and defined by symbols.

[14] In the empire, the surnames of nobles have five syllables, with the stress on the first and fourth. Here *dh* is used to represent the sound of *th* in *the*; and *c* the *ch* sound in *chew*. Thus "SAADH-rahm-bah-CHOO-rah."

[15] In the Confederation, the calendar year for every inhabited planet begins with the southern hemisphere winter solstice. The southern hemisphere was chosen as the base because Landfall, the original settlement in the Confederation, is in Iryala's southern hemisphere.

# THE REGIMENT'S WAR

This one is for GAIL

_____

Acknowledgements

I'd like to thank David Palter, Bill Bailie, and as always, Gail and Judy for reading and commenting on a preliminary draft of this manuscript.
I also want to thank Jack Jones, my black-belt son and eclectic martial artist, for reading the sections on hand-to-hand fighting.

# Prologue

The audience room was richly fitted, its hangings dark, its light subdued. Centered in it, straight-backed before the throne, Ambassador Vilmur Klens didn't notice the buzz and click of cameras. His attention was totally on the king, who stood on the dais, reading the accusations in a loud, reedy voice. Klens had heard them before; they'd been read to him by a royal envoy on the day they'd been published. He'd then read and digested them himself before wiring them home. Now, a week later, he was hearing them from Engwar II Tarsteng himself.

Engwar's tone was merely petulant, but the malice in his glance turned Klens numb. When he'd finished reading the charges, he went on to read the appended ultimatum. An impossible ultimatum because the charges all were false: cynical and ruthless, lacking even a pretense of truth. Smolen had been given twenty-one days to deliver to Komarsi justice "those persons guilty of the outrages." Fifteen days now.

Engwar Tarsteng completed his reading, then rolled the parchment and slapped it against his plump palm, once, twice, a third time. If Engwar's reading had been loud and reedy, his next words were almost purred. "I was generous," he said, "in giving your government twenty-one days. I should have realized that civilized deportment could not be expected from it. My sources assure me that it has made no slightest effort to comply. Instead you have mobilized your reserves, preparing to attack Komars."

*Preparing to attack Komars! Did the vole attack the stoat?* Vilmur Klens knew now what this meeting, this needless recitation was about, had to be about. Still emotionally numb, he felt the muscles of his chest and arms begin to twitch and tremble, and tried to control them.

The king put away his scowl. A smile curved his full lips, his remarkable cupid-bow mouth; he'd seen the trembling despite Klens's fashionably loose jacket. "Therefore," he went on, "I herewith declare that a state of war now exists between my country and yours, a war which shall not end until your evil, upstart republic has been prostrated, and its people properly punished!"

Engwar seemed to swell then. Two of his guards had stepped up beside

513

Vilmur Klens. Now they grasped his arms roughly. Klens did not resist as they manacled him. The king continued, his voice rising further:

"You, as the representative of a vicious government, share its responsibility for this war, and for its costs-to-be in blood and treasure. Therefore I herewith arrest you in the name of the Crown of Komars, and of civilized states throughout the planet." For the first time, the Smoleni ambassador became aware of the busy cameras. Engwar shifted his attention to the officer who'd moved up beside one of the guards. "Lieutenant, I want this—criminal locked securely in the block. You know the cell."

He turned on his heel then, but as he left, he spoke to his lord chancellor, loudly enough for the room to hear: "Sixday would be nice for a public beheading, wouldn't you say?"

# Part One
# THE ASSIGNMENT

# 1

Colonel Artus Romlar lay listening behind a tree. There were many sounds. Just now, none seemed meaningful.

Insects buzzed and clicked and crawled. Sweat trickled. His shirt stuck to his back. He ignored them all. It was early spring in Oven's northern hemisphere, and the late morning temperature had risen well above a hundred. At least there was forest and shade, here in the Jubat Hills.

And the T'swa would be along soon. If he was wrong about that, he'd made a serious error.

Below him was a log landing on the Jubat Hills Railroad, a long strip of open ground used periodically for piling logs. The ground sloped downward at thirty to forty percent almost to the tracks, which here had been built along the bottom of a wide draw. Farther on, the draw became a steep-walled ravine; if the T'swa were going to detrain short of Tiiku Lod-Sei, this was the last good site.

The trick was to fool them into thinking he was somewhere else, hours away. Romlar considered he'd done that. The risk in *not* being at Junction 4 Village made it convincing. It was also the principal down side of his decision.

Regimental commanders don't customarily *lead* their troops into firefights, but this fight would be pivotal, perhaps decisive. The situation had become increasingly critical, the overall odds poor. He'd long since consolidated the men he had left into two battalions. If he lost in this week's set of engagements, his regiment would be—not finished, perhaps, but so reduced as to lose much of its effectiveness. And the Condaros, the people who'd hired it, would be beaten beyond hope. On the other hand, winning here decisively could carry them a while longer, and give them some sort of chance.

Of course, the T'swa might not come. In that case, he'd left 2nd Battalion, along with his Condaro allies, in a precarious position to little avail. Though he still might be able to hit the Booly positions by surprise, and even the odds a bit. That was another reason he was leading 1st Battalion personally: Its commander, Coyn Carrmak, was the best officer he had, but to Romlar's thinking, he had to be present at this action himself, to know the result promptly, and as fully as possible.

The T'swa would come though, reportedly a fresh regiment, full strength. All he had to do—*all he had to do!*—was beat it soundly, cut it up badly with relatively few casualties of his own.

Meanwhile the Booly 2nd Division was sure to hit Junction 4 and its village today, with its two regiments of Condaro defenders and his own 2nd Battalion. Might have hit them already. If he were there with 1st Battalion . . . But if the T'swa were allowed to intervene, there was no chance at all of pulling the fat from the fire.

There were many ways to lose this war. There might or might not be a way to win it.

Romlar didn't run all this through his mind now. It was there, had entered into his decisions, and that was enough. He had committed. Now he lay quietly relaxed, waiting and watching, alert without effort. He'd been through this before. It seemed his reason for being.

He heard the locomotive now, a laboring steam engine chuffing up the long grade. Assuming he'd judged right, and he felt ninety percent sure he had, the train would slow and stop just here below him, and the T'swa would start getting out of the open-sided wooden cars. He'd open fire when about half were still on the cars and half on the ground. If the engineer started the train moving again, he'd be abandoning the men already off, and besides, the terrain became difficult along the tracks ahead, even for T'swa.

No, they'd detrain here, then try to move back under fire, and that would spring the rest of his trap. They might well see it coming, but there'd be little they could do about it except fight furiously. Which in the case of the T'swa also meant intelligently and joyously. To them, too, fighting was fulfillment, the spice of life.

He could feel his troopers waiting. There was, of course, the danger that the T'swa would feel them too. But *he* felt them knowing they were there. They were relaxed, too imbued with the T'sel to be anxious. Thus the T'swa were unlikely to sense them. Except for the T'swa, there wasn't another fighting force in Confederation Space that could lie in wait like this and not be tense, not reek psychically. And except for the T'swa, he knew of no military force other than his that might detect that sort of thing.

The locomotive poked into sight, moving slowly, resinous woodsmoke issuing from the spark arrester on its stack. It wouldn't have to brake; the slope and the heavy gravity of Oven would stop it. With their typical energy and athleticism, T'swa began to pile out before the cars had totally stopped. Romlar leveled his bolt-action rifle and squeezed the trigger, and the ridge side to both his left and right erupted with fire—rifles, grenade launchers, and light machine guns all firing blanks.

Referees with the T'swa began to move up and down the line,

shouting and pointing, and men "died"—lay down, rolled over. Others were returning fire, and the referees with Romlar's 1st Battalion went into action too. But Romlar's men had the advantages of position and cover. Some of the T'swa took cover behind the cars' steel trucks and chassis, while others backed down the slope toward the limited cover of the trees— backing toward the other jaw—two machine gun platoons.

The T'swa weren't really surprised to receive a new surge of fire from behind. The exchange continued noisy and intense; the referees contin- ued busy. After a few minutes more their whistles blew, ending the action. Most of the "surviving" T'swa were free of the trap now, having over- run the machine guns, and the real harvest was finished. The referees needed to confer, to sort out the confusion and define the casualties on both sides. Meanwhile both troopers and T'swa stopped where they were and waited.

While the referees conferred, Romlar washed down a "sweat capsule" with a swallow of warm water, then got on the radio to Brossling, who'd kept comm silence till then because their frequency might be monitored. The Boolies had hit them, Brossling said, but the assault hadn't been as bad as expected. The referees there had agreed that 2nd Battalion and the Condaro had driven them off with fairly heavy Booly casualties and only modest casualties of their own. Modest because they were dug in, and because they hadn't let themselves be overrun.

Romlar's own casualties, the referees announced, had been relatively modest too, considering it was T'swa they'd ambushed, T'swa in their prefinal year of training, most of them seventeen years old. When the whistles blew again, the surviving T'swa would regroup and do whatever their commander decided. Romlar would move his men back to the abandoned logging camp at Junction 4, fifteen miles away. A camp that, in the never-never land of the training exercise, served as the nucleus of the mocked-up Condaro village at Junction 4, whose rough wagon road gave logistical access to the principal pass through this part of the Jubat Hills. The Condaros, like the Boolies, were mostly imaginary of course, represented by T'swa veterans, survivors of retired regiments, pretend- ing to be non-T'swa. Veterans each of whom, for the purpose of the exercise, represented a Condaro or Booly platoon.

It was all as real as it could reasonably be made, but given the genu- ine and bloody fighting his regiment had been through on Terfreya, five years earlier, the difference had always been conspicuous to Romlar. None- theless, the regiment had learned a great deal in those five additional train- ing years, learned much more than simply strategy, tactics, and fighting techniques.

Romlar had lost thirty-two percent of his command on Terfreya—real deaths by violence, not pretended deaths by referees' decisions—and like

the T'swa, the "White T'swa" did not replace their casualties. But allowing for that short-handedness, he had no doubt that this regiment, under
his leadership, was as good as any regiment in Confederation Space,
whether at War Level One, Two, or Three. Which were all the levels the
Confederation condoned.

True, the T'swa were physically stronger than his men; they'd been born
to this world's heavy gravity, as had their ancestors for a hundred generations. And his men would graduate with six years less training, though
the Ostrak Procedures, and six years of work under T'swa cadres, had
brought them close. Especially given the months of bloody combat on
Terfreya. Perhaps more important, particularly in a Level Three War where
night visors were prohibited, *Homo tyssiensis* had considerably better night
vision than other humans.

*But under his leadership . . .* Numerous T'swa officers were his equals
in strategy and tactics, Romlar knew, and at spotting importances. But
no one outguessed him, out-predicted him. That was his edge. Even in
training it didn't always bring victory, but it was as good an edge as he
could hope for.

The referees' whistles shrilled again, blowing the two forces back into
action, and Romlar's buglers called a withdrawal. His major advantages
here were gone now; it was time to get back to Junction 4.

The Game Master had declared the "war" over. The Condaros had
broken, and with that the greatly outnumbered regiment had been chewed
up. First Romlar, and later Carrmak and Brossling had been "killed" in
T'swa night assaults, and Eldren Esenrok, still and always cocky, had led
what was left of the troopers.

Now the entire regiment, survivors and casualties, sat together in the
Great Hall to hear their efforts critiqued. Sat facing the Grand Master
and the board of Masters. Tiers of wooden benches, dark and smooth,
rose on three sides, holding other regiments in advanced training, those
which were on base. The hall was well lit by T'swa standards, but the
light was ruddy as a campfire. The timbered roof was high and dark,
unpainted and with massive beams, its corners shadowed. All in all it
felt primordial, despite the large viewscreen on the wall at one end.

Grand Master Kliss-Bahn was ancient, his frame still large but its
covering shrunken. His naturally short hair, long since white, had become
thin and soft, and like himself no longer stood straight. He'd commanded
the legendary Black Tiger Regiment in its time, survived its gradual
shrinkage and final destruction, and had been overseeing training in one
capacity and another for sixty-eight standard years.

His critique was direct, detailed, and generally favorable. When he'd
finished, he turned his large, luminous black eyes on Romlar, who as

regimental commander sat front and center facing him. "Now," said Kliss-Bahn, "let us hear from Colonel Romlar. Colonel, you may comment at any reasonable length on this exercise. And because it was your final exercise, feel free to address your training overall. Colonel?"

Romlar stood. He was rather tall, and massive for an Iryalan—as big as most T'swa. "Thank you, Master Kliss-Bahn. I'll keep it short. This exercise was a lesson in fighting for a losing cause of little merit, a lesson in dying with integrity." He grinned. "It was an interesting experience.

"As for our overall training—T'swa warriors have not only trained us; they've inspired us and been role models for us. And T'swa masters of wisdom have done much to expand us in the T'sel during the three years we've spent on your world. Basic to all that were the Ostrak Procedures, received from counselors of our own species in our first year of training. But even the Ostrak Procedures grew out of training in the T'sel, received by Iryalans here on Tyss six centuries ago. So it all comes down to Tyss, the T'swa, and the T'sel."

He looked around, scanning the black faces, the reflective eyes. "We are not truly T'swa," he went on. "Our scripting and imprinting have been different. The Ostrak Procedures, and our training by your lodge and by the Order of Ka-Shok, have made us close cousins to the T'swa; in most ways we have become closer to you than to our families, or to the friends of our childhood. But we remain Confederatswa, and more specifically Iryalans.

"We will go somewhere to fight soon, taking with us what we have learned from you. What we have learned not only about the art of war, but of the T'sel, of ethics, of integrity.

"As the T'swa well know and fully intended, the T'sel is infiltrating the Confederation, particularly at the top and most particularly on Iryala. In time, wars will cease; that is the direction the T'sel moves us, now that the hold of the Sacrament is beginning to crumble in the Confederation. In lives to come—perhaps not the next, or the one after that, but in some future life—we will do things beyond our present dreaming. But for this life we are warriors born and trained, and we will practice our profession as skillfully and ethically as we can, taking pleasure in its challenges and actions.

"Because we are Confederatswa, we will no doubt do some things differently than you would. But we will always act according to the T'sel. We thank you for all you have given us, and should it happen that we meet some of you in battle, we will not disappoint you."

As Romlar sat down, the T'swa regiments stood, clapping in the T'swa manner, strongly, rhythmically, large palms cupped, the sound resonant in the hall. A rush pebbled the young colonel's skin.

# 2

Elgo Valarton gazed out the broad window and unconsciously added a sixth or eighth stick of gum to the wad in his mouth. The building stood on a high rocky hill, giving a marvelous view across Basalt Strait, its water a perfect blue beneath a perfect sky, its whitecaps perfect white, the sails of its pleasure sloops bright and vivid. It seemed to Valarton that the view must be one of the loveliest on Maragor.

Appropriately, for The Archipelago was one of Maragor's wealthiest nations, and Azure Bay its richest and most sophisticated city.

The receptionist looked up from her typing. "Mr. Helmiss will see you now, Mr. Valarton."

Suddenly aware of the cud he chewed, Valarton dropped it into a wastebasket before he walked to the office door. The man who awaited him was standing behind his desk, and leaned across it to shake hands. They sat down then.

"What can I do for you?" the man asked.

"Mr. Helmiss, let me say first that the matter I've come to talk about is extremely confidential."

Klute Helmiss nodded slightly. "I treat every matter brought to me as confidential, unless otherwise instructed. What may I do for you?"

Valarton found himself reluctant to begin; there was a certain risk to his country in this mission. "You're aware, of course, of the Komarsi invasion of Smolen, and how it's turning out. And of the broader political and human aspects of that war."

"Of course."

"Krentorf would like to see Smolen survive. And to see the war cost Komars enough blood and money that she won't be encouraged to assault her other neighbors."

Helmiss nodded.

Valarton paused another long moment. "The Crown of Krentorf would like to assist Smolen, but that assistance needs to be securely confidential."

"What do you have in mind, Mr. Valarton? Or what does your government have in mind?"

"This would not be an act of government. In a constitutional monarchy like Krentorf, if this were done by the government, it would soon be public knowledge. I am here as the personal agent of the queen. She will finance the project out of her own, personal resources, if the cost is one she can reasonably meet."

The Movrik Transportation Company's station chief on Maragor leaned back in his chair, folded his hands over his modest paunch, and waited.

"Her Highness has considered various possibilities, and it seems to her that—that to provide a regiment of T'swa mercenaries could have considerable impact on the war, while being essentially impossible to trace to her. Is she correct in that?"

On several trade worlds, Movrik Transportation served as the agent for the warrior lodge of Kootosh-Lan, of the planet Tyss, known also as "Oven." It was a hat that Helmiss hadn't actually worn in his four years on Maragor, but he knew the procedures. "That is correct, Mr. Valarton."

"What might the services of such a regiment cost?"

Helmiss turned, took a letter-size sheet from a file cabinet, and handed it to Valarton, who skimmed it rapidly, then handed it back. "I'm afraid Her Majesty's personal resources will not stretch so far."

When Helmiss did not reach to take the sheet back, Valarton laid it on the desk. Watchfully, for it seemed to him that Helmiss might offer some sort of terms.

"If the T'swa are too expensive, I have an alternative to offer. A regiment, a short regiment actually, of Iryalan mercenaries."

"Iryalans?"

"Trained by the T'swa. It should be graduating about now, and because it's not well known, I suspect it's more affordable. My company is not an agent for it, but I'd act as go-between if their, um, lodge would give Movrik the transportation contract."

Valarton pursed his lips. "Her Majesty didn't authorize me to hire non-T'swa. And newly graduated? They're inexperienced then."

"On the contrary. If you were hiring black T'swa, there'd be a fair chance you'd get a virgin regiment, unblooded albeit highly effective. These Iryalans, on the other hand"—he paused for effect—"it is they who drove the out-sector invaders off Terfreya, and that as a green regiment with only a year of training. Since then they've trained five years more. And it was their T'swa trainers who named their regiment 'the White T'swa.' "

Valarton wondered how Helmiss came to be so informed. "But you don't know how much they'd cost," he said.

"I'll find out for you." He touched a key on his commset. "Aron, I'm sending Mr. Valarton back out to you. Offer him refreshment. I'll be looking into a matter for him." He turned to the Krentorfi then, stood and indicated the door to reception. "I'll be no longer than I must."

There was something about this that seemed odd to Valarton, but he got up and went to the door. When he reached it, he turned his head . . . and saw Helmiss going through a door behind his desk. He got only a glimpse, but the room Helmiss was entering seemed small, with shelves and cabinets—an office supply room obviously. Then Helmiss closed the door behind him, and Valarton went on into reception.

❖    ❖    ❖

The room that Valarton had glimpsed was somewhat wider than deep. When Helmiss had closed the door, he set the lock, and went to an apparatus at one side. It was a low platform with a tubular frame that looked like a doorway leading nowhere. There was a small console; he tapped certain keys on it, gazed at the monitor, then tapped some more. Faintly he could feel a power field develop, the generator subaudible. A green light came on beside the "gate." Looking through it, he no longer saw the wall a few feet on the other side; instead he looked into another room, seen vaguely. Without hesitating he walked through and disappeared. The green light winked out and the field died.

Splenn was the most sophisticated of the trade worlds, and one of only two with its own spaceships. Movrik Transportation owned most of them. The Movrik family was wealthy beyond any other on Splenn, though they did not flaunt it. They had more important purposes. Their influence, though mostly not apparent, was becoming ubiquitous on Splenn, while offworld they were covertly connected to the highest levels of Confederation government.

So closely connected as to have a teleport on the family's home estate, and one at most of their offworld offices. Something not known to anyone outside the loosely organized, secret society whose members called it "the Movement," and themselves "the Alumni."

A teleport needed only a transmitter, not a receiver, and gates could target far more accurately than a few years earlier. Though a matric attractor was necessary for fine precision. Movrik's various offworld gates opened into the middle of a room, on the family estate referred to as "headquarters." The same room held the gate used in returning.

This was the room into which Klute Helmiss stepped from his supply room nine hyperspace days away, with a lapsed time of zero. Except for him, it was empty. Rather than hunt through the house or disturb the domestic staff, he went to a commset on a desk, and keyed the personal communicator of Pitter Movrik himself. A moment later, Pitter's face appeared on the screen.

"Klute! What brings you to Splenn?"

"I have a potential job for the White T'swa. I need authorization, terms, a contract. . . ."

"Okay. I'm in Carris. I'm going to disconnect and call the Confederation Ministry; the minister himself if he's in. I'll get back with you as quickly as possible. Can you wait there?"

"Can I have a prediction? I left a man in reception, back on Maragor, totally bewildered."

"Under fifteen minutes."

"I'll wait."

There were books in the room, the usual hard copies. Helmiss looked at their spines, and pulling one, began to browse. Within a few minutes the commset interrupted him.

"Klute, we're going to talk with Kristal on Iryala." He gave Helmiss a destination code to key into the gate controls. It would activate an algorithm to compute the constantly changing destination coordinates of the target. Klute followed his instructions, and stepped through the gate into a room on Iryala, in the office suite of Emry Wanslo, Lord Kristal. Within three minutes, the two Splennites were sitting at a table with Kristal himself, personal aide to Marcus XXVIII, King of Iryala and Administrator General of the Confederation of Worlds.

Elgo Valarton had waited less than thirty-five minutes when he was sent back to Helmiss's office. Helmiss had an authorization and a proposed contract. The cost was negotiable, though Helmiss didn't say so. Kristal wanted the regiment employed, and as described by Helmiss, the Smoleni cause appealed to him.

There was no dickering. Valarton had been selected for his discretion and reliability, not for any particular bargaining sense, and the price proposed was a bit less than he'd been authorized to meet. He was a bit spooked though by one of the signatures on the document: Emry Wanslo, Lord Kristal. There was also a delivery deadline. How had Helmiss gotten those? Surely he didn't have a stock of signed and dated contracts in his supply room!

The queen's emissary tried to avoid thinking about it. Somehow it gave him chills.

# 3

It was late summer at the Blue Forest Military Reservation, the day a preview of fall. Colonel Carlis Voker had just returned to his office after lunch, and sat reading a report on his terminal. His commset chirped, and he reached to it. "What is it, Lemal?"

"Kelmer Faronya is here to see you, sir."

Voker glanced at the clock: 12:59. Young Faronya was prompt. "Send him in."

A moment later a young man entered, well built and rather tall, like his sister before him. He'd come to lunch from a training exercise, a four-hour run with a sandbag on a pack frame. The sweat had dried on his face, but his bur-cut hair was still awry from it, and his shirt stained.

He saluted, a trooper's casual hand flip. It wasn't necessary; he was in fact a civilian, not a trooper. On the other hand he'd trained with the 6th Iryalan Mercenary Regiment for just eight days short of a year. He'd done almost everything they'd done, although in part a helmet camera had substituted for a weapon.

Also he hadn't done the Ostrak Procedures. After the early training difficulties of the original Iryalan mercenaries, the White T'swa, trainees had been run through the Ostrak Procedures *before* their training was begun. It had saved headaches of various sorts, as well as scheduling problems. But Kristal had decided that the "regimental historian"—actually an in-house journalist—should do without the procedures. That way he could write more nearly from a public point of view.

This did cause a complication, because without having been through the procedures, Faronya couldn't teleport without going psychotic. And die without quick and effective treatment. It had probably left him feeling a bit of an outsider, too, lacking a trooper's viewpoint, and major areas of a trooper's reality.

He wasn't even spiritually a warrior as they were. He *had* been born with the basic warrior underpattern, but not in warrior phase, not for that lifetime. Thus he lacked a warrior's script, and a warrior's psychic and mental tool kits. He did have the metabolic attributes though; without them he would have washed out in training.

At a glance he looked like a warrior: A year's mercenary training, strenuous to the limits of endurance, had given him a physical hardness that, even in a baggy field uniform, was quite apparent.

"Faronya," Voker said, "I'm transferring you out of the regiment." The young man's eyes widened, and his lips parted as if to object. Voker went on. "You're familiar with the White T'swa, of course."

Faronya's objection stopped unspoken; he'd hear this out. He knew a lot about the White T'swa. His sister had been with it during part of its training, and when she'd come home had talked of little else to him. Then she'd ported with it to Terfreya as a stowaway, and ended missing in action, no doubt with her camera busy. Her loss had hurt him, but the war—the war had been so necessary, and the troopers so brave.

"Yessir, I know a lot about them. As you're well aware."

"I'm attaching you to them. They have a contract to fight a war on a trade world called Maragor. A Level Three War; nothing technical. You'll record and report on it.

"You can refuse, of course."

Kelmer Faronya's lips were parted again, not with intended rejection now, but with surprise. "Refuse? No, sir! It's the sort of thing I wanted when I applied! I just hadn't expected it to happen so soon."

"Sooner than you think. A floater leaves here in an hour. That means you shower and pack and be at reception at 1:55, ready to leave. Someone will meet you when you arrive at Landfall. You'll leave there on a hyperspace courier later today, to join your new regiment on Splenn. Now jump!"

Kelmer Faronya sprinted to his barracks.

# 4

Customarily, when a regiment had completed its training at the Lodge of Kootosh-Lan, graduation was at midmorning. For the comfort of unconditioned Iryalan guests, however, the ceremony for the White T'swa was held shortly before dawn, when the temperature was relatively cool—only 91 degrees on this morning in early spring.

Some of the guests from offworld were T'swa—the basic training cadre from Blue Forest, on Iryala. They'd ported in, more than four hundred of them, absent from their posts for a day. Their current cycle of trainees was almost at the end of their basic year and would get along very well under their student officers.

All through the ceremony, Romlar watched them from across the Great Hall, among them Bahn, his old squad sergeant; Dao, his old platoon sergeant; Lieutenant Dzo-Tar; Captain Gotasu; and his old regimental C.O., Colonel Dak-So. And Lord Kristal, representing the king; Colonel Voker, who administered the basic training program; and Varlik Lormagen, the first man to be called "the White T'swa," forty years ago on Kettle.

And Lotta Alsnor, who so far as he knew had been on Tyss all along. In his three years there, he'd seen her just once and been alone with her not at all. She was shorter than average, and considerably less than half Romlar's mass, with a wiriness apparently more the result of genetics than of her early interest in gymnastics and dance. On Tyss she looked even slighter than before, as if the heat had dried her out, which didn't bother Romlar in the least.

Perhaps he'd have a chance to talk with her alone before she went back to Dys-Hualuun. It troubled him that he might not, and the feeling surprised him. To someone grounded in the T'sel, it was illogical. Their purposes in life, his and hers, were different, at least those purposes he knew of. This evening he would rebalance himself—enter a trance and regain neutrality on the subject. On Terfreya they'd had what they'd had together. If nothing more came of it, that would be fine.

On the other hand, perhaps something more would. Perhaps when the time came—when casualties had reduced the regiment below any effective level—perhaps then they would be together. Assuming he survived himself, which in a mercenary regiment in the T'swa tradition was unlikely, even for the commanding officer.

Mentally he shook his thoughts away and focused on Kliss-Bahn. The ancient veteran, owning humankind's most admired military mind, was worth his full attention, even making a graduation address.

Because of the offworld visitors, there was a reception after the ceremony, an opportunity to mix. Lieutenant Jerym Alsnor went straight to Lotta, his sister. "Hi, sib," he said. "I was hoping we'd have a chance to talk."

"Bet on it," she answered. "I don't have to leave when the others do."

"Good. What've you been doing lately?"

She grinned. "You mean have I been monitoring Tain."

He laughed. "You read my mind!"

"Not really. And, yes, I have been monitoring Tain."

Their eyes met and held. "How is she?"

"Happy."

"Really?" The last Lotta had told him, five years earlier on Terfreya, Tain had been a prisoner on a warship from the empire. And amnesic.

"Really. She's married and has a child."

Jerym didn't answer for several seconds. "Does she—remember yet?"

"No. Not you, not me. Nothing."

Jerym thought of the out-sector marines he'd fought on Terfreya. Mostly they'd been small men, and hairier than anyone he'd ever seen before. They hadn't seemed entirely human to him. "What's her husband like?"

"He's a good person, Jerym. He's strong and considerate and loving."

"Remarkable." He wasn't referring to Tain's marriage, but to the welling in his eyes. He didn't feel sad at all, but there it was. "Anything more?"

"Yes. He's an ex-marine officer—and the emperor of eleven worlds. And he has a rare innate sense of how to treat the woman he loves." She didn't tell him the rest of it, and he didn't pick up on the omission.

His earlier reaction had receded. "Well. I'm glad, sib, I'm really really glad she's happy." A slow grin built. "I'll ask about her again in another five years. With an emperor for a husband, she shouldn't have any trouble getting authorization for all the kids she wants.

"Now. What have you heard from the folks?"

❖      ❖      ❖

Jerym was already talking with Lotta, so Romlar sheered off. Dak-So, his old T'swa colonel, came over to him and asked questions about the fighting on Terfreya. Colonel Voker came over and stood listening. Dak-So's eyes seemed to gleam with a light of their own, and his white teeth were vivid in his black T'swa face. "You are changed, Artus," he said when Romlar had finished. "Beyond the changes generated by combat."

"As you expected. They've trained us well here, not only Kliss-Bahn's cadre, but the Ka-Shok adepts under Master Rinn. We're ready."

Dak-So laughed, a deep rich rumbling. "I believe you," he said. "Your higher center had already displayed itself during your basic training. Brigadier Shiller was sufficiently disheartened that he retired, beaten and embarrassed by a nineteen-year-old commander-in-training with less than a year's service."

Voker spoke then. "Speaking of ready, Lord Kristal wants to talk to you before he goes."

Romlar's pulse quickened. *A contract*, he thought, and wondered where for. Kristal wasn't letting grass grow under his feet or theirs. He looked around, but didn't spot him in the large crowded room. Who he did see was Lotta Alsnor coming toward him. *His lordship can talk to me later*, he told himself. "Excuse me," he said, and started toward her.

She grinned at him as they met, and her touch on his arm had an electric intimacy. Her gaze was direct but her words playful. "I had to tell Jerym it was nice talking to him, but that lovers outrank brothers."

*Lovers.* They'd never used the word before. It gave their feelings a certain standing. Lotta read his reaction and laughed. He gestured with his head in the direction of Voker and Dak-So. "Lovers outrank colonels, too. Shall we go outside and talk? There'll be some privacy there."

They wove their way toward the entry, among clusters of cadre and troopers renewing old bonds. Outside, there was enough dawnlight to extend visibility, and no one was in sight. Romlar felt an urgency now that took him by surprise.

"Colonels have private quarters," he murmured. "Would you like to see? It's been more than five years."

She purred. "A long five years. Let's go, before someone else comes out."

He took her hand then and they ran, his gait an easy lope. Her slender legs scissored quickly, feet scarcely seeming to touch the ground. The regimental officers' barracks were dark and silent. In his room, enough light came through the windows that they could see each other's eyes, if not their color. Their first kiss was cool, lingering, then they sat down on his narrow bed and kissed urgently, hotly, their hands busy. Within a couple of minutes they were naked.

When they were spent, they lay side by side holding hands. "I'm lucky," he said. "Lucky we found each other."

"It was an agreement we made, before this life."

"I've always thought so. That winter at Blue Forest, it seemed more like a renewal than a new friendship."

"It goes beyond this," she said, "beyond being together and making love."

"True." He lay thoughtful for a few seconds, then asked: "An agreement to do what?"

"I think we won't know until the time comes. Or it might simply be an agreement to love each other. I've developed a lot, training under Grand Master Ku; I can see more deeply than ever into other people. But not into myself, and when it comes to seeing my own script . . ." She shook her head and chuckled. "Ku says that's typical, almost invariable, even among masters. Otherwise it would remove much of the challenge and interest from life, and the lessons of experience." She turned her head to look at Romlar. "I'm done on Tyss, at least for the present. I'm a master now. Officially. I'm going back to Iryala at the end of the week."

He grinned. "You're *my* master, I know that."

She jabbed him with an elbow then, and they began to wrestle. He discovered he wasn't as spent as he'd thought.

# 5

On Maragor the solstice was approaching, and the back-country village of Burnt Woods was in deep spring. The air smelled of forest in the flush of new growth. Birds sang, and—the flaw in the beauty—insects bit, Maragor's version of mosquitoes.

Burnt Woods was now the administrative capital of what was left of the republic of Smolen. The southern one-fourth—with ninety percent of the population and arable land—had been occupied by the Army of Komars. Except that it didn't have ninety percent of the population anymore. More like seventy-five percent. And in the north, throngs of refugees lived in scattered tent camps, while making communal shelters of logs against inevitable winter.

Burnt Woods' largest house had been turned over to the president for his quarters and offices. Not commandeered. Offered freely by the owner, the local fur broker, who lived now with his son's family in their home. The hotel *had* been commandeered—all twelve rooms of it—rented by the government for deferred rents that might never be collected. Would surely not be collected, unless some hard-to-envision military turnaround occurred. It held what was left of the president's staff. Officed them, that is, for they dwelt in tents like the refugees. And like the regiments stationed southward, prepared to meet as best they could any Komarsi strike.

A strike that might be made but seemed unneeded. There were nearly one hundred thousand people in the northland now, including troops. By next spring they'd be very hungry. There was neither arable land nor implements to grow anything like adequate crops.

The Smoleni had had a long history of oppressions, though none for more than four hundred years. And traditions had grown from those oppressions: notably doggedness, a refusal to give in. And a dedication to as little government as practical.

Most mornings, in the weeks they'd been in Burnt Woods, the president's War Council had met in his office, which for years had served as a family's dining room. His conference table had been their dinner table. President Heber Lanks was a very tall, rawboned man who'd gained weight in middle age and now was losing it. His arms were long, even for his height, their length accentuated by long, large hands. All in all, he was physically imposing, but his manner was mild.

He stood up to call the meeting to order, and on his feet studied briefly, soberly, the men he'd surrounded himself with. The night before, a floater had landed. A message had been delivered to his hand, and the floater had lifted again.

"Gentlemen," he said, "I have news from a source which I shall not identify. A couriered message. It seems we shall have some help." He paused, looking thoughtful, unexcited. "This is strictly confidential. I repeat that: this is strictly confidential. A regiment of mercenaries will be delivered to us. They . . ."

"*Mercenaries? Mercenaries?*" General Eskoth Belser had half gotten to his feet, his voice rising in anger. Vestur Marlim jerked on the general's sleeve and almost hissed the words: "Eskoth! For Tunis's sake shut your mouth! This is confidential! Have you no self-control?"

Belser's heavy features reddened and seemed to swell, but he settled slowly to his seat, jerking his arm free of Marlim's grasp. The general was a thick slab of a man, while the War Minister was small and fine-boned.

President Lanks had looked briefly pained. "Not mercenaries from here on Maragor," he said. "These are civilized and highly trained professionals from offworld. T'swa trained."

Belser's clamped jaw relaxed slightly. "T'swa trained?"

Lanks told them what he knew.

"But only one regiment! We have twenty-six regiments of our own!"

"Not as many as we need."

"Of course not! Not by a long shot! But what good will a single additional regiment do us?"

"That remains to be seen. We know the impact the T'swa had in the Elstra-Tromfel War, and at Stemperos."

"But these mercenaries aren't T'swa. Correct? They're 'T'swa-trained,' you said."

"That's right. They're Iryalans."

Belser subsided into grumblings. "I've never even heard of Iryalan mercenaries."

Colonel Elyas Fossur looked across at him. Fossur was the president's intelligence chief and military mentor. "Actually, Eskoth, I think you have, but they weren't identified as mercenaries at the time." He turned to the president then. "I presume this is the regiment that drove the out-sector invaders off Terfreya, several years ago."

"That's the information I have."

"Then they may not be T'swa, but they seem to be something quite like them. T'swa-trained indeed! The T'swa dubbed them the White T'swa."

The council sat digesting this, all but Lanks, who still stood. He'd digested it earlier, lying awake in his bed till the birds called the sun to the sky. Historically, the Smoleni experience with mercenaries had been as victims, not beneficiaries. He would make a point of welcoming this regiment as valuable friends, and hope its men behaved decently.

Belser was still disgruntled. "What we really need is for someone else to declare war on Komars," he said. "The Komarsi'd at least have to pull their troops south of the Eel then."

"There are various reasons that won't happen," Lanks said drily. "And these Iryalan mercenaries may make a difference. Meanwhile they won't arrive for at least a week, and we'll need that much time to prepare a camp for them."

He handed a thin sheaf of papers to Belser. "This is not the contract," he said. "The party who hired them for us has that. But it does include all the operational clauses, and assigns responsibility to me. I'm turning that responsibility over to the army, specifically to you. It's important that we meet the clauses to the best of our ability; that was stressed to me."

Belser took the papers with his jaw clamped. It seemed to him that this would be more trouble than it was worth.

# 6

At the Movrik family's large wildlife estate on Splenn, the weather was considerably different than at Burnt Woods. It was early winter there, and a cold rain fell steadily and thickly, drumming on the roof. The gray lake surface seemed to seethe with it.

Pitter Movrik loved that kind of weather; during the long rainy season he often visited the lodge just to experience it. But the decisive reason for being there this day was isolation. A teleport large enough to accommodate AG trucks, say, or floaters, was hard to camouflage in a populated area. Certainly it could be difficult to conceal the occasional traffic it received.

For example, 1,170 troopers plus their gear. They'd be impossible to hide or explain, even at the family's rural estate, where the sizeable domestic staff and farm crew would see them. Here, on the other hand, there were no neighbors at all, except wild animals. And the lodge staff of four, ported there as needed, were at least second generation employees of the family. They'd been educated in the family school with the family offspring, and received the Ostrak Procedures as children. As their parents had before them. And finally, as adults, they'd chosen to stay.

The regiment had already arrived, and transferred to the HS *Maryam Burkitt*, which sat parked on a gravitic vector well above the weather. Just now, though, twenty-one regimental officers, including the company commanders and their execs, sat in the lodge's dining room, with old Pitter an interested observer. They were waiting for a situation briefing by Movrik's senior agent on Maragor, Klute Helmiss. The dining room opened onto a roofed deck which overlooked the lake, a view framed by rain forest. Water poured off the eaves onto rockwork below, except where a gable provided a gap in the cataract, a sort of window through which Movrik could see a shuttle parked close above the shore, waiting to take the officers up.

Helmiss finished writing instructions into the player, then turned to face his audience. He pressed a key, and the wallscreen lit up with a globe of Maragor. Slightly to the left of center, they saw a block of yellow and one of pink, together extending from about 45 degrees to nearly 53 degrees north latitude.

"All right, gentlemen," he said, "let's start." He spoke a bit loudly, to be heard above the rain and the splashing of the roof cataract. "We're looking at what by definition is the eastern hemisphere of Maragor. The country shown in yellow is Komars, and the one in pink is Smolen. And here . . ." The two countries filled the screen now, and briefly he described their demographics, Komars with its nine million people, Smolen to the north with three hundred and twenty thousand.

Graphs showed in windows on the map, replacing each other as he talked. In terms of area, the two countries weren't too different, but they differed greatly in the kinds of land they had. Komars was mostly a fertile plain, flat to rolling. The southernmost part of Smolen, "the Leas," was similar, if generally more hilly. The Leas, along with two northward extensions and a short strip of coastland in the southeast, made up twenty-five percent of Smolen, but contained almost all its farmland and manufacturing. The rest of the country was forest, lakes, and peat bogs, broken here and there by small farm settlements which became fewer as one went farther north. It was called "the Free Lands," because centuries earlier, the Smoleni peasants, suffering home-grown oppressors, would flee to its forests from time to time. There to starve and raid until coaxed back out by promises of justice.

"Normally," Helmiss said, "the Leas raise enough food to feed the nation, but without enough left for significant export. Smolen's on-planet exports are primarily lumber, paper, and furs. Its offworld exports are entirely furs, some ranch-grown but mostly trapped."

He went on to describe the events leading up to a Komarsi attack that had quickly occupied first the Leas, then the coast, and two valleys that extended northward. "Initially," he said, "the Smoleni policy seems to have been to cost the Komarsi enough in blood and material that they'd settle for limited objectives. It wasn't a promising policy, but it may well have been the best available to them. Obviously it didn't work. Now—" He shrugged. "Now I don't think they have a policy, unless hanging on and hoping qualifies. In fact, the Smoleni prospect seems nearly beyond hope. It appears that you'll find yourself in a no-win situation there. But you'll have marvelous opportunities to fight, and landscapes well suited to the operations of small, elite units.

"I've always found war intriguing, and I've read a great deal about it. Including Lormagen's video-studies of the T'swa, prepared before he got the Ostrak Procedures. I've also read about and watched the cubes on your training at Blue Forest, and your campaign in the Terfreyan jungles, and it seems to me you can find marvelous opportunities in this war. As the T'swa would."

Listening, Romlar chuckled to himself. With a little concentration, he could see auras, and Helmiss had a warrior underpattern manifesting strongly.

A few hours later, Romlar sat in the wardroom aboard the *Burkitt*, a cup of joma by his elbow, reading a book. Lieutenant Jerym Alsnor came in and sat down by him.

"What're you reading?"

Romlar held it up. "*Historical Strategies and Tactics in Level 3 Wars: Selected Case Histories.* Carlis wrote it just recently; he gave it to me on Oven, after graduation." Marking his place with a napkin, Romlar put it down and went on. "The reason I sent for you is—" He paused for effect. "Tain has a brother. Kelmer."

Jerym cocked an eyebrow. "She mentioned that. He's quite a bit younger than her. And?"

"He's who we're waiting for here. He's following in his sister's footsteps; he's a journalist. Kristal's sending him with us to Maragor to record and describe the war, primarily our part in it. His official designation is 'regimental historian.'"

Jerym nodded. "And he hasn't been through the Ostrak Procedures, so he can't be ported. Right? Wouldn't it have been cheaper to gate us through to Maragor and have him follow in a courier?"

"He's not the reason we're shipping from here. Maragor's pretty conservative—the Sacrament's only been defused there for about twenty years—and the Movement doesn't want to draw attention there to the gates. Also, Splenn's only a nine-day jump from there, and because Movrik's agent on Maragor brokered the contract, Movrik had a fee coming from OSP. He was willing to take it in the form of a transportation contract."

"Um." Jerym repeated himself then: "And?"

"I'm assigning Kelmer Faronya to your platoon. Carlis tells me he was with the 6th Regiment through almost their full year of basic, so strength and endurance won't be a problem, and he should understand what you tell him without a lot of explanation. He trained with them as a combat journalist, not a fighting man, so on combat exercises his weapon was his camera. But he got a lot of basic weapons training, too, and the basics of jokanru.

"I want you to see he gets chances to do what he needs to do. And—" Romlar paused, frowning thoughtfully. "I was going to say I want you to keep him from taking reckless chances. But—" He shook his head. "I don't think he's the reckless type."

"Something Carlis said?"

"No. A feeling I have."

"Um. I suppose he thinks Tain's dead."

"Right. It's best that way."

"When's he coming aboard?"

"The courier arrived in-system last night. They should land him here before dark."

"I look forward to meeting him," Jerym said, and wondered if Kelmer Faronya looked at all like his sister.

# 7

The *Burkitt* was under way. On warp drive still; they'd jump to hyperdrive when they were far enough from the primary with its distorting gravity field.

Jerym shared a small cabin with another A Company platoon leader. They lay one above the other on shelflike, fold-down bunks, reading a manual on space warfare as it scrolled slowly up their wall screen. It was theoretical of course; there'd never been a space war in the Confederation Sector. But so far it was making sense.

The door signal beeped, and Jerym, having the bottom bunk, opened to a tall young man they'd never seen before. But dressed in regimental uniform, not the jumpsuit of a Movrik crewman. "Kelmer Faronya?" Jerym asked.

"That's right, sir. Colonel Romlar told me to report to Lieutenant Alsnor and get acquainted."

Jerym reached out a hand, and they shook. "I'm Jerym Alsnor," he said. "This is Furgis Klintok; he has First Platoon. Furgis, I'm going to leave you with Commander Fenner's good book, and take Mr. Faronya to the briefing room. Who knows? We might even find some privacy there."

The passageway wore a durable carpet for traction and quiet, the same carpeting that spaceships had worn since before history. "My sister mentioned you," Kelmer said. "You were her—guide at Blue Forest. Were you her guide on Terfreya, too?"

"No. On Terfreya my platoon wore a particularly dangerous hat. We were attached to Headquarters Section and did special projects for Artus. Colonel Romlar. Till almost none of us were left."

Kelmer nodded. "And afterward, when the regiment got reorganized, I suppose you got a platoon again."

"Right. Actually my platoon got reconstituted on Terfreya, from remnants of a company that—pretty much had to be sacrificed, used as the bait for a trap. Then I lost most of that one in the big night raid that closed the book and won the war there."

Kelmer Faronya paled at that. He knew the history of that war in some detail and had watched the video cubes. The story had become part of the education of subsequent regiments. He'd felt intrigued but also uncomfortable with them, perhaps because Tain had died there. (So he believed. It's what he'd been told, and he had no reason to doubt it.)

He'd also felt discomfort at the other trainees' relaxed attitudes toward the casualties, and had blamed it on their youth. Most had been sixteen or seventeen years old when they'd begun training, while he'd been twenty-two, a worldly graduate in journalism. But Jerym Alsnor was older than he was, and had been there, had experienced it all. Had seen most of his men killed, and still seemed casual.

He wondered if he should ask him about it, then asked instead: "What's it like to be in combat for the first time?"

They came to the briefing room door, even as he asked. Jerym opened it, and they entered and sat down before he answered. "For us it was exciting. Exhilarating. I can't say what it'll be like for you."

"Exhilarating? Uniformly for all of you?"

Jerym smiled. "I haven't polled the others on it, but yes, I think all of us."

*Like the T'swa,* Kelmer thought. The black T'swa, the real T'swa. "I asked Sergeant Bahn the same question once, and that's pretty much what he said. He used the word *fulfilling,* but everything considered, he seemed to feel about the same as you." He paused then, looking at it, and decided he'd ask others when he had the chance. But it seemed to him that Jerym was right, that they'd all felt pretty much the same.

Jerym watched the other. Faronya was not a warrior, he told himself, and more, he no doubt believed that a person lives just once. You die and that's the end of you. "What do you expect your first combat will be like?" he asked.

Kelmer's strong young face turned very sober. "I used to think it would be exciting. But the more I trained . . . I think it was the cubes of combat. Old ones by Mr. Lormagen on Kettle, and Tain's from Terfreya. I saw men blown apart! Saw bodies lying with their faces shot off. Now I'm not sure. I'm pretty sure it won't be exhilarating though."

"I suppose you're familiar with the Matrix of T'sel."

"Yes. We were trained on that the first week, until I could diagram it from memory."

"Where do you suppose you're at on it?"

"I'm at *Jobs,* at the level of *Knowledge.* I asked Sergeant Dao, and he asked me some questions and told me that's where I was." Kelmer found that he was sweating.

"How did that seem to you?"

"Pretty good, I guess. It seemed accurate to me."

"Anything wrong with being at Jobs and Knowledge?"

"Well, when everyone else, my friends, the guys I trained with, were at War, at the level of—of Play! . . . Sometimes I felt a little out of place."

"You don't need to be at War, or at Play. You don't have a warrior's function; you're a journalist. How did your buddies treat you?"

"Okay. No one ever criticized or belittled me. Actually, training with them was the most consistently enjoyable time of my life. The most uncomplicated and active. I loved the training! Even running for hours with a sandbag, with sweat burning my eyes, or wading in a swamp full of mosquitoes. Even doing an all-night speed march on snowshoes after not eating since breakfast. I felt—I felt like hot stuff!"

Jerym was grinning broadly. "Yeah. It's a good feeling, isn't it? Kelmer, I'd say you'll fit in with us just fine." He cocked an eyebrow. "How long was the flight here from Iryala?"

"Fifteen days."

"Fifteen days on a courier boat? How'd you work out?"

Kelmer's answer was rueful. "Not very adequately. It had an exercise machine, and I did handstand pushups, but that's not like real training."

"They fitted out the *Burkitt* with a pretty good gym. Come on, I'll show it to you. You can use it on Second Platoon's shift tomorrow."

When Kelmer had returned to the cubby he occupied, Jerym went to the wardroom. Romlar was still there, watching two others play cards.

"Talk to you privately?" Jerym asked.

Romlar got up. "Sure." They went to his cabin, not much larger than Jerym's, but private. Its primary amenity was an electric joma maker. Romlar drew two cups and handed one to Jerym. "What did you think of him?" he asked.

"I like him. But I think he's got a problem."

Romlar raised an eyebrow.

"I've got a feeling he'll have problems under fire. First of all he's not a warrior." Jerym waved off a possible response. "I know. Some of our pilots on Terfreya, even gunship pilots, weren't warriors, but had no obvious difficulty under fire. As brave as you could ask for. But Kelmer worries about it. And he never really met my eyes. I got the impression he feels inferios to us. I doubt he learned that at Blue Forest. I know there's been changes, but neither the T'swa nor Voker are strong on formalities. I assume it's him, the way he is. It came out as if he feels inferior to warriors. As if there's something in his case that makes him feel inadequate for combat."

Romlar took a thoughtful sip. "Hmm. Remind me to give you his interview analysis; it's in his folder. He has a warrior underpattern, so we can be sure he's been a warrior in some of his lives. But for this one he was definitely scripted as a non-warrior, and of course imprinted that way at home and in school. That's not much to override any past-life factors that might make him fearful and untrusting of himself.

"So we've got a guy who's strong and tough and weapons-skilled—even had basic jokanru—with a good education and a high intelligence score, yet who's afraid and a bit submissive. With his psych profile, I'm really curious as to why Kristal chose him. It's got to have been intuitive."

They sat inhaling the aroma and sipping. "A warrior underpattern,"

Jerym said thoughtfully. "That explains his aura. And he says he loved the training; without at least some affinity with the guys, he wouldn't have. Maybe with combat getting close, his case is closing in on him."

Romlar shrugged. "We'll just have to wait and see. We've both read about guys who almost shit themselves waiting, they were so scared, and ended up decorated for bravery."

Jerym nodded. Time would tell.

# 8

There was an electricity among the troopers, a deep excitement. The world of their first contract was no longer a concept, no longer even a blaze against the blackness, or a beautiful blue, white, and tan ball. "Out there" had become "down there."

The *Burkitt* was a combination passenger and cargo ship, not built as a troop transport, let alone as a transport for egalitarian forces designed after the T'swa pattern. Thus the regiment's senior officers sat in the wardroom, watching on the large screen there. The platoon leaders and platoon sergeants watched on screens in the first-class dining room, and the lower ranks in their messhalls (they ate in shifts) and troop compartments.

On the screens, flashes of silver had become lakes, often in chains, and threadlike creeks could be made out where they flowed across open bogs and fens. Some of the fens in particular were large, showing pale greenish-tan, occasionally with islets of forest looking like black teardrops. Here and there, widely separated, were the lighter rectangles of farm fields, mostly in small clusters or strings. Romlar supposed they were along roads, but at first the roads couldn't be seen.

Most of it was dark forest though. As the *Burkitt* sank lower, the horizons drew in, the view became more oblique, and the forest appeared nearly unbroken. The terrain was gently undulating, approaching flat, with here and there low ridges crossing it, wrinkles on the plain. Then someone on the bridge changed the camera, and they were looking straight downward. In the local area shown below them now, fields were prominent. A couple of miles lower they became predominant, with scattered farm buildings visible. In the center, a village stood along the north side of a stream, with a mill pond and mill. On the south side of the stream, at a little distance, were the orderly tent rows of a military camp that would house, Romlar thought, a couple of regiments.

Their descent stopped and the intercom sounded. "Colonel Romlar to the bridge, please. Colonel Romlar to the bridge, please."

It was time. Romlar got up and left the wardroom, striding down the passageway to the bridge, a room not particularly large, resembling in size and shape the bridge on a surface ship. The central monitor showed the same picture he'd seen in the wardroom, but here it was flanked by an array of other views. The *Burkitt's* captain motioned him over, and Romlar contacted the government below, to find out where to land.

As soon as Colonel Fossur's aide began to talk with the ship over the radio, the president rang General Belser's office and informed him. Then Lanks, his War Minister, his intelligence chief, and his daughter Weldi went outside. The ship hung motionless, something less than two miles above the village. It seemed very large. None had ever seen one before, and to Weldi especially, it was exciting. The four of them climbed into Fossur's open-topped army GPV, filling it, and trailing a long tail of dust, drove down the road to the landing site, to welcome the mercenary regiment.

When they got there, the ship still hovered above the village. The camp site had been prepared as agreed. Tent floors had been hammered together and stood in regularly placed stacks, with folded squad tents piled beside them. Log footings had been set, and sills spiked on them. Mess tents had already been erected, along with the tents that would be regimental and battalion headquarters, and orderly rooms. Wells had been driven and hand pumps installed, the best the Smoleni could do under the circumstances. Latrine pits had been dug.

The ship was still parked above the village.

Another GPV sped down the gravel road, to pull up nearby. General Belser's aide got out and came over to them, trailed by a master sergeant. They saluted when they got there. "Mr. President," the aide said, "General Belser sent me as his representative."

Lanks nodded soberly. "Thank you, Major."

Vestur Marlim's lips thinned. Belser wasn't coming then. He was "making a statement," no doubt; he had "important" things to do, and the mercenaries weren't worth his attention. Actually, Belser hadn't initiated a single action since the Komarsi ended their advance. As if he was willing to sit here until the food ran out, making no effort. *If I were president*— The thought embarrassed the Minister of War, as if it were disloyal. He'd long admired Heber Lanks as a historian-philosopher and teacher, and admired him now as president for his patience, his humility— and yes, his judgment. Marlim was learning not to second-guess him; the man could be right with the most unlikely decisions.

*But something needed to be done about that arrogant, surly, Yomal-punish-him Belser!*

With the coming of the other GPV, the major's reporting, and his own thoughts about Belser, Marlim had lost track of the ship. Now he became aware that the others' attention had shifted upward, and he saw the ship lowering, even as it moved toward them. Within a few minutes it had parked only two or three feet above the ground. Massive jacks extruded, sought and found the earth, and the ship's AG generator gradually surrendered the *Burkitt*'s tonnage to them.

Abruptly gangways opened and men poured out, boiled around the piles of floors and tents, and began to set up. As if they'd drilled it; no doubt they had. Others began to unload the ship's cargo holds, to set up prefabricated sheds and transfer goods to them. All this was under way before the mercenaries' commander had time to come over to the welcoming group.

President Heber Lanks watched him come, a man with thick shoulders and marked presence, flanked by what appeared to be two aides. Another man followed a bit behind them and to one side, wearing a helmet that seemed to be a camera as well; it had lenses, and a visor covered his upper face. It occurred to Lanks that he himself bore no insignia of office. Fossur was in uniform, and so was Major Oress, but Lanks wore comfortable yard clothes, with a heavy twill shirt to protect him somewhat from the bull flies, for fly-time had followed mosquito-time in the Free Lands. He looked, he supposed, more like a curious villager than an offworlder's concept of a president.

The mercenary colonel seemed to know him though. He stopped six feet in front of him, saluted casually, and spoke: "I'm Colonel Artus Romlar. This is my executive officer, Major Jorrie Renhaus, and my aide, Captain Fritek Kantros."

So *young*! "I'm Heber Lanks; I'm, uh, the president."

As Lanks had begun to speak, a bull fly had landed on Colonel Romlar's temple and dug in; clearly the young man had not applied a repellent. It distracted the president, and for a moment he'd faltered, then continued. "This is Vestur Marlim, my Minister of War; Colonel Elyas Fossur, my adviser and chief of intelligence; and Major Oress, aide to General Belser, who commands our armed forces. It seems I don't know Major Oress's first name. The young lady is my daughter and caretaker, Weldi."

The fly had continued to bite, and been joined by another at the angle of the jaw, but there'd been no indication at all that the mercenary commander noticed. Then Oress stepped forward and held out a folded paper to the young man.

"Colonel Romlar," he said, "these are General Belser's orders to you."

The young man took them, glanced at them, and handed them back. "Has the general read the contract of employment?"

Oress blinked. "I—don't know. I presume so."

Romlar smiled, his eyes steady on the major now, his voice mild but utterly uncompromising. "It is quite explicit. First we are allowed two full weeks for reconditioning and to become familiar with the situation. I don't expect it will take that long, but it's ours if we need it. Furthermore, I am not subject to the general's orders: We are here to apply our military expertise, which includes my military judgment."

Oress had gone pale at this; the general would skin him for bringing such an answer. The young colonel continued. "I'll be happy to receive the general's briefing, and to coordinate my planning with his, or with whatever representative President Lanks may care to designate."

Both bull flies had gorged themselves and flown; another had settled on the colonel's other temple. President Lanks suspected that welts would arise at the sites. "I do urge, though," Romlar went on, "that whoever I work with be thoroughly conversant with the contract. Its language is straightforward and leaves little room for interpretation."

One of the president's long hands gestured as if dismissing the awkwardness. "Colonel Romlar," he said, "I appoint Colonel Fossur as liaison between you on the one hand and myself on the other. I am quite conversant with your contract, and I'll want to be kept aware of your plans and activities. I'm sure they'll be intelligent and potent, and I look forward to your results. If you're prepared to receive a briefing now, we will go to my office for it. I'm sure Colonel Fossur can deliver it without any special preparation."

He turned to Oress then. "Major, please radio for a vehicle for the colonel's use. There are too many of us for these two GPs."

"Of course, Mr. President."

Kelmer Faronya had kept his camera on the principals. He was more aware of the president's daughter, though, than of anything else, and he positioned himself to keep her in view. She couldn't be more than seventeen, he thought, tall and coltish and astonishingly pretty. In fact, it seemed to him she was the most appealing girl he'd ever seen. *Weldi.* It seemed to him the name was pretty, too.

Colonel Romlar hadn't said anything about the journalist attending any briefing, but when the extra GPV arrived, Kelmer climbed into the back with Captain Kantros. Perhaps he'd have a chance to talk to her.

Lunch was brought to them in the president's office by his cook. Fossur kept finding more and more to tell, Romlar and the other two officers following on maps that Fossur gave them. It was late afternoon before he'd finished.

They'd taken a midafternoon break. Kelmer, going outside to move around a bit, had seen Weldi in the garden, and talked with her briefly.

He'd learned that she was indeed seventeen, and that her father was a widower. She admitted to playing the piano, and invited him to visit them some evening, when she would play for him. He'd been in a state of bliss when he went back in the house.

Among the things that interested Romlar were: There had been no significant fighting for twenty days; the Komarsi seemed content to wait— starve them out. And General Belser, who'd earlier directed a dogged defense and hard-fighting withdrawal, had not suggested any further military actions, although the president had prodded him.

The boundary of Komarsi-occupied territory mostly ran east to west along the Eel River to Hawk Lake, where the Eel curved northward, continuing west from there to a monadnock named "the Straw Stack." This line was thinly manned by Komarsi forces, thinly because they correctly evaluated that any Smoleni breakout would be short-lived and very costly.

North of the Eel River, the Komarsi had no "held lines." However, they'd established a number of brigade bases in two major valleys whose streams flowed south into the Eel. Combined, these brigade bases held more troops than the entire Smoleni Army. The two valleys had some sizeable villages, most of whose families had fled. They also had substantial farmlands, and Komarsi occupation denied the Smoleni their crops and pasturage.

The Smoleni army had inflicted and taken heavy casualties in the south. The replacements were quite largely teenaged recruits from the refugee camps, but there were also many Class B reservists from the northern districts, middle-aged backwoods farmers and villagers who logged in the winter as the markets allowed. The Smoleni Army had a leavening of trappers, many of them backwoods farmers who in winter worked so-called trapping "bounds" assigned to families. Also there was a tra- dition of solitary "wandrings"—often in winter—hiking or snowshoeing in the vast forests for days or even weeks at a time. The wanderer slept beneath the stars, or in a tiny lean-to set up where dusk found him, living largely off what he could snare or shoot or pull from the water. Most northern men, and more than a few towners and men of the Leas had done this, some only a few times in their youth, but many others repeat- edly. On occasion, squads of these backwoodsmen had gone AWOL, to bushwhack Komarsi patrols in the vicinity of brigade bases, with the tacit approval of their reservist officers. When Belser had learned of this, he'd forbidden it. To him it smacked of ill discipline.

Romlar was a very thoughtful young man as he rode to the regimental encampment. He'd already made certain working decisions, and shared them with Fossur on the condition that they not get to Belser till Romlar was ready.

# Part Two
# SUMMER WAR

# 9

A Smoleni reserve officer walked along one side of the mercenary camp, for no other reason than curiosity. He wore calf-high, laced moccasins instead of boots. That was one nonstandard thing Belser hadn't forbidden; boots were in short supply. His company was doing close-order drill, an activity he was required to order, though he thought poorly of it. His men had learned to walk in orderly ranks during their first couple of days in the army. To him it made no damn sense to spend hours at it now; he could think of lots more useful activities. But if he had to order it, he sure as shit didn't have to stand around and watch.

He heard voices ahead, more or less in unison, coming from what looked to be a mess tent. Curious, he walked toward it. A guard stepped out from behind a squad tent, an old Class C Smoleni reservist by his uniform and looks. He was a solid farmer pushing sixty, with graying hair and a rifle.

"Sorry, Cap'n. You need to go 'round. Ain't no one let to come through here."

The officer looked at him interestedly. "How come you to pull guard duty here?"

"Might's well. Belser got nothin' worthwhile for us to do. And seems there's an agreement that 'non-field personnel' will pull guard duty for the mercs."

"Hnh!" The officer gestured toward the mess tent. "What're they doin' in there? Sounds like they're chantin' Komarsi."

The guard looked troubled at the comment, and raising his rifle to port arms, made as if to push the officer back. "C'mon now, Cap'n. You ain't supposed to hear that. Move on back, or you'll get me in trouble."

"That's what they're doin', sure as winter. Must be learnin' it." Except on the planets Oven and Kettle—formally Tyss and Orlantha—Standard was the language throughout the Confederation Sector. But the vernacular differed somewhat from world to world, particularly on trade and resource worlds, where there would be different dialects even within countries. "I hear tell they learned to talk our lingo on the way here," the captain said. "That right?"

"Seems like. Good enough that a Komarsi couldn't tell the difference. I suppose it's in case they get took prisoner. They can say they're us."

The officer grunted. "Maybe they think if they learn Komarsi good enough, they can fool the real thing."

"The reason don't matter to me. I'm just supposed to keep folks away, so's they don't hear."

Grinning, the officer half turned as if to leave. "Best you don't let 'em get so close then."

The guard nodded ruefully. "Guess so. My wife's told me more'n once I don't hear so good no more. I never thought some'nd hear 'em from off here though."

The captain laughed. "Well, I won't tell nobody. They may be mercs, but they're our mercs, and I wish 'em well." He left then. He'd heard that one reason they were such a short regiment was, they'd done a lot of fighting somewhere else. He'd also heard that they weren't bound by Belser's orders. Another story was that most of them were going down to Shelf Falls, a lot closer to the Komarsi. He didn't entirely trust people who went off to fight in other people's wars, but help was help, and good help was something to be glad of. That old fart Belser had lost his appetite for fighting; maybe the mercs would go do some.

He left the camp at an easy trot. *There's them says the general knows what he's doin', that he'll move when the time's right. Shit! Time ain't likely to be any righter later than it is right now.*

# 10

It was near midnight. Kelmer Faronya lay on his belly on the side of a large stone pile, the boundary corner of four farms. Next to him lay Jerym Alsnor, and on Alsnor's other side a picked young captain, a Smoleni intelligence officer selected by Colonel Fossur. About half a mile ahead lay the village of Hearts Content, a large village, one-time seat of government for a large district. The Komarsi didn't call it Hearts Content. To them, according to the intelligence briefing, it was Brigade Base Four.

The least moon was near the zenith, and full. Another, a larger half disk, lay dusky gold on the treetops behind them in the west. Even in the light of just one, Kelmer felt dangerously exposed. Through his visor, he could see almost as well as by daylight, saw what his camera saw, and of course it adjusted to the available light. Specifically he saw Komarsi soldiers standing guard at the fence ahead of them. It had been decided by someone, perhaps Lord Kristal himself, that a journalist's video equipment, being non-military, need not meet Level 3 military restrictions. Colonel Voker had warned him not to tell the troopers what he saw through it though, said it as if he'd meant it. Kelmer wasn't sure what he'd do if Jerym asked him to.

Lieutenant Jerym Alsnor glanced back. It was time to move; the setting moon had half disappeared behind the treetops. The grass and weeds made better cover than he'd expected. The Komarsi had torn down the rail fences in the fields, presumably to prevent them being used for cover, then sent out crews with hay mowers to cut the grass and weeds. But they'd been allowed to grow up again. The responsible thing for them to have done, it seemed to him, was plow the fields, then harrow them every week or two.

Remarkable carelessness, born of overconfidence. *That'll change after tonight,* he told himself, *whether we pull this off or not.*

Scouting from a treetop at sundown, his binoculars had shown him the sentry posts around the ordnance dump, and at intervals around the rest of the camp. Now, with one hand he operated the signal scratcher he carried, heard it answered, then tucked it back into a shirt pocket. The sound they made was easily distinguished at some distance, but also easily dismissed as small night creatures. His men knew better. Then he flowed off the stone pile and began creeping toward the gate where the road entered the fenced compound.

The sentry stood with his rifle at order arms, as prescribed. His attention wasn't as prescribed though. He was thinking of the foreman's daughter back home. She'd never given him better than mild disdain, but in his imagination he enticed her into the hayloft, then grabbed and kissed her. Her eyes had widened, and she'd clutched him passionately. He'd slipped the skirt off her haunches, and . . .

An arm locked across his face, his mouth, and a heavy, razor-sharp knife drew firmly across his throat.

A moment later his killer stood in the sentry's place, the sentry's rifle at present arms. Seconds later he heard the wire cutters, kept hearing them. Now if the zone between the fences was clean, the way they'd been told . . .

At the truck-park office, only two soldiers were on duty, playing cards. There was no guard at the door. It opened. A man stepped in with a small crossbow, fired a bolt and dropped to his knees. Instantly the man behind him released another. The first Komarsi's forehead had hardly hit the table before the second was falling sideways.

Jerym walked openly down the street, followed by twelve troopers. They carried no packs, because in the village, Komarsi soldiers wouldn't ordinarily carry them. The weapons slung at their shoulders were submachine guns instead of rifles, providing heavier firepower for close range.

He'd know soon how good Colonel Fossur's informants were. At intervals he grunted a low "here," gesturing, and two men turned off to disappear into the shadow of some house. Finally there were only himself and two others. They continued to the inn, where Jerym stopped on the broad porch and sat down on a bench, as if for a chew of spice leaves before going in. The other two disappeared inside. One went on through to station himself in the back yard. The other, grenades dangling, sat down in the lobby, where he could watch the stairs and the hall beyond them.

At the ordnance dump, a man opened the gate, and a tarp-topped half-ton truck rolled out. He closed the gate behind it. So far, he thought, things seemed to be going perfectly. So far. At worst, now, they'd raise enough hell to make it worthwhile. He resumed his guard post, in case some Komarsi came while the others were stringing the det cord.

The half-ton rolled quietly, slowly down the street, headlights on but half-hooded, according to brigade policy as last known. It passed the inn, reached the village plaza, and followed the street around one side of it. The driver had thoroughly assimilated the intelligence they'd been given. He didn't review it now, didn't need to. He simply acted on it, on it and his warrior perceptions and reflexes.

At the far end of the plaza was the district government building and village hall combined, a large, two-story frame building that was now brigade headquarters and communication center. At least a skeleton crew would be on duty through the night there, and the brigadier and his immediate staff had their quarters in what had been the district magistrate's residence next door. There should be guards, but the slipshod way these Komarsi did things, he wouldn't bet on it.

The two guards at the headquarters entrance watched the half-ton approach. "Bloody strange," one of them said quietly. "The brigadier said headlights had to be full-hooded." He pursed his lips. "Somethin' mayn't be right. Get back inside the door and watch."

He moved quickly down the steps, submachine gun ready, and strode into the middle of the street, walking toward the oncoming half-ton. It slowed, stopped, and calling, he ordered the driver out. Instead of the driver, the man beside him got out and stepped toward the guard. He seemed to have no weapon. "What's the matter?" he asked, then abruptly dropped to one knee, drawing a pistol as he did so, and fired. The guard went backward, his weapon discharging into the air as he fell.

The truck jerked forward then, passing the kneeling trooper. At the same moment the other guard stepped onto the porch, firing a long burst through the windshield, hitting the driver. The half-ton rolled on, slowing, and the remaining trooper vaulted in over the tailgate.

Unsteered, it swerved, lurching to a stop a half-dozen yards from the building, and the remaining guard approached it crouching, ready to fire again. There was a tremendous explosion, a blinding flash as the truck erupted . . .

Kelmer Faronya crouched by a tree near the base gate. The men who stood guard were men he knew. Earlier he'd almost died of nerves, waiting in the grass sixty yards away, his camera tracking one of them while they'd stalked the guards who'd stood where they stood now. Whose bodies they'd dragged into the shallow ditch beside the road. It had seemed impossible they wouldn't be seen, wouldn't be shot down, bringing the whole unlikely scenario falling with them. Nothing in the training at Blue Forest provided the necessary skills. He hadn't known there were such skills.

Simply by watching, he'd recorded it all. Now there was nothing to record, but from his tree-side vantage he recorded anyway, staring down the graveled main street into the village. It was difficult to breathe. Gunfire would surely break out any minute, and the sleeping village would erupt with armed and angry soldiers. A half-ton appeared, turned onto the main street, and he watched/recorded it recede toward the village center. He knew its roles: destruction and cue. It was almost time; perhaps they'd do it yet. It lost itself in the darkness, blocking the close fan of illumination from its hooded lights, and he waited some more. And waited.

Suddenly there was a shot, then another. A submachine gun belched. Seconds later the night was split by a powerful explosion. Almost at once there was more submachine-gun fire, continuing, and the dull roars of grenades. An alarm whooped needlessly, and he imagined soldiers pouring from the village houses, each of them a barracks of armed men. Then the ground shook, and again, and again, the explosions overlapping like a string of monstrous lady-fingers as ordnance bunkers blew.

His paralysis was gone. He wanted to slip back down the road, run through the grass, find the forest, but the two troopers stood watchfully at the guard posts, and he would not go till they did. They were his friends, and he feared their disdain even more than he feared the enemy.

Minutes passed with diminishing gunfire, then two of the troopers who'd marched up the street with Jerym appeared and stood beside Kelmer in the deep shadow beneath the tree. He felt safer with them there. Soon a GPV came, headlights unhooded, and together they hid from it, bunched behind the tree. A Komarsi officer got out and walked over to question the troopers by the gate. Their answers seemed to satisfy him, because he got back in the vehicle and it turned and drove back into the village.

Three more troopers arrived, one of them Jerym. "All right," he said, "let's get our asses out of here." Seen through the visor, he seemed exhilarated. They turned and trotted down the road a short distance till they were joined by men with light machine guns who'd been placed to cover them if they were pursued. They all left the road then, loping across the field, even the men carrying the machine guns running easily and swiftly. In eight or nine minutes they reached the forest edge. Jerym whistled shrilly, was answered, and soon others joined them; the men who'd blown the ordnance dump had gotten out earlier. But of the men who'd marched into town with the lieutenant, there were only the four.

The men that were with him, though, were grinning. Kelmer stood unbelieving. Then Jerym gave the order, and once more quiet, they headed into the woods along an old sleigh road.

# 11

Half a mile back in the woods, the sleigh road petered out. The major moon had topped the horizon behind them, but even so, beneath the forest canopy it was so dark that even on the narrow sleigh road, travel had been slow and somewhat blundering. Without the road, it was too dark to travel, short of dire emergency, so Jerym set sentries, and the rest lay down to sleep.

They'd sweated off the insect repellent they'd worn, and Kelmer applied more. They were all more or less inured to mosquitoes, but it bothered him to have them biting when he lay down to rest. He wondered if the troopers really would sleep, they'd seemed so exuberant. He lay mentally numb for a time, not really thinking, disconnected images and fragmented thoughts passing through his mind. Once it occurred to him that until tonight he'd thought of himself, usually, as one of them, a trooper. Not always, but usually, for here with the White T'swa, as with the 6th Regiment at Blue Forest, the troopers were remarkably easy to be with, get along with. But tonight it seemed to him that a gulf had opened between himself and them, a gap that couldn't possibly close. That he was no trooper, could never be. He was an impostor. Finally he slept, dozing fitfully until dawn began to thin the darkness.

The sentries wakened them and they started on again, speeding to a trot when the forest became light enough. Apparently no one had followed them into the night. Kelmer wondered if indeed the Komarsi had any idea where they might be, or how many, or even what had happened at all.

After about two miles, they topped a low ridge, the highest in the vicinity, and ranged northward briefly along the crest to where they'd stashed their packs. Jerym called a halt there, and they opened their packs to eat before pushing on again.

At midday they stopped. Sentries were posted. They ate, and men lay down to nap for half an hour, Kelmer a little apart from the others. Jerym came over to him and sat down beside him. Kelmer avoided meeting his eyes.

"How did it go for you last night?" Jerym asked.

*You know how it went for me,* Kelmer thought. *You know exactly how it went for me.* "Not very well."

"Tell me about it."

There was no sympathy in the words, no consoling. But in spite of that, or perhaps because of it, Kelmer rose a bit from the mental quagmire he was in.

"I was scared. So scared, I felt like I couldn't move."

"Ah. Sounds like a bad night, all right. But you moved when you had to; moved up, moved back. And lots of people would have felt as bad." He paused. "Beyond being scared, how was it?"

The question struck some deep cord of dread in Kelmer. He put a cap on it, but it wasn't a tight seal. It seeped through. *Was it all the men they killed?* he wondered. That didn't indicate as part of it; a small part at most. No, what really bothered him was the troopers who hadn't come back. It had bothered him a bit when Jerym had talked that first night about a company being used as bait on Terfreya, bait in a trap, and getting shot to pieces. It had bothered him like a gentle prod at a ripe boil. But tonight had truly hit him, hit him hard.

Kelmer was able to look at Jerym now, at the calm face, the steady eyes. His voice was little more than a whisper when he answered. An intense whisper. "Where are Trimala and Fenwer, and Ekershaw?" It occurred to him that he hadn't sorted out who else was missing.

Jerym gazed thoughtfully at him, and to some detached part of Kelmer Faronya, it seemed that the trooper was looking for a way to put it. "Ekershaw's still alive, and so are Pelley and Kalbern. But BJ saw Kalbern go down, so I suppose he's wounded and a prisoner. The others are dead; Olkerfel died maybe an hour ago."

Kelmer's short hairs began to prickle. "How do you know?"

"When one of us dies, he joins us, lets the others know. That happened even on Terfreya sometimes. Last night it was strong. The training on Oven finished opening that channel for us."

Kelmer stared, then turned away. And began to shake, shake hard. He hadn't known any of the dead men closely, couldn't even place who Olkerfel was, but a deep grief welled up in him, a grief somehow too dry to find release in tears. He felt Jerym's hand on the back of his shoulder, a brief touch, then he was aware that the lieutenant had left.

Awhile later he heard Jerym whistle the nappers out of their sleep. Getting up, he put his pack on and joined the others. After a few minutes of hiking, he began to feel almost all right again.

# 12

The Komarsi field hospital occupied what had been a children's camp by a lake, and was busy for the first time since they'd moved in. Sunlight streamed through screened windows, floodlights for dancing dust motes. Men lay sedated on the beds. At the foot of one of them stood several officers. One was a surgeon in a pale blue gown, monitoring what went on, prepared to step in, to demand a halt if necessary. Not that he had the authority to stop it: The subcolonel doing the questioning was General Undsvin's intelligence chief. An aide stood behind the man, pen poised over a secretarial pad.

"Tell me, Sergeant, what exactly happened?"

"I was in the first truck behind the escort, three gun trucks. We was prob'ly goin' 'bout twenty-five per; not much more than regulation...."

The subcolonel interrupted. "What about spacing?"

"We—started out regs. But we'd closed up some'at. Hard to keep intervals on the road."

"All right. There'll be no action taken against you for anything you say here. Continue."

"Well—all of a sudden there was a big explosion up ahead. I think the lead truck got blowed up. Then other trucks piled into the back of 'im. My driver braked so's I got throwed into the windshield, but I had time to get my arm up. Then some'n run into us from behind.

"My door'd flung open when we hit, but before I could get out, there was a really big explosion from back t'the tail of the convoy—an ammo truck must have blowed—and pieces of truck come rainin' down. About the time they started to hit, there was more explosions, just as bad. The ammo trucks was all back in the back, per regs, and I reckon they'd been keepin' intervals better. There was other explosions not as bad, mortar bombs I think, and when one of 'em hit an ammo truck, that's when it blew. You could feel the ground jump!

"I knew that wouldn't be all of it, I knew that like I know Yomal loves me, and that I needed to get out of there. But I was too scared while pieces of truck was comin' down outa the sky. Then it stopped, and I jumped out.

"I could see 'em then, runnin' 'cross the field shootin'! I went for the ditch, but about the time I jumped, I felt myself get hit. It slammed me in the back, and I landed in the water. I just laid there then; 'tweren't deep enough to drown in, less'n you passed out with your face down in it. There was a lot of shootin' for a couple minutes. I was on my side and I could see 'em runnin' round shootin' people. I closed my eyes, hopin' they'd take me for dead, and finally I couldn't hear 'em no more. After a few more minutes I crawled out of the water. Then I donked out. I didn't know whether I was the only one alive or not."

The subcolonel nodded curtly, then turned and walked away without a "thank you," a major beside him, his aide following. Outside, the subcolonel questioned the chief surgeon. "You said they killed all but three. Who are those others in there?"

"I said fifty-six were killed and only three were wounded. But there were six ambulances with twelve medics in the convoy, going to Tekkeros to pick up overflow from the field hospital there. Nine of the twelve were injured in the pileup; none were shot by the raiders."

The subcolonel's interruption was testy. "Make sense, man! You said only three were wounded!"

The surgeon's face tightened. "Their injuries were from collision, colonel. They were not shot; they wore blue medical corps jackets."

The subcolonel bit short what may have started as an oath, and turned away without acknowledging. *The damned hair-splitter!* The chief surgeon outranked him, was a full colonel, but he was also a commoner; you could smell it. Probably the son of a merchant family—the kind that tended to think they were better than their position in life.

He led his small party to the command car they'd come in. One was another subcolonel, chief of the general's planning staff. The planning chief walked beside him. "You say these raiders are offworld mercenaries. How can you be sure?"

"Our spies at Burnt Woods reported a regiment of foreigners were landed from a spaceship there. They saw the ship themselves, saw it come down. And before the day was out, they'd heard that a mercenary regiment had been landed from it. They then went to where they could see their encampment."

"I'm aware of that."

"They're the ones who attacked the brigade bases; that seems quite evident. The prisoners we took, and the bodies we recovered, were remarkably muscular. That and the way they operate are proof enough."

"And when the prisoners were questioned?"

"There were only a few, and none said anything. Unless you count howling."

"Perhaps further questioning will be fruitful?"

"There can be no further questioning."

"Dead?!"

"Dead."

The planning chief frowned and looked away. The intelligence chief said nothing. He'd erred, he recognized that now, in letting brigade G-2s do the questioning. They'd been traumatized by the devastation at their bases. Three weren't even intelligence-trained, had inherited the G-2 hat because brigade G-2s had been wiped out. He should have had the prisoners brought to Rumaros and questioned them himself.

No doubt General Undsvin would point that out to him quite forcefully.

# 13

The raids on Komarsi brigade bases were the major subject of conversation in the Smoleni army and in what was left of government. And the information that fueled those conversations came from more than the mercenaries involved. Each raiding team had been accompanied by a Smoleni intelligence officer, only one of whom failed to return safely.

"Belser's angry about it," Fossur said.

Romlar nodded, and sipped the "joma" Fossur's orderly had served. At Burnt Woods they called it, "war joma"; it was actually made from scorched grain. "He was angry from the start," Romlar said. "He's angry because we're here."

"True." The president had had to insist, when Romlar had wanted intelligence officers attached to the raiding parties, and Belser had left the meeting in a huff. "He'd have resisted harder if he'd thought you'd be so successful. Now he says you've stirred up a hornets' nest; he expects the Komarsi to mount punitive strikes."

"Mmm." Romlar sipped again. "It's to their advantage not to. They control the territory they need to win the war, win it by starving you out. But if they make punitive strikes, they'll have to move on forest roads. In that case you can hit and run, hit and run. Bleed them badly.

"Meanwhile our raids tell your friends abroad that you're not just sitting in the backcountry waiting to run out of food. You're taking the war to the Komarsi. Consider the impact on public opinion in other countries when the cubes of the raid on Hearts Content get circulated around Maragor."

Fossur nodded. The Krentorfi ambassador had been delighted when they'd been played for him, and young Faronya had made copies for him to take back to the queen. Komars was not a well-liked kingdom, and Engwar a widely disliked monarch. Perhaps states besides Krentorf would be inclined now to provide aid. There'd already been a rumor that Oselbent and The Archipelago had discussed a mutual defense pact. If Selmark joined them, he had no doubt at all that Oselbent would provide an avenue for shipping in food and munitions. As it was, the Oselbenti feared Komarsi reprisals—the shelling of her ports.

"You haven't told me what you'll do next," he said. "You won't catch the Komarsi asleep like that again. They're already building gun towers, digging trenches, and hauling in a lot more barbed wire."

Romlar laughed. "We're working on several things. But they need to be kept absolutely secret from the Komarsi, and they almost certainly have agents here. Like you have there."

Fossur nodded; as an intelligence specialist, he took spies for granted. Romlar looked around, then got to his feet. "Let's take a walk."

They walked a meadow path along the bank of the Almar River. Romlar described his plans, most of them requiring cooperation, and they made some agreements. Fossur, who had friends and connections throughout the army and government, said he could provide the resources without going through Belser, for these were all small matters, small but crucial. "If necessary I'll ask the president for help."

He bent, picked up a short piece of branch left by flood-water, and threw it in the river. They watched it slide down the current to an eddy, where it spun around briefly, going nowhere, then emerged and floated on.

"I suppose you wonder why he leaves Eskoth in command."

"I've guessed because the general led a skilled and dogged defense in the south. And perhaps because of old friendship."

"Actually they didn't know one another until Heber was elected president, but there seems to be a certain affinity between them. You've noticed the president is invariably polite to him, regardless of how surly Eskoth might be. But when he says do such and such, Eskoth always shuts up and does it, however gracelessly. I have no doubt that if he ordered him to take his army and begin a suicide offensive on Rumaros, Eskoth would do it.

"Actually I think he might replace him, if he had someone he felt enough confidence in. I can think of several myself, and I've named them to him. But—" Fossur shrugged. "The president's a mild and patient man. Too patient, I'd say. Once he decides something though . . ." He glanced sideways at Romlar. "It helps that he's so big. And you've shaken hands with him; you know what his grip is like. He wasn't always an academic. As a boy and a youth he worked as a fuelwood cutter, felling and bucking trees, loading them on sleighs, and hauling them to his uncle's fuelyard at Collinsteth, where he'd help cut them up and split them. He's said to have been mild mannered even in those days, and usually with a book in his pocket."

When they parted, Romlar returned to regimental headquarters thinking how unusual a country Smolen was, and how unusual its president.

Kelmer sat in the president's parlor, showing the cube of the raid on Hearts Content. This was a command performance. Heber Lanks had seen it before, but his daughter hadn't, and she'd asked Kelmer to show it to her. So he'd brought the player from his tent. Initially Weldi Lanks had been more interested in seeing the rugged, good-looking young Iryalan than the video, but as he played it, she'd become fascinated.

When it was over, the president looked thoughtful and a little drawn. "War," he said, "is not an activity I greatly like."

"Me either, Daddy. But we didn't want the war! They invaded us! They forced it on us!"

"Yes, and sit safely in Linnasteth or on their estates, sending their serfs to die for them." He looked at Kelmer. "Bullets don't avoid journalists. What do you think of dying in battle, Mr. Faronya?"

"I—" Kelmer wanted to seem brave to Weldi, but he could not flagrantly lie, so he evaded the question with a half truth. "I haven't been exposed much to combat, Mr. President. But I don't find death comfortable to think about."

"And what do your comrades think of dying in battle? They've been exposed abundantly to it. Colonel Fossur studied their record on Terfreya, where they lost about a third of their number."

"On Confederation member worlds there are tests they give children," Kelmer said. "And make psychological profiles from them. Some people are born to be warriors; all of the regiment's troopers were. But I'm not, so I can't really know how they feel about things. I can only observe what they do and say."

Weldi looked interested. "What *do* you classify as, Kelmer?"

He thought of where he fitted in the Matrix of T'sel, but that was something else. "They don't tell you," he answered, "at least not ordinarily. You don't need to be a warrior to be a soldier, though; most soldiers aren't. As far as getting killed is concerned, troopers, the men of the regiment, don't seem to be afraid at all. But they're different than most warriors, too: they're T'swa-trained. And they believe implicitly that when they die, they'll be reborn as someone else."

"Really?" Weldi said. "They believe that?"

"Apparently."

"Umh," the president grunted. "How well does this belief hold up when they look down the barrel of a hostile machine gun?"

"You might ask Colonel Romlar, sir. Or maybe Lieutenant Alsnor; he led his platoon in repeated actions on Terfreya, and in time almost every man in it got killed. It was a special platoon that got especially dangerous missions."

"And does it still?"

"I'm not sure, but they made the Hearts Content raid. Company A is stationed at Shelf Falls now. I'm supposed to go there tomorrow, to rejoin him."

"You'll be gone then!" Weldi said.

Kelmer nodded. "That's right, Miss Lanks."

"Daddy, I've hardly had a chance to know Mr. Faronya, and now he'll be gone!"

The president smiled. "I have things to do in my office. Why don't you two stay here and talk."

He unfolded his long frame and left them. Weldi didn't give Kelmer time to feel uncomfortable; she began at once to talk. "Kelmer—may I call you Kelmer? You may call me Weldi. What is it like where you're from, Kelmer?"

Her gaze was intense, making him feel a little awkward. She was a very pretty girl. "I went to university in Landfall," he said. "It's a big city: more than a million people."

She nodded. "I've read about Landfall. It's thought to be the place where the first people landed in our sector. It must be wonderful to live there."

"It's nice, all right. But I grew up in a smallish town called Silver Lake. There are lots of lakes and wooded hills around there. Not wild forest, like you have here, but very lovely. Tended forest. And the trees are mostly leaf trees. One of the things I liked to do was hike and run along the roads. We use AG vehicles there, instead of surface vehicles; they run about eight inches above the ground. So the roads and highways are kept in grass, and there are beds of perennial flowers along the edges."

She put a hand on his. His collar grew suddenly tight. "It sounds wonderful. I'd like to visit there someday. In fact, I'd probably like to live there. What was it like at the university?"

They talked awhile longer, Weldi especially. Then the president came in and reminded her of her lessons; he acted as her study guide. Kelmer left bemused by her obvious interest in him. He'd never felt assured around girls, but neither was he inexperienced. And he found Weldi Lanks very stimulating. He fantasized about her all the way back to camp.

# 14

Lieutenant Rob Mesvik halted his platoon on a high, rocky bluff. They were in the rugged, mountainous western fringe of Smolen known as the High Wilds, fifty-five miles from the nearest village, and almost as far from the nearest farm. There wasn't a Komarsi soldier for a hundred miles.

Varky Graymar wiped sweat from his forehead, and looked across a gorge whose other side was in the Kingdom of Krentorf. This was the platoon's fourth day on the trail. With only brief breaks, it had been hiking since sunup, each trooper carrying a substantial pack despite the pack horses. Their packs held the gear each man would need on the mission. The horses carried what was needed on the trail and pulled the narrow two-wheeled boat carts that the troopers had occasionally needed to manhandle around switchbacks or up steep pitches. Occasionally their scouts, ranging ahead, had had to unsheath axes to clear windfalls from the trail.

The men all wore civilian clothes, rough work clothes that would look quite natural on country roads in Komars.

The river below was called the Raging River. From where Graymar stood, it appeared smooth and perhaps a hundred and fifty yards wide, flowing southward. He looked, then lay down by the trail, leaning back against his pack. Their packs weren't military either. They were of patterns that vagabond Komarsi laborers might carry.

They ate their midday ration and had time for a short nap. Then Mesvik whistled them up, and they started down a narrow crooked trail through patchy forest to the river. It was the worst stretch they'd hiked yet. Repeatedly they had to manhandle the boat carts around switchbacks, across slide-outs, and through narrow places. By the time they'd reached the boulder-littered shore, the sun had set behind the ridge on the other side of the river. The sky was clear, so they set up no tents. After supper they found the best spots they could to lie on, and slept for a time.

Their boats were a stable, durable design that had been known in a distant time and place as bateaux, used then and now on rough rivers, to carry rough men herding floating logs. The platoon and its boatmen-guides launched them by moonlight, hours before dawn. The troopers had trained briefly on smaller rough rivers, but this one was deadly in places, and the places wouldn't always be evident in advance. Thus they had river guides.

The country it flowed through was wild, but here and there were human habitations—cabins occupied mainly by trappers in winter. Occasionally, their guides told them, some would be occupied by sportsmen, but on the Smoleni side that had been in better times. So far as feasible, their guides timed the platoon's sleep so they'd pass such cabins by night. When they passed one by day, a close watch was kept for any sign of occupation, but they saw none.

Several times they'd bypassed dangerous rapids and cascades, struggling and sweating, manhandling the heavy, awkward boats around and over boulders and talus, and the wrecks of trees that had slid down from above.

For three days and nights they rode the current, speeding the trip by taking constant turns at the oars, three pairs plus a stern scull in every boat. Their guides, strong and enduring men, were impressed with the troopers' strength, efficiency, and seeming tirelessness, whether at the oars or on portage. They'd tell stories about them in years to come, coming to believe their own exaggerations.

On the last day, the country became lower and less rugged, less wild. On the last night they crossed the border, though they didn't know just when. Twice, glimpses of lamplight marked Komarsi logging camps near the river.

The current that night was smooth, and they kept near midstream, with muffled tholes so their rowing couldn't be heard from shore. Here their guides weren't as familiar as they had been with what lay along the banks. Finally they heard a sound like distant thunder, a sound they'd been waiting for: Great Roaring Falls. They rowed to the Komarsi shore then, and the troopers got out, taking their packs. After that the four boatmen rowed away, one in each bateau, staying close together. In mid-river, all four transferred into one boat, and crossed to the Krentorfi side. The other three boats they let go, to ride the current and plunge over the falls. What remained of them wouldn't be distinguishable from any other bits of floating wood.

# 15

Some two hundred miles northeast, Jerym Alsnor crouched in the forest, waiting and listening. It was night. The mosquitoes swarmed in clouds; he didn't notice. He led two platoons on this mission: his own rifle platoon, and a mortar platoon. The rifle platoon carried no rifles this night; they carried light machine guns for reach and firepower, and submachine guns for close work.

They'd been moving slowly. The word was that since the night of the Great Raids, the Komarsi ran strong security patrols in the vicinity of their brigade bases. It was very doubtful that they moved in the forest at night, but they might well leave outposts at strategic locations— platoons or even companies—their guards listening nervously in the dark, with fingers on triggers.

It was difficult enough for *his* men in the forest at night. If they'd had the night vision of the T'swa, *Homo tyssiensis,* it would have been different. Or if it had been a Level 2 War, where they could use night visors. But at Level 3 they had to make do with their unaugmented human eyesight.

Three things made it feasible. *One,* under T'swa training, the troopers had developed the latent talent of "going without knowing." That is, if they knew a location, they could go there crosscountry without map or guide. Not easily perhaps, if there were obstacles for instance, but they could find it. It was difficult to disorient them, and nearly impossible to keep them disoriented. *Two,* the major moon was riding high. And *three,* their route took them through a tract logged selectively two years earlier, leaving the forest roof with enough openings to let significant moonlight through. That same logging, however, had left branches, tops,

and cull logs lying on the ground, too often hidden in shadow, waiting
for someone to trip on them.

What Jerym waited for now were the scouts he'd sent ahead. He'd come
to the major skidway, a sleigh road through the woods, broad enough
for sleighs eight feet wide. It was a logical place for the Komarsi to cover.
If it was safe, it would take them to a preplanned firing position, a
position from which they could fire for effect without first firing ranging
rounds. He'd scaled it off precisely on a detailed forestry map before he'd
left Shelf Falls.

There was a hiss ahead of him, a pattern of them, and dimly he made
out a figure waving. He hissed back, then moved ahead, the others following: his two platoons plus a dozen Smoleni noncoms along for the
experience. And Kelmer Faronya, wearing his helmet camera. Its visor
made him the only one of them who could see decently. Each of them,
in the mortar platoon and the rifle platoon, carried a .37 caliber pistol
and a trench knife. The men in the mortar platoon also went burdened
with a mortar tube or baseplate, or a packframe loaded with 66 mm
mortar bombs, plus propellant horseshoes.

The way was clear, and on the skidway they made better speed. In less
than an hour, the mortars were set up on the abandoned log landing
where the skidway met the gravel road. On the other side of the road
were fields and pastures. Beyond them lay a Komarsi brigade base, barely
more than a mile from where they crouched. The village was on the
forestry map, rows of tiny symbols for buildings. Added to this, Fossur's
local agent had sketched in the QM dump, the ordnance dump, the motor
pool, and other military additions. He'd even circled the more important buildings. At that range, even T'swa-trained mortar men couldn't
expect to pinpoint buildings they couldn't see, but they should be able
to do a lot of damage.

His machine gunners left then, each with his twenty-pound weapon
ready, an ammunition belt in the metal box he carried. Jerym gave them
time to take positions, beginning some two hundred yards up the road,
counting off the necessary seconds in his mind. Meanwhile his mortar
men had set up their weapons, set their phosphorescent sights, and
snapped on the propellant horseshoes. He gave the low whistled signal
to fire. If the map was accurate, things were about to get exciting in
the brigade base. After that, things could get pretty exciting here, too,
depending on the Komarsi response.

Kelmer listened to the thumps of mortar rounds being launched, a salvo
of eight to begin with, targeted hopefully on the truck park. The next
salvo was a bit ragged. After that the firing was non-synchronous. He
stared; it was as if nothing had been fired, or as if the rounds had been

swallowed into hyperspace. Surely, though, the Komarsi had seen the muzzle flashes. With the machine gun towers they'd built, they could hardly avoid it. And they'd have artillery.

Then he saw the flashes of the mortar rounds landing, and moments later heard the explosions. After that, the explosions were more or less continuous.

He didn't feel particularly fearful yet, it was all so far away. But he watched for possible flashes of artillery. If they saw any, the mortar crews were to disassemble the mortars at once—a business of short seconds—and run back up the skidway. Wait out the barrage and return to expend their mortar rounds. He, on the other hand, was to run along the road to the machine gunners, to record whatever developed there.

The mortar men had expended most of their rounds before they saw a response: A long row of muzzle flashes, virtually simultaneous, flared from the base. For a long moment Kelmer crouched transfixed, forgetting his order. Then the mortar crews were running past him onto the skidway. Remembering, he dashed onto the road, and along it northward. Now he saw something else alarming: a line of trucks moving out of the base, with headlights on unhooded! He heard the incoming rounds rumbling through the night air, and they began to fall in the field behind him, fifty or sixty yards short of the road. There were a lot of them, and their crashing roars lent speed to his feet.

Inside a minute he was with the machine gunners, who were spaced along the road, among the edge trees. His heart pounded wildly. When the trucks arrived, they'd be less than forty feet away. Kelmer realized he couldn't see well from where he crouched, and what he couldn't see, he couldn't record visually, so he crept out a few feet, to kneel on the back bank of the ditch.

Southward down the road, the next salvo of shells roared into the forest with terrific crashes, producing a long rain of branches and larger pieces of trees, invisible in the night. A third salvo landed still farther back, and the fourth mostly on and along the road. Clearly the Komarsi artillery observers didn't know whether they were long or short; they kept changing the range, plowing the pasture, the forest edge, the roadsides.

The lead truck turned onto the north-south road, and Kelmer scrambled back into the woods to avoid being caught in the headlights. A minute later, the machine guns began firing point-blank into the trucks, which were spaced much too closely. Some braked; some went into the ditches, some of these tipping onto their side; more crashed into trucks ahead of them. Tracers chewed canvas canopies, metal hoods, windows. Soldiers spilled out, spilled running. Many fell wounded or dead. More took shelter behind the trucks, or dispersed into the pasture.

There was surprisingly little return fire at first, as if they were content to take cover.

Northward, a number of trucks had stopped short of the machine guns and unloaded their troops too. Some of these dispersed into the woods. With any leadership at all, they'd move to flank the machine gunners. Return fire began to increase, as the Komarsi recovered from their surprise and shock. Closer at hand, some began throwing grenades.

The troopers were heavily outnumbered, and the balance was shifting. Someone whistled a shrill retreat order, and the troopers rose almost as one, moving back into the woods. Kelmer got up too—and saw something land on the ground in front of him. *Grenade!* his mind shrieked, and with a hoarse cry he turned, starting into the forest, where he promptly stumbled and fell on some logging debris, not because he couldn't see—he could—but because he didn't see. His heart thuttered wildly, and he lay wide-eyed for a moment. The grenade had not exploded! At the same time, he realized that his rectum had spasmed, had sprayed his shorts.

Shaking, Kelmer got to his feet again. Then a row of shells exploded in the field not much short of the road, some in the farside ditch, on line with where he was, knocking him down again. As if some Komarsi officer had panicked, and radioed for artillery support, bringing the shells down on his own men. Kelmer and the others realized where the next salvo was likely to land, and despite the trees and shadow-hidden logging slash, they ran, hard. More crashes rent the night behind them, some of the shells bursting in the treetops, spraying the woods with steel and splintered wood. Kelmer, with his visor-given vision, outran the others until a fallen branch tripped him and he fell heavily, the breath knocked out of him.

A moment later, someone stopped beside him. "You all right?" the trooper asked.

"I think so."

"Good. Stay with me."

*He recognized me,* Kelmer thought. *He doesn't want me to get lost.* He followed gratefully.

They came to the skidway again and followed it. When they came to its end, they kept going, if more slowly. Soon afterward they reached the end of the cutting. The denser forest behind it was much darker. They groped their way into it perhaps twenty or thirty yards, then Jerym stopped them and posted sentries. The rest lay on the ground to sleep.

Hidden by darkness, Kelmer went a few yards apart, took out the packet of toilet paper he carried in a shirt pocket, lowered his pants and tidied up as best he could, then fastened them again. Lying beside a moss-grown log, he reviewed the experience. All in all, it seemed to him he'd done well. Or if not exactly well, he at least hadn't humiliated himself. He'd done what he was supposed to do, and had stood to the last.

*If I just hadn't fouled my pants,* he thought. It hadn't been too bad though—a spray—and he didn't stink. Perhaps no one would notice. He couldn't know till it got daylight again.

He was drifting off to sleep when it first occurred to him to wonder how many troopers had died. When he slept, he dreamed they had come to him, jollying him gently about his pants, and it didn't bother him at all.

When he woke up, he remembered the dream. He'd remember it as long as he lived.

# 16

Thunderstorms stalked the night over northwestern Komars, and wind lashed the forest. The civilian-clad troopers were soaked but not much chilled. They'd been alternately jogging and walking the forest road they followed, and the exertion warmed them. It was a good road, a major forest road, wide enough that, at night, light reached it from the sky. They could make out its edges and avoid the ditches on each side.

It was their second night on the march. They'd holed up during the day, laid low in a dense stand of young growth. They weren't ready to be seen yet. They'd already broken up into three groups, to find and follow three different roads east. This group was the larger, two squads, led by Lieutenant Mesvik.

Mesvik whistled a signal, and the men slowed to a brisk walk. Thunder rolled like some great bowling ball across the sky, to be answered by another, and another. Trees thrashed, genuflecting before the wind.

Varky Graymar paused for a moment on the shoulder to relieve his bladder; he could catch up easily enough. As he stood refastening his pants, lightning split the sky overhead, striking a tall tree, shattering it while thunder burst the night. The top snapped out. Pieces flew. The branchy top, hurled by the wind, crashed through other treetops and fell onto the roadside. A limb struck Varky, knocking him unconscious beneath it.

✧　　✧　　✧

It had been no passing convection storm. An unseasonable cool air mass had moved in, undercutting muggy, unstable air, and the storm had continued for hours. Near dawn it blew over, and the lesser moon shone through the trees, though they still dripped. The jogging troopers looked forward to the sun and a chance to get dry. Dawn had paled the eastern sky when they came to the forest's edge, and Mesvik called a halt. In front of them was farmland, open and nearly level.

"This is where we split up," he said. "You know your partners, and your order of march. Urkwal and Graymar, when the sun comes up . . ." He paused. "Where's Graymar?" There was a looking about among the troopers. Mesvik looked back down the road and raised his voice. "Graymar?"

Nothing. "Anyone got a clue where Graymar is?" No one answered. "When's the last time anyone noticed him?"

It turned out that no one had since he and Urkwal had talked on a break before the storm began. In the storm and heavy darkness, the men had talked scarcely at all with each other, and mostly couldn't see who jogged or walked beside them.

"All right," Mesvik said. "Immeros, you and Smit will lead off instead. The rest of us will move off to the south a hundred yards or so and try to get some rest in the edge of the woods. Urkwal, go back up the road and find Graymar. If you haven't found him by ten o'clock, come back. If all of us have left when you get here, catch a nap and carry through with your orders. That's it. Go."

Urkwal acknowledged and jogged off. Mesvik watched him leave. *Not a promising start,* the lieutenant told himself. *Interesting but not promising.*

When the sun rose high enough, it aligned with the road and shone down on Winn Urkwal's pack, and the back of his leathery neck. He hiked on, jogging enough to keep warm. A truck passed him headed east, loaded with logs, and after a while another. Later he heard a vehicle coming headed west, cut off from view by the brow of a low hill behind him. On an impulse he left the road, hurrying to cover behind a sapling thicket. It passed him, a sky-blue carryall with a decal on the front door. He returned to the road then and continued. Shortly a log truck passed empty, also headed west. Urkwal simply stepped off the road for it.

Minutes later he heard another vehicle coming, from ahead this time, and again he hid, now behind a convenient roadside deck of logs. It was the same carryall as before, traveling faster now. And he knew, knew as if he'd seen him, that Varky Graymar was inside, although the only visible occupants were strangers in the front seat.

He hiked on anyway, until just beyond a storm-felled treetop, he saw tire tracks where a vehicle had pulled off onto the saturated shoulder of the road. Turning, Urkwal examined the treetop. Some large branches had been chopped from it and thrown aside, their leaves only starting to wilt. Foot tracks told him that two men had carried something between them to the vehicle.

Winn Urkwal had no doubt what had happened: the treetop had struck Graymar, knocked him out and injured him. The two men had seen him beneath it as they'd passed, and had picked him up. And Varky's pack held incriminating contents: a submachine gun, broken down inside a waterproof bag; a holstered pistol; a roll of det cord; and half a dozen blocks of takite; all buried beneath a blanket, some food, spare socks. . . . If someone dug through it, an alarm would be raised.

Perhaps . . . Urkwal knelt where the branches had been cut away, to scrabble beneath limbs and foliage. And here—here was the wrapped SMG, shoved back beneath some branches and weeds. And here the bagged explosive. And here the det cord! Varky'd managed to get his pack off, rummage through it, and at least somewhat conceal the dangerous stuff.

But where was the pistol? He crawled further, groping, and found it too, in its holster. But the magazine was missing. He hunted for it awhile longer, then gave up, put the other things into his own pack, and started back eastward down the road.

Before long he saw where a tree had been uprooted by the wind. He went to it, and with his hands dug in the soil where the root disk had been tipped up. Then he buried all but the det cord and takite. He had use for them later.

That done, he trotted back to the road, and eastward to his rendezvous.

# 17

The screened dining porch looked out over a neatly tended yard in the direction of large barns. In winter they housed registered livestock. It was a beautiful summer morning, fresh and cool after a hot and humid spell. A couple sat at a flower-decorated table, drinking midmorning joma that was not made of scorched grain. Physically the man was smaller than ordinary. His features, the gray eyes especially, suggested high intelligence and an even disposition. He was dressed in a gray riding suit of serviceable material, a white shirt and black ribbon tie. And boots suitable for both saddle and stable.

Their butler entered. "Sir, Mr. Chenly wishes to speak with you. When may I tell him you'll see him?"

Mild surprise registered. His chief forester had planned to check the thinning work on Compartment Four that morning. Fingas Marnsson Kelromak glanced at his wife, who nodded. "I'll speak with him now, Kinet."

The butler's nod was almost a bow, and he left. A minute later, Chenly stepped onto the porch. Kelromak sat back, his expression questioning.

"Good morning, sir. Bobbi and I were driving to Compartment Four this morning, and we found a man lying by the road, unconscious. A drifter by the look of him. A tree had broken in the wind, and the top had fallen on him."

"Badly injured, I suppose?"

"When we got him here, he was able to take his weight on one foot. The other knee is pretty swollen, and something's wrong with a shoulder. And he's got a knot on his head like an egg."

"And?" Kelromak knew there was more to it than that, or Chenly wouldn't be troubling him with the matter.

"The storm went through in the middle of the night, and I wondered what he'd been doing on the road at that hour. Also he's a rather large man, sir, and hard, and—"

Kelromak interrupted. "Hard?"

"His body, sir. When Bobbi and I raised him up, I was surprised how hard and heavy he felt. And supporting him under the arms— He's got muscles like Big Farly, or maybe harder. A man like that could be dangerous, sir, if he's inclined to be lawless. So—" He held something up: the magazine from a pistol. "I took his pack off to lay him on the back seat, and threw it in front. And looked in it on our way back; I found this."

Kelromak pursed his lips. The forest country had always been a refuge for felons and runaways. They'd hide there till they got too hungry, or sometimes till the sheriff asked for a company or two of soldiers to sweep the forest for them.

It was Lady Kelromak who spoke then. "But no gun, Chenly?"

"No, ma'am. Just the magazine. He could have found it on the ground somewhere. I've had a magazine fall out of my pistol butt when the catch didn't latch like it ought to."

"What else did he carry?" Kelromak asked.

"A match safe, better than you'd expect, given the clothes he wore. And a horse blanket, half a loaf of cabin bread, a bag of dried *lumies*, most of a cheese, and some snare wire, as if he might take a *yansa* now and then. And thirty dronas."

*Thirty dronas! A great deal of money for a drifter. Most, if they had that much, would be in town drinking it up.*

"And a folding knife," Chenly went on, "bigger than usual and razor sharp, but something anyone might carry, especially in the woods." He dug into a pocket, drew out the knife and opened it. The blade was nearly five inches long. "I took it and the matches, and left him with Frenis in the bachelors' quarters. He was pretty much in a daze yet."

Kelromak got to his feet. "I'll talk to this drifter, if that's what he is. See what I can find out."

"Well, that's another thing, sir. You see— I asked his name, even before I looked in his pack, and he said he didn't know! He could be faking, but that's quite a knot on his head. You can actually see it, what with his hair so short."

"Hmm. I'll see him anyway." He turned to his wife. "Excuse me, dear," he said, and left with Chenly. Kelromak limped, as if from some old injury grown used to, a limp sufficient to hamper him. "Have you called the outcamps to see if there's been thefts?"

"Bobbi's doing that, sir."

They crossed a broad lawn and went through a gate in a ten-foot privacy hedge. The bachelors' quarters were on the other side, a single-story frame dormitory, painted cream with white trim, and had a lawn of its own. Only two men were inside, one a burly middle-aged man with a fire-scarred face and vestigial right ear, seated in front of a window with a book open in his left hand. His curled right hand lay on a thigh, as if the elbow wouldn't bend far enough to help hold the book. The other man, young, lay on a bed with his eyes closed. His shirt had been removed, leaving a ragged undershirt, and his right arm had been immobilized—put in a sling and wrapped to his body with a bandage.

The older man lay his book on the sill and got stiffly to his feet. "Good morning, sir."

"Good morning, Frenis." Kelromak's attention went to the stranger; the young man's eyes had opened, but they didn't seem to focus. "How do you feel?" Kelromak asked.

The man looked at him blankly. "All right."

In the undershirt, his arms were large, and considering how relaxed they were, looked extremely muscular. Also, if he was feigning concussion, he did a convincing job of it. Kelromak knelt beside him, felt the lump on his head, then took the hand on the injured arm and examined the palm. "What have you been doing for a living?" he asked.

The man blinked. "Living? I don't rightly know, sir. Don't remember."

"Well." Kelromak straightened and turned. "Chenly, call Dr. Ammekor to come by and look at our visitor. He should check Dori-Ann, too, while he's here."

They left together then. "I'd judge he's no robber," Kelromak told the forester. "His hands are as callused as any I've ever seen. He's a laboring man, or I've missed my guess, probably come to the forest to find work. Now if he'd carried a gun— But as you said, he could well have found the magazine somewhere. And the money could have been earned; not every drifter drinks his up, I'm sure."

"You don't want me to call the sheriff to question him then?"

Kelromak grimaced. "No. Not unless Bobbi learns something suggestive from the out-camps. If Sheriff Geltro got hold of him, he might well try to beat some memory out of him. And possibly beat him to death in the process."

When the lord of the estate had left the dormitory, Varky Graymar closed his eyes again. His head ached and he didn't remember anything between the river and waking up by the road. But he knew who he was and why he was in Komars, and there was nothing seriously wrong with his thought processes. He'd functioned well enough to hide his stuff and even get his pack back on, damn difficult with a separated shoulder.

*If they let me stay here,* he thought, *I'll be functional in a week or two.*

# 18

The president's War Council was meeting in his office, and Romlar was there. He had a standing invitation, though he didn't regularly attend. General Belser's expression was stoney with suppressed anger, so instead of starting with Fossur's intelligence review, Heber Lanks opened the meeting with a question: "Does anyone have anything we need to get out of the way before Colonel Fossur brings us up to date?"

Belser heaved to his feet. "Yes, by Amber, I do! And I'm going to demand that something be done about it!"

Inwardly Lanks sighed; Eskoth was a difficult man. "Tell us about it," he said.

"*He* knows about it!" the general said, pointing at Romlar, "and so does he!" He pointed at Fossur. "And I suspect he does too!" he added, gesturing at Vestur Marlim. From the way he glared at his president, he suspected Lanks knew as well. He launched on. "Last night I learned that four—four!—enemy brigade bases were attacked by two batteries each of our pack artillery! That is eight batteries *committed to action without my permission or previous knowledge! Someone is covertly trying to take away my command! And if something like this happens again, I shall resign!"*

*By all means do,* Fossur thought. The president turned to him.

"Do you know anything about this?" he asked.

"As liaison officer," Fossur said, "I've had your permission from the beginning to attach men to Colonel Romlar's units, so we and they would be closely familiar with how an elite force operates. I've been aware that the men assigned have accompanied the mercenaries into action as early as the Great Raids. I should comment also that I've questioned a number of these men, debriefed some of them in detail, and they and I all feel they learned a great deal from their experiences. In fact, they and their officers have been almost uniformly excited by what they've seen and observed."

He turned his gaze to Belser. "I do not try to keep a finger on everything that happens in operations that are established and going well. I did not know in advance about the artillery action you mentioned; I learned about it last evening, as you did. And I must admit surprise that such an operation was carried out under the guise of 'observing.' "

Fossur turned to Heber Lanks. "After the first raids, the Komarsi were forced to expend considerable effort and resources in strengthening their bases. This required different tactics on the mercenaries' part, and resulted in their mortar attacks on five bases. Since then the Komarsi have been forced to mount more, larger, and farther-ranging patrols, which the mercenaries have routinely attacked and really pretty much massacred. As I've reported to you previously. Now it seems that most of the patrols sent out, particularly those sent to patrol at larger distances, commonly go out and sit in some relatively secure position, hoping the mercenaries don't find them.

"My usual intelligence sources didn't learn this; mercenary reconnaissance patrols observed it. And decided to take advantage of it to shell the bases. Having no artillery of their own, they borrowed some—guns and gunners—from unit commanders they'd come to know. Nonetheless, most of the personnel involved were mercenaries. The guns, with mercenary escorts, were disassembled and packed to locations accurately identifiable on forestry maps, where they were reassembled. The mercenaries provided strong infantry protection for the batteries, and strong mercenary patrols ranged the vicinity. They had their own fire observers ahead to direct the fire. Bombardment was by daylight, when there were no visible muzzle flashes, and the Komarsi never located them. When our batteries had expended their ammunition, they disassembled the pieces and withdrew. They had no casualties. No equipment was lost. The enemy suffered painful losses of personnel and material.

"It seems to me that this was an excellent operation—one I recommend we repeat. My information is that the units involved are very enthused, and eager to do more of it. If the Komarsi increase their patrols, the mercenaries will eat them up. And if they don't, we can injure them at will."

As Fossur sat down, Vestur Marlim got up, a small, sharp-faced, and just now angry man. "Mr. President," he said, "I applaud this cooperation between Colonel Romlar's troops and our own. It's the sort of thing we should be doing. I applaud anything that punishes the Komarsi for their assault on our country and our people." He turned to Belser then, thrusting his face toward him. "*Of course you weren't asked or informed. If you had been, you'd have forbidden it!*"

His tone moderated then, for remarkably, Belser showed no anger, and this cooled his own. "In the south you were a lion," he said. "Since then—something has happened to you."

Normally Belser stood to speak. Now he stayed in his chair as if tired. "In the south I lost more than six thousand men, killed, captured, or disabled. And we lost all the resources we need to win this war. Our food supplies shrink daily, and we cannot replenish more than a small fraction of them. We cannot replace munitions expended. To fight with no prospect of winning is to waste lives."

The president spoke gently to him then. "What would you have us do, Eskoth? Surrender?"

Belser's voice was soft, hardly recognizable. "No. I do not know what to do." He looked away then, and Fossur stood, his voice quiet.

"Mr. President," Fossur said, "I have nothing I need to report." He looked around. "If no one else does, perhaps we should adjourn and meet again tomorrow."

"Not yet." Lanks stood and looked around the table. "We have not had an explicit, stated policy since we lost the south. That is my failure, and I'm going to remedy it now. But first let me say that I am president of the people. And the people, at least most of their soldiers, want us to fight. They'd like us to win, but that isn't the key issue; *they want us to fight.* And we are going to because they want us to, if for no other reason.

"And if we fight, we should do it in a way that grasps whatever chance we do have of winning. Using whatever works. We must show the rest of Maragor that we have heart, that we can hurt the Komarsi, that he is not the force they may have thought he was. We have already begun to do this, or Colonel Romlar has, and we must begin to take the larger role in it ourselves. We must define that role and play it to the hilt!

"Much of Maragor has seen the cube of the Great Raid, seen or at least heard of it. And much, perhaps most, of Maragor would love to see us win. Neither Engwar nor his father, nor his uncle during his regency, made many friends on this world.

"I will increase my efforts to gain their help. This will not be easy, given our geographic position, our lack of a coastline now, but I see possibilities. Ambassador Tisslor believes that, if the war becomes sufficiently troublesome for Komars, sufficiently unpleasant, Engwar will face sentiment to end it." The president paused, looking less than happy. "Perhaps not giving up all they have gained, but much of it. Enough that we can be a viable republic again, a nation that can feed its people."

Once more he paused, then went on quietly. "Who knows what may happen if we persist and strive.

"At any rate, there you have it. A policy: We will fight." He turned to Fossur then. "On your recommendation, I adjourn this meeting till tomorrow morning at eight. We will then discuss specifics."

The council got up and left without anything more being said.

Belser left the president's house and walked, rather than strode to his office. Sitting behind his desk, he looked tiredly at his in-basket. His door opened; his secretary stepped in and closed it behind him.

"General, Colonel Romlar would like to speak with you."

Belser looked up and said nothing for several long seconds, then answered. "Send him in."

The sergeant motioned Romlar in, then left them. Belser gathered a little of his old iron, though none of the fire. "What is it, Colonel? I'm a busy man."

Romlar moved a chair close to the general's desk, and sat down uninvited. "General," he said, "I have never led an army. I have never led a division, or even a brigade. Our specialty is small unit tactics against larger and more powerful opponents, tactics most efficient in circumstances like those we find here.

"In the north, the only effective way to hurt the Komarsi is with tactics of the sort I have used. But I have only one short regiment. You have in your army many backwoodsmen who can readily be trained to carry out the sort of actions we do. Readily trained because they already have the most important personal skills needed, and the necessary attitude. My regiment won on Terfreya when it had little more than begun its training, had finished just one year out of six! And we started training as unruly adolescents with none of those skills."

He paused, then leaned toward the general. "Let us select men from your regiments for their experience as woodsmen. Let us train those men, enough for a battalion to start with. And turn them loose on the Komarsi."

Belser said nothing, simply looked at him, seemingly without anger. After a long and silent half minute, Romlar got up. "Thank you, general. I appreciate your granting me the time for this talk. I hope to see you tomorrow morning."

Belser nodded acknowledgement. Romlar bowed slightly and left, Belser watching him out the door. Then the general noticed something on his desk, which Romlar must have left. He picked it up: a food bar, one of the merc's imported iron rations, honey-sweetened, rich with nuts and wrapped with chocolate. He examined the label, then unwrapped it and bit off a piece, chewing thoughtfully.

# 19

Rumaros was the farthest north of any sizeable town in Smolen, and the Rumar River was navigable there for seagoing ships. Thus the commander of Komarsi forces in Smolen, General Undsvin Tarsteng, had chosen it for his headquarters.

More specifically, he'd chosen its district courthouse for his headquarters, and the district administrator's office as his own. Its furnishings had been plain before the conquest, and remained so. Unlike his cousin Engwar, this soldier had no compulsion for the trappings and ornaments of power. For him, it was enough to have an army.

"Gentlemen," he was saying to his staff, "it is time to cut our losses. Given the recent aggressiveness of Smoleni forces, or more specifically the mercenary force they've employed, our advanced brigade bases are a needless and embarrassing expense to us. They were established to deny to the Smoleni the food-growing potentials of their districts. They've accomplished that; the summer is now too far advanced for anyone to plant and grow crops there.

"Accordingly, I am going to withdraw all military forces south of the Eel River-Strawstack line. We will burn the villages as we leave them. It is not in our interest that the Smoleni reoccupy them, and we will not need them again. By next year at this time there will be no Smoleni government, no Smoleni army, and no war.

"This withdrawal will begin no later than a week from Twoday, and will be carried out in no more than three stages. Colonel Daggit will coordinate the planning, and will report to me each . . ."

He stopped at the sound of muffled gunfire within the building, and his very first reaction was not alarm but anger: *This was the last straw! Those drunken fools had gone too far this time; he'd send them all to the stockade!* Alarm followed though, for that first gunfire was answered at once by shouts and more shooting. There was an outburst of it from the end of the corridor outside the chamber, an intense flurry of it somewhere on the ground floor, terminated by a grenade. And then, more from nearby in the headquarters billeting district. All this in less than five seconds. Undsvin drew the large pistol holstered at his side and moved toward the door despite the gunshots in the corridor. He hadn't yet reached it when a massive explosion shook the building, followed almost instantly by two others. Behind him a section of wall fell, and the floor collapsed beneath his feet. . . .

Even in the larger towns of the south, enough people had left ahead of the invaders that there were numerous empty houses. In one of them were six men in Komarsi uniform shirts. They were all more or less large and physically powerful. None of them wore trousers or shorts, for they were in the process of raping twin girls of perhaps fifteen years. By then the girls were in shock, and the soldiers resorted to occasional knife jabs to elicit movement from them.

In the distance they heard gunfire, but ignored it, were scarcely aware of it. They were off duty, drinking, and occupied. Then there was a large multiple explosion, and they paused. One of them went to his trousers and picked them up. "That's from over 'round headquarters," he said, and began to pull them on. "Get yer pants on and let's go." All but one moved to obey; he was building to a climax. The man who'd given the order strode to him, one hand still holding up his pants, and kicked the man powerfully in the buttocks, dislodging him. "Now!" he bellowed.

Drunk or not, in half a minute they were ready to leave. With a thumb, the leader gestured at the girls still lying on the bare floor. "Kill 'em," he said. "If they get home, they may tell what we look like, and it could get to the general."

One man laughed and moved toward them. He didn't need to draw his knife. His boots would do.

# 20

It was twilight. In a working-class section of Linnasteth, the capital of Komars, two drifters carrying rucksacks turned into a weedy yard and walked up a broken sidewalk to a house. One of them knocked. A large middle-aged woman opened. "What do you want?" she asked.

"We been told this's a place that'll rent a flop to an old soldier."

She cocked an eye. "You ayn't soldiers, and you ayn't old. Whadya got for me?"

"Good news and bad."

The formula completed, she stepped back. "Come in," she said, and when they had, she closed the door behind them. "We've been worried about you. Day after tomorrow's the day, and the others have checked in." Her speech had lost the twang of the shanty towns outside the city. An old man had entered the room from a hall, and she turned to him. "Mogi, fix something to eat for them." She looked the two up and down. "Damn! They picked you people for strong! I've got uniforms for you, but they're not going to fit worth a damn. I'll have to do some altering tonight." She turned, gesturing. "Come on. I want you to clean up while Mogi's heating something in the kitchen. Then I'll show you what we've got."

She shook her head. "You people have really stretched our resources. But at least for you two we don't need to make passes with photographs."

# 21

The main gate into the walled government district accommodated two wide lanes of traffic, with a sidewalk on either side. The midmorning traffic was considerable, and the gate guards busy. The workman with a tool chest stopped for one of them.

"Your pass."

The man put down his chest, took out a wallet, and displayed the pass in it. The guard waved him through without looking in the chest. The man had been told it would be that way, but his chest had a tray in the top, with tools, just in case. He picked it up and went through, glancing at his watch as he walked. The better part of an hour yet. Inside, someone hailed him, and he recognized his partner. They met and shook hands, as if they hadn't seen each other for some time.

"Security is as poor as Jenni said it would be," the first commented quietly.

"I'll take all the breaks they'll give me," the other answered. "Barrek and Norri have already gone ahead."

They moved on then, noting the names on the buildings, following the route they'd memorized on a map nearly four hundred miles away.

A van bearing the name and logo of a well-known delivery firm stopped in the horseshoe drive that curved to the front entrance of the War Ministry. Two men in coveralls got out, went to the back, and slid out a sizeable chest with carrying handles jutting out at both ends. Two uniformed armed guards followed the chest out. The two who took it were strong-looking, but even so, it was obviously heavy. The van then pulled out of the drive and stopped at the curb across the street.

They carried the chest laboriously up the steps, then set it down as one of the entrance guards came over to them. He barely glanced at the courier guards; his attention was on the men with the chest. "Whadya got there?" he asked.

"Reports from archives. For the adjutant general's office."

The entrance guard looked at it for several long seconds, as if x-raying it with his eyes, then nodded. "All right, go on in. They'll tell you in reception where his office is."

The two picked up the chest and lugged it inside. The armed guards followed them without challenge. If the door guard had looked inside it, all he'd have seen was report binders held shut with rubber bands. Unless, of course, he'd dug beneath them.

The morning was already hot. A fan on the windowsill drew in more humid air, mixing and stirring. Colonel Torey Eltrimor wished he hadn't been given a rear office. At the War Ministry, rear was south, and hot. Although it could have been worse, for this was the second floor. The top floor, the fifth, became unbearable on days like this.

Eltrimor made most of the Commissary Department's meat purchases. He bought livestock on the hoof, and was known for driving hard bargains. He liked Fingas Marnsson Kelromak, as much as he allowed himself to like anyone he did business with, but he would not bend when it came to prices.

"I don't doubt your word," Eltrimor was saying, "but the department's overbought on grade B just now. It's only used in officers' mess, you understand. I can pay what you asked for for one car of it, but everything else I'll have to buy as C, regardless of the actual grade."

Fingas nodded. It was cheaper to market to the War Ministry—it was the easy way, so to speak—but with a modest effort, he could sell all the grade B he wanted to commercial buyers, for B prices. He raised very few cattle that graded C or lower—culled dairy cows, mainly, and an occasional sausage bull.

"Fine. One car of B then, and I'll ship the rest to Brisslo. Will someone come out? Or can your man check them on arrival?"

"In your case, arrival will be fine. You've never sent me anything yet that didn't meet . . ."

He stopped in mid-sentence. From some other part of the building came the sound of shooting, muffled by distance and walls. "What is it?" asked Fingas, alarmed.

"Damned if I know. Gunfire, but . . ." A muffled boom followed, spelling "grenade" to the colonel. "Fingas," he said, heading for the door, "we'd better get out of here!"

Others were entering the hall as they did, but Eltrimor's office was nearest the back stairs. On the level, Fingas could move quickly when he had to, but on the stairs his bad leg slowed him. Eltrimor reached the first floor well ahead of him. Others passed him, jostling him as they hurried down. Sporadic shots continued, three- or four-round bursts from an automatic weapon, and he could hear shouting.

Fingas had expected to find the first floor corridor full of people, but there were relatively few. *Of course,* he thought. *There's a side exit.* The rear door was something of a bottleneck, but the press of bodies was not severe. He was carried out the door with the flow, then lost his footing on the outside steps. As he fell, there was gunfire ahead of him—a submachine gun, and screams. People in front of him fell. Someone stomped hard on his chest, the pain making him gasp; someone else trod on his hand. Someone else fell on him then, and someone else. Behind him, inside the ministry, a great explosion roared, jarring the massive stone building.

In front of him the shooting continued.


The fuses were short. It wouldn't do to have them noticed. And radio detonators that would have allowed blowing the charges from a distance weren't permitted in a Level 3 War.

The Linnos Ordnance Depot was temporary, had been set up for this particular war. And instead of storing explosives in massive bunkers, as in permanent depots, the Komarsi War Ministry had elected to rely on distance to protect the surroundings from possible accident. It saved the cost of construction, and made access far easier and quicker. They'd set it up in a poor, sandy, grazing area, four miles downstream from Linnasteth. For simplicity in handling and transshipping, materials were segregated by class. High explosives, tons of them, were held in the southeast quadrant.

Of course the area was well secured. A heavy chain link fence surrounded it, eight feet high and topped with barbed wire. Outside lay a double barrier of accordion wire, while beyond the accordion wire was sandy pasture, still picked over by leggy cattle, and providing no cover. Inside the fence, armed sentries walked their posts, and guards watched the surroundings from corner towers.

Loading of munitions was done by dock crews, who entered with the trucks. Invariably they brought their mid-shift lunches, day or night, and no one ever thought of checking their boxes or pails to see what sort of sandwiches they held.

Casual labor was provided by drafts of new recruits, looking awkward in unfamiliar fatigue uniforms. That was how Chelli Morss got in.

The depot mission was the iffiest and most challenging part of Operation Scorpion. It involved the most uncertain preliminary steps, required the most on-site decisions and innovations. For example, Chelli couldn't know in what part of the HE quadrant the charges had been set.

He'd hardly arrived when he'd been given a bucket of paint and a brush, and detailed with several others to paint a shed. A corporal had been with them, and Chelli'd had no chance to slip away. So he'd painted fast, if somewhat sloppily, to finish the job as soon as possible. They'd just finished washing out their brushes when he heard a distant boom. The War Ministry; he knew it by the sound, and the timing was right. It had been scheduled first.

No one else seemed to notice. They'd started handing out sickles to cut grass with, inside the fence and between the piles. Chelli had seen his opportunity and crowded in to get one. They'd hardly started when they heard a much greater explosion, a great thunderous roar that he knew was at the harbor facilities some three miles away. He'd felt it through the ground! Surely someone in command would think of the depot now, and take quick action to increase security.

As soon as he dared, he separated himself from the others, slipping into one of the traffic aisles between piles of boxes. Once alone, he began to scout the piles, chopping at grass now and then in case some non-com looked down an aisle and saw him. Actually he was looking for the red crayon streaks that should mark the fuse locations. Any one charge would do. He saw a red streak on the end of a box, went to it and looked around for the fuse. There! He reached into a pocket and found the small lighter buried beneath his handkerchief.

"*Hey, you!*"

He turned. "Yessir?"

A sergeant was striding down the aisle toward him, with another man. The sergeant wore a holster at his hip; the other carried a rifle.

"*Get your ass back to the trucks,*" the sergeant called. "*Now!*"

"Just a minute, boss. I dropped something." He bent, and lit the fuse.

"Yomal *damn* you Amber-damned recruits!" The sergeant came up to him and punched him. "Don't you 'just a minute' me, you son of a bitch! When I say *jump*, you better damned well jump! Now let's go!"

"Sergeant," said the private with the rifle. He was staring at the fuse. "What's that? Looks like a . . ."

Chelly hit the sergeant in the throat with a spear-hand, felt the trachea crush and saw the eyes glaze. Before the man could fall, he'd pulled the sergeant's pistol from its holster, thumbing the hammer back as he drew it. The rifleman was good. Quick. He swung his rifle around and pulled the trigger at the same moment Chelli pulled his own.

The difference was that the rifle had a cartridge in the chamber and the pistol didn't. The shock of the bullet knocked Chelli down, then the man dropped his rifle and went for the fuse. Even as Chelli hit the ground, lung-shot, he jacked a cartridge into the chamber, rolled onto his side and pulled the trigger again. The .37 caliber slug took the soldier behind the ear, killing him instantly.

Chelli raised up enough to shoot the sergeant too, just in case, then fell back.

There were shouts now. Men drawn by the shooting were running up the aisle from the other direction. The trooper grinned; they'd never make it. It was a short fuse.

# 22

The Royal Council sat around a polished table of some dark wood, the king at one end. The table was raised there, stepped up to accommodate his throne, which was on a small dais.

"Your Majesty," the Foreign Minister was saying, "it is not true that foreign confidence in us has been shaken. They were inevitably surprised by the recent Smoleni efforts, even impressed by them, especially since the widespread theater distribution of certain cubes. But I know of no foreign government which imagines that it was other than the effort of a dying state."

Engwar looked past the man, lips pinched, still unhappy. The Foreign Minister went on. "What is true is that there have been from the start— from before the start—certain factions in those countries that wish us ill. But even these do not imagine that the Smoleni might win. They'd simply like to see the war go on, see the Smoleni persist as long as possible and fight as long as possible, embarrassing us and costing us lives and money. It is these who make much of the recent Smoleni successes, small though they are. They—"

Engwar interrupted. "They were intolerable! Insolent! I'll see they pay for them, a hundredfold."

"I have no doubt of it, Your Majesty."

The king glared at him for a moment, then subsided. "You were saying."

"Yes, Your Majesty. These factions are agitating their governments to provide aid to the Smoleni, and of course most of those governments must at least pretend to listen. But I predict that nothing will come of it. First of all, of course, you have the largest navy on the planet, both in tonnage and firepower. People fear you, Your Majesty. And secondly, we isolated Smolen when we captured her coastline. Supplying her—"

Again Engwar interrupted angrily. "Someone supplied her with those mercenaries!"

"True, Your Majesty. But it is generally agreed that they are from offworld, that they were landed from a spaceship. No one is going to supply Smolen with food and munitions by spaceship. First, there is no precedent for it in practice or in law. And secondly, the cost would be prohibitive."

With that, the Foreign Minister stood silent. Engwar glowered. "Is that your entire report then?"

The man inclined his head. "It is, Your Majesty."

The king looked at the minister next in line. "And you, Dorskell, what have you to—"

He bit the words off in mid-sentence, for the Lord Chancellor had entered the room to stand quietly by the door. Such an intrusion must signify something important. "What is it, Gorman?" Engwar said testily.

"Your Majesty, word has just come from Rumaros that enemy infiltrators have attacked General Undsvin's headquarters there and destroyed it with explosives. The general has been injured, and many officers are dead. The infiltrators have all been killed or captured."

Engwar II Tarsteng stared at the man. Such an act was incredible! Intolerable! Civilized people did not do such things! They did not attack persons at high levels! "When did this happen?"

"I'm told it was at 1110 hours."

"Is my cousin's life endangered by his injury?"

"They did not say so, Your Majesty."

"*Well go ask them, Dolt! Did you think I wouldn't want to know?*"

"At once, Your Majesty," the man said, and left the room, Engwar glaring after him. The cabinet sat frozen by the news, and by Engwar's anger, for Gorman was his right hand. After a moment, Engwar took his attention from the door and looked at the men around the table.

Before he could speak again, an explosion boomed from somewhere inside the government district, startling most of them to their feet. The Minister of War, who'd already risen to give his report, hurried to the balcony door, stepping out to see what he could see. And fell backward into the room and onto the floor, a hole in his forehead. As he fell, they heard the shot that killed him.

Engwar stared wide-eyed, not angry yet but shocked. *His palace had been violated! It could have been himself who lay dead there!*

# 23

"Fingas, it's really good to see you getting around so soon. And a relief as well. Would you care to enumerate your injuries?"

Fingas Kelromak smiled slightly. "Those you can see are a broken hand and cheekbone. The more severe are less visible: cracked ribs, a broken rib, and a punctured lung. They're what kept me in the hospital." His smile turned wry. "Our country has had some remarkable experiences lately."

Lord Jorn Nufkarm grunted. "Indeed. I suppose you read of them or had them read to you; those you didn't experience personally."

The War Ministry had been evacuated for major reconstruction; eighty-four had died there, not including raiders. And of course there was the sniper killing of Lord Dorskell, in the cabinet room itself. The ship *Pride of Komars*, with a cargo of munitions, had been blown up at the dock, surely also by raiders. The explosion had considerably damaged the harbor facilities, with a reported additional 107 dead or missing. While the ordnance depot . . . "I've visited what used to be the Linnos Depot. The hole in the ground is some hundred yards long, and said to be thirty feet deep. I can't vouch for the depth; there's a small lake in the bottom."

"I understand they caught none of the raiders alive."

"That's right. There are rumors that two or more escaped from the government district, and I suppose it's possible. As for the escape or death of those responsible for the other disasters—there aren't even rumors."

Nufkarm pulled a bell rope. "I suppose you've read that they blew up three of the four bridges across the Komar, too."

Fingas nodded. "They mined the fourth, but something went wrong and only one charge exploded. It's already back in operation."

A servant entered. "You rang, m'lord?"

"Yes. Would you bring joma please, Varel. With honey and cream for Lord Fingas." He turned again to his visitor. "My physician insists I lose weight, a great deal of it. Thus I now take my joma innocent of flavorings.

"As for the problems of war—the greater problems are rather like the injuries to your ribs and lung; they're not readily visible. Nor are they discussed in the papers. They're not as impressive, and Engwar doesn't want them written about. I speak of inflation, fiscal deficits, proposed new taxes—and of course the labor shortage. Which will grow noticeably worse when harvest comes, as you know better than I. And when manpower is short, field crews can become unruly, or at least insubordinate, for only then do they have any power at all. At the very least they don't work as hard as they normally do, and at the exact time they're most needed.

"And when it's over and the army is disbanded, we'll have one hundred and forty thousand ex-serfs who've gained their freedom by enlisting. There'll be little work for them, of course, and they'll expand and overflow the shantytowns, giving rise to an increase in hooliganism. All because of one man's irrational greed."

Fingas Kelromak didn't reply, didn't nod, simply held the older man's eyes for a long moment. "And how do our peers view all this?' he asked at last.

Nufkarm grunted. "Many of them are heedlessly and self-righteously loyal to our good sovereign's ambitions, of course. To be expected. On the other hand, there are people of influence who did not like this war since before it began. More than a few of them, including"—he gestured theatrically—"you and I. But went along with it because there seemed nothing we could do to stop it, and because the war's result seemed a foregone conclusion. And of course because we were afraid of our good king."

Fingas exhaled audibly through pursed lips. "And what seems to be known of the raiders? I've read that they're supposed to be offworld mercenaries. Does there seem to be anything to that?"

"I have no doubt of it. A few prisoners were taken, wounded prisoners, in the raids on brigade bases in Smolen. But they didn't survive interrogation." He grimaced. "They're said to be T'swa-like, but white. Very muscular, quite fearless, and extremely crafty. I have no doubt at all that they're from offworld."

"And the effect on foreign opinion—what's that been? Have you heard? The papers have avoided that, too."

"I haven't heard, but I expect to have supper with The Archipelago's consul this evening. I may learn something there. Logic says they must be impressed with what Smolen's accomplished, but it's questionable whether that will translate into actual assistance to President Lanks's unfortunate people. Token assistance at most; token assistance covertly delivered. Now if the Smoleni could maintain this sort of activity— But that's scarcely imaginable. These various raids aren't likely to be repeated; they were successful only because they were unexpected, and security, apparently, was terribly lax."

Varel returned with a tray, set it between the two, and while they waited, poured for them. He left then, and after Fingas had stirred in cream and honey, so did his host.

"So," Nufkarm went on, "given the circumstances of distance and accessibility, any aid the Smoleni might receive will be ineffective. The rational thing for Engwar to do would be to ignore it."

Fingas nodded. "And of course, he won't do the rational thing."

"He might. Cairswin's advice carries weight with him. But he also might send out fleet units to harass foreign shipping, perhaps even search for contraband. Which could result in some form of concerted counteraction."

Fingas nodded thoughtfully. "So certain persons are worried."

"But will do nothing."

"Unless someone else starts it."

"I hope you're not thinking of it. You've already offended Engwar with your proposed reforms of the serf laws. And Engwar is doubtlessly inclined, just now, to take harsh action against anyone who treads on his toes. With trumped up charges, if need be.

"And really, Fingas, we need you for better things. You are one person the party might be willing to rally 'round, when the time comes."

"It might be worth the risk."

"Umm. Well—" Nufkarm appeared to consider something, then went on. "I have heard a rumor," he said. "One I tend to credit. And if it's true, broad support will surely fail to materialize. It will probably even weaken support from those you'd count on most."

"And that is?"

"That Engwar has decided to hire a regiment of T'swa. If he does, everyone will wait to see what happens."

That closed the subject, and they spoke of other things. Eventually they rode Nufkarm's elevator to his roof garden and had lunch there. After lunch, Nufkarm accompanied Fingas to the foyer, and they shook hands.

"You will keep me informed, I trust," Nufkarm said.

Fingas raised his eyebrows. "Informed? About what?"

Nufkarm smiled. "Why, whatever there is, young Kelromak. Whatever you feel I should know about. Or whatever you feel I might help you with."

The cab Fingas had called for was waiting. He went carefully down the steps, and gingerly entered it, meanwhile thinking of certain possibilities.

He was also thinking of the "drifter" he'd left behind at his estate.

# 24

General Undsvin Tarsteng entered his new headquarters building, the four-story Hotel Rumaros. One of his arms was in a cast, and he rode in a wheelchair, pushed by a corporal and accompanied by two large and formidable armed guards. As he rolled into the lobby, someone shouted "at ease," and the room went silent. Hands slapped shirt pockets in salute. He acknowledged them collectively with a scowl and a single curt nod. The general was clearly in a vile mood; no one moved, outside his small entourage, until the elevator doors had closed behind him.

A man was waiting in the reception room to the general's office. He was Captain Gulthar Kro, a rather large man, though not so large as the two guards with the general. His shoulders were conspicuous in their width and thickness; the rest of him seemed almost slim by comparison. His face was scarred as if by assault with a blunt instrument, which in fact it had been several years earlier. He'd risen when the general entered.

"You asked for me, sir."

"Damn right!" The general turned. "The rest of you OUT!" They jumped, then started for the door. He added then, more moderately, "Lersett, you stay, damn it! How am I supposed to get around?" The corporal stopped, shaken, and when the two guards had closed the door behind them, Undsvin continued, grim again. "Captain, what, precisely, is your post?"

Kro alone, among the people who'd met or accompanied the general, seemed at ease with him this morning. "I'm the commander of your personal unit, sir."

"*And isn't one of its central responsibilities to protect my person?!*"

"Yessir."

"THEN WHERE IN AMBER'S NAME WERE THEY WHEN I NEEDED THEM?"

"Two of 'em were in the corridor outside your office door. They ran to the head of the stairs when they heard the shootin' below, and got killed there. Of the rest, a third was trainin' by your orders, and—"

"*And the other two thirds were drunk!*" The general shouted this too, but it lacked the fire of his earlier outburst.

"No, sir. Not more than one third was drunk: the ones that had passes to be off base. They knaw better'n to take liberties with me."

Undsvin's lips drew in, leaving a slit. "Captain, your unit is a disgrace."

"Sir, they're your unit, not mine."

The corporal behind the wheelchair blanched at the impertinence, but Kro went on. "You had 'em recruited from stockades and jails. You wanted the toughest sons of bitches you could get. Then you asked me to tame 'em for you. I done the best I could with what you gave me." He might have added that if the general thought he could get someone better, he should try. But he didn't; Kro had integrity, not insanity.

Undsvin Tarsteng examined him long. He'd put out word that he needed someone self-disciplined and extremely tough, someone who could command respect from and control the toughest, most undisciplined men. He'd had half a dozen prospects brought to his attention, and Kro had ended up with the job. Undsvin had no doubt the man had a hidden history, an interesting one, but all he knew of him was that he'd made sergeant first class within a year of enlistment. Which was truly remarkable even then, when the army was beginning to expand rapidly.

When Undsvin spoke again, it was calmly and quietly. "I haven't paid much attention to their training. What are they good for? What can they do?"

Kro's expression didn't change. "They're strong and they're tough; that's what you picked 'em for. But most of 'em got no judgment 'cept what I beat into 'em. They're mean; they'd rather cut a man up than kill 'im, and rather kill 'im than talk to 'im. You dint have that in mind, but it's what you got.

"Physically I've got 'em hard and kept 'em that way. They hate long runs, but they don't mind speed work. I run 'em hard down one side of the track, and let 'em walk the rest of it to rest, then make 'em do it some more. They can run down just about anyone you want, up to a quarter mile; then they're used up. They'll lift weights all I tell 'em to, 'cause they like to be strong, and they beat the heavy bags bloody. I got to replace a busted leather bag near every day. And they love to rassle each other. They'd rather beat one another bloody, but I've forbid it; I'm the only one supposed to beat on 'em. And they've been happier since I had posts set in their exercise yard. They thraw knives at 'em by the hour. They don't knife each other though. You prob'ly remember I flogged one of 'em to death for that. The lesson took.

"Before the war, when we were at Long Ridge, I took 'em in the woods and tried teachin' 'em to track and sneak. Most of 'em dint learn to track much at all, but they learnt sneakin' pretty smart. Plus they did good at just about all their infantry trainin', includin' drill. They hated drill, but I told 'em when they learned it good enough, I wunt make 'em do it no more.

"Most of 'em I wouldn't trust around the corner; they're like to do anything they think they can get away with. Those what're different, more reliable, are the ones I made squad leaders and platoon leaders."

He shrugged. "And that's it."

Undsvin regarded the fingernails on his good hand, then glanced back at the man behind his wheelchair. "Corporal," he said, "wait outside the door." When the man was gone, he turned to Kro again.

"Captain, these raids have humiliated me, and more to the point, they've humiliated the king. To make matters worse, the military situation dictates a withdrawal to the Eel River. At this point in the war, such a withdrawal does the enemy no good, and it greatly reduces his opportunities to harass us. But the appearance is of a victory for him, and a loss for us.

"So I want to hurt him. Punish him. Remind him of reality." The general looked quizzically at Gulthar Kro. "Surely your men are as tough as the mercenaries the Smoleni have hired. What might they do to accomplish that?"

Kro read Undsvin Tarsteng's face, his eyes, his attitude: the general truly wanted something of him, but didn't really expect anything. "My men are at least as tough," Kro answered, and believed it. "But from what I heard, those mercs have a hundred times more discipline. They have to, to do what they did. My men only cooperate when you tell 'em just what to do, and you watch 'em. And if they figure you might beat 'em up or flog 'em for screwin' off. There's no way they could bring off the sort of things the mercs done.

"What they mawt *could* do, though, is assassinate Lanks and Belser, like the mercs tried to kill you and the king. Mawt be they could kill the merc commander, too."

Undsvin stared, and a slow smile formed on his face. "Remarkable, Captain! That's exactly what I had in mind, right down to the mercenary commander! You impress me! Now, tell me how you might carry out this intention."

# 25

Fingas Kelromak was almost always glad to get back from the capital. For one thing, his estate was home, and for another, his wife seldom went with him to Linnasteth. And of course, things invariably had come up which wanted his personal attention. Things he could actually do something about.

The evening he got home was invariably given to being a husband and father; he was not to be approached with any matters of the farm, except perhaps a screaming emergency. He did have a note placed on Chenly's desk though, to see him in the morning, in his office.

Chenly was there when Fingas walked in after breakfast. "Good morning, your lordship."

Fingas's face was still discolored, and his left hand still in a cast. The face in particular held Chenly's eyes, and his own showed dismay.

Fingas smiled wryly. "Rather colorful, isn't it."

"I read about what happened, in the paper, but . . ."

"Well. I was one of the lucky ones. I wanted to ask you how our— guest is. The drifter you found beside the road. Does he remember anything yet?"

"Seemingly not, sir."

"What did Ammekor say about him?"

"The knee was pretty badly sprained. That seemed to be all of that. Also his shoulder was separated, the collarbone torn partly loose from the shoulder blade. And he said a knock on the head like his was could lose a man his memory. But that it should come back to him sooner or later; probably sooner. That's how he put it, sir."

"And how is his recovery coming?"

"He uses both hands now, and helps around the workshop, but nothing heavy yet. As for the knee—I had him show it to me yesterday; I assumed you'd ask. It's still swollen a bit, and he limps, but he walks on it."

"Um. I suppose someone's cleaned up the broken tree by now."

"Oh, yes, sir."

"Did they, ah, find anything there?"

"Sir?"

"Like a pistol that might go with that magazine you found in his rucksack."

Chenly shook his head. "Not that I know of, sir. And I'm sure they'd have told me if they had."

"I want you to take me there this morning, Chenly. We'll go in your utility vehicle."

"Yes, sir. I'll call camp and tell them I'll look at the slow-bear damage with them tomorrow."

"Good. I'll see you at the front entrance at—" He glanced at his watch. "At 8:20. Just the two of us."

The lightning-shattered snag was conspicuous beside the ditch. They searched the grass and weeds thoroughly, and with the broken treetop gone, found something Winn Urkwal had missed: a thick roll of plastic tape, suitable for all kinds of things. For example, mending tool handles until they could be replaced. But the cardboard spool had the name of a Smoleni manufacturer printed on it, and the color was Smoleni army green. And it could also be used to tape blocks of explosive together.

Fingas looked long at it, lip between his teeth, then handed it to Chenly. Chenly examined it, then looked worriedly at his employer, saying nothing.

"Let's go back," said Fingas. "I need to speak with the man, see how he explains this. Say nothing about it to anyone. Nothing at all to anyone at all."

The forester nodded. They got into the utility vehicle and started back down the road. "Chenly," Fingas said, "there are things we need to talk about, you and I, and we need to be completely frank." He paused. "Tell me what you think of this war we're in."

Varky Graymar's remaining limp was feigned. The examination by Fingas's physician had been superficial—it hadn't seemed to warrant anything more. The actual degree of healing would have surprised him; Ka-Shok meditation had very definite medical applications.

His pack still held most of the 30 dronas cash, and over the last several days he'd stashed hard crackers filched from the table, and candy and dried fruit purchased from the estate commissary. On Sixday evening, most of the bachelors would ride in a crew bus to a dance in the nearby town. Others would visit friends. If he wasn't in his bunk when they got back, no one would pay much attention.

He had no doubt whatever that he could find his way several hundred miles cross-country to Burnt Woods.

This morning he sat cleaning the beginnings of rust from shovels, sharpening them with a mill file, and rubbing them with an oily rag. It was the sort of work a man could do who didn't get around well and was thought to lack proper mobility in his left shoulder.

Fingas Kelromak came into the tool shed, his forester with him. The forester held a pistol, and stationed himself to one side of the door. Varky put the shovel down and looked at Fingas questioningly. "It seems," said Fingas, "that you are not the only injured man about the place."

Varky nodded, completely calm. "I heard folks tell what happened to you."

Fingas's eyes latched onto his. "I suppose you've heard too of the great damage done. It's thought to be by mercenaries from Smolen. The generally accepted theory is that they were smuggled into the country on a freighter, perhaps from Oselbent. But they could have gotten here crosscountry, through what the Smoleni call the High Wild."

"Yessir, I heard that too."

"I have another theory."

Varky said nothing.

"They could have come down the Raging River in small boats. I'm sure there are Smoleni who know the river well enough. Then separated and hiked to Linnasteth, to regather there." Varky's gaze never wavered. "If they had," Fingas added, "they'd probably come through here."

Still there was no reaction.

"Our government failed to capture any of the raiders. If they had one, they'd question him at length. Undoubtedly a horrible experience."

It was Fingas's eyes that turned away; he reached into a pocket and held up the magazine. Varky knew at once where it had come from. "You see what this is," Fingas said. "It was found in your rucksack while you were being brought here, and given to me. I decided then that it was simply something you'd found."

"Could be. I don't recall."

Fingas looked long at him again. Finally he said, "I need you to do something for me: I need you to tell me the truth. And when you have told me the truth, I'll need you to do something else for me: an errand." He paused to let his words sink in. It wasn't necessary. "But first the truth—two questions. Number one, how did your hands get so heavily, and really rather peculiarly callused?"

Varky waited for three or four seconds before answering. Not making up his mind; his reaction to the situation was as quick as his reactions to physical confrontations. He simply knew without computation that Fingas Kelromak expected a lag, and it would be better to meet his expectation. He held up his hands as if examining them—and answered with a typical Iryalan accent. "They result mainly from a form of training, but partly also from the temperatures in which the training was done."

"Ah!" Fingas's face twisted, as if with some inner adjustment. "My second question is, are you able to travel cross-country now, with your injured knee and shoulder?"

"I can travel."

"Good. Now for the errand: I want you to convey for me a message to your commander."

Varky nodded. Fingas drew a thick envelope from inside his jacket, and handed it to him. "You may read it if you'd like. In fact I recommend it."

It was open at one end. Varky shook out the contents and scanned them; there were several pages.

"You can see it wouldn't do to be caught with it. If at some point you seem to be in danger, I want you to burn it. Are you sure you're willing to do all this?"

The risk this Komarsi nobleman was taking was remarkable, Varky realized, even astonishing, given what he had to lose. Romlar and the president would very much want to see this letter. He folded it, put it back in the envelope, and tucked it in his own shirt. "More than willing," he said.

"Do you think you can find your way?"

Varky let himself grin. "Like a migrating bird," he answered.

Twenty minutes later they were in the carryall, Varky in the back out of sight, traveling up the road first north, then west. Food had been provided for Varky's rucksack—cheese, bread, honey in a can— and insect repellent, which he could have done without but was happy to have.

Several miles within the forest, Chenly pulled off on a spur road and drove to near its end, where they got out. Now Fingas drew his own pistol, extending it to the trooper. "Best you take this. And—" Reaching in a pocket, he took out the magazine. "See if it fits. The design is standard, but the make is undoubtedly different."

*This,* Varky thought, *is a real man!* He removed the magazine already in the butt and tried the other. Standard didn't mean as much on the trade worlds as on Confederation member worlds, but he wasn't surprised to find it fitted. He slid the action back, and a cartridge seated nicely.

"Thank you, sir. Much appreciated."

He slung his pack, being only a little careful with his shoulder, then turned and jogged off easily toward the north without a limp.

# 26

Gulthar Kro was the grandson of freed serfs—freed for having served in the last war with Selmar. His childhood was spent in a shantytown outside Wheatland, a provincial seat. At age twelve he'd gotten into trouble with the authorities for excessive fighting in one of the poor, ill-taught schools provided for freedmen. He'd hit the road, working at whatever he could, stealing as necessary.

At age sixteen he'd been sentenced to life in prison. He'd waylaid and beaten a notoriously brutal undersheriff, would no doubt have killed him if two constables hadn't interrupted. He was already man-sized and more than man-strong, with a reputation among the drifters for ferocity in fights.

In prison he was assigned to quarrying rock. Because he was so strong, he was alternately a hammer man, whaling away with a twelve-pound sledge, and a prizer, using a crowbar to move blocks of granite. This work, imposed on an exceptional genotype, developed extremely powerful back, arms, and shoulders. The sledgehammer work in particular developed ferocious strength in his hands and forearms.

In the prison camp, fights were frequent. He soon became respected by the toughest inmates, and feared by the rest. He wasn't sadistic, but he could be ruthless, even brutal when it served his purpose.

At age twenty-two he was part of an escape that left three guards dead. Once out, he left the others, mistrusting their judgment. The camp had been in the hills that farther north became the "High Wild" of western Smolen. The others had determined to move eastward out of the forest, planning to sleep in haystacks and rob farms. Kro, on the other hand, had moved northward through the forest, stealthy and swift, disciplining his hunger, sleeping on the ground. Two days later he found a woodsmen's shack, where he stole a can of beans and two cold pancakes, but nothing else. With three men living there, so little might never be missed.

The next morning he ambushed a timber cruiser and killed him. First he ate the man's lunch, then took his belt with its knife and pistol, and hid the body in a ravine.

The next day he was across the border. Already he was becoming woodswise; it seemed natural to him. Eventually he found work as a log cutter, and got the feel of the Smoleni speech. When fall came, he'd joined with two Smoleni brothers who trapped in the High Wild.

By spring he was tired of the quiet, the lack of excitement. However, for the first time in his life he'd lived among men who were reasonable and cheerful—neither violent nor contentious—and he'd been affected by it. He traveled south again, by bus now, returning to Komars where he joined the army. The law required identification cards, but these were not ordinarily asked for, and their lack was disregarded in men volunteering for the expanding army. He was a natural warrior, his mind was quick, and he was self-disciplined. He was also a natural leader, and advanced quickly.

After being selected for the Commander's Personal Unit, he was promoted to warrant officer and made a platoon leader. Within two weeks
the unit commander was removed as ineffectual, and Kro was made acting
commander. Two weeks after that, having beaten several men severely for
insubordination, his appointment was made "permanent" by the general,
who rammed through a jump to captain for him.

The post remained his for more than a year.

# 27

A submachine gun resting on his lap, Gulthar Kro rode in a commandeered Smoleni bus, sitting next to the driver, where he could see out.
He'd selected twenty two-man teams, men who might at least attempt
to carry out their mission, while leaving the unit most of its officers and
sergeants.

For ten days he'd worked the selected teams in the forest, making sure
they could use a compass and read and follow maps. He'd made com-
petitions of it, and before the ten days were over, the men were competent and confident. Each man wore a captured Smoleni uniform; each
team had a book of forest maps taken from the captured headquarters
of the Smoleni Forest Survey, maps showing the major variations in forest
types, every creek and pond, and every open fen larger than perhaps
twenty acres, which gave them many reference points to guide on.

Finding Burnt Woods was entirely feasible with them. The question
was, how many would do it. Because it was also feasible to desert now,
hike westward to the Raging River and cross it on a raft or stolen boat,
or even travel eastward to the border with Oselbent. He guessed that perhaps half would try for Burnt Woods. They'd been shown a sketch map
of the village, with the president's house marked, and the general's, and
each team had been assigned a primary target. When they got there, they'd
have to play it by ear.

They'd been shown where, on the appropriate forest map, the merc
headquarters was, too, but he hadn't assigned its commander to anyone.
No one knew what he looked like or what tent was his, and anyway it
seemed to Kro that it would simply waste a team to try for him.

The bus had taken them west along a graveled east-west connecting
road, and he'd dropped off team after team at intervals marked on the
maps. The first stage of the troop pull-back had been completed, and

tomorrow this road would be left to the Smoleni, too. Not that they'd get any good of it; every farmstead along the road would be burned, as well as the sole village.

Now Kro was the only man left on the bus besides the driver, who'd turned it around on an old roadside log landing and was driving back eastward. Kro watched through the windshield for a landmark, and when he saw it, told the driver to stop.

He turned to the man before stepping out the door. "When you get back," he said, "tell your commander I gave you a message for the general—an important message that he's gawta get." He stopped, waiting for the man to digest that, then went on. "Tell him I'm gawn north too. And with enough luck, I'll be back.

"You got that?"

When the man had repeated it to him, Kro nodded, stepped off the bus, and disappeared into the forest. The merc commander was his target, his alone.

# 28

Kelmer Faronya had been having nightmares. He'd felt better about himself after the night of the mortar attacks. He'd done his job in the face of heavy fire, and stayed as long as the others. But on several nights since then, he'd had recurring dreams in which the grenade once again landed in front of him. In one of them, Jerym had thrown himself on it to save him, and it had exploded. Then Jerym's corpse had followed him everywhere in the dream, mangled and bloody and grim. He'd get in front of Kelmer, stand in his way, take Kelmer's seat at the table. There was no escaping him. The dead mouth moved, but no words came out. The dreaming Kelmer was sure that the message it mouthed was horrifying, that if he ever heard it, he too would die. Meanwhile the corpse decayed. Pieces sloughed off. He could even smell it! Finally, with a horrid resonance, the words would start: "Kelmer . . ." And he'd waken sweating—with the smell of putrefaction seemingly still in his nostrils! It seemed to Kelmer that odor had never been a part of his dreams before.

More terrifying, though, was the one in which the grenade landed and Kelmer ran. And running looked back—to see it rolling and bouncing after him! He would run and run, but always it followed him, getting nearer. And implicit in the dream was the certain knowledge that if it caught him—*when* it caught him—it would explode. He tired. Actually it was as if the air thickened, making running almost impossible, and his legs grew heavier, harder to move. Then, looking back, the grenade would be closer, almost at his heels. Sparks flew from it! He *knew* with dead certainty it was about to explode.

That's when he'd waken, sweating and panting, a wakening that was like a reprieve.

It was twelve days after the action, and he'd just dreamed of the rolling grenade for the third time. He lay on his cot at Shelf Falls, wide-eyed and gasping, when the thought struck him. *The dream, it seemed to him, was a warning, a premonition. In the next action, or the one after that, or perhaps one later, a grenade would kill him. And somehow— somehow he would cause Jerym's death!* There was no doubt in his mind that this was so.

So when, on the next day, a message came from Romlar that he was to come to Burnt Woods, he felt like a prisoner pardoned. For Burnt Woods was far away from combat, and Jerym wouldn't be there.

Romlar had a different kind of assignment for him. The repeated successful strikes at Komarsi brigade bases, followed by the raid on Komarsi army headquarters at Rumaros and the destruction at Linnasteth, had rejuvenated the Smoleni. Even Belser had come around to an activist position. He'd approved the training of Smoleni ranger units, men selected for their wilderness skills, their marksmanship, and their warrior auras. Troopers would be their cadre.

Kelmer was to record some of their training on video cubes as part of regimental history. Selected parts would be distributed to other countries on Maragor, as public relations for Smolen.

Beyond that, he was to record civilian survival activities. These had been underway earlier at backcountry villages, but now the refugees had joined in. He took cubeage showing trees of certain species being felled, the bark stripped from them and carried in pack baskets to village houses and refugee camps. There the inner bark, the phloem, was scraped off and pestled into pulp that would be added to flour for baking. Centuries earlier, "bark bread" had kept their ancestors alive when they'd hidden in the forest, and the process had been passed down in stories and history books.

That wasn't all. Crews with scythes hiked to wet meadows in the forest, where they cut hay and stacked it to dry on racks made of poles, so the horses herded up from the Leas could be fed that winter.

There was even a pair of crews sawing *roivan* trees into five-foot logs, splitting staves from them, and cross-stacking the staves to dry. They could be shaved and carved into bows, against the time when ammunition might run out. Still others cut and peeled osiers from stream banks and fen margins, and straightened them, to be made into arrows if the need arose.

Concussion grenades were thrown into lakes, stunning and killing fish. These floated to the surface, and were gathered in baskets for drying or smoking.

More important, it seemed to Kelmer, were activities near Smolen's northernmost village, a tiny place named Jump-Off.[1] The border lay only forty miles north, forty miles of true wilderness. The Granite River flowed out of it, south through Jump-Off; the river was the only road there. In summer the village was reached by boat, in winter by skis, snowshoes, or sleigh.

Tiny as it was, and more than two hundred miles north of Rumaros, Jump-Off nonetheless had strategic importance. Smoleni diplomats outside the country were negotiating secretly with the governments of Oselbent, The Archipelago, and Selmar for food and munitions. Oselbent was a long and mostly narrow country, mountainous and incised by fjords, living largely by its fishing boats, merchant marine, and mines. It feared Komar's army and fleet, and would like to see her militarism broken. Especially since, with the Smoleni coast occupied, Oselbent had Komarsi forces at her southern border. And it seemed to the Oselbenti that once the Smoleni surrendered, the Komarsi would be tempted to conquer Oselbent, or make a tributary of her. Besides, Oselbent, like Smolen, was a republic, of which there weren't many on Maragor.

But to antagonize Komars could be fatal.

The Archipelago was another republic. And more important, from the Smoleni and Oselbenti point of view, she had a strong fleet. If she could be gotten to sign a mutual defense pact with Oselbent . . . But she had her own vulnerabilities.

Selmar was the kingdom to the south of Komars, and a considerably more limited monarchy. No friend of her northern neighbor, she'd lost the last war they'd fought, along with some of the planet's diminishing iron mines. Potentially she was as strong as Komars, but suffered serious political and economic problems that a new constitution and king had only recently begun to ease. If The Archipelago were to sign a favorable trade agreement with her, the Selmari economy and morale would substantially improve, and Komars would find a revitalized old adversary on the south. One worrisome enough that Komars might be reluctant to extend her northern war to Oselbent.

If a mutual defense pact could be engineered between Oselbent and The Archipelago, and a trade pact signed between Selmar and The Archipelago, then surely, covert assistance agreements could be worked out for Smolen, with The Archipelago as the main supply source.

To Kelmer Faronya, a young man of the Confederation, all this seemed very very foreign—something out of a novel—and beyond photography.

The other problem of foreign supplies was getting them into Smolen, now that her coast was occupied. This was one the Smoleni could do more about, and one readily recorded on cube. Jump-Off was fifty-four miles from the border with Oselbent, and seventy-five miles from the town of Deep Fjord, which was a busy, even somewhat congested, harbor. The Falls River, which emptied into the fjord, was the site of a large hydro-electric development, which supplied the power for a large plant that manufactured nitrogen compounds, notably nitrate fertilizers. (Ironically, it was also a major supplier of nitrocellulose for the Komarsi munitions industry.) On the plateau above the fjord, and near the border with Smolen, were mines producing iron and magnesium. Thus a railroad climbed its way up from the fjord almost to the border.

Ships of many nations came to Deep Fjord, including ships from The Archipelago. It was the logical transshipment point for supplies to Smolen, if an agreement could be reached.

The problem of getting such supplies to the Smoleni army might seem to be worsened by the nature of the terrain, for that part of Smolen was largely peatlands—fens, moss bogs, and muskegs—but to the Smoleni, that provided not difficulty but opportunity.

An army engineering officer and a logging operator took Kelmer to photograph part of the supply road they were "building" to Oselbent. Actually they were building nothing, nor did they need to. What they were doing amounted mainly to staking the route, marking it with tall flagged rods. So far as possible without adding much length, the route was marked across open fens and moss bogs. Where these were absent, it mostly passed through muskegs—forested swamps. In much of the muskeg, the trees were sparse and stunted, and little obstacle. Sometimes, though, it was necessary to flag the route through heavier muskeg, where crews had begun to clear the right-of-way with saw and axe.

Over the years, trains of large sleighs, drawn by giant steam tractors, had been used in Smolen to haul logs on frozen rivers. Now, if the diplomats succeeded, similar trains would be used in winter to haul supplies from Oselbent across vast roadless swamps to Jump-Off.

Here and there, non-swamp intervened—mostly glacial till and outwash, and rarely low outcrops of the underlying rock. Kelmer visited one of these, a neck about a hundred yards wide, fifteen miles east of Jump-Off. A small crew was camped there, with axes and saws to fell trees; picks and shovels to dig with; dynamite to blow rock and stumps; and small, horse-drawn drag scoops to move earth and broken rock. They were cutting a narrow roadway almost to swamp level, so the sleigh trains wouldn't have to climb. On hard-packed snow, one great steam-powered crawler tractor could pull a whole train of large, heavily-loaded sleighs, if the road was level.

There already were steam tractors at Jump-Off, barged up the Granite. More could be brought as needed. A large crew of men was converting logging sleighs into cargo sleighs, building 20- by 8-foot cargo boxes of planks on the heavy skids and cross-bunks, which were hewn or sawn from tree trunks. The only metal in the sleighs were spikes and bolts, nuts and washers, stout chain-and-ring couplings, and stake pockets.

The only road maintenance equipment was drags made of logs split or sawn in half lengthwise, and bolted together with braces into a V-shape twelve feet wide at the tail. Dragged along the route in winter, by either horses or teams of native *erog*, they would pack the snow. Beneath soft snow, the swamps froze, but the frost was often honeycomb frost that would not bear weight. By contrast, where the snow was packed, the peat would freeze six- to eight-feet deep, and hard as concrete.

Kelmer left impressed, more by the resourcefulness and matter-of-fact attitude of the people undertaking all this than by what they were doing. He'd discovered a backwoods mentality, and hoped that the diplomats, in their way, could match it.

# 29

Artus Romlar awoke with something on his mind. He didn't know what inspired it. It simply arose from his "warrior kit," the set of talents and potentials he'd been born with as a warrior, freed up by the Ostrak Procedures and through meditation, and sharpened by training and experience.

He considered it while he dressed. It was important but not terribly urgent: certainly it could wait a few hours.

Normally he awoke earlier than his men; in mid-Sixdek[2] the sun didn't rise as early as it had when they'd first arrived, but at 0540 it was already well up in the northeast, high enough and warm enough to bring the morning's first bull flies buzzing sluggishly around him as he stepped out of his tent. His aide was waiting for him, and without speaking, they jogged together the two hundred yards to the exercise area, where they stretched and did light calisthenics to warm up. After a few minutes they did some easy work on the high bars and parallel bars—in field uniform with boots—increasing the intensity until they were sweating freely. That done, they did some mild tumbling runs—nothing very difficult for them—and went to the jokanru area. There they did some forms, then sparred for a while.

By 0645 he saw and heard the troopers of Headquarters Camp starting out on their morning run.

So far, he and Kantros hadn't spoken yet. In the wash area, bathing out of wooden buckets by a pump, he broke the comfortable silence, thick hard muscles bunching as he soaped himself. "Why was Komarsi security so lax?" he asked.

Kantros grunted; the question seemed rhetorical. "Because they felt secure. They didn't imagine anyone could get at them."

"What do you think of security around here?"

Kantros's lips pursed. They had a few guards around the borders of camp—limited-service Smoleni reservists—but that was all. They depended on distance and wild country to protect them here at Burnt Woods. "According to Smoleni intelligence," Kantros said, "the Komarsi T.O. doesn't include units that could operate through country like this. We've assumed the only way they could get here would be by an offensive over ninety-five miles of roads from Brigade Base Seven. Which they've abandoned; now they'd have one hundred and eighty miles up Road Forty from the Eel. If they had suitable personnel for a small strike force, they could try to penetrate without being seen, but it's very doubtful they could do it."

Blowing and sputtering, Romlar poured a bucket of cold well water over his head, then pumped another.

"Do you think they'd try?" Kantros asked.

"Not really. It seems more practical for them to select and train half a dozen infiltrators, dress them in Smoleni uniforms and send them north to wipe out Heber and his government. March up to the president's house as if they belonged there, maybe during a War Council meeting, then rush in with grenades and submachine guns. I don't doubt they have the necessary intelligence sources."

He began to dry himself. "But that could be tricky; uncertain. There'd be opportunities for mistakes, for being recognized as foreign, for blowing their cover in advance. And War Council meetings aren't on any real schedule; some days they hold one, while on others, like today, they don't.

"Suppose, though, you sent up half a dozen picked men, singly or in pairs. They might even infiltrate cross-country; they must have some who are woodswise. Brief them on what was the president's house, perhaps even what bedroom was his. And Belser's, say. They might even know what tent was mine. They could strike at night."

Fritek Kantros nodded thoughtfully. It wasn't the sort of thing one expected of the Komarsi, but it was conceivable. And Heber Lanks, it seemed to him, was the leader Smolen needed—the right personality, the right character with the right touch. He'd also become the symbol of Smoleni persistence, at home and abroad.

If Lanks was killed, whatever chance Smolen might have seemed as good as gone.

In midmorning, Romlar ran into town. Afoot, at an easy lope. He hadn't been running lately, and knew he'd lost some endurance, but he was surprised at how much. He completed the two miles leg-weary and sweating heavily, with the decision to start running regularly. He spoke first with Fossur, describing his thoughts about infiltrators, then went to Belser's headquarters.

Belser still was not cordial; cordiality was foreign to him. But he listened and nodded, and thanked the mercenary commander gruffly when he'd finished.

Romlar had no doubt at all that Belser and Fossur would establish some sort of security system for the village. He, in turn, would assign a company for security at camp.

Fossur and Belser consulted, and two-man lookout shifts were posted round the clock, in the bell-tower of the village hall. It gave a good view of the approaches to "the Cottage," a humorous term for the president's house. Guards would also be posted at each door. Perimeter guards were posted outside the village edge. The general's house and the Headquarters Company officers' billet would also have guards around the clock, and the occupants would sleep with weapons handy in their rooms.

They weren't really concerned, but it made sense to take precautions.

# 30

Oska Niemar knelt to examine the dung beside the trail. It was small and felted with hairs, but there were also tiny seeds of stinkberry. A female with a litter, then; nothing else than nursing female marets and some birds would have anything to do with stinkberries.

He straightened, and scanned the treetops. The nests built by marets to raise their young could be hard to spot. Usually they chose a high fork in some *roivan,* a leaf-tree, but in summer, the leaves obscured them.

He'd been seeing lots of signs. He'd left this part of his bounds untrapped the last two years, letting populations recover. The last two winters had been relatively mild, the snow less deep than usual. The deaths of furbearers from starvation and freezing should have been few; such years always built up populations.

He resumed his watchful walk then, his calf-length moccasins leaving little sign. His eyes noted saplings bark-stripped by *herva.* Fawns of the year, by the height and tooth marks. *Herva* numbers were high, too, after two mild winters, and jackwolves would have produced litters the last two springs to take advantage of it. There was always a good market for jackwolf pelts, soft and silver-gray in winter.

The problem would be marketing the furs, with the Komarsi blocking exports. But you could always stockpile them. The animals, on the other hand, you couldn't stockpile; come a hard winter, losses were always heavy. Trapped or not, many would die. And they were due for a hard winter.

A game trail circled a small bog pond, or rather, it circled the band of bog osier that girdled it, and despite his sixty-five years, the trapper speeded to a smooth trot. Off to his right an *oroval,* a small furbearer, trilled indignantly at him from a branch till he passed out of its territory. Now the game trail curved upward, crossing a low rounded ridge, and Oska slowed to a walk. Near the top, the sparse underbrush was burgeoning where a great old *kren* had been overthrown by wind, letting sunlight reach the ground. Had been overthrown that very summer, for its needles were still yellow-green, not tan. And wind had not acted alone; numerous pale stalks of *flute,* growing on the uptilted root disk, had curved to adjust to the new vertical. Obviously the old tree's roots had been badly rotted with flute in advance; the wind had defeated a giant already failing.

And something else—animal, not plant—had died nearby. Recently by the smell. And been mostly eaten, for the stench, though putrid, was not strong. He stopped, wet a finger at his mouth and held it up. West. He moved toward it. Nearby, behind an old, mossgrown blowdown, were the remains of a *herva* fawn. The jackwolves hadn't left much—bones, hooves, head, and scraps of hide. The pack shouldn't be far. It would surely have a litter this year, likely within a mile or so and probably somewhat closer, for they ranged no farther than necessary from the den-bound pups and mother.

He'd barely started off again when he heard the *nut-yammer.* At first scold he guessed it was screeching at a *maret* or *oroval*—some threat to its nest. But the scolding persisted without intensifying, and that told him it was likely a man. On what business? This was *his* bounds, and folks weren't likely doing wandrings with the war on.

He moved in that direction, and now his mode had changed: He trotted in somewhat of a crouch, soft-footed and smooth, more alert even than before. Not that he expected danger, but he wanted to observe unnoticed. He came to a tangle of old blowdowns, mostly broken instead of uprooted, as if a whirlwind had touched down there. The gap had grown up thick with saplings, head high and more, and he slid along its edge. The indignant *nut-yammer* was on the other side.

"I hate them little sonsabitches screechin' like that!"

The words startled Oska. People didn't often talk needlessly in the woods. Nor so loudly; the speaker seemed someone loud by nature.

"Goddamn it," said another voice, "dawn't shoot! Someone could hear!"

"Shit! Who's to hear?"

"I dawn't know and you dawn't neither. Now I'm tellin' you—"

The first man laughed. "Don't get your ass all bloody, Kodi. I wasn't gawnta shoot. The little bastard dawnt hold still long enough."

A third voice spoke then, a growl not loud enough that he caught the words. On all fours, Oska crept to where he could see them, some forty yards away. They wore uniforms, Smoleni by the look, but that dialect! He'd never heard Komarsi talk, but these strangers surely weren't from anywhere in Smolen. And they carried submachine guns!

He watched them pass out of sight, then got to his feet. He'd track them, and see where they were going.

Kro had sent Scrap Iron Nagel and Kodi Furn out as a team. Kodi was a corporal, so he'd been put in charge. The day before, they'd run into Chesty Inkermun by himself, and Chesty had joined them. His partner, Chesty said, had cut out for Krentorf.

The cramp hit Scrap Iron just as they crossed the low rock ridge and saw the creek ahead. The day was hot, and they were sweaty, and needed to refill their canteens, so the other two went on while Scrap Iron squatted down by a clump of evergreen shrubs to shit. Thus he was low, quiet, and holding still, when he glimpsed someone following them, a civilian slinking along with a rifle. The shrubs were between them, and Scrap Iron's head, with its green field cap, was just high enough to see over them. Slowly, slowly the Komarsi reached, picked up his submachine gun, and silently slipped off the safety. His pants were around his ankles; he left them there.

At about sixty feet he stood up, and the civilian, an old man, found himself staring into the muzzle of a .37 caliber SMG. It was kind of comical how surprised the old guy looked. "Drop your rifle, old man!" Scrap Iron called. Loudly, so the others would hear.

For once Chesty didn't talk. He came running, half a step ahead of Kodi. The old man had dropped his rifle, of course, and stood big-eyed and worried looking. Chesty laughed. "Well I'll be damned! What's that you got, Scrap Iron? Caught you with your pants down, dint he."

"I caught him. He was followin' us. He must have heard that loud mouth of yours."

Chesty laughed again, unpleasantly now, and walked up to the old man. "Now that you caught us, what you gawnta do, eh?" Without warning, he struck the old man in the face, getting leverage into it, knocking him flat, and while Kodi Furn stood watching, kicked him heavily and repeatedly in the body. Scrap Iron, meanwhile, wiped himself and pulled up his pants.

"Ayn't that about enough?" Kodi asked mildly.

Chesty turned, angry at the suggestion. "The old fart was gawnta bushwhack us!" Then he turned to his victim again. The old man was doubled up, his arms wrapped around his ribs, his neck corded with pain and the effort of silence. His face was a smear of blood. Chesty drew the trench knife from his belt and dropped to one knee. Before the others realized what he was doing, with a powerful stroke he severed the old man's left Achilles tendon.

"Yomal, Chesty! Cut his throat and have done!"

Chesty snarled, literally, all pretense of wit gone now. "Don't watch if you ayn't got the belly for it. I'm gawnta give 'im somethin' to remember." And turned again to the old man.

# 31

It was early evening at the Lake Loreen Institute on Iryala. Early evening but dark, for it was autumn there. A brisk wind blew, rattling the purple-bronze autumn leaves on the *peiocks*, throwing an occasional handful of them against her windows.

Lotta Alsnor didn't notice. She sat in trance, on a mat in her room. She'd spent the day coaching five selected students in advanced meditation. All were in their mid-teens, had been students at the institute since age six, give or take a few months. They'd grown up in the T'sel, and done the Ostrak Procedures through Level 8. They'd learned early to meditate, but only to the level of stilling the mind. The goal had not been to produce seers or psychics, simply highly stable, highly rational, highly ethical people for the Movement. And gradually to transform the Confederation. Psychic incidents occurred, but except for a very few persons, they were not regular events.

Lotta had been one of the exceptions, and among exceptions she'd been *the* exception. That, with her strong interest and intention, had gotten her sent to Tyss to study under Ka-Shok Masters there, and eventually under Grand Master Ku.

She'd become a recognized Master herself, but her progress had slowed, perhaps ceased. Ku had said she might or might not continue to expand, but if she did, it would be on her own; guidance could help her no further. She was welcome to continue at Dys-Hualuun, but she might do as well somewhere else.

The trance she was in was not meditative. She was checking on people for whom she felt interest and concern. It was in her power to help them, at times, even at a distance. But at a distance, such help was limited; mostly it amounted to "scripting" therapeutic dreams or opening exploratory dreams, and helping the dreamer through them. This evening she'd looked in on Tain Faronya, three hyperspace years away but getting nearer. Now she reached elsewhere.

Since undergoing the Ostrak Procedures, Artus Romlar didn't move around a lot in his sleep. Just now, however, he slept restlessly, his hard 234 pounds forcing an occasional squeak from the wooden joints of his Smoleni army cot.

He dreamed, a dream more coherent than most. In it he commanded a spaceship, an enormous warship accompanied by a fleet of lesser, subordinated vessels. They seemed not to be in hyperspace, because he could look around him and see the other ships, not as symbols generated by his ship's computer, but as if he were looking through the ship-metal sides of his flagship in a spherical 360 degrees.

He was not the giant ship's commander. He was admiral. The ships all were his, and somehow that admiralcy inspired a despair that enclosed and saturated him. The reason wasn't part of the dream.

It was a slow dream, almost like suspended animation. Things happened slowly, with long dark pauses, as if he were trying to hold something off, prevent or delay it. Men came to him with questions and reports, and to dream-Romlar they seemed unreal, insubstantial. Then another man entered the bridge, and with his entry, the dream accelerated to an apparent rate of something like normal. The man rode a wheelchair, and sat wrapped in an old-fashioned blanket as if the ship were cold. Attendants accompanied him. The hands folded on his lap were thin, showing sharp tendons and blue-gray, wormlike veins. Only his face was blurred, as if too terrible to see, but dream-Romlar knew it well, and knew he knew it.

"Are you prepared, Admiral?"

It seemed to Romlar he couldn't breathe, yet from somewhere he found the breath to speak. "I am ready, Your Imperial Majesty." He could see the eyes now, kind, loving. Implacable. Mad.

"Excellent. Give the command."

The dream slowed again. Dream-Romlar felt his lips part, his tongue poise. His vocal cords vibrated with the beginning of a word—

Romlar jerked bolt upright on his cot, sweat cold on his face, staring into the semidarkness of a moonlit night. There was no ship's bridge, no bridge watch intent on their monitors. Only a squad tent, shared with his aide and his executive officer. For a moment he sat breathing heavily, feeling enormous relief. The dream was fading, mere impressions, then they too were gone. But the feeling remained that it had been terrible, the sort of dream no one should have after the Ostrak Procedures, and certainly not after the spiritual training of the Masters of Ka-Shok.

He untucked the mosquito bar from beneath the edge of his narrow mattress, swung his feet out, got up and dressed. He needed activity, to walk, perhaps to think.

For awakening, he felt a concern that hadn't been there when he'd laid down. A concern that this war would waste his regiment, eat it up, that he would need it somewhere else but only a remnant would remain, too few to do what was necessary. True they were occupied largely with training Smoleni rangers just now, but that was temporary. It was also true that the Komarsi units they'd fought so far were neither well trained nor well led; casualties had been light.

But bold new actions were necessary. The status quo—even the new, adjusted status quo—seemed to lead ultimately to defeat for Smolen. And if the Komarsi brought in T'swa . . . The thought took Romlar by surprise, but once looked at, it seemed to him very possible.

Lotta had monitored the entire dream without impinging. Three hyperdrive years away, the kalif's invasion fleet had left Varatos, and at a very deep level, Romlar had become aware of it. It had touched, had stirred, a very powerful sequence of incidents in his remote past— many, many lifetimes past. In a vague and general way, Lotta had known it existed—Wellem Bosler did too—and what it was about. Both of them, in processing Romlar, had glimpsed it. Now she knew more, knew certain specifics.

She thought of communicating to him, then didn't. Troubled as he was just now, and introverted, he might not receive her anyway—not consciously. And at Artus's Ostrak level, to dream script for him might do more harm than good.

Besides, it would settle out by itself, for the most part, unless it was further restimulated.

She decided to look in on him from time to time though.

# 32

Kro preferred water from a wild creek to that in his canteen, even when the creek was amber brown tea, flavored with tannic acid, steeped with dead bog moss, fallen needles, and last year's leaves. His knees were wet from kneeling beside it, and a pair of bull flies bit his neck, but he swigged deep, his face to the water, drinking noisily uphill like a horse.

While he drank, a sound reached him, a yapping of jackwolves. When he'd finished, he listened, and though his knowledge of them was limited, it seemed to him they must have something treed or at bay.

He'd started this mission feeling a certain urgency, but four days in the forest had eased it. And he was curious. So instead of continuing due north, he angled off easterly toward the yapping. He found them less than a quarter mile off; they had something backed into the hollow base of a large old, fire-scarred *roivan*. They were so intent, they didn't notice him, and he edged around for a look at their victim.

It was a man!

Kro stepped forward then with a sharp shout, and the small wolves parted, startled, saw him coming toward them, and after a moment's hesitation fled silently.

The man stayed in the hollow base. He had a knife in his hand, its blade bloody, otherwise they'd have had him: dragged him out and torn him up. Kro was sure all the blood on the man's clothes wasn't wolf blood. And the man, he saw now, was elderly, his face blood-smeared.

"You gonna be all right?" Kro asked.

The old man laughed with irony. "I can't walk and they cut my nuts out," he said. "They cut my heel tendons and busted some ribs, too. Other'n that, I'm fine." He crawled from the hollow, gasping and sweating at the pain of it, then collapsed on the side where no ribs were cracked. After a long moment, he opened his eyes again and looked up at the newcomer. Realizing he'd confused the man, he explained. "My problem weren't jackwolves; it's human wolves done this to me." He eyed Kro critically. "Dressed like soldiers, same as you, but they talked like Komarsi."

Kro realized then that he'd spoken with the Smoleni accent he'd cultivated as a logger and trapper. He'd intended to, of course, when he got to Burnt Woods, but hadn't consciously thought to just now. His dialect wasn't perfect, but good enough to pass for someone from another district.

He knew damned well who'd done this—not specific individuals, but they'd been his men, no doubt of it. He knew them, to a large degree understood them, and had tolerated their aberrations, not happily but of necessity. He exhaled gustily. "Well shit! How far to the nearest folks?"

"'Bout six mile." The old man gestured eastward with his head. "There's a hand-plus of farms over there. I got a shack at my daughter's. Her man got called up with the reserves, and killed in the fight at Island Cove. I help her farm." As quickly as he'd said that, his voice changed, as if he'd just seen for the first time the long-term consequences of his mutilation. "Leastwise I used to help her."       .

Kro made a decision then, and took off his rucksack. "This is gonna hurt like fire," he said, holding the pack up. "But I want you to wear this. Then I'm gonna hoist you on my back and carry you. You'll have to tell me the way."

Oska Niemar eyed him, then nodded stoically. He'd had the notion that this man might be of a piece with the others, in spite of his speech. A submachine gun out in the bush like this, and a big, scar-faced man . . . But he weren't the same. "Put it on me," he said.

Just stretching his arms back while the stranger put the pack on him hurt badly, and when the man rose with him on his back, Oska nearly passed out. Then the stranger started walking. Every step sent pain stabbing through the old man's chest.

It was when he came to a pond surrounded by floating bog, that Kro realized the old man had passed out. He'd asked which way was best to go around, and got no answer. So he chose a way and slogged on, guided by intuition. Things got worse when he came to an old burn, littered with the crisscrossed bones of fire-killed trees, and choked with brush and saplings. He chose a direction and skirted around it. The sun was down when finally he stumbled into a hay field, grown knee-deep again since the first cutting. At the far end of the clearing was a log house and log outbuildings. Kro strode more strongly, now that an end was in sight.

The farmer and his family were eating, but forgot their food when Kro put down his burden at their door. Kro had begun to wonder if he was carrying a corpse, but there still was breath in the unconscious man, and a discernible pulse. The farmer made a stretcher out of two pitchforks and a blanket, and they carried Oska Niemar to his daughter's, a quarter mile away, while the farm wife followed.

The two women stripped and washed the old man. There wasn't much more they could do for him. Then, while the daughter put her two round-eyed children to bed, the farmer took a bottle of turpentine and splashed some on Niemar's wounded crotch as an antiseptic. When they'd put the old man to bed, the farmer and his wife went home again.

Niemar's daughter wiped her hands on her apron. "My name's Seidra. I guess you heard them call me that."

"Mine's Gull. Gull Kro." He looked at her straight. She was a handsome woman, strong, with strong hands and forearms.

"You must be hungry," she said.

Kro chuckled. "More like starved. I've been totin' your dad since midday. I was lost—don't know my way around here—and when he passed out, I got all tangled up with burns and blowdowns. Seemed I best not put him down, otherwise I'd a had to carry him over my shoulder like a sack of grain. And if his ribs are busted, like he thought, that mighta killed him."

She'd already eaten, she and her two children, but she fried up salt pork and boiled two potatoes, sliced some bread, and got butter and buttermilk from the well-house. For gravy, she heated some cold stew. He ate ravenously, and she kept him company with a slice of bread.

"Your dad said your man got killed."

Seidra nodded.

"How you gonna manage?"

"I got cousins here at Wolf Creek, and a nephew that's thirteen. And my husband's uncle will help when he can. And Tissy is nine now, old enough to take on more of the housework."

The talk dwindled then, as if she was sorting out the situation. When Kro had finished eating, she got up. "I'll show you Dad's cabin; you can sleep there. You'll prob'ly want to start for Burnt Woods tomorrow."

Kro nodded. They walked through the twilight, she with an unlit candle. At the door, she lit the candle with a waxed match. The cabin was a single room, with a small, sheet-iron stove. It was orderly, the old man's clothes hanging from wooden pegs. He told himself that if he learned who cut the old man, he'd show him what suffering was all about.

"This is it," she said. "There's *roivan* bark for kindling, if you want a fire. You got matches?"

"A fire starter," he said.

She nodded, still standing in the middle of the floor. "You been long from home?"

He nodded. She closed the door and began to unbutton her blouse.

"It's been a long time for me, too."

# 33

"Umm, Kelmer? I think we should go in the house."

He hated to stop. Weldi Lanks kissed very nicely, her lips full and moist and exciting, and his hand had begun to stroke the back of her thigh. But this was not a good place for further developments.

"I suppose you're right," he answered, and got reluctantly up from the narrow wooden bench in the rose arbor. It was dark, really dark, with a thick cloud layer cutting off the stars. The house was a vague something to their left, barely discernible. At least, he thought, the darkness had given them privacy, the most they'd had yet. Even the lookouts in the bell-tower of the village hall, assigned to watch the approaches to the president's house, couldn't see them crossing the lawn, he was sure.

The house was unlit, from this side at least. Maybe they could sit together in the parlor for a while, he thought hopefully; her father was a man who went early to bed and was up with the birds.

They went to the side porch. No uniformed guard was visible by the door but that didn't register with Kelmer. His mind was on Weldi. She wondered though, and looking around, her foot bumped something lying by the stairs, something heavy but yielding. Kelmer heard her gasp.

"What's wrong?" he murmured.

She hissed him silent, then whispered. "I think it's the guard!"

He knelt and groped. It was a man, and *his shirt was sticky with blood!* "He's dead!" Kelmer whispered.

He found the gun still holstered, and removed it. Then he stood, and setting the safety, shoved the pistol in the back of his belt. "Darling," he whispered, "go around to the front and tell the guard there. If he's—like this one, go to the rose arbor. I'm going inside."

He thought she nodded. At any rate she turned and started round the wraparound porch. He went to the door, then changed his mind. Whoever the intruder was, he was there to kill the president, and he'd have to find his bedroom. Kelmer decided to be there waiting for him. It was a corner room upstairs, with large windows opening onto the roof; Weldi'd given him the tour.

Getting onto the porch railing, Kelmer climbed a scrolled corner post and pulled himself onto the roof as quietly as possible, then began creeping along it toward the president's room. The roof sloped enough to give him nervous stomach, even without the tension inherent in the situation.

When he'd rounded the corner, he could see a faint paleness at the president's window; there was a night light on inside. The window was open but screened. He recalled that the screens downstairs were held at the bottom by a hook. Even the villages were primitive here! With the pistol barrel he poked a hole in the screen, large enough for his finger. Then, disengaging the hook, he opened the screen, and looked in.

There were two windows in the west wall and two in the south. The bed was near the southwest corner, to take advantage of breezes from either direction. The president lay on his side beneath the sheet. Kelmer couldn't hear a thing. Silently he let himself in. His right foot had barely touched the floor when he saw the bedroom door start to open, and froze.

A man stood in the door with a submachine gun. He seemed not to see Kelmer, as if his eyes had found the bed and stopped there. Kelmer stood paralyzed, his pistol untouched in his belt, as the man raised his weapon. There was a boom from the hallway behind him, and the man spun, firing a burst down the hall. For a long frozen second, Kelmer stared, then another boom shocked him out of his momentary paralysis. The would-be assassin pitched forward on his face, and the president, in a nightshirt, was moving to the door with a large pistol in his hand.

It was all over.

Weldi had found the front door unguarded too, but instead of returning to the rose arbor, had slipped inside. She had the advantage of close familiarity with the house, and moved with certainty. In the parlor was a gun cabinet. Groping, she'd found it and taken out the first gun her hands met with, a double-barreled shotgun of about ten gauge. Without even checking to see if it was loaded, she'd crossed the living room to the stairs, and started up. Like Kelmer, she was sure her father was the target of assassins.

It seemed to her she could sense someone in the hall above. She counted the carpeted steps, skipping the one that always squeaked. When she got to the top, she was unsure what to do. Then, at the far end of the hall, her father's door opened, letting faint light out, and not twenty feet in front of her she saw the back of a man who was not her father. She raised the shotgun and pressed on the trigger. Nothing happened. Then she thought, drew a hammer back with an audible click, and pulled again.

The weapon boomed. The man in front of her was the second of two, and the hammer she'd cocked was to the full-choke barrel. A concentrated load of number three shot drove into his chest from behind, killing him instantly. At the same moment, the shotgun's powerful recoil, taking her by surprise, knocked her onto her back.

The man in her father's doorway had turned and fired a burst down the hall, the slugs going above her where she lay. The president had started from his sleep with the sound of the shotgun, and with a single movement snatched up the pistol that lay on his bed table. He'd shot the remaining gunman in the back, through the heart.

There'd been just the two. Weldi had killed one, her father the other. No one had even noticed Kelmer still seated on the windowsill.

He followed the president to the door, where Heber Lanks switched on a light. The corpses lay in the hall, and Weldi was just getting to her feet. The shotgun lay on the floor. Kelmer crowded past the president and threw his arms around the girl, who clung to him shaking.

Downstairs voices were shouting, and lights were turning on. "It's all right," called Heber Lanks. "Everything is all right."

Half an hour later, Kelmer Faronya was trotting down the road toward camp. He had mixed feelings, mostly not good. He'd frozen at the climactic moment. Yet if he hadn't, the gunman would quite possibly have seen him and fired. He'd be dead now. As it was, everything had turned out well.

On the other hand, it seemed to him, his courage had failed utterly.

# 34

Gulthar Kro hiked the last sixteen miles to Burnt Woods on roads, the last five being on the main road from the south, ditched, graveled, and graded. The farm families in the Halvess settlement had accepted him as Smoleni; he'd continue as one.

He'd burned the incriminating mapbook; he didn't need it now.

The road passed through intermittent farmlands the last few miles, emerging finally from a short stretch of swamp forest to enter continuous fields. Across them he could see Burnt Woods, more than a mile away. A formation of uniformed men came toward him down the road, double-timing, and he stepped aside onto the shoulder to watch them pass. He knew them at once, though he'd never seen any before—mercenaries; a company of them. They wore a uniform like none he'd ever seen; the cut was standard, but the color was mottled green and brown and yellow. The rationale behind it was obvious. And they weren't double-timing after all; their pace was considerably faster, a brisk trot. They wore packs, too; not combat packs or field packs, but pack frames with what appeared to be sandbags.

What impressed Kro most about them was their sense of presence. He felt it as they passed; these were warriors, all the way. These were the men that had given Undsvin fits. To kill their commander might be even more difficult than he'd thought. As for escaping afterward—that, he judged, would be the real challenge.

The road he was on ended at a junction, and instead of turning east into the village, he turned west toward the merc camp, to have a look at it. Nearing it, it seemed to him much the same as any regimental camp might be. Near its near side, he saw activity, and went to watch. He'd never seen gymnastics before. The difficulties would not have impressed the judges at a meet, but the exercises they did there were powerful and demanding, and they impressed Gulthar Kro deeply. He'd never seen anyone do giant swings before. And while he'd learned as a boy to stand on his hands, and even walk on them, the mercs kipped up and planched into handstands on horizontal and parallel bars. Beyond that they did tumbling runs, boots flying, shirttails flapping.

He would have missed the close combat drills, because the jokanru ground was on the far side of camp. But an off-duty Smoleni had strolled up beside him, and the two of them carried on an intermittent conversation while they watched the gymnastics.

"Somethin', ain't it?" the Smoleni said.

"Yup. Sure is."

"You ever watch 'em practice fightin'?"

"What d'ya mean?"

"You know." The man stepped around as if in some dance, moving his arms. "Hand to hand."

Kro frowned at the exhibition. "Nope, never did. Where do they do that?"

The man pointed. "Round t' the far side." So after another three or four minutes, Kro trotted over there. Several pre-teen Smoleni boys were already watching. These drills were even more interesting to Kro than the gymnastics had been, and he began to grasp a concept he'd never known before; the concept of personal development technologies. The platoon he watched was sparring, the men matched off in pairs. One played the role of a man who had a knife but lacked jokanru. He'd attack using some technique, and his "victim" would counter and "destroy" him. Then they changed roles. These encounters were brief, over in a moment, but Kro's warrior eye, evaluating, saw how truly powerful the techniques were. Then they faced off as two jokanru opponents. Some of these bouts lasted as long as fifteen seconds, and were even more impressive. He saw the techniques here as for use between men who were more or less equals. Then the troopers grouped in threes, two as canny fighters lacking jokanru; the one would subdue the two. Kro recognized that such skills could only have grown from true talent drilled at length.

Finally that platoon moved on to other activities, another platoon replacing them. They started with stretching, even though they'd just come from the gymnastics area. Men stood on one booted foot, with the other leg out straight, foot at shoulder height, reaching out with their hands to pull back on their toes, stretching the Achilles tendon. After two or three minutes of stretching, they began their forms, as flowing and rhythmic and graceful as ballet, but moving ever faster. Watching them almost hypnotized Kro; this, he realized, was the basis of the fighting skills he'd just seen.

He watched the platoon through a full twenty-minute cycle, then hiked thoughtfully back toward Burnt Woods. *If they develop such skill in hand-to-hand fighting,* he told himself, *they no doubt do as well with their weapons.* To kill their commander, it seemed to him now, might best take an indirect approach. Perhaps he needed to get hold of a rifle, and a sniper scope if the Smoleni had them. Make his strike from a distance, then disappear into the forest. It was not an approach he cared for.

Meanwhile he needed to find a home, a unit to live with. After getting directions, he went to the Smoleni army camp south of the village, and presented himself to the personnel officer. The captain there frowned at Kro's coarse-stubbled face, and at the dirt ingrained in clothes and skin. The captured Smoleni uniform Kro wore had sergeant's insignia on the sleeves, and the unit emblem of a regiment from the Eel River-Welvarn District.

"Where have you been, Sergeant?"

Kro had had days to concoct a story, should he ever need one, and he knew enough about the fighting in the south, that spring, to make the story sound real. He'd been in the Eagle Regiment, he said, an outfit that had fought long and hard to hold the coast, and been pretty much shot to pieces. When his company was overrun, he'd hidden in a culvert. After that he'd picked his way west and north through occupied territory, traveling by night and hiding by day. Civilians had given him food, and at times had hidden him. Finally he'd reached the Free Lands, and made better time. Now he was here, reporting for assignment.

The captain bought it all. And looking beneath the unsoldierly appearance, he recognized Kro's strength and presence. There'd been an attempted assassination of President Lanks, two nights earlier, he said. Since then, 3rd Battalion had been scouring the woods for Komarsi infiltrators, and lost several men in shoot-outs. They'd be glad to have a seasoned replacement.

Gulthar Kro had a home.

# 35

Varky Graymar was trotting. He'd had hard country to cross, mountainous part of the time, and been living off the land, so when the terrain permitted, he went for speed. The sooner he delivered the letter he carried, the better.

He knew he was near settlement. Not only had the forest been logged through; the unmerchantable tops of fallen trees had been hauled away for fuelwood. Just now he ran along a narrow sleigh road.

He heard a gunshot some distance off, followed immediately by screams, almost certainly by women. He veered off, moving quietly. Shortly he heard men laughing. Ugly laughter. He slowed to a walk, his senses turned full on, Fingas Kelromak's pistol in his hand.

One thing he would not do was endanger the mission Kelromak had given him—to deliver the letter to Romlar. But he'd take a look.

He glimpsed movement ahead through the trees and undergrowth, lowered himself to hands and knees and crept to where he could see. Several *happa* trees lay freshly felled, and large baskets stood near. There were two men there. And two—three women. Two they'd bound, and seemed to have gagged. One of the men was holding the third, while the other raped her. He saw two army packs with guns lying on them, submachine guns.

Varky scanned the vicinity and saw no sign of any other men. It seemed highly unlikely that there were any; they'd be with the two. He crept forward on his elbows, pistol in his right hand, belly on the needle mat, pushing with knees and feet. The rapists seemed to be soldiers, perhaps Smoleni. He'd give them a chance to surrender.

At eighty feet he rose, pistol leveled with both hands. "On your feet," he shouted, "hands in the air."

He didn't expect compliance, and wasn't surprised at what happened. The man doing the holding half rose and dove for a gun. Varky's shot burst into the soldier's temple and blew half his forehead away. The other man pushed away and turned in a crouch.

"Hands in the air!" Varky repeated, and this one too dove for a gun. A bullet burst his upper mandible from the front, and destroyed the second and third cervical vertebrae. The woman who'd been on her back sat up staring, her face a smear of blood from someone's fist. Varky had crouched again, following the second shot, and scanned around, listening intently. He spied a fourth woman then, surely dead. After a moment he trotted over to the women who were tied, and with his knife cut them free. The cords they'd been bound with had cut deeply. They too were bloody-faced, and more or less in shock. One had lost her front teeth; the other, luckier, had had her nose broken. It took a moment before either got up. Then the one with the bloody mouth rolled to her knees, got up, and with a cry ran to the one who'd been raped. They clasped each other and wept. They were young, Varky realized, hardly more than girls.

He went to the two army packs and scouted the contents, found the mapbooks and suspected what they meant.

Then he waited, letting the women help each other, not questioning them. For whatever reason, they'd been peeling the bark from *happa* trees. Apparently the two men, seemingly Komarsi infiltrators, had heard them.

He relaxed, and undertook to commune with the spirits of the three dead. He could sense them in the vicinity of their bodies, but at first none of the three acknowledged him. They were too deeply in shock.

Then the spirit of the woman responded, and he perceived through her what had happened. They'd been collecting bark for bark flour, only a mile or so from home, when they'd been attacked. She was older, an aunt. When she'd tried to stand the two men off with an axe, they'd gut-shot her. She might have lived, but the bullet had cut a major artery, and she'd bled to death internally.

She gave her attention to the surviving women then, but they weren't aware of her, and after another minute she left. Varky didn't notice when the spirits of the two men left. They'd been there, then were gone.

The girl with the broken teeth helped the naked girl put on her cut and torn clothing, and when they were done, they all started home. None of them said a word to Varky till they stopped at a creek to wash the blood off. Then the girl with the broken nose came over to him. The blow had caused her eyes to swell; she peered through slits now. She told him essentially what the dead woman had shown him. She also said that the men weren't Smoleni, she'd known that at once from their speech. "Komarsi," she said. "They'd got to be Komarsi."

They passed the first farm, going on to the one the two sisters were from. The people there had heard the shots, but occasional gunshots weren't alarming in the backcountry.

At the farm the girls were from, Varky was an instant hero, the man who, with a pistol, had shot two Komarsi soldiers armed with submachine guns. And saved the girls' lives, there was little doubt.

They questioned him more from curiosity than any demand to know. He sounded Smoleni, but his work clothes weren't those of a woodsman, and his accent wasn't quite what they were used to. He told them a version of the truth: that he was one of the Iryalan mercenaries, "the white T'swa." He'd been spying in Komars, and was returning to Burnt Woods when he heard the shot and investigated.

✧          ✧          ✧

Varky would not have to run the last thirty-four miles to Burnt Woods. After they fed him, they put him on a horse, and two men rode with him, rifles across their horses' withers, in case they ran into any more infiltrators.

# 36

The Smoleni platoon sergeant dismissed his men to wash up for supper, and went to his lieutenant. "Lieutenant, you know the new man? Kro? I had 'em all to the range, shootin' at jump-up targets, and that son of a gun shot a perfect score. Tough-lookin' cuss, too, but he seems to get along all right. Just don't talk much. And gettin' here like he did, all those miles through Komarsi territory . . ."

"So?"

"Him already havin' sergeant's stripes, I heard the cap'n say he was gonna make a squad leader out of him, if he worked in all right. But seems to me he might better be transferred to one of the ranger units the mercs are trainin'. They're trainin' up officers from scratch, in the ways they do things, and from the way Kro acts, and what little he says, seems like he'd make a good one. Appears to be smart, and he's the kind that, if he told me somethin', I'd pay attention. A born leader's what he is."

The lieutenant shook his head. "If he's that good, I'd hate to lose him. And we're short now; two men killed moppin' up infiltrators, and already seven gone to the mercs for trainin'."

The sergeant nodded. "But we're gonna lose him anyways. We don't need a squad leader. He'll get assigned to some other platoon; maybe even some other company."

The lieutenant looked at that for a few seconds, turning it over in his mind. "Mm-m. I'll talk to the captain about it. If he's willin', I suppose that might be best. If this Kro is that good, that's prob'ly where he oughta be."

# 37

Romlar had read Fingas Kelromak's letter and carried it personally to President Lanks. Lanks had read it, gone over it with Elyas Fossur, then radioed Romlar's headquarters: He wanted him to attend a War Council meeting in the morning, and he wanted Corporal Graymar there to describe personally what had happened.

Scrubbed, shaved, and wearing a clean field uniform, Varky described his experience briefly to the council. Then the president spoke. "I'll read the letter to you," he said, and adjusting his half-moon spectacles, he began. After brief self-identification, Kelromak had written that a large part of the Komarsi public—perhaps a majority—were badly disillusioned with the war, and that numerous persons of economic and political influence even said as much. But not publicly; their discontent was not strong enough to make them so bold.

And if the wealthy were unhappy with the war, the laboring classes would be at least equally unhappy, for they were particularly hurt by the shortages and currency inflation of war time. Thus there seemed to be a potential for civil disorders that could well bring agitation by the nobility and merchants to end the war.

After that, the letter included pages cut from a Reform Party journal, reviewing the class of freedmen. Serfs were bound by law to the estate they were born on, and under ordinary circumstances were not accepted by the armed forces. But commonly during war and the preparations for war, they were, and satisfactory completion of their military service gained for them the status of freedmen.

Some newly freed serfs found employment quickly enough, and became part of the general commons, more or less, though there tended to be a lingering prejudice against them. Most however, gathered in shanty settlements at the edges of the larger towns, where they provided a body of casual labor, and made a more or less precarious living. The movement of shanty-towners into the population of general commoners was slow, and in general they were chronically discontented.

The freedmen also provided most of the subclass called "drifters," men who drifted about the country doing casual labor wherever they could find it. Shanty-towners and drifters contributed much, and probably most, of the crime in Komars.

Following the cutout pages, Kelromak suggested an action; the raiders who'd struck targets in and around Linnasteth had proven themselves resourceful men who could pass for Komarsi. Judging by the courier, they were also bold, physically impressive, and had presence—the sort of men who could become dominant in harvest crews, which consisted mostly of drifters. And Kelromak believed that, properly incited and led, the freedmen could be brought to disorders, even insurrections here and there. Which might be as effective as an army in bringing the war to an end with Smolen surviving.

His final item was quite different. And troublesome. It was rumored, he said, that Engwar had sent an agent to The Archipelago to contract for a pair of T'swa regiments. He considered the source reliable.

When the president had finished reading, the room was quiet for long seconds. Then Vestur Marlim had a question for Varky Graymar: "What do you think of this Lord Kelromak?"

"I trust him. And the people who work for him like and respect him. Also, he was injured during our hit on the War Ministry, so apparently he has business with them."

Fossur spoke then. "Kelromak's a leader of the Reform Party. His father was Marn Kelromak, who led the party till he got so radical he frightened them—worried them at least—and they elected someone else to the job. The family has a history of reformist causes."

The president looked thoughtfully at the tabletop, then across at Varky. "And he gave you his pistol. Did you have the slightest urge to shoot him?"

Varky looked surprised at the question. "None whatever, Mr. President."

"Any discomfort at being given the gun?"

"No, sir. I wasn't even surprised at it, though I hadn't foreseen the possibility."

Lanks looked at his council. "It is my observation that our mercenaries are unusually perceptive. I give Corporal Graymar's impressions more than a little weight."

Belser looked at Fossur and spoke. "Elyas, have your agents picked up anything about a T'swa contract?"

Fossur shook his head. "Not a hint of it. All we have is this letter."

"Perhaps it's not true then."

"Possibly not. But given Komarsi wealth and Engwar's pride, and their recent embarrassments, I rather suspect it is."

Heber Lanks spoke then: "Colonel Romlar, do you have any comments?"

"Yes. Regarding the T'swa: They won't send him two regiments, unless they're greatly reduced regiments, somewhat smaller than mine. It's lodge policy. And considering scheduled graduations, they're very unlikely to get a new and unreduced regiment. In fact, they may very well have to wait a bit for any at all. What they can expect is a short regiment—at least somewhat short."

Belser interrupted. "Colonel," he said slowly, "could you defeat a T'swa regiment?"

Romlar leaned back and folded thick arms over a thick chest. "One not much larger than mine—maybe. Note that I didn't say probably. I also consider the reverse to be true: they could quite possibly defeat us. But I don't consider that the key issue here. They can play a more important role by attacking you, and I have little doubt they'll tell Engwar that. Just as I can make the greatest difference by attacking the Komarsi.

"Regarding their importance to this war: They are *very* good, very dangerous. But their advantage over you is less than our advantage over the Komarsi." Romlar paused, looking the room over, and repeated himself before elaborating. "You have many troops well suited to traveling and maneuvering in the forest, troops who respond quickly to situations. They're not likely to panic or freeze if surprised. All in all, they're a lot better suited to fighting the T'swa than the Komarsi are to fighting my men. This is particularly true of the units we're training now, the ranger units. They're not equal to the T'swa, not at all. But the T'swa will find them dangerous opponents, opponents to tell stories about in their old age—those few who live to old age.

"The T'swa can't destroy you by fighting us. They can only destroy you by fighting you. And we cannot defeat Komars by fighting the T'swa, but we can strike the Komarsi and hurt them deeply."

It was Belser again who questioned. "Then you don't expect to fight the T'swa?"

"I don't expect to seek out the T'swa. Nor do I expect them to seek us out. But will we fight each other? I have no doubt of it. Circumstances will see to that. We'll meet; sooner or later we'll meet. And then we'll fight."

He leaned forward now, resting his elbows on the table. "We haven't talked about Kelromak's suggestions yet. If Colonel Fossur thinks they might be worthwhile, we need to act, to get agitators into Komars before harvest."

The meeting went on to other matters then. When it ended, Heber Lanks watched thoughtfully as the others left. His mind was on the comment he'd made after listening to Corporal Graymar: that the mercenaries seemed exceptionally perceptive.

No doubt it was that perceptivity, as much as their fighting skills, that made them so effective—enabled them to do what they had. It would be useful in battle and in planning. And Colonel Romlar—so often when he thought of him, it was with the shadow label "the boy colonel"— Colonel Romlar undoubtedly brought that perceptivity to the War Council.

He'd make a point of asking him to attend more often.

✧    ✧    ✧

Romlar didn't leave at once. Instead he went with Fossur to the intelligence chief's office, where they discussed how to insert troopers into Komars as agitators. Fossur seemed to have sources of information everywhere, and remarkable recall for details. His orderly brought lunch for both of them, and when Romlar finally left, it was with a written plan.

Carrmak would lead the infiltrators. Esenrok would take over Carrmak's battalion.

Driving himself back to camp, something else surfaced in Romlar's mind. The T'swa would come, he had no doubt. His men were able, and as a commander he'd shown himself equal to the T'swa. At least equal. But the prospect of fighting them troubled him.

Well. Every T'swa regiment got used up sooner or later; it was the other side of being warriors. It hadn't bothered him on Terfreya, when he'd lost so many, and he'd seen no sign that it troubled his troopers. Not even Jerym, who'd been sent repeatedly to lead men into no-return situations.

And his old cadre—Sergeant Dao, Sergeant Banh, Captain Gotasu—they'd all been through it. Found fulfillment in it. After four wars on four worlds, Colonel Dak-So had lifted from Marengabar with fewer than two hundred men of what had been the Shangkano Regiment.

Was there something that different about losing men on Maragor?

If Lotta were here they'd sort it out, he had no doubt.

# 38

Council meetings in Linnasteth were quite different from those in Burnt Woods. Different as the personnel were different, especially the central figures, Engwar II Tarsteng and Heber Lanks.

General Undsvin Tarsteng had never attended one before. His role in the war had been limited entirely to carrying out the king's edicts, and that was the way he preferred it. As a first cousin of Engwar, they'd been childhood playmates periodically, and sometime associates in adolescent mischiefs. It had been Undsvin, two years the elder, who'd introduced Engwar to the pleasures of having serving girls available, an activity not unusual in many noble households.

But he'd never been an adviser—hadn't even seen his cousin since the war began—and wondered what this "invitation" meant.

He arrived by floater and was escorted limping to the council chamber by a sycophant he would willingly have done without. He found Engwar's entire council waiting, and waited with them. They were expected to be early, and to wait without conversation; it was a foible of Engwar's. Eventually a marshal entered, and announced, "His Majesty the King!" Everyone got to their feet, and Engwar entered, well guarded. He was pale, his expression strained; Undsvin wondered if his cousin had been ill.

The king said nothing as he walked to the head of the table. He took his seat stiffly, and without even calling the meeting to order, made an announcement that stunned all of them.

"I am going to end the war," he said. "I am going to requisition every floater in my realm and drop bombs on the Smoleni government, every Smoleni supply depot, and on the mercenary camps!" When he'd finished, his expression dared anyone to disagree.

Undsvin stared. He couldn't believe what his cousin had said. Currently the war in Smolen was the only war on Maragor, which meant that all three Confederation monitor platforms would be parked over this part of the continent. And the Confederation Ministry in Azure Bay reportedly had more than its share of agents planetwide, their ears everywhere.

It was the Foreign Minister, Lord Cairswin, who broke the silence, after first rising, as protocol required. "Indeed, Your Majesty, that would certainly break the Smoleni ability to resist, and no doubt weaken their will. How did you plan to keep this action secret from the Confederation?"

"The Confederation be damned! They cannot dictate to me!"

"Of course not, Your Majesty. But after the deed is done . . . do you have a plan for that?"

Engwar didn't answer, but his eyes seemed to bulge with anger. Undsvin eyed the Foreign Minister, a man tall and lean and calm. He had guts; he was taking his life in his hands. "They'll probably let you choose your successor," Cairswin went on, "but whoever you select, it would be best if he has a plan of government when the Confederation task force . . ."

"SHUT YOUR MOUTH!"

Cairswin bowed and sat down. Again no one spoke. It occurred to Undsvin that if Engwar insisted on this—and he was nothing if not obstinate—it could well bring on a coup before he could carry it out. And the coup would be justified. For aerial bombardment—even aerial reconnaissance—was banned in Level 3 wars. And a Confederation takeover would ruin every family involved in top government levels; it had happened before, elsewhere.

Undsvin found himself on his feet then. "I've heard, Your Majesty, that you're bringing in T'swa. Two regiments in fact."

"They'll only let me have one! And it won't be here for deks!"

"Ah! But bombing—Heber Lanks would hardly live to crow, but later, when the Confederation marines arrived, the remaining Smoleni would be enjoying victory, while we'd be eating ashes and drinking gall. Komars would be stripped to pay reparations and penalties. A shame, when there are alternative means of breaking Smoleni insolence. Of burning their hopes and costing them blood and supplies."

He bowed to his cousin then. "You are the king, of course; your will be done. But truly, Your Majesty, I hope that in your wisdom you'll reconsider."

Engwar stared narrow-eyed at his cousin. "Indeed! And what is this alternative means of breaking Smoleni insolence?"

"I've given it careful thought," Undsvin lied. "I propose a destructive strike deep into Smoleni territory, with mounted infantry and mobile artillery. Not to capture more territory, but to strike and destroy Smoleni supply depots. Their supply situation is desperate, as you know, and they'll have to defend them with everything they can bring to bear."

The ideas had begun to flow for Undsvin as he spoke, and his assurance infected the others, even Engwar. "We succeeded early in the war, when we forced them to defend fixed locations. We could bring our strength to bear on them then. More recently, facing the vast Smoleni forests, we ceased to attack, and they brought what force they had against fixed positions of ours. I'm simply proposing to reverse this again. We can bloody and rout their defending forces and capture their supplies. Next winter will be hungry for them at best. This move will leave them truly desperate, while the capture of their munitions will make them less able and less willing to fight."

All that was left of Engwar's earlier rage was a jutted jaw. *He's given in,* Undsvin thought. *But he'll want to save face with these others.* "Indeed!" Engwar said. "You should have told me in advance."

"I'd thought to use the T'swa in this, as well as forces of our own."

"Umh! When will you start?"

"It will take some preparations, Your Majesty, notably logistical." Engwar's brow pulled down. "But four weeks should do it."

He'd prefer more time, but better to say four weeks and strive for it. After four weeks, Engwar's attention would have gone to something else, perhaps the approaching arrival of the T'swa. A request then for two or three more weeks wouldn't seem like much.

"Very well." Engwar looked around the table. "All right. Arlswed, give us your intelligence report."

The room seemed almost to lift with relief.

On the flight back to Rumaros, Undsvin examined possible resources and tactics. And possible uses for his personal unit. He knew where he'd gone wrong there. Strength and fighting qualities (among which he included arrogance) were more easily recognized in hooligans, but most hooligans lacked other necessary qualities.

He wondered how many Gulthar Kros there were unrecognized in the army, men deadly yet disciplined. Very few, he suspected. But surely there was a sizeable number who more or less approached Kro in soldierly qualities. Perhaps when the war was over, he'd make a project of finding them, perhaps even enough for a battalion.


# 39


The train rolled through a shallow valley whose sides curved mildly up. Sheep grazed its grasses. Beside the tracks, a considerable river surged and roiled, the color of clear tea.

The train was mostly ore cars, full of reddish earth and stone, but behind the engine was a single coach, such as might take bachelor miners to town for the weekend. This, however, was Threeday.

There was no long plume of coal smoke trailing behind, snowing acid soot, for this train rode an electrified track. Thus the coach wore a pair of cupolas, with seats for those who wished to watch. Coyn Carrmak sat absorbing the scenery. Behind the train, the late sun lowered in the rounded notch that was the valley. Ahead, the ground disappeared into a much sharper, deeper notch—the fjord.

They rolled into it, and the grade steepened. To the side, the valley walls had become emerald green scarps, with dark wedges and strips of trees. The stream no longer flowed. It leaped, foamed, plunged toward the hydroelectric plant, dropping far more steeply than the tracks. Afternoon was left behind, replaced by false evening born of shadow, the shadow of the walls themselves.

A few miles ahead and a thousand feet lower, Carrmak could see larger water, Deep Fjord, with its harbor and nitrates plant.

And unless something had gone wrong, a ship from The Archipelago that would carry him and his forty troopers to Linnasteth, unarmed. Their weapons there would be their minds and tongues.

# 40

They left Deep Fjord in moderately rough seas, the wind out of the southeast at first, shifting round to the east, then to the north of east. Thus the SS *Agate Cliffs* took the seas more or less broadside. She rolled heavily, and in their hidden compartment, the troopers were crowded. Most of them were seasick, too, a condition contributed to by the sickness and stink of those who got sick first, and by the honey pots.

For there was no fresh sea air where they were. Their narrow compartment had been built into the starboard trim-tank, hurriedly and specifically to accommodate them. At the dock in Deep Fjord, in a single night, by the chief engineer, no less, with the help of his first assistant and four Oselbenti. Most of the crew had been ashore or asleep.

The idea was that no one, especially no crewmen, should know who didn't have to. Light was provided by two drop cords. Sanitary facilities were three steel drums, each cut off at about twenty-two inches, with a top welded on, and baffles, and a seat and hinged lid. Handles of steel rod had been welded to the sides for carrying. Drinking water came from pails with dippers. Holes had been cut in a bulkhead, opening into the portside fuel bunker, thus what air they got smelled of coal dust.

It hadn't been feasible to bring mattresses aboard, not secretly. So for beds they had folded tarpaulins—old, worn hatch tarps stored overhead in the boiler room to supply tarp patches, and hand rags for the firemen. They were softer than the bare steel plates.

Their only heat was body heat. When they'd first slipped aboard, about three o'clock one morning, the night had been chill. The seawater was cold too, and the ship. But after a time their compartment warmed up, from their bodies and the poor ventilation.

Food, for those who could eat, and water was passed to them through a hatch by the four A.M. to eight A.M. deck watch. Twice a day: once before dawn, just after he came on his morning watch, and once after dark, not long after he got off his evening watch. At first, he was the only one aboard who had any contact with them, and one of only five who knew they were there. For obvious reasons, the food required no preparation. It was loaves of sliced bread, cans of jelly, a pot of beans, and fruit. On his own, the deckwatch passed them an unofficial jug of whiskey, too. He was also the ship's medic, and the whiskey was part of the closely guarded medicinal supply. They ate little, even those who weren't sick, and drank almost none of the whiskey. Mostly they slept and meditated, waiting.

Coyn Carrmak was one of those who hadn't gotten seasick. What he had gotten was a chest cold, one of several, before the ship had ever left the dock. Faintly the deck watch heard their coughing as he crossed overhead, and passed a warning message to them later. From that point the coughers huddled under a piece of tarp and did their coughing there. They still could be heard, but the sound was faint, and not easily identified.

What worried the *Agate Cliffs'* captain was Komarsi paranoia from the Day of Destruction. In Komars, the authorities didn't even allow ship's crew ashore, not even to handle lines on the dock! Longshoremen were assigned to that. He'd been warned to expect ship inspectors aboard as soon as the *Cliffs* tied up, hunting for possible infiltrators. If they heard the coughing, they'd surely investigate.

The chief engineer provided a possible solution. He personally strung a cable over the grating close above the boilers, tightened it with a turn-buckle, and hung a tarpaulin over it to form a sort of tent. There were two boxes to sit on. In the dark of night, the coughers were led from their hideout two at a time, and hustled to the makeshift sauna to spend an hour baking. It was hotter than a summer afternoon on Tyss, and weakened them temporarily, but their coughing lessened.

This project required that two more crewmen become privy to the secret: the stoker on the twelve-to-four watch, and his coal trimmer. It was unavoidable. They were told only that these were four Smoleni spies, and were sworn to secrecy. *No one else must know, not their messmates, no one. Not now, not later. Their grandchildren perhaps, if they ever had any.* Like Archipelagons in general, the crew didn't like Komars, and liked even less their assault on Smolen, so the two swore willingly, and their oath was readily accepted. They didn't know about the other thirty-six troopers.

On the third day, the rolling ceased. Carrmak was awake, and noticed it at once. The ship still rose and fell, but the seas were from the stern now, and he realized they'd turned, were headed west into the Komar Gulf. To the southwest would lie Komars, to the northwest what had been the Smolen coast. A few hours later, all wave motion was gone; they'd entered the Komar River. Occasionally, through the deck plates, he heard the ship's whistle as they met outbound ships in the river. Then he slept.

The trimmer, on break from his wheelbarrow, came to take them again to the dark boiler room. On deck, Carrmak saw sparse lights on both sides of the river, but mostly on the south where Komars lay. They moved silently to the boiler room door, heat flowing sluggishly from it as from the entrance to hell. Inside was scarcely less dark than night. They entered, and descended a ladder to the grating and their sauna tent.

Inside the tent, Carrmak relaxed, became semicomatose. Soaking up the heat, breathing the dry hot air, he lost track of time. From the other side of the bulkhead, the dull booming of pistons lulled him. From the

boiler room itself came little more than the sound of the shovel ringing on the deadplates, as the stoker fed the fires, and the sound of coal
being dumped from a wheelbarrow.

At one point he heard bells jangle. The ship slowed, stabilizing at half
speed. He'd almost dozed again when the jangling repeated. The speed
slacked even more, and he became aware of another change in sound:
the great induction fan had ceased turning, ceased sucking air through
the boiler fires. Close at hand, a chuffing sound began, somehow alarming.

*Abruptly the safety valves blew, first on the starboard boiler, a second
later on the port. The sound was stupendous, overwhelming, driving both
troopers to their knees, hands over their ears. Seconds later the deckwatch
was crouching in the opening of their tent, face a twisted grimace at the
sound, beckoning them to come.*

They followed him quickly, down another ladder into the stoke-hole.
Usually it was semidark, lit only by two small tubes. Now the four big
fire boxes added to the light, their doors open to cool the backheads and
help draw down the steam pressure. The stoker stood alone, eyes
squinched, jaw set against the sound, frowning questioningly at them.
Speech was hopeless in the thunder of the safety valves. In response, the
deckwatch gestured and shook his head, then hurried the two troopers
to the far bulkhead and into the bunker alley. There a single tube gave
light enough to work by. At the far end, the sinewy coaltrimmer stood
by his big-bellied wheelbarrow. Speech was possible there by shouting.

A Komarsi guard boat had pulled alongside, the deck watch told them.
They were going to put inspectors aboard now; that's why the ship had
slowed to slow-ahead. Unexpectedly, which had caused the valves to blow.
The two troopers would pretend to be trimmers. "Get in the stokehole,"
he told the trimmer. "Grab a shovel and pretend to be a stoker." The
trimmer, a teenage boy, grinned, nodded, and hurried out.

"You!" the deckwatch said, gesturing at Carrmak, "take the shovel!"

Then he left the alley, shooing the other trooper ahead of him. The
trimmer had been filthy with coal dust, so Carrmak buried his hands
in slack, then rubbed them on his face, his shirt, his thighs. Behind him
the safety valves cut off, the sudden silence a lifting of oppression. He
heard clashing then, as the stoker and trimmer closed the heavy furnace
doors. After a couple of minutes he heard voices, one interrogating, the
others answering. With his shovel he began to load the wheelbarrow,
tossing the coal to make a maximum of dust. It billowed 'round him.
He became aware of someone blocking the door to the bunker alley, and
looked up. A strong flashlight caught him in its glare. He grimaced, and
raised a hand to shield his eyes. Then the light was gone. He finished
filling the barrow and stood for a long two or three minutes. The trimmer came back in, still grinning.

"They've gone," he murmured. "Stupid fookin' Komarsi lubbers! They think it takes two to fire a watch on this bucket!" He shook his head at such ignorance. "Stay here awhile, till we go to half speed. That'll mean they've left the ship."

He grinned again, and thrust out a filthy hand. They gripped and shook.

Ten minutes later, the deck watch led the two troopers back to their covert, and came inside long enough to talk. "They took us by surprise," he told them. "It's occurred to them that a ship could send someone ashore by boat or raft, so now they check when you first enter the Linna.

"Be ready. I 'spect the skipper'll want to unload you before too long. In case there's more surprises ahead."

Actually they didn't leave till near dawn. The freighter slowed briefly to slow ahead, and put a life raft into the water through the fantail gangway. Half a dozen troopers got onto it, and the deck watch let go with the boat hook. The ship was passing only fifty feet from the channel's edge, so they didn't have to row. They were on a rope end, which gave them velocity, and used the steering oar to slant them ashore. Then the raft was pulled back to the gangway for another load.

It was the right side of the river, too. Linnasteth was upstream on the far side, and that's where security would be strongest.

They were spread along a mile of riverbank, of course. But they didn't need to rendezvous; in fact, to do so would be unwise. And they all knew what they were supposed to do.

# 41

Kelmer Faronya had spent six days recording the trooper-directed training of a ranger company. The emphasis was on small-unit tactics in T'swa-type actions. The trainees learned quickly. And enthusiastically, for this was the kind of tactics that felt right and natural to them.

They'd been six good days for Kelmer. Days and nights, for there'd been night exercises too. But through it all he'd had a piece of his attention on Weldi Lanks.

Seemingly neither father nor daughter had realized his funk that night; hadn't been aware that he'd stood unable to move when the Komarsi infiltrator had pushed the door open, prepared to gun the president down. Weldi had even regarded him as a hero, for having been there. Particularly for having gotten there as he had, climbing a pole and working his way along the sloping roof.

He'd said nothing to disillusion her. Inwardly he even agreed that she had a point; he'd made the effort, and put himself at serious risk. He wasn't even sure that he might not have acted, tried to shoot the gunman, if the circumstances had been slightly different. And as it stood, he'd done the right thing. But he remembered the fear and paralysis he'd felt when the Komarsi had pushed the door open. Thus he found little solace in that rightness.

Despite his self-invalidation, he had sense enough to realize that in life as a whole he was competent: intelligent, diligent, and generally ethical. And when the war was over, his production here would make him a celebrity video-journalist at home on Iryala. His income would be quite good.

Weldi clearly dreamed of living on Iryala someday. A dream very difficult to realize for a citizen of a trade planet, even the daughter of a president, because immigration visas to Confederation member worlds were few and hard to get. Except for spouses of Confederation citizens.

He told himself that when he'd finished his week with the ranger trainees, he'd visit Weldi. And if the time seemed right, he'd ask her to marry him.

Weldi had observed some training that week too. With Colonel Fossur's wife, she'd gone to the mercenary camp and watched their morning workouts in gymnastics and jokanru. And been very impressed. Could Kelmer do those things? she wondered.

When he came to call, the next evening, they'd walked together along the millpond. She'd left the house without saying anything; otherwise her father would have sent armed guards with them. It seemed to her that if any assassins had survived the sweeps, they'd have shown themselves by then or fled the district. Besides, Kelmer carried a pistol on his belt now.

He told her what he'd seen, while he'd been away, and she told him of seeing the troopers train. "Can you do those things?" she asked, and having asked, wondered if she should have. For if he couldn't, it might embarrass him.

He grinned and nodded. "Not as well as they do, though. They trained for six years; I trained for one. In the first year you only learn the basics of jokanru—of hand-to-hand combat. But—" He stopped, stripped off his shirt, and crouching, planched into a handstand, then walked on his hands for her on the uneven ground, ending with a dozen handstand pushups. In a tanktop, his muscles were quite impressive. She watched delighted. When he was back on his feet once more, she asked to feel his bicep. He flexed his arm and she squeezed it, first with fingertips, then with a whole-handed squeeze.

"Oh!" she said. "It's so hard! And so *big*!" Then blushed delicately.

Kelmer blushed more vividly. And somehow, that evening, couldn't bring himself to propose. It hadn't been fear, he insisted inwardly on his way back to camp. After her comment, it just hadn't been the right time for it.

Weldi watched between the curtains as Kelmer trotted off up the graveled street. He'd been so sweet, blushing as he had. She guessed he'd be good in bed; he had a wonderful body. He'd be surprised how good she'd be. Not that she'd had experience, but she'd daydreamed of making love often enough. She'd even done some heavy petting with a younger cousin, a couple of times. She'd been fifteen then.

She wouldn't go that far with Kelmer though. He wasn't thirteen, and she wasn't stronger than he was. Besides, if they made love before they were engaged, he might not propose.

# 42

They were an entire brigade, the 3rd Mounted Infantry. And they'd arrived, they thought, to take part in maneuvers. Five miles west was another brigade, the 6th, with the same idea, prepared to be their opposition. The mounted infantry were proud units, proud and privileged—*ride* to battle, then fight on foot—and the 3rd and 6th were judged the two best brigades in the Komarsi army. Their troops were the sons of yeoman farmers, sturdy, self-reliant young men who considered themselves much better than units manned by serfs and freedmen, and willing to prove it if asked.

Maneuvers were to begin the next morning, and surprisingly they'd been allowed to lay around camp all day; no drill, no fatigue duty. And like all soldiers, they knew what to do with slack time: sleep. So that day, napping was the principal activity of two brigades, some twelve thousand Komarsi soldiers.

Only a few hundred had pulled duty, loading caissons and light but rugged campaign wagons. The brigades' packs and saddlebags were already packed, ready for the next morning.

They were three miles south of the Eel River, the boundary between Komarsi-occupied south Smolen and the Free Lands.

Autumn was pending, the nights much longer than they'd been. It was twilight when bugles blew, calling the men from the tents they'd occupied. Within the hour they'd struck camp and were riding north toward the Eel through moonless night.

The 3rd Brigade stopped a mile from Mile 40 Bridge, and were told that this was no exercise. The same was happening to the 6th, near Mile 45 Bridge. They were going to strike deeply into Smoleni territory. Very deeply. A thrill passed through the young soldiers, spiced with a tinge of fear. This promised to be a different kind of action than the drive to the sea that spring: more venturesome, less predictable.

They were to wait till *Eliera* rose, then ride most of the night. With luck, the Smoleni wouldn't know they were there till after daylight.

# 43

The squad of young Smoleni soldiers had made their hidden out-camp as comfortable as they could. They were recon cavalry, an outpost with radio, set to watch Mile 40 Bridge over the Eel. There was a similar squad watching every other bridge. It was isolated duty, but included no drill or make-work. Nor was there any commissioned officer, just Sergeant Murty, though Lieutenant Hoos checked on them every day or two.

They had a small lookout platform in the top of a tall, clean-boled *jall*, with a rope ladder to climb it. A pair of side branches had been removed in its top, giving a clear view of the bridge, but the platform itself would be hard to spot. The tree stood on the riverbank two hundred feet downstream of the bridge, and it seemed unlikely that the Komarsi knew it was there, or that they were.

Private Tani Berklos had stood a number of lookout watches so far—he'd lost track of how many. You stood watch one hour in eight, theoretically so you wouldn't get bored and careless. By day, watching was easy. By night, if it was cloudy enough or there was no moon, you listened and imagined. Of course, by night, two other men watched from a thicket near the base of the bridge, too. He'd pulled that duty, they all had, and preferred the platform.

Just now there was no moon, and clouds dimmed the starlight. He could sort of make out the bridge, but he couldn't have seen anyone crossing it.

Off watch they were allowed to sleep as much as they wanted, on the assumption that they wouldn't then get sleepy on watch. And there was some truth to that. But just now, Private Berklos was fighting sleep. There weren't even many mosquitoes to help; their numbers had dwindled greatly through the drier than normal summer.

Even standing he'd dozed, and stand you must, for there was no place to sit. Unless you sat on the small platform itself, which was strictly against orders. There was a safety line around it, about waist high, so you wouldn't fall off, but Tani didn't trust it. He feared that if he fell asleep standing, he might fall and be killed. So in spite of orders, he sat down with his back to the trunk and his knees drawn up. He had no doubt at all that he'd fall asleep, so he draped one wrist over a ladder step. If Sergeant Murty came to check, or his relief started up, he'd feel the ladder jerk, and waken.

To his credit, he tried hard to stay awake. He pinched himself, rubbed his bur-cut with his knuckles, and thought about girls. It wasn't enough. His lids closed without his realizing it.

It was the ladder that woke him, and he jerked to his feet. Enough time had passed that *Eliera* had risen, and he could see the bridge plainly despite the clouds. Nothing was there but the timbers and planking. Meanwhile his relief climbed faster than he'd expected, and when the man stepped onto the platform, Tani turned to say something. And realized, even in the cloud-dimmed moonlight, that the grinning face before him was one he'd never seen before.

A trench knife struck deeply into Tani's abdomen and thrust upward into the heart. He didn't even have time to scream. But then, none of his squad were alive to hear him if he had.

# 44

Third Brigade had ridden till after daylight before they met opposition. Till then there'd been no evidence that it had been detected. The lead battalion was crossing an open field when a Smoleni force estimated at two companies of infantry opened fire from the cover of forest, with rifles, machine guns, and light mortars. The Komarsi dismounted and advanced. Fighting was heavy but brief; the Smoleni were flanked and routed. Two miles up the road, another small Smoleni force repeated the performance.

The apparency was that they were trying to gain time, to bring more forces and no doubt prepare some sort of defensive positions.

Private Marky Felkor knelt behind a fallen tree, one of many felled across the road, more or less crisscross, their tops pointing generally south, toward the enemy. And not just across the road; the barrier stretched on each side of the road for two to three hundred feet, though it was deepest in the road. It would be hard to flank, too. One flank of the barrier was guarded by fen, the other by moss bog, in either of which a horse would sink to its knees.

The Komarsi were coming, supposedly a whole division of them, and 2nd Battalion, 5th Regiment, was supposed to hold them here as long as they could.

Fifth Regiment had taken heavy losses defending the coast that Fourdek, and many of its replacements were like Marky, less than eighteen years old, without combat experience, and short on training. But Marky was from the back-country; his ax had felled a number of the trees in the barrier, and he was at least as good with the rifle as the ax.

Ahead he heard a rattle of rifle fire, as Komarsi scouts met Smoleni skirmishers. Gradually the noise grew, coming nearer. On the flanks, along the open fen and bog, mortars thumped, preregistered on the road ahead. *That'll slow 'em,* Marky thought. Moments later he heard the crashes of mortar bombs landing, hopefully among the Komarsi. Ahead, the rifle fire slacked. Either the skirmishers were being overrun, or the Komarsi had backed away.

Another sound overrode the spatter of rifle fire then, a thundering sound not too far ahead. A muted rumbling followed, like nothing Marky had ever heard before. But he'd heard it described, and fear spasmed in his guts.

Then the earth shook with explosions. Dirt flew, and branches, and sections of tree trunks. Marky was raised from the ground and thrown down again. The crashing continued, though not as concentrated as the synchronous opening salvo, but nothing more hit as close as the shell that had lifted and dropped him. Eyes bulging, rifle still clutched tightly, he no longer knelt. He hugged the ground, as low and flat as he could make himself.

After about two minutes the shelling stopped. Though Marky didn't know it, the Komarsi batteries were well ahead of the brigade's supply column, and were being frugal with their shells. Ahead, the rifle fire picked up again. The lieutenant shouted, and Sergeant Torn called: "Steady, boys. They're comin'. Don't rush now. It's *aimed* fire we want! *Aimed* fire!"

✧          ✧          ✧

Clover Meadows was a considerable village at the meeting place of Road 40 and a major east-west road, which was why the army had located a major supply dump there. There were also two large tent camps, one military, the other of refugees.

It was a beehive now, with soldiers and civilians, more women than men, loading boxes and barrels onto wagons, all the wagons they'd been able to scrounge, to send it north up Road 40. They'd even started loading boxes into crude slings across the backs of horses and cattle.

Because the Komarsi were coming. During the preceding four days they'd moved eighty-four miles north from the Eel. The people loading wagons could hear distant gunfire—artillery. The fighting was too far away yet to hear the rifles and machine guns.

The last of the wagons moved off, and people flopped down on the ground to rest. More wagons were supposed to be coming from both west and east. There'd better be; there were still a lot of supplies stacked there, and supplies were life, and the means of resistance.

After six days of fighting, the brigade had stopped. It had stopped before, briefly but repeatedly, to fight and to clear the road of fallen trees. The entire thrust of the offensive had been speed. They'd even pushed ahead by night, when the Smoleni fire was not so damnably accurate. They'd slept in snatches, mainly while they waited for the artillery to catch up, and the supplies.

This time, however, they were to stop for the night, and Rumaros be damned. The men desperately needed sleep.

B Company, 9th Regiment, had drawn picket duty, and Captain Jorn Vilabo had posted his company in five-man fire teams, with orders that at least two in each team should be awake at all times; most would manage that, he thought. He had no illusions that they'd stay alert though. The solution, such as it was, was to post *lots* of pickets, and the brigadier had assigned several companies to the duty.

Hopefully things would get easier from here on. Maybe they'd even capture a supply dump, which they'd been told was the main purpose of this operation. So far the Smoleni had left little for them. It seemed to him that had been the hole in the plan: The advance hadn't gone badly, although the big brass in Rumaros were probably dissatisfied. They hadn't expected the Smoleni to muster the wagons and labor and energy to move the dumps the way they had.

Trooper Karly Nelkrim lay in the shadow beside a stone pile. Low shrubs grew around its base, where the hay mower had failed to reach. It was night, but moonlit, and he was looking at Komarsi soldiers sleeping no more than twenty yards in front of him.

The tricky thing had been getting through the pickets unobserved. It had taken more than an hour of careful movement.

The Komarsi hadn't pitched tents. There had been no rain during the offensive, and this was the first night with appreciable cloudiness. The clouds helped. Here in the open you moved when the moons were hidden, lay still and plotted your next move when they weren't. Fortunately the two moons up were only six or eight degrees apart; when one was hidden, usually both were.

They were shining now. The Komarsi were dark oblong lumps in separate small groups, probably squads. He'd have preferred they weren't lying so close together. He hadn't spotted a sentry yet, but surely there were some.

Another slow cloud hid the moons, and Karly moved forward smoothly but quickly till he came to the nearest Komarsi. Reaching down, he drew the knife strapped to his leg and cut the man's throat. The body spasmed once. Then he moved to the next, wondering how many he could kill before an alarm was raised. And whether any of the others had reached the sleepers yet.

Sergeant Pitter Pross was unhappy: The paddock guards fell asleep faster than he could circle the paddock and wake them up. He hoped the pickets were doing better, and wondered how he'd been able to stay awake himself. Or for how much longer. His eyes felt gritty, and he'd caught them sliding shut a couple of times, even as he walked.

He felt ill at ease about this night. He'd overheard the C.O. telling the lieutenant that they should have made a stop like this one two nights earlier, when everyone wasn't unconscious on their feet. That the decision to keep pushing had come from Rumaros, from some sonofabitch who slept between sheets eight hours a night, plus a nap after lunch. Men so short on sleep not only had trouble staying awake, Pross told himself. Their judgment went bad. They fell asleep on their feet or in the saddle, dreaming they were awake. They were short on rations, too, and on grain for the horses. Thank Yomal! The brigadier had passed the word that they'd wait here till the supply train caught up.

Somewhere a man screamed. The sound stiffened Pross for a moment. Then it was quiet again. Nightmare, he told himself. And it would take more than a single scream to wake most of them.

Abruptly a machine gun began to fire, and another, and another, firing into the horse herd from close up. Abruptly Pross was wide awake and swearing, looking around for the muzzle flashes. He couldn't see any; they seemed to be on the far side of the horses, which were milling wildly now, crowhopping with their hobbles on, some of them screaming. Abruptly randomness became direction, away from the machine guns and toward him. Horses charged through the rope fence, the whole herd coming his way with an up-and-down, hobbled-horse gait.

There was no chance to run. Pross crouched till the first one was virtually on him, hoping to clutch its mane and pull himself onto its back, but its clumsy gait foiled him. It struck him with a shoulder, knocking him down, and the horses behind it trampled him to rags.

Kelmer Faronya listened to the staccato of machine guns, the rumbling of hooves, and felt a distancing, a separation of himself from the event. Looking out from the forest's edge, he could see the oncoming horse herd. They were nearing, but also, hobbled as they were, slowing. At a hundred yards, Jerym's hand clapped his shoulder.

"This offensive's been running on borrowed time and borrowed energy," he murmured. "Now it's time to foreclose the mortgage."

Tired, and confronting the dark forest, the foremost horses slowed to a hobbled walk, the momentum and energy of those behind insufficient to force them. At about thirty yards, Jerym whistled a command, and A Company trotted out in a line, armed for this mission with grenades and submachine guns. They began a butchering, while Kelmer, neither frightened nor excited, recorded it all. Tired as they were, it took time for the horses to turn around and flee again. There was a great squealing and dying before those behind got turned around. Then slowly, heavily, the survivors began to run again, back the way they'd come.

It seemed to Kelmer that they should not show this cubeage.

# 45

It had been raining for a day and a half, and rivulets of cold water trickled down Colonel Renvil's slicker as he watched his brigade straggle by. He wore no insignia of rank. He'd cut them off after a sniper had killed Brigadier Lord Willing, leaving him in charge.

*Commanding officer!* He grunted. Spectator was the word. The brigade had been misused, the men overspent. Willing had known it, and had argued on the radio with Rumaros, to no avail. Now the mortgage had been foreclosed. (If he'd known that a mercenary officer had used the same metaphor, two nights ago, he'd have thought it a fitting irony.)

At the beginning, Willing had tried to make it a fighting retreat, though mostly the men had lacked the energy for it. Then the downpour had begun, no transient summer convection storm, but a slow-moving, pre-autumnal cold front undercutting warm moist air. All fighting response had dissolved in it, and the men rode soddenly southward, hoping the snipers would sight on someone else.

Where the land was suitable, stretches of the road were flanked by narrow fields, mostly no more than two hundred yards wide. The fields were glacial till. Generations of farm boys had picked rocks in them, and each year frost heaving provided a new crop, to be piled as fences along the edges of the field, especially along the back edge, the forest margin. It was there that sniping was the worst, especially when the rain thinned a bit, for the Smoleni could shoot in safety.

More often, though, the forest came up to the ditches, and the sniping was much less heavy there.

The men were desperate for sleep, and if they'd been on foot, it would have been worse. Many more would have lain down beside the road, rain or not.

As it was, they still had to walk from time to time to rest the horses. Rather often, in fact, for they were short on horses. They'd lost enough, that first night, that they'd started back with many carrying two men. And some of the snipers seemed to target horses; even indifferent marksmen could easily hit them. (It never occurred to Renvil that the Smoleni looked at his horses as food, to be smoked and stored for winter.) Doubling up became more common, almost the rule. Men had broken discipline, cutting artillery horses free to ride them, leaving the caissons and guns in the ditches for the Smoleni. In the rain, the caissons wouldn't even burn readily.

Troops afoot sometimes took cover in the shelter of a roadside fence, mostly not to shoot back, but for a reprieve and a nap. Willing had forbidden it. The column had to keep moving, and once a man fell asleep, even on that cold wet ground, it was nearly impossible to wake him. Sometimes, enticed beyond resistance by the shelter of a roadside stone fence, they lay down despite orders and threats. At one stretch, the Smoleni had violated such a shelter with mortar fire, throwing the column into confusion, and causing more concentrated casualties than sniping did.

Men slept on horseback, but that wasn't really effective. Occasionally one fell out of the saddle without being shot; some didn't even wake up when they hit the ground. Some who'd lain down and refused to get up, Willing had had shot, and the problem had abated somewhat till nightfall. When daylight came, they were hundreds of men short. Much of this was certainly due to night ambushes by submachine gunners, who struck, then quickly withdrew, but as certainly, many had simply gone back in the woods a bit and lain down to sleep.

He had no doubt that the Smoleni had made that sleep permanent; they had no facilities for prisoners.

The night before, they'd passed the remains of the supply column— corpses and broken wagons. With the heavy cloud cover, it had been necessary to use battle lamps to stay out of the ditch, and by their light, it seemed the fighting had been heavy there. That might have been the Smoleni's major effort, with supplies the incentive and prize. He hoped they'd paid heavily for them.

He'd never believed in Yomal; educated people didn't. But just in case, he prayed they'd meet a relief column before night fell again.

# 46

Major Jillard Brossling commanded the White T'swa's 2nd Battalion, his office a squad tent shared with his E.O. and Master Sergeant Hors. Hors, once a platoon sergeant, had had a knee smashed on Terfreya by a shell fragment. Even after repairs it hampered him, and he'd been given an administrative job. His desk faced the entrance.

Brossling was not long back from "the south"; 2nd Battalion and its ranger trainees had been part of the gauntlet along Road 45, and the scourging of the Komarsi 6th Mounted Infantry Brigade.

A large man in Smoleni uniform looked in. "Sergeant Gull Kro reporting," the man said. "At the major's request."

Hors motioned him in. Brossling had looked up at Kro's words, and gestured toward a folding chair across from his own. There was no salute. Kro had learned that the mercs had no rules about saluting. They saluted when they felt like it, and most often as an acknowledgement and conclusion, seldom as a greeting. Even in form it was different: They touched their cap instead of clapping hand to heart.

"Kro," said the major, "your cadre keeps saying good things about you: how quickly and how well you learn, about your talents as a ranger and your abilities as a platoon leader . . . and how well you operated down south last week." He paused, examining Kro's aura. It showed little reaction; the man handled praise easily. "They've also told me you tended at first to be overbearing toward your men, and learned to tone it down. Anything you'd care to say about that?"

These last several weeks, Kro, still young himself, had grown used to officers above him who were little or no older. "Yessir," he said. "My old outfit was mostly from towns. They needed pushin' sometimes, and some would try to get away with things. These rangers are different; got different attitudes. They need to be handled different. And I seen how you people operate."

The major grinned. Kro still wasn't entirely used to how often the mercs grinned, or at what. "Good," said Brossling. "The reason I called you in is to give you a conditional promotion. I'm trying you out as trainee company commander, starting tomorrow. If at some point I decide to give someone else a chance at it, it won't mean you're not measuring up. We might just want to see how he does. If one of us thinks you're fucking up, we'll tell you about it."

He stood, and the two shook hands. Then Kro saluted and left, thinking again what hard damned hands the mercs all had. Brossling, he thought, was as strong as he was, pound for pound.

# 47

It was not the usual War Council meeting. There were guests: the ambassadors from Krentorf and Oselbent, and an envoy from The Archipelago. They'd come for a summary report of the Komarsi offensive, its accomplishments and defeat, and for a status report. Meanwhile, quiet orderlies entered at intervals, replenishing their cups of "war joma," and the cookies deliberately made with "bark flour"—actually three parts wheat flour mixed with one part bark flour. The refreshments were almost the only purely PR act, to demonstrate the make-do resourcefulness of their hosts.

The battle summary began with a map showing the launch points of the two Komarsi strike forces, the location of Smoleni supply depots, the rates of Komarsi advances, and the sites of major fights.

Video cubeage was shown of people, mostly women, old men, and adolescents, laboring furiously to transfer a supply depot. It gave the diplomats the sense of an entire people united in resistance to an invader. They saw the night assault on the Road 40 spearhead, the decimation of its horse herd, and the hundred-mile gauntlet the 3rd Brigade had suffered through. For the two brigades combined, the count of dead Komarsi was 5,437, almost half their total strength! It was hard to imagine.

They also saw the butchering, the wholesale cutting up of dead Komarsi horses; the smoking of horse meat on hundreds of improvised racks; the salvaging of Komarsi supplies, of ammunition from the belts of dead Komarsi soldiers, and the boots from their feet. Little was wasted.

Kelmer Faronya hadn't gotten a whole lot more sleep than the Komarsi soldiers.

The diplomats weren't shown Komarsi prisoners. There were only a few hundred of them. The Smoleni troops were inclined to shoot anyone wearing Komarsi brown, especially the severely wounded, because facilities and medical personnel, like supplies and food, were seriously short. The prisoners who were taken were stripped of clothes, all but their boots, and a shallow *x* was cut on their foreheads to leave a scar. An oath was required that they not again serve against Smolen. With the understanding that if they broke it and were captured, the scar on their forehead would be a death sentence. Then they were herded south on foot.

The overall strategy and battle plan had been Belser's. The tactic of attacking the horse herds had been Romlar's.

There was no exultation, least of all by President Lanks, whose face was grave. Belser had a satisfied look, which was new to him, but that was all. Romlar was calm and matter-of-fact as always.

Vestur Marlim summarized the overall military situation, which actually hadn't changed much. The Komarsi still had far more power, but an all-out Komarsi offensive would be risky. The north was too big, too wild, and the Smoleni could not be pinned down. While on Komars's southern and western borders, Selmar and Krentorf remembered old wrongs. At the same time, however, the Komarsi could not be driven from the Leas or the coast, where their army could see and target the enemy, and maneuver its large forces more or less freely.

And the Smoleni supply situation, while eased a bit now, was still poor. By winter's end, unless supplies were brought in, there'd be serious hunger among the people, and next summer would see it worsen despite some limited acreage of crops. Unless events intervened, a second winter would bring wholesale deaths from the combination of hunger and sickness.

Elyas Fossur gave an intelligence summary then. His new material was more political than military. There was widespread, if generally subdued, discontent in Komars with the war. People of every class were unhappy with one or more aspects of it: cost, taxes, shortages including labor shortages, overwork, and the increased disobedience, even insolence, of the laboring classes, which went with the labor shortage. If the discontent was to worsen substantially, pressure by the nobility and merchants might well result in a Komarsi offer of terms.

"What terms would Smolen consider?" asked the envoy from The Archipelago.

Fossur turned to the president, who answered. "During this emergency, I rule Smolen, subject to impeachment by popular referendum. But I would not sign a peace without its approval by my Council of Ministers. I can say this much unequivocally, however: All Komarsi forces would have to withdraw south of the legal boundary—the Komar River. We would not, I think, demand reparations, but I would probably want a trade agreement as well as a treaty of peace."

The ambassadors from Krentorf and Oselbent contemplated the president's strong words. Only the Archipelagon seemed to take them without discomfort. After a moment the Oselbenti said, "Mr. President, Engwar would never accept that. He is too proud."

Heber Lanks answered mildly. "Proud? I would have said 'arrogant.' But if his nobles and merchants are sufficiently unhappy with the war, his power may be diluted against his will. There are few kings on Maragor with power as nearly absolute as his. Yet almost every kingdom whose people enjoy a decent constitution was once as his is. And until the time came, it no doubt seemed inconceivable that they would change.

"Indeed, it may be that in attacking Smolen, Engwar has set in motion the downfall of his power. His merchants and nobles may trim his wings, or even depose him."

The president paused, his expression not entirely clear. To the envoy from The Archipelago it seemed somewhere between reflective and glum, but with an underlying doggedness. He would listen closely to this Heber Lanks. Even if his own government decided not to involve itself as Smolen's covert supplier, there'd be food for thought in this man's words.

"For that to happen, though," Lanks went on, "we here in Smolen must survive and fight on. Many of us will never surrender. We will eat what we can find, and fight with bows if need be. But we cannot be effective eating bark and fighting with sticks. If it comes to that, and we die, it will stand as a reproach to the rest of Maragor."

He sat back then. It would have been an effective note to close with, but the ambassador from Oselbent cleared his throat and spoke almost apologetically. "Mr. President, have you heard that Engwar has contracted for a regiment of T'swa?"

"I've heard he was trying to."

"Our ambassador to Komars was recently invited to meet with Engwar's Minister of War, who showed him a signed contract with the Lodge of Kootosh-Lan. A regiment will arrive in—" He frowned, calculating mentally. "In about six weeks."

Lanks knew the mystique of the T'swa. These diplomats and their governments might well consider that with T'swa in the equation, Smolen could not last long. And that to help a hopeless cause was both dangerous and wasteful. "Colonel Romlar knows the T'swa intimately," he said. "For six years, he and his regiment were trained by them. He's engaged in maneuvers with them. Colonel, what effect do you think a regiment of T'swa will have in this war?"

Romlar stood to speak. "Less than you might suppose. They're as good as you've heard, but there will be only between about eight hundred and seventeen hundred of them. And they will fight only soldiers, not civilians, unless the civilians take arms against them.

"Against the Komarsi or any usual army, they would be a major element. But here they will not dominate as they usually do. The Smoleni are much better suited than most to fight them, especially the Smoleni ranger battalions we've been training. Many of the Smoleni troops are woodsmen and sharpshooters, self-reliant and self-assured. All of the rangers are. And the tactics the rangers are being trained in are well-suited to fighting either Komarsi or T'swa in the wild country. You'll hear more of these rangers. They do not hesitate to act, do not fear to act, and they act skillfully. And like the T'swa, and like ourselves, they hit what they shoot at."

He shook his head. "The T'swa are better; you need to know them to know how good they are. But the Smoleni, especially the rangers, will make them pay in blood. When the T'swa survivors return to Tyss, they will tell stories about the Smoleni and their fighting skills."

He sat down then, and when he was seated, the envoy from The Archipelago spoke. "And you, Colonel, you and your men—how do you compare with the T'swa?"

"Ask again a year from now. We've never fought them. We've beaten them in maneuvers, but those were maneuvers, however realistic. We're as good as they could make us, as good as we can be. They're the ones who named us the 'White T'swa.'

"I guarantee, though, that here in the north, in these forests, our advantage over Komarsi troops is much greater than the T'swa advantage over Smoleni troops."

The president followed Romlar's commentary by having Kelmer show cubeage of the mercenaries' own training routines, and of rangers in training. He then ended the meeting by reminding the diplomats of the cubeage they'd seen at the start of the meeting, of the devastation along Road 40. He didn't want them to leave with the T'swa on their minds.

With his training and the Ostrak Procedures, anxiety had become foreign to Romlar, but he'd felt a pang of it when the T'swa were mentioned, and it was still there, a deep psychic bruise. And with it a thought: *He was in danger of wasting his regiment!* But a regiment of warriors lost in battle wasn't wasted; not if seen from a neutral viewpoint. Not if winning or losing was unimportant, and warplay itself the purpose.

Yet it seemed to him he *was* basically neutral regarding the outcome of this war. He would use his skills to the utmost for the Smoleni not because of his liking for them, but because it was part of the T'sel. He did like the Smoleni, liked and admired them and wished them well, but if they lost, he would not grieve. The past was past. The spirit ensouled a body to experience, to learn. When the spirit was released and the body left behind, soon enough it would ensoul another.

So why the anxiety? He hadn't felt it on Terfreya. He hadn't felt it the first weeks here. The T'swa seemed the key. When T'swa regiments fought on opposing sides, sooner or later they'd fight each other. It wasn't so uncommon. And when they did, their casualties were often heavy: over several engagements they could chew each other up.

Of course, it was customary for warriors to be chewed up sooner or later, if they were fulfilling their warrior nature. And the prospect of death—his or others—didn't feel like the key to his problem.

No. The problem was, it felt to him that he'd need his regiment for some other purpose. Then was there some purpose, waiting in the future, about which he did not feel neutral? He examined the thought, consulted his feelings, and decided that that wasn't it either.

He snorted. *Enough of this wallowing,* he told himself. When the time came, he'd know. Meanwhile he had a war here to fight, and probably a regiment of T'swa before long.

And with that, the anxiety faded. Though its root was still there; he could feel it.


That afternoon, after the diplomats had left in their separate floaters, Heber Lanks sat down with Marlim and Fossur. And concluded they'd probably get the level of supplies, that winter, that they'd earlier felt encouraged to hope for. Not as much as they needed—the limitations of wilderness transportation alone prohibited that—but enough to make a difference. It would extend their efforts, and allow more time for something truly favorable to develop.


# 48


On the great estates of Komars, two kinds of men worked the harvests. One was serfs, part of the real estate, legally bound to the farms they were born on. The other, the crews brought in, consisted of "casuals"—mostly freedmen: shanty-towners and drifters. Many worked the grain harvest in midsummer, picked fruit in late summer, and in autumn harvested potatoes and sugar beets.

The Iryalan infiltrators had dispersed, placing themselves with different labor brokers so they'd be with different crews, working different estates. They wanted to agitate as widely as possible.

On the first farm he'd worked at, Major Coyn Carrmak, alias Coyn Makoor, hadn't said a lot. Certainly nothing contentious. He'd learned the ways, the thinking, and the temper of the casuals; absorbed the situations; and learned the work of the potato harvest—all things he needed to know. Besides, on the first estate the conditions were relatively good, and the men didn't complain among themselves. They even commented that the cots and pads were better than at most places, that the barracks windows were screened, that there were even bathing facilities and brooms.

And that the food was better than they usually were given. They had fried potatoes and pork for breakfast, with bread, butter, and jam, and an apple. For the midmorning and midafternoon lunches, bread and butter, boiled eggs, and apples. And after work, wheat and beans boiled with beef, boiled greens in broth, and pickled beets, again with bread and butter. All you wanted of them.

The work was simple enough, but hard. There were men who wielded spading forks, digging up the potatoes, and more men who bagged them. And there was an elite who were paid a bit more: the men who followed the rows of sacks, accompanied by horse-drawn wagons. They'd pick up the heavy bags and throw them aboard. It was the hardest labor, and the foremen assigned the stronger-looking men to it. Carrmak was made a loader on the first morning, and was an immediate success. For where the other loaders on his crew hunkered down and lifted the sacks in their arms, Carrmak simply half squatted, gripped a sack with a pinch-grip, and with an easy-seeming swing, threw it on the wagon.

Some of the others tried it then. It looked easier, and it was, for those with exceptional hand strength, because it wasn't necessary to squat as deeply or bend as low. Most who tried it gave it up though. Either their grip wasn't strong enough to do it at all, or after a bit their strength gave out.

Meanwhile it made Carrmak an instant special figure on the crew. It also drew the quick attention of the foreman, because the technique was faster. He made Carrmak, alias Makoor, the strawboss—a man who worked like the others but had authority over them to see they neither loafed, nor interfered with the work of others. It also earned him an additional half drona a day, and provided status.

He was careful not to exercise his authority beyond necessity. Actually he didn't need to; men tended not to cross him. And during the lunch break, and after work, he made a point of being one of them, a quiet, unobtrusive one of them. Only one man challenged him, a large aggressive drifter named Kusmar. Carrmak threw him heavily to the ground, so quickly and decisively that everyone stood astonished by it. Then he helped the man up, clapped his shoulder, and said he wasn't half bad, not at all.

The next estate was something else; the men began to grumble at once, about the barracks, the food, the foreman. Almost everything about the job was substandard. After the first job, the broker had hired Carrmak out as strawboss. It would be his job unless the foreman demoted or fired him.

On the second day, word of the grumbling reached the foreman's ears. Their mid-afternoon lunch had been a baked potato each, and they'd shouted their complaints. One of the estate's teamsters told him about it. He went over to check it out, and rode up to Carrmak. "You're the strawboss, right?" he said.

"That's right," Carrmak answered. The foreman knew at once he'd erred in riding up to this man, because Carrmak had gripped the bridle, taking control of the horse.

The foreman looked at him and decided a mild approach would be best. "I like the way you work, Makoor, but you gotta keep your crew in line. They're wastin' time and energy complainin'. We can't have that."

The entire bucking crew, the strongest men on the whole harvest crew, paused in their work to watch. Carrmak looked the foreman in the eye and drawled: "Well, tell the fuckin' manager to get his head out his arse then, and give us decent food. That'll cut the yawpin' by at least half."

The foreman blanched. He was a large, thick-bodied man himself, physically powerful though somewhat porky. But Makoor, he realized, was dangerous. As foreman, he wore a truncheon on his belt and carried a bullwhip coiled on his saddle, but it seemed to him he'd have little chance to wield them against this man.

Yet he couldn't let the challenge pass. He jerked the reins, trying to cause the horse to rear, to jerk free. It danced but didn't rear. Then one of the other workmen was there, grabbing at him. Cursing, the foreman drew his truncheon to strike at him, but another man ran up to him on the other side, grabbed his stirruped boot and heaved upward. He lost his seat and fell to the ground, where workmen's stout brogans kicked him into huddled submission.

The crew looked to Carrmak then, excited but scared. They'd gone too far to stop, and wanted to be told what to do. He still held the bridle. The horse had quieted.

"Well shit," Carrmak said, "the fat's in the fire now. Let's bust this place up. Who's with me? Kusmar?"

It was Kusmar who'd dumped the foreman from his horse. He was grinning from ear to ear now. "All the way, Makoor."

"Good. Let's go!" Carrmak swung into the saddle then and led them to headquarters. They trashed the barracks, throwing stools out the windows and smashing benches. They were stacking the sleeping pads in the middle of the floor, prior to setting fire to them, when they heard someone bellow.

"Come out of there or we start shootin'."

Inside, the crew stopped, looking around at each other, suddenly sober. They recognized the voice: it was the overseer, a bull of a man known for the beatings he'd delivered. With him he'd have his three enforcers, large dangerous men also known for their fists. Their gaze stopped at Carrmak, who stepped to the window for a brief look, then turned to the others. "He's got a shotgun," he said. "The others only got billies."

He turned back to the window then. "All right. We'll come out." He was grinning when he looked at the others again. "I'll take his gun from him," he murmured. "You follow me, with stools and that like. We'll beat shit out of 'em, and then we'll torch this place."

"Quit your stallin'!" the overseer boomed. "This is your last warnin'!"

Carrmak waved the others to the front wall, then called with a sneer in his voice. "You ayn't got the 'thority!" With that he stepped quickly to the side of the door.

He expected the overseer to enter first. He'd grab the man's shotgun and take it from him. But the overseer was cautious; he sent one of the others in, truncheon in hand. Carrmak's foot drove into the man's ribs from the side, sending him sideways to the floor, then the trooper was out the door headfirst, and landed rolling. The shotgun roared, sending a load of birdshot too high, and as the overseer jacked another shell into the chamber, Carrmak was on him, disabling him quickly and efficiently. One of the enforcers attacked with his truncheon, but the collapsing overseer was in the way, and Carrmak recovered the fallen shotgun. Meanwhile the crewmen, after initial hesitation, were pouring out of the barracks. The remaining enforcers fled toward the manor house, calling a warning ahead of them.

After they'd taken out their packsacks, the laborers touched off first the barracks, then other outbuildings, but left the stables alone, and sheds with livestock, and the cabins of the serfs. The hay barn began to blossom with flames. One of the crew suggested they grab some serfs' women and have a little fun. Carrmak said none of that; they had nothing against the serfs. Instead they looted the headquarters building. No one offered to loot or torch the manor house though; that would be suicide. One of them had backed a large truck from the equipment shed before they torched it. They piled into the back, most armed with pitchforks, some with axes. Most were flushed with excitement, though two or three looked as if they wished this wasn't happening. Carrmak, with the shotgun and a pocketful of shells from the overseer's desk, spoke to the driver.

"Where's another place around here as bad as this one? Or almost as bad. You know?"

"Lamskor Place," the driver answered, grinning.

"How far?"

"Six or eight miles."

"Let's go then. We'll fuckin' burn it too."

The driver waited for Carrmak to climb aboard. When he banged the cab roof with his hand, the man shifted gears and drove from the yard.

They'd only driven half a mile when the hay barn collapsed, sending a great puff of flame high into the air. The men cheered.

They trashed the Lamskor place too. The overseer had been warned— word had spread by phone—but Carrmak had faced him down, shotgun to shotgun, and told him to go in the house. With his enforcers, the man had retreated into the manor then. On the way, Carrmak had assigned teams to certain tasks, and they finished their destruction more quickly. By now it was clear to him that most of the managers here didn't know how to cope with violent rebellion; it was outside their training or reality, perhaps even their concepts. He sent two men in another truck with another shotgun, to recruit another crew and go wherever they thought best. He put Kusmar in charge. Kusmar was a dominant; they'd pretty much do what he said. He'd be less fastidious than Carrmak about what he did, what he burned, but that was part of insurrection.

It was late now, the sun nearly down and dusk near at hand. Carrmak told his driver to drive to the district seat. That's where the hiring hall was, no doubt with men waiting to be tabbed by brokers, maybe even crews waiting for transportation. They should be able to recruit a small army there, a platoon or more. Five miles short of town though, they saw an enclosed truck coming toward them. Even from a little distance they could see the sheriff's insignia on it.

Carrmak thumped the cab roof and yelled down, "Ram the sonof-abitch!" The driver slowed a bit but kept going, while his riders crouched low, bracing themselves as best they could. The driver of the sheriff's truck realized too late what was about to happen. He hit his brakes, and a moment later the farm truck hit him head on at about twenty-five miles an hour. Metal tore, glass broke, and the farm crew piled out. The posse had locked their doors from the inside. A crewman hacked the sidewalls of the tires with his ax. Then they all stood looking at each other.

"There's a place half a mile up the road," Carrmak said. "We'll get another truck there—two or three of 'em. We won't stop to burn the place. Just get trucks and go on into town, like we planned!"

From the hiring hall, three truckloads of laborers spread into the countryside, each with someone more or less in charge, each with ideas of which estates to hit and which to pass by. Carrmak stayed at the hall to see what would happen. Sometime after midnight, soldiers arrived by rail and surrounded the hiring hall. The handful of men still there were arrested and handcuffed. They complained that they were innocent, that the men the soldiers wanted were out attacking estates.

"We'll get them too," the lieutenant said. Then the men arrested were hauled away to the provincial capital. The next day they were put on a railroad car, under armed guards, and taken to a military prison near Linnasteth.

# 49

Major Rinly Molgren glowered first at the morning report, then at his master sergeant. "What's this shit about? Dumping civilian prisoners on us!"

The sergeant had learned patience years before. He'd also learned to recognize a hangover; the major had one, not too bad, but bad enough. What the officer wanted to know was all written in the report, but no doubt the pain in his forehead, and the queasy stomach, got in the way of reading it. "They're charged with rebellion," the sergeant answered, "assault, destruction of property, and a few counts of murder. The first few were jailed at Millinos, but more kept bein' brought in, and they considered 'em too dangerous to keep there."

The major sat back and exhaled audibly in exasperation. "Shit!" He looked up at the sergeant again. "Have you seen these new prisoners?"

"Yes, major."

"What do they look like?"

"Dirty, hungry, and worried, sir."

The major grunted. It was after ten o'clock; he should have been in two hours earlier, and knew it. He was going to have to cut down on this damned partying, unless he found a whiskey that didn't leave him feeling so wretched in the morning. "Assign them to cells, did you?"

"No, sir. We never had civilian prisoners before, so I left 'em in the holding pen till you could decide how you wanted 'em handled. I did have a couple removed for questioning though."

"Did you question them? Or did you leave that for me, too?"

"I questioned 'em. They're in a cell now; it didn't seem smart to put 'em back in with the others."

"Umh." Wincing, the major heaved himself to his feet. "Let's look at them, Sergeant. Blasinga can take care of things here for a few minutes. And bring the records on them."

They went downstairs to the ground level. In the holding pen, the prisoners looked as the sergeant had described them: handcuffed, slouched, and hangdog. Most of them didn't look dangerous at all. Molgren was willing to bet that if they were sent back to work on condition of good behavior, they'd be no trouble to anyone. But it was too late for that. Rebellion! They'd likely end up in the rock quarries, those who weren't executed.

One of them stood a little apart from the others, as if no one wanted to be too close to him. "Sergeant," the major said quietly, "who's the one by himself? The one standing straight?"

"The men we questioned say he's the instigator, sir, the one who started it. Seems he ran it like a military operation—gave orders and assignments. They say that in a fight, the man's a one-man army."

"Hmm!" The major was remembering a request that had come down lines from command a few deks ago. More than a year ago. "Have him brought to my office under guard, Sergeant. Right away. Leave the rest in holding for now." He turned and left then, thinking. If the prisoner seemed suitable, he just might be able to get a bounty for him. An extra hundred drona was always nice to have, and it never hurt to do a favor for a general.

# 50

The Assembly of Lords was scheduled to meet again, and Fingas Kelromak was back in Linnasteth to attend. As usual, when he arrived, he came to the townhouse of Jorn Nufkarm, to be updated on the capital and the activities of the Crown. When he sat down, though, it was Nufkarm who asked the first question.

"How went the harvest?"

"Mine? Overall quite well. The potatoes went nearly two hundred bushels per acre."

"Indeed! I take it that's good."

"Surely you know the answer to that," Fingas said playfully. "Your estate grows potatoes."

Nufkarm gazed blandly at him. "I'm trying to raise a crop of reforms; I therefore cultivate politicians. My familiarity with potatoes ends at the table." He patted his impressive belly. "I leave the farming to my dear brother, who considers himself to have the best of the arrangement. Did you have any, um, troubles at your place?"

"None; I was fortunate. It was no doubt useful to have a reputation for decent quarters, good bedding, and good food."

"Any in your neighborhood then?"

Fingas's expression was a partial answer, his features tight, his face slightly pale, and he didn't answer at once. "Trouble?" he said at last. "Rather more than one might wish—certainly on Rorbarak. They burned the serfs' hamlet there, and violated some women. On most estates, though, serfs weren't molested. What have you been hearing?"

Nufkarm shrugged his shoulders. "You read the papers: *The Herald* at least. It's the worst outbreak of violence in a millennium."

"And what response from our peers?"

"Hmh! One proposal is to have the army discharge a large number of serfs. To get away from hiring so many casuals. Get them home, back into the fields."

Fingas's eyes sharpened. "Remarkable! Somehow overlooking the fact that by enlisting, they are no longer serfs."

"Not overlooking it at all. Arbendel has proposed that the manumission act be abrogated by royal decree. His argument is that practically all the unruly casuals are manumitted serfs, or rather their descendants. Ergo, free no more serfs."

"Good god!"

"Exactly. They think we have troubles now! That could produce not only uprisings in the provinces, but insurrection in the army. Which of course has something to recommend it from our point of view, but it's entirely too dangerous. As it happens, wiser heads recognized this and quashed the proposal. Not all conservatives are fools.

"Meanwhile, the war and Engwar have taken the blame again, though people don't say this publicly. And coming after that terrible fiasco recently, where our good general left some five thousand corpses along the roads in northern Smolen . . . If he wasn't Engwar's cousin, he'd be fired by now, though the rumor is that he only did it under pressure from Engwar. And Engwar, of course, defends him. I'm afraid our good sovereign will definitely not get the special war tax renewed, unless something quite unforeseen happens.

"On the other hand—"

"Yes?"

Nufkarm waved at the radio on a table. "Just this morning he announced a special sedition act. We'll need to tone down the *Bulletin* substantially."

"He can't do that!"

"Of course he can. We're at war, and the Conservatives control the Assembly."

"But the Charter!"

"Indeed the Charter. But there is precedent, and I repeat, the Conservatives control the Assembly. Think about it. And I strongly advise you not to publish underground leaflets to fill the gap. Given your social inheritance, you'd be the first one Engwar would suspect. Be prudent, dear Fingas; hold your peace. Engwar is digging his own grave, or rather constructing his own political—shall we say castration?

"Do nothing rash. Stand ready. Take whatever *safe* steps present themselves. When he makes a serious mistake, we'll make whatever use of it we can. With patience we will bring him down. If we are impatient, someone else will bring him down later, but we won't be privileged to see it."

# 51

Subcolonel Jomar Viskon sat frowning at the papers he held: an invoice and a bill of particulars. "Who in Amber's name is Major Rinly Molgren?" he asked exasperatedly. With all he had on his desk today, he didn't need some off-the-wall crap like this.

The sergeant major resisted telling him it was there on the sheets he held. "He's the C.O. of the stockade in Linna Commune, sir."

"We haven't been looking for men like this for more than a year now."

The comment hardly rated an answer, so the sergeant major said nothing for several long seconds, waiting. Finally he broke the silence. "The prisoner's in the waitin' room, Colonel. Manacled and guarded."

"Well crap!" The colonel looked at nowhere, then focused and took a deep breath. "Have him brought in."

"Yessir."

The sergeant major left, and Viskon sat drumming his desk top. Ten seconds later a staff sergeant pushed the door open and held it. A rather large, hard-looking man stepped in, wearing manacles on his wrists, and followed by a corporal holding a pistol. Anyone who had to be guarded that closely wasn't going to be of use to anyone, Viskon told himself. When all three were inside, he spoke with exaggerated patience. "All right, Sergeant, seat your prisoner and close the door."

He looked the prisoner over, scanned the bill of particulars again, then glanced up and found himself matching eyeballs with the man for a moment. The fellow was genuinely unperturbed, and he'd swear there was excellent intelligence behind those eyes. "Your name is Coyn Makoor?"

"Yessir," Carrmak answered.

"It says here that you were arrested for inciting to riot, assault on authorities, arson, grand theft, assault with a vehicle, murder, and inciting to murder. Is that right?"

"I ayn't seen what you're readin', sir. So far's did I do those things; I dint murder no one, and I dint tell nor ask no one else to. The rest of it sounds about right."

"Murder or not, I suppose you know what's likely to happen to you. What your sentence will be."

"I can guess, sir."

"And what would you guess?"

"Likely they'll cut off my head."

"They will indeed." The prisoner still didn't seem perturbed. Interesting. Perhaps he was someone to whom the future is unreal until it's at hand. "The officer who sent you to us was under the misapprehension that we were still recruiting for a special fighting unit. We are not."

The man didn't respond. Viskon found himself wanting him to, and asked a question. "Why do you suppose Major Molgren thought you'd be suitable for such a unit?"

"Umm. Four reasons: One, I'm dangerous in a fight. Two, men gen'ly do what I tell 'em. Three, I'm gen'ly in control of myself. And four, I understand what I'm told, else'n I ask questions."

Viskon stared, then looked again at the invoice for the name. "Makoor," he asked thoughtfully, "were you ever in the army?"

"No, sir. But I was with the Red River Sheriffs Department for three years. Promoted to senior sergeant. Then three sheriff's men 'rested my dad; brawk his face and knocked out an eye. Dint knaw who he was; said he'd been spearin' horse pike in the spawnin' season. Not that him and me got on so good, but I half killed the one in charge. Off duty it was, but they had to fire me for it."

Viskon had never heard of the Red River District, didn't know where it was. But the training in sheriff's departments was partly military, and there was something about this man . . . He looked at the staff sergeant.

"Sergeant, keep him here for a few minutes. I'll be back." He left then, walking down the hall to the general's office. When he returned, he had the prisoner taken to the local stockade and confined, until he could instruct Lieutenant Hesslor, the commanding officer of the Commander's Special Unit. If the new man proved to be an unacceptable problem, or lacked sufficient training to function in the unit, they could always imprison or execute him then.

# Part Three
# WINTER WAR

# 52

The leaves had mostly fallen in Linnasteth when the T'swa arrived. Their transport put down on Engwar's estate a few miles outside the city. Engwar wasn't there to meet it—it would have been unseemly—but he had the T'swa commander flown to the palace to a reception.

Colonel Ko-Dan arrived without an entourage, beyond Captain Ibang, his aide. The T'swa have no dress uniform, but even walking through the palace in field uniform, Ko-Dan was the nearest thing to true royalty it had seen, though his father was a farmer and his mother a blacksmith's daughter. The servants glimpsing him (they hardly dared to stare) were awed, even a little frightened.

Engwar's entourage included, besides attendants, his council and certain aides currently in his special favor. And Undsvin, who if not back in his cousin's good graces, was at least partly out of his doghouse. And as Commander of the Komarsi Army in Smolen, it was appropriate that he attend.

The greetings were formal, held in the smaller receiving room. Then the participants relaxed, more or less, though first conversation with the guests was reserved for the king. The two T'swa unobtrusively ignored the canapes and drinks. Engwar noticed, but decided not to be offended. They were, after all, from a barbaric world, and presumably didn't do it to insult.

What troubled Engwar more was their youth. It was unseemly that a regimental commander be, apparently, in his early twenties, regardless of how formidable he might appear physically. But if he was as good as the T'swa reputation . . .

"You are not," Engwar commented, "the only mercenaries in this war, Colonel. We've been severely irritated, not to say injured, by the activities of a mercenary regiment employed by the Smoleni. My first job for you is to eliminate it. Wipe it out!"

Ko-Dan smiled slightly, his large T'swa eyes unreadable. "We were told they're here, Your Majesty, in the situation briefing we received before we left Tyss. In fact I know something of them. They were in training on our world when we graduated. And had earlier earned a reputation in combat on Terfreya, though they'd trained only a year at the time."

Ko-Dan's casual attitude irritated the king. "Yes? Well they're here now, and I want them gone! Killed, captured, driven out, whatever. But preferably dead. That is my first order to you: Get rid of them!"

"Ah," Ko-Dan answered gravely. "Has Your Majesty read the contract he signed with our lodge?"

"Read it? That's what I have a secretary for."

"Did he read it to you?"

Engwar's gesture expressed impatience. "I seem to recall that he did. Yes."

"I'm sure Your Majesty signs many documents and can hardly be expected to remember each of them. Let me make a suggestion. Captain Ibang and I need to leave quite soon to see to the proper disposition of our troops." That wasn't true. They could make camp quite well without their commander, but Ko-Dan foresaw an awkward situation developing if he stayed. "I'd like to meet with you late tomorrow afternoon, or evening if you prefer. After we've had a military briefing, perhaps from General Tarsteng or one of his staff." The T'swa commander paused, just for a moment. "Meanwhile you'll have had a chance to review our contract again, perhaps with the general.

"I should tell you now, however, that my regiment can be most effectively occupied in the demoralization of the Smoleni army. A regiment of mercenaries, even as capable a regiment as the Iryalans, will not defeat your army. If any force available to Smolen is able to do that, it is the Smoleni army itself."

He bowed then, slightly. "Captain Ibang and I are most honored to have been so royally received, but we must return to our men now. Let us know when, tomorrow, we may meet with you to discuss business. We will be ready for your transportation at any time after 0800." He turned to the officer who'd escorted them. "Lieutenant, please return us to our encampment."

His mouth slightly open, Engwar watched them leave the room, then turned to his secretary. "What's in that contract?"

"It's in my office, Your Majesty. Would you like to go over it now?" He flashed a hopeful glance at the general. "Perhaps Lord Undsvin could review it with us."

Engwar turned to his cousin. "By all means do, Undsvin." He turned again to look at the door the two T'swa had left by. "Those strange black men are damned inscrutable." *Or is it insolent?* he added silently. "I wonder if they realize how much I paid for them. They damned well ought to do what I tell them to! Especially isolated here, a very long way from their home world."

Undsvin had done his homework. "Cousin," he said mildly, "the T'swa are not only the best fighting men in human space, they are the smartest. At least half of their value to anyone is their military judgment. I might say their military wisdom."

He paused, assuming a more clearly respectful and subordinate attitude. "As for their isolation here— About four hundred years ago, I forget on what planet, some kingdom hired one of their regiments, and for whatever reason, the ruler there became angry with them. So he had them surrounded and shelled heavily and at length, then sent troops in to kill the survivors. Not the sort of thing we'd do, of course.

"About a year later, several T'swa regiments descended on the kingdom with Level Two weapons, and with cold ferocity destroyed the king's army. The king himself they delivered to his enemies, who, as I recall, executed him publicly."

Engwar looked at his cousin alarmed. "Really!" he said.

"It's described in a book I have, if you'd care to read it. They are not an offensive people, nor do they easily take offense. Their interest is only in fighting, never in cruelty, and they have no fear at all of death."

The king frowned, not angry now but a bit bewildered. "Remarkable! I will take your word for it." He turned to his secretary. "Let us look at that contract together. Bring it to my office now. Undsvin and I will be there momentarily." He looked around as the secretary left, and beckoned to the first butler, who was in charge. "Aljin, these others may stay as they please. Undsvin, I've decided I feel quite sanguine now, with the arrival of these T'swa. I believe my fortunes are about to turn."

# 53

Sergeant Jak Fenssen was not your stereotypic informer. About five-feet ten, he was a brawny if somewhat overweight 230 pounds. His face showed the marks of fighting, mostly during his younger years. He seldom fought now. Not that he was unwilling, when it came down to it. Rather, over the years, while developing his fighting reputation, skills and insights, he'd also shed any hesitation to kill or maim. He was seldom challenged.

Nonetheless he informed; it was a duty assigned him by Colonel Viskon.

Fenssen was first sergeant of the Commander's Special Unit, which had been having particular difficulties since Gulthar Kro had left as its commanding officer. He therefore reported to Viskon, confidentially of course, on how things went there. Its current C.O., the third since Kro, was a Lieutenant Hesslor, arguably the strongest man in the unit. Hesslor had begun his command by having two men executed, which had established his willingness. The effect had worn off, however. Now the unit existed in a kind of tension bordering on murder.

If Viskon could have, he'd have disbanded the unit and had most of its men imprisoned for various good reasons. Which would have ended the headache. But that wasn't an option Undsvin had given him. Actually, Undsvin had decided to do just that, more than once, but the basic idea of an elite unit at his personal call still held a strong attraction for him. He no longer had any illusion that this collection of men would work out, but he'd keep it, for the time at least, tinker with it, and perhaps learn from the experience.

From time to time Undsvin would have an idea, which he'd have Viskon translate into action. Viskon was a bright young man; the challenge and exasperation both would do him good. Viskon, in attempting to cope with the responsibility, occasionally proposed an idea of his own, such as the possibility that Coyn Makoor, already Sergeant Makoor, might be the kind of material from which a commander could be molded.

That week two things had happened in the unit, which was down to only forty-two men. Hesslor had killed a man with a table leg—a man who'd given him particular trouble—had smashed his skull. Later the same day, the man's two best friends had cornered Hesslor with knives, undoubtedly to kill him. Hesslor, however, had a small pistol in his pocket—perhaps he'd foreseen the confrontation—and had killed them both. It's impressive how deadly even a small caliber slug can be when fired at the breastbone at point-blank range.

Judging from Fenssen's comments, morale was at its lowest. Viskon and Undsvin had discussed the deteriorating situation, and Viskon had had a suggestion. Undsvin had told him to go ahead with it. Now Viskon looked at Fenssen appraisingly. Fenssen felt the gaze and sat unperturbed. He was a rock, exactly as the first sergeant had to be in a unit like his. "Anything new about Makoor?" Viskon asked.

"No, sir," Fenssen answered.

There was seldom anything anecdotal about Makoor. The man had no cronies and no enemies. He stood apart without seeming aloof, and for whatever reason, no one had seen fit to pick a fight with him. There was something about him. Fenssen had already told Viskon all those things. He'd also told him that, inexperienced or not, Makoor was the best soldier of the lot. An opinion which he, Fenssen, kept to himself was that Makoor had been in the army before, and deserted. Perhaps as an officer, despite his freedman dialect.

"The general has something different he wants you to do for him."

Fenssen didn't reply, just sat stolidly, waiting.

"Incite Hesslor to fight Makoor. Do you think he'd do that?"

"If he could catch him off guard, or had enough advantage." Fenssen grunted then, with a sort of grimace, as close as he ever came to laughing. "Maybe another table leg."

"Who do you think would win?'

"It'd depend on Hesslor's advantage. He's bigger and meaner, but in a straight fight, Makoor would prob'ly win."

"How might you go about getting Hesslor to attack him?"

Fenssen didn't hesitate. "I'd tell him Makoor said he was going to be C.O. himself some day."

"That would do it?"

"Prob'ly."

"What sort of advantage do you think Hesslor would create for himself?"

"No way to know."

Viskon sat pondering. He preferred not to waste Makoor, and felt uncomfortable with such a large degree of uncertainty. Nor did it help that he didn't understand men like these.

"Do it," he said.

Fenssen nodded. "Yessir."

"That's all for now, Sergeant."

Fenssen got to his feet, saluted, and left the room. Viskon watched the door close behind him. It seemed to him that the first sergeant would make a good C.O. for the unit, and he'd suggested it to the general. Who'd refused to consider it. That had been just before Hesslor. "Men like those," the general had said, "need a good first sergeant more than they do a good C.O. Any company does, and these men more than most. But what they really need is both. We've got the one now, and I'm depending on you to find me the other."

The subcolonel hadn't expected it to happen so soon. The next afternoon, the report came that Hesslor had been killed in a fight. His killer was in custody. Viskon called Fenssen in and asked him what had happened.

"I did what we agreed on: told the lieutenant that Makoor was after his job—that he'd told me so. The lieutenant went in his office and didn't come out for about an hour. When he did, he had a bat he'd took to carryin' sometimes, and ast me where Makoor was. I told him off duty, prob'ly in the barracks.

"Bisto came in about ten minutes later. He said Hesslor had gone in the barracks with the club in his hand and told Makoor to go outside with him. He motioned that Makoor should go out first, which meant

Makoor had to turn his back on him. While they were going to the door, Hesslor raised his club to hit him from behind, and Makoor killed him."

The sergeant shrugged, and grunted again. "I questioned four different men, separate; they all said the same thing. 'Cept for how Makoor did it; nobody agrees on that. What Bisto said was, it was so quick, it took 'em by surprise."

"Surely someone must have said something. Warned Makoor what was happening."

Fenssen shrugged again. "I ast 'em that separate. They all said no one did."

"Do you think they were telling the truth?"

Fenssen shrugged again. "They all agreed. And they'd had no chance to talk to each other from the time I questioned the first one till I'd done with 'em."

"Umm. All right, Sergeant, you can go now. And thank you."

A written order from the general got Sergeant Makoor's prompt release, and Fenssen told him the colonel wanted to see him. Standing now before Viskon's desk, Carrmak seemed as calm and unruffled as when he'd first been questioned, weeks earlier. Viskon wondered if such calm might be a symptom of something pathological.

"None of the witnesses seem to agree on how, precisely, you killed Hesslor. How did you?"

"It was too quick to think abawt," Carrmak answered. "I din't trust him, so I give a little look back over my shoulder and seen him raise his club. I spun and moved inside the swing, and did whatever it was I did."

Viskon regarded him thoughtfully. It sounded reasonable. "That makes four men killed in the unit inside a week. You seem like an intelligent man, Makoor. What do you think is wrong?"

A slight smile curved Carrmak's mouth before he answered. "Colonel, a dozen or so of 'em are flat crazy, and some of the rest ayn't much better. Put 'em all together and you've got trouble."

"Hmm. What would you do about that? If it were up to you."

"Me? I'd cull the outfit. Keep maybe a dozen and a half. That's abawt how many's worth it."

"Interesting. Are you one we should keep?"

Carrmak definitely smiled then. "I think so."

"Given the list of charges against you, when you were brought here, I'd have said you were a violent psychotic. A troublemaker at the very least."

Carrmak pursed his lips thoughtfully. "At most farms I was their best worker. Where the food and the treatment was even halfway decent. At this one place though— After a few days there, we were all of us like gunpowder. And when the foreman hit this old gaffer in the face with his stick, that was it for me. It was like the gaffer was my dad again."

"Umm. I suppose you read and write?"

"Yessir."

"Sit down and make me a list of who you'd keep and who you'd let go."

Viskon shoved tablet and pen across his desk. Carrmak sat and wrote. When he was done, Viskon looked the sheet over and almost marveled. The man had not only made the lists; he'd done it alphabetically! "Thank you, Makoor. Return to your barracks now. Stay there until I send for you."

When Carrmak had gone, Viskon phoned the unit's orderly room and told Fenssen to come over. He told the sergeant what Makoor had suggested, and asked him to provide a list of who he'd cull. Fenssen's list agreed quite closely with Carrmak's.

The next day, Makoor was promoted to warrant officer third class, and appointed unit commander. The unit, to be culled promptly, would henceforth be known as the Commander's Personal Guard.

Carrmak had a private room again, a place where he could meditate. He discovered that his body wasn't as flexible as it had been; a half-lotus would have to serve for the time being.

Instead of meditating, he contemplated his situation. Why was he here? What use could he make of his position? Kill the general? There'd be a new commander within a day or two. Listen and learn, and somehow get information to Burnt Woods? To do that, he'd have to make effective contacts. It might be possible. What seemed most feasible, though, was to desert and get back to the regiment. He was sure he could do that.

On the other hand, it seemed to him that here, he was in a position with potential. The question was, potential for what?

*Relax,* he told himself. *Don't push it. It'll come to you. It'll show itself.* After that he did meditate.

# 54

Colonel Ko-Dan and his aide stood by the railing of the excursion liner *Linna Princess,* watching the farmland of northern Komars passing on both shores of the Linna. They weren't alone; the railings were lined with

T'swa troopers in a calm yet somehow festive mood. They were going to war. The contract allowed them two weeks for conditioning and acclimating, orientation and briefings. Ko-Dan had decided that one had been enough.

The sun was bright, the sky blue between scudding white clouds, but the wind was chill. The trees along the banks and roads and around the farmsteads were mostly bare. There were scattered evergreens, and some species of deciduous trees still bore remnant brown leaves, but overall, the aspect was one of impending winter.

Ko-Dan had just commented on a dubious Komarsi decision. "But you declined the general's request to advise him," Ibang observed.

Ko-Dan regarded the surface of the river. "Advice has purposely been omitted from the contracts," he replied. "And we are neither trained nor experienced in directing large units. As I pointed out."

Ibang's teeth flashed white. "He was disappointed none the less. Particularly since he knows that the Iryalans have been advising and training the Smoleni."

Ko-Dan's answer was serene as he watched the Maragoran version of a gull dip a small fish from the surface of the river. "We are T'swa, and therefore visibly quite strange. To the general, we are an enigma. As for the barbarous Engwar II Tarsteng, I shall give him everything the contract calls for, but little if anything more."

Ibang chuckled, then changed the subject. "The Iryalans are sure to challenge us."

"Very likely, sooner or later. It will be a pleasure to contest with them, especially after the inept drafts we faced on Carjath." The colonel's gaze became remote then, as if contemplating some other realm, some other reality. "This war will be more than strenuous. I believe we will find it stimulating in various respects. There will be surprises, things one can hardly foresee."

Ibang nodded, his smile beatific now. Meanwhile, perhaps within ten days, they'd test the Smoleni and see what kind of fighting men they were.

# 55

Tomm Grimswal stood by a tree in the darkness. Stood because orders said to; you weren't as likely to fall asleep on your feet.

Wintry temperatures had arrived on schedule in the Free Lands;

nothing severe yet, but seasonable. Only the snow delayed. A cold night wind moaned through the treetops and rattled the leafless *roivan* branches. Tomm had been a high school student in Rumaros before the war. He didn't like the wind, and he'd decided too late that he didn't like the army. He especially didn't like picket duty at night.

For one thing it seemed unnecessary. The Komarsi weren't going to come in the night. In fact, they weren't going to move this far from their lines day or night. Besides, clouds hid the stars, and the moons if any of them were up now. You couldn't see ten feet, and all you could hear was the wind.

He was tired of holding his submachine gun, too. A rifle was long enough that you could lean on it, but on night duty you got SMGs because any fighting would be at short range, and you couldn't aim at night anyway.

He'd sit down and maybe catch twenty winks, except Marky was on the other side of the tree, and he'd tell the sergeant. Marky Felkor was unreasonable about orders, even when the orders were obvious bullshit. He thought because he'd been in the fighting along the . . .

From just around the tree from him, Tomm was startled by a burst of submachine gun fire, and then another. His immediate thought was that Marky had fallen asleep and fired by accident, maybe from a dream. He heard Sergeant Tarrbon call out: "What post is that?"

"Fourteen!" Marky shouted back. It was the last thing Tomm Grimswal ever heard, because just then a large hard hand closed over his mouth, and a razor-sharp knife slit his throat nearly to the spine. It might have been soundless, except that when he'd felt the hand, the youth's thoracic muscles had spasmed, driving air from the severed trachea with a rude and liquid noise. His submachine gun fell to the frozen ground unfired, its safety catch still set, its only sound a thud.

Corporal Il-Dak realized at once that the soldier's comrade had heard the noise, and instead of lowering the body quietly, he dropped it and jumped sideways six feet, landing in a crouch. Overhead a flare popped, and another, flooding the forest with brilliant white light. Though he didn't look up at it, the brightness blinded him, blinded all of them for a moment. Then he spotted his partner, sprawled where the first shots had found him. He bounded forward like a night cat to find and shoot the other picket, but someone fired from behind another tree, a burst needlessly, wastefully long. Five slugs tore into Il-Dak's torso. And his own burst tore into frozen ground as he fell. All around, the T'swa slunk forward, avoiding the glare so far as possible, keeping to the inky shadows. More shots were fired.

✧    ✧    ✧

From here and there came gunfire. *These aren't Komarsi,* thought Lieutenant Joran Bannsfor. Not deep in the forest in the dark of night, sixty miles north of the Eel. Which meant the T'swa had arrived! He peered hard and saw nothing.

The flares, on their parachutes, had been swept southeastward by the wind. Bannsfor fired another, off somewhat to his right, then glimpsed movement among the trees just ahead, coming toward him as he reloaded the flare pistol. Marsoni's rifle banged beside him. *T'swa or whatever,* he thought, *these people know how to move.*

And thought no more. Some of the T'swa had infiltrated unnoticed, and one of them fired a burst from behind him. Bannsfor fell dying. Private Marsoni spun even though hit, and fired a single round from his bolt action, the bullet finding nothing, before a T'swa round took him in the face.

Major Hober Steeg had wakened to a call of nature, and been standing beside a straddle trench when the first burst had ruptured the night. *T'swa,* he thought. Before he'd even buttoned his fly, there was firing from here, there, seemingly everywhere, and he dropped into a crouch. The first flares had almost blown away already, but more were being fired; the T'swa night vision, it seemed to him, wasn't an advantage to them any longer.

He held his pistol in a white-knuckled fist and peered around with no idea what to do next. Meanwhile the firing increased. "Shit!" he said aloud, and started for his nearby command tent. Then a different sound assaulted his ears as a grenade blasted the tent ahead of him. A bullet plucked his sleeve, and he threw himself onto the ground. He could see his on-duty radioman sprawled in the tent door, and wondered if he'd gotten a message off. A man in black ran past in a crouch, a submachine gun in his hands. The major, prostrate, twisted and fired. The man didn't pause, but before Steeg could shoot again, someone else had, and the man in black fell, half spinning. The face was black too, the eyes large in the flare light: a T'swi for sure! The black man rose to his knees and fired a burst at something, then dropped to his side, drawing another magazine from his belt, slamming it into his weapon. The major shot again, once, twice, and the T'swi went limp.

The major got to his feet and headed for the radio.

Artus Romlar sat in his winterized command tent at base camp. Morning lit it through the fabric roof. The T'swa were more than an intelligence report now. A force of them, probably a company, had hit 2nd Battalion, 5th Smoleni Infantry, shot it up and withdrawn. Fairly standard T'swa procedure: When you arrive in a war zone, you engage the enemy in a small action to test his fighting quality and learn what you'll be dealing with. *Then* you plan.

A stocky, middle-aged Smoleni woman popped into the tent with breakfast. There were snowflakes on her shawl. She put the tray on his table and he thanked her. More bodies might be found later, he thought, and some of the wounded would no doubt die, but the initial count was encouraging: 42 T'swa bodies had been counted. The Smoleni Battalion had lost 96 killed and 152 wounded. The T'swa would be impressed and pleased with the quality of their opposition.

Where were they quartered? Or bivouacked? He should have something on that soon. Since the big Komarsi strike of Sevendek, Colonel Fossur had set up a field recon network of converted fur trappers, with iron rations and forestry maps. They ranged in threes through the forests in the zone north of the Eel, watching the roads. Each trio had a radio that would reach Shelf Falls.

This snow, if it stayed, would complicate things for the recon network, disclose its presence and force them to keep moving constantly. But it should make them more effective, too, because enemy movements would leave far more conspicuous tracks. The biggest danger was that the T'swa would hunt them down.

He had no doubt that as soon as the snow was deep enough, the T'swa would be out learning to snowshoe.

# 56

By day's end there were four inches of snow on the frozen ground. The next morning the weather station at Burnt Woods registered eight below zero, and it had scarcely topped zero at noon. It was sixteen below the next morning, and colder still on the morning following. Test holes found the river ice up to eight inches thick.

Then the weather moderated. Marine air moved in from the southeast, and midday temperatures rose well above freezing. The next cold front moved in four days later, and before the sky cleared, what was left of the old snow was covered by twenty-five inches of new—an unusually heavy fall—and the temperature was near zero again. It wasn't truly winter yet, the locals assured Romlar, but with the solstice little more than six weeks away, a major thaw was unlikely.

✧     ✧     ✧

Kelmer Faronya had ridden a freight sleigh thirty-five miles to Jump-Off. This fall no trapping parties had moved into the Great North Wild; most of the trappers were in the army. But several parties of old ex-trappers were preparing to trek north for something more important now than furs. They would hunt meat—*erog* and *porso*—and send it back on sleighs. Kelmer was there to record their leaving. Such a hunt was a violation of the rules governing the Confederation reserve, but the meat was badly needed, and the game populations would recover quickly enough from a single year's heavy hunting, just as it recovered from the heavy die-offs of the occasional extreme winter.

So said his guide, the local fur broker, an old man called Hanni. And Kelmer had no reason to disbelieve; these people had lived intimately with the land and its creatures for generations.

Each party had a sleigh to haul its supplies and gear. Just now they were parked before the combined store and fur warehouse, loading supplies: flour, beans, and dried fruit mostly, and cartridges. Beyond that they'd live off the land. Most of the village was there: fifty or so besides the hunters.

What impressed Kelmer most about the hunting parties were the animals hitched to their sleighs: long-legged *erog* geldings, their heavy shoulders higher than a man's head, with long necks that raised their antlers ten feet above the ground, and prehensile noses to aid in browsing. He'd glimpsed them before, in the forest and along the roads farther south, and been awed. They were even more impressive up close.

"What's their advantage over horses?" Kelmer asked.

"Well, first off their legs are so much longer. Helps in deep snow. But mostly, horses need hay in winter; they can't make do on twigs, 'specially *jall* 'n *fex* twigs, which along with *kren* is what we mostly got up 'round here."

"Why don't the farmers use *erog*?"

"They ain't no farmers up here."

"I mean farther south. Around Burnt Woods, for example."

"Ah. *Erog* ain't no way tame as horses. These here was either took as foals or dropped by a penned mare. And gelded. Ain't nobody could harness an *erog* stallion; the geldings are bad enough. One of them big old hooves hits a *loper,* his head is broke right then, maybe 'long with his neck. They'd do the same to you. And they bites worser'n a horse. Horses'll bite, sure, but them boogers"—he gestured at an *erog* calmly chewing its cud—"can truly take a chunk outta you. You don't go up to *him* and stroke his nose."

"Do people ever ride them?"

Hanni crowed with laughter. "No how! Too mean!"

"Horses can be mean, but people ride them."

"Sure. But these long-neck critters could reach around 'n bite you in the saddle. Maybe take yer knee off!"

Kelmer nodded thoughtfully. "I don't suppose all the hunters will go to the same place."

"No no. They'll go up the river together 'bout thirty mile, then a party'll peel off every ten, twelve mile up different side branches to different trapping bounds. All told, they'll hunt over a big territory. They'll hunt *porso* a lot more 'n *erog*, 'cause *porso* runs in bands of twenty or thirty, sometimes more.

"One man in each party'll keep camp while three cast around till they come on tracks. Then one'll go back 'n fetch the gelding and sleigh, while the other two catches up to the *porso* and kills all they can of 'em—maybe five or six—'fore they scatter too bad. Then they'll leave the guts and heads for the jackwolves, use the gelding to drag the carcasses to the sleigh, and haul 'em to the river, where one man'll camp by 'em. Some fellers'll go up the river every couple weeks with big sleighs and teams, and bring back what's out."

The sleighs were ready, and the hunters. Men who seemed mostly to be in their sixties, tough old men with their earlappers up in the zero cold. They climbed together onto the sleighs, and the men at the reins slapped their geldings on the rump. The *erog* started off, mostly with a jerk, drawing the sleighs down the riverbank and onto the ice. Kelmer watched them through his visor, recording.

And wished he were going with them, to live and record a week in their life. He wasn't a warrior, he told himself, he was a photojournalist. He'd gotten into this job to record an interesting way of life—interesting and exciting scenes and events.

"And they'll hunt all winter?" he asked.

The old fur broker raised an eyebrow at the question. "Not likely. They'll come out when they ain't much *porso* or *erog* left 'round where they're huntin'. When what they ain't killed has scattered, maybe moved out of the district."

Kelmer lost himself in visualization for a moment. "They'll have killed a lot of animals."

"Son," Hanni said, "with all the folks down in them refugee camps, all we can kill won't begin to be enough. All we can do is help. Make a difference."

# 57

Colonel Ko-Dan and Captain Ibang walked into the reception room outside Undsvin's office. Both of them saw the guard standing beside his door, and knew him at once. He knew them, too, and knew he'd been recognized. They saw it in his aura, though he never twitched.

Twenty minutes later they'd finished their business, and started back to their billet in the GPV assigned to them by the general. "You noticed Undsvin's guard," Ibang said.

"Yes. Major Carrmak. I must say I was surprised."

"The Iryalans are remarkably resourceful. I take it you don't intend to tell the general who his guard is."

"We are contracted in a military role, not as a counterespionage service. If his cousin was a different kind of man, and I thought better of their cause . . . As it is, we will give Engwar his money's worth of fighting—show him the value of a T'swa regiment—but provide him no bonuses." Ko-Dan chuckled. "Whatever Carrmak is doing, it's nothing he learned in the lodge. His commander had a reputation for imagination."

Ibang laughed aloud. "Imagination or not, none of us could masquerade as a local, here or on any world but Tyss."

The general's elite guard, now only a section with two ten-man squads, had been moved to a single large two-story house. Though twenty-two men shared it, Carrmak, as commanding officer, had a small, second-story room for himself.

He'd put together items that would be useful, when the time came, for escaping to Smoleni territory. They were in a pack which hung in his closet, with his greatcoat hanging over it. Tonight his web belt, with its holstered pistol, was also in the pack.

He hadn't known what to expect when the two T'swa walked past him into Undsvin's office. But he'd decided to stay, see what happened. By the time they'd walked out, twenty minutes later, he'd become optimistic. When his shift ended, twenty minutes after that, and nothing had happened, it seemed clear that they hadn't said anything. And if they hadn't then, they weren't likely to later.

Nonetheless he was prepared to go out the window, jump into the back yard, and run for it if anything seemed to threaten. For a while he waited ready. After an hour, he undressed and went to bed with his pistol in easy reach.

# 58

Undsvin had never intended to fight the Smoleni in the northern forests. From the beginning, his strategy had been to shut them off from effective supply sources and starve them out. That was the reason he'd allowed his troops to abuse the local populations as they captured one southern district after another. And why he'd allowed refugees to move north, even though they were an impediment to his advancing army: Stories of murders and rapes would spread with them, and many in the towns ahead would flee northward, putting much greater pressure on the limited Smoleni supplies.

Meanwhile the serfs who made up more than half the Komarsi army had broad competencies of their own. They'd worked with their hands from childhood, doing almost everything there was to do on the estates they'd been part of. Besides field work and barn chores, they'd built and repaired almost everything required, except the manors themselves and their furnishings. And there was no shortage of lumber in Smolen: the sawmills along the Rumar and other major rivers had had many stacks of it dried or drying when the war began. Thus by summer's end, the Komarsi army in Smolen was housed mostly in barracks it had built outside the towns. In-town billeting was limited largely to headquarters personnel; discipline and training were more readily maintained in units barracked in the countryside.

Now that winter had arrived, the troops stayed close to their camps. They were drilled enough that, along with camp chores, they were kept busy, but their main function now was to be there, to occupy southern Smolen. For one thing, they weren't equipped to operate in the northern winter. Their supply of snowshoes was limited, although that was being remedied, and skis were nonexistent. Units along the Eel-Strawstack border with the Free Lands skirmished rather frequently with Smoleni raiders—particularly rangers practicing their new, T'swa-style tactics—but they took no offensive actions.

Even the T'swa were not particularly aggressive now. On Tyss there'd been no opportunity to train in snow and cold. Here they'd been issued snowshoes, and were learning to use them. They were discovering the nature of the landscape in winter—what the operational problems and opportunities were in different landscape types. But T'swa learn fast, and even before the solstice they were out hunting and destroying Smoleni recon teams.

# 59

With the war essentially on hold, Undsvin had gone home for the first time since before the invasion began, to spend the solstice holidays with his family. His daughter had given birth to his first grandson, whom he hadn't yet seen, while his younger son, who'd turned sixteen, had grown what seemed like four inches.

Then, on his second week back at Rumaros, a royal order had come, to fly to the palace at once. It didn't say why. Undsvin felt ill at ease about it, but the king was the king; the general was in the air inside an hour.

It was sleeting that day in Linnasteth. Streets were glazed with ice, and traffic was nearly nonexistent when Undsvin's floater arrived at the palace. The guards who met him stood beneath large umbrellas, to whisk him up the cindered walk and through the ornate entrance.

The king didn't meet him in a reception hall or audience chamber. They met in Engwar's office, just the two of them. (Engwar's bodyguard didn't count; he was a necessary cipher.) Undsvin knew at once that Engwar was deeply agitated. The pouches and dark smudges beneath his eyes told of hours spent rehearsing and dramatizing his troubles instead of sleeping. Still, the king was clearly making an effort to control himself.

He gestured at the chair before his desk, the motion a nervous twitch. "Sit, cousin, sit!"

Undsvin sat.

"What are you doing to win the war?"

"I'm depriving the Smoleni of their farmlands and goods, forcing them to use up their limited supplies."

"They are getting supplies through Oselbent! Both food and munitions! By sleighs over the swamp country!"

"I'm aware of that, Your Majesty. But all that buys them is an extra dek. Two or three at most. They can't bring in enough to begin feeding their people."

Engwar sat heavily, contemplating what his cousin had said. Then, more calmly: "What are the T'swa doing? Why don't I hear of them attacking the Smoleni?"

"T'swa companies have begun harassing Smoleni units weekly now. And they've effectively eliminated the Smoleni surveillance system."

"I didn't hire them to harass, or to destroy surveillance systems. I hired them to destroy the Smoleni."

"Engwar," Undsvin said almost gently, "the T'swa are marvelous fighting men, but they are human. Their world has no snow or cold; they've had to learn to travel and fight in the northern winter. They are already damaging the Smoleni; in time they will demoralize them. And they may yet play a decisive role in shortening the war. But they cannot destroy them."

Engwar gnawed a lip. "The Assembly is complaining about the war. The treasury has shrunken badly, existing taxes are far from adequate, and the Assembly has refused to authorize new. Rich though they are, they have cried and complained at the inflation of currency. They care nothing about their king or country, only their own wealth! So I froze prices, and the merchants rose up screaming! Some have even publicly burned stacks of their goods in protest, while others have closed their doors. Supposedly withholding their goods from sale, though I have no doubt they are selling them on the black market and getting richer than ever."

He exhaled tiredly. "The freedmen have rioted in their disreputable townships, and that fool Nufkarm has publicly urged our royal assistance for them. While that greater fool, Arbendel, has stated that no one should receive assistance without signing an agreement of serfdom. The upshot of that was a wave of arson that resulted in merchants distributing food, a terrible precedent that will have who knows what long-term effects."

The king paused then and looked beseechingly at his older cousin. "Dear Undsvin, I need a victory. I truly need a victory. Something that will excite people, make them glad for the war."

*My god, dear cousin,* Undsvin thought. *What world do you live in?* "Your Majesty," he answered, "I will come up with something. Let me have a week, and I will let you know what my plan is. Though it may well require a dek or two to carry out."

He left the palace wondering how he could have said that. But by the time he landed again at Rumaros, he had the basic idea.

# 60

Undsvin appreciated the potentials of enemy spies, especially in occupied territory. Potentials some of which were positive.

In Rumaros, about seventy percent of the people had stayed when the Komarsi took over. Their situation was poor. There was poverty and hunger. An important part of their income came from the taverns and girls who entertained the Komarsi soldiers, and from those who kept house and cooked and otherwise served the officers. Thus there were abundant opportunities for careless talk to reach the Smoleni intelligence lines that the general had no doubt existed.

So he told no one what he really had in mind, not even Viskon, who in most matters was his confidant as well as his aide. There'd be time enough later to let them know. Instead he called his staff together to give them orders, and false premises for those orders. The T'swa commander was requested to attend.

It was not a conference: opinions weren't asked for; joma wasn't even served. When they were all seated, he gaveled them needlessly to order in a way that was quite bizarre: he rapped the table with the butt of his pistol. What, they wondered apprehensively, was going on with their commander?

"Gentlemen!" The room fell silent. "I've brought you here to tell you about the coming offensive!"

The groan was silent, a psychic protest. Every one of his officers agreed with Undsvin's so-called siege policy, of waiting and letting the Smoleni starve. And they all remembered the ill-fated strike northward in early Sevendek, that began so well and ended so terribly.

"By late winter the Smoleni will be hungry, their morale and their physical strength low, and their guard down. They won't expect us to move before the snow has melted and the roads dried out. Also, by the equinox, the severe cold will be past, and the days longer. But the roads will still be frozen, and the Eel will be locked beneath at least twenty inches of ice, more likely thirty or more. The rivers in the north perhaps fifty.

"We will move at the equinox, striking northward with perhaps five divisions, up every road between the Kumar and Road 45. Snowshoes for five divisions are being produced in Komars even as I speak, made of a cold-resistant plastic."

His officers glanced at one another out of the corners of their eyes. By then there might well be four feet or more of snow, on the roads as well as in the woods. To move and supply artillery—to supply large forces at all—would be a monstrous task. And even at the equinox, subzero weather could be expected—not thirty, forty, or fifty below, but bitter weather for large-scale operations. None of them had operational experience or training in such conditions. And if breakup came early, the snowpack melting before operations were complete . . .

"Other forces will follow," Undsvin continued, "to secure the territory taken. We will continue in this manner all the way to Burnt Woods, capturing the refugee camps on the way. The people will either submit to us, or be forced north past the last villages and camps, to freeze and starve in the snow. If the Smoleni government doesn't surrender then, a force, perhaps of brigade strength, can be sent north up the Granite River, the north branch of the Rumar, to the hamlet of Jump-Off, to close the supply road from Oselbent."

He looked them over, his expression implacable, and they ceased exchanging glances, though none of them met his eyes.

"The planning and preparations for this offensive will be much more demanding than any to date. We'll need to build up major supply and ordnance depots on the Eel Valley Railroad, probably near the villages of Meadowgreen and Eel Fork."

His voice became more conversational now. "I realize there are problems inherent in this. We will develop plans to deal with them. Anoreth, you will prepare a basic operations analysis. Have a draft of it in my hands by next Twoday. On Fourday we will have another meeting to discuss that analysis. Between now and then, the rest of you will give thought to this. I expect you all to take a useful part in that discussion. Afterward I'll assign a planning mission to develop a complete operating plan, from which we'll go to logistical planning."

His voice became imperious again. "I'm going to demand the utmost in careful speed in the whole planning operation. And it requires speed! The equinox is less than a quarter away! You will work harder than you ever worked before. If anyone lags, obstructs progress in any way, I'll find other duties for him. Specifically he'll be leading a penal platoon in the offensive.

"Any questions?"

Faces had paled. Middle-aged staff officers grown fat and soft, leading penal platoons into combat? If the Smoleni didn't kill them, their own soldiers were liable to! Such a threat to noblemen was unprecedented.

Among the Komarsi staff officers, only Colonel Sharf, Undsvin's intelligence chief, seemed unflapped. "The Smoleni will learn of these depots," Sharf said, "and may very well deduce from them the basic features of our plans."

"It will be your responsibility to see that they deduce incorrectly," Undsvin answered, and looked them over. "Anything else?"

No one spoke.

"Very well. Sharf, Colonel Ko-Dan, please remain. The rest of you are dismissed."

When they'd gone, Undsvin said to Sharf: "Colonel, regardless of what I said before the others, *I do, do* want the Smoleni to learn of this. And I have no doubt that some of the gentlemen who just left will feel constrained to talk about it to their friends. Particularly stressed as they are by my threat of penal platoons. Word will spread. Let it. *Do you understand?*"

"Yes, sir."

"Good. You are dismissed."

He watched Sharf out the door. *You understand enough to follow orders. Beyond that you are utterly mystified, and burning with curiosity. Well. Enjoy!* He turned to Ko-Dan. "Colonel, what is the status of the Smoleni surveillance system?"

"It no longer exists, General. We tracked down and killed most of the men they had operating. A few escaped us; we lost their tracks in a snowstorm. However, the Smoleni may simply discontinue it temporarily, expecting us to withdraw our hunter teams."

"Exactly. I'm depending on it. When they do, I want you to leave them alone. Do not visit the north shore of the Eel. Raid northward along the Upper Rumar if you wish. Any questions?"

"None whatever, general."

Undsvin looked at the T'swi curiously. "Well then, I believe our business is over for the day."

When Ko-Dan had gone, Undsvin sat wondering. Did the T'swi have no questions because he wasn't curious? That seemed unlikely. Surely his orders regarding the Smoleni surveillance system must have seemed strange to him. Just what had he surmised?

In his own office, Ko-Dan had described the meeting to his aide. "You realize what he plans, of course."

Grinning, Ibang nodded. "The Smoleni will learn of the big depot at Meadowgreen, and with their supply problems will be greatly tempted to raid it. No doubt bringing a sleigh column down the road to carry away what they get. And presumably moving major elements of their army with them to protect the sleighs.

"This will, of course, require considerable effort on the part of the Smoleni, and the commitment of much energy and resources, of which they have little to spare. Once their columns are well underway, say past Shelf Falls, they'll be increasingly reluctant to discontinue, except for compelling reasons. Then I suspect the general will want us to clean out their surveillance teams again. After which he'll situate forces at the Eel to ambush their strike force and destroy their sleigh columns.

"That accomplished, he may or may not launch an offensive at the Equinox. I suspect he will not."

Ko-Dan nodded, smiling. "Anything further?"

"He will, of course, have to take certain commanders into his confidence, but that will be quite late in the sequence. His assumption will be that the Smoleni will not learn of the planned ambush." He reached for his cup and sipped the joma, grown tepid during their talk. "Through his Smoleni employers, Colonel Romlar will learn of the supposed offensive. And as deeply as he obviously perceives, will suspect that something is amiss, and send scouts to investigate. A probability our general may well overlook. It is quite possible then, even probable, that some of them will avoid our re-inserted hunter teams, discover the Komarsi ambush forces, and warn the Smoleni away."

Ko-Dan chuckled. "An apt analysis. But there is another possibility, let me say probability. Because the Smoleni truly need supplies, and I suspect they need successes to nourish their spirits. I visualize Romlar warning them in advance that they are being baited, and the Smoleni deciding to try the raid anyway. In which case they'll plan a surprise attack on the Komarsi ambush force."

He got to his feet and replenished his joma from the pot on his sheet-iron stove. "Consider that the Iryalans are training Smoleni woodsmen as what they term 'rangers.' In some numbers. From our own limited experience, there is no doubt that these so-called ranger units will prove much better than anything General Undsvin can field. Much more mobile and confident in the forest and the snow, much more energetic and responsive to situations, and more skillful with their weapons." He sat down again. "And of course, the Iryalans are likely to involve themselves. I would rather expect the Komarsi ambush force to be savaged."

"Ah!" Ibang's eyes brightened. "And we will prepare a counter-ambush of our own. Perhaps even engaging the Iryalans in a decisive fight!"

The colonel's upper lip dipped cautiously in the scalding drink. "Exactly. Of course, we've made a long and involved series of assumptions, any of which may be in error. But it feels right, as right as the T'sel gives me to feel about something that hasn't yet set up in the reality matrix."

# 61

Kelmer Faronya took off his skis and leaned them against the porch rail. Then he stepped up onto the porch, spoke cheerfully to the guard, and rang the president's doorbell. The butler answered.

"Good evening, Mr. Faronya. Step inside please." Kelmer did, and the butler closed the door against the cold. "We haven't seen you for a time. Shall I tell Miss Lanks you're here?"

"If you would, please." He waited while the man left. A minute later, Weldi came smiling down the stairs and put her hand on Kelmer's arm. As always, the touch speeded his pulse.

"Kelmer, dear," she said as she guided him toward the guest parlor, "we've missed you. I've missed you." She frowned. "And when I heard about the attack on the supply train . . ." They sat down on the settee. "Were you in danger?"

"*I* wasn't. Not really." He looked back at the experience. He'd gone to Jump-Off again, this time to record a sleigh train coming with supplies from Oselbent. "Hanni Distra took me out the supply road in a cutter pulled by an *erog*. We'd gone about twelve miles when we heard rifle fire about half a mile ahead. We stopped, of course; couldn't see what was going on. There was a stretch of tall reeds in the fen just ahead. After the shooting stopped, we waited for a few minutes, not knowing what to expect. Then there was more. This time it sounded like machine guns and rifles both. Soon after that was over, there was a big explosion, and after that two really big ones.

"We talked about whether to go back, or stay awhile and see what happened next. There was a radio with the train, and a company of infantry at Jump-Off, with skis. So we waited. When nothing more happened, I skied on ahead, listening hard. After a while I came to bodies in the snow—our own people and some T'swa. I didn't hunt around and count, but I saw more than half a dozen bodies, including two T'swa. None of them were moving. It looked like the train had had scouts ahead on skis, and the T'swa had ambushed them where the road passed near a stand of *fex*.

"The T'swa wore snowshoes instead of skis, and from their tracks, they'd gone on to attack the train. There were a lot of them, maybe a company. What I didn't know was, were they still there? Maybe waiting to hit any relief party that might come from Jump-Off?"

He stopped, his expression abstracted. After a moment, Weldi asked, "Then what?"

"Then I went ahead a few hundred yards, following the T'swa's snowshoe tracks, till I passed through a narrow neck of muskeg. There were several dead T'swa there, too, and I could see the train ahead, out on the open fen. And where the T'swa had spread out along the edge of the trees, as if they'd been firing from there. I found out afterward there'd been machine gunners with the train, and they'd started shooting when they saw the T'swa. Then the T'swa had taken cover and picked off the machine gunners before going on. They're marvelous marksmen.

"I couldn't see any activity at the train, so I kept going, and found a couple more dead T'swa before I came to it. They'd blown the tracks off the steam tractor, and blown up a couple of sleighs loaded with ammunition. Then they went on east along the road. There were a couple of guys with the train that weren't dead, just wounded. And suffering from exposure; they'd been lying in the snow too hurt to move much. They were lucky it wasn't cold; not a lot below freezing. So I hurried back and brought Hanni with the cutter, and we started west with the wounded.

"After a little while we met troops skiing out from Jump-Off. They'd heard the explosions from thirteen miles away! When we told them what happened, they went on east. They wanted to catch the T'swa before they hit another train.

"I'd recorded everything I saw and heard. Then today I got a real early start and skied back here. I met two more infantry companies on the way, headed for Jump-Off. I haven't heard what happened to the company that followed the T'swa."

Weldi took one of his hands in hers. "Oh, Kelmer," she murmured, "I worry about you so when you're gone. I'm never sure..." She stopped then, and kissed him. He put his arms around her, and they kissed some more. His breath labored as if he'd been running upstairs. After a minute she pushed him away. "Not here," she said.

"Where then?"

She didn't answer at once, her gaze troubled. "Not anywhere. I—I love you too much. I'm afraid we'd do something we shouldn't." They sat looking soberly at each other for another minute, then embraced again and kissed some more. Finally she pushed him away and got up. "I think—you should go." She fluttered her hands. "But don't stay away. I just need to, to think."

Kelmer nodded, backing away. "I'll come back tomorrow if I can."

His mind was spinning as he put on his skis and started back to camp. He thought how much he loved Weldi Lanks, how lovely she was, how desirable. *And she loved him!* Halfway to camp he stopped, a decision made without even looking at it, and turned back to the village, kicking hard. He stepped out of his skis, bounded up the porch steps, and rang the bell again while the guard eyed him quizzically. The butler's eyebrows arched when he saw who it was.

"Mr. Faronya! Did you forget something?"

"I'll say! Something important," Kelmer answered as he went in. "I need to speak with Weldi again."

She met him in the hall, her expression troubled. "Is anything the matter?" she asked.

"Marry me!" he said. "Marry me and nothing will be the matter!" She stared.

"Marry me and I'll try hard to make you happy. All our lives."

She stepped into his arms then, looking into his eyes. "Oh yes, Kelmer, yes, I'll marry you." She kissed him, then stepped back. "We'll have to talk with Daddy, though. I'm not of age."

He nodded, suddenly unsure of himself. She went upstairs while he waited. A few minutes later, a disheveled president followed his daughter down the stairs, wearing slippers, and with trousers pulled on over his nightshirt. He looked grave, as he often did.

"My daughter tells me you want to marry each other," he said.

"Yes, sir. Very much, sir."

"I presume then that you love her."

"Yes, sir."

He turned to Weldi. "And you love him, I take it."

"Yes, Daddy, very much."

"Hmm. Well. And when did you want this wedding to take place?"

They stared at each other, unsure what to say, then Kelmer looked at the president. "We haven't talked about that, sir, but . . . soon. I could be in a firefight next week, and—that could be it for me."

Heber Lanks's long face grew even longer, and he turned to his daughter again. "When would you suggest?" he asked.

"Tomorrow," she said, without hesitation.

He pursed his lips, looking to Kelmer again. "How long have you been talking about this?"

"We, uh—just since this evening, sir," Kelmer said.

"Ah. Well. Let's set a tentative date for some day late next week. That will give you both time to think about it some more." He raised his hands defensively. "And to get a wedding dress fitted and made."

"Father!" Weldi said, "we're in a war! And this is Burnt Woods, not Cliffview! I don't need a gown; I'll wear my best dress. And I've known for deks that I want to marry Kelmer; *I'd* have asked *him* if he'd taken much longer." She shook her head. "Next week isn't soon enough. Colonel Romlar could send Kelmer to Shelf Falls tomorrow, and who knows . . ." She cut her sentence short.

The president's expression was rueful now. He looked at Kelmer. "I suppose you've been thinking about this for deks too."

"Yes sir." Actually he hadn't. He'd been wanting for deks to take Weldi to bed, but he'd thought seriously about marriage only a couple of times. Now, though, he had no doubt. He did want to marry her, and be married to her forever.

"Well." The president stood regarding the carpet for an endless half minute. "Today is Twoday, the twentieth of Onedek. How would, um— Fiveday the twenty-third be?"

Weldi startled them both; she laughed. "Daddy, you're hopeless. Fourday!"

"Um." He waggled his head, clearly not in denial. Perhaps in self-commiseration. "Fourday afternoon then, if Colonel Romlar agrees. That will give you time to move things into the guest bedroom. The one you have now hasn't got room to add anyone else's things, not even a soldier's."

She threw her arms around her father's neck and kissed him, then hugged Kelmer and kissed him much differently. Her father looked more lugubrious than ever.

Kelmer skied back to camp almost without touching the snow.

# 62

Surprisingly, the wedding hadn't much interfered with presidential duties. Because Weldi, to the president's surprise, had insisted there be no advance announcement and no guests. Colonel Fossur served in the semiformal position of groom's uncle, counseling Kelmer in advance on how to treat one's bride, particularly in bed. Idrel Fossur had served as the bride's aunt. At the ceremony, it was the president, of course, who solemnly reminded the bride that her marriage would have priority over the parental family. Colonel Fossur, in turn, reminded the groom that responsibility to his wife had precedence over his relationships with other friends. Colonel Romlar had stood beside the groom, suppressing his tendency to grin, while Mrs. Fossur had supported the bride. The mayor of Burnt Woods presided.

When the ceremony was over, the newlyweds, with their skis, some food, personal luggage and precious wine, had been loaded into a cutter drawn by the mayor's handsome harness horse, an animal which he loved and never allowed anyone else to drive. So it was the beaming mayor who'd taken the newlyweds and their skis to his getaway cabin on Owl Lake, and left them there.

Thus on Fiveday the twenty-third, the War Council met in the president's office almost as if nothing unusual had happened the day before. Colonel Fossur presented and evaluated information received on two large new supply depots the Komarsi were building: one at Meadowgreen, on the railroad three miles south of Mile 40 Bridge across the Eel, and the other near the village of Eel Fork, where the river flowed into the Rumar, some twenty-five miles north and west of Rumaros. He felt they might presage a spring offensive to deny the Smoleni the production of northern farming settlements.

The president examined the statement. "You say *might* presage a spring offensive. What are the other possibilities?"

"I was coming to that, sir. I've had a report from two agents in

Rumaros that Undsvin plans an equinox offensive, a very large one, supposedly using six divisions plus followup forces. My agents found that hard to credit, too. The story is that Undsvin made heavy threats to ensure compliances from his staff."

"Why should they mount an offensive in spring or any other season?" Belser growled. "The smart thing to do is sit back and starve us out. It would cost a lot less, and save a lot of young men's lives."

"Most of those lives would be serf lives," the president pointed out. "And I doubt that Engwar worries about serf lives. Elyas, at our last meeting you reviewed Komarsi civil unrest and other economic and political problems caused by the war. Could it be that Engwar wants an offensive to take his people's minds off the problems at home?"

Fossur shook his head. "It's conceivable, but I've seen no evidence that things are that bad there. And considering how badly it went with their last bold stroke . . ."

Belser interrupted. "Have you heard what they're stockpiling in the new depots?"

Fossur looked surprised at the question. "As a matter of fact I have. About what you'd expect: Munitions ordinary to a campaign, plus fodder, barrels of hardtack, and cases of dried fruit. Presumably other foodstuffs will come later."

The president spoke thoughtfully. "An equinox offensive by a large army might make sense, if they're properly equipped. We'd have much more difficulty safeguarding our supplies. We'd have to disperse them, and they could follow the sleigh tracks. And if they drove us out of our villages and refugee camps—drove us all into the forest with three or four feet of snow still on the ground—for all intents and purposes the war would be over."

Vestur Marlim replied before the general could. "Mr. President, such an offensive would cost the Komarsi heavily in material and blood. I can't believe they'd do it when our condition will be critical by early next winter at the latest."

They all sat quiet then. It was Belser who broke free of it. "Let's raid the depot at Mile 40," he said. "We need the supplies worse than they do."

Marlim stared. *And this was a man who, last summer, lacked fight! But . . .* "Eskoth!" he said. "You can't be serious!"

"Certainly I'm serious! If we pull it off, we'll not only ease our supply situation—particularly munitions—we may also dislocate the Komarsi plan, whatever it is."

The War Minister shook his head. "It's altogether too dangerous. We'd never get away with it."

Remarkably, Belser didn't get angry. "If your house starts to burn when you're sleeping on the second floor, it could be dangerous to run down the stairs or jump out the window. But it's absolutely fatal to stay in bed."

"What if your neighbor is on his way with a ladder?"

"And what if he's not? What if his brother-in-law borrowed it and didn't bring it back?"

"Gentlemen!" Lanks said, and they stopped. "Colonel Romlar, you haven't said anything yet."

Romlar smiled ruefully. "That's because I don't have anything to say yet."

Lanks looked at him, still with a question in his eyes, then turned to the others. "I'd like both of you—Elyas, Eskoth—to sit down and draft an analysis. By tomorrow. And for security reasons, minimize the staff involved. Then bring copies to Vestur and me. We'll discuss this further on Oneday."

Fossur completed his intelligence review then. One of the data he mentioned was that companies of Komarsi infantry had been observed practicing on snowshoes. Which fitted the rumor of an equinox offensive.

Romlar still said nothing. He wanted to let the ideas ferment awhile.

# 63

On Oneday the War Council met again. They discussed Belser's idea at length—he'd provided a basic operating plan by then—and decided: As dangerous as it was, and as much as it would cost their limited and shrinking supplies, they would do it. It was time, said Heber Lanks, for daring.

It was a simple plan, as military plans go. An infantry brigade on skis would move down the 40-Mile Road, followed closely by a sleigh column—all the logging sleighs readily available. Details of troops would cobble together cargo boxes, spiking them to the log bunks.

The brigade would assemble in the forest near Shelf Falls, where presumably no one would see. Converting logging sleighs for package freight was not unheard of; these would be prepared wherever they happened to be, which would conceal their significance. They too would be brought together near Shelf Falls.

The brigade would suppress Komarsi troops protecting the Meadowgreen depot, and load the sleighs. The Iryalan mercenaries and two battalions of the newly trained rangers would scout ahead and on the flanks of the column, and would cover the withdrawal, once the sleighs were loaded. Speed, even haste, was emphasized.

Romlar then developed a plan of his own, compatible with theirs. But kept it secret even from the War Council; reviewing it only with his own battalion commanders. There'd be time enough to coordinate with others, especially with the commanders of the ranger battalions, when they approached the Eel.

# 64

On his side of the road was forest. On the other side lay a field, and beyond it more forest, all deep in snow. Kelmer Faronya tromped a place for himself in forty inches of it, then released the toe-bindings of his skis and stood one of them upright. With the other he swept the snow from the leaning trunk of a blowndown *jall* and clambered onto it, steadying for balance against a stout branch stub. From there he had a view of the troops moving south along the road. The Smoleni wore army green. Rifles slung, one company after another skied by, as silently as an army ever moves. Occasionally Kelmer murmured to his camera, sometimes narrating, sometimes verbally switching it off or on. After several minutes he cut it off, and waited till he saw the guidon of Battery C, one of 7th Regiment's howitzer batteries, the last unit before the sleigh column. Then he switched the camera back on and watched them pass, their guns with the wheels mounted on broad flat runners.

The sleigh column came into view behind it. The horses were not in good condition, though better than they may have looked to most eyes. They were shaggy against the season's cold, and unkempt like the old men who drove them. And somewhat gaunt, which was particularly undesirable in winter; it had been most of a year since they'd tasted grain.

Fortunately for the horses, the weather was mild. Just then, in early afternoon, it was about twenty-five degrees, not a lot below freezing. Had the weather been severe, it would have been much harder on them than it was.

The sleighs they drew were mismatched and crude, their runners and bunks rough-sawn timbers, or in some cases ax-hewn. Their cargo boxes were partly of boards, but mostly of slabs with bark on one side. Just now the cargo on each was only a pile of hay bales. They'd started out with more, had eaten some and left others in piles along the road for the return trip—hopefully a return trip. The cargo boxes would hold other than hay then, if things went well.

He watched the whole long column pass, 114 logging sleighs drawn by 228 horses, with a small herd of spare horses trailing. When they were by, Kelmer jumped down and donned his skis again. All he had to do now was pass the entire sleigh column and most of the brigade, and catch what was temporarily his outfit—Headquarters Company of the Smoleni Army's 2nd Brigade. Before dark if he could.

The Iryalan 1st Battalion was along, but operating at a little distance. And with the brigadier's ready agreement, Romlar had detailed Kelmer to 2nd Brigade, had said it was more important to get cubeage of the column than of the troopers in this raid, at least until the sleighs were loaded and the return underway. Kelmer felt a certain resentment at this—to him it seemed rejection—but mostly he felt relief. Around regimental headquarters, he'd felt a deep current of excitement, as if they'd be going into some particular and unusual danger. Which it seemed to him could only mean they expected to fight the T'swa. And if, in the past, he'd felt a deep visceral fear of combat, he'd added to it now an intellectual fear. For he'd gained a wife, someone he very much wanted to return to.

And there was something more. At Blue Forest he'd trained for a year under T'swa cadre, and felt a strong affinity with them—with their whole species. An affinity which he couldn't reconcile with killing them or being killed by them.

The weather held unseasonably mild, which helped progress. Troop morale was stronger, too. The packed snow was slicker, and the sleighs, growing ever lighter as the hay was eaten or loaded off, pulled more easily and rapidly.

Second Ranger Battalion was the point force, scouting the route in advance of the brigade. The Iryalan 1st Battalion was ahead on the right, and the 1st Rangers ahead on the left. There'd been no sign of Komarsi, nor of T'swa patrols. There'd been no recent tracks of anyone, only traces of old snowshoe trails buried by later snow.

Finally, on the next to last day of the trek south, Romlar sent a courier to Brigadier Carnfor, saying he planned to visit him in camp that evening, needing to speak with him.

Wearing the regiment's white winter field uniform, something new to Maragor, he arrived after nightfall, after camp was made, and they hunkered on an area of tramped-down snow around a fire. There was no joma, not even war joma; grain was too precious now to scorch for drinking. There was hot tea though—melted snow boiled with *fex* buds to make a brew that was hot, bitter with tannin, and rich in vitamins.

Very briefly they traded trivia and sipped. Then Romlar turned to business. "In the morning," he said, "the Third Ranger Battalion will take over the right flank. My battalion has something else to do."

The brigadier raised his eyebrows. "The Third? I thought they were at Shelf Falls."

"They've been following a mile or two behind the sleighs. My analysis is that the depot is bait for a trap. There are reasons to suspect there'll be concealed forces on the south side of the Eel, waiting to jump you after you've crossed. If so, the T'swa will be involved. If I'm right about this, they plan to chop you up badly. I'll take my battalion, along with the ranger battalions, and surprise their ambush, hit it from behind."

Carnfor stared. "A trap," he echoed. The brigadier had foreseen that as a possibility, but to have it set before him with such seeming confidence . . .

Romlar unfolded a forestry map of the area. The depot had been inked in on it. Contour lines showed a respectable ridge a mile west of the depot; a green wash showed it forested. "I expect they'll have artillery here," he continued, pointing, "along the ridge top. They'll probably let you cross the bridge, then knock it out. And besides the predictable units emplaced to guard the depot, they should have a strong infantry force hidden here." He pointed to the stretch of forest between the ridge and the open ground the depot was set in. "There's woods enough there for a brigade."

He pointed to the open country south of the depot. "This would be a logical place for their artillery, especially if they expect you to answer with some of your own. But I don't think that's where it will be. And odds are they'll have no forces north of the river. Our scouts would almost surely find them, and that would spoil their trap.

"Also, there'll probably be a freight train parked at the depot, a long one. If there is, it will no doubt be full of concealed troops, waiting to jump out when you've been cut off south of the river. Be ready for that."

The brigadier gazed into the flickering campfire, his drawn face ruddied by its flames. "How sure are you of this?" he asked.

Romlar shrugged. "I have no explicit evidence; I'm basing it on hints—peculiarities and anomalies in the situation. But I'm reasonably confident there'll be something of the sort. The reason I didn't bring this up in War Council was the danger of spies. You people need all the supplies you can get, and this is an opportunity. And if you're to get them, it's best the Komarsi don't know we suspect.

"If I'm wrong, well and good. You should get the supplies without too much fighting. If I'm right, you should get the supplies anyway, and we should be able to surprise and shoot up their ambush force."

"What makes you think you can do that? Especially if the T'swa are involved."

Romlar didn't elaborate on his plans. He simply said, "The Rangers will coordinate with us."

The brigadier gazed long at Romlar. *He looks so damned young,* Carnfor thought. *And it seems too pat! But so far he's pulled off everything he's tried. And if confidence means anything . . .* "Thank you, Colonel," he said. Grimly now. "We'll be ready."

They discussed coordination then, and Romlar left. *We do need supplies,* Carnfor thought, *munitions even more than food. But can we afford to risk so much for them?* He watched Romlar ski away, perhaps finding some slight assurance in the boy-colonel's broad white back and his easy skill on skis.

Romlar's battalion broke camp early and set out well before dawn. They crossed the ice early the next evening, more than eight miles upstream of the Mile 40 Bridge. South of the Eel much of the country was open farmland, but between it and the Welvarn Morain were areas of forest, some of it rather thin from long-time summer grazing. The troopers then moved eastward, mostly under cover of woods. After a bit they came to an abundance of ski tracks they took to be those of the 3rd Ranger Battalion, which had crossed before them, as intended. At a point just east of Road 45, the troopers camped that night in a stretch of ungrazed forest along the west slope of a little ridge.

Romlar traded his skis for the snowshoes he'd carried on his pack, and scouted cautiously ahead with two men. When he reached the ridgetop, the moonlight showed him the larger ridge a mile or so ahead, on which he expected the Komarsi artillery to be set up. Between the two was another ridge, smaller than either. If he was correct, the T'swa would be on the middle ridge. The map indicated that all three ridges and the ground between were wooded, and as far as he could see, that was right.

The 3rd Rangers should, he thought, be ahead and well to his left, waiting for morning, and for the sounds that would cue them into action, sending them up the higher ridge to attack the Komarsi artillery ambush. The T'swa, hearing the firefight, would hit them from behind, hopefully thinking they were his troopers. The 3rd, meanwhile, would be expecting them.

A lot of ifs—more than he liked. His genius as a commander was that his ifs almost always worked out; his attunement to the reality matrix was remarkably good. The trick was to get the necessary hard evidence as well, or as much as you could, and put it all together. But sometimes hard evidence was short when you wanted it.

Tomorrow would answer his questions, he told himself. As for wasting his regiment—his fear, any fear, was aberration. He'd do what he had to, what the situation called for.

Beckoning, he backed down below the crest, then followed a contour southward till he came to a brushy saddle. There he crossed the ridge, watching carefully ahead. Moonlight and starlight on the snow provided excellent visibility. In the near-level bottom between the two ridges, he saw ahead of him the broad, heavily tracked trail of many men on snow-shoes. He gestured the other two to stop, and alone slipped ahead to where he could see the tracks better—close enough to see their direction. Northward; it fitted. Turning, he started back to camp, to brief Major Esenrok and his company commanders on what he'd found.

While they slept, an overcast developed, and at first dawn it was warmer than it had been the previous afternoon. When the officer of the guard made out the faint beginning of day, he woke Romlar, then sent men to waken the company commanders, who in turn had their men wakened. The troopers crushed heat capsules and dropped them in their canteens, that they might start their day with hot water instead of eating snow. Then they sat hunched in their sleeping bags, munching cold iron rations while the sky paled. One by one they stood, swinging their arms, running in place, bending, getting ready for the day. Somewhat before full daylight, they had their packs and snowshoes on, rifles ready. Romlar moved them to the top of the first ridge. It was the warmest dawn they'd seen since autumn.

There they waited—longer than they'd have preferred, but patiently, calmly. Anxiety was something they'd banished years before, primarily in Ostrak sessions. At 1007 hours, Romlar's radio brought him a code phrase that told him the brigade was in place, about to come out of the forest and start across the bridge.

Then nothing, and more nothing, then distant rifle fire that quickly increased. Machine gun fire followed, also distant, swelled briefly, then leveled off. Ahead, the 3rd Rangers would be slipping through the trees now, ready to begin their assault of the ridge. Romlar whistled, not shrilly, and gestured, then started forward on his snowshoes, white-painted skis and poles strapped on his pack. His whistle was echoed by others.

Abruptly there was nearer rifle fire that intensified; the 3rd Rangers had engaged the infantry protecting the Komarsi artillery ambush. Now the troopers moved quickly. From the main ridge ahead they heard the sound of light mortar bombs. Almost at once, howitzers began to thunder, and the troopers moved still more quickly, down the slope through deep soft snow, from time to time sliding sideways till they reached the bottom. There they began to trot. Quickly they reached the T'swa tracks, and still they trotted. The sound of firing was closer. Then scouts saw T'swa ahead, and knelt. The line of troopers drew even with them and moved forward; they hadn't yet been seen.

They opened fire before they were noticed, aimed fire, deadly fire, and at once the T'swa began returning it. But dressed in white and kneeling in the snow, the Iryalan troopers were not good targets. They pressed forward. Romlar visualized the 3rd Rangers dropping two companies back to hold off the T'swa, who had to press uphill against them, slow heavy work on snowshoes. The other two ranger companies should be pressing on to reach the artillery at the top. The howitzers continued to boom, but mortar bombs should still be dropping among them, reaping gunners.

Then, from the left, Romlar heard more rifle fire. The 2nd Rangers, he thought, or companies from it. His whistling now was loud and shrill, as he ordered his battalion to shift to the right, to flank the T'swa right if they could.

Kelmer had reached the timber bridge with the first elements of the 2nd Brigade. His stomach was nervous, his bowels knotting, but he felt no great fear. There was no hint of paralysis. He stood beside the north end of the bridge, recording the troops crossing, the depot visible in the distance. The first Smoleni platoons were across before there was any sign that the Komarsi knew they were there. From outposts came first the popping of rifle fire, then the crackling of machine guns. At first it was at long range and not heavy, so not many men fell. The Smoleni companies continued to cross. It was warm enough that, with the exertion of the march, they went with earlaps up and coats open, their mittens in their pockets.

Kelmer was almost the only one on skis. The Smoleni infantry had stacked skis, poles, and bedrolls along the road in the forest, to cross the bridge on snowshoes. Through his visor, Kelmer watched and recorded the first companies deploying and advancing under light fire. The Smoleni riflemen had the cover of deep snow, which, along with distance, made them poor targets. They were not returning fire themselves. They might have if their ammunition supply had been greater; as it was, they were holding off till they were nearer, and could aim their fire.

Thus there was no nearby gunfire to cover the sound when more intense fire began to the west. Kelmer guessed that the White T'swa were involved. That would be the action Romlar had left him out of.

The artillery commander listened nervously to the small arms fire on the slope behind him. He was protected by three rifle companies and four additional machine gun sections, which seemed like a lot, crouched as they were behind log parapets with cleared fields of fire. But the firefight hadn't slackened in what seemed to him five or six minutes of furious exchange. He didn't hear the Smoleni mortars thump, and the first bombs arrived without warning, some exploding in treetops, some on contact with the ground.

He panicked then. His orders were to begin fire on a radioed command, but fear froze his mind, fear that his crews would be decimated if he waited. He gave the firing command at once. The howitzers bellowed, sending a salvo toward their initial targets—a salvo very premature.

More mortar rounds exploded. A fragment bit him and he yelped, sat down abruptly in the snow and rolled backward, grabbing at his right arm.

Kelmer pulled his attention to what was happening in front of him. A battalion had crossed, and another, and the beginning of a third, almost as if drilling. Only the lead units were receiving enemy fire. It seemed to him too easy, that something was bound to happen.

He heard the first artillery salvo—first the booming of the guns, then the sound of the shells in flight. The guns had been registered in advance, and their rounds hit on or near target, one striking the bridge span between the center and north-bank piers, the explosion throwing Kelmer bodily backward into the snow. Others landed on the far side. Two fell short and another long onto the thick river ice, throwing chunks of it into the air on geysers of water. More landed in the woods on the north, rending trees, flinging snow and frozen earth. Fragments of steel and wood whirred and warbled. Men screamed, shouted, fell shocked or bleeding or died.

Kelmer realized he wasn't hurt, and untangling his skis, struggled to his feet. For a moment then he hardly moved, not from fear but indecision. Cross the river on the ice? Or drop back along the road into the forest, to record what was happening there? He chose the forest.

More than a mile away, the howitzers roared again, this salvo with time fuses, targeting the troops who'd crossed.

A Komarsi intelligence agent had reported by radio, the day before, that Smoleni scouts had passed the Valar Road. Colonel Ko-Dan had led his regiment into position a few hours later. He'd assumed that the Iryalans would attack the artillery ambush, and planned to strike them against the anvil of the emplaced Komarsi defense. But now, the word passed to him was that the force engaging him from behind was dressed in white, and he realized at once that *they* were the Iryalans. He'd been outguessed and set up. The troops assaulting uphill ahead of him must be rangers.

He assumed that the entire White Regiment was behind him. He couldn't know that Romlar, hedging his intuition, had left the Iryalan 2nd Battalion at Burnt Woods, in case Ko-Dan had outguessed him and sent a force by some wide-swinging route to attack the Smoleni government there.

Neither confusion nor hesitation were any part of Ko-Dan. He ordered one company to strike hard against the new pressure on their left, and another at the Iryalans behind him. The rest would continue uphill. It was important that the batteries on the ridgetop not be overrun.

He knew the ranger units were good. He didn't realize how good.

Among Komarsi veterans, the Smoleni already had a reputation for marksmanship, but the Komarsi infantry protecting the artillery had never experienced the kind of accuracy these rangers showed them. To expose yourself enough to use your weapon was deadly dangerous. Nor was all the mortar fire directed at the batteries on the ridgetop. Rounds were detonating in the treetops above the infantry, and on the ground among and behind them. Thus the rangers were able to press on uphill despite casualties.

The Komarsi had built their parapet with trees cut from the field of fire, and in the process, trampled the snow heavily. Thus the leading ranger elements had removed their snowshoes. When they began to come over the Komarsi parapet, the Komarsi broke and tried to flee uphill. It turned into a slaughter.

The ranger battalion C.O. radioed to the mortar sections to discontinue their fire on the hilltop and direct it against the T'swa. It was too late. The mortars, protected by machine guns, had been set up in a glade where they wouldn't have to fire through a screen of treetops. Their machine guns were under heavy attack by the T'swa, whose accurate fire had decimated the gunners, and before the mortarmen could reset their sights, the T'swa were overrunning them.

When the rangers reached the ridgetop, most of the gun crews fled down the east side of the hill. The rangers took no prisoners; the gunners who didn't flee were shot down. The Komarsi wounded were left unmolested but untended; the ranger medics were busy looking after their own.

The first company commander to reach the top called for any men with experience in artillery. There were three in his company. He gave a fourth man a compass and sent him up a tree to give him azimuths and range estimates as needed. The three ex-artillerymen became instant gun commanders, showing others how to load, aim, and fire the 4.2-inch howitzers. Within a couple of minutes he had five guns manned, each with three instant crewmen. Most of the 3rd Rangers, though, manned the parapets lower on the slope, to hold the top against the T'swa pushing upward.

The captain's attention was on the man in the tree. "Can you see a train from up there?" he shouted.

"Yessir! A great long sonofabitch!"

"Gimme an azimuth on it!"

The man sat on a branch, holding himself in place with one arm, and sighting through the compass, gave the captain the reading. The captain decided the present range settings were good enough to start with, and had his novice gunners traverse their guns to the new azimuth. Then he ordered what he'd dubbed gun number one to fire for range. It boomed, stunning the gunners, who had no ear protection.

They waited. After a few seconds the observer called down, "She 'sploded in the air 'bout two degrees left of the train and 'bout even with the locomotive!"

*Good,* the captain thought. *They've got time fuses, and the range they're set at is good enough to start with.* "Add two degrees more azimuth," he called to the gunners. "Gun number one, add one degree to your elevation; number two add two degrees; number three add three . . ." He shook his head when he'd finished, not knowing if he'd made any sense at all. He didn't even know whether elevation was set in degrees. "All guns fire when ready."

Again the number one gunner pulled the lanyard, again the gun roared. After a few seconds, the others began echoing it raggedly. Briefly they waited again. Then, "Holy shit!" the observer shouted. "It blew 'bout fifty or a hundred feet above the train! Yomal! There's another, and—guys are jumpin' out like fleas!"

"Keep firin'!" the captain shouted. "And Ingols! Keep tellin' me what's goin' on!" He shook his head while the gunners reloaded. *We may not know what we're doin', but we're doin' it.*

The 2nd Royal Komarsi Grenadier Brigade was a show unit, yeomen drilled to the highest parade sharpness. Just now they stood on snow-shoes in the woods east of the ridge, almost crowding them. Waiting, they listened nervously to the firing in the open fields ahead and on the wooded ridge behind. Their brigadier jumped at the sudden sound of the howitzers' first salvo. So soon! He barked a command to his trumpeter, who raised his long ornate horn and blew. His battalions surged out of the woods, into the field, well before the plan had called for.

When the artillery had stopped firing, Ko-Dan realized the Komarsi gunners had been overrun. And when, scarce minutes later, they began to roar again, he knew what that meant, too. Meanwhile he was taking casualties on all sides. His purpose in being here had been to trap the Iryalans; instead his own men were caught between forces, beset by what seemed to be three regiments, all of them dangerous. It was time to leave.

His right flank was taking the least fire; that was the side to break out on, before the Iryalans could get more men there. He gave the order, and almost at once his men moved, striking hard. Briefly the firing intensified, but the Iryalans in position were mostly riflemen. Some were overrun and killed, while others fell back out of the way, to fire on the T'swa as they poured past.

When the T'swa had gotten out, Romlar ordered his men not to pursue. They were outnumbered. If the T'swa became aware of that . . . After a minute's breather, he ordered his men up the hill. They had artillery training; it seemed likely that the Smoleni on top hadn't. He'd leave gunners there. Then, along with the ranger battalions, he and the rest of his troopers could move down the east side of the ridge and hit the Komarsi infantry he assumed were still in the woods there.

By midday, the Komarsi defenders, though considerably more numerous, had been routed. They'd been hit by their own artillery, by the light Smoleni howitzers on the north bank, and by the Smoleni infantry, the mercenaries, and the rangers. Nor were they allowed to reform and harass the loading of the sleigh column.

The empty sleighs had crossed the river on the ice and been driven to the depot, Kelmer with them, camera busy. Men worked furiously loading them, while at the river, the brigade's engineers worked equally furiously rebuilding the broken bridge span. The horses could never pull the loaded sleighs up the river's considerable bank, not without at least triple-teaming them, which would slow things unacceptably.

A handcar had been parked on a siding. Brigadier Carnfor had sent scouts with a radio, pumping it eastward. They were to warn him of any Komarsi reinforcements approaching.

The brigade had approached the job of loading with priorities and a plan, but given the delay, their considerable casualties, and the obvious fact that the Komarsi had expected them, they'd loaded hastily. They took almost solely foodstuffs and munitions, but not as selectively as planned. When the handcar scouts radioed that another train was coming, the final sleighs were loaded almost at random. Then the sleigh column started for the river while artillery ranged on the tracks eastward, destroying them. The three ranger battalions and the mercenaries moved east on skis to meet and discourage the Komarsi reinforcements.

Some of the munitions sleighs were too heavily loaded for the horses to pull easily, and men had to throw off cases of ammunition or shells as they went. The first to reach the river had to wait briefly while the engineers finished decking the new, temporary span with corduroy, manhandling the logs into place. They tied them down with Komarsi detonating cord.

The sleighs began to cross, while engineers chopped holes at intervals into, but not through the river ice, and set charges of Komarsi explosives in them. In the distance eastward they heard gunfire, but it grew no nearer. When the last sleighs had crossed, the brigadier radioed the battalions under Romlar's command. The brigade artillery was remounted on its skis and pulled away, and its infantry regiments began to cross the bridge. The rangers and mercenaries would cross on the ice downstream of the destruction. When the entire brigade was across, an engineer lit the det cord, and with a vicious, cracking explosion, the decking fell to the ice below. After that they blew the ice.

As the brigade moved north into the forest, a drizzle began to fall, thick and cold.

# 65

The column didn't make camp till after dark. The temperature was falling, and the drizzle, after wetting everyone and everything, had turned to snow that fell thick and silent onto the trees and the ground between.

On the march, Artus Romlar's headquarters tent was simply a larger shelter tent, made with six panels instead of three, providing room for three men to function with map books and radio. They banked it with snow for insulation.

Arms behind his head, Romlar lay awake, not anxious but depressed. Depression was foreign to him, but there it was: He'd been wasting his regiment.

The thought was irrational. The regiment had been formed to make war. Its troopers had been born warriors, who'd volunteered and trained to make war. And the usual end point of making war, certainly for T'swa, was dying in one. Other people died of other causes: mercenaries customarily died in or from combat.

*Wasting his regiment.* In the fighting south of the Eel, he'd lost just thirty-seven killed, and eighteen unaccounted for. They'd also been able to bring out twelve wounded and unfit for action, who now rode on sleighs assigned as ambulances, atop plundered Komarsi supplies. Even for so brief an action, those were moderate figures, considering they'd fought T'swa.

The T'swa! He had no doubt he'd see more of them on this campaign. They wouldn't miss the opportunity for a good fight on their own terms. They'd follow, and his troopers were the rear guard; he'd volunteered them.

They'd hardly catch up this night, but in case they did, his troopers were sleeping fully clothed. And given the snow, the pickets he'd set out could see almost as well at night as the T'swa did.

*Wasting his regiment!* At least he hadn't held back from committing his men to combat, and they'd done very well. *He'd* done very well; his aberration hadn't affected his muse. His predictions had very largely been accurate, seemingly more accurate than the T'swa commander's, and the Komarsi had ended up badly bloodied.

*Yet I'm lying here depressed.* Kantros lay next to him, jackknifed in his half-zipped sleeping bag, his breathing soft and regular. Romlar sighed and sat up. The lotus posture was out of the question in a sleeping bag, so he knelt to meditate. It didn't last long; he fell asleep in just a few minutes.

When they broke camp at dawn, fifteen inches of new snow had buried the trail the sleighs had packed on the trip south. And still it snowed. It quit about midday, leaving a storm total of twenty-three inches atop the old. Units changed their order of march with every hourly break, so that the same men weren't breaking trail continually.

By the time they made camp again, some time after dark, the temperature had fallen well below zero. Kelmer Faronya, who'd been taking cubeage of the column on the move, joined the battalion again, attaching himself to Jerym Alsnor and A Company, as before.

The brigade chief surgeon carried a standard Weather Office thermometer, and when they broke camp next morning, the temperature was −48 degrees. The horses walked through a cloud of their own freezing breath, whitening their bony sides with rime. Men wore ice on their week-old beards, and rime thick on their eyebrows and collars. Their eyelashes threaded delicate frost beads, and their noses and cheeks were waxy gray with frostbite.

An hour after the column hit the road, the T'swa caught up with the rear guard, Romlar's White T'swa. The T'swa, on snowshoes, could fire with only a momentary stop. The Iryalans, on skis, had to turn and put their poles aside to fire; fighting on the move wasn't practical for them. So they stopped, and knelt behind such cover as the trees provided there, removing their skis and donning snowshoes. It was a drill they knew well.

They were considerably outnumbered, and the T'swa, fighting on the move, seemed likely to flank and surround them, so when it seemed to Romlar that everyone but his couriers would be on snowshoes, he ordered a flank retreat westward. If the T'swa chose to pursue them, well and good. If they chose instead to continue pursuit of the Smoleni and their supply train, the Smoleni were well warned by the shooting. The rangers would already be moving to cover the rear, and his troopers could then attack the T'swa flank.

Ko-Dan chose to pursue the White T'swa, who stayed ahead of him. There was not a lot of shooting, but the T'swa did most of it, for they didn't have to stop and turn to find targets. Their targets were always in front of them; they needed only to pause to fire. And gradually, despite their white uniforms, the troopers accrued casualties.

It seemed to Romlar that his men had an advantage though. They'd undoubtedly gotten more rest, more sleep. The T'swa, on snowshoes, must have pressed hard well into the night to catch the column traveling on skis.

They climbed a low ridge and made a brief stand there, taking advantage of the terrain cover while shooting downhill at the T'swa in brown Komarsi winter uniforms. But they stayed only briefly, enough to give the T'swa some casualties, then turned again and hurried on. For several minutes there was no firing, and Romlar wondered if the T'swa had, in fact, broken off. He'd wanted to draw them farther from the column if he could. Then he heard a shot, and another, and more, and knew that the T'swa were still coming.

He knew where he was going, had chosen it on his map. He'd give them a bloody nose there, and escape.

Toward noon they crossed another ridge, this one little more than a wrinkle in the earth, just big enough to show on his map book. Now the critical terrain was less than a mile farther. He sent orders to two machine gun platoons to move ahead.

The two platoons came to the miles-long stretch of open fen, a mortal danger but also a near-perfect opportunity. The difference lay in sacrifice— their sacrifice. Their shrill whistled signals, passed on, told Romlar they'd arrived. In the fen, knee-high sedge-like graminoids and clumps of dwarf shrubs had prevented the snow from settling normally. Snowshoeing into it, they sank knee-deep, which slowed them markedly. Forty yards out they stopped, turned, and dug themselves into the snow, where they waited, catching their breath.

At the whistled signals, the rest of the battalion had speeded up to disengage. It took the T'swa a minute to realize what was happening, and to speed up themselves. The troopers bypassed the machine gunners, galloping past them as fast as they could. The men in the lead, breaking trail, had heavy going in the deep fluffy snow. When they fagged out, they slowed, and others moved ahead to take their place.

When the T'swa reached the fen, they'd have clear shots at the fleeing troopers, all the way to the other side. It was nearly five hundred yards across to the forest, and the first troopers made it in about two minutes, sweating heavily at the violent exertion, despite the arctic cold. They stopped within the screen of trees, and formed a firing line.

By that time the rest of the battalion was halfway across; all but the machine gunners, who'd already begun to fire at the T'swa arriving at the fen's edge. Their fire allowed much of the battalion to get across before the T'swa could direct appreciable fire at them, and at such long range, in their white uniforms, not many were hit. The T'swa, who'd also been running, were breathing hard; thus their aim wasn't up to standard, and at any rate much of their fire was aimed at the machine gunners.

It took the T'swa about half a minute to silence the machine guns. By that time, for them to start across the fen would have been suicidal, and suicide would serve no function for them there. They stayed back within the forest's edge.

Meanwhile, on the far side, the battalion donned skis again, and all but a small rear guard moved on. A few minutes later, when the T'swa showed no sign of following farther, the rear guard left too. But as far as the T'swa could tell, they might still be waiting in their white uniforms.

At their next break, the platoon leaders checked their men to see who was still with them, then informed their company commanders. Jerym Alsnor, now Captain Alsnor, looked around, tight-mouthed. "None of you see Faronya then?" he asked.

No one had since before they'd crossed the fen.

"Shit!" Kelmer wasn't a combatant, though T'swa riflemen could hardly know that, certainly not at a distance. And it was inappropriate that non-combatants die in combat. On Terfreya they'd lost Kelmer's journalist sister, Tain. Now here they'd lost Kelmer. Hopefully he was still alive.

He carried the word to Romlar himself. Not that there was anything to be done about it.

The fallen T'swi still had an aura, but it was shrunken and faint. The man could not live long. "Can you hear me?" Ibang asked. His pistol was in his hand.

"Yes." The answer was faint, little more than a hiss. The eyes had not opened.

"Do you wish to let death find its own time? Or shall I bring it to you?" Ibang had bent near the man's lips, that he might get the answer.

"I will wait, and contemplate."

That was the customary response. Today it seemed invariant among both T'swa and Iryalans; he hadn't heard one pistol shot. Mortally wounded T'swa normally preferred to have the complete experience of death, pain and all, rather than have it truncated. But when time and circumstance allowed, it was customary to offer the death stroke. And on a mission of this sort, any wound that disabled a man from travel-ing on his own feet was a mortal wound.

Ibang straightened. "Captain," someone called, and he turned to see a corporal looking at him. "Here is an Iryalan who does not seem badly hurt. His aura is not a warrior's aura. You may wish to deal with this one."

Ibang went over to them. The Iryalan wore skis, and lay sprawled sideways, legs twisted. His helmet was specialized for some purpose not immediately apparent. It was not protective, and had a hole in the back, near the top. *A spent round,* Ibang told himself, *probably a ricochet. Otherwise he'd be dead, or near it.* He removed the visored helmet and the thick woolen liner to examine the wound. The Iryalan groaned, stirred, and tried to raise himself. The soft snow made it impossible without more effort than he was ready to make. The bullet had scored the man's scalp, and his hair on one side was clotted with blood. It seemed evident to Ibang now that the helmet was a camera of some sort. The man wore a pistol with its holster snapped shut, but there was no rifle by him. Clearly then a noncombatant, a journalist of some sort. Given his stunned condition and the deep snow, the man would have serious difficulty getting up, with skis and pack on and his legs twisted as they were. Ibang unclipped the man's pack from his harness, unbuckled the ski bindings, then put a hand on the man's shoulder and shook it gently.

"My friend," he said, speaking Standard, "you must get up if you can. Otherwise you will freeze here."

There was no visible response for several seconds, then the head turned, producing a wince. The blue eyes were open, the expression confused. Ibang took the man's hand. "I will help you stand," he said.

The Iryalan groaned, turned his body, and made the effort; Ibang raised him to his feet. It was obvious from the grimace that his head had hurt when he'd gotten up. Meanwhile he was up to his buttocks in snow. Whether from the pain or an awareness of something missing, his hands went to his head and found dried blood instead of his camera helmet. Ibang shook snow from the torn and blood-caked woolen liner, and handed it to him.

"Put this on," he said, "or your ears will freeze."

Kelmer stared at it blankly for a moment, then comprehension dawned. He took the liner and put it on. Ibang turned to the corporal and handed the T'swi the camera helmet. "Keep this and stay with him. I will bring Ko-Dan."

Ibang left. When he'd found his colonel, they went together to the Iryalan, who was alert enough now to look worried. Ko-Dan removed the liner and examined the wound. "Corporal," he said, speaking Standard, "he carries an aid kit. Use it to bandage his wound." While the corporal bandaged, Ko-Dan questioned Kelmer. His answers verified what observation indicated.

"Can I have my helmet back?" Kelmer asked when they were done.

"Certainly," Ko-Dan said, and Ibang handed it to Kelmer, who wiped the visor and lenses, then adjusted the helmet's suspension to allow for the bandage. Clearly he was able to think. When he'd put it on, he activated it by voice, and found it still functional. He looked around, recording.

"I suggest you put your snowshoes on, instead of skis," Ko-Dan said. "Your injury may affect your balance for a time, and snowshoes will be easier to use."

Kelmer squatted and awkwardly strapped the snowshoes on, then stood on them. The pain in standing had been slight this time, and he had not dizzied. Ko-Dan had watched him. "You are not one of Romlar's White T'swa," he said. "They were chosen as warriors, and your aura is not a warrior's aura. Yet you are able to keep up with them physically. How is that?"

Aura? Kelmer didn't know the term. "I did the basic year of training with the Sixth Iryalan Mercenaries. Then the government sent me here with the First, to record the war."

"Ah! Then you have come to know some T'swa intimately, in their role as training cadre. That explains your ease with us. So. You are indeed a noncombatant. I am going to let you go, to follow your people. Assuming you feel able to travel alone. Do you?"

"Yes, sir."

"Good." Ko-Dan took off his own pack and removed two rations from it. "I suspect you can make good use of these. In cold such as this, it is well to have all you need to eat." He watched Kelmer tuck the rations in the inside pocket of his coat. By feel, keeping his lens focused on the colonel. "In turn," the T'swi continued, "I will ask a favor of you. I am Colonel Ko-Dan. Please tell Colonel Romlar for me and my men that he has a very fine regiment, and his leadership has been outstanding. It has been a pleasure to contest with them. I also suspect he has had more than a little to do with preparing the Smoleni troops we fought on the ridge. They are truly exceptional for troops which, unlike his and mine, lack the T'sel."

He stripped off a mitten then, and extended a large black hand. Kelmer shook it, and Ko-Dan grinned. "Yes," the colonel said, "you are T'swa-trained; you have the calluses and strength."

He began to turn away.

"Colonel?" said Kelmer.

"Yes?"

"May I record your troopers before I leave?"

"Certainly. We shall not do anything very interesting though. We shall eat, and return the way we came."

The T'swa commander turned away then, ignoring Kelmer utterly, as did the others. Kelmer knew that odd T'swa trait, from the training cadre at Blue Forest, and was neither offended nor puzzled. He recorded them eating and talking—laughing despite the dead around them—and wished he understood Tyspi. Then they got up, slung their packs, and snowshoed off southeastward.

He turned and started off northward across the fen. On the far side, he saw where the troopers had changed from snowshoes to skis. He switched too—he felt steady enough, and on snowshoes he'd fall farther behind instead of catching up. Then he set out following them.

# 66

Briefly the troopers continued northwestward till they hit Road 45, which they followed north till after dark, taking advantage of its freedom from obstacles. Then Romlar had them dig into the snow again and pitch their shelter tents, after posting pickets of course. He'd let them sleep till daylight, assuming that nothing happened, and it seemed to him that nothing would. It was his intuition that the T'swa no longer followed him, and this was supported by several facts or apparent facts: The T'swa must have traveled much of the night before; they'd snowshoed very hard for several hours during the day, in pursuit; and to catch up again, they'd have to snowshoe much of the night without sleep, for their snowshoes were slower than skis.

No, it seemed highly unlikely that the T'swa still followed.

He had every reason to be pleased with 1st Battalion, his leadership, and the performance of the Smoleni rangers. But he found no joy in it, which was irrational. With today's casualties, notably the two machine gun platoons, he'd lost 189 troopers on this operation alone. And his White T'swa now numbered fewer than nine hundred.

Call it wastage or something else, his regiment was shrinking, and rational or not, that troubled him. It didn't keep him awake though; not this night. He was too thoroughly tired. He ate a high-fat ration, stretched out in his sleeping bag, and fell asleep at once.

To dream. He was in a spaceship, not as a passenger, but as commander. Colonel Voker was with him, looking as he had at graduation, old and wiry and tough. And Varlik Lormagen, as young as he'd been in the old cubeage from the Kettle War. And Dao, his platoon sergeant from basic training, big and hard and black. They all looked serious except Dao, whose mouth and wise T'swa eyes smiled slightly.

*We all have the T'sel now,* Romlar thought, *but Dao more than the rest of us. Maybe it's something in the T'swa genotype.*

"We are different," Dao answered. "We are the T'swa, the true T'swa. We differ genetically, and especially culturally. But you are as deep in the T'sel as I." He eyed Romlar knowingly, and chuckled. "Though yours has slipped a little lately. That sometimes happens."

It seemed to Romlar that the others hadn't heard any of this conversation. Voker said, "Artus, the Imperials are out there. You hear them, don't you?"

He did. They were knocking on the door. He looked out the window, and the front porch was full of imperial marines.

"I want you to take your regiment and drive them away," Voker ordered.

"I'm sorry, Colonel, but my regiment is all dead."

"All dead! What did you do to them?"

"I got them all killed on Maragor, Colonel."

The knocking had loudened to booming. *In a moment,* Romlar thought, *the door will burst open, the air will rush out, and we'll all have to recycle as new-born slaves. Not just Voker and Lormagen and I, but everyone in the Confederation.*

There was a gunshot in the dream then, and Romlar jerked awake. To realize immediately what had happened: a tree had split from the intense cold. He'd heard them do that before, here and once at Blue Forest, and in training in the Terfreyan austral taiga after the war.

He'd been dreaming something unpleasant, and the dregs remained in his subconscious. Something about—Voker. And Dao. He lay silently trying to pull those slight threads and bring the rest to view, but fell asleep again before he'd made any progress.

The sun went down. Dusk faded to twilight, and twilight to dark, and still Kelmer hadn't caught up with the troopers. He was bushed by then, but had only a single shelter panel, not enough for a tent. And as cold as it was . . .

He pushed on. He'd never felt so alone, so abandoned. After a bit he was wobbling, knees weak, and finally he fell. It seemed to him he could go no farther—that he would die there of the cold. He thought of Weldi. Tears filled his eyes, and he was gripped by a sudden fear that they'd freeze there, perhaps blinding him, so he covered them for a minute with his mittens, blinking furiously.

Then he forced himself to his feet and pushed onward. The battalion might be camped just ahead; a hundred yards on, he might be challenged by a sentry. He wasn't. At Blue Forest, he reminded himself, they'd spent a night in the snow without any panels at all. They'd dug depressions and lay down in them in their sleeping bags, covering each other with snow. But the last men down were covered by sentries, who were covered in turn by their relief. Here he didn't even have someone to bury him. And that night at Blue Forest hadn't been this cold; not nearly.

He'd skied only half an hour more when he collapsed again. After lying in the snow for a minute, he unsnapped his pack, and with one of the snowshoes strapped to it, dug himself a narrow hole in the snow, deep into the old base. He lay the panel in it then and sat down on it, wondering what the temperature was. He'd eaten both the T'swa rations already, and it seemed too much work to open one of his own. Instead he took out his sleeping bag and crawled in, leaving one arm free to pull snow over himself. When he was covered, he pulled his arm in and lay there, afraid to go to sleep.

Nonetheless, within two minutes he slept.

He awoke having to urinate. Faint daylight penetrated the snow. He undertook to sit up, and found himself held. Warmth from his breath had melted a small space around his head, and the cold penetrating from outside had frozen the moisture into a shell of ice. For a moment, fear swelled in his heart, then subsided. He moved his legs; they were free. So was his torso below the chest. He worked his bag open, got his arms out, and with mittened hands broke the ice around his head, then sat up.

It was another bitter arctic morning, colder, he thought, than the morning before. He broke off a piece of his ice mask and put it in his mouth to melt, surprised that he was no colder than he was. *Actually,* he thought, *I've slept colder when the temperature wasn't nearly this low.* Then he dug a ration from his pack, and sitting up in his bag, ate it. Exposed to the air, he was quickly colder than he'd been in the night. He put the rest of his rations inside his coat, crawled out of his bag, put his boots on, and relieved himself against a tree, watching the urine form a mound of amber ice on the bark.

Finally, working clumsily in mittens, he donned pack, skis, and helmet, then continued on the trail of the battalion. With a remarkably light heart. Not only had he not frozen to death. He'd discovered that the danger was not so great as he'd thought. Half an hour later, he found where the battalion had camped. And decided it was just as well he'd stopped when he had. Otherwise he wouldn't have learned what he had, wouldn't have discovered that he could survive alone.

# 67

First Battalion left Road 45 that morning, angling northeastward toward Road 40 and the Smoleni column. The weather remained brutal. Even near noon, when Romlar spat at a tree, the saliva hit like a pebble, frozen. The cold sucked the heat from them, and the high-fat rations they gnawed from time to time weren't adequate, pressing as they were. By early afternoon they'd eaten the last of them. Such a speed march itself would burn more than ten thousand calories a day, and their bodies carried no fat to draw on.

More than the virgin snow made travel slow. Instead of roads, they found tangles of blowdown, occasional swamps of bull brush to push through, soft-snowed fens and bogs to cross. Twice they came upon old logging roads, but never in a suitable direction.

The impulse was to press, press, press, to reach the column and the captured Komarsi rations. Yet they needed to rest from time to time, and no one grumbled when Romlar called a five-minute break each half hour. Five minutes wasn't enough to cool down seriously.

They reached Road 40 near sundown, and followed the tracks of the column. It did not gladden them to find the bodies of several horses along the way, frozen rock-hard. They kept going until, soon after dark, a sentry challenged them. Minutes later they saw campfires.

Night held the forest in an arctic fist when Kelmer reached the road. He'd slowed the last hours, his reserves exhausted, and was weary almost to the point of collapse. He might have laid down in the snow an hour earlier, but his confidence had slipped, replaced again by anxiety and thoughts of Weldi. The road gave him new life, and briefly he speeded up, but it was only surface charge, and within the next hour he twice fell to the snow, to struggle up tight-jawed and push on.

Finally a ranger sentry challenged him. The Smoleni directed him to where the Iryalans had made camp, and trooper sentries directed him to the colonel's buried tent. The camp seemed dead, its fires cold and dark.

Kelmer stood his skis up by Romlar's and Kantro's, set his pack beside them, then opened the entrance flaps. Romlar wakened when he crawled inside. "Who's that?"

"Kelmer Faronya reporting, sir."

"Great Tunis!" A moment later a battery lamp lit the tent. "What happened to you?"

Kelmer took his helmet off. "I got hit. It was superficial. Enough to knock me out though."

There was a moment's silence. "Who bandaged you?"

"The T'swa. They found me unconscious, and recognized me as a noncombatant, so they let me go. Colonel Ko-Dan asked me to congratulate you for him. He said—" Suddenly Kelmer found himself thick-witted again, from exhaustion. "It's all on cube. He said fighting you had been a pleasure."

Romlar chuckled. "He would." Then, "You're bushed. Drag in your pack and bed down with us."

Kelmer found it a heavy effort to crawl back out and get it. When he'd laid his sleeping bag out, he saw the colonel's boots standing by the end wall, and took off his own. Romlar watched. "Here," he said when Kelmer had crawled half into his bag, and handed him a ration. Kelmer stared. He was so tired, he was asleep before he'd finished eating it.

# 68

They suffered two more days of arctic cold, though that second day was the worst. Almost a third of their horses died from the combination of cold and exhaustion, contributed to by the total lack of grain. Brigadier Carnfor did not press for speed, but he kept the pace steady.

At first, when a horse died, it was hastily cut up before it froze solid, but that slowed the column. After that, when a horse went down, it was simply dragged out of the way and gutted; it could be salvaged later. Horses from the replacement herd replaced them, and when there were no more replacements, sleighs without a team were left by the road. They too could be picked up later, in weather less severe, with fresher horses.

The constant brutal cold numbed the minds of some men, and there were suicides, none of them troopers and none rangers. Frostbitten noses and cheeks were general. The medics cursed men who froze their fingers, for they'd been given procedures to avoid the problem. They cut off fingertips, even whole fingers, so they wouldn't become gangrenous when they thawed.

A few men, discovering their fingers frozen, hid the fact to avoid the knife, keeping them secret till they began to rot and stink. As a result, several hands had to be cut off. Even before the weather eased, though, morale was improving. Jokes could be heard, coarser than usual. Fires were made at night, and horse meat stewed. It was tough and stringy, and lacked fat, but it was edible, and the broth was hot.

❖     ❖     ❖

The regiment stayed with the column for those two days, the easier pace resting them. Then they left it behind, speed-marching to Burnt Woods. En route they passed horses being driven south to begin the recovery of abandoned carcasses and sleighs. Nothing was to be wasted.

Although the supply situation, critical in the long run, was not so severe as earlier forecast. Once The Archipelago had committed itself and began to send supplies, it had been relatively easy to send more of them than originally planned. Thus long trains of sleighs arrived at Jump-Off fairly frequently. Not enough to cover needs, but enough to stave off, somewhat, the time of serious hunger.

The Krentorfi ambassador would be leaving for Faersteth in three days, and the president asked Romlar that Kelmer be allowed to accompany the ambassador in his floater, taking video cubes and an audio report of the depot raid to the queen and her court. After that they'd be made available to theaters in a number of countries.

Kelmer asked that Weldi go with him; the ambassador said it was an excellent idea. Kelmer spent the three days editing and narrating. But he worked only till eight in the evening. He would not neglect his bride.

# 69

Despite the cold of northern Smolen, the troopers wore their hair short. Thus when Kelmer sat at his keyboard, and Weldi came into the one-time storeroom assigned him to edit in, she would eye the broad, still-livid scar that parted his scalp from the right rear almost to his forehead. She'd been that close to widowhood! She didn't consciously intend to interrupt his work, but on one occasion she allowed her finger to trace gently the path across his crown.

He turned and smiled, then stood and kissed her. She looked at him thoughtfully. "You're a very brave man, Kelmer," she said, "and I'm proud of you."

He kissed her again, partly to cover his discomfort at her words.

First Battalion was on light duty for a few days, resting from their mission, and that evening after supper, Kelmer took time to ski to the Iryalan camp and visit Jerym Alsnor. The evening was balmy, about 20 degrees, with a very few snowflakes drifting down lazily. Jerym put aside the tattered book he was reading—he was perhaps the thirtieth to read it—and grinned at Kelmer when he came into the winterized squad tent that housed A Company's six officers.

"Just couldn't stand it, eh? Had to get back to bachelor quarters."

Kelmer smiled back, then glanced around at the four other officers there at the time, two reading, two meditating. "Actually I came to talk to you," he said. "Is there somewhere we can go?"

Jerym stood up and took his garrison jacket from its peg. "Yeah. We can go for a walk." They left the tent, with its snowbanked outer walls of small logs, to saunter the well-packed snow between the rows. When, after a minute or two, Kelmer had said nothing, Jerym took the initiative. "What can I do for you?" he asked. "I warn you though, all I know about married life is what I saw growing up."

*Though your sister and I discussed it seriously enough. But I'm not going to talk to you about that.*

"You know how I used to wonder how I'd react to combat, to the danger of getting killed."

"Yeah. It seems to me you've done pretty well."

Kelmer grunted. "Jerym, it scared the shit out of me. One time literally, when a dud grenade landed almost at my feet. And I still get scared. Really scared."

The White T'swi shrugged. "There's nothing wrong with that. You've been in combat a number of times, and did what you were there to do." Jerym looked him over. Tain had been the warrior in the family, he had no doubt, though when he'd known her, he didn't see auras, except perhaps subliminally. "You weren't born to be a warrior," he went on. "Your aura shows it. And you haven't had the Ostrak Procedures or Ka-Shok training." He paused. "Why do you doubt your bravery?"

"Because I feel so damned afraid sometimes."

"Okay. Could it be that bravery has to do with action, with behavior, instead of with feelings?"

They continued walking, the photojournalist thoughtful now. "How do you feel," Kelmer asked, "when you're in combat? Or getting ready to go into combat."

"Differently than I did on Terfreya. On Terfreya, getting ready, I'd get excited. I lost that doing Ka-Shok meditation. In general, in combat, I feel highly alert, very quick and responsive, very vital and alive. But that's a consequence of having been born a warrior, and six years of learning how to handle it and do it right."

From a mile or more off to the west came the howl of a *loper*, the Maragorn great wolf. The sound was a high-pitched keening, as sharp-edged as the ringing of a wine glass tapped by a spoon, belying the long-legged, thick-necked, two-hundred-pound predator that voiced it. It was answered by another almost at the edge of hearing. The two men stopped to listen. The reclusive gray predators were uncommon, perhaps had always been. When the brief duet was over, their listeners walked on in silence for a bit.

It was Jerym who broke it. "So you came out here to talk about bravery and fearfulness?"

Kelmer nodded.

"What specifically brought it up?"

"Weldi told me I'm a very brave man. It made me feel like a phony."

Jerym grinned, and suddenly hugged Tain's brother. "She's right, Kelmer! She's right!" He thumped the journalist's shoulder. "It's okay not to believe her, but she's right!" He looked around. "Come on to the messhall with me. There's always a kettle of hot water on the stove, and canisters of *fex* buds. We'll have a cup of tea and talk about other stuff. Then you can go find someone prettier than me to be around."

That night after Weldi had fallen asleep, Kelmer lay thinking for a while. He'd come to the conclusion that he was, if not actually brave, at least no coward. Jerym had been right: men differed, and the proper criterion was behavior, not emotion.

# Part Four
# T'SWA VICTORY

# 70

The latter part of the winter alternated between further extreme cold and unseasonably mild weather. Neither of the combatants showed any interest even in minor harassments, let alone substantial operations. Fossur's spy network had little to report, nor did Undsvin's, though Fossur continued to get political information via the Krentorfi ambassador.

The word was that General Lord Undsvin Tarsteng was in disgrace again, but that Engwar had left him in command, perhaps because of political agitation for his replacement. At any rate, Undsvin was his cousin, and no one else had demonstrated particular promise in a command role.

The equinox brought thawing temperatures, and the snow began to settle, but there was a great deal of it to melt, and the ice was massive on lakes and rivers. Spring would not arrive overnight. It would be weeks before the supply road from Oselbent would become impassable to sleigh trains.

The White T'swa continued training: running and marching on skis and snowshoes, practicing their tumbling and jokanru on the packed snow of their exercise areas. The Smoleni army, on the other hand, aside from the ranger battalions, pretty much laid up. Men with families in the north, in villages or refugee camps, were furloughed to be with them. Even in the ranger battalions, a third of their men were on leave at any one time. It was a season of rest and renewal, as it had always been in Smolen's north country.

By the end of Threedek, the spring thaw was at its peak. Snowmelt ran gurgling downstream over the river ice, and formed a foot-deep layer of icy water atop the frozen lakes. The remaining snow, hardly crotch-deep now and shrinking, was wet as water, except that usually a crust froze at night. The rawhide thongs of snowshoes soaked it up like blotters, and became thick and soft. It was time to hang them up. Used much in that season, they'd require restringing.

Security fell slack; it seemed needless. Conditions were obviously impossible for military operations, even by the seasoned backwoodsmen of the Smoleni rangers.

✧     ✧     ✧

A long line of armed, white-clad men alternately walked and trotted through a forest, their gait seemingly tireless. Their snowshoes were of tough white plastic, and when the snow had shrunken enough, they would abandon them. Their packs too were white. Their mortars, machine guns, and supplies were in white bags that rode on white toboggans. Their route took them up the eastern side of Smolen, where settlements were absent over large areas. The region was predominantly shallow-soiled rock-outcrop terrain, with peatlands and numerous lakes.

They followed a predetermined map course, crossing lakes on rubber boats, paddling through shallow water that lay atop three to four feet of rotting ice. Thirty to sixty percent of the drainage lengths consisted of lakes, so it was rarely necessary to cross the swollen and often dangerous streams. Near the end of their march, they were able to abandon their snowshoes, but it became necessary to detour around peatlands, where the remaining snow was underlain with a foot or so of icewater. Their trek was mostly over by then.

These men were black, not white. After the Battle at the Depot, Engwar himself had seen to it that white field uniforms and gear were provided them; he considered them his own special regiment, even if they did not take his orders. They appealed to the romantic in him, and surely they were more interested than anyone else in actually fighting. Besides, when he'd been under pressure to replace his cousin as commander of the army, it had been Colonel Ko-Dan who'd spoken up for the general.

Neither Engwar nor Undsvin knew where the T'swa were now, though; Engwar didn't even know they were gone. Ko-Dan was taking a big risk, and secrecy was vital.

# 71

Gulthar Kro had settled into the Smoleni 3rd Ranger Battalion more comfortably than in any family or group he'd ever been part of. For a day and a half, the battalion had hiked the graveled road from Shelf Falls, where they'd been replaced by the 1st. Where there were fields along the road, the ground was mostly bare. In the forest, there was still a foot or so of granular snow. Flocks of spring birds wheeled and whirred. About midday the forest ended on their right, and some distance ahead, Kro could see the village of Burnt Woods, its houses flecks of color in the spring sun, red and blue, yellow and white.

The battalion turned off the main road a mile or so before they reached the Almar, and hiked a half-mile east to the army encampment, halting in ranks on the drill field. There the battalion C.O. turned it over to its company commanders. Kro turned his company over to his 1st sergeant—he had business of his own—and began walking alone toward town.

During the company's period of intensive training, and during the Great Raid, he'd been occupied, physically and mentally. After resting briefly at Shelf Falls, the 3rd had gone south again, patrolling the district along the north side of the Eel for several weeks.

But since the equinox they'd loafed a lot, and Kro had always had a problem with loafing: it made him brood. He'd looked again at his reason for coming north, the challenge he'd set himself. He felt no loyalty to Komars, nor to Undsvin any longer—in fact, he'd admitted to himself that he liked the Smoleni better than his own people—but he did not easily abandon a challenge.

So he'd left camp with a purpose in mind: to find and kill the merc colonel, whom he now knew by name if not on sight.

Kro had great confidence in his own physical strength, which might well exceed the merc commander's. He was a truly formidable street fighter, too—had exceptional natural talent and savagery to go with his strength and quickness, and had learned some valuable techniques over the years. But he had no illusion that he could beat the Iryalan colonel in a hand-to-hand fight or with knives.

On the other hand, his face and form were familiar to a number of the mercs, and as an officer of a merc-trained outfit, he might gain access to their colonel. The first trick would be to kill him, the second would be to escape. But if he could cultivate him, he could catch him alone some time, perhaps even sleeping. And with surprise and his service pistol, or his knife if possible, kill him. Then escape into the forest. They'd have to catch him, and tracking would slow them.

Those were some of the thoughts that ran through his mind as he trotted easily north on Road 40. He crossed the Almar, normally thirty to forty feet wide. Just now it was bank-full and more, a hundred feet wide in places, all of it squeezing forcefully between two bridge piers only twenty-five feet apart. A short distance to his right lay the millpond, roofed gray with massive rotting ice. At the junction with the river road, he turned west toward the merc camp.

Patience was the key, he told himself. Don't grab at the first opportunity unless it's a very good one. The mercs at Shelf Falls had relaxed their security during breakup, and spent more time in camp—had slept till after sunup, took long noon breaks, and didn't run field exercises that took them far from camp. It was probably the same here. If their colonel wasn't in camp today, there would still be this evening, and tomorrow, and the next day. Meanwhile he knew approximately what he'd say.

The snow had melted in the merc camp, except for shrunken piles where it had been banked along the tent walls. The ground was trampled mud. Kro looked into one of the squad tents. "Afternoon," he said. "I'm lookin' for yer colonel. Where'll I find his tent?"

One of the mercs was sitting in a strange cross-legged sort of posture on a little rug, and didn't look up. A couple were napping. One of those who were reading got to his feet. He was a small man—five-six and a hundred and fifty, Kro guessed—but in a fight, could have destroyed any of Undsvin's brawlers, he had no doubt.

"I'll take you there, Captain," said the merc. "It's simpler than telling you."

A row of muddy boots stood at the entrance, and the man paused to put on a pair of them, tying the laces around his ankles. "It'll be nice when this mud dries," he commented. Pleasantly, as if it didn't really matter to him. Kro had repeatedly been struck by how good-natured the mercs were.

"Yeah. I just come up from Shelf Falls. It's even worse down there, seems like. What kind of man is yer colonel?"

"Smart. Artus is smart. You should have seen what he's brought us through, here and on Terfreya."

"Tough?"

"Where it counts. Easy to get along with though. There; that's his tent: his, his exec's, and his aide's. If he's not there, his command tent is right through there."

The trooper pointed, then left. Kro went to the tent and looked in. Its furnishings were similar to the one he'd looked in a minute before, except there were only three cots. Only one man was inside, a large man, napping. Kro's heart jumped; he could see a small colonel's sun sewn on one sleeve. He could cut his throat right now, and no one the wiser, for a few minutes anyway.

The colonel turned over. His open eyes were on Kro, and for a moment it seemed to the Komarsi that the man had read his thoughts. He sat up then. "How can I help you, Captain?"

Despite the moment just past, the answer came easily. "Sir, my name is Gull Kro. I've come to make an offer. You took some casualties down below the Eel, and a bunch more, I heard, when you led the T'swa away, comin' up Road 40. I'd like to be a replacement."

Romlar raised an eyebrow. "What would your C.O. think of that?"

"I think I could talk him into it. I can learn more from servin' with you. And maybe you could teach me things about command. Then, when you leave, I could help train others."

The merc colonel smiled. "Maybe you could at that. But it's at odds with T'swa tradition to take replacements. Besides, we all started out together, my men and I. We were recruits together as teenaged kids. We trained for six years together, and fought two wars together. We're closer than brothers; we think alike. I don't have to tell them much, mainly just what our objectives are. They take it from there; they know how to get it done."

Kro shifted gears. "Well then," he said, "last summer when I got here from down south, I watched you guys train in hand-to-hand. I never seen nothin' like it before. Could you teach me that? So I could teach my men?"

"Hmm. I'll tell you. It took us . . ."

Sudden rifle fire to the north cut him off in mid-sentence, and from his sitting position, the colonel seemed to pounce to the door. In five seconds his boots were on, the laces wrapped and knotted 'round his ankles. He snatched his ammunition belt with pistol attached, buckled it and grabbed a rifle, then was out the door before Kro fully grasped that it was the flurry of distant shots which had so galvanized this man. Somewhere in his burst of activity, the colonel had also put a helmet on.

Kro found himself running behind him as if on a tether. To his astonishment, the camp was full of running men, a few barefoot or shirtless, all of them armed, most galloping northward between the rows of tents. As they fanned out of the tent area, Kro saw men in white running from the forest some 300 yards ahead. With no order given, the foremost troopers dropped to kneeling positions and squeezed off aimed shots. Others ran between them, and in perhaps fifteen yards these too knelt and fired. All had grabbed weapons—rifles or the twenty-pound, one-man machine guns they used.

It was as if the whole regiment had realized instantly what was happening and what needed to be done.

Meanwhile the men in white were firing back, and mercs too were falling. The current first wave of troopers had reached the ditch on the south side of the road, and lay on the side of it, legs in the water, squeezing off round after round, while the rest ran up and hit the ground among them. Kro found himself lying beside the colonel, pistol in hand. It didn't seem like the time to shoot him though, despite the noise and battle focus. Somehow it wouldn't be right.

The damned water was ice cold.

The attackers, those in the open, lay prone now too, returning the fire. Others, he couldn't tell how many, were firing from the edge of the woods. Those in the open were easy to see, white against the wet ground; he was willing to bet they'd all be casualties quickly. Those in the woods, on the other hand, he couldn't distinguish from the background.

The fire from the woods was shockingly accurate. With only heads for targets, the enemy had killed a number of troopers in just a minute or so of fighting. Then mortar bombs began to crash along the forest's edge, some as air bursts detonated by branches. The mortar men hadn't run out into the field; they'd set up back among the tents. Bombs began to fall along the road, too, in and behind the ditch. For a moment Kro thought they were short rounds fired by the mercs in camp, then realized they came from the forest ahead. It seemed to him that he and the colonel would both die today, side by side, comrades at arms.

The T'swa—they had to be T'swa—seemed uninterested in pressing the attack, as if they were satisfied to chew the mercs up from where they were. After another minute, he wondered how many there were of them, because merc mortar rounds continued to burst along the edge of the woods and in the treetops, but no more seemed to be coming from the forest. He became aware then that other mercs had run not out to the ditch, but west from camp, into the woods that crossed the road nearby. Those mercs were flanking the T'swa now. The merc mortars stopped firing, and their colonel whistled several shrill shrieks. The men in the ditch jumped up and charged, their colonel with them, across the road and toward the woods. Willy nilly Kro charged too, wondering if the colonel knew what he was doing.

More mercs fell, crossing that last hundred and fifty yards. Most, though, plunged into the edge of the trees. A grenade hurtled toward him, and Kro's gut spasmed. He snatched the thing in mid-air, and side-armed it back. It exploded no more than twenty feet away, and he felt a fragment strike his chest, burn across his ribs and take a nick out of his upper arm. It seemed to him trivial, made him feel somehow invincible. A T'swi in front of them showed enough of himself to aim his rifle, and Kro pulled his pistol trigger, felt the recoil through his wrist, once, twice, a third time. The first shot bit, the other two knocked bark from the side of the tree. He was aware that the colonel was down, and looked around for someone more to shoot, someone wearing white. Instead, someone shot him through the face, from the side. Kro went down as if clubbed.

Two ugly grenade fragments had hit Romlar, one in the right thigh, the other high on the chest, knocking him down. The wounds were nasty but not severe, and he got up again in seconds. By that time the fight was all but over, and the surviving T'swa were pulling out.

That told him something—that and what he'd already seen and heard. Even before they'd left the ditch, Romlar had been aware by the sound that there was fighting in the village. But by the time he'd limped back out of the trees, the shooting had all but ended there too. The major T'swa force, he realized, had occupied Burnt Woods, with the intention of capturing the Smoleni government. Only a small force—perhaps just a single company and not more than two—had engaged him here, as if they were more than they were. Their function had been to prevent his intervening in the village, in case it was seriously contested.

Clearly the T'swa had traveled overland during breakup, probably taking an easterly route to minimize the risk of detection. They'd have crossed the Granite south of Jump-Off, and swung around to strike from the north, the side from which certainly no one would attack.

There was no point in further action. The T'swa would have captured the president and his people already, unless they'd died in the fighting. Either way, the war was effectively over.

The way it felt to him, though, Heber Lanks was alive, alive and a prisoner. He shouted orders. At least he had the opportunity to salvage the wounded for a change, his and the T'swa's.

# 72

A squad of T'swa, well-spaced, sprinted across the back yard of the president's house. From a window, someone fired bursts from a sub-machine gun, and one, then another of the T'swa fell. They did not shoot back. From the porch, a guard's rifle banged, just once, then he fell dead. The first T'swi to reach the house bounded onto the porch, shooting the glass out of a window, and jumped through. Another followed. A third crashed through a door. Others had run to the back of the house. They could have thrown grenades in but didn't, as if they wanted to take the occupants alive.

Kelmer Faronya had been in his editing room when he first heard shots. He'd gone to his window then, concerned, wondering what was going on, and had seen T'swa dash around the corner of the barn on the next property north. Without taking time to consider, he ran up the stairs to the room where he hoped Weldi would be. She wasn't there. Then where? He ran back out and went down the whole flight of stairs in three bounds, wheeled and ran for her father's office—to run bodily into a T'swi coming out of the study. They went down together, Kelmer trying for a throat block, but fingers dug his carotids, and he blacked out almost at once.

The president had come out of his bedroom, pistol in hand. For a moment he'd hesitated: It was him they'd come for, had to be. If he gave himself up, it might save lives. So he tossed the gun on the floor, walked to the stairs and started down, hands raised to shoulder level, palms forward. A T'swi darted into the foyer, they saw each other, and the T'swi lowered his submachine gun. The president didn't hesitate; he continued down. He'd never seen a T'swi before, except in Kelmer's videos. The face was the color of a gun barrel, the large eyes calm. The T'swi met him at the foot of the stairs and took his arm, firmly but not hard.

The voice was deep and had no edge. "Mr. President," said the T'swi, "you are a prisoner. Please lie down on the floor, in case there is more shooting."

When General Eskoth Belser heard the first shots, he was examining a map. He turned in his chair. "Arkof! What is that shooting?"

"I'll find out, General."

He didn't turn back to his map though, because the shooting continued, now from more than one direction. For a moment he simply sat upright, looking out his office door, frowning and waiting for Arkof to learn something.

There was shooting nearby then, and getting abruptly up, he stepped to a rack and took out a submachine gun. A magazine was already seated, and he jacked a round into the chamber as he strode out into his reception room. The sergeant major had been outside and was just coming back in, a submachine gun in his hands. "It's T'swa, sir. Arkof's lying shot in the street. Best you keep low." He turned then and hurried back out.

Belser paused for a moment. There was gunfire in every direction. Then he realized; they'd come for the president. He strode out the door.

The house was set behind a small front yard with a waist-high picket fence, shrubs, and last year's dead flower patches. A massive *kren* stood in each front corner, remnant snow in their shade. He'd started for the gate when four soldiers ran down the street. A submachine gun clattered harshly, a long burst, and all four fell to the gravel. Belser ran to one of the *kren,* his gun held chest high. A man in white uniform ran from behind the house across the street, and for just a moment Belser thought it was one of the Iryalans. Then the black face registered. He stepped out far enough to fire a short burst, but failed to hit the T'swi. Before he could curse, bark and splinters burst from the side of the tree, head high. Just enough of him had been exposed. The general fell dead, reddening the snow.

Ko-Dan sat in the president's office. The president was there, and Fossur, and Weldi and Kelmer. And the Krentorfi ambassador, standing white-faced. A sergeant, the president's secretary, sat at the shortwave radio.

"Call the commanding officer of your local military forces," Ko-Dan ordered. "I will speak with them."

The sergeant looked questioningly to the president. "Do as the colonel asks," Lanks said calmly, then turned to Ko-Dan. "Let me speak with them first. They'll be more receptive."

The T'swi nodded. The sergeant pressed the microphone switch. "NC-1, NC-1, this is the Cottage, this is the Cottage. Over."

"This is NC-1. Over."

"The president wants to speak with Brigadier Carnfor. Over."

They waited for a long five seconds. "This is Carnfor. Over."

The sergeant handed the microphone to Lanks. "Elvar," said the president, "I am under military arrest, in the custody of Colonel Ko-Dan of the Black Serpent Regiment. T'swa. My cabinet is also under arrest, and General Belser is reported dead. I hereby appoint you commanding officer of the Army of Smolen until otherwise notified. Colonel Ko-Dan wants to talk with you. Please oblige him. I am giving the microphone to him now. Over."

Again there was a lag. "All right," Carnfor said. "I'll talk to him. Over."

"Brigadier Carnfor," Ko-Dan said, "I have your President Lanks, his cabinet, daughter, and son-in-law in custody, along with Colonel Fossur and other key persons. We see no purpose in shedding further blood, and propose a cessation of hostilities. Over."

"Colonel," Carnfor said, "you may have the government, but we've got you, and you're a long way from the Eel. You should know us well enough to realize that if we choose, we can wipe you out. It may cost us, but we can do it. Over."

"Indeed, Brigadier Carnfor. But if you attack us with any effective force, you will quite probably kill our captives. I'm sure you do not wish that. Over."

"We're a free people, Colonel. We can always elect a new president, and he can appoint new officials. This may sound strange to you, but we can. I'll make a deal, though: You let your hostages go, and I will personally give you a safe conduct out of the country. You'll be free to leave, and take your weapons with you. Over."

"Brigadier, that is not the kind of agreement that the Lodge of Kootosh-Lan allows me to make. And if you know anything about us, you know we do not object to dying. I can guarantee, however, that the president and his people will not be harmed, unless by yourselves. Over."

"I don't doubt you, Colonel. But when you get them to Rumaros, you and I both know what'll happen to them. That sonofabitch Engwar will either execute them publicly or parade them around Komars in chains and rags, on exhibition. No, I can't do that. Over."

Ko-Dan's thick eyebrows arched. He wasn't that familiar with the historical behavior of some Komarsi royalty. "If we arrive safely out of the present de facto boundaries of Smolen," Ko-Dan replied, "I guarantee their safety, and reasonable conditions of captivity. Over."

"That's a guarantee you can't make good on. You people are tough, but not that tough. Over."

Ko-Dan pursed his lips for just a moment, then answered. "I suggest you call Colonel Romlar of the Iryalan Regiment. He and his men know my people and my lodge better than anyone on Maragor except ourselves. Ask him what force my guarantee carries. Over."

The company mess tents in the Iryalan camp had been replaced, the previous autumn, with low log buildings. Two of these were being used as de facto hospitals, with tables for beds. That's where the runner found Romlar, not as a patient but as a commander checking the wounded. His own wounds had been dressed, and he was walking.

At a rapid limp, he followed the runner to the command tent, and sat down at the radio. "This is Romlar. Over."

"Artus, this is Elvar. We've got a situation." Carnfor reviewed what it was. "How good is the T'swa guarantee? Over."

Romlar knew what the brigadier hadn't said—couldn't say, under the circumstances: If they lost the president, their cause was basically lost. In Komars, unhappiness with the war would subside, and that was a key factor in Smoleni hopes. Also, while they could elect a new president and persist for a time, they'd have lost their credibility with the rest of Maragor, and without increased support from abroad, they could not long survive, as a nation, or ultimately as a people.

"Elvar, it's as good a guarantee as you'll find. If the Komarsi try to take the president away from the T'swa, there'll be a bloodbath. They'll have to wipe the T'swa out, which will bring every regiment the lodge can round up, and with Level Two weapons. And the Confederation won't say a thing. The Komarsi government will be out, and the reparations will make their nobility weep bitter tears. Engwar will either end up dead in combat, or a suicide, or they'll deliver him to you for trial. There's precedent for all this. Over."

There was silence for several seconds, as Carnfor assimilated Romlar's words. "Thank you, Artus," he said simply. "NC-1 out."

"White T'swa out." Romlar sat back and let his eyes close. He had no surgeon; the Smoleni had several. He'd call them back in a few minutes, and see if he could borrow one or more of them.

In the president's office, Ko-Dan had had the radio tuned to the White T'swa's frequency, and everyone there had heard what Romlar said. Heber Lanks couldn't help but think that, were it not for his daughter, he'd wish the Komarsi *would* try to take them from the T'swa. Seemingly it would guarantee the long-range restoration of Smoleni territory and independence, and reparations as well. But he doubted it would happen. Engwar wasn't that insane; surely Undsvin wasn't.

"The Cottage, the Cottage, this is NC-1. Over."

Ko-Dan thumbed the microphone switch. "This is Colonel Ko-Dan. Over."

"Colonel, I will accept your guarantee if the president approves. Let me speak with him. Over."

Ko-Dan handed the microphone to Heber Lanks. "Elvar," the president said, "we overheard what Colonel Romlar told you, and you have my approval to accept Colonel Ko-Dan's offer. See that he has free passage. If the new government wishes to renew hostilities with the T'swa afterwards, it will be free to do so, of course. Meanwhile, Ambassador Fordail of Krentorf is here, witnessing all of this. We must hope he can influence the international community to continue their support. Over."

"Your message received, Mr. President. If you'll sit tight for a bit, I'll get messages to every unit I can contact. My love and best wishes go with you, sir. NC-1, out."

Ko-Dan waited half an hour, then radioed NC-1 again to arrange truck transportation for his regiment. The reply was that the Smoleni had insufficient trucks and fewer power slugs. A large carryall and several trucks could be provided, however, along with a section of engineers to repair culverts and bridges washed out by breakup. Agreements were come to.

The T'swa waited till daylight the next morning, then left for Rumaros, most of them on foot and heavily loaded. Their captives rode in the carryall.

# Part Five
# CLOSURE

# 73

The regiment's medics had administered synthblood, opiates, and antibiotics, had sutured wounds and splinted limbs—pretty much the limit of their skills. Instead of sending a surgeon, Carnfor had sent ambulances to take men in emergency need to his field hospital, and to the small district hospital in Burnt Woods. They also took the ranger with the badly damaged face, Gull Kro. Kro's wound wasn't life-threatening, but he was one of Carnfor's own officers. Covered trucks picked up the T'swa wounded who were fit for the ride to Rumaros.

Romlar had left those matters to his executive officer, Jorrie Renhaus, and gone to bed in his tent. He'd lost Fritek Kantros to a T'swa bullet. Eldren Esenrok had lost most of a leg and too much of his blood to a T'swa mortar round; his survival was uncertain.

With Fritek dead and Jorrie spending the night in the command tent, Artus was alone, which was how he preferred it just then. He'd declined to take anything for his pain. It wasn't that bad, and he preferred not to dull his mind if it wasn't necessary.

He allowed lassitude and depression to settle in though. *How many men do you have now?* he asked himself. The question was rhetorical. He knew how many: 733, including wounded whom he judged could return to combat effectiveness after proper treatment. Or 773, if he could salvage all of the men he'd sent into Komars as agitators. Depending on how you defined "waste," he'd gone a long way toward wasting his regiment.

That was the sort of thoughts he fell asleep to.

On Iryala, Lotta Alsnor sat in a lotus in the *ghao* at Lake Loreen, in deep meditation. She was preparing to monitor Tain Faronya, riding through hyperspace in the imperial flagship, accompanied by an invasion fleet. Before she reached, though, an image, a being, appeared to her. Eldren Esenrok: she knew him at once. Her immediate thought was that he'd died.

*Nope,* he told her. *Maybe later tonight. Maybe tomorrow. Just now, the body's still hanging on, what's left of it. It's close enough to gone; I seem to be sort of in-between. I suppose that's why I could come here like this.*

*Is there something you want me to do?*

*For Artus. He's pulled in a bunch of shit; something the Ostrak Proce-dures didn't reach. It's gotten to him. We've had a couple of big bouts with the T'swa, and he's lost quite a lot of us. No fault of his; he's done a helluva job. You might want to help him out.*

He was gone as abruptly as he'd arrived. Briefly Lotta adjusted her focus and perception, then projected. . . .

Romlar awoke as he would have if someone had come into the tent. And found that someone had: Lotta. When she'd come to him before in the spirit, she'd always seemed just that, a spirit. This evening she looked physical, except for the aura. Ordinarily he had to make a certain effort to see auras, but not hers this evening. She stood clad in a glow of auroral blue that sheathed her thinly below the chest, expanding upward, flar-ing around and above her head like the flame of a Bunsen burner. It seemed to him it would have been visible to anyone.

But it illuminated nothing. He could see no sign of it on the tent walls or ceiling.

Then it struck him. "I'm dreaming." He said it aloud.

"No, I'm here all right."

"I didn't know you could travel—like that. In a form that looks physical. I'll bet anyone could see you."

"I didn't know I could, either. Eldren told me you could use some help."

Eldren. Another gone; this one a close friend. Closer in his way than Fritek. "He's lost his body then," he said.

"No, it's still alive; it might still make it."

Tears threatened, growing out of some undefined emotion. Relief perhaps. He grinned through them. "You don't have any clothes on."

She laughed. He wondered if anyone but himself could hear it. "So I don't," she said. "But in this form there's only one way I can help. Regardless of appearances. Shall I?"

"Let's do it."

"Are you comfortable?"

"Not bad, considering I took two grenade fragments today."

"Warm enough? It's cold in here."

That surprised him. How could she tell? "Yep."

"Need to go to the bathroom?"

"The latrine, you mean. Nope. I was there just before I came to bed."

"Good. I've sat in on some of your dreams, so I've got a starting place. All right to begin?"

"Go ahead." He closed his eyes. For him, sometimes the Ostrak Pro-cedures worked better that way.

"Okay, here goes. Is *wasting* a good subject to start with?"

He chuckled ruefully. "A very good subject."

His aura had verified it for her before he'd answered; it had thinned and darkened. "Good," she said, and her mind settled into a psychic posture from which she could monitor and support him. "So say the words 'to waste,' and keep saying them until something happens."

This was a procedure he hadn't done before, something new perhaps. "To waste. To waste . . ." He said it several times, then got an image of the open fen he'd used to break the T'swa pursuit, and the machine gun platoons fighting their bloody rear-guard action. She watched his recall with him, like a holograph, heard the gunfire, even felt the iron cold. "There was no other way," he said, as if he knew that she watched too. "It was that or take a lot more casualties. I had to sacrifice . . ."

He stopped. Cold waves of gooseflesh washed over him, intense, electrifying, and he abandoned "to waste." "To sacrifice," he murmured, "to sacrifice," repeating this until he got another image: Tain Faronya aboard an imperial warship, being questioned. A gate stood before her, the teleport the imperials had captured without knowing what they had. An officer—he felt like an intelligence officer—held an instrument in his hand. He pointed it at Tain, and though there was no sound with these images, Romlar saw her scream with pain, recoiling. *Where did this come from?* he wondered. *How can I be seeing this? I wasn't there!*

The image dissolved. "Keep saying it," Lotta told him.

"To sacrifice. To sacrifice . . ." It returned. This time he heard Tain scream, and heard the officer speak to her. The words, in Standard, seemed not to come from his lips but from a computer vocator. They exchanged words, while seven years later in his tent on Maragor, Romlar watched and listened. Then some uniformed men tried to push her into the teleport gate. Abruptly she wrenched loose from them, lunged forward into it—*and went berserk, bounding from the platform with a wild and guttural howl, crashed blindly into one of the uniformed men, knocking him sprawling, then charged into a table with men sitting behind it, rebounded, still howling, staggered, lunged, and fell over a chair onto the deck, where she lay thrashing and kicking.*

The image snapped out of existence, leaving Romlar staring at nothing, his hair on end. After a long moment he spoke: "Where did that come from?" he breathed.

"You're doing fine," Lotta answered. "Keep saying it."

"To sacrifice. To sacrifice." He paused. "You know what?"

"Tell me."

"She did sacrifice herself. For us. For all of us: the regiment, the worlds as she knew them. . . . She assumed it would kill her to enter the gate, or at least leave her mindless. And if she was dead or mindless, she couldn't tell them what it was."

His aura had cleared, but it hadn't flared. "Right," Lotta said. "Keep saying it."

"Sacrifice. Huh!" He saw himself talking with Lotta, not a three-dimensional image of her, here in his tent in Smolen, but the flesh-and-blood Lotta in his command tent in the Terfreyan jungle. And repeated the words he'd spoken then: "I wouldn't bring in more gunships; I don't want air superiority that way. I want to drive them off with inferior numbers and inferior weapons. That will stamp us with the mystique we want them to remember the Confederation by."

He shook his head. Lotta had watched the images with him, he knew, images colored by the events that grew out of that decision. The events and the casualties. Half of all the casualties he'd had on Terfreya.

But it didn't affect him now; he looked at it as if it was just what it was: a decision intended to produce the best result with the least cost over the long run.

"Keep saying it," Lotta ordered.

"To sacrifice. To sacrifice. To sac—*un-n-nh!*" He saw people, men and women, on the bridge of a spaceship. And shuddered. Lotta saw his aura flare, then collapse, and the image dissolved. He continued without prompting: "To sacrifice. To sacrifice . . ." Gradually, as he repeated, the image formed again, unmoving, like a still photo or a freeze-frame. It was a large bridge, ringed with instrument and monitor stations, while above them screens showed space, ships, a world—*Home World!*

"To sacrifice. To sacrifice." The image took life, became a sequence. There was no sound. One of the people on the bridge, tall, aristocratic-looking, was clearly the commander, and it seemed to Romlar that he'd been that man. It also seemed to him he'd seen these people, this bridge, in a dream. Perhaps only in a dream? Was that all it was? Another sat facing him, sat on an AG chair, wrapped archaically in a blanket, looking as if in the final stage of some degenerative disease. The man's gaze was powerful though, powerful, gentle—and compelling. He was pointing at the monitor that showed Home World, and his lips parted. Though Romlar didn't hear the words, he knew them. "*Destroy it!*"

He saw himself, the figure that seemed to be him, step to a console and touch a series of keys. In the present, in his winterized tent near Burnt Woods, his eyes were squinched tight. His aura had contracted almost to nothing, as if it were his skin that glowed murky yellow. Then the picture he watched flew apart in a blinding flash, and chills rushed through him more intense than any orgasm. His aura flared and contracted in a sort of irregular pulsing, as the chills continued. He writhed on his cot as if trying to escape.

This went on for nearly twenty seconds, then faded. His aura swelled, clear gold again with flecks and sparkles of red. His eyes opened and he laughed. "Speaking of sacrifice," he said, "I had a crew of nearly seven thousand on *Retributor*, and blew them all up. With the emperor and myself. He'd ordered me to destroy our Home World." He shook his head ruefully. "No wonder the ancients developed the Sacrament. There were *weapons* in those days."

"Okay. How do you feel about sacrifice?"

He shook his head again, but the grin was still there. "We'll come up with something better before we're done. Better than sacrifice, better than sacraments. We'll call it sanity."

"Okay," she said. "You're looking good. Are we done?"

There was no hesitancy in his answer. "Yep." His aura glowed pure and steady.

"Good. We're done then."

"And you're leaving now?"

"I need to. This isn't easy for me."

"I love you. I haven't told you that for a long time."

"I'll remember. I love you too."

She faded then and disappeared, to find herself back in the *ghao* with moonlight shining through the window. *We didn't get it all,* she told herself. *We may have taken care of "wasting" and "sacrifice," but there's something still there that we haven't touched. He's not ready yet, and I'm not either.*

When she'd rested—moved around and swung her arms a bit—she tranced, then reached to Eldren Esenrok. The ravaged body had stabilized; Eldren had returned to it, and slept. It seemed to her he'd live, but she stayed with him awhile, helping him communicate with his stump, with its nerves and blood vessels. They could look into other matters later.

# 74

In Linnasteth, spring was far more advanced. A fragrance wafted in through open balcony doors, the sweetness of *Syringa vulgaris*, the lilac, which had accompanied man to many worlds in his ancient expansions.

Engwar didn't notice. His round face turned grim as he listened to his justice minister. "The entire Reform Party is in outcry at Fingas's arrest," the minister was saying. He held out a copy of that day's *Bulletin*. "They insist that the offending issue does not constitute sedition, and—"

"Yes?"

"Several of the Conservative Party have publicly agreed with them."

"*What?! Who . . . ?*" Engwar stopped, got hold of himself. "Never mind," he said petulantly. "I can name them without help." He paused to blow gustily through his narrow, full-lipped mouth. "We're at war! I'll give them something to chew on! Arrest his editor as an accessory, and then . . ." He scowled at the worried-looking minister. "Then find some further crimes he's guilty of. Create evidence if necessary. We will have a great trial before the nation, and I want . . ."

His commset buzzed, and he slapped its flashing button angrily. "Yes?"

"Your Majesty, General Undsvin is calling. He . . ."

"*I told you I did not want to be interrupted!*"

"That's what I told the general, Your Majesty. He said you'd want to hear this. He said it's what you've been waiting to hear."

For just a moment, Engwar's face went slack, then, "Connect us!" he said, rapped the privacy switch and picked up the receiver. "What is it, Undsvin?"

He listened open-mouthed. "Really? Really? Great Amberus, Undsvin, this is marvelous! Truly marvelous! Where are they now? . . . This afternoon! Look, sweet cousin, I want to be there. I'll fly up today. . . . Yes, I insist. Have suitable quarters prepared. I'll have you called later with anything further you need to know."

He turned, a man transformed, beaming excitedly at his justice minister. "The T'swa have made a raid—*and captured Lanks!* Isn't that marvelous? He'll arrive in Rumaros later today! I told people! I said the T'swa were worth the money! Now they have proven me right!

"Do not arrest Fingas's editor. I may even release Fingas himself when I get back, as an act of magnanimity and celebration.

"Go now! Go! I have things to see to!"


# 75


Undsvin gnawed his lip and paced; he wasn't thrilled with Engwar's resolve to come to Rumaros. For several reasons. Most compelling, there was an element of risk. Rumaros was an occupied town, still with more than twelve thousand Smoleni, some of them undoubtedly having weapons hidden away. But the risk was something he could take steps to counter. More unpleasant and far more certain was Engwar's anger when he learned that Lanks had been taken five days earlier and he hadn't been informed.

Of course, Undsvin hadn't been informed himself till this morning. Ko-Dan had explained calmly that he hadn't reported it because he'd guaranteed the hostages' personal well-being—it had been requisite to the arrest. And because the Crown would wish to take Lanks from him if it knew, and Lanks was his safe conduct through Smoleni territory. Also, his regiment had needed to cover most of the distance on foot—the Smoleni lacked adequate motor transport.

Ko-Dan had finally called when he'd reached the Rumar River Highway. The colonel had gotten Smoleni approval to arrange convoyed truck transport from Rumaros, to pick up his regiment there.

More troublesome was Ko-Dan's insistence on sharing custody. Clearly he was serious about the hostages' well-being. *Well-being.* A term subject to interpretation.

At least Engwar's displeasure would be directed at Ko-Dan, though he'd be impossible to get along with afterward. He'd be angrier at Ko-Dan's guarantee to Lanks than at the delay, for there was no doubt that Engwar would want to humiliate the president publicly, while causing him pain and anguish privately. He'd probably be rehearsing his plans for that on the flight north.

The general sighed, a sound unusual from him. He'd taken steps to ensure—or nearly so—that the capture would not be leaked by his people, and hopefully the prisoners' arrival would go unnoticed. That should avoid public demonstrations. He'd taken comparable precautions to keep Engwar's arrival secret. The safest place to put him up would be in his personal apartment, on the upper floor of the building, which was well fenced and well guarded. But suppose word did leak? Certainly Smoleni intelligence was active in Rumaros. Suppose one of them had a mortar secreted in the city, or several of them!

Undsvin had done all he could. Now only the waiting remained. Lanks and his people, with their T'swa escort, had been landed on the roof, and taken by lift to cells in the cellar. Ko-Dan's arrogance had been an aggravation. He'd gone down with the prisoners, examined their quarters, and insisted they be made more comfortable. At least he hadn't objected to the heavy guard there, but he'd left men of his own to supervise, to see to the prisoners' "well-being."

Engwar, of course, would never consent to be landed on the roof. He'd be landed on the lawn, and received as properly as secrecy allowed. The staff had been told that Lord Cheldring was arriving to inspect headquarters, a believable lie. Cheldring, uncle to both of them, had been more than simply regent during Engwar's childhood. He'd also been Engwar's guardian, and still served him occasionally in special capacities.

Undsvin had considered posting snipers on the roof, but decided against it. It would be noticed, would draw attention and curiosity, and so far it wasn't necessary. If evidence of a leak developed, he could order it then.

The general glanced at the clock. Engwar had said he'd arrive at 2000 hours, and Undsvin had thought that, as eager as his cousin had sounded, he'd be on time for once. But it was 2007 now. He fidgeted, then took a report from his pending basket and tried unsuccessfully to read. Which irritated him: He was one of the senior nobles of Komars and the ranking general of the army, yet here he was dithering like a debutante.

At 2051, the general's command radio broke the suspense. It came on the air with: "Commander in Chief Komarsi Military Forces in Smolen, this is His Majesty's floater. This is His Majesty's floater. His Majesty will land in your courtyard at approximately 2100 hours."

Undsvin put hand to forehead in dismay. After his efforts for secrecy! Now he could only hope that no one was monitoring the command frequency. He sat like a stone for several minutes, then stood, turning to his two guards. "Lord Cheldring will soon be landing. We'll wait outside for him."

*The king was coming here! Into his hands!* It seemed to Coyn Carrmak that his face had surely betrayed him, had anyone been looking. But Innelmo, sharing the shift with him, showed his surprise at least as much. And clearly Undsvin had been unnerved by the call; as if he really had expected Cheldring, rather than the king. Carrmak took a slow breath, moderately deep, and then another, calming mind and body, counting the seconds of inhalation, the seconds of holding, the seconds of letting it back out.

He wondered if the king's arrival had anything to do with Burgold's behavior earlier. Ordinarily Burgold had at least something to say about his shift. Today he'd said nothing, and Carrmak had wondered then if something confidential had happened.

Undsvin led them outside. It was dusk and getting chilly, and they were dressed for indoors. Carrmak didn't crane his head around watching for the aircraft; that wouldn't have been acceptable to the general. He did glance around the courtyard though. Sixty yards away, the "open" end had been closed by a privacy wall about ten feet tall, with a bored guard at its gate, a submachine gun slung over a shoulder. Beyond that, the only people he could see were Undsvin, Innelmo, and himself. But Engwar would surely travel with bodyguards.

Undsvin was looking upward, waiting. More minutes passed. His head began to move, as if he watched something coming from south to north. Carrmak waited stolidly. He judged the craft's approach by watching Undsvin, until it was in his own range of vision. It wasn't as large as he'd expected; there couldn't be a lot of people on board. Given the size of the magazine in his pistol, even half a dozen would stretch things if they were armed, because he'd have to deal with Undsvin and Innelmo as well. He'd see.

It landed some eighty feet away. After a few seconds, steps extruded, and the door slid aside. A large man in uniform appeared, a bodyguard perhaps, came down the several steps and stationed himself at their foot. Then a boy emerged, in cape and tapered trousers, to stand at the other side. The king came next; Carrmak knew him at once by the richness of his cape, evident even in evening light. He was followed by another burly man in uniform—carrying baggage in each hand!

They were all on the ground, their attention on the king, whose attention was on Undsvin. One more man appeared in the door then and started down—the pilot, Carrmak decided. Then the king and Undsvin walked toward each other, Innelmo and himself a stride behind the general.

"Your Majesty!" Undsvin said.

"Dear cousin!" said the king.

Carrmak had his pistol in his hand with no one aware of it. His first shot struck Undsvin in the back, through the heart; the second took Engwar through the breastbone. The third struck Innelmo through the chest as he began to turn. Two more felled the bodyguards, one of whom got off a shot of his own, hitting Carrmak in the guts as he dropped into a squat, striking only soft tissue but burning like a red-hot poker. The pilot had started back up the steps. Carrmak shot him too; with a cry, the man fell backward. Carrmak was running then, jumping bodies. He dashed up the stairs and inside before the guard at the gate had gathered his wits enough to shoot.

He moved quickly to the pilot's compartment and sat down. Except for customized add-ons, he found it standard—almost everything made in the Confederation was standardized. Flying it was simple, and he'd been given basic flight training in their last year on Terfreya. The gate guard was shooting now; Carrmak heard slugs strike the floater. He touched the switch which closed the door and retracted the steps, then raised the floater vertically and abruptly to sixty feet and swept away across the roof in a course that curved northward. He was beginning to feel his wound.

His hair began to bristle, and he turned. Hardly five feet behind him was the boy in the cape, pointing a submachine gun at him. Carrmak heard the firing mechanism click, and saw the look of shock on the boy's face; there had been no round in the chamber. By that time Carrmak was half out of his seat, his pistol drawn. In the split second available, he decided not to kill him. His shot struck the thin shoulder, knocking the boy backward into the cabin, the submachine gun clattering onto the deck.

Carrmak gave his attention to the floater again, setting a course in a northerly direction and locking the controls. He took a moment to partition off the pain, then turned on the ceiling lights and stepped into the passengers' cabin. On the wall separating the two compartments were a medical chest, a fire extinguisher, and a rack that hung open, no doubt where the submachine gun had come from. Carrmak picked through the medical chest, then knelt to tend the boy he'd shot. Young, about thirteen he thought. And conscious, though dazed. As he bandaged, the boy jerked.

"Hold still," Carrmak said. The boy's eyes were large, and vague with shock. The pain hadn't really hit him yet.

"You—shot the king!" he said.

"Right. What's your name?"

"Jemi Kelisson Arkenvess." With that he seemed to gather his senses somewhat. "You're a traitor! A regicide!"

"I'm a regicide, right enough, but I ayn't no traitor. I'm not Komarsi."

"What are you then?"

Carrmak realized he'd been using the freedman dialect, and switched to Iryalan. "I'm a mercenary. Like the ones who blew up the munitions ship at Linnasteth last summer, and did other things like that. He finished his bandaging and began to tape the boy's wrists together. "What are you? A squire?"

The boy ignored the question. "You'll never get away with it!" His voice was weak but fierce. "They'll hunt you down and shoot you like a dog!"

"Let's hope not." As he lifted Jemi Arkenvess to put him on a seat, the pain broke through the partition he'd set up between his mind and his ravaged gut and damaged back. His knees gave with it, and he half dropped the boy onto the seat. For a moment, everything went black, and he kept from falling by clutching the back of the seat. When the pang had passed, he taped the boy in so he couldn't fall out or get out. Then he turned toward the pilot's compartment, intending to see what sort of navigational aids he had. "It won't do you any good, because we've caught the Smoleni president! We've got him locked in a cell in Rumaros! And Lord Cheldring will be regent again."

*Lanks a prisoner? Could that have been what Burgold wasn't talking about? Could it be why Engwar had flown there?* He paused, composed himself against the pain, then began to pump the boy for more. "Do you expect me to believe a lie like that?" he asked.

"He is! His Majesty flew to Rumaros to see him!"

"Nah! They wouldn't keep something like that secret. They'd tell the whole planet."

Carrmak's ploy had played out: The boy's mouth pinched shut, angry that this murderer didn't believe him. It occurred to Carrmak that, if it was true, maybe the Komarsi *would* keep it secret for a while. Who knew what considerations might apply from their point of view.

He returned to the pilot's seat and called a map onto the screen. It provided little detail north of Rumaros, but it did show villages. One of them was Burnt Woods. It also showed his present flight course, with his existing location. He read the bearing he needed, and reset his flight controls.

Pain brought beads of sweat to his upper lip. Bent over by it, he went into the cabin again and explored the medical kit further. The only powerful painkiller there was also sleep inducing. The tablets were scored. Judging that Jemi Arkenvess weighed a little more than a hundred pounds, he broke one in two and gave a half to the boy, with a cup of water. Jemi could afford to sleep.

He watched while Jemi washed down the pill, then said, "The reason I know you're lying is that President Lanks is way up north, where your people could never get their hands on him."

"That shows how much you know! The T'swa caught him! They went up there through the wilderness and caught him in his palace—his house! I heard His Majesty tell Lord Cheldring!"

"Really! Hmm! Maybe I believe you after all."

The T'swa! He wasn't sure if there was a precedent for their capturing a head of state, outside of retribution for treachery. And that couldn't apply here; Lanks wasn't the contractor.

The T'swa looked for ways to cut wars short, though, and capturing Lanks would no doubt shorten this one. Just as shooting Engwar . . . Another pang hit Carrmak's guts, and he turned away so Jemi Arkenvess wouldn't see. When it passed, the level of pain left behind was worse than before.

The boy was already sleeping, he realized, and Carrmak wobbled back to the pilot's seat. He'd see what they knew in Burnt Woods. Another pang struck, and he ground his teeth against it. This one left him less than clearheaded. He hoped he wouldn't vomit; that would be bad. *Maybe the president's in his office right now,* he told himself, *or in bed. Maybe the kid's lying after all. Maybe—* He grimaced, then managed a chuckle. *Maybe I'll pass out before I get to Burnt Woods.*

# 76

The Komarsi corporal was heavy-bodied from overeating and little physical activity. But he was also conspicuously strong—a freedman who'd followed the harvests for several years. Just now he was peering through the bars at Weldi Faronya, and smirking. "Yer a pretty thing, ya knaw?"

She darkened. Kelmer was on his feet at once; the corporal pretended not to notice. "I likes them long legs, too. But what I like best is that fuzzy thing up atween 'em."

Kelmer strode to the bars and gripped them, face tight with anger. "I'll report this," he said.

The corporal snorted. "You? Yer a prisoner! Report all ya likes." He looked at Weldi again. "You knaw what's gawnta happen to ya when His Majesty's done with ya? He's gonna give ya to us to play with. And I'll be first, 'cause I got the biggest one in the army."

He guffawed then, hooted with laughter, as Kelmer began to shout curses at him. When his prisoner had run out of curses, the smirking corporal opened his mouth to taunt him some more. The words never got out, because Kelmer spat in his face. The Komarsi stepped back, wiped the spit from his cheek and looked unbelievingly at it on his fingers. With a sudden oath he reached to his holster, ripped open the flap and drew his sidearm.

He'd been unaware of the T'swa sergeant coming up behind him. He'd entered the cell area in time to see and hear the entire performance. As the corporal's weapon cleared its holster, hands gripped his wrist from behind and jerked across and up. He squealed, almost screamed. The pressure threatened to rupture the ligaments in his shoulder, and the pistol clopped onto the concrete floor. Then a hand gripped the corporal's collar from behind. Grimacing and white-faced with pain, he was jerked around and frog-marched out into the corridor. Sergeant Ka-Mao eased the pressure only a little on their way to the lieutenant's office.

The Komarsi lieutenant was tall and rawboned, a surly, lantern-jawed man with a nose broken in a tavern fight years earlier. A yeoman farmer's son, he was proud of his commission and jealous of his authority. He'd been a shift officer at the military prison in Rumaros, and the provost marshal had commended him in inspection reports. That had resulted in a transfer to Command Headquarters as a shift officer in the head-quarters security company.

General Undsvin had had the cells installed for civilian prisoners, but they'd been empty for more than a dek. When he'd learned of the Smoleni government's capture, he'd thought of them at once, and the provost marshal had put the lieutenant in charge. From the beginning, the man had resented the presence of T'swa on his turf, outsiders with loosely defined but seemingly absolute oversight authority. He considered it a deep personal insult. It would have been bad enough if the T'swa inter-lopers, one on each shift, had been commissioned officers. But these were enlisted men, and rejects at that, men to some degree disabled, unfit for combat.

When Ka-Mao shoved the corporal in through the open door, the lieutenant stood so abruptly, he knocked his chair over. "*What in Yomal's name is going on here?*"

The T'swi released the man, thrusting him sharply aside, and recited calmly what had happened. When he was done, the lieutenant stepped around his desk and slapped the corporal's face, backhand and forehand, the sounds like shots. Then he turned to the T'swi, scowling. "You can go now, Sergeant. I'll take care of this piece of shit."

"Thank you, Lieutenant." The T'swa veteran was completely matter of fact. "This man was nearly the cause of at least three deaths. Including yours as the officer in charge. He must not be returned to the cell area." Ka-Mao saluted then and left, closing the door behind himself. The lieu-tenant stared after him, then turned and slugged the corporal in the mouth, knocking him down, splitting his lips. "Yomal *damn* your ass!" he snarled. "If this ends up on my personnel record, you stupid horse turd, you'll wish you were never born." Without sitting, he rapped keys on his commset, calling the provost marshal's office, and arranged to have the corporal taken away under guard.

Ka-Mao, of course, included the affair in his shift report, a copy of which went to the general's office. Since Undsvin's murder, headquarters had been in near chaos, and Colonel Viskon, as acting commander, was overloaded with demands from Linnasteth. When he'd worked his way to Ka-Mao's report, the next day, he swore vividly. He too phoned the provost marshal's office. Afterward he called the lieutenant, questioning him, then told him to expect his replacement in an hour. He'd hardly hung up when Colonel Ko-Dan radioed him.

"When will the security apartment be ready for the president and his family?" Ko-Dan asked.

Viskon hadn't checked since ordering it. "Tomorrow," he said. *And it damned well would be; he'd check out progress as soon as this call was finished; skin some asses if need be.*

"In the interim, what privacy has been provided for the president's daughter?"

"A portable screen has been provided for the sanitary facility in each of the occupied cells, as you requested. Required."

"You have, of course, seen the report of yesterday's extreme insults to her, and of the threat to her husband's life."

"Yes. The offending corporal has been replaced. He's being held in the stockade pending a court martial. The officer in charge of the prisoners has also been replaced."

"Thank you. I have confidence in both your intentions and your competence, Colonel Viskon, but it was necessary that I call to ensure that the situation has been fully corrected. That was a very close thing for Komars. Please inform me when the president and his family have been moved into their apartment."

After the call from Colonel Viskon, the security lieutenant was so angry, he didn't trust himself to leave his office for a few minutes. Basically he didn't blame the corporal for what he considered his humiliation, nor even the T'swi. It was that aristocratic *pig* he blamed. When he'd regained some composure, he went to the cell area. Ka-Mao wasn't there. Walking to the bars of the Faronyas's cell, the Komarsi glared in at Weldi. He said nothing, but as she stared back white-faced, he made a movement with his right fist as if disemboweling her with a short sword. Then he turned and stalked away.

Breath frozen in their chests, Weldi and Kelmer watched him leave, not knowing what had caused such hatred. This man seemed to them more dangerous than the corporal, and they were left with their imaginings. Weldi's were sick with fear. Kelmer's were a mixture of fear and violent intentions.

# 77

General Lord Heklos Erlinsson Brant was a small man with a spine like a steel rod, a learned posture reflecting neither rigidity nor any special toughness. In fact, he was a pliant man, within limits, bending readily with shifts in policy and power, always heedful of politics. The youngest general in the Army of Komars, he'd been commander of the Infantry Training Center at Long Ridge until, on the second day after Undsvin's death, the new regent had appointed him Commander of the Army of Occupation, and he'd been flown at once to Rumaros.

Heklos was, in fact, a competent organizer and administrator. But his appointment had resulted at least as much from his pliancy, and from the fact that Lord Regent Cheldring Tarsteng Brant was his paternal uncle. Cheldring had been regent for and guardian of Crown Prince Engwar while Engwar was growing up, and at Engwar's death had declared himself regent again. The Komarsi Council of Ministers and the Assembly of Lords had ratified Cheldring's self-appointment by a slim majority. Under the circumstances, his supporters insisted, a strong man was needed quickly on the throne, and Engwar had died without acknowledged offspring.

Despite Heklos's new appointment, which was also a promotion, he was not fond of Cheldring. He remembered his uncle from childhood as generally disapproving and sometimes caustic. So in this the second week on his new post, he was less than happy at Cheldring's unexpected arrival in Rumaros. Cheldring had left his bodyguard in reception, outside Heklos's office, and invited/ordered Heklos to send his own guard out. Then they sat alone together over joma, and talked.

"You are wondering why I came," Cheldring said.

"Indeed, Uncle."

"I have come to end the war." He dipped his upper lip in his cup and frowned, not at the joma but at his thoughts. "The kingdom is in serious trouble. It was in trouble before, and the malcontents are taking advantage of Engwar's death. The Assembly of Lords is being notably uncooperative, and as regent I lack the leverage to coerce them. They approved me, they said, because they needed a strong man to lead the kingdom. But now they do not want me strong. The merchants and many of the industrialists rail because of inflation and shortages. The reformers try to destroy the country. The freedmen are more rebellious than ever, as if a fire had been built under them and they were stirred with a spoon. The serfs are insubordinate. And I, as mere regent, cannot declare martial law without approval by the Assembly.

"Meanwhile the capture of the Smoleni government has not had the result one might have expected. They have appointed an acting president, and he a cabinet of shit-boot farmers. Who have stated their determination to continue—*and win!*—the war. Empty bravado, of course. But by humiliating that bungler Undsvin, and through him the army, they have gained a certain credibility, in Linnasteth as well as abroad."

He scowled down at his bony hands, studying them as if to learn something. "So I will discuss possible peace terms with President Lanks. This will tend to undermine the authority of their acting president, and a man in prison is likely to be more reasonable than one who is not."

Heklos hadn't looked forward to directing the war. To cover his relief, he asked, "What sort of terms do you have in mind?"

Cheldring grunted. "I will offer him independence and a treaty of peace, with a new boundary along the Welvarn Morain. That will give us most of the Leas—the more fertile eighty percent of them."

"What if he declines?"

"I will point out the hopelessness of the Smoleni supply situation. And tell him we have an agreement with the Lodge of Kootosh-Lan for another regiment of T'swa; he'll have no reason to doubt me. And if it comes to it, I'll offer to return the coastal strip to him.

"In either case, it will leave them in a weak and irreparable economic situation: They'll be dependent on imports for most of their food, which will badly tilt their export-import balance. And along with their lack of resources for industrial development, they'll discover the taste of real poverty." He sat back, looking self-satisfied, pleased with the images. "They will develop severe internal stresses, and before long, internal strife. I will not be surprised to become their master in economic fact, if not in name."

Heklos poked at the idea with his mind and wondered. He could imagine the obstinate Smoleni clearing more plowland in the north and feeding themselves despite the loss of the Leas.

Cheldring wasn't troubled with such thoughts. He dovetailed arthritic knuckles over his brocade vest. "Once the peace is signed, I will use the Leas to heal our internal wounds. I'll offer small yeoman holdings there to serfs who've earned sergeancies, and small estates to yeomen's sons who've become officers. That will end the demonstrations and quiet the reformers. The rest of the Leas I will claim for the Crown, then offer it as land grants to the younger sons of Conservative nobles, estates large enough to qualify them as Assembly candidates. That will strengthen my position substantially."

*And allow you to claim the Crown as well as the Throne,* Heklos thought wryly. *Shrewdly planned, Uncle!*

"I will meet with Lanks after dinner," Cheldring went on, "and feel him out. What sort of conditions do you keep him in?"

"He shares a small—apartment, you might call it—with his daughter and son-in-law; three rooms on the ground floor in back. His government occupies cells in the basement. The T'swa commander insisted that he have better quarters than our cells provide, so I had bars installed. . . ."

Cheldring interrupted. "*The T'swa insisted?!*"

"One of the conditions of his surrender was that he be treated respectfully."

The regent's grimace gradually relaxed to a thoughtful frown. He'd been briefed on the T'swa guarantee, and it seemed to him they'd carried it too far, but still . . . He grunted. "Perhaps it's just as well, given my purpose for being here. Anything else about their living conditions?"

"A basement room has been provided with mats on the floor, and dumbbells. They're taken there once a day for exercise and recreation, which also allows those in different quarters to see each other for an hour. This was at the insistence of the T'swa commander, who's appointed sergeants to supervise the prisoners' treatment. As a matter of fact, he's had two guards removed for showing disrespect to the prisoners."

"Hmh! Well. Let us eat. I will meet with Lanks afterward."

Accompanied by a private, a Komarsi lieutenant strode down the corridor, a tall, rawboned security officer with a lantern jaw and a scowl. On their way, they'd been joined by a thick-shouldered T'swi with a limp. The door they stopped at was different than those they'd passed; it had a small, unglazed window with bars, and instead of a knob, a handle and a heavy deadbolt. The lieutenant looked sourly at the T'swi, then knocked firmly on the door and called through the barred window. "This is Lieutenant Walls! I'm comin' in!" With key in one hand and pistol in the other, he unlocked the door and pushed it open. The private too held a gun in his hand. The T'swi stood relaxed, his pistol in his holster but with the flap loose.

There were three prisoners in the room. All had been reading. Without rising from his chair, Heber Lanks put his book aside. He recognized the man. "What may I do for you, Lieutenant?" His tone was correct but cold.

"General Heklos has sent me to take you to his office."

"Indeed? To what purpose?"

The lieutenant bit back what he wanted to say. "Lord Regent Cheldring will speak with you there."

"Ah! That is kind of the lord regent. But I am President of the Republic of Smolen, and this is my country. If the Lord Regent wishes to speak with me, let him come here to my home. I'll be happy to give him an audience."

The lieutenant turned away red-faced and angry, and gestured the private out ahead of him. His pistol stiff in his hand, he turned to the prisoners. His eyes swept them with a look of cold hate, ending on Weldi. Then he followed the private out. The T'swi left last. He'd have stepped in front of the lieutenant, had it come down to it, and drawn his own gun, but the Komarsi, he knew, hadn't intended to shoot.

When the door closed behind the T'swi, Weldi began to shake violently. Kelmer knelt by her and wrapped her in his arms. "I'm all right," she whispered. "I'm all right. I'm all right." But still she shook.

Her father had left the room, feeling helpless. It seemed to him that Kelmer was the one to comfort her, and that for him to stay might constrain them.

Kelmer held her, stroking her shoulders, her neck. "He can't do anything to you," he murmured. "He can't do anything to you."

After a minute the shaking stopped, but he continued to hold her.

❖    ❖    ❖

The two Komarsi walked quickly to Heklos's office, one floor up in a corner suite; the T'swi had stopped at his own desk, in what had been a room service alcove when the building had been a hotel. At Heklos's office, the lieutenant, stony-faced, told the general what Lanks had said, being careful not to look at the lord regent.

Heklos, on the other hand, had little choice; he had to look. "What is your wish, Lord Regent?"

Cheldring's wide mouth was a slash. "I will go to this insolent Smoleni." He got up. "Stay, nephew," he added. "Lieutenant, take me to him."

The lieutenant retraced his steps, the lord regent following, his bodyguard and the private two strides behind. As they came to the alcove, the T'swa sergeant got up and followed them. This time the lieutenant did not call through the barred window. He simply unlocked the door, pushed it open and walked in, pistol in hand. Cheldring followed, and the lieutenant stepped aside. The bodyguard and the private entered behind them, followed by the T'swi.

Heber Lanks got up from his chair. "Lord Regent," he said, and stepping forward, shook Cheldring's hand with cold formality. "Welcome to my temporary headquarters." He stepped back and gestured. "My daughter, Weldi." She stood up, still pale, her eyes dark smudges. "And her husband, Mr. Kelmer Faronya."

Kelmer's face was without expression. He stepped forward as if to shake hands. Suddenly he ducked, and pistoned his left leg sideways with all the power of a strongly muscled thigh. The lieutenant was standing obliquely sideways to him, and Kelmer's heel took the man explosively beneath the ribs, smashing the liver, bursting the peritoneum, rupturing the intestine. Air whooped hoarsely from the lieutenant's lungs as he flew sideways, flaccid. For Kelmer, time slowed abruptly as he watched the pistol fly from nerveless fingers. He dove for it, heard the roar of a gunshot but felt no bullet. His fingers closed on the pistol's grip before it struck the floor, and he rolled onto his side, firing upward, once at Cheldring, then at the bodyguard whose shot had missed him, then at the private, who'd broken and was turning to run.

Cheldring was dying when he hit the floor, his aorta torn. Kelmer almost missed the bodyguard, who'd been moving; the bullet smashed through the right elbow, and the man's gun thudded to the floor as he howled. The private he lung-shot, sending him sprawling. Finally he shot the lieutenant, just to be sure he was dead.

The young journalist lay panting. The entire action had taken about three seconds. The T'swa sergeant stood with eyebrows raised, his pistol in one large black hand.

Kelmer became aware of shouts from down the corridor. Getting to his hands and knees, he vomited.

# 78

Heklos had taken over the situation with unhappy efficiency, first safeguarding the prisoners. Colonel Ko-Dan had made clear to him at the beginning what T'swa protection meant. Now Ko-Dan's sergeant also pointed out that the two nations being at war, the lord regent was not a murder victim but a war casualty. Heklos gave orders to suspend exercise privileges, and the T'swi did not object. The two off-duty T'swa guards now posted themselves on either side of the president's door, with submachine guns.

Ka-Mao reported the sequence of events to Ko-Dan. Heklos, he said, seemed intent on containing the situation, to avoid confrontation with the T'swa.

Heklos was concerned that some elements of the army would try to exact revenge. He'd notified Linnasteth of Cheldring's death, and what had led to it. While he waited for instructions, which he was prepared to ignore if necessary, two T'swa companies double-timed into Rumaros and took positions around the Komarsi headquarters.

In Linnasteth, Cheldring's death leaked at once, and before nightfall, embassy row had spread the news across Maragor, including to Burnt Woods via Krentorf. From Azure Bay, Pitter Movrik's agent sent off an official summary of events, so far as he knew them, to Splenn, via pod. With a copy, of course, to the Confederation Ministry, also located in Azure Bay. Then, unofficially, he went into his supply room, stepped through the gate, and reported personally to Pitter Movrik, who did much the same thing to inform Lord Kristal on Iryala.

Over the next ten days, a lot happened. Engwar's queen claimed the throne. The Council of Ministers rejected her out of hand. Lord Nufkarm proposed that Fingas Marnsson Kelromak be crowned. Fingas was descended on his mother's side from King Ferant II Blundell, who'd been deposed a century and a half earlier, giving rise to the Tarsteng Dynasty. The relationship was thought close enough to satisfy the less extreme formalists. While the matter was under debate, the sedition charges against Fingas were thrown out as invalid; Cheldring had already released him from prison. A rumor spread that if Fingas was crowned, a convention would be called to write a constitution. Meanwhile, large and surprisingly orderly freedman demonstrations were taking place in Linnasteth and other major towns. (Carrmak felt reasonably sure who'd provided the leadership.) It was also reported that some units in the Army of Occupation were refusing to drill.

The Council of Ministers, deeply worried by all this and seeking to relieve its intensity at least, appointed Lord Nufkarm regent. He in turn ordered a schedule drawn up for the return of army units to Komars, a de facto abandonment of the war. Smoleni farmer refugees had already begun to move back into the districts abandoned by the Komarsi the summer before, to begin their spring plowing.

The Archipelago requested permission to ship relief supplies up the Rumar when the river was free of ice—the lower reaches were already—and Nufkarm approved it. Through the Krentorfi government, he then proposed a truce, with representatives of the two warring nations to meet in Faersteth and discuss armistice terms. Although he could hardly say so, Nufkarm intended to offer a favorable trade agreement.

Both governments agreed to release their offworld mercenaries. Movrik's agent in Azure Bay, representing the Lodge of Kootosh-Lan as well as the Iryalan Office of Special Projects, sent a pod to Splenn with notification. Romlar began work on getting his infiltrators out of Komars.

The next day, Heber Lanks, with his daughter and son-in-law, arrived back at Burnt Woods in a Komarsi floater.

When the troopship arrived from Splenn to remove the regiment, Romlar still hadn't accounted for all his infiltrators. Brossling had flown to Komars to sift through the jails there, and question leaders among the freedmen. Carrmak would have been sent, but he was still recovering from abdominal surgery.

Over the several weeks since his last fight with the T'swa, Romlar had visited the little hospital in Burnt Woods from time to time, and the army's field hospital, talking to the wounded, both troopers and T'swa. And Gulthar Kro. Kro's face had been substantially disfigured. The bullet had torn through his upper jaw, palate, and cheekbone. His speech was somewhat impaired.

By the time that Brossling had returned with the last infiltrators, Kro was in reconditioning camp. Romlar visited him there. "Gull," he said, "I owe you for grabbing that grenade."

Kro snorted a harsh laugh, and in his awkward speech said, "Colonel, you owe me nothin'." He peered hard at Romlar. "You know what I went to you for?"

Romlar shook his head. "What?"

"Undsvin sent me up here last summer to kill you. Then I kind of forgot about that. Finally I decided I better do it, so I went to your camp."

Romlar half grinned. "Really?! Well I'll be damned! Hmm. But you didn't—kill me that is. And out in the woods, you may have saved my life. You saved me getting wounded a lot worse than I was, anyway. And you were out there fighting alongside the rest of us. So I still owe you."

Kro clamped his jaw as best he could. The fit wasn't very good. The merc commander was beyond understanding.

"How'd you like your face fixed?" Romlar asked.

"Whadya mean?"

"We've got doctors on Iryala that can remake your face."

Kro's gaze was intense now. "How'd I get there?"

"I'll load you aboard with my men. After we get you there . . . I've got pull. I'll tell you what. It seems to me—it seems to me we've known each other before. Long ago."

Kro looked at him more puzzled than ever.

"Do you want to go?"

"Sure I wanna go."

"Okay. I'll go to your C.O. and get you released. We're leaving tomorrow."

# 79

The regiment arrived at Splenn by ship. There Romlar arranged with the Confederation Ministry for Gulthar Kro's passage to Iryala. Kelmer Faronya and his wife would ride home in a courier. The regiment gated home, arriving at a security area of the Landfall Military Reservation. They were quartered overnight there, and given a reception next day by the OSP, with the king himself attending briefly. *Interesting*, Romlar thought. *Why the king?* Colonel Voker had flown down from Blue Forest, which was a lot easier to understand, and Varlik Lormagen, the original "White T'swi," from the school he and his wife operated on the coast.

The next day the troopers were given new paycards that accessed the credits they'd accrued, and they dispersed for a dek, most to visit their families.

Romlar, however, was taken by limousine to Lord Kristal's handsome home on the royal estate. Lotta Alsnor met him at the horseshoe drive, and they faced off, holding hands between them, looking at each other. He grinned broadly. "How come I get to have such a pretty girl?" he asked.

She laughed. "Bullshit, Artus; I'm a scrawny little minx. Wiry anyway. But say it again; I like it." She paused for a moment, squeezing his thick hands. "I suppose you're wondering why you were brought here. And what I'm doing here."

"It has crossed my mind."

"Well then, let me take you to Emry and we'll uncross it."

She led him inside and through halls, his attention not on what he might or might not learn there, but on the beauty and harmony of the art and other furnishings he passed. He'd never imagined a home like this before.

It was more than a home. One wing held Kristal's staff—offices with people sitting at monitors, dictating to computers, talking with each other. Kristal's receptionist didn't seat them. "Just a moment," she said, then spoke quietly to a commset and disconnected. Smiling, she motioned toward a door to one side. "Go right in."

The old man was on his feet to greet them. He took Romlar's thick hard hand in both of his slender ones, and shook it. "Artus, it's good to have you back. It's spring where you've come from, right?"

"Spring going on summer."

"Well. And here you find summer half used up." His deep bright eyes examined Romlar's. "I have a new assignment for you. To start when you've had your leave." He paused. "And when I say a new assignment, I mean a *new* assignment.

"I take it your regiment came home in good mental and spiritual condition?"

"Absolutely. Most of them better than I did."

Kristal nodded as if he knew what Romlar alluded to. "Good," he said. "Good.

"Your regiment will not be contracted out again. The Confederation has its own need for it. An imperial invasion fleet is on its way, little more than two years distant. I want you to be part of a secret royal commission to develop strategies and tactics to counter it. Defuse it if possible. This will mean turning over regimental command to someone else—whoever you consider best suited to the job."

Romlar wasn't smiling now, but his face was relaxed, his answer casual. "Coyn Carrmak," he said. "He's my best battalion commander, and the smartest man I've got. Men tend naturally to listen to him and do what he says, and beyond that, he's the luckiest person I know." He glanced at Lotta then. "With the exception of your brother. Jerym's come through more than anyone else in the outfit, and unscratched."

He turned back to Kristal then. "You said the regiment isn't going to be contracted out again. What are you going to do with it?"

"Train it. That's partly where you come in. Over a period of time the commission will develop strategies and tactics, as I said. Your regiment will learn and train in tactics and techniques no one's invented yet.

"Are you willing to have the job?"

Romlar grinned. "I'm your man. It sounds interesting."

"Fine. It's yours. To begin with, you'll work here at the capital. Part of the time just down the hall."

Romlar put a hand on Lotta's arm. "And where does Lotta fit in?"

The king's personal aide laughed. "She'll take you to lunch and tell you about that. Meanwhile, I have a great deal to do here." His gesture took in not only his desk and monitor, but the whole wing. "We'll talk again, very soon. Perhaps over dinner this week."

Lotta led Romlar to his lordship's conservatory, and the small staff dining room there. They sat in a private corner beside a bank of Iryalan tropical flowering ferns, their fronds soft green. A waiter came over, described the menu and took their orders, then left.

"So what hat do you wear in all this?" Romlar asked.

"I'm Emry's psychic resource and special intelligence section."

"Then we'll both be working here."

"That's right."

"If you'll marry me, we can take an apartment together and save on rent."

"I'm afraid I can't share an apartment with you."

His eyebrows raised. "Why not?"

She laughed. "Because Emry has assigned me a small house on the hill, as free from psychic disturbances as you can get near the capital. Free official housing for his special assistant; I'm one of a kind, he tells me. To be more exact, he said: 'Lotta, you're like Artus. You're one of a kind.' "

Her smile softened. "There's lots of room for two, if you'd like to share it with me. Our schedules won't always match, but we'll be together a lot more than once every few years."

Romlar chuckled. "I love you, Lotta. Very much. I'm sure I've told you that before."

"I seem to recall something like that. Would you like to see the house? Before we fill out the marriage application?"

He laughed aloud, then leaned across the table and they kissed.


### ~ THE END ~

## AUTHOR'S NOTE:

There are two other novels in this series. One, the
longest of the five, is the wrap-up story: *The Three-Cornered War.*
I think of it as Lotta's book, although it contains several
subplots and a number of riveting characters.
(And of course the White T'swa and the T'swa play important roles.)

The other, *The Kalif's War,* is somewhat tangential to the three you've
just read. Following directly upon *The White Regiment,* it is set almost
entirely within the old Home Sector. It continues the Tain Faronya
subplot, and contributes strongly to *The Three-Cornered War.* Niccolo
Machiavelli would have approved mightily of the kalif.

To include those two stories in the same set of covers with these
three would have made this book more than 60 percent longer,
thicker, and heavier. Either that or resulted in tiny type,
and numerous optometrist appointments.

# Notes

[1] North of the border was "The Great Wild," a wilderness reserve established by the Confederation, which made modest annual payment to the three bordering nations on the south. Controlled fur harvest was allowed, and Jump-Off was the base from which licensed Smoleni trappers left in autumn for their territories.

[2] In the Confederation Sector, the year on each world is divided into ten "deks" of equal or nearly equal length. These are numbered in order from the winter solstice, however slight it may be.